THE BASTARD FACTORY

The Bastard Factory

CHRIS KRAUS

Translated from the German
by Ruth Martin

PICADOR

First published 2022 by Picador
an imprint of Pan Macmillan
The Smithson, 6 Briset Street, London EC1M 5NR
EU representative: Macmillan Publishers Ireland Ltd, 1st Floor,
The Liffey Trust Centre, 117–126 Sheriff Street Upper,
Dublin 1, D01 YC43
Associated companies throughout the world
www.panmacmillan.com

ISBN 978-1-5098-7908-3

1 3 5 7 9 8 6 4 2

A CIP catalogue record for this book is available from the British Library.

Printed and bound by CPI Group (UK) Ltd, Croydon, CR0 4YY

Visit **www.picador.com** to read more about all our books
and to buy them. You will also find features, author interviews and
news of any author events, and you can sign up for e-newsletters
so that you're always first to hear about our new releases.

Similarities with persons living or dead are coincidental.
The actions of historical figures are in part public knowledge,
and in part invented.

Author's Note

Many of the situations, historical events and catastrophes of the twentieth century that feature in this book will be familiar to readers. But not all. Some may cause astonishment and head-shaking, and seem so very like the material of a novel that you may take them to be pure invention.

Although sometimes that may be true, only a small proportion of the events and political affairs described here are wholly invented. And very few of the people who appear in this book (even the maddest of them) never lived.

But the actors depicted here and their actions belong to the book's fictional world. Outside it, things may have happened as described, or they may not.

There are no secrets that time does not reveal.

JEAN RACINE

Contents

I

The Red Apple

I

Sometimes he places his hands on my shoulders and looks sadly into my face. He tells me in the simplest words how sorry he is for what happened, and for what is probably still to come.

But he has no idea what happened.

And even less of what is still to come.

He's a genuine hippy, in his early thirties, I would guess, with long blond curly hair, when he's lying to the right of me. But when he shuffles past the left-hand side of my bed (to stare down from the window at the babies on the floor below) then I see – and I marvel at it afresh every time – that above his ear they have shaved a perfectly round, mother-of-pearl-coloured patch the size of a saucer into his Botticelli haircut. At its centre gleams a titanium screw, the thread of which ends somewhere under his skull and prevents it from falling apart.

The Hippy has troubles of his own.

He has been lying there – for weeks, now – beside me, more Orient than Occident, lying there without any impatience, a threadbare rug with traces of Indian influence.

Be at one with the universe, he says.

Be at one with yourself.

That's his mantra.

But when, from time to time, the Hippy is jolted out of his being-at-one, it's by the babies who doze downstairs.

And of course, I mustn't forget the fits.

The orderlies will wheel him out at the least sign of an eruption. And when he comes back, he's unconscious for hours. Then they fit a catheter onto his screw, which is actually a kind of pressure valve. One of these beeping devices starts up. And to prevent any damage to his head, excess fluid is pumped out of his skull through the catheter and into a plastic beaker.

The plastic beaker is the property of the night nurse. Her name is Gerda. Her beaker has a handle and a pattern of black Mickey Mouse heads on a red background. When the fluid reaches the third Mickey Mouse, the night nurse tiptoes into our room and carefully pours it into a large thermos flask, without spilling a drop. She taps the four or five other skull fractures on the ward in the same way. She looks into the plastic beakers and is happy.

But when she does that, her mouth is not attractive.

Later, she smuggles the thermos flask out of the hospital. The liquor is used to feed Night Nurse Gerda's house plants. They must be terrifically fruitful. There are photos of her winter garden on the pinboard in the nurses' station. It's a jungle of plants both useful and ornamental, you have to take your hat off to her, with vines and forget-me-nots growing in between. All of them huge and green. A baroque glory, just as Night Nurse Gerda herself is a baroque glory, all exuberance and expansiveness, which is her temperament, too.

It's no wonder, then, that Night Nurse Gerda once brought the Hippy a home-grown, tennis-ball-yellow tomato that she had nurtured with his brain fluid. He ate it with pleasure and pride and, typically for him, tried to give me some as well.

He is a wonderful person, I'm sure, just as you imagine hippies to be. He uses the informal '*du*' with almost everyone – even me. It doesn't trouble him in the least if people don't respond in kind. He doesn't use titles in the conventional sense, and won't address people as 'Herr' or 'Frau', or anything else. If he really must, he will call them '*compañero*'. The senior consultant is 'chief *compañero*'. Conventional courtesy means nothing to him. He also takes a very different view of names from you or me. He believes everyone should be named after their dominant characteristics, as they are in Papua New Guinea, where over the course of a lifetime a person will acquire three, four or more names that sometimes contradict one another. Or so the Hippy tells me. He lived there for quite some time. And in Australia, too, where he prospected for diamonds. Later he left that line of work and took jobs in a kindergarten and at Munich-Riem Airport. He robbed the Rolling Stones' luggage there last year, and still has a pair of cufflinks belonging to them.

Of course, I didn't know what the Rolling Stones were.

I do now, however, because he sang me one of their songs. He would have been snapped up straight away all those years ago when St Petri was looking for singers – do you remember? – because half the cathedral choir had been shot dead by the Bolsheviks (first and foremost the basses, of course).

He can't comprehend the fact that he is sharing a room with someone who was born in the Russian Empire. I can scarcely comprehend it myself.

Some time ago, when I was transferred here from the intensive care unit, he asked me to give him a name based on my first impression of him. I recalled a visit to the Prado, where I once copied Francisco Goya's portrait of the degenerate Spanish royal family, who had also been blond and frail. That was what I said to him.

He thinks 'Bourbons' means several glasses of whisky.

His name is Mörle. Sebastian Mörle. I am to call him Basti if I can't think of anything more fitting.

I am Konstantin Solm, I told him. And just one day later, I added (with complete indifference, a smoke ring from my peace pipe) that a lot of people call me Koja.

The Hippy replied that I wasn't a Koja for him. And that Konstantin Solm wasn't me at all.

Rusty nails.

Coldness.

Distance.

That's what I was.

But also a wonderful person.

He does make me laugh when he says things like this. Ten times a day he whispers what a wonderful person I am, in his Chiemgau accent with its Bavarian burr, although he finds me 'proper posh' and takes exception to my manner of speaking. It's too Baltic for him, I think, not crude enough, and better suited to a more expensive single room – in which, of course, I wouldn't say anything at all. Perhaps that's why they put me in a two-bed room. To loosen my tongue. That might be it.

But I don't talk. The Hippy is the one who's always pouring his heart out. My age doesn't put him off talking to me, and unfortunately most of what he says is rather facile. I am the repository for his very few worries. He calls the ward room, with homely affection, 'our pad'. He gives effusive thanks to the universe for every dish of cold milksop they feed him when he's had a fit. And he has no reservations about the fact that I was in the war. He never asks what I did. In all creatures, including me, he sees intimations of the World Peace that is to come. Ever since he found out that I once drank champagne with David Ben-Gurion (and even sipped from his glass), he has shared my standpoint on the Israel question in general and on Golda Meir in particular, at least on her first name, which is truly charming. On this, we agree.

However, he is disappointed by my attitude towards marijuana (which, in my view, would be an even lovelier first name for this intoxicating prime minister).

Without drugs, the Hippy feels incomplete.

He has therefore given Night Nurse Gerda a tip-off, cleverly organized, on where to obtain cannabis plants. And they have come to an arrangement.

Sometimes she brings in photos of the seedlings; photos which, of course, she can't pin up in the nurses' station. And sometimes she brings not just the photos, but a whole plant, which has shot up in no time. Then the Hippy offers me the resinous, multi-leaved opiate, grown in flowerpots in suburban Schwabing and fed with his cerebrospinal fluid, which I naturally decline, along with all the extracts from it.

'You know hash?'

'I know hash.'

'You know hash, *compañero*?'

I never answer questions that are asked more than once, and so after a while the Hippy says, 'Fancy a guy like you knowing hash!'

'What do you mean?'

'It's like me knowing Kaiser Wilhelm.'

A few days ago the Hippy and Night Nurse Gerda chewed some leaves together, almost ceremonially. It was two o'clock in the morning. Her heavy body swayed back and forth on his bed as she sat shoulder to shoulder with the Bourbon-like Hippy, and the squeaking sound kept me awake.

All the same, I must say: things could have been worse. Much worse. He could have been one of those crazy types who set fire to Frankfurt department stores and go on Vietnam protests and are anti everything. My shock-headed roommate isn't anti anything. Because being anti impairs being at one. He believes in goodness. Not in superiority, as ideologues do. But in goodness. Like Mahatma Gandhi.

His interest in my goodness isn't feigned, you can see that in all kinds of details. When I have visitors, for instance (he almost never has visitors), he listens wide-eyed to what is being said, even shuffling closer, like a pet, as if he's part of my story just because he happens to be in the next bed. I believe it's a hippy tradition to accept whatever beach fate washes you up on.

The Hippy simply can't believe his ears.

As soon as my visitor has gone, he asks me to explain everything, his eyes filled with impulsive emotion, a sentiment that is both broad and deep. He believes I deserve his sympathy for the projectile that I am carrying around inside me. It's under my skull, lodged in my cerebral cortex, that protoplasmic mass made up of countless millions of neurons. A medium calibre, 7.65 millimetre bullet; sometimes when I close my eyes I think I catch a glimpse of it. It bobs like a ship's hull in the ocean of my thoughts and memories. Doesn't sink. Doesn't hurt. Can't be salvaged.

Inoperable, the young registrar says. He's Greek, incidentally, and a little googly-eyed (as they say in Chiemgau). Be thankful it's 1974, Herr Solm. Three years ago, we wouldn't have been able to get the inflammation of the cerebral membrane under control.

Dr Papadopoulos is kind to me because he thinks I'm sad.

I must inform you, Ev, that I really have become a sad person. I think I am always sad, but not in a conscious way: great sadness has nothing to do with one's day-to-day condition, it doesn't cloud my mood; it lies miles below the surface, which means I always have the same cheerful demeanour, and I understand that you can't write to me, I do understand that. But I have to write to you, even though I'll probably never hear from you again, and at this moment, as I set down these words, I'm sure no one can see your silence in me.

I am all right, in any case.

I can talk, albeit rather slowly. At best, I just seem pensive. I can sit upright and am eating more sweet things than I used to. Pure sugar is my favourite, compressed into those little crystalline cubes that rumble like a storm over my inoperable shipwreck when I crunch them between my teeth. The bullet seems to have sent my taste receptors haywire. My left eye has lost four dioptres, but the right eye is fine, and I can read perfectly well, although I can no longer manage without glasses. Hardly surprising for a man in his mid-sixties. Unfortunately, I do need a crutch to walk and it takes me three minutes to get to the lavatory. Sometimes I talk about you, Ev. And when I talk about you, the Hippy forgets the babies screaming on the next floor down. But only for a brief moment – I never say more than necessary.

Whenever his condition permits, the young man wraps himself in his old, threadbare dressing gown. He pushes his feet into a pair of slippers that give him very little purchase on the floor, and shuffles down-stairs to the maternity ward. And there he pumps his heart full of the nameless life that bubbles out into the world day after day. Sometimes he tries to take me with him. But it wouldn't do anything for me. He loves looking into the bright terrariums where the maggot-babies lie with their shining halos of trust, love and hope. Most of the time he does nothing more than sit in the corridors, watching pregnant women puff and pant, and explaining his titanium screw to fathers who are interested in technology. Now and then he steals a few of the birth announcements pinned to the walls and brings them back up to our 'pad'. Then he either shows me the photographs of the mothers' faces, which he says remind him of orgies in the South of France – or he marvels at the babies' names.

'Max. How can you call a boy like that Max. How is that little lad supposed to become an individual? Doesn't he look fierce? Just look at that expression, like he's lying in wait. I'd call him "Wary". Don't you think?'

You can imagine how difficult it is for me to maintain my cheerful demeanour at such moments. How much my great sadness does affect my day-to-day condition after all. How close Anna feels. How present. Grief clasps me in her little fist.

The Hippy doesn't have any children. That pains him. And I don't say a word about what it's like to have had children. He doesn't think you can 'have' children at all. Or cufflinks. Things seek you out. Not the other way round.

If only we had named Anna 'Wary'.

*

The Hippy respects my sadness. The visits have enabled him to work some things out. Especially the visits from police officers. A few of the firm have been, as well. Even after all this time, there are still some trivial matters they want to ask me about. I thought people would let things lie.

But that's not how it is.

You haven't shown your face even once, Ev. I understand. No phone call. No letter. I understand. Who is it who knows the sound of your breathing now? Who lays his face on your body, on your collarbone, who counts your ribs, like I once did, do you remember? Do you remember, Ev? And now I come to the reason I am writing to you, the awful reason I have started this long letter.

Here it comes.

Because one day, as my bullet-dulled mind was busy wading around in old do-you-remembers, Hubsi suddenly appeared in the room.

You don't believe me.

At first I thought it was a memory that had materialized in front of me. That happens, sometimes. But it really was him, filling the whole doorframe in his bulky, wet trench coat. Water dripped from his hat, and it was only the small puddle forming on the floor beneath him that made me realize it was raining outside.

Since Hub was merely a silent, damp silhouette framed by the passepartout of the doorway, the Hippy sat up in bed and – using the informal '*du*' – asked him in friendly tones, 'Who are you looking for, *compañero*?'

You can't call Hubsi *compañero*. That is a thing of impossibility. You can't even call him Hubsi.

So he stuck his hands into his coat pockets – his hand, I mean. He only has one hand now, of course. I keep forgetting that. He didn't shift his weight towards us even a centimetre. He is still a proficient user of body language, a language the whole world understands. And he doesn't know how else to express himself, either.

'Koja,' he hissed, 'I'm sure you can't help the fact that you're sharing a room with such a person.' It was the voice that gave his presence the necessary depth and menace. 'But please make it clear to this long-haired ruffian what will happen to the pathetic remains of his pigtails if he says '*du*' to me one more time.'

I turned to my baffled roommate and told him what he needed to know about Hub and the intimate '*du*', and their relationship to one another.

'That's your brother?' In his shock, the Hippy forgot himself for a moment and used the polite form of address.

'Hubert Solm,' I nodded. 'Do not under any circumstances call him Hubsi.'

'No, no. I'll call him sir!'

Then we are alone, Sir Hub and me. We scuttle out into the hallway like two mutilated insects, towards a window as tall as we are. On the other side, silver threads of sleet form a curtain, turning the outside world into a blur like one of those modern carwashes. I don't take his remaining left arm, how could I, it has a hat and briefcase clamped under it. With my crutch, it takes forever to reach the billowing cold front of the window. Before it stands a small Formica table with some strawflowers on it. And a basket of hospital apples.

We sit down.

An amputee and a man with a bullet in his head. Together, our age amounts to over one hundred and thirty years. We have four legs, three arms and one woman. (It isn't just the fleeting nature of your existence that a hospital shows you, but the daily progress of the same; in dance-halls, for example, you don't notice how quickly you are deteriorating.)

Hub has been treated well, but he has come to visit now because his prison sentence is about to start. He still doesn't speak, and I don't know what to say, either. He swore he never wanted to see me again, but now he *is* seeing me, and he doesn't appear to like what he sees.

'I'm sorry about what happened to you,' he mutters.

'Just tell me what you want.'

'I'm sorry,' he repeats.

'Then why don't you look like you're the least bit sorry?'

'Your slate has been wiped clean now.'

'My slate has been wiped clean?'

'Don't twist my words.'

He hasn't changed a bit. He is coarse and self-righteous, a fossil of himself, from his petrified skull to the soles of his feet.

'All right,' he adds. 'You aren't twisting my words. But I know you will. You're going to twist them.'

'Fine,' I say.

'You've already won your victory, anyway.'

'Won? Look at me. Your friends shot me in the head.'

'They aren't my friends. They're your friends. And they're putting me behind bars, as well.'

Outside: drumming, thundering, burbling water; inside my head, silent halls stuffed with artworks – that museum in Syracuse, do you remember? The wonderful, violet peak of Etna, high above it all.

'How is Ev?' he says after a while, as if he can read my mind.

'She hasn't been to see me.'

'She will. She's won, too.'

'Did you come here to talk about winning?'

'I've always protected you, Koja. You were under my wing.'

'In your hands.'

'Under my wing. That's what it means to be family.'

He smiles, in that cold, gloomy way he has.

'But now it's all dirty. I'm dirty. You are. Our honour. Everything.'

'Our honour. Don't make me laugh. What honour do we have?'

'Loyalty.'

'Stop it.'

'*Our honour is called loyalty*. Isn't it?'

'You surely can't have come here to talk about the SS.'

'Do you remember that time we sat down with Heydrich in his office? Right at the beginning? He had a first-rate understanding of people. He could sniff out penetrating minds and strength of character.'

'Character, Hubsi?'

'Yes. Not really necessary in our profession, of course. But still. He told me later that he'd chosen you for your intelligence, not your character.'

'Evidently with you it was the other way round.'

His face keeps all emotion well below the surface. He refuses to take offence; not even his lips react. Despite the rain they are drying out, unmoving, like beached sea reptiles. He has grown old, old and grey, older and greyer than his sixty-nine years. But when he gets up, I see that he can still move as though he's in an arena. He bends down to his small, sodden briefcase, opens it with great dexterity (for a person with one arm) and pulls out a rust-brown A4 envelope. He places it carefully on the table in front of me and sits back down.

He sighs, his gaze falling on the envelope.

'Ev needs to know,' he says.

What does Ev need to know, Your Unbearableness, stop trying to be so interesting, stop sitting there like you did aged twelve with a frog in your lap, showing me how to inflate it.

I listen to the endless rain, at the same time still hearing the silence of Syracuse, which must be twenty years back now, ah, it was so lovely, and finally he says, 'I didn't show any of this to the court. It's no concern of theirs. But Ev needs to know.'

I haven't looked in the envelope, but I now know what it contains. And without a second thought, I take one of these red hospital apples out of the fruit bowl in front of me, an Edelborsdorfer, I think, some kind of Reinette in any case.

'Don't you dare,' Hubsi whispers, almost tenderly.

For those few seconds when I am rubbing the Reinette's shiny red skin, I can't help but think of you, Ev. I see you not as you were in Syracuse, but the way I saw you when we were children, a very thin little girl from the distant past, your sabre-toothed-tiger teeth biting into everything you set your sights on, including of course (like Snow White) the apple that was our family's Holy Grail. And once, biting into my arm, because I had caught you and was trying to tie you up: you were the robber and I was the policeman – and when, almost passing out from the pain, with you piercing my flesh like a moray eel, I told you not to bite so hard, you let go and said, with a laugh, But I'm a robber, and robbers can do whatever they like, and anyway your skin tastes funny, you should wash more often.

'Put that down,' my brother murmurs.

I don't put the apple down; I bite into it with the strength of a sabre-toothed tiger, and as I do I feel all the events and moments that make up my personal history come rushing down on me like the rain outside, like the rain of a real life, that is. My brother snatches the piece of fruit from my hand and hurls it away angrily, towards the vending machine, I think – my God – while uttering curses that relate to my impermissible consumption, and I don't know how long I have been sitting there, looking into the black slits of his hate-filled eyes, when the Hippy appears beside us and hands me back the bitten apple.

'What *is* this gentleman doing to you?'

I just shake my head violently – although of course I'm not allowed to shake it violently – unable to see anything through the curtain of my tears, and take a second bite out of the bruised fruit flesh.

'One more bite!' Hub threatens me.

'But why shouldn't your brother have an apple?' the Hippy wonders, and Hub barks that it's none of his business.

The Hippy refuses to back down. 'He needs vitamins.'

'Get out, quick march, back to your room!'

'This here is a place for wonderful people – so it might be best if you leave.'

Given that the Hippy isn't anti anything, he is worryingly anti Hub.

'Are you trying to say,' Hub asks scornfully, 'that I am not a wonderful person?'

'I am trying to say that you should go now, or something terrible will happen.'

'Oh yes? What terrible thing might that be?'

'I'll call Night Nurse Gerda.'

In the silence that descends, all you can hear are my jaws grinding, for I am gradually demolishing the whole damned apple, and my brother's rage swells with every bite.

'Listen to me, you little pansy,' Hub says to the Hippy. 'You need to have a think about the word "wonderful". A long, hard think about what the word "wonderful" has to do with people like this man here!'

'Your brother has good karma.'

'Karma? What's that supposed to mean?'

'And maybe I should think about the word "pansy" instead.'

'If by karma you mean the soul, the immortal soul suffused with the Holy Spirit: this man doesn't have one. He has no heart. He's a monster!'

'You really need to chill out, *compañero*!'

'Please, Basti, stay out of this,' I mutter anxiously, my mouth full, as my brother's fingers begin to twitch, even the ones that were blown off.

The Hippy has had enough; he does the breathing exercise that will allow him to break off all contact with Hub. He learned it in an ashram, where they also taught him to make bread out of stones. He closes his eyes, stands up straight and spreads his arms.

Hub stares at me, open-mouthed.

'Go ahead and show this lobotomized idiot the brown envelope. Show him just how "wonderful" you are.'

'Basti, please go back to the room. I'll be there in a minute, all right?'

'Oh yes, change the subject! You're changing the subject so you won't have to tell him you betrayed everything and everyone.'

The Hippy lowers his arms. 'And who exactly is my *compañero* supposed to have betrayed?'

'Yes, go on Koja, tell us: who did you betray?'

'The whole world.'

'The whole world?'

'In other words, everything and everyone.'

'I knew it!'

'What?'

'You're twisting them! You're twisting my words!'

'No, I'm just repeating your bloody words. I'm just telling you what you want to hear. The whole world is suffering because of me! Satisfied?'

'Yes, sarcasm is the only weapon you have left. But we fought for freedom and against the ultimate evil. We fought for the rights of an idiot like this to follow his Buddha and poison our children with drugs.'

'You are insulting, sir,' the Hippy objects.

'I speak the truth. That's all. I've only ever spoken the truth, and that's why I'm going to prison. You, Koja,' he says, turning to me, 'you lied and betrayed and sold out, and now the only thing people like this can see is your blank slate. You should be left to rot for it. You even betrayed Grandpaping.'

'That I did not do.'

'You betrayed nineteen-five.'

'I did not.'

'*Annus mirabilis!*'

'No!'

'You dare to scoff an apple in front of me, you bastard!'

'Stop it!'

'And you even betrayed your whore.'

He is so close to my face that I manage to strike him on the chin with my crutch – with a suddenness you might not expect from a cripple. It makes a crackling noise, quite soft, actually, like someone crushing dried flowers. He shouldn't have brought you into it. Not like that. He stumbles backwards, trips over the chair, throws his arm out, but not in the right direction, topples like a tree, hits the ground and stays lying crookedly by the glass pane, bent into an S-shape, rain falling at his back.

'Night Nurse,' I hear the Hippy's voice crying, but before it can add, 'Gerda!' Hub is back on his feet. He gives his arm a little shake, like an elephant shaking its trunk, and launches himself at me. I see the Hippy move into his path, his gestures urging non-violence, and then his head flies back, his beautiful Dürer head with the pallor of the 1498 oil portrait, and I think there's no way the titanium screw can survive this, and suddenly people appear – though they might have been there before, just waiting for a definitive signal, and in this place what could be more definitive than a patient with a brain injury shouting for help?

2

Although I find it easy to recognize her in the old photos – I just look for my own profile in hers, since we both have the same slightly unfortunate Roman nose that leans a little to the right – I can't imagine my mother as a young woman.

But she was still very young, and had already brought pathos to our family, when she came up with the red apple ceremony.

It was all because of nineteen-five and the teetering Russian Empire in which we grew up. My mother always said *annus mirabilis*. That's what nineteen-five was for her, and we never called it nineteen-o-five, because only Reich Germans said that. Time was always an organic thing for Mama, a thing with a will and an aim of its own, which could be good or evil, almost like a person. And in the eleventh year of the reign of His Most Awkward Majesty Tsar Nicholas II, any kind of order our homeland had known went up in smoke. Russia burned, from St Petersburg all the way to the most distant provinces.

The picturesque Baltics, my parents' home, were also torched by the revolutionaries. The Hippy doesn't know what the Baltics are or were, and I say: just imagine a watery Claude Lorrain sky – fine, you won't have heard of the painter, so let's not make it too complicated – a beautiful blue sky. Beneath it, a miniature edition of Canada, on the Baltic Sea, with endless wheat fields and large farms in the process of being abandoned by their fearful ranchers, who are fleeing in caleches and Sunday carriages, chased by the Vietcong. That's exactly what it felt like at the time. The rebellion was in full swing. The German estates all lay fallow. The Russian troops were off in Japan, busy losing an unlosable war. Latvian peasants marauded through the defenceless provinces, allying themselves with the poorest of the poor, surging onto land that belonged to the nobility, felling the trees, mowing their hay, storming the abandoned German manor houses and leaving heaps of dung on and under the oriental rugs.

Unlike the other pastors in his region, my grandfather, who was always known as Grandpaping, couldn't make the decision to flee. He would never have deserted the community entrusted to him by God – for then he would have been deserting God himself. This Grandpaping, Hubert Konstantin Solm (Huko to those who dared) is said to have been working happily in his fruit garden one warm August evening when a troop of bellowing scythe-wielders came marching towards him across the meadow.

This was a familiar sight. For months, his church had been afflicted with demonstrators from Riga almost every weekend. The strangers often forced their way into the house of God carrying red flags, drums and axes, and belted out 'The Internationale' in front of the altar. My Grandpaping would thank them for the lovely song and carry on quite impassively with his service. The Latvian peasants loved him because he could preach in their language and drove about the frothing provinces in his bone-shaking carriage and pair, refusing to let worldly imponderables keep him from his burying and mourning, comforting and admonishing, or from the obligatory come-again-soon tot of firewater.

Once, he calmly removed one of the revolutionaries' edicts from the church door and pinned it to the door of the pigsty; that was where it belonged, he said.

Grandpaping's portrait, done by my father two years before these events, used to hang above our dining table. It was a sombre picture in

pastels of an old man with bizarre side-whiskers. The balding head –
framed by this snow-white chin curtain – was topped with a little
pastor's cap. His features: the pale, arrogant ice-water eyes, the broad
cheekbones and the half-open, almost sensual mouth beneath his clean-
shaven upper lip, reminded me of the way Moses was depicted on page
54 of our Schnorr von Carolsfeld Bible: serious, brutish and ready to
bring Jericho's walls tumbling down at a moment's notice.

Beside the portrait hung the little sword that Grandpaping himself had forged and always wore under his cassock when he ascended
the pulpit. He didn't want them to take him alive (for 'take' he said
'kriech', in the East-Prussian-Yiddish dialect of my homeland), and
he once brandished this rusty home-made article at the revolutionaries
when they threatened to test their axes on the crucifix, as you might
ward off vampires with whittled birch stakes.

Grandpaping would certainly not have hesitated to ram the blade,
coram populo, into his own neck if anyone got too close to him or to
the crucified Christ. But a pastor's blood in the font wouldn't have
been a good advertisement for the revolution at that point, particularly
as Grandpaping would have made a bella figura as a martyr, of that I
am certain. It was from him that I inherited my dramatic talent, though
I have always lacked the defiant courage, the lonely loftiness, envers et
contre tout, that has remained so prevalent in our family and to this day
still causes endless misfortune.

Grandpaping's precaution – preaching the word of God with a
sword in his belt – was both grotesque and sensible. A revolver in his
belt would of course have been even more grotesque, and even more
sensible.

But when Grandpaping was standing in the violet glow of his garden
on that aforementioned summer evening, beside and beneath the fruit
trees, and saw the mob swarming towards him like a plague of mosquitoes, he had no weapon to hand but a basket of freshly picked red
apples. Svaigiaboli they are called in Latvian, what a lovely word.

Perhaps the situation might have ended differently if my grandfather had used that word, or some other from this rich, wonderful
language that knows no swear words, since 'black snake' is the worst
thing you can say to another person in Latvian. If my grandfather had
stayed quiet, humble and modest, if he had acceded to the delegation's

demands (which sounded almost like polite requests) with a show of humility – or at least, in the Latvian manner of speaking, accepted them as his inevitable fate, then who knows, perhaps everything might have been different.

But that was something his temperament did not permit.

He chose German, hissing out psalms that sounded like curses. And when the leader, spattered with the most improper parts of the Lutheran Gospels, lost his patience and demanded with a tiny pinch of surliness that Hubert Konstantin Solm give him the key to the sacristy, *nekavējoties! nekavējoties!*, the old man hurled an apple at him, a red autumn Calville, from three metres away. Which was really an astonishingly silly thing to do. But the lad ducked. The red autumn Calville flew past him and hit the girl standing behind him in the face, like a stone, breaking her little snubbed fifteen-year-old nose. Blood spurted onto her pinafore, or perhaps it was just the pink juice from the mashed fruit flesh.

All the same, one delicate girl's scream later they laid hands on him.

They kicked down Grandpaping's front door, and before his eyes they gathered up the pictures and sculptures of Jesus, the Bohemian crystal and the good English china, as well as the death masks of his two late wives from the parlour, and smashed them all to smithereens. Then they pushed the family grand piano, on which my father had first encountered Mozart and Chopin as a little boy, out onto the veranda and demolished it, sharing out the ivory keys among themselves. Once the considerable store of Bordeaux that had been discovered in our wine cellar had reduced everyone to gurgling hallelujahs, they devised a *sodīšana* for Huko, a very special *sodīšana*, which was to be less honourable than the ancient Roman suicide that his little sword might have effected.

At that time, my parents were living in Riga, in the heart of the art nouveau quarter. On Albertstraße, a brand-new street that was an operetta of architecture, entirely unique in Europe, Papa had rented an aria of a studio. The city's few military units were concentrated quite close by, to the west of the city pasture – most of them belonging to the listless infantry. This meant that the city, but especially Albertstraße, which was otherwise guarded only by French butlers and English pugs, was considered relatively safe despite the seething revolution.

Papa gave shelter to the relatives who had fled the countryside. Only Grandpaping demurred. He stayed where he was in Neugut, in the region of Courland, stubborn as his fruit trees and the only German for miles around. Papa sent letters with humorous illustrations, then telegrams that were at first cajoling and eventually desperate, delivered by world-weary postilions, begging Grandpaping to see sense and up sticks as soon as possible. But sense, as I have learned, cannot be got by begging, because fashion cannot be got by begging.

The fashion for cowardice, Grandpaping wrote back.

And so the old man not only ignored all calls for demission; he also assumed pastoral care of five other abandoned congregations in the area. The deserting shepherds of these flocks, having slunk back to their families in Riga, came to my father at regular intervals, pale with shame, to ask if all was well with Huko. Though asking if all was ill would have been nearer the mark, since this was, to put it mildly, something for which they ardently hoped.

When one of these hypocritical priests eventually told Papa that 'alas, alas, my dearrr man', a train had been derailed very close to his father's parsonage, the telephone masts chopped down and – 'you know, I hheeard it first hhand' – the police station attacked, Papa had the carriage brought round. He had resolved to go himself and fetch his stubborn father from where the uprisings were taking place, a mere fifty versts away.

But in the end my mother forbade it. Or rather, her condition forbade it. That summer she was nine months pregnant, and Mama's swelling body was quite a sight when she laid it across the street. Her husband, of course, did not dare storm such a barricade.

It was not that Mama would have felt defenceless without Papa; no, she was worried that without her supervision on such a dangerous journey he might get into terrible trouble. He was – and I suspect this was a side-effect of his artistic talent – a veritable magnet for debacles, fiascos, catastrophes and extraordinary complications (of which Mama herself was certainly the most extraordinary) – although ultimately he was still a man favoured by fortune, which is in no way a contradiction.

Every day, Mama took her globe of a belly on a walk to the market, past the public rallies held by the socialists, spooky, oil-flecked figures whose eyes wiped her and her spawn off the face of the earth: Anna

Marie Sybille Delphine Baroness von Schilling was born into the aristocracy, not just a lady but a m'lady who came into her dominion as an infant on a floating, moated castle near Reval. She was certainly no stranger to fear, though she was not accustomed to showing it. She could get extremely cross when people didn't know how to behave. But I never saw her in a state of panic. Panic simply was not proper.

She saw the Russian Revolution of nineteen-five as a lapse of human decency. She had the same degree of respect for radical political views as she had for rape or child murder. And so even as a foetus my brother was imprinted with his mother's rage against communist overthrows, which no hippy movement in the world will ever dispel, my dear pacifist roommate.

I know how interested you are in births of all kinds. But the notable thing about my brother's birth was that it happened in the midst of chaos and hysteria. It was really more of an emanation than a birth, since it took place on the same evening and even at the same hour that our grandfather was lost to this world. Buddhists like you would call such a thing reincarnation, and perhaps as my brother was pushed along the birth canal he really did feel the torment of his luminous Grandpaping, who was just then awaiting his fate, half a day's ride away.

They kept the German preacher locked up in his own church for two hours so that he could watch from the sacristy, champing with rage, as the parsonage that had survived four generations went up in flames. Then they meted out a punishment reserved for the priesthood, which requires nothing more than a nearby pond, an empty potato sack and an expectant audience. All these were present, and so they fetched the roaring Huko from his church, cut off his beard and forced him to eat the red autumn Calville with which he had committed his outrage. In contempt, he spat the raspberry-coloured flesh – a pomological curiosity – at the red flag which had been planted on his land and was now fluttering just a couple of feet away.

Then his hands were tied, and they pulled the sack over his head and bound it to his ankles. Finally a local farrier, who would be hanged for it a year later, lifted the helpless, struggling bundle into the air and threw it into the parsonage pond. The Latvian onlookers applauded as the absence of divine intervention became starkly evident. Particularly unexpected were the high-pitched screams that could be heard from the floundering sack, which continued for some time: the drowning process kept being interrupted so that no one would miss anything.

It was only the next morning that the body was recovered.

My grandfather's Russian housekeeper Anna Ivanovna, with whom he had lived (occasioning much gossip) since the death of his second wife, took off her outer clothes, swam across to him in the dawn light and pulled the dead man, on whom apparently a frog was sitting, back to the bank by his bare foot, which was protruding from the water. Later she became our Mary Poppins and our childhood governess, and she told us how the villagers gathered silently around the wet, jute-wrapped body as people might around a stranded whale, and wept bitterly over it. For half a century, Hubert Konstantin Solm had presided over baptisms and weddings, births and deaths, the first prayer and the last rites in his village. Even to those who had hollered for it the previous evening, his fate was an incomprehensible thing.

For my brother and me, his end marked the beginning, the Archimedean point of our world. Nothing that would happen in later years can be judged or even contemplated without the apple thrown in rage, the house in flames, the red flag spat upon and the corpse drying beside the pond.

The whole world changed for my parents, becoming an Armageddon of pain and guilt. Even when my father was close to death (tolerating the life around him, but unable to participate in it), he was still reproaching himself for that long-ago omission; you could see it in his eyes.

There was really no choice but to give my brother the best of all names: that of the grandfather so magnificently reincarnated in him.

Hubert.

I was given the second best.

Konstantin.

And in this way, our relationship was fixed for a long time.

Which is not to say that he was first and I was second. Let me rephrase that: he was the first and I the last; he the good luck and I the bad; he cosseted by fortune and I struck down by fate; he loved by Mama and I dropped on the marble floor by her three days after my birth (leaving me with a slightly damaged hip that is not making my current learning-to-walk-again situation any easier). No, it's nothing, I'm just moaning or being silly. But one thing is true: the stars were aligned quite differently for Hubert and Konstantin, even when they were still Hubsi and Koja. I was born neither on the day of my grandfather's death, nor on his birthday. It was not a Sunday, a holiday, or a day that had some significance for my family. I was not even an August or December Solm like two thirds of my relations, who came into the world almost exclusively in these two months.

When we were small, my brother always needled me about the meaningless timing of my arrival in the world. Yes, we even came to blows once, and I lost of course, four years weaker than he was.

And yet there was not the least reason to be glad at having been born in the *annus mirabilis*, that holy terror of a year. Is it really a desirable thing to celebrate your birthday on the day when, as soon as the presents have been opened, everyone has to go to the graveyard and weep bitter tears? Every second year it was also the day of the martyrs' memorial service in St Petri, for all the priests of Latvia's Lutheran Church who died at the hands of the Bolsheviks. Hub had to stand at the front by the altar for hours holding a fat white candle that symbolized the light of Grandpaping's life.

When I was once allowed to take over this honour, I accidentally blew out the flame, then got a desperate fit of the giggles because the bishop had a love bite on his neck, at least according to Baron Hase (known to us for obvious reasons as Spotty Hase), who was standing beside me with his candle, quaking with hiccups. No, I never really wished I'd been born on such a day.

I was actually very glad that my inevitable anniversary belonged to me alone: it was the ninth of November when a storm caused my mother's waters to break two weeks early and I became her second son. On the calendar, the ninth of November was a very insignificant day, quite suited to my needs. Grey. Underestimated. Open to interpretation.

That did not change until nineteen-eighteen. In the final months of a year that was so significant for Europe's fortunes, Riga was already (or perhaps one should say: still) occupied by the Reichswehr, and was in effect no longer Russian territory. In the evening, as we were running sack races – sack-racing was another thing strictly prohibited on Hubsi's birthday because of its dreadful potato-sack associations, and we could hardly go swimming on such a day, either – as we were hopping around the living room like kangaroos, then, Papa's cousin who worked for the *Rigaer Rundschau* dropped by, having raced over to tell us that Kaiser Wilhelm of Germany had abdicated early that morning and a republic had been declared in Berlin. Hubsi latched on to this straight away: 'A great man died on my birthday,' he whispered to me as we lay in our beds. 'But a whole country kicked the bucket on yours.'

I wept a great deal, for by this time we were committed Germans. We had long since stopped loving Russia. After the Revolution was defeated, from nineteen-six onwards, Mama and Papa had gone back to living a very grand life. My early memories are of overloaded interiors, rooms stuffed full of cushions, a silver Russian samovar, with which I once only half accidentally scalded our cocker spaniel Puppi – one of my many mishaps. We were coddled by three serving Annas: Kibbi-Anna (our nursery maid), Kocka-Anna (a fat cook), and our beloved Anna Ivanovna. She was always singing the praises of our Grand-paping, the tragic saint with whom it was said she'd had a dissolute arrangement, though Mama was furious whenever Papa hinted at this, with a wink that said it wasn't really all that bad.

Mama did think it was bad – but then, she thirsted for panegyric, for ceremonial glorification. And so the red autumn Calville became the family sacrament, the *magnum mysterium* of my early childhood. Mama instructed Anna Ivanovna that we were to treat the red autumn Calville as the Catholics treat their host. My father, however, refused to eat the body of Grandpaping, and did not appreciate Mama's papist leanings (though of course I certainly don't mean to, how shall I put it, denigrate the beliefs of your Chiemgau home, my dear Hippy).

There was a set ritual for the way we sons had to consume an apple – no, each and every apple we ate. It would be cut down the middle, and while this cut was being made it was important that we stood in abso-lute, respectful silence, thinking very hard about Grandpaping – for which reason I often used to cry as a small child when the apartment smelled of baked apples. Afterwards, the two halves were ceremoni-ously handed to Hubsi and me. We were never allowed to throw away the core; we had to polish off every last bit, including the stalk and all the little pips that tasted of marzipan, in honour and remembrance of

Grandpaping. Before we were allowed to bite into the apple, we had to cross ourselves, although Mama wouldn't let us call it 'crossing ourselves' (Protestants don't cross themselves, they make the sign of the cross). At the bottom of her heart, Mama was a good Lutheran, but she had her superstitious side just as Luther did; he believed you could chase away the devil by farting. We were not allowed to tell Papa, but before the eating of the apple she made us murmur, 'Hosanna in the highest', which in later years was reduced to nothing more than a garbled 'Anna', much to Anna Ivanovna's delight.

One crucial precondition for the sacred repast was high moral integrity; any fibbing, stealing, waywardness or dilly-dallying would lose you your apple privileges. Mama was unyielding on this matter.

Since the red autumn Calville ritual was carried over not only to every kind of apple known to man, but also to the products made out of them, we had to treat apple cake, apple compote, apple juice, cider, and even the apple-scented hand soap that Mama so loved to buy with the same religious reverence. We even had to make the sign of the cross before our first Calvados. As Mama felt an affinity with the French cultural milieu, she initially considered giving the same ceremonial treatment to potatoes, which of course are *pommes de terre*, and were also known as 'earth apples' in our Baltic German. This consecration would have made potato soup, roast potatoes, the then unknown *pommes frites*, croquettes and of course potato pancakes (with sacrosanct apple compote) into liturgical fare as well. It would also have elevated potato-starch products like ethanol or paper to the status of devotional objects. To take the process to its logical conclusion, every newspaper would contain a bit of red autumn Calville.

Papa found it all terribly fanciful and told Mama she was merely using this semi-Catholic circus to try to compensate for the guilt she felt at having thwarted Grandpaping's rescue so theatrically.

Doors were often slammed.

But then, we had plenty of them.

All the same, for Hubsi and me the apple always remained the symbol of our unwavering intimacy. When we finally became inseparable – he the strong, dauntless hero of my childhood, who always managed to rescue me; I his rather chubby Sancho Panza – we got into the habit, after winning a playground fight or dancing with girls at a school rub, of slaying an apple together, as we called it. The apple of honour and loyalty and of time and eternity.

Anna Ivanovna encouraged us in everything that kept Grandpaping in the collective memory. From the way she looked at us, I could tell that she had loved him very much; she searched for him in our features. She moulded us with her dramatic disposition, her large bosom and her laughter. She really did laugh as loudly as a muzhik, and used the formal mode of address with the droshky drivers for some unfathomable reason, which no one else in the whole of Riga did. Even thirty years later, when she was on her deathbed, we still had to call her Mademoiselle: she spoke excellent French.

But most importantly, she taught us Russian, for we were to be prepared for careers at the Tsar's court, following in the footsteps of Mama's ancestors, who had made names for themselves in St Petersburg as admirals, generals and illustrious diplomats.

Mama's father was not commemorated in our household as Grandpaping was, with apples, or even with reverence, in fact not at all. He had made the error of falling victim to fish poisoning just a few months after Mama's birth, on his first (and last) visit to the Orient – together with his wife Clementine (née von Üxküll), my grandmother, who didn't even like fish, but had tasted his spoiled Nile perch out of misplaced loyalty to her husband. Their daughter (my mamushka), left behind in Reval at six months old and fed by a Latvian wet nurse, was brought up by her grandfather, whom we all called Opapabaron (though Great-opapabaron would have been more accurate).

Opapabaron, whose real name was Friedrich Baron von Schilling, had been born during the Napoleonic wars and had circumnavigated the globe several times as an admiral. The stories he told my mother, his granddaughter, of gliding blissfully along under sails swelled by the warm trade winds, had been so vivid that she in turn was able to conjure up for us the glow of the sea, the swarms of flying fish, an attacking sperm whale, contrary storms and waves as high as mountains – and for a long time Hubsi and I thought that she herself was an admiral (she behaved like one, too).

Opapabaron had brought back all manner of souvenirs from his voyages as a ship's captain and explorer: the scalp of a Tlingit chief, for example, which was kept in our good drawer along with other precious things, and felt like a bicycle inner tube on the side without the hair. Or a shred of skin from a brontosaurus, which he had found at the foot of a volcano in icy Kamchatka and which hung on the wall beside Grandpaping's sword.

There were two animal species that had shaped Opapabaron's fate: he had the mammoths to thank for dying in Siberia, where their cadavers were preserved for ten thousand years under layers of snow (which is why he received the imperial commission to hack them out of the permafrost in search of their ivory). And sea otters took him and his wife Anna (née von Montferrant), who was ten years his junior, to Alaska, where as governor he was tasked with securing millions of sea otter pelts for the Russian crown and protecting them from Indian raids. He was quickly promoted to admiral and became a close political adviser to the Tsar, though his advising consisted first and foremost of playing bridge with His Majesty.

Mama knew the Romanovs too, of course.

At the age of ten, she was walking in the park of Tsarskoye Selo with her grandfather when they bumped into the Tsar and Tsarina. She was introduced to them by the now shrunken-headed Opapabaron, made a nice curtsy as her heart beat wildly, and received an invitation to come and delight the princesses with her unusual liveliness. Mama had kept a snow-white Arctic fox muff from that time, a very impractical winter fur for young ladies, useful only for putting one's hands in from either side and standing around with nothing to do. To increase its elegance, the animal's head and paws had been left on the pelt, so that from above the corpse of an Arctic fox seemed to look at you rather reproachfully with its dull eyes. We always used the muff as the big bad wolf in our puppet theatre, though it had been a gift to my mother from Xenia, the Tsar's daughter, who was her own age and had spent two days playing with her in Gatchina Palace during the winter of eighteen eighty-five.

It is quite astonishing that Mama was able to wrest permission from the proudly aristocratic Opapabaron to marry a bourgeois drifter and have-not like my father, who had nothing better to do than become a painter, much to the disappointment of both my quasi-grandfathers. While one thought it wasn't a proper job, the other didn't consider anything a proper job (because normal people had huge tracts of land and captain's licences, not *jobs*). Opapabaron was horrified. Grandpaping went so far as to consider disinheriting my father. To his mind, Papa had been born primarily to take over his father's ministry and with it the saffron-yellow village church where four generations of my family had preached on a hereditary lease since the time of Catherine the Great. The Solms were the Windsors of the Baltic German clergy, one might say.

And yet my papa, Theo Johannes Ottokar Solm, who had a life ready-made for him in the remotest parts of rural Latvia and was Grandpaping's contribution to shaping the world according to God's wishes, refused to be guided by these wishes. He had his own: a desire for artistic expression, for instance. The desire for a variety of sexual adventures (which was to be more than fulfilled on his painting trips to the Mediterranean). The desire for psychographic experiences. For happenstance. Beauty. And, for lack of any tyrannical qualities, a strong desire not to become a pastor.

Although I might be giving the impression here that Papa was particularly strong-willed, that was never really the case. He was only able to desire things, not will them into being. All the same, he saw the death of his mother (Huko's first wife) from meningitis as an opportunity to escape to Berlin on his modest inheritance, despite his father's fury, and to study painting at the Academy of Arts there. Having passed his diploma with the highest honours, he instructed two members of the Hohenzollern dynasty in life drawing (first getting a waft of imperial favour as he knelt before them, then a little bohemian air as he knelt before others) and finally, following trips to Rome and Florence to further his education, returning to the Baltics and Gut Stackelberg, where he became my mother's very worldly drawing teacher.

Mama quickly fell in love with his serenity and his easy manner. She worshipped his posture, which was very proud and upright as the result of a spinal injury from a riding accident in his youth. She was infatuated with his age – he was twelve years her senior – perhaps also with his charming, irresistible and often entertaining indecisiveness, most certainly with his artistic talent, which was prodigious, even by a European standard, and not least, of course, with his occasional soft, velvet-black periods of depression.

Without question, he could have achieved more in the art world. But Faustian striving was foreign to him, and the poverty that went hand in hand with the quest for personal expression held no attraction. Under constant pressure from both my quasi-grandfathers to justify himself, he longed for social recognition first and foremost. And so he finally settled on portrait painting, the least rewarding genre artistically and the most rewarding financially, as well as the most socially acceptable. I, too, would one day learn to love it. And through her contacts, Mama persuaded half the nobility of the Russian provinces on the Baltic Sea to sit for him.

But that was all over in nineteen-eighteen, which was no *annus mirabilis*; it was an *annus horribilis*.

I still have a clear memory of that October day when a short-statured count came into my father's studio. He went straight to his half-finished portrait which, because Papa always left the hair until last, still looked bald and defenceless, cut it off the stretcher with a little knife, rolled up the canvas and, with the words, 'Ey'm afraid we haff to flee, deear boy,' hurried back out past my deathly-pale father, leaving behind just a fraction of the agreed price. The aristocracy no longer needed distractions; they needed passage on a ship. The Tsar had been executed by firing squad. Blue-bloodedness was a deadly disease and Germany, which had annexed the Baltics, looked like it was about to lose the war.

In Moscow, Lenin had taken power and his armies were making inroads into our blessed little country – though believe me, I don't intend to bore you with general knowledge. One thing must be said, however: the trauma we had felt in nineteen-five seemed to be repeating itself. Now, though, it was many times more potent.

For as the last of the occupying German troops withdrew on New Year's Day nineteen-nineteen, and the Bolsheviks marched on Riga with a huge bow wave of refugees and terrible rumours surging ahead of them, Papa spent a long time standing in the living room in front of the pastel of our drowned Grandpaping, slapping himself on the forehead again and again and finally deciding to put a bullet there – but not before he had put bullets in the neatly combed heads of his two sons.

Mama was not there; she had joined the desperate crowds fleeing on the few available British steamers, whose crews were already stoking their boilers in the harbour. Using all his savings and despite her protests and fits of weeping, Papa had managed to secure her an iniquitously expensive diplomatic ticket and an even more expensive British exit visa. She was the daughter of a baron, and could not be allowed to fall into the hands of the Reds. Yes, the atmosphere was something like it was last week in Saigon. We watched it on the news, downstairs in the television room, do you remember, my dear young friend? Those people trembling with fear as they packed their suitcases, with the Vietcong at the gates, and the newspapers can say what they like, everyone knows the city is about to fall. That's how my parents felt on New Year's Day nineteen-nineteen, when they had to say goodbye, because the Lord may have parted the Red Sea for Moses, but he did not part the Baltic for Theo Solm.

Papa wrote Mama a letter of farewell (which was a fruitless exercise, strictly speaking, in the absence of any way to post it), had a final shave, checked his gun and called us into his studio. He beckoned my big brother to him first, and Hub glowed so fiercely in the light of the January sun shining across the rooftops, a golden meteor, at once there in the room and burning itself out somewhere in the universe, that my father sank into a chair, his courage gone.

'What are you doing with the pistol, Papa?' Hubsi asked.

'I don't want them to take us, darling boy.'

He said '*kriechen*', just as Grandpaping once had.

'*Cher Papa*, Koja is still so little.'

My father looked over at me. I really was still so little, I had just turned nine, a boy with a slight limp who loved to play with puppets, and I set Mama's muff, the wolf, down on the floor.

'Come here, Koja, go to Papa and hold his hand.'

Even then, my brother had great power over me, and at that moment he looked wonderful, serious and smiling at once, like an adult, while my father was a mere dragonfly. I stumbled eagerly over to hold his hand, so that he wouldn't fly away on the quivering dragonfly wings that were his eyelids.

'What's all this in aid of?' Papa asked sullenly, irritated by the unmanliness of my behaviour.

'I think he has an Attic influence on other people,' my brother explained cryptically (probably meaning the Periclean age), and I watched Papa, already under my Attic influence, gradually crumple. He pressed his thumb and forefinger against the dragonfly wings over his eyes as he amended his plan, deciding to carry out only the final part, the third (if you count in bullets).

He had never been a manly man, not nearly so manly as Mama, and a few years later he dressed up in women's clothes in his studio – to make sure his feminine side would not fall short, either, as he told Hubsi after the latter opened the door when he'd been told not to and caught Papa in a chiffon dress. But that time Papa was in a different mood, with no intention of killing himself.

'You must look after him, Hubsi,' Papa said, pushing my hand aside gently with the barrel of the pistol, cocking it and preparing himself.

'But, Papa, aren't *you* going to look after us?' my brother asked softly.

We could hear people shouting and screaming outside, the Bolsheviks were only fifty kilometres from the city limits now, the British ships were blowing their horns in the harbour, and as so often happened, Papa couldn't decide. He pressed the loaded and cocked pistol into Hubsi's hand and walked away to paint a hyacinth.

Ultimately, my mother's return took us back to square one.

She was overcome by a terrible fit of anxiety (the kind of anxiety that caused her to hit a sailor in the face as he was taking her below decks, much to his astonishment), managed at the last second to leave the steamer that would save her, and ran through the seething, wailing, weeping crowds that stank of fear and time, back to her doom, to her children whom she simply could not leave, but above all to her husband, who had an overactive imagination, *quod erat demonstrandum*.

A few days later, Hubsi and I were out with a sledge, hoping to scavenge some cabbages that we'd heard about from a cellar somewhere, when we ran into a gang of Red cavalrymen. They came from the direction of the racecourse, an ice-grey bank of cloud looming over them, beneath which they trotted towards us on their shaggy little steeds, their weapons the only thing that identified them as soldiers. One grey pony had a rolled-up rug slung over its back, but as it came swaying towards us the rug was revealed to be a corpse wrapped in a green tarpaulin, identifiable only by a pair of dangling boots. One of the boots was torn open, and I saw blood trickling out onto the snow, drawing a thin line that froze instantly.

One of the riders grinned and waved at us, and I raised my hand in return, a reflex for which my brother punished me with a week of contemptuous silence.

The death mill began to grind that same day. In the blink of an eye,

Mama and Papa and Hubsi and I, and Anna Ivanovna and almost all our friends and acquaintances became satanic vermin, insects to be wiped off the face of the earth.

Baron Hase, the mischievous Spotty Hase, was one of the first to prove this, when he made an overly loud joke at school – not about the Bishop's love bite this time, but about the visage of our comrade headmaster. The authorities decided to spare the fourteen-and-a-half-year-old this unedifying sight in future by considerately executing him. Revolutionary tribunals were working hard, firing squads too, proscription lists were going around, and it seemed only a matter of time before they knocked on our door.

Papa almost fainted when, on top of this, Mama forced him to hide some of her aristocratic relatives in the apartment – the ones for whom arrest warrants had been issued – while they grew their beards in order to pass through the front unrecognized. Beards take time. If anyone finds them here, said Papa, then *finita la commedia*.

The Cheka had set up their office in nearby Schützenstraße, and in its cellar resourceful Mongols flayed the skin of imprisoned aristocrats from their wrists down to the nail of their little finger, a unique feature of these interrogations.

Hunger was then added to the immediate terror, as the food supply lines had broken down. Every day I saw snow-covered human bundles lying on the streets and in entryways, starved or freshly frozen, fingers clutching at their final dreams. An extremely cold winter swept through the country. In order to survive, Papa claimed to be a medical orderly, though he couldn't stand the sight of blood. He was permitted to work for a doctor friend of his in a Red Army field hospital, where he fainted all the time, but still brought home a few roubles now and then. Otherwise we lived off stolen potatoes and potato peelings, and Mama was very glad that the consumption of potatoes did not require any ceremonial offices in honour of Grandpaping.

When our neighbours were arrested and then hanged a few days later, Hubsi and I broke into their flat via the balcony and found a barrel of salted mushrooms in the kitchen. It became the main source of our sparse protein intake, and without a doubt saved our own lives and those of the very slowly growing Beards.

Then the shortages took on unbearable forms.

*

On one of those days, which to us as children seemed colourful and strange, and also unpleasant because of the constant hunger and all the corpses – but not truly threatening, because *we* would never die – Anna Ivanovna arrived at our door accompanied by a visibly distressed, bearded Russian named Vladimir, who was leading a child by the hand. Anna Ivanovna, tears running down her cheeks, talked insistently to Mama while Papa sat in the armchair, recovering from having amputated a completely healthy leg in error. It was a Bolshevik leg of course, and – as the Beards who were clustered in the kitchen assured him – this act ought to be regarded as God's work, since the leg might have gone on to do even greater injury to civilized people.

That evening, Mama swept into our room and told us that our household had a new member. It was the child I had seen that morning, a little girl, thin, with watchful, coal-black eyes that never seemed to blink and scrutinized everything around her with both frightening intensity and a remarkable ease.

Hubsi had to move out of the bed that we shared now that all the other beds, sofas and divans had been claimed by our aristocratic guests. Mama decided that it would not be improper to let me and *la petite* 'bunk' together, since my young age, my girlish features, and the fact that I was a courteous and (most importantly) an unassertive young man meant that I would not commit the sort of improprieties she already expected from Hubsi – particularly since his tongue was similar to Grandpaping's, as Anna Ivanovna had incautiously remarked. He was banished to the hallway, where the general snoring made sleep almost impossible.

La petite slipped into bed with me. I marvelled at how similar the size of her body was to that of Puppi, our tiny spaniel who now ate only rats. She received a goodnight kiss from Mama and then lay motionless beside me. She wasn't at all tense, and I could feel the warmth of her skin under the covers. Her hair smelled of camomile.

'You have a lovely bed.'
'Thank you.'
'You're welcome.'
'Who are you, then?'
'Eva. But you can call me Ev.'
'I'm Koja.'

'May I pee in your pot, please, Koja?'

Her foot brushed against mine.

'You can go and use the lavatory if you like,' I suggested. 'It's still early.'

'But then I'll have to walk past all these people I don't know.'

'Oh, I see.'

'I think you're nice.'

'Thank you.'

'So can I pee in your pot?'

'Yes, of course.'

She got up and sat on the pot in front of me – I had no idea you *could* sit on it. I sucked in my cheeks, studied the pattern on the wallpaper and wondered where she might be looking. When she had finished, she slid the pot alongside the bed.

'You have to put it underneath,' I explained.

'Yes, in a minute,' she said, 'but it's your turn now.'

'I don't need to go.'

'Nor did I. I just wanted to see if I could trust you.'

I was incapable of saying anything. She smelled like a chemist's; it wasn't just the camomile in which her hair had obviously been washed, but also the fresh, astringent scent of urine rising from the floor.

'I think I can trust you. You looked away the whole time. You're a gentleman.'

'I'm definitely not having a pee.'

'But *I* did.'

'Yes, but you can sit down, and your nightshirt stops anyone seeing anything. I have to hold the pot up, and you'll be able to see everything.'

'I'll look the other way, like you did.'

'But you'll still hear me.'

'I can put my hands over my ears.'

'So what's the point?'

'Then we'll be brother and sister.'

And so Eva, known as Ev, became part of our family, wafted to us on the madness of the moment. Her parents, a German doctor and his sick wife, refugees from Dünaburg, had been arrested by the Cheka without any stated reason and executed the following day. Her father had hidden little Eva along with two sausages in a secret cubbyhole, just in time, before the Cheka's henchmen broke down his front door.

A while later she was found by their Russian manservant, a cousin of Anna Ivanovna's. He had a second key to the apartment and his heart was in the right place. First, he took the girl home and hid her there, but when he learned of his master's death he knew he had to act. A German-speaking child in a Russian servant's family was an indication of counter-revolutionary activities that could cost them their lives. Added to which, Vladimir was struggling to feed *la petite* in the midst of the famine. What could have been more obvious than to turn to his resourceful and charitable cousin Anna Ivanovna? And she decided – having wrongly assumed that a baroness like Anna Marie must still possess some remnants of her former wealth – to ask us for help.

'The girl is an angelka,' Anna Ivanovna swore to my mother in her heart-melting dialect. 'She cared for her mamushka, her poor mamushka, as you care for a sick pony – her mamushka had the nerves and the despair' – but probably cancer, my father said – 'and she washed her mamushka every day, washed away the slime and dried her' – cleaned the shit off her, my father said – 'and instructed she was by her poor papashka, who was a doctor with a very full sick room always' – I don't know him, my father said – 'and then the Cheka came for him – him and his sick, sick lastatshka – and they brought her out in a wheelchair and for her probably the bullet was a release, but oh God, little Eva heeared it all. Isn't she just good enough to eat? And she is a lovely dancer, too.'

Ev's relationship to the weed-like functions of the body (as Papa disparagingly called them) was shaped by an unusual empathy, perhaps because medicine was in her blood; it certainly wasn't in mine and Hubsi's, to say nothing of Papa. I could well imagine the complete lack of disgust with which she had cared for her mother.

From the very first, people succumbed to her; she simply conquered them with her direct and largely unafraid manner, and her eyes that took wing like ravens. This was her only chance of survival, and she fought for love like a wild beast. We liked each other from the beginning, and on only her second evening with us she put an arm around my shoulder and told me I had lessened her loneliness. We always prayed to God in Heaven and then peed together, and she decided she didn't want to be an orphan any more, but a real Solm.

She even brought a secret language into my previously colourless life. As we were consuming our daily portion of three mushrooms, which tasted of old aspic, and I complained of my ravenous hunger, she pulled a piece of mouldy bread that she had begged from the Red Army soldiers out of her jacket. She gave me half and whispered with a smile, so that no one else could hear, 'It isn't much, but *a bisl un a bisl – vert a fule shisl!'*

I was shocked. Among genteel Baltic German children like us, knowing Yiddish was frowned upon. It was the vagrant language of Riga's street urchins, a language that Mama loathed even more than Latvian, just as she loathed the Jews even more than the Latvians, who at least had the decency to leave the beautiful family of Germanic languages alone.

'*Bistu a yid?*' I exclaimed in my bad street-Yiddish.

'*Bistu a goy?*' she laughed brightly, a laugh like the smallest bell of St Petri. I can still hear it today, the way she squeaked a little coloratura into the '*goy*', using all her charm to soften the question about my idiocy. And then she said, in the best High German of a Dünaburg surgeon's daughter, 'That's how I used to talk to all my girlfriends when there were no adults around. Shall I teach you, Koja?'

And so she taught Koja the language of her girlfriends, and instead of being horrified, I enjoyed stepping into the realm of the forbidden and the feminine with her, and when we were in high spirits, we prayed like street-rats, reciting the words from the start of Genesis, when *in onheyb hot got bashafn dem himl un di erd. Un di erd is geven vist un leydik, un finsternish is geven oyfn gezikht fun thom, un der gayst fun got hot geshvebt oyfn gezikht fun di vasern.*

If anyone had heard us in those days, if anyone had realized the progress I was making in this joyful carnival language, if one of the Beards had believed what he was hearing (for sometimes, as we were whispering, we would attract uncomprehending looks), Ev would have had to pack her three or four things and leave (she owned a few clothes and a silver Jesus on a little chain, that was all). Mama and Papa and Hubsi – who was fed up of sleeping on the floor beside one of the snoring Beards and wanted his bed back – had already begun to feel

quite resentful towards our little guest. They came up with all kinds
of objections and pretexts, of which the material ones of course held
the greatest sway. I myself pestered my parents to be allowed to keep
Ev, the way some children beg for a little dog. Ev seemed to have no
blood relations, and Dünaburg, where she came from, was impossible
to reach because volunteer militias had formed there in an attempt to
liberate the city from the Soviets.

But even after the Baltic Army retook Riga in the bloody battle of
May nineteen-nineteen, we were still none the wiser about Ev's background. In all the confusion of that troubled spring, there was nothing
unusual about people who had been uprooted and scattered far from
all certainties.

After five years of war, Latvia was a picture of destruction. Whole
stretches of it were depopulated. The loss of inhabitants took on
Carthaginian dimensions, particularly in relation to the size of the
country – its small size, that is. People in Europe knew hardly anything
about this ravaged Lilliput, in which we Germans felt like a little gang
of Gullivers – and I see from your face, my cataleptic friend, that you
know nothing about it, either. And yet after the war, forces began to
develop there that have persisted to this day. Because everything you
see on television at the moment – Gerald Ford's cowardice, Brezhnev's
forward surge, Mao's Cultural Revolution, Ho Chi Minh's legacy and
so on and so on – to this day all these things are supervised or opposed,
furthered or undermined, but above all, investigated, by a few of these
Baltic German Gullivers.

We hated this new state, the Latvian Republic. And the Republic
hated us. The Lilliputians condemned Gulliver to death (for urinating
in public) and then planned to blind him instead and let him slowly
languish, and that was exactly how the Latvians treated us. We were
meant to gradually starve and die of thirst.

When the Latvian State came into being in nineteen-twenty, Mama's
family were forcibly dispossessed. Their lands, an area the size of
Andorra, were distributed among two thousand delighted Latvian
farmers. Opapabaron's moated castle became a boarding school. Many
Sirs and Excellencies emigrated.

Papa ran out of solvent customers for his portraits, and my parents were struck down as if by lightning. The Solm family, there is no other way to put it, became desperately poor. 'Poor as a church mouse,' Papa always said, with a strange satisfaction in his voice, as if a church mouse were still a nice creature, pious, offering unconditional solidarity. We could no longer afford servants. Mama, who had never washed a plate or ironed a shirt in her life, doggedly learned the necessary skills, even trying her hand at cooking, when there was anything to cook. But even stinging nettles can be prepared in a palatable or less palatable way. Mama's always tasted freshly picked.

I must say: the war, the Revolution, Bolshevism, the founding of the Latvian State and the demise of my social class brought very little that was positive for me personally. The only thing in which I whole-heartedly supported the Latvian Republic was its new and extremely laissez-faire rules on adoption. Essentially, any child found looking confused and abandoned could be snatched off the street and claimed by a family as their own. The country needed all the workers it could get. And thus we were permitted – without any bureaucratic compli-cations, since not a single one of Ev's relatives could be traced in the devastated city of Dünaburg – to turn our little wartime visitor into a kind of Fräulein Solm. My brand-new sister, this girl with her three summer dresses and her silver Jesus and her fondness for forbidden things and proscribed languages.

It was not only her tragic lot as an orphan that convinced my par-ents to feed another mouth despite their own misery. Ev also had an instinct for making herself indispensable. She was very down to earth, and never complained. And she brought with her skills that a little girl from a good family really should not have had. She even knew how to use a sewing machine, and made terrible suits for Hubsi and me out of the good living-room curtains. She taught Mama what a flat seam was and a chain stitch. And for Christmas nineteen-twenty, she made me some new, white winter boots out of my mother's Arctic fox fur. They looked rather peculiar, like giant snowballs, and I was teased at school over them. But it was better than walking barefoot through the snow, and I still have them today. I kept them with me through all the wars and expulsions, through terror, mass murder and dictatorship, and I particularly love the shaft of the left boot, to which an Arctic fox paw is still attached.

Ev was aware that she had not only to impress Mama, but also to conquer Papa. He was initially less enthusiastic than my mother about the idea of adoption, and took it to be a new manifestation of Mama's guilt complex. He even floated the idea that this scrawny little Eva-child nibbling away at the last of our provisions was Mama's application for a letter of indulgence from Grandpaping in the hereafter.

Mama took to slamming doors again – the ones that had not been turned into firewood, that is.

Ev responded with meekness. She never showed any overly great devotion, except to me: she called me her big sister, while Hubsi became her big brother.

There was nothing false about her; she never curried favour, and she didn't go in for flattery. In her coy, sometimes cheeky way, she simply made herself essential. She had a sixth sense for what the person she was with sought most desperately, and in her arsenal of ways to help she often found what was needed, and we regarded it, gratefully, as emotion, although that emotion may well not have existed. We hoped she would see us with her heart. And who can do that.

She managed, in any case, to hit the mark with Papa as well. She thrust herself upon him as an artist's model – something he resisted strongly at first, but ultimately without success. Papa had received his first major post-war commission: illustrations from the Kama Sutra to be painted as frescoes in a new war profiteers' brothel on Elisabethstraße. It was imperative that Mama should never find out about this, and she never did. The commission was far beneath my father's dignity; it drove him to vodka and fed us in secret. Above the necks of women's defoliated and bacchanalian bodies he painted angry white ovals, since in his opinion the whores who sat for him possessed snouts, not faces. Ev, on the other hand, who despite being only ten years of age had a clever, circumspect and largely unabashed profile, second not even to a young Mata Hari in her radiance and her rosebud mouth, had so many faces that each one found a home on a different woman's body. Papa concentrated on her variety, her wealth of expressions, her eyes, and all the incarnations of ecstasy that little Ev was able to put on like masks. In the studio, she often had to tense her facial muscles for half an hour at a time, while Papa arranged them with delicate brushstrokes on the *Catherine Wheel*, the *Fantastic Rocking Horse* or the *Nirvana*.

*

'Do you know what a position is?' Ev asked me one evening.

I knew about social position, military positions on the battlefield and sporting positions on the football field, our own financial position, and of course the relationship of one thing to another, like the stars, for instance, though that was usually called a constellation.

'No, Koja, I'm talking about sexual intercourse.'

'You're not allowed to say things like that.'

'Why not? Papa explained it to me.'

She was now permitted to call Theo 'Papa', although at first he had favoured 'Father' and occasionally even 'Uncle'.

'Why on earth would he do that?' I asked, taken aback.

'Well, you know, there are sheets hung over all the walls. And a little while ago when he was painting me, one of the sheets fell down and then he had to say something.'

'Uh-huh.'

'Yes, because there was an Indian woman on the wall wearing pearls and nothing else, with a naked Indian man crouching behind her like a dog. Like this.'

She showed me.

'Papa was very embarrassed, and said I mustn't tell anyone about it. He told me what a phallus is.'

'A what?'

'A phallus. When a penis grows, it's called a phallus. You'll get one too, when you're older. But I really mustn't tell anyone.'

'So why are you telling me?'

'I mean, I mustn't tell anyone *else*.'

'That must have been a terrible sight.'

'It was. Do you want to see?'

'No.'

'I know how to get in without a key. I mean, it's a building site, after all.'

'Papa would beat me black and blue.'

'I looked at everything. There's a picture where an Indian woman has a phallus in her mouth.'

'I don't believe you.'

'I swear.'

'So someone's peeing in her mouth?'

'No, peeing is what you do with your penis. It's only your phallus that you put in someone's mouth, not your penis.'

'That's disgusting.'

'No, it's a perfectly normal position.'

'Papa doesn't paint those things. No, Papa doesn't paint those things.'

'Oh, Koja, why are you crying? I'm sorry. Please forgive me. Let's put our arms around each other and pray, we'll *davenen zu dem gutn got, yo*?'

Years later, as a student, when some members of my corps and I visited that discreet establishment, the exotic name of which changed as frequently as the women who worked there, I saw for myself that all the rooms were adorned with shimmering wall paintings, temple dancers with many arms, topped with the unmistakably childlike countenance of the young Ev. My father's brushwork was also unmistakable. Her innocence more evident than his. I chose a room with an image of cunnilingus and a buxom Slovakian girl.

When I told Ev about it later, I thought she would laugh. But this time she was the one who grew dejected. And I had to *davenen zu dem gutn got* with her, our arms wrapped around each other as before. For there was no more innocence, there was just guilt and guilty people, and we would all have to be painted as centaurs – Ev, me and Hub – as mythical creatures born out of a dark cloud, hot-headed and wanton, siblings wedded to one another.

And thus we really did become the raging of the whole world.

3

The Hippy doesn't respond. He is lying on his back, his eyes open and staring at the ceiling, not moving, not breathing, a mute fish, an ear for my innocence, not my troubles. Perhaps he's waiting for me to go on. But there's nothing else I want to say, and so eventually his pupils slide towards me.

'Why have you stopped?'

'From now on, it gets complicated. It's hard to explain.'

'You're stopping just because it's hard to explain? You don't stop when something's hard to explain. When something's hard to explain, that's when you really get started. I don't even bother to listen when people are explaining easy things. I get bored straight away. But hard things are great.'

'I just wanted to tell you what that business with my brother was about.'

'Red autumn mandrill.'

'Calville! Not mandrill. Red autumn Calville.'

'What's a mandrill, again?'

'A kind of monkey.'

'Right.' He thinks for a moment. 'That's why he, your brother I mean, didn't want you to eat that apple, right?'

'I shouldn't have done it. Then none of this would have happened.'

'Are mandrills the ones with the red arses?'

'The monkeys, yes.'

'With red monkey arses?'

'Correct.'

You can almost see the lively jungle scene the Hippy is projecting onto the screen in his mind, and then he laughs softly, because laughing loudly is painful for him. For me, too. There isn't much laughter in our room. If something really tickles us, we can smack our hands on the bedcovers several times in succession; that muffles the shocks, but unfortunately also the noise. The Hippy can't stop himself now, it has to come out, he giggles helplessly.

'Be careful: don't go having a fit, now,' I say.

'I'm being careful.'

'And it's not even that funny.'

Hub caught him right on the frontal lobe. The blow caused nausea, vomiting and visual hallucinations, real photopsia. Night Nurse Gerda and the Greek registrar are very worried (possibly for different reasons), but the Hippy waves it off. The visions remind him of really great acid trips, he says.

No question, my Attic influence on other people has waned. My brother didn't deign to look at me as the police took him away. Breach of the peace, coercion, grievous bodily harm. All chalked up to his account. He'll be sitting in a cell by now. Three metres by three, that's the standard. They might let him out again in ten years' time. It will be nineteen eighty-four by then. What will things be like in those far-off days? Will Germany still be divided? Will the Yanks have a colony on the moon? Will George Orwell be proved right? We often played that game as children: looking into the future. Another way of saying: we had high hopes. But Hub will be seventy-nine by then. And the only hope he will have left is that he'll make it to eighty.

With a bullet in your head, even that hope is gone.

A police officer is sitting outside our room now, leafing unhurriedly through a magazine, licking the leafing finger before turning each page as he waits for his shift to end. They might have guessed that it wouldn't be difficult for someone to slip into a hospital unnoticed. It isn't difficult for Hub, or for anyone else. The police guard is supposed to provide me with reassurance, but he just makes everyone nervous and prevents Night Nurse Gerda from bringing the Hippy his cannabis plants.

Since my wheezing roommate can hardly get up, I limp downstairs to the maternity ward for him, watch the newborns, flash them in the face at close range with his Polaroid camera. I feel as though the babies need police protection, too: I am able to creep into their room entirely unchecked, and could snatch whichever one I wanted and carry it off in a sports bag: the lively Rage-Enough-For-Two, say, or Sunny-With-Light-Cloud, Afternoon-Tea, Let-It-Be, and whatever else the Hippy calls them.

These worms wear me out. I have hidden my brother's brown envelope with the photos inside upstairs in my locker. Those photos are of a baby, too. Whoever took them must have been a perverse swine. Down on the second floor, when I press the shutter-release above the newborns' glass cribs, the flash goes right through me, as if it were detaching my retinas. I can't stand it for very long, and nor do I want the Hippy to spend forever looking at the Polaroids.

I can't sleep at night.

The wind moans in the branches outside the window. Though there aren't any branches there. The nearest tree, a caricature of a beech, is a long way off, and would be impossible to hear even if it shouted. I am assailed by illusions and dark dreams that attach themselves to this one hundred per cent reality: the beeping, buzzing, whining, ticking, squawking, sighing and puffing of all the machines that surround us, measuring and guarding us like overzealous angels. Under your wing, Hub. Yes, that's where I was.

'Koja!'
  'Hmm?'
'Koja! You're having a nightmare.'
  'Nonsense!'
'You were shouting bang bang bang bang.'
The Hippy looks at me wide-eyed, as I wake up feeling like I'm in a coffin. The silence of the hospital surrounds me. Then the beeping, buzzing, whining, ticking, squawking and so on. Then the voice, which seems to come straight out of his eyes.
  'I'm worried about you, Koja.'
'No, you were the one who was punched. Not me. It's you we should be worrying about.'
  'You know what? You really are a wonderful person.'
I roll sideways and vomit on the blue linoleum floor. It flows out of me like water pumped from a well. The Hippy wants to call Night Nurse Gerda, but I would rather he didn't. Eventually the police babysitter would come in as well, and that's the last thing I need. The Hippy offers to help me clean up my vomit. These hippies really do take things to extremes.

I'm sure Basti must be an extreme case. But there have been other people in my life – men, women – who felt drawn to my integrity. Not many. But they did exist. Though they never actually asked me whether this integrity existed. I had no illusions on that score, of course; I always knew what had happened to me. But it did *happen* to me. Things befell and were visited upon me. I reacted to a world that had gone to rack and ruin, not the other way round. I was deeply sincere. I was deeply insincere, too. But that was part of my job; my true self was honest. A skin that couldn't be peeled away, the very last skin of honesty, paper-thin, perhaps, but there was no tearing it. Beneath it lay my flesh, my bones, my heart. I never let the deceit penetrate my guts. That's what I always think. Or used to think. Of course, that's what everyone in my position thinks. Deception is my currency. The hardest currency of all. But just because you pay with it, I say, doesn't mean you're false through and through.

I walk over to the window, open both casements, hear the rustle of the branches that aren't there, that only exist in my head. I climb up onto the windowsill, and am pulled back by the Hippy, who has rushed over, devoted and inconvenient, refusing to believe that I just want to feel the fresh air on my skin, from top to bottom, from my broken head to my bare feet.

Two days later, we are sitting on the hospital roof.

At night, this is the one place where the Hippy will not be interrupted while he smokes the dope that Nurse Gerda has cultivated for him. This section of the roof is only accessible via the fire escape, and it took us almost thirty minutes to tiptoe up here. The Hippy wants to celebrate the fact that he can move again. The midnight air is warm, late-summer warm, with a trace of loss in the warmth. The city lies at our feet, its lights distant enough for the stars to come into their own above our heads, a thousand little splinters of magnesium.

Night Nurse Gerda, who is now a seasoned drug mule, has even smuggled in a hash pipe, right under the nose of the police Cerberus. It is called Bamboo, and my protector is now explaining its advantages at great length, whether I like it or not. The Hippy crumbles the dried hemp leaves into pieces as he talks, even his hands are an irritant. His croaky voice fills my heart with bitterness, and I get angry when, as he did a few days ago, he tries to free the doctors from taboos and constraints through the grand gesture of flushing not just his own medication down the lavatory, but mine, too. In short: he is unbearable, he bores me to death with his esoteric terrorism, and almost everything about him makes me furious.

But he is the hereafter made flesh, and God knows, he is not unkind to me. In his tremendous complacency he is as loyal-hearted as a poodle, and his view of the world would make me smile, if I felt like smiling. He is always considerate, always asking if I'm all right – and, in a touching gesture, he regularly gives up his hospital sausage sandwiches to me (dead animals!), and gratefully accepts my dessert in return, which is not sweet enough for me. He is especially fond of reading terrible Buddhist primers to me, but he also loves Hindu tracts and Ayurveda guides that suggest healing projectiles in one's head with oils and scents. He has assimilated all the Indian doctrines of salvation, believes in the holy cow, in the divine power of Brahman, but also in

Buddha, who does not fit easily into this company. Even a few tantra techniques, something I had never heard of before, have gained a foothold in his energy centre, the brainbox (as he calls it) so often juiced by Night Nurse Gerda. He is flooded with immense love for his fellow man, and now also hands me his hash pipe, refusing to accept that I don't even want to try it.

'But why not? It'll relax you.'

I begin with the simplest of all truths, the one about hash.

Twenty years ago, we were involved in Project Artichoke. This was the code name for the CIA's attempts to test drugs like heroin, amphetamines, sleeping pills and LSD, the last of which had only just been discovered. The programme was carried out in Germany, principally in Kronberg, in the lovely Taunus Mountains, and so our organization was brought in. We took over parts of the project, which was so secret that, unfortunately, everyone talked about it out of sheer excitement. The aim was to develop an interrogation technique that we named the Hammer of Witches.

The Hammer of Witches was supposed to be a merciless truth serum. Under its influence, no one would manage to keep their cover story straight when they were questioned. As part of this experimental programme, seven prisoners from the Nuremberg Correctional Facility were pumped full of hash and LSD for seventy-seven days in the autumn of nineteen fifty-two. Seven was the lucky number of the man in charge of the programme, a pharmacologist from Philadelphia. You can imagine what went on in that prison. But there was nothing more to marvel at than brightly painted cell walls and good-humoured lifers. So we called for seven volunteers, but could only find three in the whole firm: me and two other officers from the operational division. Three is not seven, and the head of the drug trial later said the whole sorry business was down to that cursed number. We were given the marijuana intravenously, and I'd prefer not to say too much about my rather reflexive reactions. But a week into the trial, my colleague Frank Burmeister jumped out of the third-floor window of his apartment block, intending to use his wings to fly across to the Stachus Cinema. Lauren Bacall was over there waving to him, stark naked and as big as a Tyrannosaurus rex. The fall was only eight metres, but the ground below Frank was solid asphalt. It took him three days to die.

After that, we destroyed almost all the Artichoke files; the ministry would have finished us if anything about German involvement had become public knowledge.

That is where I know hash from, and that is why I don't particularly like it, especially not on a roof with this view, where it's so easy to spread your wings and fly away.

'Herr Solm,' says the Hippy – it's a long time since he's addressed me so formally, but now he starts again. 'Have I understood you correctly? Are you saying you work for the government?'

He is holding the hash pipe in the same way Ev used to hold her cigarette, with daintiness and concern.

'You don't need to worry about that.'

'But you said that stuff about the CIA.'

'I can't talk about it.'

'Are you a secret agent or something?'

'Look, I told you: I can't talk about it.'

'And you shouldn't talk; you should *confess*.'

'With the best will in the world, Basti, you're not a priest.'

'I'm a swami.'

'Excuse me?'

'I teach courses in dynamic meditation. I've been to Bombay three times, and there they call me Swami Deva Basti. In any case, I see your seed, your potentiality, and I don't understand how you could have strayed so far from the path of your true destiny.'

The Hippy may be incredibly childlike, and he may understand very little of the crystalline purity of evil (and even less about its stupidity), but all the same, I want to feel that it can be normal for people to engage honestly with me. Tectonic plates of emotion are moving within me. And on these plates, little candles of childhood are being lit. It's true, even back then, blessed be the memory, I had moments of spiritual potency. After all, I do come from a long line of pastors. Even Papa was forced to study theology before he became a painter. It had been a commandment from the severe Grandpaping, who so desperately wanted an heir to take over his ministry. Papa even passed his trial sermon with flying colours, before taking refuge from his despotic father in art. So there are four and a half pastors in my genetic history, and perhaps it is no coincidence that I am coming full circle here in this hospital, stumbling across my true self in the presence of an infantile amateur guru. No, it can't be coincidence. The Hippy doesn't believe in coincidence, either; he thinks everything follows certain rules. Everything is connected to everything else, he says. We just have to see it. When you've got the connection, what seems unnatural becomes natural. If you want to find yourself, you must find your story. Tell me the beginning and then the middle and then the end of your story. Then you'll have the connection.

He says something along these lines.

'The beginning is very complicated! I've already told you that,' I say hoarsely.

'That's why the two of us have been brought together, so that you can tell the beginning of the story. You hardly ever get a chance to tell the beginning. It's so difficult. People only ever want to hear how things end.'

The Hippy shakes his head slowly and sadly, and the long hair on its left side tangles itself around his pipe.

And so I carry on with the beginning.

4

In the twenties, things seemed to start getting better for us.

Papa hired himself out as an art teacher to German-speaking private schools, and on the side, he created cycles of paintings with titles like *Aphrodite's Embraces* or *Sappho in Bed*. In order to keep these a secret from Mama, he often went away in the summer months for weeks at a time on 'portrait trips' to Jutland, where he was supposedly capturing the likenesses of old Danish aristocrats, though in reality he was sating their appetite for amorous and more than amorous pastoral scenes. Mama exploded once or twice because he would come back with a deep suntan, and one memorable Sunday morning she even set light to an oil painting entitled *In Flagranti*, as a result of which Papa's studio caught fire. And as if it were the most natural thing in the world, she extinguished the blaze by throwing all the burning paintings out of the window.

But otherwise she made *bonne mine à mauvais jeu*, simply pretending she didn't know about any of it, and her aristocratic countenance was a great help to her in this. She saw us through the first hard years with great diligence, and though her cooking never improved, she loved the gardening that was limited to our twelve-square-metre back courtyard, loved each one of her roses. She never had a philosophical or lofty air about her, while Papa always looked pensive, even when he was sitting silently at his easel, adding colour to nipples.

We might have fallen a long way, but Mama clung tight to her breeding and remained an embodiment of the old Baltic German qualities; even in the depths of misery, she was still a baroness with some aristocratic pride. But she never seemed ridiculous; she just lived firmly in this world, while Papa also had something of the next world about him, something that soon became an air of morbidity. He took children seriously. It was he who said that children always know more than they can say, and adults always say more than they can know. Perhaps that was one of the reasons he'd taken Ev on as a model at such a young age. He probably sensed even then that she would be inspired rather than offended by it. He sometimes also spoke to me in a way that authority figures seldom speak to eleven-year-old boys. Once, we were fishing together on the banks of the elderberry-red Düna, and after half an hour of stoic silence he said in very dignified tones, 'One cannot know whether fish piss. Below the surface, you can't see it, and above the surface, they don't do it.'

Of all the objects in which his sensitivity was embodied, I loved his canvases most of all, which he whitewashed and primed himself with great relish. His egg-yolk primer was only ever mixed in the presence of our old cook, Kocka-Anna; the egg yolk had to be beaten as if you were making a perfect omelette. And for his famous white 'Solm' primer, he used a centuries-old recipe that supposedly originated with Jan Vermeer, and included marble dust and quartz crystals. It reflected the light into Papa's paintings and made them dance. It may well have been this shimmering white that finally sparked my obsession with becoming an artist myself, because the proper association with white is innocence, and being an artist means being the most innocent person in the world.

Papa taught me that the self-consciousness of our age comes from our devotion to this world; the devotion to the hereafter that shaped our ancestors, the pastors – and even him, the half-pastor – was being replaced by material things, by the tangible and immediate, the experience of which is what first leads us to ourselves. 'Individuality, my son,' Papa often said, 'means believing in what you see.' It follows that you cannot learn to paint. You can only learn to see. Everything I can see I learned to see from Papa. It didn't do Picasso any harm, either, that his father was a freelance painter and a teacher at the San Telmo School of Art. And just as, under his father's tutelage, Pablo learned to see his dog Clipper at the age of seven, so Papa taught me to see my beloved Puppi from every possible angle, so that when Puppi saw my portrait of him, the similarity elicited a joyful bark. Papa was very proud of me: I was a fast learner, and although I would never a achieve a blue or a rose period (at most, I had a black one), in terms of technique I was never a worse painter than that wholly overrated Spaniard, as evidenced by the fact that, decades later, I was able to forge his work with highly profitable results.

Hub passed his exams and went to the University of Latvia in Riga, and so did I. Following in Grandpaping's footsteps, he began studying to be a Lutheran theologian, even though – much like the rest of us, in fact – he didn't want anything more to do with the hereafter. We both joined the Curonia: a striking connection. My brother blossomed in the academic fencing club, duelling with anyone who appeared before his visor. He celebrated his first 'smite' like a lottery win, tearing off his helmet and padding, shouting 'Hurrah', and leaving the fencing physician standing there in the hall. He ran, bleeding patiently, to a nearby hotel, where Ev was already waiting for him. She stitched the gushing wound, having first licked off the blood, and thus made fun of the whole thing in her usual way. She was by then in her first semester of medical school, and wanted to show what she could do. Above all, she wanted to show Hub, who regarded female students as unladylike bluestockings, just as most of us did. He played one of our boys' songs on the guitar to tease her:

> All the clever-clever things you know, it
> Will not do you any good with us.
> Women have no business being poets;
> A woman should aspire to be a muse.

At university and in the Curonia, Hub was known as 'Gob'. That was his official nickname, because he had a big mouth and wouldn't take any nonsense from anyone. At that time, the idea that priests-in-training should cultivate an especially peaceable temperament was seen as unworldly, at least in the Baltics. Even Grandpaping had lost half an ear in a student duel, and was proud of it all his life.

I myself had no great love for the duelling loft, the fug of beer, sweat and old leather that you walked into every morning, hungover, to practise your parries, quartes and tierces. I was never challenged to a duel with sharp blades, so unfortunately I have no scar to remind me of Ev. In later years, I sometimes felt a pang of jealousy when I saw Hub sitting, lost in thought, running his fingers over the vein-like white line on his cheek. I must confess that, sadly, I was never as hard-working as Hub, nor did I even come close to his legendary success with women. I didn't have his magnificent and completely unbroken self-belief, either. Hub had a natural authority, conveyed simply through the way he spoke and sparkled, and he exuded an immense energy that won everyone over.

I was largely self-contained, keeping to my paints, books and intellectual elective affinities, while he had a highly developed social streak and loved the harmony and cooperation of groups, which in his mind existed primarily for him to excel in or to lead. His favourite words were 'fabulous' and 'terrific', and this vocabulary was also a fair description of his university career.

When we were in Jugla, in our little dacha on the shores of the Stintsee, he would badger us into playing all kinds of communal games: charades, cards, ludo. He usually won, and when he didn't win, he acted as though he had. But he always found the time to look out for those who practically never won, in games or in life. When it looked as though I might fail my school-leaving exams, because Latin was cooking my goose, he helped me cram Caesar's *Commentarii de bello Gallico*. 'You just have to make a terrific effort, Koja!' That was the key, a terrific effort.

Without being a swot, Hub sailed through every theological exam as easily as Jesus once walked across the Sea of Galilee; but I was an academic idler who might easily drown.

My gossamer dream of becoming an artist like my father was quickly snared on the brambles of reality. Papa continued to support me, however; he claimed that I was gifted, and everyone believed him. Ev in particular seemed convinced that they would have to name the next century after me.

But as a Baltic German, I couldn't be admitted to the Latvian Academy of Art, although I passed the exam with the best marks in my year. An angry Papa took me to see the Latvian president of the academy, Celnins, to complain. Professor Solm was a luminary of the art world, so even though he wasn't a professor, Celnins still addressed him as such out of respect – a respect that contained within it the regret that Germans and Jews were not now permitted to take student places away from talented Latvians.

And so I was forced to transfer my artistic ambitions to architecture, although I found houses about as exciting as a heap of rubble. I could already see myself designing coal cellars and firewalls for the rest of my life.

'Firewalls sound interesting, what are they?' Ev asked me.

'It's the wall between two buildings that stops a fire spreading from one to the other. A protective wall.'

'I'm sure there must be some beautiful protective walls.'

'You can't see them, Ev!'

'Just make an effort,' she laughed, 'you must always make a terrific effort!'

But I found that hard.

Whenever I had a free minute, I got out my brushes and canvas. Like Papa, I preferred to paint people – or more precisely, beautiful people, which meant women.

After Puppi died (who was, in a way, also a woman), Ev gladly offered to model for me. My seeing her naked didn't seem at all strange to either of us, and not just *seeing* her naked; as I painted, I studied every fold of her body, every shadow on her skin, even the constellation of her moles, which she strictly forbade me from painting.

We had been familiar with each other's bodies ever since she was a small girl, when she crept into my bed on her first night in our house. That didn't change as we grew to adulthood. During puberty my skin was not particularly clear, and she loved to squeeze my spots, with a look of great concentration on her face as if she were walking a tightrope. She would always show me the little yellow newly slain worm of pus curling on her fingernail, expecting praise. Once, when Ev was seriously ill, Mama and I were the only people she would allow into her room. She had pulmonary tuberculosis, an 'infiltrate in the left middle lobe', the doctors said, and although her life was hanging in the balance, her primary concern was the way she smelled. It was strange, when disgust was usually so foreign to her. But she was ashamed of her own plight, even with me, although not as greatly. As soon as I entered the room, she would ask me to open the window wide, which I did not do because it was the depths of winter – and, feigning revulsion, she would wrinkle her nose, and I would reassure her, stroke her damp arm and read aloud to her.

I liked the sour, resinous smell she gave off, the subtle scent of urine, although to this day I am repelled by illnesses and am eager to leave this hospital in which we are now compelled to vegetate, my dear, scruffy friend. But Ev's smell told me she was still alive, and that made me happy – while the cologne that Mama dabbed on Ev's forehead and throat every day would have smelled exactly the same on a corpse.

Although Ev and I treated each other like Amazonian Indians, and would have happily pierced rings through each other's noses, there was a kind of Anglo-Saxon prudishness between her and my brother. When we were getting dressed and undressed on the beach, for instance, their mutual modesty was nothing short of crippling. But when Ev and I were lying on Riga Strand, and no one else was around, she would sometimes strip completely naked and together we would leap, shrieking, into the sea.

As soon as Hub turned up, her otherwise flirtatious soul was completely thrown off kilter. She only got changed in his presence if there was no possibility of indecent exposure. There was also a period of time when she would turn as red as a Chinese lantern at the least provocation, but only in the presence of Hub or one of her ardent admirers, who could be an embarrassment to a young lady.

With me she remained completely at ease, retaining her usual porcelain pallor as if I were nothing more than a pet cat. She would never have squeezed Hub's spots – not that he had any. His skin was smooth and flawless, just like his body. And he seldom played the 'Gob' with her. He liked to tease her, it's true, but he always kept a gentlemanly distance, from which he even began to exhibit a bashfulness similar to hers.

It was clear to me that there was a hidden, perhaps even sinister attraction between them, as if Ev were a kind of Lorelei to whom Hub was blocking his ears, a siren who would lure him to his destruction.

When I asked Ev why she and Hub were so funny with one another, quite unlike the two of us, she said, 'He's the papa. I'm the mama. And you're the child.'

I didn't speak to her for a week after that.

Ev didn't care. You couldn't provoke her with your silence, just as you couldn't provoke her with your absence. Shouting and being present were her parameters, but I only learned that later. In any case, this attitude explained why she was the driving force when it came to exploring the mysteries of the sexual maturity that was engulfing us, and to which we were both in thrall.

One evening, when my parents had taken Hub out to a concert – he was four years older than us and already a member of the student corps – she darted into my room, locked the door behind her and declared very firmly that she needed to examine me. I was to take off my nightshirt, lie down naked on the bed and let her look at my penis. She remained fully dressed, still wearing her daytime clothes: a red checked dress, a light-coloured shawl and white socks. She sat down beside me, without touching me, and looked at my nakedness in the same way I looked at her when I was painting. Thoroughly. Then she cautiously wrapped her hand around my penis. Within a few seconds it had her full attention.

'Does this embarrass you?'

'A little bit.'

'Oh, come on. I'm your sister. You don't need to be embarrassed about anything in front of me.'

'It's fine.'

'It's getting really big.'

'Don't let go.'

'Well, what should I do?'

I showed her. She shuffled closer, leaned over me, and I could feel her breath on my stomach. When I looked down at her, I saw that she was observing everything with an almost scientific zeal, as close up as possible. She was determined not to miss anything important. She didn't flinch when I ejaculated, just blinked a little. Unfortunately, her mouth had the same keen look about it as when she was squeezing spots. She was already, to some degree, the doctor she would later become. She dipped her forefinger into my meagre ejaculate, probably intending to see what it tasted like, but then registered my utter horror and allayed my fears with a slight smile tinged with sadness, before taking off one of her socks and passing it to me discreetly.

Later we lay side by side, doing what we always did at times like this: praying in our secret language to the silver Jesus she wore around her neck. She made me swear on my favourite painters, Albrecht Dürer and Sandro Botticelli, never to tell a living soul about the frothy examination, which overall had passed off entirely to Ev's satisfaction.

She snuggled up to me and murmured that she had found the love of her life. I was very content.

'Yes,' she whispered, 'Hub is the best, he's so splendid, so wonderful, so dangerous.'

'Hub?' I spluttered.

And she described to me, entirely unselfconsciously, the kitschy and ridiculous things she longed for from my brother, longings that must have been kindled by distance, quiet respect, a strong mistrust and all the teasing that went on between them. I, on the other hand, despite being a faithful servant to her every whim, was demoted to the role of pillow, into which she pressed her face and confided her dreams. Human gratitude is not exactly a rock on which you can build.

'So, do you think he likes me too, just a little?' she asked.

'Mmhmm.'

'Hey, what's wrong? Why are you being such an ox?'

'It's late. Mama and Papa will be back soon.'

'You're not jealous, are you?'

What was I supposed to say to that?

'Hub is just a member of a different race. We two will never come close to him. Oh Koja, my dearest Koja, we're so alike. And you love him too, don't you?'

'Yes, I love him.'

'If you like, I'll take my clothes off. Would you like that?'

It's hard to believe, but all of this seemed completely normal to me, unspoiled and pure, although at that time Woodstock and 'Penny Lane' were not our guiding stars, my noble and possibly bored friend. You may be wondering what all this has to do with my work, with the secret service, the government, the bullet in my head and the world out there. But you wanted to hear the whole of the beginning, and believe me, a beginning is what this is.

Ev and I felt we were not of this earth. We might have admired heroes like Hub, and lusted after them, too (I am taking Ev's perspective for a second), but unlike him or our parents or Anna Ivanovna, we didn't live *with* or *among* people, but alongside them, out on the periphery. While they regarded the world as solid and unalterable, we saw that it was hanging from loosened screws, and the wind was rattling it. We were outsiders, but we both had the gift of not seeming like outsiders; we gave each other strength, and yes, perhaps this harmless touching was part of that, like chimpanzees grooming one another. But it was this very chimp-like quality that would have shocked everyone we knew. Siblings at that time simply did not masturbate one another. Ev might have been sent off to boarding school or disappeared from our family entirely if this pleasure, this *freyd* (as she called it), had been discovered.

The fact that she gave me the power to destroy her welded us together for all time.

This was something that happened from time to time; our roles might change, but we never overstepped the boundaries we'd set. Sometimes months would pass between these episodes; once it was even a whole year. I probably would have been able to carry on like this forever. I might even have grown accustomed to enduring her singing Hub's praises, describing his strength of character in extravagant detail, which so to speak went hand in hand with these secret bacchanals that lacked any strength of character whatsoever.

But on her twentieth birthday, Ev told me that she had fallen in love with a newly qualified doctor of jurisprudence. She was quite beside herself.

'We have to stop it. I'm sure he'd think it wasn't right.'

'But we're not doing anything.'

'He says he would never marry a girl who had so much as kissed anyone else.'

'Do you want to marry him, then?'

'He's crazy about me. He's the most wonderful man an alien could wish for. And I want to free myself from Hub.'

'Do you think you'll be able to?'

'I will if I have lots of children.'

'How many is lots?'

'He says eight.'

'Well, that really is a lot.'

'He says we have to Nordicize our race, because otherwise we'll be overrun with Semites.'

'Ev?'

'Yes?'

'That's utter nonsense.'

'I know. But he's so wonderful.'

'And we've never kissed.'

It was in this way that something very significant happened.

Erhard Sneiper came into our lives. He was the man whose blood-shot eyes would hypnotize us all into the National Socialist paradise, a paradise of which we knew nothing at that time, a non-existent paradise in which Ev and I would not have been interested even if it had existed, with or without red autumn Calville, snake and poison. The two of us were interested only in our own marvellous household, we were inward-looking like oysters, which never come to know anything in their lives but the little white pearl they weave from their own shells.

Ev had met Erhard Sneiper at a student ball, and although he couldn't dance to save his life, they were engaged in no time, and if I didn't know about the scandal in which this would all end, I would have to admit that Erhard, although no Adonis, was quite a catch. His narrow face, with its watchful expression and a hint of rat-like cunning about it, had the same intelligence that you can see in images of Cardinal Richelieu. He was thin, scholarly, and wore spectacles (he favoured the kind that Mr Lennon wears now, that mop-top man you talk about so much). With his consumptive appearance, Sneiper was the very opposite of Hub, whose build was powerful, athletic, almost mastiff-like. Erhard's distinguishing qualities were a sonorous tenor voice, an unusual eloquence – a great help to a man starting out in the legal profession – a tenacious memory, and an outstanding talent for politics. He knew everyone who was anyone, and could pull all kinds of strings. He also loved Ev, which made me hate him. I sugar-coated my hatred, sweetening our day-to-day dealings with warmth. But I still hated him.

Hub, who at first glance seemed so much more charismatic than Erhard, fell for this man two years his senior on the spot. To this day, I can't understand it. Until that year, nineteen thirty-one, none of us had ever heard of Adolf Hitler. But Erhard talked about him as if he were King Arthur, and I was a little surprised that years later, the Führer turned out to be not a great king, but a mixture of King Kong and Charlie Chaplin – who were, at least, two film stars I admired greatly.

I myself very quickly became a good Nazi. Not that I was aware of it. Many of us became good Nazis almost without realizing, for becoming a good Nazi was like becoming a good Christian. 'Good Nazi' was tautological. There was no other kind, and it seemed to happen all by itself.

Our political situation was not rosy. This perhaps needs to be said. A global economic crisis is never nice, but after Wall Street was detonated, the fragments of asphalt that rained down over the whole planet destroyed the last shreds of optimism that a German in Latvia could cling to. Erhard agitated against the Latvian government, both openly and behind closed doors. Soon, he also began to receive financial support from one Herr Himmler, whose name I first heard from Erhard's lips. He met with Himmler in Berlin and the two conspired together. Erhard was working to build support for a populist party, which was referred to as 'the Movement'. And Hub, of all people, became his right-hand man – a pastor-in-training, from a long line of priests, accustomed to dispensing benedictions wherever he went.

My brother was first and foremost an idealist, the opposite of pearl oysters like Ev and me. His focus was not really on his own advancement; he wanted to help save the world, as men from church families often do. His defiance, which had skipped from Grandpaping down to him, was transformed into zeal. He loved to get excited over a mission that required his steeliness. Rumination, inconstancy and indecision had always been my talents, not his. Believing in an absurd goodness that was actually nowhere to be seen in the Movement (except when, drunk, we saw it in ourselves), he went to stand at Erhard's side, and I was surprised to discover that being second was enough for my brilliant, extraordinary brother – though being second was really what I was for.

Erhard came to me, too. He walked into Papa's studio one morning without knocking; I had closeted myself away to despair over the landscape sketch of a Palladian villa. When someone is speaking, I look at his mouth, not into his eyes. As a painter, I can tell when a mouth expresses indifference or hints at tenderness, for these are the things I need to draw. You can only ever draw an eye as a marble covered in gossamer-fine leather. An eye reveals nothing to me but a chance reaction to light – but when Erhard's lips opened with a smacking sound, and he planted his bony backside on my drawing table, what I saw was self-importance.

'Koja,' he said by way of greeting, breathing between the syllables. 'Ko' – breath – 'ja.'

I put down my pencil and did what he wanted: I looked up at him.

'Ev tells me that you don't have a very high opinion of this uniform business.'

'What uniform business?'

'The sometimes rather primitive way in which people address problems in Germany. That uniform business.'

'It's possible.'

'Believe me, I understand. I went to a party conference in Munich once' – he lowered his husky voice, raised a hand, and his mouth showed me that he wasn't sure how to start a conversation amid all these saucy pictures of Theo's – 'and I found it re-vol-ting.'

He slid off the table to stand beside me, and I felt his hand clap me on the shoulder. He was trying to be jolly, sounding me out.

'But please don't forget that the very survival of our people is at stake here, something very good that is being challenged by something very evil.'

'Erhard—' I began, but he interrupted me at once, his hand still on my shoulder, now gripping it more tightly.

'Yes, your family is no stranger to this evil. I know what the Latvians did to your grandfather. It's what they're trying to do to all the Germans who remain in this country. And that is why we must defend ourselves, Koja. Do you understand? We must resist!'

He paused for effect in the earnest way that was so very popular among would-be demagogues at that time. Then he whispered, 'Resist,' twice more, almost dreamily, his lips very close to my ear, like Count Cagliostro trying to con people into buying occult love potions – before saying in a low, oily purr, 'There is only one man in all of Europe who is doing more than just watching this happen.'

He let go of me then, and strode around the studio, feigning interest in all the pastoral scenes and *fêtes galantes* that crept up the walls. He paused to study a jar filled with red powder and asked me what it was. I said it was crushed insects from South America that the conquistadors had brought to Europe as a pigment five hundred years ago, which threw him off course for a few seconds. But he didn't give a damn about the story of carmine red. There was no way on earth he and Ev would last, I was certain of that, and so I was just starting to feel a little better when he finally said, with endearing tenderness, 'Your brother told me what the sight of an apple makes you all feel. Whenever you decide to do more than merely sympathize with our cause – more than just eat an apple – come and see me.'

He beamed at me auspiciously, and said, 'Your life will get an awful lot more exciting.'

I can't remember, have I told you already how much I hated Erhard Sneiper?

But he was right about one thing. In the years leading up to that point, my life had been anything but exciting. It had been one long siesta, in fact. I'd let my studies and my architectural drawing slide, had my fun in the Curonia, and in my many free hours discovered a passion for sailing. I read a great deal, learned to ride a motorbike, and in summer I killed time by painting in Jugla, where I had designed and built a little log cabin in order to assuage my parents' worry: it was the only tangible result of my many years of study, which were paid for out of my father's dubious income. My artistic ambition had hit a dead end, but neither Papa nor I wanted to see it.

The city of Riga had plenty of distractions in store for failed students: an almost tsarist nightlife of vodka, champagne, Gypsies and droshkies, which waited with their coachmen outside the bars and restaurants; cabarets, variety shows, all kinds of thrilling parties in the Foxtrott-Diele or the Alhambra; and beautiful brothels, where I frequently happened across my father's frescoes. That might have been the best time of my life, although like all periods of indolence there was also an air of melancholy about it. The old-fashioned rattling trams, the baleful whistle of the little steamers on the Düna, the cry of the Baltic seagulls that sailed above the boulevards – the city had become a kind of Barcelona of the North, with the kind of metropolitan atmosphere you might have seen in Paris. It was impossible to imagine that, just a few years previously, thousands of people had starved and frozen to death on these streets.

In the Old Town, Kalkstraße was a hotchpotch of Latvian, Jewish, German and Russian shops. The Beck shoe shop was famous for its English imports, and opposite was Schaar und Caviezel, the excellent Swiss-Jewish merchant of colonial wares and wines. To the right, on the corner, was the Ulei Russian Cultural Centre, and a little further along was the AT Theater, a cinema with an elaborate facade where you could see all the terrible Lilian Harvey blockbusters. Finally, there was the sweet corner, with Kuze, the Latvian chocolate shop on the left, and the famous Baltic German patisserie Otto Schwarz on the right – and opposite, the huge Laima clock, the meeting place for Riga's young people, for all of us.

All the same, the Latvian capital was not a melting pot, or a picture of assimilation. No, Riga was not New York. It was more like Cape Town. Apartheid, I mean. The nationalities remained strictly separate. Each culture stayed stubbornly in its own kraal, had its own administration, its own representatives in the Saeima, its own schools, its own sports clubs: there was a Latvian, a Baltic German and even a Jewish yacht club. The school caps were not the same everywhere either, but coloured according to where you came from. At the German schools we had green caps; the Jews' were light blue, the Russians' dark blue, the Latvians' dark red, autumn Calville red, to my mind (the colour of their flag), and there were Estonian and Polish caps, too.

This explains why Hub and I never really left the Baltic German world in Latvia. We lived in an enclave with no Negro dances, no French *chansons*, Latvian folklore or Jewish choral music. It was only ever German songs, German dances, German classics, German literature and German history, in our entirely German city.

The cultural evening at which my life changed forever was dedicated to this Teutonic spirit. A sentence that sounds wrong, my dear Swami, but isn't. Hub and Erhard had hired the Salomonski Circus on Elisabethstraße. In place of circus artists, tightrope walkers, clowns, lions and costumed elephants, regiments of strapping singers from the Movement would give renditions of uplifting pieces such as 'Und wenn wir marschieren'. The whole of Baltic German society was invited – the upper ten thousand, that is, anyone who was anyone.

That afternoon, Papa complained that he felt unwell. Ev gave him a camomile infusion, took his pulse and advised him to stay in bed. But my father didn't want to stay in bed. He wanted to go out, particularly as a lot of the nymphettes from his art class were due to perform. Naturally, he taught at a girls' school, and received a lot of lavender-scented love letters, even though he was approaching seventy and looked like Mark Twain.

I had decided to do something thoroughly stupid; hatred always has a trace of idiocy *in petto* – but so far, no one suspected anything. Erhard's white shirt, a typical cultural-evening shirt that Ev had brought back to our flat and washed with such love, was hanging up to dry for the day on the washing line right outside my window. Perhaps I was annoyed that my view was blocked. Perhaps I was also pricked by the usual barbs of resentment. Perhaps I simply didn't like this dishonest white. In any case, the previous week Papa and I had had a stir-up day, as he called it. On stir-up days, he taught me the old masters' techniques for making paint. He loathed tubes of ready-mixed paints and had his own recipes that used walnut oil, egg, wax, lime, crushed insect wings, slaked lime, borax or turpentine to turn pigments into emulsions that could go on shining for centuries. That day he'd shown me a tincture made almost entirely of lemon, salt of hartshorn and boiled linseed oil, which served as a primer. Once it was painted onto a white canvas, the odourless and colourless mixture dried slowly over a number of hours, and only then did it turn a rich, warm brown, of the kind that Rembrandt, for example, used to prime his canvases. Erhard's white shirt, which gleamed like a blank canvas and was practically begging to be daubed as lavishly as possible, had now been rubbed with Papa's tincture as a result of my devilment, my jealousy and a sudden impulse – in short: by me and no one else. My future brother-in-law had not slighted me in any way. All he had done was take away my sister, who, whistling cheerfully and giving me a friendly wave, took the shirt down from the line, still blossom-white, without noticing any sign of the nefarious deed that I already deeply, deeply, deeply regretted.

To open the cultural evening at the Salomonski Circus, with its smell of toasted almonds, sawdust and horse dung, Erhard gave a rousing and thoroughly populist speech. He had positioned himself in the circus orchestra's gallery and was flanked by stout-hearted buglers, who kept blowing into their instruments on his command, producing something like the fanfares at the Mainz Carnival. But what neither he nor the musicians could see was that, over the course of several minutes, his snow-white collar was turning into neatly ironed excrement, as if God himself were personally defecating on Erhard's shirt. A few small children in the stalls began to giggle; the rest of the audience froze. And the members of the Movement's youth wing, standing to attention in the crowd, no longer stood quite so stiffly. Out of the corner of my eye, I saw Ev press her hand to her mouth in horror, her hand that had ironed with such care.

At that moment, my father straightened up. A practised lip reader, I read a thoroughly uproarious lust for life between his lips, where little spit bubbles were forming. They were framed by a twisted smile that looked strangely out of place, particularly against his rigid cheeks, and the prominent jawbone that stuck out beneath them. I cannot know for certain, but I fancy that my father looked over at me before he toppled forward, clearly surprised by the stroke that made him tumble onto the people sitting in front of him. Erhard's dung-brown shirt was forgotten amid the shouting.

From that day on, Papa was paralysed down one side.

His forehead, that high forehead criss-crossed with veins, remained the only constant in his face, the rest of which was a melted candle, lopsided, his mouth hanging open; he could no longer speak at all. He was confined to a wheelchair, and Mama fed him like a baby. I had always been closer to my father, while Hub had been closer to our mother, the soft-hearted and hard-headed elements of our family forming two lines that crossed in Grandpaping's fate. My father had believed in me, and in losing him, I lost my messianic calling.

I withdrew to my bed and spent three days trembling there in the half-light.

No one learned of my brainless impertinence, for which one would have been reluctant to forgive a twelve-year-old, let alone a Curonia member fit for sharp challenges, a student in his fourteenth semester. But nor did I know whether the calamity had been brought about by my hand: the clandestine, tincture-dripping hand trained by Papa, which I now wanted to hack off, at least for a minute.

Mama looked like she'd been turned to ashes. Ev was at least partly distracted by the medical necessities. Hub took refuge in drinking and trying to help Papa drink, too. I convinced myself that Papa held Hub's hand longer and more lovingly than mine, to which he never clung. And in his eyes, which looked soupy and pastose, I saw no trace of the immense warmth that had always enveloped women and children and anyone else who was weaker than him, but particularly me.

That was gone now.

Overnight, we became penniless. Bankruptcy broke over us like a natural disaster. It wasn't just that my father's medical care cost a fortune; all his sources of income were gone, too, both the official and the illicit. The family had no others.

Ev was forced to give up her medical degree. Despite his excellent grades, Hub had found only a lowly position as a hostel manager with the Christian Pathfinders, which barely fed him, let alone us. All Mama could do was sew gloves, though for a while she did entertain the devastating notion of working incognito as a washerwoman. I was studying architecture without any prospect of qualifying. It was clear to me that I too must abandon my studies and find a job to help see us all through. I was desperate for Ev not to give up her training.

'Oh, come on,' said Hub. 'Erhard will take care of Ev once they're married. She's a woman, and a pretty one at that. She doesn't need a degree. You do.'

'She has the best marks in her department, and I have the worst.'

'Well, then that needs to change.'

But my situation was hopeless, as even Hub had to recognize once he was in possession of all the facts. I'd taken hardly any of my exams, and the professional diploma alone would require another two semesters, for which there was nowhere near enough money.

Ev was fully prepared to sacrifice herself for us, and had already found a position as a secretary with the White Star Line, with which she intended to support the family.

'Koja,' she told me gently, 'your parents took me in. They saved my life. Now I have to do my bit to save them. I'll manage. And you must manage to graduate, all right? Otherwise Mama will be even more unhappy than she already is.'

I was so angry that I turned her into Salome, working on the canvas at night and filling it with browns and reds, an eruption of brown hair with golden butterflies dancing around it and, in her outstretched hand, the severed head of John the Baptist, which bore my features.

And, now that I had no choice, I went to Erhard to remind him of the offer he'd made me and to ask for a meeting.

It took place two days later, right at the back of the Otto Schwarz Café – in the presence of Hub, which I had not expected. Their silhouettes approached me between the tables and sat down opposite me; their faces remained in shadow, too, shaded by their hats. Only their hands were bathed in the sunlight that poisoned the whole tabletop.

'It's wonderful to see you, Ko' – breath – 'ja,' Erhard Sneiper began, as I tried hard not to read his shadowy mouth. 'Yes, we might find something for you to do. I have influential contacts in Berlin who'll ensure you a handsome salary, with which you can support your parents and yourself.'

'What's the catch?'

He laughed, and as he laughed I thought that this was probably how he laughed with Ev in the evenings. He had a gold tooth, and she'd told me that his orgasms were brief and almost spasmodic.

'There is no catch. You just have to pledge yourself to National Socialism. Because if you don't pledge yourself to National Socialism, then National Socialism can't pledge itself to you.'

I didn't know what to say; Hub came to my rescue.

'Not everyone can see Koja's euphoria, Erhard, but inside he is brimming with it, I know him very well.'

'And, Ko'– breath – 'ja, do you know yourself well, too?'

'Without question,' I said. 'And what I know of myself is on your side.'

Erhard was not pleased with my answer. He clasped his sunlit hands together, tilted his head a little to one side and adjusted his glasses on the bridge of his nose. It almost looked rehearsed. He appeared to be mulling things over; he glanced at Hub and cleared his throat reluctantly. 'Very well then. Our movement is growing by the day. We need professional leadership for our young people. Too many of our German girls and boys are Christian Pathfinders or scruffy Wandervogel scouts without any political robustness.'

Yes, you may laugh, my revered roommate, but 'robustness' was far from being the most ridiculous word spoken on that memorable day.

'What we have need of is a powerful instrument. An organization with a common purpose for all the young Germans in Latvia. A Hitler Youth, though without any Hitler, of course: the Latvians mustn't grow suspicious. This requires some subversive – or shall we say diplomatic – skills.'

'You mean, disband the Christian Pathfinders?' I asked. 'But don't you work for the Christian Pathfinders, Hub?'

'It's not about disbanding anything,' my brother said through gritted teeth, 'it's about unification. The opposite of disbanding.'

'That's why there is no better man than Hub to lead our young people into another dimension. He's very persuasive.'

Erhard's enthusiasm was scratching at the hard shell of my loneliness, but it couldn't crack it open. Never had I felt more guilty, never had I been less keen for any person to help me, and in an attempt to distract myself I looked across the café, wondering whether I shouldn't become a waiter, a bar pianist, or a drunkard.

'What Erhard is trying to say is that I'm going to serve the Movement full-time,' Hub said pointedly.

'You're not becoming a pastor?'

'No. I'm not becoming a pastor.'

'He's becoming a German!' Erhard put in, as if he were saying something especially weighty.

'Exactly. I'm becoming a German. And you could start out as my deputy.'

'A deputy German?'

Erhard stiffened, and for an instant a furrow appeared on his forehead. His voice acquired a metallic sheen.

'Let us be quite clear about this, Koja.' (No breath this time.) 'There are others in our movement with greater merits than you. The position is very decently paid. You came to us so that we could help you out of a difficult personal situation.'

He pulled his chair into the table like a vet preparing for an insemination, and his face was struck by a monstrous flood of light.

'The Führer expects proficiency from his people first and foremost. You don't seem to have been very proficient in the last few years. The second thing he expects is loyalty. And your jibes strike me as too foolish to be loyal. So if you don't want to help your brother shape the

German youth of Latvia into great men and women, you just have to say so. But' – breath – 'you must say so now.'

I looked at his white shirt, and honestly, despite the magic, tragic circumstances in which we found ourselves, I once again wished heartily that it would turn brown. There were various drinks on the table that might have helped with that.

'Koja, please let's do this together!' my brother urged me. 'We both need these positions, otherwise we're finished. And our parents, too. And think how pleased Ev will be!'

And so, at the age of twenty-four, I became a full-time Nazi youth leader. Hub was the face of our organization, and he gave the speeches. I steered the course. Neither of us had ever been members of a youth organization, except for Hub's brief tenure as a hostel warden. Now, at the age of Methuselah, we had a lot of catching-up to do: camping, campfires, putting up the German black tents, morning roll-call.

Hub explained to me that very soon we would be going on a training course in the Reich, at the Hitler Youth leaders' academy in Potsdam. In the meantime, in order to acquaint ourselves with the scouting life, we went on a few Baltic German camping trips. Hub was in his element. He'd always loved groups.

The only thing that bothered me was the frequent rain.

It quickly became clear that I should stay in the background and look after the organizational side of things. I submitted to this plan. I wanted to appear reliable – but 'reliable' was all I could manage. Being a member of Latvia's German Youth meant marching in columns, not hiking in groups. Discipline. Obedience. No skimping, no lolling about, no slovenliness. No dawdling and no claptrap, no magazines, no popular songs, no excuses. No consolations. No happy endings. And no painters or would-be painters, either, no literary types, no erotomaniacs. No hash. No LSD. And no rock 'n' roll. None of the things that you, my flower-powered Swami Basti, do with your incense sticks and batik kaftans would have met with any enthusiasm at all. With pogroms, more likely.

I took over the cultural programme, making sure that the young Spartans also went to the theatre from time to time, or put on plays themselves, ensuring that they strummed a guitar and drew from nature; periods of Attic leisure, in other words.

Hub's main focus, by contrast (apart from being in charge) was on jiu-jitsu and religion, a combination that made both physical and spiritual demands on him, but which I found irritating. For the first time, there was something like friction between us. Until that point we had always had the same opinion on things, or if we didn't, then at least one of us hadn't cared one way or the other.

One of our first tasks was to reorganize the separate sub-groups of the youth movement, which from now on were to be called 'clans' and were given extremely patriotic names. There was Hagen Clan, Siegfried Clan, Schlageter Clan, Andreas Hofer Clan, Blücher Clan, Bismarck Clan and Arminius Clan, which was later rejected as being too Roman and renamed Hermann the Cheruscan, though following the pact between Hitler and Mussolini it was re-Latinized in a spirit of international friendship.

I requested that there be at least one clan named for the intellectual and spiritual rather than the martial aspects of our fatherland. Hub promised he would come up with one. After two weeks during which all my suggestions were batted aside (Faust Clan, Martin Luther Clan, Bach Clan, by which of course I meant Johann Sebastian), he finally strode beaming into the office, flung open my door and cried:

'Apple!'

'What are you talking about, apple?'

'Apple Clan! It has everything: German fruit, German sentiment, and so on!'

I just blinked at him.

'Yes,' he went on, 'and Grandpaping is in it too, of course, which means Baltic history, Baltic courage, Baltic spirit.'

'Don't be an idiot.'

'What do you mean?'

'Apple Clan? That's ridiculous.'

'What's so ridiculous about it?'

'It sounds like apple flan, for one thing.'

He considered this for a while, shook his head slowly and thoughtfully, and then said, with the sudden joy of a eureka moment, 'A traditional German dessert! That's in there, too!'

I pinched the bridge of my nose – a gesture that I missed seeing Papa make since the stroke had paralysed him.

'You can't seriously want to call a group of people who are potty-trained and over three years old Apple Clan.'

'Erhard likes it.'

'You talk to Erhard before you talk to me now?'

'Not by design, honestly. I saw him downstairs on my way in.'

'Listen, Hub. It's a symbol of something that only we understand. You and I. It's our pain. It's something that all those who don't know or share that pain will just think is an apple. Apple Clan is undignified.'

'Undignified? You suggested Minna von Barnhelm Clan!'

'What objection could there be to Lessing? What objection to the dignity of German women?'

'So our lads will feel better mincing about as Minna von Barnhelm than as a symbol of the Reich and beauty and virtue?'

'Then let's call it Red Autumn Calville Clan. At least then no one will know what it means.'

'Calville means "winter hat" in Finnish, you dolt!'

We argued as we had seldom argued over such a trivial thing before. Eventually we agreed on Reich Apple Clan, but I had the feeling that all the original intent had been lost.

Some time later, months after Hitler had taken power, Hub and I caught the express train to Berlin. In the application for our exit visas, we had to state our destination. And under 'intentions' we had written 'visiting museums'. The flabby border guard looked us up and down with mistrust and told us gruffly that in the name of his government, once we'd crossed the border we weren't to commit the offence of visiting any anti-Latvian museums. He waited for us to nod innocently and then banged the stamp down in our passports.

We spent a thoroughly traitorous week in the beautiful town of Potsdam, at the spick-and-span Hitler Youth leaders' academy, learning how to lead and engage young people, attending lectures on race science, geography, sexual hygiene, even on flag-raising protocols, and at the end of the week we were given a whole pile of fanfares for our marching bands. 'How are we going to get all this stuff back through customs?' Hub sighed.

On the last day, he suggested that we skip the timetabled programme to meet up with some of his friends in Berlin. Did I have any objection to missing the seminar entitled 'Live with loyalty! Fight with ferocity! Die with a laugh!'? I had no objection. The day was bright and warm, and I had not seen anything of Babylonian Berlin beyond a station platform.

We alighted from the S-Bahn at Potsdamer Platz. You cannot imagine it. At once we found ourselves in an Amazon Basin of human droplets, a current sweeping us away in one direction or another, it didn't matter which. Noise all around us and above our heads, urgent voices, metre-high words like 'Chlorodont' and 'Bolle' painted on gigantic double-decker buses that slid past like moving cliff faces. There wasn't a single horse-drawn droshky still rattling along the street here, as there was in doddery old Riga. Instead, a whole Big Band of engines played, and the trams sprayed sparks as they performed a mystifying ballet before our eyes.

Hub was reluctant to tell me where we were going, but I didn't really mind. We still had a little time, and we gulped down a lemonade with our backs to the great, five-sided traffic light that stared down at us like a robot. After that, we fought our way to the other side of the road and into Haus Vaterland. We were almost knocked over by the giant ventilators that blew a mixture of smoke, cologne and beer fumes out onto the street. And around the interior. Two grinning Hereros with rings in their noses thrust leaflets into our hands, directing us to the world's largest ballroom. The café one floor down had two thousand five hundred and thirty-two seats, none of which were vacant for two good provincial Baltic German Nazis, who reeled wide-eyed through the Spanish bodega, the Turkish coffee house, the Viennese wine bar, the Arizona bar, and cavernous rooms decorated like harems from *The Thousand and One Nights*, with frescoes that could easily all have been done by Papa, if he'd been given too much vodka. For people who didn't want any lolling about, slovenliness, dawdling or claptrap, any magazines or popular music – in short, any kind of amusement – this Haus Vaterland was absolute hell on earth.

Hub dragged me back out. I trotted beside him, dazed and sheeplike, almost getting run over when I stepped off the pavement for a second. Hans Albers' 'Flieger, grüß mir die Sonne' blared from a shop selling radiograms. And at my side there appeared a dancing girl fresh from the hairdresser's, who smiled at me and belted out, 'Greet the stars for me, greet the moon,' before vanishing again just as quickly into the crowd.

You fly away, way up high, to a place that no one calls home.

We walked five hundred metres or so down Saarlandstraße. Then we turned off into Prinz-Albrechtstraße. At first, I thought that Hub was heading for the Museum of Prehistory and Early History, which housed the treasure of King Priam and would have given a pleasing element of truth to our Latvian museum-visiting visa.

But we walked past it to the building next door, an even larger, even more exquisite five-floored, north-facing building. A highly polished brass sign (in which I could see the reflection of an SS man standing to attention) soon told me that it was the Gestapo Headquarters: Geheimes Staatspolizeiamt Berlin.

I came to an abrupt halt, my head still filled with snatches of melody that had done nothing to prepare me for such a sign. Hub took me by the arm and dragged me through the door.

Inside, the building was cool and silent. It was all bronze sculptures, stucco and dramatic wall paintings. Along with an array of majestic pot plants, the decor gave the hallways an air of blasé refinement, which was topped off by the crossed legs of Erhard Sneiper, who was sitting on a leather sofa in the foyer with a smile on his face. He was expecting us. He stood up politely, as gentlemen in British gentlemen's clubs do, and in fact laid aside a copy of the London *Times*, which you could probably only study without raising suspicion if you were in the Gestapo, though you wouldn't find one in their offices.

So where had he got it from?

'Eva sends her greetings. She's at the Adlon.'

We knew very well where he'd got *her* from.

'Ev is here?' I asked stupidly.

She hadn't said anything to me. Hadn't so much as dropped a hint. I looked at the two gentlemen. The elegant bow tie (Erhard). The cheap tie (Hub). The feeling that crept over me is hard to explain. Indignation isn't the right word; it was as though I was in the Caribbean, and instead of tropical abundance, I had just encountered an iceberg.

'Didn't you prepare him for this?' Erhard said to Hub, with a slight edge to his voice.

'He wasn't ready.'

'What is going on here?' I asked.

'We're meeting our employer.'

'You mean the Reich youth movement has its headquarters here, too?'

They both stared at me. Despite all the potted palms, there was nothing Caribbean about this place at all. Erhard tactfully stepped to one side so that Hub could lean towards me.

'Koja, you surely can't believe,' he began in a low voice, 'that someone is paying us such a princely salary for organizing outdoor games and singing "Die Fahne hoch"!'

Faster and faster still.

'Can you?'

The propeller spins, the pilot thrills.

'Really? Do you believe that?'

You're free as a bird up there, mein Herr, so away you fly.

Ten minutes later, I met Reinhard Heydrich, a man with very clear ideas and a surprisingly high, almost shrill voice, who spent the time that remained before afternoon tea explaining to us how the SD might be established in Latvia, the kinds of reports, research and results he expected, and which political opponents we were to observe, infiltrate or, potentially, liquidate.

5

'The secret service?' says the Hippy.

'Security service,' I reply. 'SD stands for Sicherheitsdienst.'

'Heydrich. Wasn't he that total bastard?'

'Yes, but he was a cultured bastard. Later, he moved his office into the building next door. Prinz-Albrecht-Palais. Mahogany floors. A late-baroque residence built for French silk merchants.'

The Hippy doesn't move.

'There could not have been a more beautiful setting,' I say, 'for the slaughtermen of Europe to sharpen their knives in.'

'Gruesome,' he comments limply.

'Yes,' I say, 'you may be right there.'

'I'm glad to hear you talk like that, man. How can you say you were a Nazi? And a good one, at that? It really is gruesome.'

'It's the truth. And it's going to get a lot more gruesome yet.'

'But you didn't liquidate anyone, did you? Herr Solm, tell me you didn't do that?'

We are lying there on a clear Munich night, moonlight pouring down over all the machines that are keeping us alive. I am exhausted. The Hippy turns his troubled face towards me. He looks like he wants to say something else, but doesn't. I close my eyes, and without opening them again I say, as if speaking into a lightless tunnel, 'If you want, we can stop this now.'

I listen for an answer.

The building's breathing draws closer.

The Hippy seems to be rustling something, the bedcovers perhaps, and then he lies still.

I get no reply, but I interpret this as agreement. It could also be refusal, of course. Silence can mean anything. Perhaps he just died. Perhaps at this very second Shiva is gathering up his swami soul, and I'm talking to an empty shell, a shell that can be burnt, ground into dust and thrown into the river once it has heard everything, into the poor, poor Isar River.

I find that reassuring.

6

I didn't speak a word to Hub for two weeks. My silence grew inflamed and swelled until the pus oozed from every pore.

But when I looked silently at Hub with this pus in my gaze, his pupils slid away. He didn't want to see anything. My festering eyes were telling him that he should come and ask me what was wrong. But he didn't want to see anything. Or to ask any questions.

We no longer acted as one flesh and one blood.

All the same, I had to ask the disguise-and-deception question. Had it just been our financial cataclysm, the crisis surrounding our father, that had given Erhard Sneiper the idea of putting us forward to Herr Heydrich as secret scouts? Or did Hub already have some experience in the disguise-and-deception business? After all, he had disguised himself and deceived me, his own brother. That had never happened before. Nor could I imagine that Ev knew what we were getting our-selves into.

'No,' he told me, when I managed to catch him at the right moment, just before the third week of silence. 'Women have no business in any of this. Ev doesn't know. And you must swear to me that it will stay that way.'

'I don't have to swear anything to you.'

My voice was weary and guttural, thickened by the pus that was lodged in my throat.

The signs of distress I saw on Hub's face left me cold. The tempera-ture fell in my guts, that's what I mean by cold. I got no answer to my disguise-and-deception question. There is no other way to say it: I had been led into a trap, and there was nothing that bore any resemblance to a discussion between us. Hub acted as though I must always have known that the 'League of German Youth' was just a disguise for the sale of our dignity.

Until that day, I had seen my brother as more of a titan than a man; as a Prometheus, bringing fire to the mortals and having his liver pecked out for it, the whole thing sculpted in marble in the style of Adam de Jeune – really, that's how I had thought of this man who hit you in the face last week, my unfortunate Swami.

Our mission was quite clear. We were to make extensive observations. Latvians. Jews. Political opponents within the Baltic German camp. Herr Heydrich had also instructed us to record economic and political movements, personnel and personalities in Latvia, to characterize them and prepare index cards and documents for a potential intervention in Latvia. Hitler's potential 'intervention' in Latvia – a remarkable word, which had previously entered my life only as a term from Ev's medical textbooks – was the first state secret to which I was party. While my brother went on to collect state secrets like rare stamps, they never gave me a thrill of pleasure.

I must admit that Hub did his best to look after me. He was trying to heal things – but in looking out for me, he refused to look back and acknowledge what had happened. It was a kind of retrospective blindness that he regarded as mercy. Above all, he wanted me never to reconsider my position. Our parents were too dependent on the money the SS was paying us.

We had to lead a double life: to the outside world, we were not much more than overgrown teenagers, petty Nazi officials without much power. Underneath all that, however, we were part of the hidden power that was transforming the whole world. We became initiates, we were in the know. It was vital that no one who was uninitiated, uninformed, ever discovered our secret. On our journey back from Berlin to Riga, I realized that the sporting attraction of being a spy lay in hiding the very existence of this secret, even from your nearest and dearest. All the stages of deception lay ahead of us, and we began to go through them one by one.

As was Hub's way, he suggested taking on the dirty work himself. He would compile the archive and run the blacklists. He would recruit spies from among our young people and cast an impressive net of agents out across the Baltic German population. The particularly unpleasant task of evaluating the pedigrees and views of our own neighbours, the other people in our apartment building – ancient Fräulein von Pilatier on the ground floor, for instance (who was an unreliable Aryan, a Huguenot, though she claimed to come from an old Roman consular family with a legionary eagle on its coat of arms and a lineage that could be traced all the way back to Pontius Pilate) – all of this fell under his remit.

I, meanwhile, was responsible for spying on Latvia. The fun part, in other words.

All I really had to do was read the Latvian newspapers every day, travel around our homeland over the months and years to come, and map the locations of any garrisons and restricted military areas I came across. To read and write and draw: all things I enjoyed doing. This was a clever move by my brother to spare my scruples – by which I was frequently tormented, and he never was. His world view was entirely secure. In his opinion, he was acting for what was good and right, since he was working against the Bolsheviks and Latvians, the people who had drowned our Grandpaping. I could see the same absolute faith that had characterized Grandpaping and the many other men of God across the generations of our family taking on a new shape in my brother. It didn't frighten me yet, but I did find it unsettling, for with the best will in the world I could not share it.

*

I arranged to meet Ev, to show her the pus, perhaps in the hope that she could wipe it away. Hub had forbidden me from uttering a single word about our activities, but I was planning to give away my very first state secret before I had even properly understood it. I didn't care. And in any case, it would have been impossible to keep anything from Ev; I'd never had any secrets from her, not even the smallest thing. She knew whom I loved and with whom I was sleeping, and I knew that she loved Hub and was sleeping with Erhard, even if she put it in terms that were more (though admittedly not much more) romantic.

'Hub is my castle; I look at him from afar. And Erhard is so sweet. He's my cave, where I snuggle up.'

'And me?' I asked. 'What am I?'

'You,' she smiled, 'are my firewall.'

That was very much the sort of thing she said.

No, not much more romantic.

We agreed to meet at Café Puschkino, a plush, sleepy place not far from Freedom Boulevard, where the Russian émigrés veiled their despair in the smoke from their papirosi. No German Balt ever set foot in there.

It was late evening. She was sitting in the furthest, brocade-red corner, wreathed in smoke and lit by the milky glow of an electric light bulb. I was surprised to see her in a low mood; the chin cupped in her hand looked as though it wanted to flutter away, together with the restless fingers on which it swayed. I gave her a hasty kiss, sat down on the other side of the table and complimented her outfit, which was yellow with black polka dots – though the compliment came with a hint of sarcasm, just the way she liked it. She gave me a pained smile. Her darting eyes avoided me more than sought me out as they usually did.

I began at once to reveal my new, murky secrets, but the disclosure, or the revelation, or whatever you want to call it – yes, the confession – had no effect. Ev looked neither amused nor repulsed. She seemed fragile, and somehow absent.

'Ev?'

'Yes?'

'Are you listening to me?'

'I'm listening to you.'

'You're being so strange.'

She shifted her chin into her left hand, reached for a small spoon with her right, and made it turn tiny pirouettes on the tablecloth.

'I already know all of this,' she whispered hoarsely. It was noisy in the café and I could barely hear her.

'You already know?'

She nodded.

'You mean Erhard told you everything?'

'Not Erhard.'

'No?'

'Hub.'

Now I was certain I'd misheard her.

'Hub? He's not allowed to say anything. He strictly forbade me from telling you, too. All of these things are state secrets.'

She looked at me sadly, with a heaviness that I'd not seen in her before.

'Hub and I .. ...' she began. 'Oh well, you know.'

The waiter came and brought me a beer. Hub and her? What was that supposed to mean, Hub and her? I tried to refocus my confused mind on my beer, which sloshed in front of me like some kind of sea creature, like a yellow jellyfish – might it, too, have feelings, hopes, fears, I thought – the kind of thing you think in moments of purest bafflement.

'I'm an adulterer.'

Yes, my beer had fears; it was terrified of being drunk, for one thing. I stared at the yellow dress in front of me, the polka dots that I had a sudden urge to count, every last one of them. The castle and the snuggly cave and even the firewall began to rearrange themselves. One of the Russians opened the lid of the out-of-tune piano and began to intone 'Along the St Petersburg Road'. Everyone on the next table joined in.

'Koja?'

'I'll admit, that is news to me.'

'Yes.'

'You and Hub . . . ?'

'Yes.'

'Does Erhard know about this?'

'For God's sake.'

'Does Hub know about us?'

'Are you mad?'

'Does anyone know anything about anyone?'

Half the room was now emitting this useless old song, as tears welled up in Ev's eyes.

'I knew you would condemn me.'

'I'm only asking.'

'It just happened. Listen, I didn't provoke it. I feel bad. And Hub feels bad, too.'

'Well, so do I, now. And your fiancé isn't going to jump for joy, either.'

The Russians had their arms around each other, *na zdorovie* here, *na zdorovie* there, sentimental, joyful, angry, proud, passionate and lost. I took a deep breath and downed my fearful beer. A kind of fog settled over me and made me feel calmer.

'All right. I believe if we look at this objectively, dear Ev, there is some hope. I really do.'

I tried to conceal the fact that I was trembling by pressing my fingers against the empty glass.

'You know,' I went on, 'Hub isn't committed to anyone else. He has a lover now and again, but nothing substantial. And as for you, it's not possible for you to be an adulterer. All you are is engaged. You just need to break off the engagement. And then you can marry our Hub . . .' My voice failed for a moment, but only for a moment, before I pulled myself together. 'A . . . and you'll be happy, and you won't need to have eight children, just two or three. Like the Solms usually do.'

I know I have the tone of voice one needs at such moments. A tone with which you help ladies out of their fur coats or hold doors open, including – let's be honest – church doors. All the same, Ev's expression didn't brighten, it became more serious, more forlorn.

'I'm not an adulterer. But I will be.'

Her raven eyes settled.

'I'm marrying Erhard.'

The jellyfish in my stomach wanted to climb back out.

'In two months' time,' she said. 'He asked me yesterday.'

'Ev!'

'I have to, Koja.'

'But you love Hub! You have done for years! You love him! And now that idiot castle belongs to you! What are you talking about?'

'Don't you understand? Hub's whole career is tied to Erhard. And so is yours. If you lose your jobs, what will become of Papa? And Mama? What will become of you, Koja?'

It was absolutely necessary for me to leap up and run out, to run half-way down Kalkstraße. It really was necessary. A droshky swerved to avoid me, the driver almost catching me with his whip. A dog chased after me, but I shouted at it. That was necessary, too.

When I got to the town hall square, I couldn't go on. I bent over, panting, propping myself up on old Roland, or rather on his plinth, and wishing the man of granite could just lend me his heart. Mine was beating so hard it hurt, pumping blood back into my brain, which is the last place I wanted it when I felt like my mind was going to explode.

The most upright man I know. Starts a secret service. Manipulates his brother. Goes behind the back of his superior, his friend and confidant, to fuck his fiancée, who is also his own sister. And agrees that this superior, friend and fiancé should marry her anyway. A wedding that, if everything is taken to its logical conclusion, he might even perform himself, asking for God's blessing on this marriage, playing the good priest.

Blessed be the Solms, praised be their name, anointed be their fate.

And as if this weren't horrific enough, I now knew all of this and supported and encouraged and even needed it.

For ever and ever.

Amen.

A Latvian policeman, taking me for a drunkard, came over and asked if I was all right, and I uttered a few coherent sentences to him in Latvian. I don't need to sober up in a cell. I don't know what I need.

How could all this have happened?

That, my esteemed and morally far superior Swami, is something I have often asked myself. The story I am telling you is not the history of the German secret service, but of me in it. All I can give you, to quote a famous phrase by T. E. Lawrence, is a narrative of mean happenings and little people, who long for trivial things, for recognition and influence, for love and even for trust. No one should listen to the unimportant odds and ends that a man with a bullet in his head thinks are worth mentioning, and mistake them for history. We were dwarves. And in our calculations, our actions and decisions, we were immensely dwarfish. Though not in our planning and ideas. Never. The questions of our time overwhelmed us, the greatness of that historical moment, the proximity of war, the taste of mystery and danger. We were high on our own destiny, even when, leaning on the plinth of a Roland statue, life seemed like a nightmare, an ant's nightmare of burning anthills. You cannot seriously blame us for being Nazis then: it makes sense to live in the future, and you can't always choose the future, because, until it congeals into the sordid present, all it can be is hope, the hope that things will improve in time.

No, it was that we couldn't manage to keep the lie out of our lives, although – I swear – Hub, Ev and I longed for truth. That was what brought the dwarfishness into our existence, and later the depravity, and after that, crime, and finally death.

Perhaps it was the same for most Nazis.

But I can't comment on that.

The wedding of Eva Solm and Erhard Sneiper was quite an event.

There was not a single seat free in St Petri. Hub and Ev had had to employ all their powers of persuasion to talk Erhard into a church wedding. The admirable leader of our movement would have preferred a Germanic marriage ceremony, without a priest, beneath crossed legs of mutton.

I expect that would have finished Papa off; as it was, he sat propped up in his wheelchair, spitting out little crumbs and oat flakes during the chorale. That was his hallelujah. Mama wept. Everyone threw their hats in the air. The grins on each and every face were unbearable.

It was only Anna Ivanovna's perturbation that should have made me stop and think. But that took me another five years, and I will come on to it later.

Comrades in white shirts and white socks formed a guard of honour, though they didn't dare give the Hitler salute. The Latvian secret service had their trench coats there, too, monitoring the jubilant singing for signs of subversiveness.

Hub had chosen not to assume the role of pastor, thank God. But – and this was almost worse – he was forced to walk his sister, clad in innocent, glacial white (thoroughly snowed-in, in fact) to the altar and her proud bridegroom. I had roundly refused to play the father-of-the-bride role. Hub had begged me on his knees to do it. He was deeply shaken by my No. He couldn't understand what was wrong. Ev hadn't told him anything, and I kept my secret knowledge to myself, acting the innocent to keep from shaming him. And so the distance between us increased, the distance between the glistening castle and its shabby firewall, which was no use to anyone now and thus collapsed. No, not even that. Disintegrated. Turned into sand. Nothing but sand.

Ev moved out of our apartment and in with her husband. I gave her a fraternal goodbye kiss. In the years that followed I saw her often. On official occasions, at Christmas, at the party to celebrate her doctorate, or events organized by her husband. But never again was it just the two of us.

7

It was obvious that the affair was still going on. In the office, Hub would sometimes sit staring nervously at the clock at odd times (11 a.m. on a Monday, with the spy from Libau waiting in reception), and then go out walking for an hour, setting off towards the Petersburger Hof Hotel. When he came back, the smell of Ev clung to him, childhood camomile or the perfume that her husband (afflicted with a sudden blindness) regularly brought back from Berlin.

As soon as Hub had thoughtfully dropped his brother-in-law off at Spilve Airport, from where a plane shot the cuckold through the air to the conspiratorial capital of the German Reich, his happiness became tangible. Hub would wander back into our office whistling cheerfully, start spouting some kind of nonsense that was probably meant to sound like innocuous chit-chat, and then take the rest of the day off, asking me not to tell Sneiper about it. He was just feeling a little tired.

It was no wonder he needed me. His pathetic game of hide and seek, in which I aided him without his knowledge, was made transcendent, as it were, by the strong passion behind it, and seemed almost justified.

Meanwhile, our shadowy work was beginning to take shape.

My own heart had frozen, and I now sensed how conducive that could be to professional advancement.

We were extremely successful.

At a fair in the city, I met a charmless girl named Mumu; she was a pudgy Latvian from Dünaburg who worked as a secretary at the war ministry. My mind was so dissipated and I felt so lonely that I made use of the girl, and it was my first piece of malicious deceit, since Mumu was guileless and good-hearted. I soon stopped being alarmed by the extent to which sexual activity loosens people's tongues: they take it for intimacy, but it's just warmth, or at best a fever.

In summer, I rode my motorbike all over the country, at top speed, with a large quantity of drawing and painting equipment riding pillion. I held exhibitions in Riga, mostly watercolour landscapes; I concentrated on studies of plants, managing to capture a birch's every mood – the birch is Latvia's national tree. Under this pretext, I spent many happy hours outdoors and in the vicinity of large army training grounds, for it was there – and within sight of barracks, military airports and bunker complexes – that the most enchanting of all birch trees grew. I soon managed to dispatch detailed military maps and statistical materials to Germany. Heydrich himself sent me his regards, and rather than sending back a birch, which of course is just a tree, I gave him an oil painting of an oak, the Teutonic uber-tree.

Although I had left university without a degree and had never acquired any respectable skills, I still enjoyed a certain esteem in Riga society. My reputation was excellent and my social rank, calculated by multiplying the ranks of my ancestors, remained untouched. On top of this, I was now in a good financial position. No one guessed at the real source of my income. My disguise was an air of capability, various painting commissions, and a job as a youth leader. At that time, all that existed for me was work, nothing but work from morning till night, and I cannot claim it bored me. Everything was a useful distraction, as I tried with all my might to forget my sister, who sometimes appeared in my dreams as I was falling from the gallows, just before I cried out.

Into this period of personal unrest there burst a coup orchestrated by a man whom everyone has now forgotten. On the fourteenth of May nineteen thirty-four, I went to bed in a Latvian republic, and on the fifteenth of May nineteen thirty-four I woke up in a Latvian dictatorship. Overnight, the right-wing peasant leader Kārlis Ulmanis had blasted himself to the top of the government; ten years later, Stalin would send him to Siberia to starve to death for his actions. Tanks were stationed in all of Riga's big public squares. The arterial roads were controlled by large military units, and I cannot deny taking pride in my ability to recognize almost every vehicle from my summer excursions.

That morning, Mama wheeled Papa into the nearby city park, as she did every day, for the fresh air. And so she was witness to a small group of communists, hands in the air, being marched off by soldiers and forced onto a lorry – though this did not prevent my mother from addressing the bewildered commando leader politely and asking him, using the Baltic German parlance, to move his machine gun a few metres further along; his men were pussivanting about on Papa's favourite spot, with the splendid view of the cathedral.

Latvia had ceased to be a parliamentary democracy.

This was to have consequences for me and my family: the Ulmanis fascists who were now in power did not like Baltic Germans. There were even calls to round us all up and throw us on bonfires, to make our lovely blue blood boil and cause explosions, which Papa would have watched like new year's fireworks, but which Mama took as her cue to sharpen Grandpaping's home-made sword and place it under her pillow.

In the end, it was only our pride that was castrated. We lost rights both old and new: there were no more political parties; there was no freedom of assembly or of the press, and of course, no Movement, either. All property belonging to Baltic German associations was seized, the club funds confiscated. Even the centuries-old Guild Houses, palazzos built with Italian elegance and Lübeck craftsmanship, were occupied and decommissioned by the police.

It was as if Al Capone had come to Riga, with his army of Sicilian looters.

Erhard put on his wolfish grin and telephoned Herr Himmler.

The Movement, which had been persecuted to no small degree in Latvia even when the country was a democracy, now moved into the realm of illegality. Hub and I would have moved into this realm, too, but we were already spies, and there is nothing more illegal than spies. So we just prepared ourselves for seven lean years.

But what Hub, Erhard and I got were seven fat weeks. The lawlessness, the public humiliation and the loss of all their remaining influence drove a stampede of angry Balts into our arms. Our little party was fattened up out of sheer indignation.

The authorities quickly began to take an interest: when I looked down at the street from our window, I could see that our building was under surveillance, from a dark green Ford V8 saloon which occasionally emitted cigar smoke through an open window.

The democrats among the Baltic Germans avoided a confrontation with the ruling powers. They believed an open uprising could only end in catastrophe. I can't deny that I took a different view. As willing as I was to let the world take its course, theft, robbery and piratical behaviour raised my hackles. And when a turncoat member of the dispossessed guilds, a Baltic German hairdresser, publicly hailed the Latvians' criminal actions as a long-overdue corrective to antiquated ideas, and even urged the dictator Ulmanis on to further modernization, I couldn't fight off a bilious feeling.

That same evening, in a state of high excitement, Hub and a few spirited lads from the Reich Apple Clan went into the woods in search of thick clubs. They put on Italian carnival masks and entered the overzealous hairdresser's salon at midnight, without using a key.

I assure you, I was not with them – at least, I would love to say that. But I *was* with them, my distraught Swami. In fact, acting in a kind of trance, I was the first to summon up the mental and physical energy required to cross the threshold of decency (an axe may have helped, too). Our visit did not last long, but it did mar the beauty of the window-panes, the furniture and the wig mannequins. Hub rolled a barber's chair out into the street, someone placed a pig's head on it – and before I had a chance to be upset by the aesthetics of this act, two flaming torches were thrown in through the shop windows. Afterwards, we alerted the fire brigade. 'Get high! Defy! Terrorists are good guys!' Isn't that what your long-haired friends sing? We sang songs that were just as idiotic.

The Latvian press got wind of the incident. Our liberal countrymen poured scorn on what they regarded as our Jacobin methods. It was splendid. And it was hideous. It was splendidly hideous.

To everyone who hated us, we were the Sneiper-Solm gang. A lot of people hated us. Even Mama, who stood speechless outside the smoking ruins of the hairdresser's, wondering where she was going to get her wash and set now, gave a loud cry of, 'Phooey!' and thus reprimanded the Sneiper-Solm gang without even guessing that she was condemning her own sons.

8

I knew it.

I knew that the Latvian government would act. Knew that the dictator was beside himself with rage. Knew that there was no way Ulmanis could allow a small gang of boys to torch a collaborating hairdresser's business. And of course, I knew that the pig's head had been a particularly bad idea.

I knew all this because I got it first hand from my pudgy Latvian Mumu, who had heard unpleasant things about me at the war ministry and was growing sadder and sadder each time we met. Even her orgasms got sadder, and eventually stopped altogether.

'You're not pumping me for information, are you?' she asked, as we sat in a booth on one of our regular outings to the Petersburger Hof, over a bowl of the strawberry ice cream she loved so much.

'Mumu, what makes you think that?'

'Your lot are enemies of the state. They talk about it in the ministry quite openly. Sneiper and Solm are the worst names.'

'I'm not a bad person.'

'If they get wind that we're courting, I'll lose my job.'

'Then they mustn't get wind of it.'

'And you do honestly love me? You're not using me?'

It was the last I ever saw of her. The next time we arranged to meet, Mumu didn't turn up. When I tried to telephone her at the ministry, a cool voice told me that Miss Dalbeniks had resigned.

And who was calling, please?

The blow fell a few days later.

The Movement's secret apartment down by the harbour, known only to our innermost circle of mandarins, was stormed by the police during one of our meetings there. 'Well then, gentlemen, meeting adjourned!' Erhard cried, before deftly stuffing a closely written strategy paper into his mouth and chewing it patiently, like a goat, as the police broke the door down with a hatchet. Then we lined up against the wall. It was my first arrest.

Although they didn't find anything illegal there – weapons had been hidden and incriminating papers eaten – we were taken to the Schützenstraße remand prison on suspicion of 'pan-Germanic activities'. On the night we were locked up an inspector, subduing a yawn, revealed to me that I had been taken into custody under the Kerenski Decree, a law from Russian times permitting prisoners to be held without trial for up to seven years. I was placed in a single cell, which in Latvia doesn't mean that you have it all to yourself. I shared five square metres of stone floor with Mortimer MacLeach, a hoggish Falstaff of a man who proceeded to lose weight quite spectacularly, melting away before my eyes like a pat of butter in a pan. His brother was the only Baltic German traffic policeman in Latvia, possibly because the family had originally come from Scotland and therefore could not be suspected of having wiped out any indigenous Latvians.

Despite this connection to the state, none of us found ourselves in Latvian jails more frequently than Mortimer MacLeach. He was the head of the Movement's stewards, who liked to get into fights, especially with the communists. I learned all manner of useful things from Mortimer: the Kochumer Lohschen, for instance, a Yiddish robbers' alphabet that allowed us to communicate between cells through a system of knocking. This made it easy to agree things amongst ourselves right under the noses of the police. Later, he suggested an even more cunning ruse: Erhard's wife, our leader's beautiful spouse and therefore a person with some privilege, should bring us provisions. That was the full extent of the plan.

Ev really was allowed to come and visit us, pale with worry but putting on a brave face, and the three of us met her in the visitors' room: the fortunate Solm, the unfortunate Solm, and Erhard, fortune's deaf and blind fool. We were separated by a barrier, and Ev blew her husband a kiss across it. Her faint radiance grew brighter when Hub smiled at her. And faded again as she nodded to me, as to a rather unreliable accomplice who was yet to prove himself.

What she brought – along with the scent of lemon soap, which now wafted from her hair in place of the camomile and seemed to hang on the air for days all over the damned prison – was a food parcel, at which the guards laughed themselves sick, since it consisted solely of crabs and apples.

The sight of the red autumn Calville almost made Hub weep. The hungry Mortimer almost wept, too, but for different reasons. The crabs with their delicate, refined but very scant meat did little to sate our hunger. But my skilful cellmate made their claws into little fountain pens. Using urine, which turned into a blackish ink when left in a tin can, and a small hole bored into a crab claw, you could fashion a passable writing implement. You just had to regulate the flow of piss a little with your forefinger. To begin with, this requires a person to overcome a certain squeamishness, particularly if it isn't his own piss he is writing with. As we only had one tin can, we used Mortimer's piss, which was unusually dark. It enabled us to write countless secret messages on hard toilet paper, hide them in toothpaste tubes and distribute them to various recipients in the washroom. We felt like Baltic gentlemen, barons and counts of Monte Cristo, sitting on a rock with the waves crashing around us.

I can bear witness to the fact that European prisons would soon be much more on the qui vive. In the cells of the Gestapo, and the basement torture chambers of the NKVD's Moscow Lubyanka, food parcels were never proffered by unfaithful wives, certainly not parcels containing fresh crabs.

As I was writing, and even drawing in piss (I made a caricature of Mortimer as Oliver Hardy, to whom he bore a passing resemblance), I undoubtedly thought of myself as a Scarlet Pimpernel: streetwise, cunning and intransigent, while the officers of Latvia's security services seemed like cretinous natives, who hadn't the least idea that the scheming Nazis were leading them a merry dance in their own prison.

Unfortunately, however, the reverse turned out to be true.

The Latvian secret service was naturally aware of every move its prisoners made. It had rounded up the obstreperous Nazi functionaries for the specific purpose of intercepting their top-secret plans. Not only were the officials wise to the auditory Kochumer Lohschen (at night, a dyspeptic interpreter disguised as a guard typed up everything we said); the crab-claw notes, delivered by the renal mail, to put it in a roundabout way, were also brought to the secret service's attention.

Interrogation Officer Second Class Peteris Petrins knew all about me; he was aware of each contact I had made in the previous few months, and had even learned that I thought he was 'a cretin who believes any old nonsense', 'a disgusting toerag' and 'too stupid to piss on snow'. Although he knew all of this, he greeted me before each of my many interrogations with courteous cordiality, shaking my hand and asking if I would like to take a cup of hawthorn tea with him (he always had a rapid heart rate). Then, slurping his tea from time to time and exhibiting extraordinary patience, he would allow me to serve up the most opprobrious and fantastical pack of lies hour after hour. Although he saw through all this drivel, he never interrupted me; in fact, he assumed an expression of almost breathless interest. His must have been the most interested face in Riga – with the exception of mine on that rainy, dirty-yellow Monday when I happened to get a look at his papers.

Herr Petrins was unexpectedly called out that day for a brief consultation with his superior, an Interrogation Officer First Class. He left only the stenographer in the room, who just at that moment, or a moment later, had to make a very urgent visit to the lavatory. Since she was absolutely forbidden from leaving the interview room, she asked me to remain completely silent and, in the minutes when both she and Herr Petrins were absent, on no account to look in the folders behind the desk, particularly not in the one marked 'Centra'. I promised her I wouldn't in the same tone of loyal and prudent maturity that had made poor Mumu think so highly of me. She thanked me, *paldies jums*, with a smile of relief, and flitted away.

Hardly had the door slammed shut behind her before I was scrambling over to the 'Centra' folder. I pulled it out, paused for a moment, listened, heard nothing – and then opened it.

I didn't know what had hit me, as they say. 'Centra' is Latvian for 'centre', and centre is a code name, and the code name is code for a job, and the job is that of a spy, and the spy comes from our movement, and he is at the centre of our movement, and the centre is Centra, and Centra's real name is MacLeach. Mortimer MacLeach was an ND, a *neformālās darbinieki*, 'a secret informant' as the Latvian secret service called its most unpleasant employees. I saw his formal declaration of loyalty on the first page, then flicked through the rest of the file in disbelief. Saw dozens of reports. Familiar names. Surprising names. Above all, my own, the amputated form of which (K.S.) danced through the documents, appearing in every third sentence.

K.S. is a snobbish intellectual, who doubtless has a broad education and solid artistic skills. But he believes himself more talented than he is.

Likes apples. [Right beside this was the Oliver Hardy caricature that I had made of him just a few days earlier.] *Attachment: likeness of the informant Centra, cartoon by K.S., pen and ink drawing (special ink).*

Or: *K.S. says that Interview Officer P.P., with his thick-framed glasses and strikingly large nostrils, resembles an assistant executioner. P.P., he says, is a cretin who believes any old nonsense.*

And finally: *In ideological terms, K.S. is not yet a committed National Socialist. Has nothing against Jews. Has nothing against art. Were it not for his brother H.S., who is more indispensable, he would be thrown out of the Movement.*

I hung, bent double like a hook, over the bundle of documents. I looked out of the window and couldn't tear my eyes away from the rain. A curtain of streaks.

The executioner and his weak-bladdered stenographer might return at any moment. I tore out my cellmate's most recent report, shoved it into my trouser pocket, replaced the folder and dashed back to my seat, not a second too soon; just then, the door opened and the stenographer came back in, now fully relieved and thanking me effusively once more.

When Herr Petrins entered the room, he found an unaltered, conceited, speechifying snob, who was not yet a committed National Socialist, but who was so deeply shaken to find himself the object of secret-service infiltration, penetration and observation that he now saw the world through entirely new eyes.

I will linger for a moment on this point in my life because what it taught me was tremendously useful in my later work. It is not at all easy to encounter a person again when he has changed his inner form. Until then, I knew the werewolf principle only from Ovid's *Metamorphoses*. There, the Arcadian King Lycaon is transformed by the furious Zeus into a wolf who howls, claws and speaks Ancient Greek. And when I was taken back to my cell, I saw a fat werewolf dozing on his plank bed, where just an hour before there had been a fat man dozing on his plank bed. In the intervening time, the moon had risen and transformed me, too. Now I had to play with this puppy, feed it stories just as I had before, give it truths and details, talk things over with it and laugh and under no circumstances rip its fur off. Mortimer

MacLeach still looked like Mortimer MacLeach, of course; he still liked to make good-natured jokes and was friends with absolutely everyone, so it wasn't too hard to put on an act with him. The most difficult thing was to carry on writing with his piss. But I had no choice.

I kept up the facade for three weeks, listening to stories about his brother the traffic policeman (which sounded different now; I deduced a number of things from these stories), complaints about his financial situation (aha) and a few unhappy love affairs, which he revealed only to me, because he felt so comfortable in my indulgent company.

'A feeling of friendship flows through me, Koja,' he sighed. 'I can trust you, and that's such a precious thing.'

I agreed with him absolutely.

At this point, I could not let anyone know that we had a mole in our midst. At least no really sensitive information was being exchanged: Hub and I didn't go blabbing about secret Reich matters in front of our brothers-in-arms, who had no idea about our true function. And nothing but propaganda went into the toothpaste tubes.

When they were finally forced to release us – they couldn't prove anything, and the Reich had also intervened on behalf of its hoplites through the German ambassador – I went straight to Hub's office and told him everything. I thrust Mortimer's spy report, smuggled out in ways you don't want to know about and therefore not in the best olfactory condition, into his disgusted hands. In the meantime, I had begun to wonder why there hadn't been a raid. Had no one missed the report I'd torn out of the Latvian security service's file? Could the confused Peteris Petrins have seen that Centra's statement was no longer in his file, and put it down to his own slovenliness? Might there be some other explanation that my wise older brother would pull out of his hat?

No, there might not. Hub listened to the madness with his lips pressed firmly together, and simply said, 'We need to see the boss.'

Ev opened the door to us, already wearing her coat. She and Erhard lived in a villa in the Kaiserwald. Jugendstil. Large grounds, wind-buffeted pines. She smiled. It was different to her prison-visiting smile. Now she was the one being visited, and it pierced her very soul.

'Lovely to see you,' she said with rather exaggerated haste, kissing us absently, as if it wasn't us, as if it wasn't even Hub. She was on her way out.

'He's not feeling well. Maybe you could come back another time?'

Neither of us knew what to say, but then Hub shook his head slowly and seriously. I saw her take fright, I could see it in her hands, I knew her so well. But she just gave us an airy nod and another false smile, pulled her hat firmly onto her head, and as she turned to leave, fastened the belt of her coat more tightly.

'I'm so sorry, I'm needed at the hospital,' she called out, and then she was gone, blown away like autumn leaves. Hub watched her go as if she were fleeing from us.

Then we stepped through the door, which she had left open in her alarm. Erhard was standing in the drawing room with his narrow back turned towards us. He was barefoot and unshaven, looking out of the window. When he turned round I found myself looking into a grey, uprooted face protruding from a light-coloured dressing gown, the left sleeve of which had been dipped in soft-boiled egg yolk. On the wall behind him hung all four pictures I had painted for Ev: a bunch of cornflowers; Ev as a twelve-year-old, asleep in my bed wearing a blue nightshirt; the judgement of Paris; and a watercolour that I had entitled *Melancholy*, although she found it life-affirming.

None of these pictures made a fitting backdrop for Erhard's face.

'What is it?' he asked.

Hub explained that a problem had arisen; it was something that could not be put off and had to be discussed immediately.

'Yes, yes, yes . . .' Erhard murmured reluctantly, and then was silent for a long time. He was quite plainly drunk.

'Can we discuss it?' Hub pressed him. 'It really is serious, it's a really serious problem.'

Erhard didn't seem interested. He made a dismissive or perhaps an inviting gesture towards the three-piece suite. We sat down and watched our boss lurch over to a bureau, take out a brown envelope, pluck a vodka bottle from the shelf and bring them both back to us.

'Let me show you something.'

He flopped down into an armchair in front of us, pulled a photo out of the envelope and slid it wordlessly across the coffee table with his right hand. With his left, meanwhile, he was pouring us each a large measure of vodka in a less than coordinated manner.

The photo was an enlargement, grainy and not very clear. It had been taken from a rooftop or a balcony some distance away from its subject, which was a large, open window. The woman leaning on the windowsill, with an air of exhaustion about her, was unmistakably our sister Ev. She was naked from the waist up. Her arms were folded across her chest, and she was smoking a cigarette. She was staring into space. Behind her you could make out a bed on which a man was lying, also naked, his member white and erect. His face, however, was shaded by a newspaper; the shadow concealed it and merged with the darkness of the room.

In my confusion, I was still trying to grasp the full significance of the image when Erhard handed us another snapshot. Now Ev had disappeared from the window, and she and the man were a tangled potpourri on the bed: limbs, a veiled eye, a wide-open mouth, tousled hair, almost all of it belonging to Ev and not the man, whose face was still turned away and whose shimmering body was so flawless and muscular that it absolutely could not belong to the drunken twig of a man sitting in front of us, swaying to and fro as if being teased by the wind.

So: Erhard was now familiar with the werewolf principle, too.

Beside me, Hub leapt to his feet, pale as chalk. He cried out that, naturally, he would accept any challenge like a man. Erhard should choose the weapons.

His words met with total incomprehension.

'Why should we duel, Hub?' Erhard asked. 'For your family honour?' He shook his head. 'It's your sister who has been unfaithful to me, not you.'

In Hub's iris I saw a flicker of consternation, while Erhard sank back into himself and stared absently at his bare legs. I had to do something.

'Who took these photos?' I asked in a low voice.

'A private detective.'

'Why did you have a private detective follow Eva? You should have informed us about her indiscretions.'

'Indiscretions? She's cheated on me, taken me for a damned fool!'

Baltic German has many words for cheating, but the word he used – 'brietschen' – is one of the harsher ones. 'I think she's been doing it ever since we got married. The little slut.'

'Erhard, with all due respect, you are talking about our sister,' I said pompously.

'And that's why I couldn't say anything to you,' he nodded. 'You're good friends. You're family.'

'Above all, we're the Movement's security service. *We* should have taken the matter in hand.'

'You should have taken it in hand, of course you should. But still, she is your sister.'

'What does she have to say about it?'

'She doesn't know yet.'

'She doesn't know yet?'

'No.'

'Hub, she doesn't know yet.'

'Yes, I heard the first time.'

'But why doesn't she know?'

Erhard brooded darkly to himself, his mouth a straight line, completely unreadable to me. Hub's lips were even thinner. One might have read commiseration in his waxen face, and it's true, he was commiserating. But certainly not with his cuckolded brother-in-law.

'I'm sorry, Erhard,' I pressed on. 'But you had Ev followed by a private detective for weeks, you've got these photos – and she doesn't know yet?'

'No. I want to get my hands on the bastard first.'

Hub tipped the vodka down his throat and poured himself another.

'So,' I ventured hesitantly, 'do you have any suspects?'

He merely grunted. I could see dandruff in the hair through which he'd just run his hand, and when no answer came at all, I felt a sweet sensation spreading through me, a cloud of gratification and a deep sense of well-being.

'I mean, do you have even the faintest suspicion of who it could be?' I went on, refusing to let the matter drop.

Erhard raised his head; he was close to tears.

'The detective caught a glimpse of his beak once, but the camera didn't work, it was out of film. He's not bad-looking, apparently, around your height, Hub, wears English clothes, sunglasses, a hat. He's very cautious. Shame we couldn't get a good shot of him here.'

'We'll catch him, my friend!' I promised.

'Yes,' said Hub, and it was the first thing he'd said in a long time. 'We'll catch him.'

We all had another vodka, silent and sighing and lost in thought, while outside the wind blew little grains of sand against the front windows. Eventually Erhard looked up at us, like a meerkat spotting a hawk in the sky.

'So, what's this problem you came to speak to me about?'

'Oh,' I said dismissively. 'There's no real problem.'

Hub glanced sideways at me in surprise.

'There's no real problem?' he croaked.

'No, it's not all that serious.'

'I thought it was a very serious problem,' Erhard said.

A second son is never short of cunning. There is a depth to the way he thinks; it's the only way of prevailing against his older brother. Hub would have made a great preacher (he always liked to preach), but sermons don't need to be orchestrated, arranged, plotted, manipulated, concocted or even worked out. You just give a sermon. Cunning is something you build slowly. And then it becomes a plot.

'Oh no, it really isn't serious,' I said breezily, determined not to introduce the subject of Mortimer MacLeach under any circumstances.

'But, Koja, we have to tell Erhard what's going on with the Movement's leadership, it's a scandal.'

I shuffled to one side a little, attempting to distract Erhard from Hub and his awkward insistence with my shoulder. Then I leaned over to my brother-in-law.

'Yes,' I murmured, 'it's an unpleasant business, but nothing compared to this.' I pushed Erhard's photos towards him. 'Might it even be possible, Erhard, and this is just conjecture, but might it be possible that the man who is causing both you and us such pain is someone very close to us? It isn't out of the question that there could be some connection between what we came here to tell you and what you have just told us.'

No one understood what I was trying to say.

'I'm trying to say that a certain person from our political movement is doing everything he can to destabilize us.'

Erhard stared at me. For a moment he looked like he was in a trance.

'By fucking my wife?'

'I wouldn't put it in quite those—'

'You mean a man from our movement, a German man with German sympathies, is fucking my wife?'

'I find it hard to imagine, too, but . . .'

'And he isn't just fucking my wife, he's fucking us all, he's fucking you, and Hub, and me, he's fucking this garden here, he's fucking the seagulls out there, he's fucking the grass and the stars, he's fucking the German Reich – and our Führer, too?'

'Please don't upset yourself, Erhard, it's just an idea.'

'Of course, that must be it!' He clapped his hands together. 'Only a spineless traitor fucks his leader's wife! I'm the leader of the ethnic Balts!'

'You are, Erhard, there's no doubt about that.'

'I AM!' he shouted, taking his vodka glass and hurling it against the glass cabinet, which shattered loudly. 'I AM THE LEADER OF THE ETHNIC BALTS!'

'Erhard, please sit down.'

'I DON'T DESERVE THIS! I TOOK HER UNDER MY WING! UNDER MY WING! AND SHE'S FUCKING MY OWN PEOPLE!'

He wept. The sobs made his shoulders shake like a blancmange, and as if that were not enough, Hub now broke down, too. A tear rolled down his heroic cheek, and I had my hands full.

Later, my brother and I went to the Bilderlingshof Beach and sat in the dunes. He seemed to have aged years. The wind gusted around our ears, and storm clouds billowed on the distant horizon.

I pretended never to have heard a word about Hub's affair with Ev, and he now confessed it to me with great contrition. I then began to explain my plan to him. The facts were devastating and multifarious; the options few. 'Either we all get out of this with our hides intact,' I told him, 'or we won't have any hides left, or flesh, or bones.'

All the same, Hub hesitated, thinking my plan irresponsible.

For the first time in my life I was able to tell *him* that he needed to pull himself together and make a terrific effort.

It was a very simple and sure-fire plan, and so Hub had no choice but eventually to give in.

We went to visit Mortimer MacLeach, alias Centra.

He lived in the Moskauer Vorstadt, a rather run-down area near the market halls. I rang the bell beside a door covered in peeling green paint. Hub kicked it in without provoking a reaction from anyone else in the building. We dragged MacLeach off the lavatory, stuck his head in the bowl, pulled the chain, heard him bubbling and choking, explained exactly what had happened (look, he said, he really hadn't wanted to), held his informant report in front of his eyes, which were crying out in panic – and as he fell to his knees and begged for his life, we put forward our suggestion. Either we would expose the fact that he was the enemy spy in our movement's ranks, who had given away our organizational structure, our weapons cache, our contacts in Germany, and betrayed every last one of us. Just like Ephialtes, the scum of Thermopylae. He knew, we said, what the National Socialist German Workers' Party had done with traitors during the time of its struggle. He could expect to suffer the same fate.

Or we could exercise Periclean magnanimity and keep his disgrace to ourselves. But in that case, we would require his assistance in a certain matter.

'What matter is that?' the werewolf whimpered.

I explained to him that, firstly, he had to cease all cooperation with the Latvian security services right away. And secondly, he had to admit to being my sister's lover – to Erhard, her rather irate husband who was looking for answers.

'Are you mad? He'll kill me!'

Without any warning, Hub hit him in the face. There was a sound that I'd heard once before at the doctor's, when he was popping my dislocated shoulder back in. Mortimer's nose was broken. A fountain of blood sprayed over his lips, but he seemed not even to notice. Instead, he begged for mercy and pointed out all kinds of things we had to consider, among them the fact that he was much too fat to be the unknown Adonis in the photo.

In this, Mortimer had hit upon a significant weakness in our plan. He had indeed lost so much weight on a weeks-long diet of prison food that it might just about be possible to claim a physiological resemblance between him and the man in the photo (my brother, just to reiterate that fact). But the idea that one of the most beautiful and highly educated women in Riga would go to bed with an Oliver Hardy double, an endomorphic thug and notorious layabout who slouched listlessly on the periphery of European intellectual life, might cause even Erhard to smell a rat.

All the same, we had to risk it.

Love makes you blind.

Nothing is impossible.

We informed Erhard by telephone that he had no further need of his private detective.

He hung up without saying a word.

We met two evenings later in our apartment. It was still September, and Mama had taken Papa off to spend a week at a sanatorium in Kemmern. The four of us sat at the kitchen table in our long coats and hats, and the werewolf played his part decently enough. In the meantime, Hub had spoken to Ev. She refused to play along with the whole farce, which she found undignified. But at least she agreed to remain silent about her supposed affair with Mr MacLeach – she would say nothing at all to Erhard, in other words, and hope for a merciful divorce.

Once Mortimer had made his confession and begged our beloved leader for forgiveness, the latter, much to everyone's astonishment, pulled out a revolver and held it to the forehead of his wife's lover, asking him in measured tones to say the Lord's Prayer.

'Erhard, what are you doing?' I asked tentatively.

'I'm doing what needs to be done!'

'You can't shoot him here. This is my parents' kitchen.'

'Your parents aren't here!'

'This rug came from the Peterhof Palace. The Tsar once stood on it!'

'Mortimer, step away from the rug!'

'Please don't lose your head.'

'Yes, don't lose your head,' Hub agreed. 'The Movement needs you as a free man, not a prisoner. He's not worth it.'

Erhard hesitated.

'Please, Erhard,' I said gently. 'There's still so much you can do for our fatherland.'

His mouth told me of the turmoil inside him; his upper lip quivered, and I could see little beads of sweat forming.

'All right.' He finally ground the words out through his teeth.

Erhard de-cocked the revolver with tears in his eyes, and put it back in his coat pocket. 'But the bastard must be punished.'

'Of course,' said Hub, interrupting the cascade of Baltic curses that Erhard was pouring over the partially innocent traitor (cretin, cur, scrub, clodpoll, slabber). My brother went over to the likeness of our

Grandpaping and took down the home-made sword that hung beside it. He placed the sword on the table in front of the werewolf and told him to cut off one of his own fingers.

'But you promised me I wouldn't get hurt,' Mortimer whined.

'You've got five minutes. We'll wait outside.'

'Hub, shouldn't we consider a hefty fine instead?' I cried out. This development was a long way from being part of my plan.

'No! Either his finger or his cock! Something the little scurf has stuck in her!' Erhard sputtered.

'Please, comrades, let's be sensible!'

But at that moment, Mortimer MacLeach shouted, 'You stupid Hun thugs! I despise you all!' Grimacing, he snatched up the sword, raised it above his head, aimed at his outstretched left hand, cried, 'Rule Britannia!' and struck. His little finger flew across the kitchen and landed on Mama's crocheted tablecloth, where it looked quite natural – it even appeared to curl up, at least from where I was standing. No one said a word. Quietly, Mortimer started to hum an English song, and from then on he refused to speak anything but English, and I marvelled at the fact that nothing flowed out of the stump where his finger had been.

Thus the thirties ended in a curious kind of harmony.

Of course for you, my supreme astral court, the word 'harmony' belongs in a very different context. It makes you think of cosmic balance, the magic of unity, and maybe even what you feel when you take a drag on your hash pipe. But if you take harmony to mean things or events that are entirely incompatible and should really be causing chaos coming together to form a symmetrical whole, then the terrible confusions around Hub and Ev, and Erhard and Mortimer, detectives and spies, love and politics, really did come together in a very harmonious conglomeration.

The nine-fingered Anglophile Mortimer MacLeach emigrated to the Reich a few months after these events. He had been extremely lucky. It was Ev, of all people, who'd had to clean and treat the wound – she was working as an emergency doctor at the Knorr'sche Hospital when we brought her former lover, whom she'd never laid eyes on before, into her department in the middle of the night. Her eyes had a rock-like, impenetrable weight, which fell on us from a tremendous height – and if she had learned the true story behind the accident, she would never have forgiven Hub or me. Fortunately, Mortimer was terribly afraid of us (it was an almost obsessive fear) and so he lied to her and said he had slipped while chopping wood.

But who chops wood in September?

Mr MacLeach kept his mouth shut. Most importantly, he stopped talking to Interrogation Officer Second Class Petrins, as we gathered from the fact that not long after the accident Mortimer's brother was forced to give up his privileged job as a traffic policeman. To my knowledge, Petrins never became an Interrogation Officer First Class, either.

Our work as the Movement's security service was therefore bearing fruit. That fruit was not always palatable; in fact, sometimes it was as bitter as strychnine. It was not a pleasant job, amputating digits, spying on people, noting their habits and recording their dislikes, especially when those dislikes related to us.

Hub assembled all the information he'd collected and sent regular reports to the Wannsee Institute in Berlin. This institute was Heydrich's Grail Castle, a political SD laboratory disguised as a civilian 'Academy of Archaeology', to which I was summoned several times a year. It was housed on the shores of Wannsee in a villa that the Gestapo had confiscated from its Jewish owners and made entirely secure, with splendid grounds that featured animal sculptures, greenhouses, a rose garden, a boccia court and even an SS riding arena.

The sinister Baltic department that looked after us was headed by a cousin of Erhard's whose leg had been torn off by a shark in the Red Sea. 'Sharks are the Jews of the fish world,' the cousin hissed, as tenacious as Cato, when we handed our notes over to him. He hobbled away on his wooden leg to the other exiled Baltic German fascists, who got to work on our material at once. I felt rather like a seahorse swimming through this school of Baltic German secret-service men, who snapped at each other and attacked as one, a veritable band of brothers even then, subversive, dogmatic and very well paid.

By now I could see the attraction of belonging to the select club of the SD elite, this group of cool, brilliant academic minds that combined the elegance of the British secret service with the cold pragmatism of the Cheka.

But really, it was only the facade that I liked. I was overwhelmed by these people's powerful images and bold disguises; to me, they shone in the colours of Caravaggio, so much light, so much shade – and then what lurked behind the facade slowly pulled me in and opened up in me that hidden, suppressed desire for deception, power and solitude that we all share. Once a secret-service man, always a secret-service man, as we say in our business. Only someone who has experienced the almost familial feeling that exists between conspirators can appreciate the truth in this facile statement.

Erhard never found out what really happened back then.

He thanked his faithful companions (us) effusively, calling us his Burgundians, who pulled chestnuts from the blazing fire for their Dietrich von Bern (him). (We never did know what the chestnuts were supposed to signify – his masculine pride, perhaps. Of course, in truth we were the blazing fire, or rather Hub was, though Erhard still had no idea about that.)

Erhard filed for divorce at once, much to Ev's relief, and she made no objection. Very soon afterwards she told me that getting involved 'with that gnome' had been the greatest mistake of her life. She had spent summer, autumn, winter, spring and another summer with someone who planned to tie her to the kitchen sink and was hoping to breathe eight children into her womb by means of a goodnight kiss: sex had become too much for him, even with his own wife. She said he had actually taken greater pleasure in showering with sixteen-year-old boys (Youth Leader Solm, Konstantin could confirm this; he himself had been a little surprised by Erhard's eagerness in that department) and fulfilled his marital duty just once a month, when his sexual organ – on the condition of which this duty naturally depended – was able to perform for two to three minutes. He'd also made an outrageous demand on her by asking her to give up her position as a doctor, which she did not do, and this situation caused him unbearable mental anguish. 'And you know, Koja, this whole Nazi business is completely ridiculous. I realize you and Hub subscribe to it, too. But it all just seems childish to me.'

Her divorce brought us closer again, and since she had never been one to mince her words, and had never been ashamed in front of me, she wasn't embarrassed by the photos her husband had commissioned and I had seen, nor by what they showed. Erotic desire was the by-catch of her wilfulness, and she was used to asserting her will. She had never taken too much notice of social conventions. She had told me herself that she and Hub had entered into a relationship. And I had known that sex was important to her since the youthful dreams we had dreamed together, illusions of a full life that still had a hold on me, though I would never confess that to her. For I felt that my longing was for these ancient memories, which none of us ever escapes. But memories are not life, they are the death of all that exists now.

I didn't know that then.

I knew only that the way was now clear for Hub and Ev. After a decent interval they could commit to one another (perhaps even without incurring Erhard's wrath), become man and wife, have children, grow old together, and I wished that for them with all my heart – a heart that bore some teeth-marks, admittedly, but was still strong enough to wish the people I loved most the greatest happiness on earth.

And so fate took its course.

9

I'm worried.

The Hippy seems to be showing signs of a melancholy that I didn't notice at the beginning.

He was always cheerful, happy as a Negro. I don't mean that in a derogatory way. People don't say Negro like that these days, which I find odd. What's so bad about the word? Chink is different – Asian sounds more polite. So perhaps I should say African instead of Negro. But Black? I don't know.

It's something I would like to discuss with the Hippy, but he's listless. He used to display a real curiosity about me, which now seems gradually to be wearing off. Just a few days ago his interest in me appeared so urgent, and it pains me to sense its intensity waning. This much is clear from the fact that the Hippy is now much less forthcoming, and much less keen for me to be forthcoming.

Sometimes he just stares gloomily straight ahead, like a wet blanket. This melancholy isn't like him at all; melancholy and high intelligence are two sides of the same coin, and the Hippy certainly isn't highly intelligent.

I am highly intelligent, and therefore I am melancholic.

In fact, Kant once pointed out that melancholics have an excellent sense of the noble and elevated, because their attention is always drawn to difficulties first. Hippies, of course, don't do that. Hippies never turn their attention to difficulties, but towards rolling cornfields, and so they are constantly singing 'Happy Sunshine' and saying 'Take it easy'. Hippies see difficulties as mosquitoes to be swatted – though that image isn't quite right, because hippies would never hurt a fly; they imagine instead what it would be like to be reborn as a fly a thousand years from now. Thoughts of this kind certainly do not radiate nobility. Long, unwashed hair and Jesus sandals are also a very long way from being noble. The egocentrism that comes with melancholy and nobility is something the Hippy doesn't possess, either, or he wouldn't always be staring at strangers' babies and delighting in them as if they were his own. So I have no idea why he is making a face like that.

'All right, why are you so monosyllabic?' I ask.

'What?'

'Why are you so monosyllabic?'

'Oh, I'm not really.'

'Have you run out of cannabis?'

'No.'

I tell you, the Hippy is somehow different. I wonder if my story might be what has done this. The truly terrible things are yet to come, and I really don't want to leave them out. Yes, I must admit that, in a way, I feel enlivened. It is terrific and fabulous after all, as Hub would say.

'Can I ask you something?' the Hippy says finally, though without looking at me, meaning that I am blinded by the little yellow ray of sunlight reflecting off his skull-screw.

'Of course.'

'Why are you in such a good mood?'

'Am I? I don't know about that. But then, Night Nurse Gerda is looking after us very attentively. The doctors are nice. I'm haven't had any more headaches. And the two of us are getting along splendidly, aren't we?'

'Yeah, but you're telling me these really disturbing things, man, it's a real downer. That poor guy chopped his finger off? And you were spying on everyone you knew?'

'My brother did that, yes. My job was more to . . .'

'I know.'

'One thing every secret service has in common is its peculiarity.'

The Hippy turns his head and looks me in the eye.

'And is it leading somewhere, all this stuff you're telling me, or is it just a series of really not cool things?'

'What I am telling you now,' I say, and then I pause for effect in an imitation of Erhard Sneiper. I sense a desire to make myself and my story appear interesting, because I want to – no, I must – carry on with it. 'The story I am telling you will become a ballad from the wild days of the Cold War. A lesson in politics, if you like, which will reveal the continuities of contemporary international history. Before you lies a man who helped to steer this country's fate to a degree that you can't even imagine.'

'Stop pulling my leg!'

'I'm not pulling your leg.'

'This is bullshit.'

'Ask the policeman sitting outside the door.'

'Your brother went on the rampage, *that's* why he's there.'

'You will find out why I've got this bullet in my head.' I point to it. 'But you asked me to start at the beginning. And this is still the beginning.'

He turns away, reaches for his Buddhist-Vishnuist-Shaktist-Shamanist primer. Perhaps the easiest thing for a hippy to believe in is enlightenment, in a moment where the Lord God or whoever it might be flicks a light switch and bang, all at once everything is illuminated. But that's not how the progress of knowledge works. Knowledge grows out of an endless series of defeats. It is only when we sustain damage that we wise up. This projectile in my frontal lobe must be making me ludicrously wise, because that's the greatest possible damage one can imagine. And perhaps that is also why I am slowly starting to assemble the stones. The stones that used to keep on rolling away, as if Sisyphus had dragged them into my life. These meaningless stones, with which an architect like me now starts to build his house. His house of knowledge. I can already tell that the Hippy doesn't want to live in it. Who would.

Yes, I am the one who has made him melancholy, no doubt about it. He has been waking up much earlier than he did in the first few weeks. He has no appetite. He doesn't want my dessert any more; he can't even manage his own. (I, on the other hand, have more of an appetite now, and this morning I even ate all of my semolina porridge.) He is feeling disproportionately guilty, I think, for listening to me.

'Are you feeling guilty for listening to me?'

'Shall I tell you something? You think I'm stupid.'

'No, not at all.'

'You think I'm unintelligent, but you think you're intelligent, because you went to university and failed to get a degree and your aristocratic parents stuffed you full of oil paintings and Goethe. I didn't get my school-leaving certificate, and my father threw himself off a tower block because he was so depressed, and all the same I believe in the sevenfold path. I became a swami because the European path is rubbish, it's all about the will. I believe in not having a will. You're like most Europeans, you believe the will is what it's all about. But if you have a will, you also have a standpoint. You don't let God speak to you in all his manifestations. You don't groove. I'm not condemning you for what you've done. And I think my lack of a standpoint is the main reason you've condescended to spend so much time with me. Because actually, you think you're superior and that I'm only worth something because I'm enduring your biography.'

'It troubles me that you see it that way.'

'How else am I supposed to see it? You're a wonderful person, because every person is wonderful. But you're telling me things that I don't want to take in, I don't want to have a standpoint on them, and that's why I'm exhausted.'

His sadness is so terribly transparent. I would like to get out of bed and bow down to him, but my pride won't permit it; he's thirty years younger than I am.

'Perhaps I'm in such a good mood,' I begin, 'because you're letting me talk.'

'Yeah, I'm your therapist, and that's fine, but it's all just so stressful.'

'But you want to know what happens next?'

'Of course I want to know, because *you* want to know.'

'I know already.'

'No one actually knows themselves. Only God knows everything about you.'

10

The summer of nineteen thirty-nine was the hottest in living memory.
The city melted as if in a furnace. The fire-fighting pond in the park
began to seethe. Dead carp floated to the surface, and horse-drawn
cabs got stuck in the liquid tar on the roads. When I went out onto
the balcony at night, unable to sleep, I could see forest fires in the
distance, eating into the horizon. To escape the heat, I often drove the
new DKW – my pride and joy – out to the long beach at Wezahken
to go swimming.

From time to time, I would take Donald with me. Like many
Americans, he hadn't the slightest idea where he was. Donald had
been working as the *Chicago Tribune*'s Russia correspondent for many
years, without ever setting foot in Russia. He had once refused to guarantee positive coverage to the Soviet authorities, which lost him his
accreditation for Moscow, and ever since he had been lurking in what
he regarded as an eerie border town, waiting for news. He hated Stalin
so much that he thought the dictator might have caused the roasting
temperatures in Central Europe himself, out of malice and boredom.
'The Reds are burning half of Siberia to terrorize the earth's atmosphere. Carbon dioxide, you know?'

I fed him many an anti-Soviet horror story, breadcrumbs from my
secret-service work. Of course, I also opened a file on him; as a foreigner, he fell within my remit. I used the light-blue index cards that
Hub had given me for this purpose, entering the desired information
into each field. Not knowing what to put under 'racial appearance',
I finally plumped for 'Nordic-aquiline' on the grounds of his Irish
potato nose, adding 'congeneric' in brackets, because you never knew
who was going to be reading these things. There was little else to note.
Donald Day had a peculiar name; he was a bullish and blustering Yank
from Philadelphia, who loved to hunt little crabs on the beach. He was
my neighbour in Vorburg, where we rented apartments in a swanky
building full of bachelors like ourselves right next door to the US
Legation. I had been living there for the past two years.

*

Sometimes Donald dragged me out to the bars frequented by Riga's small American community, and one evening he introduced me to a dancer, a Negress – all right, an African, though she was from the Caribbean. Her name was Mary-Lou and she taught me a little English, which would prove useful to me later in the CIA. Mary-Lou smoked like a navvy; she had curly steel wool on her Nefertiti head, and everything about her was relaxed, even her anthracite-black skin, which looked to me like a beautiful dress. She didn't have an ounce of fat on her, and each one of her muscles was clearly defined. We had nothing in common but a desire for one another, and we would leave the house principally to recover from that desire or to prepare ourselves for it. She had funny names for me, called me 'Schnitzel' when I came into her dance bar with a tan, or 'Fried Chicken'. She loved meat dishes more than anything, so these were pet names.

I liked her, I liked her very much, especially when she was in a bad mood. Then she would sit in the kitchen wearing my huge white dressing gown, smoking one of my equally huge cigars and, when I asked if she would like to go for a stroll with me, she would say, 'Don't give me a *Kopfschmerzen*, baby. Give yourself a *Kopfschmerzen*.'

When she was in a good mood, she never wore my dressing gown; she liked to walk around stark naked all the livelong day: naked as she sat at the kitchen table, naked as she drank her coffee, naked as she waved to the little boy in the building opposite, who stared at her as if she were a Fata Morgana.

I had some fierce arguments with Hub over Mary-Lou. He said I was impossible, strolling along the Düna promenade for all the world to see with 'a mongrel from a foreign race'. This was not a healthy attitude, he told me. They'd already got wind of it in Berlin, where what I was doing fell under the Nuremberg Laws.

Well, I'm not doing it in Berlin, I said; I'm doing it in my bedroom, and there are no such laws there.

Hub was worried that the SS wouldn't take me when war broke out and the Wehrmacht marched into Latvia, which was something he expected at any minute. He had a lot of worries, and they had begun to write fine lines around his handsome lips. He was now thirty-three years old. The age at which Alexander the Great died. And Jesus

Christ. My brother, who so far had founded neither an empire nor a religion, grew nervous, wondering whether his time would ever come.

I, meanwhile, couldn't imagine a better time. I lived in a rhapsody of meaningless and delightful activity, and still found plenty of time for acts of treason and painting nudes (Mary-Lou turned out to be a gifted model). I liked to rise late, and then without much effort organized scouting games, marching exercises, small-calibre shooting practice, map-reading, stalking, commando-crawling, distance estimation, communications and camouflage exercises for our young people: all the things that were favoured by children and dictators at that time. By everyone, in fact. The National Socialists had long since won over the Baltic German population. Across the board. All traces of liberalism had vanished. The Latvian state was waging war on us.

But what did the Latvian state matter.

That idiot Erhard Sneiper had risen to become president of the ethnic German community. Kārlis Ulmanis didn't dare take him on. I repeat: the dictator didn't dare take that idiot on. Just imagine that (usually it's the other way round).

No, without doubt it was a great time.

Hub was the crown prince, and really he should have felt triumphant. But that was when something like wrath crept into his character for the first time.

I'm sure it was also partly related to the uncertainty of his relationship with Ev. He avoided the scandal of openly being his own sister's sweetheart. It wasn't just that Papa would have had another stroke and Mama would have attracted contempt from every baroness around, whether she was related to them or not. Erhard would never have forgiven him, either. He still called us his Burgundians – but Ev was the beautiful, lost rose garden that he had cursed like the dwarf king Laurin had once done: neither by day nor by night should man ever set eyes on it again. And although Erhard had remarried – a dull blonde, who was a stranger to anything remotely animalistic – and although on the surface his social encounters with Ev were perfectly cordial, in secret he still obsessed over her with a tenacious, all-consuming hatred. I saw it in his face, a face in which I also took a certain pleasure, for he had truly earned it.

But for Hub and Ev, this face spelled danger, and they had to be on their guard.

They lived in a little house surrounded by high brick walls, which Ev mockingly referred to as 'our Sing Sing'. Outwardly their life together was perfectly innocuous; they were simply cohabiting as siblings sometimes do. Hub said he wanted to provide a degree of stability for his sister after the divorce, which had left her feeling fragile and in need of some psychological support.

Nothing could be further from the truth. Ev had certainly preserved a talent for hypochondria from her childhood; she liked to complain of headaches and immediately suspected a tumour every time her stomach hurt. We also had to listen to her endless concerns about a particular liver spot below her left armpit, and to feel the liver spot and read every article about liver spots that she recommended. Once she brought me an X-ray of her left hand, because she'd got it into her head that this hand would soon break. She even showed me where the fracture would be: the arc of her thumb.

But when it came to the suffering caused by the loss of her marriage and of Erhard, there simply was none. She just wanted Hub by her side, and hoped that their game of hide and seek would soon be over, because as it was, she could never be close to my brother in public. There could be no kisses, no lovers' rituals, and she had to be very careful not to get pregnant.

When Ev did get pregnant all the same and Hub forced her to have an abortion, a gauze-like veil descended between the pair of them, so thin that even I barely noticed; a pained distance to the kindness with which they usually treated each other when I came to visit, the only person who knew their secret.

Professionally, my sister was making progress. She was a successful doctor. Once, she was even awarded a medal, the Latvian national Three Star Order, for performing an emergency operation that saved the life of a fat Latvian minister. The operation had to be performed at a public lido in front of five hundred gawping swimmers, that was the unusual thing about it.

In herself, she seemed to me to have grown less playful and much lonelier. Her smile did not appear so frequently, though it could still set a whole room ablaze. She liked people, she liked her patients above all. Whether she still liked herself – something that had always been a feature of her inward-looking nature, and which she liked to joke about – I could not tell, although we talked about everything, at least about most things, at any rate about all her illnesses.

When something did not go her way, she usually gave her temper free rein, making vehement objections, wagging her bold little hand at us, just as she used to.

She got very upset, for example, when Hub refused point blank to let Mary-Lou visit Sing Sing. She thought it was narrow-minded, and said so as well.

And so she came to meet my girlfriend and me in the café by Wöhr-mannscher Park, and the three of us had a fine time together. As we were sitting among all those haughty, decadent snobs who looked to be dressed for the golf course, Mary-Lou said in English, 'Sorry, I have to go to the bathroom,' got up and glided very elegantly towards the ladies' lavatory. Everyone, every last person there, watched her go, as you might watch the elephant man.

'I'm jealous,' said Ev, and in the way she pulled the corners of her mouth down as she smiled, I glimpsed a kind of surprise at herself beyond the Himalayas of her coquettishness.

'Why on earth would you be jealous?' I asked in alarm.

'It must be good with her.'

'Yes, we get along well.'

'Come on, you know what I mean by good, don't you?'

'The love?'

'And the orgasms.'

I didn't say a word.

'Does she have a lot of orgasms?' Ev asked, with the stupendous thoughtlessness she so often displayed. She sipped her Campari and orange as if nothing were the matter, and I was itching to tell her that the colour of her drink came from the same boiled cochineal insects as Papa's carmine red, because who wants to drink crushed insects.

'You're impossible,' I said instead.

'How am I impossible?'

'What would you say if I enquired about Hub's orgasms?'

'You wouldn't do that. You never have done. It doesn't interest you. And anyway, you're not a doctor. I, on the other hand, am asking purely out of medical interest.'

'Purely out of medical interest?'

'Though I expect you don't believe my interest is purely medical, and I'm just saying that because I'm so funny and ghastly.'

Usually I loved it when she went back to being the little girl whose role was simply to be lovable and to make her brothers eternally unhappy. But this time it didn't work. I was filled with a tender sadness, just for a brief moment, and Ev sensed it, as she always sensed everything, and she took my hand and said in a different tone:

'Forgive me, please forgive me, dear Koja. She is quite enchanting, really. You're a lucky man. And she is a big, bright rainbow.'

Mary-Lou came back from the lavatories looking pleased and brandishing the café's German address book, which she had found beside the telephone. 'Will you look at this!' she cried, before sounding out the word on the front: 'Furn-spreck-tail-nummer-vur-zaik-niss.' She gave a gleeful yelp. 'This isn't a phone book, it's a poem!'

Ev couldn't help but laugh, her heart was so white. Between this white and Mary-Lou's bright rainbow was where I wanted to idle forever, to play the wastrel and the good-for-nothing that my brother took me for. It was a dreamy idyll, amid these silent, joyful colours that I was desperate to memorize – but later, as I stood before the easel, they slipped away from me like my own life.

In reality, at that very moment and throughout that summer, we were sitting on a powder keg. Adolf Hitler was at the pinnacle of his power, having annexed a whole series of countries without firing a single shot – the Austrians, for example, were delirious with happiness. Added together, these countries constituted a land mass the size of Great Britain, with twenty-five million inhabitants. It seemed to be just a matter of time before it was little Latvia's turn.

And in our circles this expectation grew from one week to the next, as the days became ever more tropical. I can still recall the weather report buzzing shrilly through the ether: 'Warm and humid to begin with; cooler weather approaching from the west later on.' Donald Day told me his government was weighing up whether to evacuate its legation in Riga, leaving the minister behind, and that was the only cooler weather from the west he could feel.

'My heart aches when I think of the Baltic states,' he sighed, casting his eyes around the seedy Latvian bar where we were sitting with two glasses of vodka in front of us – and then he suddenly yelled at the few other customers in English, 'We're all dead men drinking!' He succumbed to one of his wheezing, helpless fits of laughter, doubled over, squeezing his eyes shut, and then, still laughing, knocked back the vodka.

On Hub's thirty-fourth birthday, I drove out to our dacha on the shores of the Stintsee. It was only supposed to be a small party, but it changed our family forever.

Mama and Anna Ivanovna had baked a Baltic birthday ring.

Papa spent almost the whole day asleep under the large apple tree, on which dozens of unripe, red-cheeked autumn Calvilles gleamed, glorifying our Grandpaping as they did on each of Hub's birthdays. The family visited Grandpaping's grave in the morning without me.

For I had decided to introduce them to Mary-Lou, not because I thought our relationship was a serious one, but because I saw no reason to hide a love affair that for once was simply doing me good rather than driving me mad.

Mary-Lou had been under the impression that I was the birthday boy, and three hours before, while everyone else was making the pilgrimage to Grandpaping's grave, she had danced a wild birthday boogie just for me, wearing nothing but my oil pastels, with which she had artfully painted her body. There was still a trace of ultramarine on her face, and a silver shimmer to her ankles, when we finally pulled up outside the dacha.

Ev was a real treasure; she took Mary-Lou's arm in friendship and showed her our sailing boat and the crystal-blue lake, perhaps to remind her of the Caribbean. Mama was unwelcoming. She could only imagine Africans on cotton plantations, and perhaps wasn't entirely sure what my relationship to her was.

'Is he trying to show us he can afford servants now?' Mama asked later.

Papa, by contrast, visibly livened up, perhaps recalling old habits, and attempted to wheel himself out from under the apple tree to see us. Unfortunately, he had been tied to the trunk for his own safety. Donald was moderately pleased that we had some 'Negro blood' in the party, while the reactions from Erhard and a few other comrades from the Movement ranged from neutral to incredulous.

*

Hub, however, turned into an icicle in the sticky, humid air, or perhaps it would be better to say a pillar of salt. He then disappeared behind the house, which was where I found him.

'What were you thinking of?' he hissed at me. 'Are you trying to make a laughing stock of us on my birthday and Grandpaping's death day?'

'There's nothing in the Nuremberg Laws,' I retorted. 'I checked. You can't marry a mulatto, but everything else is fine.'

'When the war comes, the world is going to turn, Koja. Then no one is going to keep paying your bills just for going out boozing with an American and going to bed with a Sarotti Moor.'

'What are you trying to say?'

'Your behaviour is un-German. And your sole life insurance policy is *being German*. Do you know the meaning of the words racial defilement?'

'Do you know the meaning of the word incest?'

He blinked, and for a moment I felt he wanted to hit me. But then he just wiped the sweat and my impudence from the back of his neck and gave me a dark look.

'You have no education, Koja. You haven't learned anything. You're painting the odd watercolour and going to seed, that's all. You're arrogant and you lack commitment. Erhard has told Berlin he doesn't trust you with more important assignments.'

'Erhard is an arsehole.'

'He's the only arsehole who's going to help you. And me. That's why we invited him to my birthday.'

'It was you who invited him, not us.'

He took a step closer and laid a hand on my shoulder, but there was no comfort in the gesture, only urgency.

'Our only future lies in the SS. Don't fuck it up.'

Now I realized that he was talking about himself. About his own worries. Not mine. He was a failed theologian; I was an unqualified architect. He was afraid that I was going to rob him of his glitter, perhaps of his whole career, a glittering star of a career. The chance to become Alexander the Great and Jesus. Because I wasn't staunch enough. And slept with the wrong people.

All at once I was conscious of how much he had changed, more than I'd ever thought. We stood silently, facing one another in the burning glare of the sun, and then Mary-Lou bounded round the corner and sang 'Happy Birthday' in English, a song that no one but she knew, and told us it was time for Hub to unwrap his presents.

We all gathered on the veranda to watch. My brother received a pair of motorbike goggles made of nappa leather, Hörbiger's *Glacial Cosmogony*, some biscuits, a hunting knife, a Finnish knife, a pocket knife (it was a good time for knives), a tin of lampreys, a bottle of single malt (from Mr Day), another pocket knife, but with a small pair of nail scissors attached, two double egg cups (emblazoned with Pompeian or Greek swastikas) and a Norwegian pullover knitted by Mama, which he had to try on despite the heat.

He opened Mary-Lou's present last, a board game in original American packaging. It was called Monopoly and was really intended for me. A friend of hers had brought it over from New York: you couldn't buy it in Latvia.

'Honey, it's the hottest game in town, believe me,' Mary-Lou trilled in my brother's ear, opening the lid. It had something to do with land and building houses and was on the list of banned games in Germany. Apart from the Americans, everyone around the table knew this, and the general mood reflected that knowledge.

Breaking the dismayed silence, Ev said bravely, 'All right then, let's earn some money.'

The birthday boy snatched a bundle of paper money out of the box and threw it in the air, and we all watched as what must have been the first breath of wind for hours whirled the fake dollar bills around like confetti, making our garden rich. Then Hub got to his feet and said, 'It's a Jewish game.'

He turned round and stalked off, in his much-too-small Norwegian pullover. Ev smiled very faintly, plucked a pink hundred-dollar bill from her collarbone, excused herself and went after him. After a while we could hear him shouting something at a suitable distance. She shouted back. I concentrated on the lush chestnut trees rustling above the awkward silence around our table, and then I thought of Grandpaping and imagined what it must be like to be held underwater, to hear people laughing as you die in torment.

'Koja, did you enjoy the party?' Mary-Lou asked me on the way home.

'Did you?' I asked her back.

'Well, I don't think it was a party at all.'

It was only later, as I was tossing and turning in the heat, sleepless and troubled by getting older, that I realized it was the first time my brother and I had not chosen an apple together following a serious argument, blessed it with the sign of the cross, shared and eaten it, murmuring 'Hosanna in the highest', the conciliatory, soothing and inappropriate words that Mama had taught us. The thought frightened me and, looking back, I believe that this omission carried within it the kernel of all the discord that followed.

A week later, the war broke out.

The Wehrmacht squashed Poland. 'Like a soft-boiled egg,' said Donald Day. Erhard flew to join Herr Himmler in occupied Krakow, and Himmler explained to him that Latvia, too, would soon cease to exist. It was not the Reich, however, but the Soviet Union that was planning a ceremonial takeover of this territory. Hitler had guaranteed it to Stalin in a secret treaty, he said.

We were dumbstruck at the news. A 'secret treaty' with Stalin? What was that all about? Another term for perverse gift-giving? Hub, who hated the communists more than anything in the world, reacted with disbelief and the Russian exclamation we had inherited from Opapabaron: '*Ves'ma zamechatel'no!*' – how very remarkable. For several nights he couldn't sleep, wondering why his beloved Führer had permitted such a thing. Although Hub had long since turned away from his faith in God, he even went to the cathedral and knelt to say hours of silent prayers. How could our Grandpaping's murderers be allowed to return, to come back to Riga, back to the Neugut parsonage, back to St Petri's Cathedral, where this year the Lutheran martyrs of nineteen-nineteen were being commemorated for the twentieth time?

And as always, a candle would be burning there for Hubert Konstantin Solm, who had died for his faith, an upright, truthful, proud, unbending man drowned in a potato sack. We found it impossible to inform our parents about the impending disaster. Nor were we allowed to, for this top-secret international agreement was known only to Erhard, Hub and me, the Movement's blond triumvirate (though now plagued by hair loss), who had long since quashed any opposition within the Baltic German community.

*

To save our countrymen from the Red Army, the Reich scrambled to organize a gigantic express migration. All eighty thousand Latvian Germans were to break down their tepees like an Indian tribe and set them up again in occupied Poland, though without being permitted ever to see the old hunting grounds again.

There would be no return from this exodus.

As the most senior leaders of the ethnic group, Erhard and Hub took over the preparations. All the newspapers carried articles about them. Mama was so proud. Through all her grief at the unexpected loss of a homeland that our distant ancestor Wolfram von Schilling had wrested from the natives in the twelfth century under the cross of the Lord Jesus (and they remain 'natives' in Mama's mind to this day), through all the anguish that could be plainly read in her face, her eyes sparkled with joy whenever she spotted her marvellous Hubsi, yes sometimes even her forever-my-little-Hubsikin, in the latest edition of the *Rigaer Rundschau*. The caption beneath a photo that showed him in half-profile said: 'Evacuation Commander Hubert Solm addresses the assembled evacuation teams in a dockside warehouse.'

In the photo, the evacuation commander looked like Clark Gable, not least due to his dashing new pencil moustache. He might not yet be Alexander the Great – a position that Erhard claimed for himself, as evidenced by the even larger photo of him in the *Rigaer Rundschau* – but, at least in Mama's eyes, my brother was well on his way to becoming Alexander the Small.

Hub was in charge of all the mass transport. He was essentially the head of a huge haulage company with a thousand members of staff, which had to transport eighty thousand people and complete fifteen thousand house-moves involving millions of pieces of luggage and furniture, all in the space of four weeks.

Germany sent a fleet of passenger and freight ships to handle the exodus by sea.

In the meantime, I was to gather as much data as possible on Latvia's fortifications, gun emplacements and so on. Heydrich's adjutant gave me the order over the telephone. Before hanging up he said 'Heil Hitler', and for the first time I said it, too.

Mary-Lou was distraught. She went so far as to shut herself in the kitchen (to prevent me from taking any sustenance) and wore my white dressing gown for days (in the end, I gave it to her). I couldn't tell her what was going on, but I did urge her and Donald to book themselves passage on a ship back to the United States as soon as possible. Mary-Lou pursed her lips defiantly and said, 'Poland must surely be very sad. Don't they need a dancing queen?' Then she said, 'I'll miss you.' And finally, very quietly, 'I'm your smile and you're my sadness.'

But by that point we were at the export harbour.

She was the most free-floating, nonchalant and musical lover I've ever had. Perhaps not the most confidently stylish. I will never forget the time she sang the Horst Wessel Lied to me in the middle of the night, in her throaty voice – without knowing the song's meaning, just because she liked the melody and believed it would please me. Amid the gibberish, instead of: 'The flag on high, the ranks are massed', I made out the words: 'The flagon I, the rats are messed'. And the tears streamed down her cheeks, and she even danced as she sang.

All our apartments had to be emptied, all the inventory packed up, and anything surplus to requirements sold or given away. Pets were not permitted to board Hitler's arks, and the streets of Riga were filled with the wailing and lamentations of all the children who had lost their Putzis and Rexes, Snuffies and Mogs, Blackamoors and Stinkies to a substantially increased rate of cat and dog mortality.

Mama wrapped all our things very neatly. Opapabaron was the only one to get his own sea-chest, which was filled with the Apache jewellery and the tusks he had once brought back from distant lands.

Hub was entirely occupied with the emigration, so in my few free hours I pulled together the various documents we would need to become citizens of the German Reich. At least, I tried to. It was a devil of a job to turn up all the necessary birth certificates, baptism certificates, death certificates, land register records, marriage certificates and attestations from within the impenetrable Solm dossier, in which documents had been filed away with all the precision of stacking firewood. I reproached my mother gently for her carelessness with her own history – she was an old Balt and didn't understand the bureaucratic zeal of the Reich Germans.

'Yes, but that isn't history. What do we need all this palaver for?' she asked me, shaking her head.

'Well, to get our Aryan certificates, for one thing.'

'What's an Aryan certificate?'

'We'll need them to find good jobs in Germany. Hub and I have to prove that our German ancestry goes back two hundred years.'

'But our ancestors aren't German!'

I put the file I was holding down on the desk and looked into her lined, somewhat distracted face.

'Aren't they?'

'We're descended from the Ynglings!' she exclaimed. 'That's why your Opapabaron's name is von Schilling.'

'Remind me: what are the Ynglings?'

'Yngvi was the grandson of Odin.'

'Are you telling me we're descended from Odin?'

'If you need it for that Aryan certificate, then yes.'

'Mama, we can't tell the officials at the Reichssippenamt that we're descended from gods.'

'Why not? They're Germanic gods. Who could object to that?'

'Is there any kind of record of this, Mama?'

'No, but I can swear to it.'

My parents had never kept their books with the necessary care. They also looked down on bookkeepers, since that work required neither brains nor talent, as they sometimes sighed – and they responded to official requests for tax returns with fits of the most slovenly indolence, simply because they found figures terribly ordinary. 'Numbers are hell, they're the death of the human spirit,' Papa had always said, and true to form he would forget each of our birthdays.

My parents felt weighed down by official forms and genealogical archives, which is why I found myself rummaging through a disordered heap of dusty files on the hunt for proof of our German descent. At some point, Papa had blithely begun to use them as scrap paper for his preliminary drawings. Both he and Mama were fundamentally artistic by nature, and in Riga it had always been a family's reputation rather than their paperwork that had gained them respect, even from the state.

I suspected that this listless approach to record-keeping was why I could find barely anything relating to Ev. Her passport listed Anna Marie and Theo Solm as her parents. The old adoption record from nineteen-nineteen, which I found sandwiched between two recipes

('Ah, how wonderful, Kojashka, my darling, I've been looking eeeeverywhere for those') did at least contain the names of her birth parents, one Marius Meyer, a paediatrician from Dünaburg, and his wife Barbara Meyer, no profession given. Try as I might, there was nothing else to be found. Not even a birth certificate. Nor did Ev herself have any further information. She had never given too much thought to where she came from, and didn't want to think about it now, either: she was too busy helping to pack up the hospital.

I searched Hub's secret archive of Balts who were suspicious or under observation. But of course, he hadn't recorded anything about his own family.

I was annoyed, for in the midst of all this drudgery and the hysterical pressure to get everything done before our departure, I had no choice but to travel to Dünaburg myself, two hundred kilometres across a country that was being rapidly dismantled. On the streets, I encountered columns of invading Red Army soldiers en route to their bases: ex-territorial Soviet plague boils that president Kārlis Ulmanis was permitting to grow and fester in his country, a last-ditch attempt to avoid or at least delay the complete dissolution of Latvia as a nation state. It was like opening the henhouse door for a fox to stop him eating.

It was in Dünaburg that I began to worry.

In the church books, I found a record of the marriage between Marius and Barbara Meyer, née Muhr. But there were no entries for Meyer or Muhr in all the decades before. The same in the register of births and deaths. It looked like both families had only just moved to the area, and I might now have to search for the origins of these families all over Latvia, perhaps even the German Reich. And while there were so-called genealogy lawyers who could be tasked with this kind of painstaking research, there was every likelihood that Stalin would take over the country very soon. And once our homeland had become part of the Soviet Union, I wouldn't be able to carry out my family research at my leisure. I knew that Ev would never get a job as a doctor without the full Aryan certificate. Time was short. I decided to ask around in Dünaburg for people who had known the Meyers. Given that Herr Meyer had been a paediatrician, there must be friends, neighbours, former patients here.

*

I stayed overnight at a hotel in the old town, and the following day managed to sniff out a German notary who was sitting on a pile of suitcases with nothing left to do but mourn the passing of his office. He praised my brother ('Capable man! Did you see the photo in the newspaper? Like Clark Gable, my wife says, terrific!'), hurried over to city hall with me, looked through the relevant collections of files and after ten minutes, politely explained to me that there had never been a paediatrician called Meyer in Dünaburg.

When I offered no response, he suggested gathering every possible clue from the city archives, in the hope of finding some kind of lead. We went through all the Lutheran church records again, with great care but no success. Then we turned to the books of the Orthodox churches, because in Dünaburg many Baltic Germans had been lured away by the Pope. Again, there was nothing.

By this time evening had fallen and we'd eaten nothing all day. The notary looked up at me, his hunger-soured breath hitting me like a waft of putrefaction, and he asked humbly and with pursed lips whether the Herr Youth Leader had any desire to take a look at the Hebrews' register, probably not, of course, he just thought he should check.

The Herr Youth Leader was more surprised than he could say. He felt his jaw drop in the most literal sense; he walked out into the soupy evening where twilight gnats danced around him, sat down in the Dünaburg grass and remained there until darkness had fallen, doing nothing but hugging two bony knees, the damp lawn cooling the haemorrhoids that had been tormenting him since Mary-Lou's departure.

That night he was plagued by horrible visions, visions of endless complications. He got out of bed, swallowed an aspirin, considered that even this aspirin tablet, such a help against headache-inducing problems, had been invented by a Jew, Herr Eichengrün, as Ev had informed him just a few days ago, but why, why – and he saw it as a sign that 'wicked Jews' had done more than just commit crimes against humanity over the long course of cultural history, though for the most part that *was* what they'd done – and then the acetylsalicylic acid took effect and he fell slowly into a delicious sleep, sweetened by a Jew.

The next day, I decided to take a look at the synagogue's records.

The notary had brought a colleague with him, an ancient Israelite named Moshe Jacobsohn, who wore a skullcap as he checked through the Hebrew records.

To my great relief, we found no Meyers or Muhrs there. We took a lunchbreak in order not to repeat the errors of the previous day; Herr Jacobsohn treated us all to gefilte fish, and my mood improved.

We returned to the archive, just to make sure we had exhausted every possibility. The Jew hesitated over one particular name, and asked the notary when Frau Barbara Meyer née Muhr had come into the world. The fourteenth of July eighteen seventy-eight, the notary replied. On the fourteenth of July eighteen seventy-eight, Moshe Jacobsohn said with some surprise, a Jewish child had in fact been born in Dünaburg, but the child's name was Bathia, not Barbara, and the surname was not Muhr but Murmelstein, and there was no entry in his books for this Bathia Murmelstein's bat mitzvah, and he had no recollection of her, either. It was quite possible that her parents had converted to Christianity.

And then his face suddenly lit up like a shining sun, and he said yes, now he remembered, of course he'd heard of a Meyer, but Meyer hadn't been a paediatrician, and his name was Marian, if memory served, not Marius, and he had been a waiter, a head waiter in fact, at that very fine hotel where the Herr Youth Leader had been well advised to take a room, and poor Meyer had been killed by the Bolsheviks, all those years ago, struck down like a dog, and they'd even killed his wife, too, because she'd looked like such a fine lady next to her husband's smart livery, it was only the little girl who'd survived – or maybe not, those were terrible times, and Meyer hadn't been a Jew for a long time, his parents had converted, so everyone said, but the little girl, the poor little girl.

It may not seem worth the effort to you today, my chief therapeutic justice, to waste any sympathy on a well-meaning man whose world was turned on its head in the space of twenty-four hours. Of course, today you would say: what does it matter if someone is a Jew or a tennis player or catches fish in a Malaysian village.

It is so hard to find an explanation for it.

If you say 'at that time', you've already lost. 'That time' is a country very far away from where we are now, but this country lies in here, my dear fellow traveller, here in this old heart; I enter the land of 'that time' as I speak about it, it is my time, not yours, and at this unpleasant moment I am tied to it. I myself cannot conceive that the young man I once was felt what you might describe as anti-Semitism. And even though it feels so foreign to me, at this unpleasant moment I am right there, in the land of 'that time', watching myself *be* anti-Semitic, so to speak. I can see myself sitting before the tactful notary and this old Jacobsohn with his stomach complaint, in the synagogue office, which is a part of the synagogue itself, as the earth opens up in front of me and I tumble into a deep hole, merely at having discovered something that would be of no consequence to anyone your age, which is to say, of your generation. I will go on, but that had to be said, since you suddenly appear so familiar with melancholy, my dear young (and briefly underestimated) friend.

Two days and several aspirins later, I was at Anna Ivanovna's house, listening to her version of the story. She wept as only Russian women with guilty consciences can weep, in other words heartrendingly. Twenty years before (she sobbed), her cousin Vladimir had come to her in the midst of the Bolshevik occupation, holding this little malyshka by the hand. How dear the little dove had been and half-starved already, and if the solnyshka's life was to be saved, we would have to find her a family, the cousin said. But who would give their last calories away to a little Jewish kitten? That was what I asked myself, my Kojashka. She was the daughter of a dear man, a waiter who had been friends with Vladimir. We asked her what her father's job was and she said she didn't know, he had always been away, and then we turned the waiter into a doctor so that the Cheka couldn't trace it back, and that's how it happened.

I didn't want to lie to the good lady and the good gentleman (she went on), but it was a matter of life and death, and the good lady had once told me, no Jew is ever going to set foot in my house, not even a baptised Jew, of course not, Kojasha, my angel, the Jews are bad people, your Führerkin is right there (I interrupted to tell her that she mustn't say Führerkin – like all Russians, she loved diminutives); of course, Kojinskaya, the Jews are criminals, but this little thing, this sweet girl, what big eyes she had, we couldn't just let her die, so please don't say anything to the good lady, she was so full of generosity, for the sake of God in Heaven, don't say anything.

*

One hour later, I rang the doorbell and Hub answered. There was a napkin tucked into his collar. He was chewing.

'I'm sorry, I thought you'd be down at the port,' I said.

'No, Koja, come in. There's some roast meat left. It's good to see you.'

Then I sat down with them, not knowing where to start. The light from the lethargic kitchen lamp above us gave all faces a warm tone, but evidently not mine.

'Koja, are you unwell?' Ev asked, sounding worried. 'You look so pale.'

'Well, there's a lot going on, so many things.'

'Shall I fetch you some tablets? I've got some left over from my last migraine.'

'Aspirin isn't Jewish at all, you know, half-Jewish at most, if you think of Bayer AG as a person – a German, that is,' I babbled.

'What a great age this is, dear brother,' Hub said – it was as much of a non sequitur as my own remark – and added, 'So, your girlfriend has left, has she?'

'Yes. Found a little place in Marseilles. She wants to go to Paris eventually.'

'And you're still writing to each other?'

'To be honest, she can barely write.'

'She was a nice girl. I behaved like a real cad with that Monopoly game. She meant well.'

I had no idea what might have caused this belated outburst of contrition, but I was sure it wasn't his own insight.

Ev cleared her throat, dabbed her lips with her napkin and picked up her wine glass.

'Well, whatever it might be that brings you here, dear Koja,' she said, raising her glass with a smile, 'forget your poor little head and let's drink a toast to this evening!'

No, I most certainly did not want to toast that evening, nor any of the evenings that would follow it, which I saw as an inescapable series of catastrophic events rolling steadily towards us.

'Of course,' I said, and we clinked glasses.

Hub had been in an unapologetically good mood from the second he'd opened the door. He was very solicitous towards me, and even more so to Ev, stroking her hand and then smiling at me, like a person who knows that something delightful is about to happen.

'I got word today,' he said, almost bursting with joy. 'I'm being made a Sturmbannführer. And Erhard will be a Standartenführer.'

His beaming smile rose like a New Year's firework into the night sky, and I realized he hadn't finished yet.

'Of course, that remains a secret until we're no longer Latvian citizens.'

He still hadn't finished.

'But what's far more important,' he went on, 'is that we're getting married!'

After that he said nothing else, no one said anything, until Ev murmured, 'Yes, Koja, we're getting married, we're going to be man and wife.'

They both looked at me in anticipation, and I really don't know what on earth they were expecting, a burst of tremendous enthusiasm and my blessing, I suppose, and I couldn't decide whether to say, 'Wonderful!' or as is more common in the Baltics, 'No, how terribly splendid!' or even, 'All these years I've yearned for nothing more dearly!' or in a more prosaic vein, 'Why? Are you pregnant, Ev?'

In the end, I just said, '*Nu, a khasene ken efsher zayn zeyer shver.*'

A silence as sharp as barbed wire.

'*A khasene?*'

'Mmhmm.'

'Is that Yiddish?'

'Yes, Hub, it's Yiddish. It means "wedding".'

'Where did you learn Yiddish?'

'Ev taught me. Didn't she teach you?'

'No.'

He thought for a moment. The firework fizzled out and fell back to earth.

'Ev – you can speak Yiddish?'

'Well, yes, it was the language all the children in Dünaburg spoke. The children were Yiddish.'

'And why didn't you teach me?'

'You weren't a child any more, Hub.'

He put his hand over his mouth, realizing that he had long since stopped chewing. He shifted a forgotten piece of meat into his left cheek and asked, 'What did Koja just say?'

'Well, a wedding might be a bit difficult – that's what he said.'

Ev brought her glass back to her lips, just for the sake of doing something, her eyes fixed on the potatoes I had left on my plate. Hub swallowed, nodded and took a more formal tone.

'Koja, I know our parents won't take it well. You're right about that. But I'll explain it to them very gently.'

'And Erhard,' Ev whispered.

'And I'll explain it to Erhard, of course. I mean, we're both grown men.'

This lamp really does give off an exceptionally beautiful light – I don't know why that thought suddenly popped into my head, but I actually considered buying one myself, preferably straight away.

'I'm so glad that Hub is taking a stand for our love,' Ev said, disconcerted by all the silence emanating from me. 'It's a big decision. But now that we're setting off for a new country and a whole new life, the stupid Balts will have hardly anyone to spread their malicious gossip to. And if they do, we'll just drink it all away.'

And with these words, she swallowed down an entire glass of red wine.

'Yes,' said Hub. 'We're not the same flesh and blood. Did you make any progress in Dünaburg?'

'That's right, you haven't said anything yet, how was it?' Ev asked. 'Do you have the papers?'

And I stared at them both for a while, and then I said, '*Nu, shturmbanfirer vet ir zikher lang nit blaybn, mayn Hubsilayn.*'

I don't want to mislead you, best Swami of all Swamis: of course I didn't say that. It was impossible to tell him he wouldn't keep his SS job for long, not in this atmosphere of endless bliss, hope, fatalism and abyssal depths.

But I said it to myself, silently, with an almost ridiculous sense of superiority – and when I imagined the face of Clark Gable Solm, the mouth that usually brimmed with disgusting ambition suddenly hanging open, I couldn't suppress a giggle, like a child who can't help giggling in church without really knowing why. An irrepressible desire to laugh filled my insides, loosened my whale tongue, unclenched my jaw and – I can't think of a better word, my friend, but in any case this describes it most honestly – encircled me.

'What is there to laugh about?'

I began to snort uncontrollably, fell into paroxysms of laughter that bordered on insanity, my mirth was inconsolable, and thank God Ev's bafflement was discharged in a laugh of solidarity, until eventually even Hub, who seldom laughed, and when he did, laughed almost silently, drove my despair to a fresh climax with a goat-like bleat.

And I got drunk on red wine and lied my head off to them, slurring my words as I was eventually forced to say that the papers had been found in Dünaburg, first-class papers, first-class Meyers and Muhrs of impeccable Aryan stock, going back hundreds of years, yes really.

The rest of that tale is quickly told.

Over the next few days, I forged and misappropriated everything that had to be forged and misappropriated. Moshe Jacobsohn received our good buffalo-leather three-piece suite, with free delivery, so to speak, and in return allowed a few pages of the Dünaburg synagogue's books to go up in flames. Under the Holy Russian Empire, Jews and their records had been burned time and again, so it wouldn't surprise anyone.

The tactful notary said that he was prepared to make the Lutheran church books of his home city available to me for a few hours, without afterwards casting an excessively forensic eye over them.

The talented painter, watercolourist, caricaturist, but of course also re-toucher, typographer and calligrapher Konstantin Solm himself made a few necessary additions to those books, with a skilled hand and artificially aged ink.

Finally, the notary was persuaded (with the help of some old tsarist gold from Mama's strongbox) to attest to a first-class lineage of non-existent but still very dead-seeming ancestors on the basis of the official church records, people who would help their direct descendant Ev Solm keep the trust of any Sturmbannführer she wanted.

On the evening of the fifteenth of December nineteen thirty-nine, Mama, Papa and I left Riga on one of the last evacuation ships.

As a man with profound disabilities, Papa had been allocated to the transport for the disabled and psychiatric patients, but Mama had refused to leave him alone with four hundred lunatics, as she put it.

We were given a luxurious cabin next to the captain's, thanks be to the evacuation commander. The evacuation commander himself had already departed on another ship, the *Deutschland*, with his new fiancée – partly, I suspect, to avoid burdening his still shocked parents with the tender endearments of the almost married.

Our steamer, the *Bremerhaven*, had been fitted out in Danzig with various modifications, expressly agreed with Hub, which turned out to be padded cells.

That evening, Mama stood on the promenade deck, which she referred to disparagingly as the 'mixed' promenade deck due to the unclear family ties of her fellow travellers. Leaning over the railing, she looked back at the skyline of the illuminated city, and she – she of all people, who had never wept when faced with the Bolsheviks or any other worldly danger, out of fear or great emotion – wept and wept. Even Papa wept, sitting beside her in his wheelchair and emitting small wails that sounded like distant seagulls.

The *Bremerhaven* weighed anchor at midnight, taking the mad and the demented, the mentally impoverished and the downcast out onto the silent sea, accompanied by thirty orderlies, a hundred nurses, a genuine professor from Wittenau and two brightly lit warships.

Despite all these efforts, almost every patient on this transport would be dead within a year, having succumbed to starvation, lethal injections, gas or poison, the work of my own office – but we will come to that later.

II

The Black Order

I

Thank you for exercising such Brahmin-like restraint. Perhaps, some-times, just carrying on is the best thing to do. And that's exactly what I thought at the end of nineteen thirty-nine. Keep your eyes fixed straight ahead, don't waver, just let yourself be carried along by forces that are stronger but also better than you. Isn't the heart monitor over there stronger and better than we are, too? The quicksilver thing? The blood-pressure-checking tabernacle, or whatever it's called? Do these gadgets not keep tabs on our condition more reliably than we ever could ourselves?

Anyway, I was thinking something very similar when I arrived in occupied Poland after a two-day crossing on the *Bremerhaven*. Poland had been admitted to a giant sanitorium. A Pole-sanitorium, do you see? The country was to be cured – first and foremost of its former inhabitants. And we Balts were the serum that would make everything good and blond again.

And so the Solms were flushed down a cannula into the Warthegau, a chamber of the Polish heart that had been transplanted using surgical implements (curative tank divisions) into the German Reich.

Our ship sailed into the great Baltic port of Stettin in the middle of a snowstorm. All the lunatics stumbled down the gangway, to the blare of a brass band that was frozen blue and encrusted with a rime of frost that looked like sea-salt. Ecstatic Valkyries from the National Socialist People's Welfare ministered to the new arrivals. As a welcome gesture, they pressed framed photographs into the hands of these baffled idiots, photographs of a madhouse doctor staring grimly into the falling snow. The patients were now to call this man 'Führer', and at once they began to lick the snowflakes from his stub of a moustache. It was all so slick, so patronizing and fawning that even my parents and I felt like castaways.

At least we had a personal Mercedes at our disposal, though the driver whom Hub had commandeered seemed even madder than the arriving madmen. First, he took us to a reception camp instead of the SS-requisitioned luxury hotel that Mama had been expecting. Then, out on a rural road, he ran over a dog with words that went down in our family history: 'It was only a Polish one.' And he refused to let a flat tyre, however troublesome, dampen his optimism.

After a spectral, meandering two-day drive through snow and ice (the land was a shroud beneath our wheels), we reached our destination: the Gau's capital city, Posen, where the cathedral that held the remains of the Polish ruling dynasty – a building almost a thousand years old – was due to be blown up 'next week, most likely', as our driver cheerfully assured us.

I say this without any ulterior motive, but I will say it all the same: the cultivated Baltic Germans of the SS like Hub and Erhard were the ones doing their utmost to prevent this kind of urban renewal. In this case, they succeeded, by pointing to the cathedral's Westphalian master builders and its mausoleum, designed by Christian Daniel Rauch (oh, aren't you familiar with Rauch? His tomb of Queen Louise? His Valhalla busts, which Hitler was so fond of?).

In the midst of a bitterly cold winter, and even colder people, we went looking for an apartment in Posen. It was anything but simple. No one had any choice about who they lived with. Most of our friends and relatives were accommodated at first in factory buildings, army barracks, and even in the unheated catacombs of the city stadium, where icicles hung from the ceilings, since the authorities couldn't dispossess, deport and execute the indigenous population (whose houses we had been promised) fast enough. Old ladies shivered in the overcrowded Baltic German camps, and rebellious boys with blowpipes fired spit-balls at the stout camp commandants, who patrolled the corridors armed with riding crops.

In order to escape this mass internment Mama, Papa, Hub, Ev and I had to apply for family accommodation, an idea at which Ev initially baulked.

I must have drawn her twenty times back then, secretly, in profile, her face turned away from me and looking lost. All I could see in her eyes were riddles, for I couldn't get close enough to her, and her dark looks enclosed the light ones that I often dreamed about. She didn't want to live with all of us; she wanted to be alone in her new-found land of love, alone with my brother. 'But snails live alone, my darling,' I heard his voice booming through the wall of the hotel where we were temporarily quartered, 'and in these times we cannot be snails.'

Our house, which Hub's SS influence finally conjured up for the family, was one of the suburban villas that had been vacated by the previous tenants with sixty minutes' notice and not a second longer.

When we put the key in the lock and went in, we saw just what sixty minutes allowed you to do. The inhabitants seemed to have been vaporized in a matter of seconds, like the people of Pompeii and Herculaneum, leaving behind the most intimate impressions of their lives. The apartment was still warm and furnished, all the drawers and cupboards stood open, and the floors were strewn with clothes. The evicted Polish family's damp towels still hung in the bathroom. There were photos of their baby on the walls, a delightful, laughing little princess playing with a wooden digger on the shores of the Baltic Sea. That digger now lay on its side in the nursery, gleaming red, along with some stuffed toys.

Mama went at once to the local SS office, explained that her son had been the evacuation commander in Riga, and asked what had happened to those poor people who'd been living in her accommodation. The SS-Scharführer in charge there told her coolly that she should be glad to have a roof over her head and no blood on the wallpaper.

And that was the reality.

Neither my mother nor any of the other Baltic German refugees, whether they were descended from Odin or not, had any say in what happened to them from the minute they arrived. We were trophies that you hang on the wall. We were Himmler's stag antlers. And even then, we were only twelve-pointers, not sixteen like the Sudeten Germans. Or twenty-four like the Reich Germans, who were flooding into the Warthegau week after week, greedily snatching up all the bounty that the deportations left in their wake.

In a very short space of time, Hub also discovered that as Alexander the Small, he had to set his sights very low in this pan-Germanic Cockaigne. Even Erhard Sneiper, who for years had been permitted to drink buttermilk with Himmler and Heydrich (much healthier than a snifter of cognac), was now redundant. The SS grandees stopped paying any attention to him and his deputy Hubert Solm. The pair were no longer indispensable superspies in enemy territory; they were just ordinary officials.

'They expect me to be a pen-pusher now,' Hub moaned. Erhard, with his hopes of becoming the grand inquisitor who would reforest a whole province with true Germans, was given a mandate as a so-called Member of the Reichstag (a name-only position that came with the instruction to refrain from all expressions of parliamentary opinion). But in practice, he was merely stagnating in a kind of registration office for Balts, which he managed sullenly without the aid of the treacherous Solm brothers.

Hub was assigned to the SD building on the Bismarckring, the road that encircled Posen's Old Town. He was given an office, a buxom girl typist, the mad chauffeur, and his own department – though it was only one of many. He was responsible for the eviction of the Poles and Jews from the Posen district, and found the job deadly dull (though of course, it was also deadly in a very literal sense). Despite this, he made an effort to take me with him.

'I don't know,' I said. 'There might be a job for me at the city theatre.'

'As what, King Lear?'

'They're looking for a set builder.'

They already had two by the time I enquired – though they were a pair of dyspeptic dilettantes, as I was informed in a whisper when I laid out my portfolio, which was greatly admired. But when the theatre management discovered that my brother worked for the SS security service – and they discovered this because he was waiting for me in the foyer, heavily armed and decked out in his full death's head regalia, as I had expressly forbidden him from doing – the dilettantes were suddenly no longer dilettantes, but marvellous masters of their craft, irreplaceable, and in perfect health, and unfortunately they no longer had any use for the talented Herr Solm, at least none that might come with any form of remuneration.

I had to earn some money, however, for our parents, for me, for the house – it didn't leech rent from us, since we were the leeches here, but it did need a new hipped roof: the existing communist-style flat roof offended the aesthetic sensibilities of a Sturmbannführer.

Just a few weeks later, I therefore became an administrator in a department of the SD that called itself 'Baltic German surveillance'.

I had a desk in a large office at the Gestapo headquarters in Posen. I was the only civilian there, and along with twelve colleagues I analysed all the data that Hub had spent years meticulously gathering on our fellow citizens in Riga. It was up to me to judge which of my countrymen had a good record, which of them we should continue to observe, which were racially suspect and should be shunted off into the Old Reich, and which should be sent to a concentration camp on the grounds of criminal or social abnormalities.

I did not find this work edifying. However, my ill humour did allow me to spice things up with a dose of extreme subjectivity. I eventually went so far as to send my old maths teacher, who was apparently suspected of being a Social Democrat sympathizer, to Dachau for a year (an establishment heartily recommended by colleagues, with a parade ground that was both imposing and exposing). The fact that he had flunked me in my fourth year a decade and a half previously was still firmly lodged in my memory.

Unfortunately, following this act of defiance I was unexpectedly plagued by misgivings. And three weeks later I therefore had Twitchy Hannes, as we used to call him, fetched back from the camp (without citing any reasons) and merely banned from his profession (again, without citing reasons). Two weeks after that (citing reasons would have been positively Freudian at this point) I recommended him for a well-paid position as headmaster of a selective school in Schwetz, in an attempt to do penance before God by showing sensitivity and good intent.

How Twitchy Hannes must have marvelled at these twists of fate, which evaded the strict logic that he also used to find so painfully lacking from my differential equations. Even as a schoolboy, I had told him that he placed far too much value on logic.

Although I occupied a very subordinate position, no one seemed to have a problem with me making to-be-or-not-to-be decisions about those members of our ethnic group who seemed suspicious – or rather, had seemed suspicious to my brother. My immediate superior, Hauptsturmführer Schmidtke, a portly, cheerful, Rhenish soul with a harelip (I had no idea harelips were permitted to join the SS, Hub said indignantly) – Hauptsturmführer Schmidtke, then, took the view that neither he nor anyone else needed to monitor our decisions too closely.

He was a great believer in people using their initiative. He instructed us only that we must not drop below a certain quota of public enemies to be exterminated, for aesthetic reasons. ('Af an artift, Eff-Eff candidate Folm, you know the fignificanf of aeftheticf!')

I must confess that, although I felt regret for these delinquents, I never considered failing to meet the necessary quota. And so I took pity on only two asocial groups: firstly, the Baltic German whores, especially the pretty ones, and in particular those pretty ones I recognized from their photos (I have always had a good memory for faces, a common trait in sentimental ladies' portraitists); and secondly, Jews who had tried to pass themselves off as Aryans by means of forged documents, but had been exposed when ancestry experts went through the baptism records with a fine-toothed comb. Here, I developed a pronounced stubborn streak. There were some ludicrously brazen cases of self-Aryanization that I claimed were entirely above suspicion.

'Do be more careful,' a surprised Schmidtke told me. 'For an Eff-Eff candidate you are fertainly very credulouf about the Jewf. You have fuch a good nofe for a pederaft! Why not the fame for a Jew?'

At that time, I truly wasn't a pure person, and certainly not a wonderful one, as you still have the generosity to say. In a subtle way, I was trapped by the expectations that were placed on me. And so I helped the Jews, I fear, not primarily out of Christian charity, but to sow the seeds of lenience, if not forgiveness, with regard to you-know-who.

It was a few weeks before my SS application was accepted, with Hub's help. Thanks to his loyalty as an employee of the SD's foreign secret service, the painter Konstantin Solm was officially inducted into the Schutzstaffel in the spring of nineteen-forty. He received a document from Heinrich Himmler appointing him to the rank of SS-Obersturmführer, two ranks below Hub (which I thought was tactfully done).

As fascist world domination was dawning around us, this job signalled the start of routine for me. Routine with a little dash of madness in it. After the years I had spent lounging in a hammock with a Bohemian air, the rhythm of my day was completely rewritten. Hub woke me every morning with a shout. I then turned over in bed as he marched into my room and did his morning exercises, panting away in an attempt to rally us both. Chin-ups. Press-ups. Knee-bends.

Always seven of each. Seven was Ev's lucky number. And Hub loved Ev. As I forced myself upright and sat for a moment on the edge of the bed, lingering over the final shred of a dream, he was already washing himself in the adjoining bathroom, as he is probably washing himself right now in jail, with his one remaining hand, briskly and very thoroughly. It looked like a religious observance.

I shuffled into the bathroom, yawning, just as he was on his way out, whistling.

When I came back into my room, wet and badly towelled, Ev had already laid out my freshly ironed uniform on the bed.

For Hub, this outfit was the armour of authority. Whenever I saw it, I couldn't help but think of a legendary quote from my father, who had once claimed that a uniform was a pair of tits for a man. The shirt with its black leather buttons did strike me as similarly signal-like and sexually charged. And all the rest of it. Black tie. Black jodhpurs. Black riding crop. Black jacket: three silver buttons, two parallel silver stripes on the epaulettes, and on the left arm a red, white and black swastika armband. Black pistol holster belt. Black peaked cap with a silver death's head and the party eagle emblazoned on it. I stared at myself in the bedroom mirror. A listless SS-Obersturmführer stared back. The cap didn't particularly suit me. I preferred the soft field service cap, which reminded me more of seafaring. But at least it covered the beginnings of my premature baldness.

Finally I picked up my service pistol from the dressing table, a 9 mm Luger (Hub favoured a Walther PPK), checked it, slid it into the holster and went downstairs. There I met my brother, and we took our breakfast armed to the teeth. There was cheese, ham, dried sausage, a mountain of black bread, milk, cups of steaming coffee. Made with real coffee beans, not ersatz stuff. There wasn't much conversation in the morning. Mama fed Papa. Ev played the role of housewife as if it were only natural, perhaps because this facade was the easiest way for her to turn her dissatisfaction with the housing situation into submission to her fate (although she found any form of submission difficult). In any case, she was much better at sewing, cooking, mending and jam-making than Mama was – the latter had learned everything she knew, literally everything, from her daughter. The only thing Mama had not yet learned was that her daughter was now set to become her daughter-in-law as well.

*

Routine. And a dash of madness. That description could be applied to the whole of our new life in Greater Germany. The migration was soon complete. The furniture soon arrived from Riga. The winter was soon over. And the obligatory wedding had soon taken place, as well.

Ev and Hub began their married life right there in front of their incredulous parents, to whom it had come as such a surprise – and it tormented me more than I had anticipated.

They had both named me as a witness to their marriage. But I didn't want to be any kind of witness beyond that. Not an eyewitness, or an ear-witness. Or a *Knallzeuge*, a 'bang-witness'. Do you know what that is? Someone who only realizes there has been a car accident when they hear the crash. A bang-witness was what I felt like during my brother and sister's occasional arguments, which would flare up out of nowhere in another part of the house, sparked either by one of Ev's mood swings or my brother being a stubborn know-it-all.

Even worse was hearing one of them bring the other pig's ears (some call them *palmiers*) in bed, or hearing their mutual desire at night. Sometimes, through the wall, I could hear Ev letting herself go during sex, or rather abandoning herself entirely. She really didn't show any restraint: Mama was hard of hearing, and Papa was grateful for any sign of life from the people around him. And my spirited sister-in-law gave me no consideration at all. I knew Ev's melodies better than Hub would have wanted: familiar, fond sequences of notes from years before, from that long-buried age when we helped each other to reach erotic maturity. Seeing Ev with wet hair in a steam-clouded mirror was painful enough, even when she didn't open her dressing gown for a wide-eyed moment, pretending she was just tightening her belt.

But I knew her well.

One evening, an incident took place that gave our life together a different undertone, which from then on was a soft but constant hum in our temples. Our parents had gone to bed early. We had lowered the blackout blinds and the three of us were lounging on the living-room sofa as we used to in childhood. Two standard lamps provided the only light. Hub and I were sitting at either end of the sofa, each leaning on an armrest, each reading his own copy of the almost orientally florid *Ostdeutsche Beobachter* in the two meagre islands of light.

Ev had flopped face down across both of us, into her big brother's arms. But her legs were lying clumsily across my lap. By means of a ser-ies of furtive movements I managed to shuffle away from her aimlessly rubbing feet, but like little rabbits they kept hopping after their moving hutch to warm themselves – or to warm me, that was how it seemed.

An ashy feeling came over me. I considered getting up, but it was already too late. My excitement had become obvious – I was only wearing pyjamas – and at least while sitting down I had the *Ostdeutsche Beobachter* to shield me, a page-long article about Dunkirk as I recall. And so I sighed and wedged myself as far as possible into the right-hand corner of the sofa, hoping to come to my senses. The next thing I knew, Ev was turning halfway over and whispering something to Hub, who began to read out details of the victory at Dunkirk to us from his copy of the paper, and her wonderfully soft calf landed like a cushion, as if by chance, against my now helplessly erect penis. I was in a panic. But Ev, suddenly a smooth, innocent creature, pretended not to have noticed anything, since the British forces making their escape in little cutters and paddle boats was so terribly interesting. Her leg, which at first merely pressed a little more firmly on my pulsing loins, soon stretched out a little and lost a slipper. The second slipper went as well, and her right big toe began to roll the sock off her left foot, very slowly, creating rubbing, pressing, stroking, twitching and swaying vibrations that took my breath away. I studied her now bare ankles, the only bare skin I could see; the rest of my field of vision was occupied by lines about the southern side of the English Channel, into which the German Army Group A was plunging, lines that I was also hearing, though they sounded distant, for it was not Hub's sonorous voice that was sharpening my senses.

When the German artillery had defeated the guns at Gravelines, my sister stretched out again to take an apple from the table, a red one – if only it had been green, at least – and I was certain that Hub would not miss this opportunity to instigate our old apple ritual, which I had never been less keen to perform. I glanced over at him anxiously, but he was oblivious to everything as the Royal Air Force was losing a whop-ping one hundred and six fighter planes over the Channel. I couldn't see Ev's face – it was either glowing or turning pale somewhere under Hub's newspaper – but I heard her teeth crunching into the apple. He was laughing about something, probably Churchill's anger, which he could well imagine, and Ev laughed too, and as the laughter tipped me over the edge, I meant to allow the convulsion that pulsed all the way back to my spinal cord to ebb away in empty space. But she suddenly shifted her whole purring body half a metre down towards me, to give Hub an apple-scented kiss, and I couldn't help it, I was trapped and had to spill my seed against her right buttock, which she pressed very briefly to my twitching member, shielded only by my pyjamas and hers, two millimetres of cotton between us, that was all.

At once, she rolled off the sofa and leapt to her feet. I could see a touch of red in her cheeks. She ran her fingers through her tousled hair as she chewed, and her eyes flitted over me as idly as if I were a cleaning rag. Her mouth full, she said, 'Come on!' took Hub's hand and pulled him up, not even giving him a chance to say goodnight to me, and they both stumbled off and disappeared into their bedroom like lightning, or like a happy child.

Then it was quiet, and all I could hear was the ticking of the large mantel clock.

A damp patch formed on the Dunkirk article in my lap, right above the fierce bridge of Field Marshal von Rundstedt's nose. I switched off the lamp and sat motionless for a long time in the dark. It was only when I heard two shots being fired somewhere in the city, a long way off (something that happened often at night), that I got up and crept, stained and mortified, into my room.

That was the only incident of this kind.

It never happened again, and there was never any lewdness between Ev and me – if there wasn't a lewd quality to her mere, enchanting presence, that is, her whole being oriented towards immediacy and charm. She was shy now when we saw each other, particularly on the morning after the Dunkirk offensive, which neither of us mentioned. And perhaps her own offensive hadn't actually been carried out with the overwhelming, aggressive determination I had felt from her. Perhaps I had just imagined it all, I don't know.

All the same, from that evening on, there was an awkwardness between us that was never really expressed. I simply tried to avoid being alone in a room with her, although when it happened – and it happened often – I had no objection to it.

She was always the first to leave.

We got along well. She liked to tease people, and I found it easy to make her laugh, certainly easier than with Hub, who had such a tremendous presence and vitality that he simply didn't need this social tool – though he, too, had a sense of humour.

'Yes, he has a sense of humour. I think I can go through life laughing with him. Though he doesn't always have the laughter I need,' she told me – a cheerful, throw-away remark – as we were planting strawberries in the garden together.

'Don't you need every kind of laughter to even begin to get by?' I asked.

'The laughter that can trigger the same thing in me. The same emotion.' She got up and wiped a soil-covered hand across her features, which were restless and at the same time calm, like an ambling tortoise. 'He doesn't have a laugh that asks.'

I could have spent half the night talking this nonsense over with her, like we used to, and that's what she wanted, too. But I just lowered the strawberry seedling into the soil and bedded it in pensively.

I simply no longer felt there was solid ground under my feet. Do you know that feeling, when everything is swaying and pitching and one feels almost queasy all the time? I once caught myself, in an unguarded moment, picking up Ev's little black boot and pressing my nose into the shaft, hoping to smell not sweat but something heavy and tremendously surprising, and that was precisely what I did smell. But when I put the boot down, dazed with the scent of leathery sweetness, I saw Papa, whom someone had wheeled into a doorway, sitting three metres away, and his wise, benighted eyes gave me a quizzical look.

I missed Mary-Lou, and so, even in something as innocuous as a blown light bulb (which I changed, with Ev holding the stepladder and my left leg) there was a burden and a tension that very slowly began to rub me raw.

On top of this, I was aware of her racial vulnerability, and by remaining silent I was protecting her day after day, which created a bond that went far beyond any previous intimacy. Though only on my side, of course. She didn't know it, but she was exposed, perhaps even under threat, for no one could know whether Hauptsturmführer Schmidtke or someone else in my own elegant SD department might spot something fishy when checking Ev's racial purity (there were no official documents; the only proof of her identity was a notary's declaration that he had inspected a church register). I felt responsible for her. I wanted to be near her in case anything happened. That was the only reason I didn't try to escape the torment that her ungainly beauty represented for me, her dreamy way of slicing the top off an egg at the breakfast table, the warmth of her body stored in the lavatory seat and soaked up by the cheek that I pressed to the wood when I rushed in straight after her, scenting her urine, which a few minutes after flushing still hung in the air as it had done on those chamber-pot nights of old.

But it was her kitchen apron, too, flung down in annoyance at unsuccessful biscuits; her throaty, boyish laugh drifting in from the garden; the clenching of her soapy fist; her lamentations over all the ways in which she thought she might die at any minute – she would get stuck in the modern lift at my office, and there would be a sudden fire in which she would perish – any of these things could occupy my mind for hours.

It was only then I realized that one part of her variegated personality was melancholic. Sometimes a whole abyss of sadness lurked within her, and she hid it behind more or less psychosomatic illnesses: migraines, stomach aches and flu-like infections, symptoms of a vague disgust at life that I understood only too well. And finally, there was her inconstant and fickle concern for me and for my own affairs (which at bottom didn't interest her very much), pricking me like a thorn in my flesh.

Even if I had wanted to, it would have been almost impossible to move out and escape this situation. I wasn't entitled to my own housing permit, since I had been provided with living space in the family home. The tremendous number of new arrivals was still causing a great housing shortage in Posen. Hub could no longer keep pace with demand by evicting Poles and Jews. He'd told Ev that his job was to look after the German immigrants and find accommodation for them, which of course was true from a certain angle: he 'found' one apartment after another.

Presenting everything we did in an entirely positive light was one of his great skills. And every day he looked at me with eyes larger than life itself, while I felt nothing but dust in my veins. We were responsible only for what was great about National Socialism, he was convinced of that – and I parroted those sentiments because it pleased him.

Yes, sir, we were the good guys.

*

Unfortunately, however, early one morning during this period, a track worker at Posen's railway yard discovered a freight train parked in a remote siding, from which he could hear quiet whimpering. It was still dark. Once he had opened a carriage that had been sealed from the outside (a decision that would later cost him his job: no one was permitted to open a sealed carriage unbidden, just because they could hear people dying inside), dozens of human forms emerged, stinking of faeces and rot. They fell on their knees and, like cattle, began to drink from the puddle the man was standing in. It emerged that a transport of Polish deportees, who were due to be shunted off to the General Governorate without food, water or clothing, had been forgotten about by a careless railway official. For six days.

At daybreak the surviving women, still clutching the stiff bundles that had once been their children, were forced to load those bundles onto a lorry parked in the street by the train tracks. And as this scene was playing out, my sister happened to pass down that very street on her way to the hospital. She had started a job as a registrar there two days previously. And since Ev was already wearing her white coat, and in the blue dawn light could only make out a lot of people crying, she asked Hub's insane chauffeur, who was taking her to work that morning, if he would be so kind as to pull up alongside the lorry.

I am certain that the SS men would have seen off any other civilian quite brusquely; civilians had no business poking their noses into internal administrative processes. But no one dared stop the beautiful young doctor, who was obviously grimly determined and (most importantly) getting out of an officer's car. She ducked under the cordon, bent down to the half-starved women, and cast a glance at the grubby little baby-maggots, lying in the back of the lorry like a cargo of turnips.

Then she asked the commanding officer who was responsible for these depths of satanic inhumanity. And the man, looking rather cowed, replied quite truthfully that it was the Frau Sturmbannführer's husband, namely the Herr Sturmbannführer himself, whose orders they were following.

I might not have described yet what happened to Ev when she was angry. A lot of women can't get angry at all; they just turn spiteful. But Ev was transformed. Her eyes tore you to pieces, eyes with nails in them, terrible, frightening eyes. All the colour drained from her features, giving the many facial muscles one needs for anger an impressive pallor. I might turn red with anger; cholerics do, you see it every day. Ev, by contrast, looked as delicate as Snow White. People who don't know what is coming might be put in mind of porcelain. Because pallor can signify so many things. Once, when I was twelve and was getting a thrashing from two lads from the parallel class, down on the quayside by the Düna, they thought something similar: Will you look at that, who have we got here, then. She approached very quickly, though without appearing to be in a hurry. Her chalk-white face gave no warning of the elemental storm that was about to break. 'Two against one?' she said, like the Queen of Sheba. '*Tsvey akegn eynem, ir zent mer nisht vi drek.*' And then, despite her bloodlessness, she punched one of these dumbfounded apes on the nose, and at that time it was not an especially common experience to be assaulted by a grammar-school girl with a fine porcelain complexion speaking street Yiddish.

By the time Hub, having naturally been informed of this incident by his driver, came home that evening with a huge bunch of flowers and two tickets to *Rigoletto* in his sweaty hands, Ev had been pacing around the requisitioned villa for hours, as white as plastic explosives.

Mama was at a complete loss. She was unfamiliar with such unbridled rage, knowing only the bridled kind which she considered to be the correct way for civilized people to express their dissatisfaction. But Ev told her that she was not dealing with civilized people here; she was dealing with her brother and husband, a combination that Mama found challenging each time she encountered it.

Believe me, I was eyewitness, ear-witness and bang-witness in one that evening, yes, I was truly a witness to history, for it was an epochal bloodbath. All Hub could do was to stammer at Ev, asking her to please calm down – and my God, that really is the stupidest thing you can say to an angry assassin in the final stages of arming her bomb.

'Of course, it's . . . well, it's a catastrophe, Ev. But there is a war on, my darling. A war. Every day hundreds of our men are dying on the front lines. You have to put it into context!'

'I have to put it into context?'

'Yes.'

'I have to put it into context? What are you *doing* in the SD?'

'I'm keeping people safe. And so is Koja!'

'Leave Koja out of this. Don't you try and tie him into this shitty business!'

'Language, child, we're not in the gutter!' my mother exclaimed in alarm.

'Oh yes we are, Mama, we *are* in the gutter!' Ev said indignantly. And then, turning back to Hub, 'You told me you were finding accommodation for the Balts! I thought you were helping people!'

'And I am. Believe me, in my job I'm sure I save more lives than you do!'

'You should have seen those babies! You say you want to have a child with me, and all the while you're killing children?'

'Now, darling, don't start comparing apples and oranges.'

She walked up to him, took the bunch of flowers from his hand and hit him in the face with it.

'Never do that again! Never do that again!' she screamed. 'Never again, do you hear me? Apples and oranges?'

She tried to stuff the flowers into his mouth.

'Ev, have you gone mad?'

'You look at these little creatures who have died of thirst, and you think of apples and oranges? We're not talking about fruit, Hub! Have a little respect!'

She was weeping with rage, and both she and Hub were speckled with a confusion of the most beautiful petals.

'Is that true, my son? Little children died?'

'Yes, Mama. It was a terrible accident.'

'Oh my.'

'But we do take very good care of the Poles. This is becoming a German province, and that means they have to move out, you know that, Mama.'

'Of course.'

'They will all be given very nice apartments in the General Governorate, they'll be well looked after there.'

'Eva, child, you see? Very nice apartments!' Mama sighed with relief, and added, '*Tant de bruit pour une omelette!*'

'I know what I saw!'

'You must have a little faith in your . . .' Mama couldn't find the right word to describe Hub, so she just looked at him hesitantly, while he cleared his throat with evident emotion.

'It was a terrible accident; I will admit that. It was extremely unfortunate. Those responsible will be brought to justice,' he promised.

'Swear to me that it will never happen again!' Ev hissed.

'I swear.'

'You hear so many awful rumours.'

'Really? What rumours?'

'That life is not at all good for the Poles and the Jews. That dreadful things happen in the ghettos. I never believed it until now! How *can* you believe such a thing?'

Hub pointed up at Papa's portrait of the tragic saint Hubert Konstantin Solm, whose stern, Moses-like gaze dominated the kitchen.

'Just look at Grandpaping! He was a pastor! His father was a pastor! His grandfather was a pastor! In the last one hundred and fifty years, my family has produced only men of God! Ev, even I'm a theologian!'

'And I'm on the church council,' my obliging mother put in.

'And Mama is on the church council! Do you think that I, or any one of us, would join the SS if its mission were not to serve the good of humanity?'

'What happened to the people who used to live here?'

'They were given a nice house in Krakow.'

'Just as nice as this?'

'Nicer.'

'Get me the address! I want to write to them. I want to know.'

'I'll see what can be done.'

'You'll get me the address?'

'I can't guarantee it will be possible. But yes, I'll try.'

'I want the damned address! I want the address, Hub!'

'All right, I'll get you the bloody address. But you mustn't individualize human suffering like this.'

'What are you talking about? Suffering is always individual!'

'But the point is the overall picture. Compared with the suffering of a whole nation, this terrible accident is just a drop in the ocean.'

'Hub, don't start this again.'

'Forgive me. But aren't you thinking about joining the SS yourself, as a doctor?'

'After what I saw today?'

'You really should. Yesterday I heard that they need a huge number of medical staff. In the concentration camps, for instance. Then you'll see the high ethical standards to which we National Socialists work.'

'No,' I said, in a daze, 'I don't think Ev would want to become a camp doctor.' And then I added hastily, 'I mean, you wouldn't be together, then. The concentration camps are such a long way away.'

'This really isn't any of your business, Koja!' Ev hissed at me. 'I'll join the SS if I want to! Even if it's just for the hell of it!'

'Heaven!' my father said. He hadn't spoken a word for years, but now he was sitting in his wheelchair as if he were about to get up and leave. We could scarcely believe that a sound was able to escape the pit of his twisted mouth. But again, we heard him croak, 'Heaven, heaven!' as if my father were trapped inside my father, shouting with all his might for us to pull him out of his own throat, past the vocal cords that were knotted up like shoelaces. You could even hear a familiar tone in his voice. That 'heaven' sounded light-footed and rather surprised.

We all looked at him, and my mother began to rub his back. 'He's talking, he's talking,' she stammered, marvelling at him as if he were a baby uttering his first 'Mama'. She stroked his ageing cheek, and the white beard that she tended like one of her flower beds. She was making an affectionate attempt to give him a cup of tea when his face was suddenly flooded by an inner light, his lips curled into a smile, and he toppled contentedly forward and hit the tabletop hard, his eyes open and blissful. Later, Ev wiped my father's final motion, his last *voilà* against mortality, off the wheelchair as if it were a true gift from God. An ultimate act of love for the man who had once taken her in and made her his daughter.

And with that, of course, the terrible argument was over.

When we met for breakfast in the weeks that followed, we were all dressed in black: in plain civilian black, in elegant SS black, in whatever black happened to be to hand – that was Ev – or in the hundred-and-twenty-year-old black of my distant ancestor Grand Duchess Mishkova's blond-lace mourning veil, which my mother favoured. She wore that veil every minute of the day, even in the bathroom and during meals, although it was a hindrance.

Beneath all our black there lay unhappiness. For although Papa had ostensibly been nothing but a breathing shadow for years, his spirit had still settled over and around us.

The funeral at the New Cemetery in Posen was like a procession from the tsarist Riga of old. Even the long since banned Curonia was permitted to don its full regalia one last time thanks to a special dispensation from Erhard Sneiper, and to unfurl the immortal flags that were lowered over Papa's grave.

When I was eight years old, I had painted a portrait of him as St Nicholas, with an overly large nose – though Papa had always said that a beautiful nose could never be large enough. And I buried this Nicholas with him.

Every night we heard my mother weeping, a woman who had never wept in her life, excepting that one moment on the *Bremerhaven*. The shock had made her thin-skinned, and now all the tears that had built up over six decades behind her composed facade poured out by the litre, as if a dam had burst. She wept over death and life, the loss of her homeland, the murder of the Tsar's beautiful daughters, but also over a poor man wearing a yellow star who had to move out of her way in the street.

By day she mostly seemed as hard-headed and self-possessed as usual. But in the evenings she would make Theo his camomile tea, put the steaming cup down in his place at the table, realize her error, sigh, 'Ah, my dear Theo,' and pour it away. Then the tears came, and they would keep flowing until long after midnight. It went on like this for months. Sometimes you could hear her through her bedroom door, talking to Theo, sobbing quietly, and the words she spoke were often reproachful or even harsh. It was something she had been doing for years, and Papa had never been able to answer her before his death, either – but now, it sounded disturbing. She left the soap-scented wheelchair parked at the kitchen table and held discussions with it, appearing to listen as well as talk. It didn't seem to be a revenant of Papa, however; it was more like some additional household imp (this was new, too: perhaps it was the lover that Mama had never permitted herself).

She often asked us what Papa might have meant by his final 'heaven': could he see the eternal light already, or was it the voice of God speaking through him? Once, I heard her praying, asking Theo to forgive her for Grandpaping, for that warning she had given by lying down in front of his carriage, a warning against riding out to the parsonage and rescuing his stubborn father. This plea was accompanied by a long ribbon of sobs, one woven into the next, and for the first time in my life I wondered if my parents, tangled in a web of guilt as we all are, had really loved one another. Why didn't Mama's all-consuming love for Papa, which came as such a shock to us, manifest itself earlier? Do we only ever become conscious of love when it's too late?

I wondered the same thing about my sister. Papa's death had clearly taken a heavy toll on her, and she wanted to be near me constantly, seemingly unaware of the discomfort I felt in her presence. The unbearable state of mind into which she had been plunging me at every turn for decades now, a state that tasted of doom, was something I couldn't and wouldn't discuss with her. But the more I withdrew, the closer she came.

Naturally, the loss of my father, my mother, who was becoming somnambulant, the wrong house, the dead babies, the Poles toiling away to save their lives, and the war, had caused all those electric discharges of passion in Ev and Hub's still-fresh, still honeymooning marriage to sputter and possibly even age. But perhaps Ev also had no desire for the eternity which, when you think about it, a marriage always signifies. In any case, since the day of Papa's death I'd heard barely any noises from the marital bedroom, none of those high-pitched sighs, no begging 'aah's and 'yes's and groaned commands, which six months previously had tormented me night after night. That surprised me. Our house was ruled by *pietas*, it's true – but Mama couldn't hear anything, and I had never cared about such formalities. Still, the silence didn't trouble me; it actually pleased me. Can you understand that?

When Ev and I drove to the cemetery one day, to take Papa some flowers – it was early, before she and I both had to go to work, in the half-light of dawn – she asked me to sit down on a cemetery bench with her: she had something to tell me. She looked exhausted, as if she hadn't slept a wink all night, and when I asked why, she just said that Hub still hadn't given her the address in Krakow.

I knew at once which address she meant.

But that wasn't why she wanted to speak to me. Instead, to my horror, she told me that she had applied for a job advertised in a medical journal. A position as camp doctor in a 'women's re-education camp' in Ravensbrück. It was an SS facility. She showed me the carefully folded advertisement. She had not yet spoken to Hub.

'But he's the first person you should ask.'

'He might be against it, though. He did *say* he supported the idea.

But I don't believe that. And you know, perhaps a little distance will do us both some good.'

She leaned down to the gravel that marked out the cemetery paths, picked up a small yellow stone and held it up, trying to see through it, before dropping it again. Then she sighed and looked me in the eye.

'Hub is such a strong person. Being with him is hard.'

I nodded.

'Perhaps I should do something for others for a year or two and build my self-confidence before we start a family.'

'But how on earth would a concentration camp build your confidence?'

'I want to do my bit. For the victims, you know. I'm certain they don't have any good doctors there. I want to help the prisoners.'

'In a camp?'

'Yes – they *are* prisoners there, aren't they?'

'Hub says those places aren't like the pictures you always see in magazines.'

'He's told me that, too. But he does want to prove how well the SS treats its opponents.'

'Please, Ev, don't go,' I begged her. 'You've got a good job here. You have a beautiful, big house. You'll be very happy here with Hub, soon enough.'

Hub was dumbfounded when I relayed our conversation to him. He told me our sister had grown increasingly fragile in the past few weeks. 'If only one thing was straightened out, this dull fear and this heaviness would be lifted from her,' he told me. 'It's this business with the babies. She still can't get it out of her head. Now she's set on making the world a better place.'

He shook his head and said that she wouldn't get the camp job, he'd make sure of that. Then he fell silent, though the silence was not an unfriendly one.

Since we found it difficult to ask each other questions, we only ever talked about other people, most often Ev. We frequently went for several days without talking at all, and when we travelled to the office together in the morning, in the back of his car, we each stared silently at the city out of our own side window, looking at the cowed Poles, seeing the self-confident Germans wearing their uniforms like courtship plumage, yes, like a pair of tits, Papa had been right about that. There were no kaftans now. The city was free of Jews.

Our daily route took us past blue advertising pillars covered in posters that proclaimed the weekly shooting of hostages at Posen Fortress, and the Wehrmacht's tremendous military victories. A provincial city swaddled in a gentle orderliness, peaceful, sedate and deadly at the same time, but above all: a *provincial* city. A sleepy word in a world that was all superlatives, speed, lightning flashes, all-time records. World domination. In the midst of this great age, Hub was not leading a heroic life. I could feel his misery. In his eyes, he was a pen-pusher, trapped in a gristmill and being ground down by an increasingly depressed wife whom he had only ever known as the midday sun. He told me he suspected Erhard of assigning him to this unedifying job. This was his instant revenge on Hub for marrying Ev, he was certain of it.

It worried my brother that he could only present Ev with a prettified version of the truth. He thought himself energetic and decent. An energetic and decent man. He thought she had no head for politics, and that made it impossible to properly acquaint her with the philanthropic core of our beliefs. She never saw generalities, the bigger picture, only ever the specifics. And her lifestyle was too individualistic (as was mine, in his opinion); she couldn't see that, while there was a worm in people, there was a dragon in *a* people, a nation. Every time he tried to point out National Socialist correlations, she reduced the world to the question of where the family who used to rent our house had gone.

'Someone from our department is going to have to forge that letter,' he sighed, looking at me with a fraternal plea in his eyes. Could you do it?'

'You want me to pretend to be the previous tenants of our house?'

'Exactly. You live in Krakow and you are perfectly content.'

'I don't speak Polish.'

'Write it in bad German. Mangle the language a bit, you know? I thank you much, madam.'

'Hub, that's not on. You're lying to your wife.'

'No. I'm reassuring her.'

And as he said this, he realized how imbecilic his own words sounded, though he still believed in them. Reassuring, placating, soothing, playing things down. The arsenal of his affection. He loved Ev very much, perhaps even more than she loved him. Of course, he was not honest in the proper sense of the word. But he remained loyal in an almost perverse way: to his saint, who had pushed God from his throne; to me, though my passivity incensed him; even to Erhard, who had forced him to bring inescapable perdition to so many people; but most of all to Ev, mournful Ev, whom he so wanted to make happy, down there in the well of his best intentions where she was now drowning.

'You know what our last really, truly pure moment was?' my brother asked me one morning on our way to work. He didn't look at me, but I could sense his voice box battling the emotion in his heart. 'It was when the three of us were lying on the couch, like we used to, and I read you that article, you remember, about Dunkirk.'

At the end of July nineteen-forty we were invited to a country estate in West Prussia for the weekend, to attend the wedding of a cousin I had never particularly liked. I was writing up my final report on 'the surveillance of Baltic Germans', which was gradually drawing to a close, so I couldn't spare the time in any case and had to stay at home.

Shortly before Hub, Ev and Mama were due to leave, Ev complained of feeling unwell. She came down with one of the migraines she had been suffering lately, and took to her bed. Hub was understanding. He moistened a flannel and pressed it to her forehead, making water trickle down over her closed eyelids in the way she liked. He made her some tea, put an empty bucket beside the bed and closed the curtains. I saw him kiss her tenderly on the mouth. Then he and Mama had to go without her, taking his official car. He had given the mad chauffeur some time off. He hugged me goodbye. That was unusual.

She didn't emerge for most of the day. Once, I went in to check on her. She had vomited, what looked like several hours ago, but hadn't called for me.

'Do you need anything, Ev?'

'Does the room smell of sick?'

'That doesn't matter. Do you need anything?'

She didn't.

That evening, mountainous clouds gathered in the west. I could feel a change in the weather approaching, the air quivered and the birches swayed. The block warden rang our doorbell and told us there was a storm warning in place for the next twenty-four hours. They were expecting some severe weather.

I went into the garden and took the washing in, protected the little greenhouse from falling tree branches, brought the sun loungers inside and bolted all the window shutters. As I closed the door behind me, I saw the first raindrops hitting the flagstones, but the thunder was still a long way off. I buttered a few slices of bread and left them by Ev's bed. She had fallen asleep. Her mouth was open, and a string of saliva hung between her lower canine tooth and her upper lip, as if spun by a very precise spider that must live somewhere in her throat, or maybe deeper down, in her heart.

I removed the bucket with the fresh vomit in it, tipped the grey-green contents down the lavatory, rinsed the bucket out and put it back in the broom cupboard.

By now, all the windows had begun to rattle and shake, and the storm's advance guard was whistling and howling outside. I went to bed early, intending to read for a while. But then the electricity went off all over the house. The room went dark. Soon after, a bolt of lightning struck somewhere nearby, splitting a tree in two. It sounded like a bomb falling.

Five minutes later, the door handle tilted down and then Ev was standing in my room. I couldn't see her, only hear her; I was lying with my back to the door, pretending to be asleep.

'Can I get into bed with you?' she whispered.

'No.'

'No?'

'I don't think that would be a good idea.'

I knew exactly what face she was making. When you've known someone a long time, you only really look one another in the eye as a courtesy.

'I just wanted to say thank you, for taking my sick away.'

'You're welcome.'

'I don't smell of sick any more, though.'

'Good.'

'I brushed my teeth.'

Her voice was as thin as paper. I turned over and saw her standing in the middle of the room, a spectre with her white nightshirt and tousled hair.

'I'm sorry, but you can't get into bed with me, Ev. I don't want you to. It isn't right.'

'That's fine.'

She just stayed where she was, rooted to the spot. A flash of lightning lit up the room for a moment, colouring her nightshirt, and I saw wide eyes and disintegration, as if there were nothing of her but dust or molecules, and just a few seconds later there came a rumble of thunder.

'I'm frightened of storms. You know that.'

'Yes, I know that, Ev.'

'I can sit in the armchair over there. You can't forbid me from doing that.'

'Of course not.'

She spent half an hour sitting peacefully in the old wingback chair. I thought she had fallen asleep.

'Koja, I'm cold.'

'Well, that's because you're sitting there with no covers on.'

'What's so wrong about it? I'm sure Hub wouldn't mind.'

I didn't say anything.

'Koja, I'm still your sister.'

'That's as may be,' I shot back. 'But *I'm* not your sister any longer.'

She got up, walked over and slipped under the covers with me.

'I'm going to be really cross, Ev.'

'Please just be cross tomorrow, all right? Please let me sleep now.'

And with those words, she really did fall asleep at once.

I listened to the world raging outside, and to the raging within me. She had thrown her right arm across my chest. She couldn't put the slightest weight on me without injuring me with memories, not even her narrow wrist. She was lying on her side, her face pressed into the pillow, the way she always used to lie beside me, as if she were not married, not my sister-in-law, not Jewish. Her breathing was soft and regular. I concentrated on the sound, and very gradually my eyelids grew heavy, and the bluster and roar carried over into my sleep, like a galley drum, and I was manning the rudder.

It was cold, but I couldn't work out why. I woke up. The wrist had gone, and I was lying there naked. Ev was lying furtively beside me, also naked, her head resting on her arm. She was watching me – she might have been watching me for hours. I sat up with a start.

'Why have I got nothing on?'

'I undressed us.'

'Are you mad?'

'We were sweating.'

I pushed her away.

'Koja, please!'

I switched on the standard lamp. The electricity was back on. The rain had stopped. I looked at her. Our nightclothes formed a little molehill on the floor.

'I just wanted to lie next to you one more time like we used to.'

'I'd like you to go back to your room, right now!'

'No.'

'Get up this minute!'

'No, please don't . . .'

'I'm going to carry you back there.'

I pulled her up by one arm, but she clung to the bedpost with the other. I tried to prise her loose, which sent her into a rage, and she bit my shoulder. I cried out. When I attempted to shovel her up with both hands like a mechanical digger, she stepped aside and hit me in the face. My lip split open, and I stopped where I was, dazed. We were both panting. We were completely naked – I've said that already. Finally, Ev sank to the cold floor, struggling for breath.

'I'm afraid, Koja,' she gasped.

'You can't be here. You need to be with Hub. But you can't be here.'

'Where else am I supposed to be, you're my only friend.'

'Is this the kind of thing you do to your only friend?' I pointed to the molehill of my clothes.

'It's what we used to do!'

'You don't take anything seriously.'

'I need you. Everything is so confusing. I'm completely confused. Nothing is more confusing than a moral defeat.'

'Yes, and now you've come looking for another one.'

'I don't know whether I might have made a mistake with Hub.'

'Papa always said,' I blurted out, 'if you're not sure whether you've made a mistake, then just wait a bit!'

She bent down, plucked her nightshirt from the pile and pulled it over her head. She was crying.

'I don't understand that man,' she whispered. 'He's so different to how he was as a child.'

'I'm different to how I was then, too.'

'But I didn't marry you.'

'Exactly. And have you ever, in all your self-absorption, in all your *I-I-I-I need someone to laugh with me-me-me-me*, has it ever crossed your mind just what that means for me?'

'What are you talking about?'

'I'm talking about the fact that you didn't marry me.'

'Oh, but you're much too nice.'

It was one of those things that only Ev could say, a statement that fell like irresistible fruit from a poisonous tree.

'Maybe I am too nice, that's entirely possible, nobody's perfect,' I whispered. 'But I love you.'

She didn't say anything.

'I've been in love with you since the first moment I saw you. I've loved you for twenty years. I loved you back when we pissed in the same pot.'

She still didn't say anything; she was looking at me in disbelief, her eyes floating like oil on water.

'But as much as I love you: I'm not about to cuckold my own brother! And certainly not with someone who causes me pain every day. Who just gets into my bed when I don't want her to. Who strips me naked like a baby. Who hits me. I'm a whore to you, and believe me, I know what whores are. You can be tremendously fond of a whore, and that's exactly how you feel about me, I'm like a nice whore. It's exactly how you feel about my cock.'

'Stop it, stop it, Koja.' She crumpled at my feet.

'I'll show you just how nice I am.'

I bent down, grabbed her leg, and dragged her across the floor like a side of bacon. She wasn't defending herself any more, just crying, crying and screaming, and her nightshirt slipped up over her backside, and I thought, no, I've seen better backsides than that, and I pulled her out of the door and she cried out, 'Please don't, please don't, Koja, I'm sorry,' and then I left her lying out in the hall and closed my door and turned the key twice in the lock from inside and all night I could hear our old vows shattering inside me.

2

I had an urgent need to take a painting trip.

Travelling with an easel and sketchbook, moving joyfully through the world, is the only way to refresh a visual artist's most vital organ: the eye.

Papa always advised us to favour yellow and red hues at times of inner imbalance, and otherwise to trust in what we could see at a given moment, in other words to let light into our brains, nothing but light. That is the important thing on a painting trip, to delight the brain with the brightest reflections and otherwise to spare it completely and just let it rest, to lay colours down while avoiding the merest hint of a thought, to paint and draw and paint again in the same way a sheep grazes.

The day after his return from what was apparently a jolly wedding in West Prussia, which had at the very least put the brakes on Mama's despondency, I went into Hub's office, greeted him in the proper manner and asked the Herr Sturmbannführer for an immediate transfer. Reasons were requested. I invented some, also mentioning my desire for a painting trip to ease my soul. I lent some urgency to the request by taking my Luger from its holster, cocking it and placing it against my temple, a rather drastic method of letting light into the brain.

My superior rolled his eyes and cursed his siblings' penchant for melodrama, though in this instance he also had the tact not to point out the state of my gun (unloaded). He'd always regarded his little brother as highly strung, but had never let him down, and so in the space of three days he managed to find an opening for me. By way of thanks, I turned his generous, only slightly unctuous expression into my first portrait sketch in months. I drew it with my father's good old graphite pencil, in my office, before clearing out my things.

And then I was on the train to Berlin. As a senior SD officer, Hub himself should have been travelling in this comfortable first-class compartment, on his way to oversee the next SS-led resettlement in Eastern Europe. But he refused to go.

For one thing, it was impossible for him to leave Ev alone for three months. When he came back from West Prussia, she had grazes on her stomach and a bruise on her hip. 'Probably from a fall, some kind of collapse,' he murmured. I pretended great surprise ('No, there was nothing out of the ordinary at the weekend, Hub. She just had a headache'). He paid no attention to my own split lip.

There was another, even weightier argument against his participation in the resettlement campaign: he would have been compelled to dine and drink vodka with Soviet officers, rather than having them shot, and he could not do that to our poor drowned Grandpaping.

And so I arrived at the sunlit Reich Main Security Office in Berlin in his place, and slotted myself into a role that carried far too much responsibility for a lowly Obersturmführer.

Or you might say I was advancing my career.

No one knew, of course, that I was really on a painting trip, under the guise of conducting everyday SS business. In Berlin, my first port of call was Heppen & Pelzmann artists' supplies on Friedrichstraße. I bought Faber-Castell pencils, drawing chalk, China ink, China-bristle paintbrushes, flat and round brushes (Siberian weasel). I bought up half the shop, in a kind of frenzy.

As I sat in the Stahnsdorf barracks, covertly caricaturing a rather leathery adviser with a new 6B Faber-Castell, he explained to me and the other agents of Office VI that we were to proceed with all haste to Bessarabia on the Black Sea coast, and assist in bringing home a hundred thousand Swabian colonizers. The adviser kept calling them 'splinters of the fatherland', summoned by the Tsar a hundred years before and strewn across the Moldovan steppes all the way down to Odessa. Now the Soviets no longer wanted them, and these splinters had to be swept back up into the land of their fathers.

I was greatly looking forward to the exotic scenery, the allure of a Karl May wilderness just waiting to be painted. But I was also very aware that for the first time I was a commanding officer, with my own little troop of foreign secret-service men. We were disguised as resettlement officials – civilians, in short. My title was 'Authorized Representative, Mannsburg District'. Officially, our task was to manage the logistics on the ground, but unofficially we would be mapping the whole country and searching for Soviet military bases. Soviets and Nazis were working together to relocate the Bessarabia Germans.

'So we can expect all kinds of fun and games,' the far from playful adviser told us in conclusion.

I was given a personal assistant, Untersturmführer Möllenhauer, a rather soft-looking Hanoverian with slicked-down hair and a face that looked like it had been dusted in flour, reminding me of the French clown Pierrot. Later, he actually did hold his rifle like a mandolin.

In addition to Möllenhauer I was allocated a kind of bodyguard, a bear of a man from Saxony who looked like a secret drinker, which was therefore what he came to be called. He never spoke a word. I enjoyed the Drinker's company for that reason, and drew his portrait in the style of Goya's *Los disparates*.

Möllenhauer and the Drinker held together my little SD detachment of sixteen men, with whom I was dispatched to Vienna. There, we met hundreds of other resettlement workers from every corner of the Reich: paramedics, doctors, lorry drivers, telecommunications engineers, Waffen-SS men disguised as tourists, ministry officials, race researchers, so-called war reporters, photographers, journalists, illustrators, and even a magician who had no real idea of what his role in this enterprise was and kept our spirits up by performing card tricks.

We sailed down the Danube on a snow-white pleasure steamer, passing Budapest (where I painted the Franz-Joseph Bridge in watercolours), finishing the stores of Tokay just after we crossed the Croatian border (resulting in an incomplete still life of two glasses with fruit and peel), sailing through Vukovar, where thirty-four of us urinated into the middle of the mighty river (something I did not depict), gliding slowly past Belgrade (a beautiful city, for which I had pastels and hand-made paper at the ready), and on through Serbia, where we waved to a decomposing, rust-red steamer anchored in the middle of the river, a vessel that was supposed to be taking some Jews to Palestine but had run aground (an impudent soldier snatched my sketchbook, wrote: 'Death to the Jews' on it and brandished his artwork at the starving Antichrists). All the way along the Bulgarian border we sang over and over, 'There are angels on vacation in Vienna today.'

Finally, our Danube steamer came into port in the Romanian city of Galatz, where the Soviets were expecting us, and I had to put away my sketchbook and pencils for the time being. The temperature was pleasantly Mediterranean, but the greetings were frosty. The head of the

Soviet resettlement commission came aboard with two of his men, but immediately suffered a heart attack. Our doctor diagnosed and treated him for severe alcohol poisoning. It took more than an hour to negotiate what luggage checks would be carried out. The Soviets insisted on searching everyone's bags for weapons, and in the process confiscated all the maps on which we were supposed to mark the enemy bases, meaning that our mission had failed before it even began.

Amid all this excitement, I was introduced to my Soviet counterpart, an NKVD major whom I met down on the quayside in Galatz Harbour. He was standing with a group of his people, hands in pockets and a cigarette clamped between his teeth. He approached me with an outstretched hand. I recalled my Curonia code of conduct and deliberately ignored the hand, waiting for the other to be removed from the trouser pocket and the cigarette politely taken from the mouth, as befits a greeting between gentlemen.

Unfortunately, this was not to be. Hand and cigarette remained where they were, and the NKVD major was evidently taking some pleasure in the slight. In a flash, I reached into my bag, pulled out the sketchbook and made a thirty-second caricature of him in the style of the Nazi newspaper *Der Stürmer*, for his face was stereotypically Jewish. This portrait, which he immediately asked to keep and showed proudly to his colleagues, earned me his respect and set the tone for our future relationship.

The major's name was Uralov. He was short and wiry, a good-natured bloodhound. Not knowing that I spoke perfect Russian, thanks to Anna Ivanovna's many years of instruction, he allocated me a female interpreter, whose job it was to pump me for sensitive information, and to have intimate relations with me for this purpose.

I took up the offer at once, which started tongues wagging among my team. My assistant Möllenhauer, looking anxious and snow-white around his Pierrot nose, asked me if I knew what I was doing, and said he should really report this to our superiors in Berlin. Go ahead, be my guest, I said, but was he not aware, I added, that this sacrifice – conducting sexual relations with sub-humans – was one of the hardest, but also the most useful sacrifices one could make for our people's cause: the bedroom was the secret service's battlefield, as Talleyrand had said (he knew who Talleyrand was!), so I was just doing my damned duty. I advised him to take the same course of action, though I already suspected he would prefer to concentrate on the beefy hauliers from Vladivostok.

The interpreter's name was Maya; she was only eighteen, and in some ways still a child. Everything about her was the exact opposite of Ev. She was not coquettish or complex or strong-willed or conflicted or hypochondriac or depressive or my permanently festering wound; she was the balm I put on it, and she smelled wonderful, just like the little flowers of the steppe that she picked for me, presumably on Uralov's orders. This girl was as light as a paper chain and as clear and transparent as water, and I drank her up like a man dying of thirst.

I liked to draw the details of her more than the whole: I sacrificed half a pastel pad to her arse, her neck, her eyes with their *Plica Mongolica*, her left ear (the lobe of her right ear was attached, which I didn't like), her large but still weightless breasts, her vulva, which was almost invisible amid dense vegetation, so that I had to ask her to trim the bushes (though when she did, it looked more like a mown lawn). She had a friendly, foxy face and questioned me so guilelessly and at such inopportune moments that I was quite touched by her devotion to her work, and invented some truly splendid stories for her. Major Uralov's ears must have fairly rung with them all.

Every day Maya accompanied me and the Drinker, who drove my official car with great stoicism. We travelled through an almost oriental landscape dotted with derelict mosques that had been abandoned by the Turks as they fled a hundred and fifty years before. The Germans we met spoke a late-baroque version of the language. They were unfamiliar with electricity, tractors, telephones. They still mowed their fields with the same scythes their ancestors had brought with them from the Swabian Alps. The whole place looked like a piece of South German folk art painted on Arabian silk. I collected some of the weather-beaten faces we encountered in my sketchbook, along with a few of the cats that lived there in their thousands, probably because this was the land of mice. Maya didn't like me constantly doodling away, as she called it. And since there are plenty of other ways to let light into the brain, we also enjoyed a great deal of kissing.

Sexual relations aside, however, this joint mission to evacuate the Bessarabia Germans went anything but well. The Soviets not only made very original assessments of the emigrants' property, to ensure that they left as many material goods in the country as possible; they also had our compatriots moved out at gunpoint, quite literally making them pass between canons, tanks and barbed wire. Sometimes a chance occurrence was all it took to set the guns firing.

We lived under the same roof as Major Uralov's troop, and used the same faulty telephone, which was unscrupulously tapped by the NKVD. I threw a fit and ordered Möllenhauer to have another line put in, so that we could talk amongst ourselves and listen in to the Russians' conversations as well. When Uralov got wind of this, he stationed two of his cudgel-wielding guards in our breakfast room, which had such an effect on our appetites that I had to ask the Drinker to escort these gentlemen out through the glass door, without opening it.

As the resettlement progressed and the first of the Bessarabia Germans were transported to the harbours of the Danube in picturesque horse-drawn wagons and endless convoys of lorries, the rainy season set in. The dusty roads, which were more like farm tracks, turned into metre-deep quagmires. Maya had found a little half-ruined hut in the mountains about an hour's walk from our hotel. We met there often, since I didn't really have anything better to do; I was relying on Möllenhauer's eagerness to see the mission through. Of course, the Russian girl didn't tell me she wanted to escape from the camera in the hotel room next to ours that captured all our movements. I knew about the camera, though, and it didn't bother me in the slightest. Neither shame nor tenderness, nor any form of fear, could touch the subtle, deep black afflictions within me.

But Maya seemed to be attracted to that. Incurable conditions always hold a great power.

'You sad,' she sometimes whispered to me in her bad German, stroking a blade of grass across my cheek – but I never said anything. The rain hammered on the ramshackle roof, my silence made her affectionate, and she began to take our intimate evening sport for the real thing. She was as childlike as a puppy, and her heart had the perfect, biscuit-like consistency for breaking. I don't suppose she ever told Uralov that I spoke better Russian than he did; if she had, I am sure he would have withdrawn her services.

Sometimes we would sit naked under a blanket in the old mountain hut, looking out at the rough, almost poetic beauty of the country spread out at our feet that glittered with its frequent overthrows. The wind brought the scent of an approaching rain shower up to us before the rain itself: the smell of wet earth and aromatic plants. The steppe was endless, and at night a great dome of clear, star-studded sky spread across it, beneath which unusual creatures – bearded vultures, wolves, pelicans, great bustards, and two spies consoling one another – followed their animal instincts. Or their orders.

We were in the car one day when I thought I saw a calf sitting at the side of the rutted road. As we came closer, the animal got up, spread its wings and hurtled towards us. It was a giant steppe eagle; one of its wings brushed the windscreen as it flew over us. The whole car went dark, and Maya clung to me as we instinctively ducked. At the wheel the Drinker, whom I never once saw drinking, didn't so much as flinch.

When I had dropped Maya off at the hotel, I was driven to our office, which had been set up in Mannsburg at a former village inn. These were our final days in Bessarabia, and my closest colleagues and I had to write up the meagre results of our espionage. Möllenhauer went out, I don't recall why. In any case, he came back a minute later with the Drinker and a briefcase. The briefcase belonged to Maya; it was the one she always carried with her.

'Look what we found on the back seat of the car,' Möllenhauer crowed triumphantly. He was almost dancing.

'Yes. The interpreter must have forgotten it.'

'What an incredible piece of luck, Obersturmführer!'

'Private!' I said to the Drinker. 'Take the bag back to the lady.'

'Shouldn't we see what's in it first?' Möllenhauer asked, clearly taken aback.

'Why? It's just make-up and her interpreting gear.'

'Yes, but shouldn't we take a quick look inside?'

All eyes turned towards me. Our instructions from Department VI of the Reich Main Security Office made it very clear that we were to scrutinize every last speck of enemy property we could find. And making an exception for a briefcase belonging to an NKVD agent assigned to keep tabs on me would place me in the immediate vicinity of a firing squad.

'Of course,' I said.

Möllenhauer opened the case and pulled out a scarf (which just hours before Maya had slung around my neck), two stenographer's pads, a drawing of her forlorn profile (made and given to her three days previously by her beloved Obersturmführer), a German–Russian dictionary, two handkerchiefs, a ladies' pistol (well I never) and finally, a thin folder. Möllenhauer stared at the cover for a second too long.

'I can't read Russian that well. But I think this will very quickly transform my Herr Obersturmführer into a Herr Hauptsturmführer.'

He showed me the folder proudly.

The Russian words on the front said: 'Top Secret'.

Underneath: 'Classified documents! Do not carry on your person!'

We opened the folder and saw an overview of every member of the Soviet delegation to Bessarabia, with real names and aliases. It was a perfect 'wanted' list. I had no idea why Maya was carrying it. But the fact that she was not permitted to carry it was clear from both the form and the content.

I gave an instruction to copy the information at once, and shouted at my baffled people to please be quick about it.

Two hours later, I raced up the hill to our hotel with the briefcase and the original document.

But Maya's door was bolted.

I ran to our mountain hut, covering the distance in twenty minutes and vomiting from the exertion when I finally arrived.

Maya was not there.

I lay awake all that night, hoping for a knock on the door.

The next morning, the Drinker and I waited in the car outside our accommodation, as we had done every morning in the months we'd been there. The Drinker left the engine running. Eventually, the front door of the hotel opened. An unfamiliar, short-legged raven of a woman, about forty years old, hopped unsmilingly towards us and croaked that Comrade Maya Dzerzhinskaya was ill, and she had the honour of acting as my interpreter for the remaining few days.

She blithely got in beside me.

Trying not to appear nervous, I recalled why I was really there and turned my attention to the area's endemic plants, to which I had not yet done illustrative justice. I drew little sprigs and nuts, a stump and a single dog rose, as autumn fell over the immense steppe. All the life seemed to have gone out of it. Cleared of almost all its inhabitants, it was now a wasteland covered in hundreds of abandoned villages. The drama of the bulging grey rainclouds was tempered by the monotonous Mongolian grey sky. When I sat outside for any length of time, my clothes grew damp and the paper wrinkled.

Möllenhauer could see that I was stricken. He was a tactful man, and took over all the organizational duties. We received a telegram conveying congratulations to our troop, and to me in particular. An imprudent telegram, since it was doubtless intercepted by the Soviets.

All the same, there was no change in Major Uralov's attitude towards me. The farewell banquet was certainly a cheerful affair.

To cap it all, the major finally escorted me back to the ship himself. By the harbour wall, where we had first met three months previously, he embraced me with tears in his eyes. He said he had grown very fond of me, German bastard that I was. Then he sang me a verse of 'Katyusha' and, as a parting gift, presented me with a brown envelope marked 'Top Secret'.

And underneath: 'Classified documents! Do not carry on your person!'

It was probably meant to be funny.

My hands trembled as I took out the snapshots of Maya and me, documenting a brief erotic diversion in black-and-white, thirty coital memories at least.

Uralov let out a good-natured laugh, clapped me on the shoulder and told me not to worry, the negatives were in the envelope as well. Nothing would be used against me. He was my friend until his dying day, and the interpreter had been a good choice. He rounded both hands appreciatively in front of his chest, the international men's code for nice tits. There was an impatient shout from the ship, where was I, everyone was waiting for me.

I went on board, or at least was heading up the gangway when I stopped and plucked up the courage to take a few steps back and ask my new friend-until-his-dying-day whether he knew how my interpreter was doing now.

He looked at me with puppy-dog eyes, took a deep breath and put all his humanity into his hoarse, booze-soaked voice as he said, 'I'm afraid that your interpreter has ceased living.'

3

In war, outrage always comes with a kind of insight. No one knows how it happens, but guilty and not guilty are very difficult to tell apart in these times; they merge into one another like watercolour paints, blue and red, for example, washed together. Serving in the underground is a wet-on-wet technique: there are seldom any clear dividing lines, and you have to take care that everything doesn't end up violet, the most dreadful colour I know apart from mummy-brown, which is extracted from embalmed Egyptian bodies, or at least used to be. Papa showed it to us when we were little, with a degree of pride. He used this bitumen-like substance in portraits because it was brilliantly suited to depicting shadows on skin. Little Ev was so horrified to discover that the colour contained essences from human bodies, and so eager to right all wrongs, that she secretly purloined the tube from Papa's studio, took it down to Mama's garden and gave it a decent burial.

I don't really want to talk about Ev at all. I wanted to wipe her from my memory in nineteen-forty, as well, but death invariably drew me back to her, even Maya's death. I could not comprehend it, and it made me jump into the ice-cold Danube – we were traversing the Hungarian border – in the middle of the night. But the guards on the bridge saw me, all the boat's engines stopped, they fished me out of the river and decided it was the alcohol that had got the better of me. I had in fact been three sheets to the wind. My rescue was celebrated, people crowded around me and again and again and again they sang, 'There are angels on vacation in Vienna today.'

As you might suppose, that was the end of my painting trip.

No wall is more insurmountable than the one you build around yourself. My brain would never receive another ray of light, I was certain of it.

I barely noticed what was happening to me.

Eventually I found myself back in Berlin. I was greeted by a lot of friendly faces. They kept me on in the Reich capital as 'an agent for special deployment' and put me on a four-week training course, my only memory of which is the housefly that came and sat beside me on the window every day, without fail. She was pleased when I was awarded a War Merit Cross 2nd Class for the personnel files I had obtained in Bessarabia by such original means – or at least, she set her ugly little legs proudly on the medal and sat there for several minutes, perhaps wanting one herself, the patriotic little fly (those shimmering wings, like old gold).

Not long after this I was summoned by Walter Schellenberg, the head of foreign intelligence. Möllenhauer, with whom I went to the cinema from time to time, was quite beside himself: 'Oh, Herr Obersturmführer, it's like the gods coming down from heaven. They must have big plans for you – what am I saying – . . . magnificent plans!'

I was, at least, driven to the Prinz-Albrecht-Palais in a limousine. A brusque adjutant was there to welcome me. We glided along red runners down endless marble hallways, past rows of doors, until I was finally handed over to a surprisingly fat secretary who was intently focused on painting her nails.

After a few minutes' wait, the double doors were flung open and I entered an office that seemed to have been designed to resemble a Viennese coffee house.

Herr Schellenberg was sitting on a Louis Quinze couch in front of a full-length gold-framed mirror. The way he got to his feet was something I had never observed in any other SS general. He approached me like a perfect host; he was slim, with a spring in his step, verging on solicitous, and full of hidden intentions. Instead of a hand I shook an empty glove, or so it felt to me. I marvelled at his face, which was soft and tense at the same time, at the rosy flesh in which his mouth, slack and sensual, had settled into a perpetual arrogant smile. The exemplary manners, the attractive hauteur and the aristocratic, expressionless visage of an ornamental guppy created quite an impression.

We sat down at an ornate little table and he remarked, his high voice reproachful but kindly, that for my age I was still in a rather junior position. There was something unexpectedly pushy in the condescending way he mentioned my age – the tarnished crest of thirty-one years – which is not only your own, my seasoned Swami, but at that time was also his (the most powerful secret-service chief in all of Europe, *Eheu fugaces postume postume labuntur anni!*).

This impression was reinforced when the Brigadeführer first asked me to guess and then showed me where the listening devices were hidden all over his tastefully furnished office. I guessed the ones in his desk, in the standard lamp, in the crystal chandelier. But I had not reckoned on the microphone under the ashtray, nor the one behind the wall, which sounded hollow when he knocked on it.

His desk looked like it had come from Renaissance Florence. It had two machine guns built into it, which could fill unwanted guests full of holes in a trice – 'They hold a thousand rounds,' he said reverently – and he showed me the button to press on the middle drawer. The lever beside it would trigger an alarm that automatically sealed all the building's exits.

I didn't really know what to say to all of this.

And so Schellenberg cleared his throat, congratulated me on my coup in Mannsburg, and proposed that I undertake a particularly delicate mission to Paris. There was a man there who was extremely important to the German political establishment, he explained, a Georgian cheese manufacturer by the name of Kedia, who was gathering Russian émigrés around him and worked for the SS. Unfortunately, he was also thought to have made treasonous contact with the French Resistance. They needed to get to the bottom of this rumour at once, and that meant putting a reliable agent on to Kedia's wife, his Achilles heel.

'You want me to place this woman under surveillance?' I asked.

'No, no, I want you to sleep with her,' Schellenberg smiled.

'But why?'

'Because you're good at it.'

Human egotism – reprehensible, transient – had now truly manifested itself in me in many respects. But the fact that, in my superior's eyes, that egotism had transformed me into a Don Juan (and a mercenary one, at that) filled me with revulsion, rage and a strange kind of melancholy. The decomposition of Maya's body could not yet be very far advanced; it was winter, after all, and no matter what part of Russia she was in, the earth would be frozen along with everything buried in it. Every day I looked at the photos of us, shadows of our bodies, always discovering some new detail that I tried to reconcile with the many drawings of her extremities that I had made. Yes, I had the feeling that only now did I understand who this girl had been, only now did I really see her. And I saw her and spoke to her, saying: this is bone of my bones and flesh of my flesh.

As I sat in this office of Schellenberg's, a room infected with listening bugs and machine guns, which looked more like a brothel or a French gaming salon than a respectable workplace, I felt the biblical force with which Maya, who had once been three grams of paper chains, bore down on me. And at the same time, it became clear that I was stepping through all these vain looking-glasses into a world where nothing carried any weight. Nothing was so far-fetched as to be impossible. Every visitor was a potential murderer. Some advantage lay behind every friendship. Acting without an ulterior motive was regarded as bizarre. A sexual act with no ulterior motive was simply a waste.

Talleyrand had been right.

Please do not misunderstand me. In the end, I accepted Schellenberg's offer. I was much too vulnerable to refuse an offer that promised me any form of social betterment. But I was determined to do no harm to this Madame Kedia, on whom my sexual organ, my education, my talents and my kindliness were to be let loose: there would be no false intimacy, not even real intimacy. I just had to get away, out of this perfumed office, out of Germany, to somewhere a long way from Posen.

And a long way from myself, too.

It was imperative.

Paris seemed like a twinkling galaxy, a Milky Way full of strange life forms and undreamed-of diversions. A promise.

All the same, I couldn't bring myself to burn Maya's photos, nor all the drawings and sketches. I couldn't part with her ear lobe (the one that wasn't attached), a life-size, cross-hatched copy of which was acquiring creases in my wallet. I looked inside her briefcase, which I always carried with me, at least once a day, picking up the little Russian ladies' pistol, which sometimes spoke temptingly to me when I'd had too much to drink. Three or four beers a day, half a bottle of red wine, a good measure of corn schnapps and a lot of sweet French rotgut were my constant companions. I dived into the reverse side of things, behind the scenes, down into the machinery. And then, in the window display at the Moulin Rouge, I came across Mary-Lou. A yellowing photograph of Mary-Lou, to be precise.

This encounter was followed by a meeting with her boyfriend, the Breton ticket taker, and we both seethed with jealousy.

Nor will I ever forget sitting in my room hours later, drinking Cahors wine by the light of a candle and digesting the news that

Mary-Lou had left for the States three months earlier, seemingly without ever having spoken of me, not even once.

All this was topped with convivial dinners in Palais Maubrid with Monsieur Kedia and spouse, a scrawny, man-mad goat of a woman who put her hand on my trousers once, but found only snail meat.

At the weekends I amused myself in an establishment where you could purchase optical hallucinations. Around midnight, little Vietnamese women would strap you to a dentist's chair, while a colonial doctor injected Merck mescaline, derived from peyote, into your expectant veins. Afterwards, you suddenly understood Vietnamese.

However, my commanding officer, Sturmbannführer Lischka – terrible even with a croissant in his mouth – spoiled these moments of French *savoir-vivre* for me. Again and again, with increasing impatience, he instructed me to do my work.

And so, in a drunken state, I wrote surreal and entirely insignificant surveillance reports about the Kedias, who were kind enough to keep inviting me round to discuss a triadic project (an erotic triad, to be exact). The proposal was made quite openly, but it involved certain quirks that did not interest me. I was still welcomed at their soirées even after demurring, because I spoke good Russian and improved Madame's complexion – with the watercolours I was coerced into painting, I mean. I included a few of these in my dispatches to Berlin, and on one occasion, a rendering of an SS raid that I happened to have the pleasure of observing on the boulevard de Sébastopol.

I made a careful list of all Frau Kedia's lovers in my weekly reports. Everyone, literally everyone seemed to stand a chance with her, except me, I cabled gloomily to Berlin. I could find no explanation for my lack of success (aside from my own reluctance, which of course I could not mention). And so I put it down to my bad breath, and visited a costly dentist at Schellenberg's expense. I could neither confirm nor deny that Monsieur Kedia had contacts in the French Resistance, but since the whole world was sleeping with his wife, that would naturally include the whole of the French Resistance.

And that was the extent of what I achieved.

My head felt like sand, and my sex life remained entirely monastic. I gave the brothels a wide berth and forgot reality as one only can in Paris.

Unfortunately, reality did not forget me in return.

*

In May nineteen forty-one I was summoned to the Gestapo headquarters, entering for the first time through the front door rather than the backstage entrance on the rue d'Alsace. I was received by a tight-lipped Sturmbannführer Lischka, who told me not to sit down. He actually said, 'Please do not take a seat!' Nor was I offered one of his cigars.

After a few pointed questions regarding various restaurant and dentistry costs, and a reference to the efforts and the suffering of the German people, which were what allowed certain individuals to live this life of luxury, which was what I was doing – goodness, all this which-ing and what-ing, those Sturmbannführers spoke the most appalling German, now where was I? Anyway, after this prologue Lischka explained that Schellenberg was disappointed in me. 'Extremely disappointed, one might even say.' I would henceforth be relieved of my SS special mission and should instead report immediately to Sturmbannführer Solm.

'Sturmbannführer Solm,' Lischka said, interrupting himself, 'is that some relative of yours, Obersturmführer Solm?'

'Yes, sir, we're related,' I said.

'Well I never,' he murmured, his tone still as hostile as ever. 'In Saxony,' he added. The Pretzsch border police academy. I would receive further instructions there. My marching orders were enclosed. Heil Hitler. Dismissed.

When my train had crossed the border into Germany, the locomotive had to be recoupled at the Stuttgart terminus. I got out onto the platform in time to hear a special broadcast from the Kroll Opera House in Berlin. Everyone stared up at the loudspeakers hanging high above their heads and heard Adolf Hitler bellowing that this day saw the start of Operation Barbarossa across a huge front: we were now in a life-and-death war against the Soviet Union and he would never capitulate; he would only take off the field-grey jacket he wore every day when the final, hard-won victory over the enemy was ours.

On that day, no one in Stuttgart Central Station would have believed that the Führer and chancellor of the German Reich, ruler over half the world, would one day have this plain uniform doused in two cans of petrol and would go up like a torch, just a few hundred metres from the jubilant enemy – me, least of all.

4

As a child I was convinced that everyone needed some kind of lifelong quest. And I'm not talking about Heinrich Schliemann and all that Troy nonsense. I don't mean a burning desire for action, or a Holy Grail. I just had the sense that we were all abandoned in the dark forest like Hansel and Gretel and had to work out how to get home.

But when I was older, I realized that, in fact, no one ever makes it out of the forest. We all just stumble around, getting tangled in the undergrowth, and rather than searching we simply want to be found.

That was the position in which I now found myself.

But what do you do when the whole bloody forest is on fire?

I didn't know what awaited me in Pretzsch. But it couldn't be anything good, beyond the prospect of seeing my brother. I missed his ability to turn the people around him into an audience for his genuine, irresistible dignity, which now made him appear rather stiff, but also made others want to confide in him. He couldn't lead you out of the forest, but he could guide you to a clearing – that had always been my image of him.

Images of Ev also surfaced when I thought of him, deeply buried images, over which my desire to forget her, the tragedy with Maya, and the Paris hallucinations had all settled like silt. Her childlike manner and her childish attitude towards life had always been a comfort to me. The fact that she was constantly aware of the effect she had on people had also been cheering, for someone who had no idea what effect he was having. It was only the effect of her words that she seemed completely unaware of. 'You're like Baron Münchhausen,' I had once told her, when she tried to feed me another of her impossible stories. 'In what way?' she asked. 'Was he pretty?'

I couldn't help but smile when these memories floated to the surface of my mind, shimmering in all the colours of Ev's sudden moods, the steps she danced in the middle of the street, her infuriating and brilliant ideas. And then the gloom, the deliriums of purest unhappiness where we had abandoned ourselves – it was a year ago now – pulsed behind my temples, extinguished the images, and my smile vanished.

How was she doing now?

Not a single letter had reached me, not even a postcard, in Bessarabia or Berlin or Paris. We three didn't write to one another, gave no sign of life. That was a relief on the one hand, but on the other it was a new development. We had always been within reach of one another; *that* was the symbol of our relationship, not this permanent unreachability.

It was only through Mama's old Baltic love of correspondence that I learned the essentials. 'My dear Kojashka,' she wrote in her swift, unornamented hand.

It is starting to look much less homely here at home. Truly it is. The empty house is large, the garden needs digging over. But my silly fall on the cellar steps has turned me into a lame old duck (don't go gadding about on it, Dr Blumfeld says!). And I need an electric man for the lamp in the kitchen, for I am all at sea with it. The idea of not always having children under my feet is heaven, but I still miss you all terribly. You are off causing some ledden with the Frenchmen, so I hear (how we loved the madeleines with Papa!). And just imagine: Hubsikin has been transferred from here to the front and is hunting down communists, he will wipe them out once and for all. And little Eva, dear as ever she was and a touch foolish with it, dithered for a long time over what to do. But rather than lowster down and be a help to her old mother (all that rubbish in the cellar to be thrown away, and I won't get far on that wreck of a bicycle with my peg leg, to say nothing of the rhubarb), she signed up for war service. So unwise. Don't you think? Your sister has too many bees in her bonnet. She needs a baby! She has just been assigned to a hospital near Krakow, which she says is awfully interesting. I don't know any more than that because they censor the field post. But before she left she had lost weight and got quite thirl, and started wearing her hair severely again. She was very quiet as well, perhaps because she was missing Hubsi.

When I reached Pretzsch in Saxony and reported to the border police academy, the officer on duty just stared at me. He looked quite taken aback; he glanced left and right down the empty hallways, shrugged helplessly and said, 'But they've all left already!'

I learned that the trainees had spent weeks in this beautiful place (a Renaissance palace that served as accommodation for customers of the nearby mud bath as well as for optimistic SS-Einsatzgruppen) looking forward to the campaign, but it had begun several days ago and my unit was already hot-footing it after the German army, heading towards the

Soviet Union to clean up the filthy hinterland. Those were the exact words the officer on duty used, quite unselfconsciously: clean up the filthy hinterland. I had been sent to help sweep out Latvia, Lithuania and Estonia – and the ferocious cleaning squad, Einsatzgruppe A, was already on its way there, a thousand eager fumigators made up of every SS unit you can think of (they bore the strangest names: you will have heard of the Gestapo, and the Kripo, the criminal investigation division, but perhaps not the Orpo, short for order police – and 'Popo' may seem scarcely credible, but that was my unit. I was glad that Himmler had spared the political police this moniker by calling them the SD).

The duty officer handed me my marching orders an hour later. He was wearing a thick rose-gold wedding band on his finger, which obscured the line that said where I was being deployed. He tapped this line several times, and it was only when he rubbed his nose that I could see where I was going: Riga.

The city was about to fall, and it would be horribly filthy.

And so, two years after we emigrated and twelve months after my hasty departure from Posen, on the second of July nineteen forty-one, I reached the outer suburbs of the city where I was born. The tower of St Petri was blazing fiercely. A hundred-metre-high yellow-and-orange torch that could be seen from several kilometres away. Like a Bunsen burner, it burned away the rain above the cathedral, which fell on us instead, angry and warm, 'Like God is pissing on this whole mess,' as one of the NCOs in the car grumbled.

The fighting had ceased only a few hours earlier. The place was littered with Russian corpses, lying unheeded along the roadside. One man's head had been run over by the tanks. Red soup, from which a single intact eyeball stared up at the burning cathedral tower. The sappers sitting beside me made their jokes, one even wanted to jump out and take the eye with him, but the other held him back, laughing. I was sitting in the back seat of the automobile, which had been speeding after my troop for the past two weeks. Now we were rolling over human entrails, moving forward at a snail's pace, hemmed in by the seething chaos. The Wehrmacht was bringing endless convoys of reinforcements to the front lines, but the roads were also jammed by great crowds of prisoners of war. The rain had set in hours ago, transforming dirt tracks parched by the hot, dry weather into quagmires and welling mud.

At a crossroads, I finally saw a member of my unit. I had the car pull up alongside him, wound the window down, and only then did I see through the pouring rain that the man, an SS-Scharführer with an SD rhombus on his sleeve, was standing guard over a large number of civilians with his sub-machine gun. They looked frightened. A petite woman with short white hair, dressed in light blue, vomited onto her husband's hand as he held her upright. Out of the corner of my eye I thought I saw another sentry thrusting the butt of his rifle into the crowd.

The Scharführer stood to attention. I asked where our registration office had been set up. At the prefecture, he said. And might the Obersturmführer be familiar with the Petersburger Hof? That was where the officers' quarters were. The small woman's husband wiped her mouth. She was weeping, and the rain tore her up like onion-skin paper. And yes, the shocked Obersturmführer was familiar with the Petersburger Hof.

Have I mentioned how much the SS loved luxury hotels?

The following morning, I met my brother in the Empire dining room, which had suffered only a single broken windowpane in the house-to-house combat. He was sitting alone at a white-clothed table. Although it was little more than a year since we had last seen one another, he had completely changed. The little Clark Gable moustache had gone, making him look not younger but harder. His blue eyes were still those of a man who hadn't the faintest idea what dishonesty meant. But I also saw determination in them, nervousness, and not even a hint of curiosity.

'Koja,' he said warmly, getting up and embracing me, and we sat down together.

A solicitous waiter came hurrying over, poured coffee into the wafer-thin porcelain cups and gave us a broad smile. Forty-eight hours earlier he had shot dead three retreating Russians. You could see as much from the Latvian cockade on the sleeve of his hotel livery. Three embroidered black crosses.

'He told me that himself, too,' Hub said with an air of indifference, before ordering our breakfast from the sharp-shooting waiter.

We acted as though nothing had changed. We may have been wearing uniforms, but we talked as if we weren't – like tourists, friends, or affectionate brothers. I wanted to find out what had become of Hub; I was in no mood for empty chatter, and began to stare vacantly over at the golden pheasants and SS snobs who were enjoying their food around us, and to praise their greed, their stupidity and their instinct for good honest corruption, giving full vent to my bile.

Hub asked me to keep my voice down. He didn't want to argue with me, but nor did he encourage my rant. The only time he ventured to criticize the regime, it was with a cryptic pronouncement: 'The government always believes that sunshine will follow rain. But sometimes rain follows sunshine, too. No one here wants to acknowledge that.'

When he was a little boy, Hub had been compared to Grandpaping, to a German admiral, a Russian tsar, an angel, a baby sparrow, a warship and an Alsatian. But now he was writhing; he had become an eel (no one had ever compared him to an eel), slithering away from things, surviving by means of camouflage.

'I can't see you,' I said, after half an hour.

'What do you mean?'

'You're evasive. You seem strange. As if your mind was elsewhere.'

'The war changes you, Koja. The war changes everything. You don't know that yet. I'm sure Paris by night is very different to what awaits you here.'

He reached for his glass of breakfast juice, raised it and said in a conciliatory tone, 'At last!'

'At last what?'

'At last, the Bolsheviks are getting it in the neck!'

I thought of Major Uralov. I thought hard. Pictured Uralov's grin as he stood on the quayside in Galatz that day, choosing his words about Maya. About Maya's remains. Yes, my girlfriend had ceased living. Yes, I clinked glasses with my brother. He took a slice of pumpernickel bread, spread it thinly with butter and told me that Ev was doing better now. She'd started a new job.

I didn't want to hear anything about Ev.

'I saw a few of our people in the Dünaburger Vorstadt yesterday,' I said, trying to change the subject. 'They had rounded up some civilians.'

'Yes,' my brother replied. 'Bandits, communists. They've been liquidated now.'

He shovelled a large quantity of elderberry jam onto his bread.

'Why did you have me brought here?' was all I said.

He took his time biting into the pumpernickel and explaining things to me calmly. In a low voice, his mouth full of bread and jam, he told me that he'd heard about my success in Bessarabia, but unfortunately also about my abject failure in Paris. The collapse of my mission there had brought me within a hair's breadth of being transferred to Auschwitz. He'd been told that in confidence.

I didn't know what he meant. I hadn't heard of Auschwitz. And nor did I want to know what it was. In any case, it seemed to be something he couldn't talk about while eating: he laid down his knife and fork, dabbed his lips with a napkin and leant forwards over the table.

'If Auschwitz hadn't been the alternative,' he whispered, 'then I most certainly wouldn't have brought you here. I'm afraid it isn't going to be a bed of roses here, either. We're dealing with the enemy. As you've already seen.'

He took a sip of coffee, his eyes fixed on me over the rim of the blue-and-white onion-patterned cup, then set it back down and leaned even further across the table towards me.

'I know you're an aesthete, Koja. A lover of theory and the Russians. You won't approve of everything that goes on in our Einsatzgruppe. But this is nothing compared with Auschwitz. Nothing at all. I swear to you.'

I was silent for a moment.

'Ev is at Auschwitz.'

I stared at him.

'I couldn't stop her. I mean, you know what she's like. She's serving in the field hospital and helping where she can. But she wrote to tell me that I mustn't allow them to post you there for camp service. And that's exactly where you were headed.'

He gave me his most winning smile.

'So just be glad that we were able to get you here.'

I stayed in the hotel for four days, left to my own devices; Hub was still busy setting up his office. He had become the leader of the local SD, the head of Department III under the commander of the security police in Latvia. A lot seemed to be expected of him.

There was a kind of carnival atmosphere in Riga at that time. Latvians and Germans promenaded around the city in the evenings, the glow of the midsummer night at their backs. I strolled the boulevards along with tens of thousands of others, mostly in small groups, sometimes arm in arm. Communism had been driven out, the defeat of the Soviet

Union seemed guaranteed, and the promise of a new age hung in the air. People were hoping that Latvia would be reborn.

And that hope, which was still floating over the nation, coming down like a parachute from a great height (soon it would hit the ground at full speed and shatter on impact), often caused mass singing and dancing to break out in the streets. Once, I even saw a half-naked fire-eater spit flames onto a red flag, and we danced around that burning flag like Tlingits around their totem pole. The lindens were blossoming, and even the last remaining wrecks of tanks and the flattened corpses that were cleared away by singing street-sweepers seemed to smell like summer.

A few days later, Hub showed me around our workplace at the prefecture. I breathed a sigh of relief. The corridors were clean, the large windows open, and the aroma of freshly brewed coffee was in the air. Pretty young typists teetered up the broad staircases. The adorable little Fräulein Paulsen took care of the new employee, her boss's brother, me – and I purred like a cat. She showed me to an office with a southern aspect, painted in fresh linden green.

I shared this office with Obersturmführer Dr Grählert, a very courteous ancient philologist who spoke in a genteel Cologne accent and bit his nails from overwork. Grählert was the head of the SD culture section (SD-D-III-C), and staff shortages meant that he also oversaw the areas of literature (SD-D-III-C1) and theatre (SD-D-III-C2). His decisions were based on nothing but the evidence of his weary, intelligent eyes. I was responsible for the 'architecture, folk culture and art' sub-section (SD-D-III-C3), which consisted of me and a Latvian interpreter whom I didn't need.

I was primarily tasked with the observation and surveillance of all Riga's visual artists, their organizations, exhibitions and personal relationships. In my youth, I had got to know the *haut monde* of Latvian painters and illustrators through Papa (they expressed heartfelt joy at seeing me again, though the joy was largely at seeing the extra rations of butter, bacon and honey I brought with me), and this provided me with informants who would sing like birds. My job was to keep a close eye on the Latvian art market, run my network of informants and spies, and pass on information to other departments, who then acted on my suggestions.

In short: it was, of course, a terrible demotion for someone who for a few months had been regarded as the great hope of the German secret service. Brigadeführer Schellenberg was probably regretting ever having shown his sharpshooting Renaissance desk to a cockroach like me. But Hub pretended not to be embarrassed by it. And I was as happy as a clam; for the first time in half an eternity, I felt I could breathe freely again.

With my colleague Grählert, whose brief also covered surveillance of the theatres, I attended some marvellous plays, met inhibited actors and less inhibited actresses, and had a good time. It began to remind me of my best pre-war days with Mary-Lou, and I occupied a very attractive and tastefully furnished flat on Wallstraße.

Hub's department had excellent manners. The vast majority of the SD members it employed turned out to be highly educated, poetically minded metaphysicians, former orchestral musicians (a very good viola player was oppressing the Latvian choral societies), defrocked pastors or ex-geography lecturers. I now found myself in an entirely new and different SS world.

All employees took their meals together, and because our department was so notably courteous over lunch, we were known as the please-and-thank-you table.

Some of the other diners, however, made a very unfavourable – even a repellent – impression on me. Particularly the members of Department IV, the Gestapo, who gave no consideration to etiquette or good manners.

One of these colleagues, a Viennese Obersturmführer named Bertl, greeted me every morning in his Austrian parlando with the words, 'All right there, fegga!' It sounded friendly, so I greeted him politely in return. I never asked what 'fegga' meant, taking it for the Austrian equivalent of an 'isn't it' or an 'eh' from Swabia or Bavaria. It was only after several weeks that Fräulein Paulsen asked why I continued to put up with this, and it emerged that 'fegga' was not one of these verbal tics but a noun. It was in fact a contraction of 'fucking egg-head'. Later I learned that Bertl was principally used for interrogations and executions.

More and more irritations had begun to creep into my otherwise picturesque daily life. When I hurried back the office late one night to work through a few important files for the next day, I was bothered by a strange whining noise coming up through the heating ducts. I asked the night watchman to check on the heating system in the cellar. The caretaker, when summoned, just shrugged and said that the lower floor of the building was where the Gestapo conducted their intensive interrogations, which they did as discreetly as they could. This was only possible at night, when the building was empty. They couldn't do it any more quietly.

In mid-July the Gestapo sealed off the Kaiserwald, Riga's villa quarter. All the wealthy Jews were arrested, to free up their houses for senior SS officers. I only learned of this because one of the participants in the raid happened to sit beside me at the please-and-thank-you table. 'There were some very plush interiors, oh boy, yes,' he said, whistling admiringly through his teeth. 'We had to go into every room to herd the Jews out onto the street, which gives you a pretty good impression of these places. But you wouldn't believe how long it takes to get them all on the lorries. And then all the way back here.'

'The Jews were brought here?' I asked, dumbfounded.

'They certainly were!' the man said, smacking his lips. 'Two hours, they spent standing down in the courtyard. And we had to guard them, in the midday heat. Full uniform. That rich villa crowd – all their lives, they've been parking their arses on leather sofas. Well, then I heard they were going to be shot. How did you manage to miss all this, friend?'

I had not the slightest idea how I had managed it. My brother had sent me off to an art exhibition in Bauske on that particular afternoon. Perhaps that was it. And suddenly it dawned on me: all the enjoyable excursions that came with my job, on which Hub often sent me at very short notice, served no purpose other than to make an idiot of the over-sensitive, highly strung Obersturmführer Solm.

Within twenty-four hours I had got hold of all the necessary information (I was in the secret service, after all). It told me that the prefecture was the nucleus of the most horrific, unconscionable crimes, the products of a perverted mind – and the please-and-thank-you table could talk about the spiritual and the material world in Descartes all it liked, it did nothing to change those facts.

'Now just calm down, Koja,' Hub said, in the same tone he had once used to justify a lorry heaped with dead babies at the Posen freight station. I told my brother very plainly that he should not dare to take his own flesh and blood for a fool, and he must swear on Opapabaron's honour and Grandpaping's holy fury that he would tell the truth, the whole truth and – as they say in court and on the high seas – nothing but the sordid truth. Hub nodded glumly and took out Opapabaron's silver cigarette case, an heirloom handmade by Peter Carl Fabergé, Opapabaron's world-famous Easter-egg nephew, as our family always said with a slight air of disdain (in a sophisticated combination of pride and envy). Anyway, the sight of the case made Hub sigh indulgently. He pulled out a Reval cigarette, lit it with a match and took a long drag. Hub never used to smoke, and it seemed to me that he hadn't quite got the hang of it yet.

'Very well then. I'll tell you the truth.'

He looked back at his cigarette, as if the truth of the world was in there, and then spoke three brief sentences, taking a hasty drag after each.

'I just didn't want to burden you.'

First drag.

'What with your nerves.'

Second drag.

'We're doing important work here—'

I interrupted him with my retort, making the third drag significantly longer than the two before it. 'Apparently,' I said, 'apparently we are shooting three hundred Jews every day up in the Bikernieki Forest.'

'They're Bolsheviks. The carriers of this intellectual plague.'

'And they're being shot without trial?'

'It's a direct order from the Führer.'

'The Führer ordered that three hundred Jews a day be shot in the Bikernieki Forest?'

'No, he ordered that all Jews be shot.'

Another drag.

'Not just three hundred.'

Another drag.

'Everywhere.'

Another drag.

'Not just in the Bikernieki Forest.'

His skull was now swathed in a fog that obscured his features, I could hardly see him, and perhaps that was the intention.

'Are you mad?'

'Himmler told me this himself.'

My eyes darted sideways and I saw the photograph. It was standing on Hub's desk, behind glass and framed in silver, and it showed my sister in half-profile, the dark Ev – or was it the dark Shulamith, whose lips are a strand of scarlet? And her mouth so lovely, and the temples behind her veil a slice of pomegranate? And I had to take a seat and think of nothing at all, and just look at this girl, her lover was an apple tree among the trees of the woods, she desired to sit in his shade, and to look at apples and apples and apples, to honour Hubert Konstantin Solm, your cheeks are lovely with ornaments, your throat in the pearl necklace, and behold, you are fair, my sister, yes you are fair. I charge you, O daughters of Jerusalem, by the gazelles or by the does of the field, do not stir up nor awaken love until it pleases.

'Put the photo back, Koja.'

'You don't know her.'

'Put it back!'

'You have no idea who she is.'

'What's this about? We were discussing politics. Not personal matters.' And then he said something else he had said before, and shouldn't have. 'Don't start comparing apples and oranges.'

As I lapsed into a kind of swoon, which made me instantly, immensely tired right down to the tips of my fingers, my brother told me I was not going to be granted a redeployment to the front lines or anywhere else after my failure in France. Riga was a punishment transfer. 'My God, why didn't you just fuck that woman in Paris?'

I suddenly realized that there was no way out of this ill-fated place for me, it was impossible. Schellenberg had quite deliberately tipped me down the drain of the empire. 'And you're surprised by that, Koja? Did you think you'd get through this war by helping old ladies onto the emigration bus in Bessarabia and throwing your guts up in Parisian opium dens?'

But Hub promised to keep me out of the darkest depths. I would not have to take part in any operations, he explained. I didn't need to know that these operations were taking place, I didn't even need to know what the word 'operations' referred to; a lot of people didn't know or simply forgot, people like that nice Fräulein Paulsen.

In the end I just sat there, my fists pressed into my eye sockets, wanting a cigarette as well.

As that summer went on, the tensions in our office became increasingly clear. I and the rest of the please-and-thank-you table mostly sat at our desks composing secret messages, or sat in cabarets criticizing couplets, and the muffled, barely audible screams from the prefecture's cellars were the only troubling hint we received of the hellfire being rained down day after day upon the carriers of the world plague. Meanwhile, other departments were already up to their knees in blood.

And every day, the Gestapo executioners saw that their sensitive SD comrades were busy evaluating newspaper supplements, having to dirty neither their hands nor their souls; *they* weren't scraping brain matter from their boots or wearing blood-flecked uniforms. The bitterness began to grow, and eventually, complaints were made. And when Bertl, with his sub-machine gun hanging from its shoulder strap, passed the open door to my office and saw me adding delicate lines to a sketch of sweet Fräulein Paulsen, he no longer called me 'fegga', but 'stupid bastard'.

Hub ushered me into his office.

You could hardly breathe inside the cloud of smoke he was creating.

He looked perturbed; he had something to tell me, and didn't know how. Well then, he began, before pointing out that I had so far not met the Einsatzgruppe's leader, Brigadeführer Stahlecker. A Swabian, he was impulsive, temperamental, pathologically ambitious, unbalanced, arrogant, vain, erratic, odd, and a textbook neurotic, for which reason Hub had done everything in his power to keep him away from me. But now this was no longer possible. The executioners of Department IV were adamant that they should not be left high and dry in their laudable cleansing efforts. Yes, they had come here to clean the place up, to scrub, polish, scour and rinse. They were happy to dispose of the rubbish. But not alone. Not without any helping hands. Not without any expression of real solidarity.

And Brigadeführer Stahlecker, their considerate and perfidious commander, had listened to his men's complaints, telephoned Himmler and received the paternal order that every member of the Einsatzgruppe, in particular every SS officer, including the artistically inclined ones, had to participate in a minimum of one 'special treatment' of Jews. Himmler had explained that the *esprit de corps* required everyone to play his part in at least one such operation.

'I'm sorry, Koja, I can't exempt you from it. You'll have to meet Stahlecker now. But we've come to an agreement that all your department will have to do is watch. I promise you that.'

'What on earth does "special treatment" mean?' I asked.

'All you have to do is watch,' Hub repeated, undeterred. 'Please just think about something else. The best thing to do is hum a song in your head. Believe me, it helps. Keep humming.'

You know, the German word for *esprit de corps* – *'Korpsgeist'* – isn't used at all now. But back then, we understood it to mean a kind of consideration. Consideration of each individual for the good of everyone.

And that is precisely why I was ordered to participate in this special treatment.

To show consideration.

I can still see that day in my mind's eye. A warm August day, it was, full of branches. A heavenly harmony, a blue harmony, shone through a wedge-shaped gap in the crown of a summer-green oak tree, and fell on earthly mud. For as I lowered my head and looked down, I saw the pit that I did not want to see, a deep, freshly dug pit ten metres long, two metres wide, gleaming almond brown from a summer rain shower of ten minutes since. Hub stood beside me, smelling of aftershave and humming for all he was worth. From time to time he glanced at me. It was probably supposed to be encouraging.

The woods were still quiet. But the delinquents would be here at any minute. Branches waving in the wind always sound like a waterfall, or heavy rain. I read somewhere that the soundwaves made by water and wind are the same length. For me, they will always sound like waiting.

To our right stood three Gestapo officials, whose names I cannot for the life of me recall, except for Bertl of course, who had brought a red air bed with him, I don't know why. To our left was the whole of my SD department, pale and quaking.

And in front of us stood Bridagefführer Stahlecker, hands on hips, a rough-hewn boulder of a man with a riding crop in his fist, which swung back and forth behind him like the thin tail of a monkey. It was the first time I'd seen him, and I knew at once that he was someone I would never forget.

The Latvians' commanding officer was waiting behind him.

The blue of the bus that had come out from Riga shimmered through other branches. It had brought a platoon of Latvian specialists from Dünaburg. They skulked about; some of them dug up an anthill for fun. There were plenty of shovels.

Finally, we heard the sound of lorry engines rumbling towards us. They stopped out of sight, just a few hundred metres away. The troop began to grow restless. The Latvian commander walked off and sat down behind a bush a short distance away. In plain view, he took out a Bible. Hub followed him and asked why he favoured the Old Testament. The officer replied that the New Testament contained no suitable passages. A brave answer. Then he admitted that he preferred not to show himself. There was no further explanation. I assume that he had acquaintances among the Jews. Stahlecker left him to it.

They were now led towards us through the trees, flanked by their escort, none of them speaking a word. Men, women, no children. They were made to take off jackets and overshirts, skirts and trousers. All the clothing would be washed and reused later. I tried to focus my attention on the quickly growing mountain of cloth. A few of my favourite colours were assembled there, looking out of place in the woods, and they provided me with a distraction: there was ultramarine, and a beautiful gold, thin threads of which were woven through a woman's suit.

The first shot had not yet been fired, and it seemed to everyone that what was to come could never happen. There was no screaming or weeping. The fear was as clearly present as the scent of the trees – but neither could be seen. The world seemed immutable. Birds twittered. Ants fled their ruined anthill. Again I heard the branches, the leaves; I even felt I could hear the light itself, rustling and dripping through the canopy of twigs. Perhaps the only disturbing element in this scene was not the hole in the earth but the containers of chlorinated lime. They had been placed near the pit, and an occasional light breeze whirled up little white clouds, dusting the ferns and moss.

Then I saw Moshe Jacobsohn. The old man from Dünaburg. And the taste of the gefilte fish he had once served me was on my tongue, almost better now than it was then. The short Jewish man was standing on tiptoe in the second row, staring intently past the people in front of him and the guards, straight at me. I'm not saying I was blinded, I'm not saying that. But for a moment I was truly blind. When I was able to use my eyes again, Moshe Jacobsohn was still in the same place, and was now croaking, 'Herr Youth Leader!'

The three Gestapo officers, following the old man's gaze, stole sideways glances at me. Brigadeführer Stahlecker's monkey tail froze in the air as he turned with deliberate slowness and fixed his eyes on me. Hub hummed away, uncomprehending, I stayed silent, and Jacobsohn called out again, louder this time, 'My dear Herr Youth Leader! Do you remember?'

A guard strode over to him.

'Do you remember? Meyer and Murmelstein?'

Then he was struck in the face. He fell to the ground and two of the others had to pick him up. I heard the words 'Meyer and Murmelstein' fall from his bleeding lips once more. I tried to make myself blind again, but I couldn't do it. What I wouldn't have given for a glass of water to take away the taste of fish.

A handful of marksmen got into position. Someone looked at his watch. They lined up, five metres from the pit.

Ninety seconds.

The guards singled out the first ten delinquents.

Sixty.

Ushered them towards the edge.

Thirty.

A few of them tried to resist, sitting down, refusing to walk to the pit.

Ten seconds.

And then there they were, all the same.

Five seconds.

Including Moshe Jacobsohn.

Three.

The usual orders.

One.

And zero.

Close-range executions usually make the victims' blood and brain matter spray in all directions. And that's just how it was. Splinters of skull flew twenty metres, like shrapnel, some of them hitting me. There were death cries. Dozens of litres of blood seeped into the earth, impregnating the summer air with the scent of wet iron and mixing with the smell of terrified sweat, excrement, urine. A new set of victims was called up and driven forwards, the guns were loaded, aimed and fired. Each time, the whole process took two minutes. It was accompanied by an incessant volley of shouts and blows, and I wondered how the Latvian commander could read his Bible amid the din. Finally, quiet descended.

But it wasn't deadly silent.

We could hear a muffled, rattling voice. It was coming from somewhere in the depths of the pit. Hub tried to take the initiative, but Stahlecker stopped him with a shrill command. 'Let your brother do it,' he said. Hub had already taken four paces towards the pit, his hand resting on his holster. Now he paused and turned to the commander with a look of disbelief. 'Brigadeführer, it would be an honour to perform this duty.'

'And I'm sure it's an honour for your brother, too.'

I looked at Hub, knowing that the decision had been made. But defiance was stirring within him. He lowered his voice to avoid openly defying an order: 'Obersturmführer Solm has only been instructed to watch, Brigadeführer. I respectfully request permission to deliver the mercy shot.'

'Enough!'

'But—'

'This is not up for discussion. Step back!'

The Latvians had already begun to shovel chlorinated lime into the grave, despite the audible wail that was rising from the confusion of bodies at their feet. I drew my Luger, stepped up to the edge of the pit and looked down.

In the middle of this still life of jumbled corpses I saw a twisted, white-dusted body whose feet were still twitching. The head was trembling, too. The skull had been blown open and was lying like a lid beside the forehead. Beneath it, the alert, pleading eyes of a young woman looked up at me. She had a baby in her arms, and it seemed to be sleeping, quite unharmed. I hadn't noticed the child before. Behind me I heard the click of a camera. My first impulse was to shoot the photographer down, but of course I didn't. My second impulse was simply to run away – to throw the gun down, turn and run, but that didn't happen, either. There were no more impulses. The rest was emptiness.

And then suddenly, I saw the baby move, too. The woman was still gurgling blood, a few bubbles forming through the chlorinated lime that was burning her mouth – she looked at the tiny bundle as well, and before I could vomit at the sight of her exposed brain, I did something that would later cause Stahlecker great amusement, yes, would even make him joke about taking me to task for wasting ammunition: I fired off the whole damned magazine.

5

The Hippy is lying in bed, holding tight to Night Nurse Gerda's hands. I can hear him asking to be transferred to another room. No, he isn't asking. He's begging.

But my dear Basti, we don't have another room, I hear her say. What's troubling you all of a sudden? You're so fond of this view, with all that green outside the window and the promise of squirrels. And the well-mannered sun, which does you such a world of good! And the new emergency button for the toilet, which you can reach lying down if you pass out – we put that in especially for you. And no other room has an extractor fan. Or a lime-green wall. Or such a lovely, charming Herr Solm.

I can see the frightened Hippy giving Night Nurse Gerda a sign. He draws her closer to him, she can feel his breath on her ear, and then all I can hear is whispering.

Oh no, Night Nurse Gerda suddenly says with a bright little laugh, I'm absolutely certain Herr Solm never killed a baby. That's an absurd thought. You know, I think we should reduce the cannabis a little. We mustn't forget the hallucinations. And of course, we mustn't forget the Greek registrar, mistrustful Dr Papadopoulos. We mustn't forget the narcotics act. And my job at this hospital, please let's not forget that, either. You're going to end up jumping out of the window on me, dear Basti. How can you think so badly of poor Herr Solm? He's a consul, for goodness' sake! (I am not a consul.)

And he gave you a set of pyjamas!

And painted that pretty picture for me!

And he captured my likeness so well!

*

Yes, I made the good lady ten years slimmer and conquered her horse heart, and now she can't begin to understand why the Hippy is bursting into tears. He spends hours at a time downstairs with the babies now. It has taken a lot of gentle persuasion on my part. He was only prepared to go on listening if I found a baby on the maternity ward who looked like the baby from nineteen forty-one, the child in the pit. I think this is another of those crazy swami things, migrating souls and suchlike.

But I played along with it.

There is one down there identical to that baby, I said: rubbery lips, a flat little nose, sparse hair (and red, as well), with a look of defiance in his eyes, he's down there, and his little basket has the name Maximilian written on it.

The Hippy and I crept into the crib room at night and did some Indian business in front of Maximilian. I had to kneel down before the baby and conjure up his dreams (innocence, first and foremost, and a little desire for his mother's milk). I also prayed for forgiveness and made a red dot on Maximilian's forehead (with Night Nurse Gerda's lipstick, borrowed without her knowledge).

But all in all, and strictly between us, of course it was a lot of nonsense. There never was any doppelgänger for that baby in the Bikernieki Forest. All babies look alike to me, in any case. I only went along with the whole rigmarole because I'm so keen not to lose the Hippy's sympathy. He calls the things I tell him 'bad vibrations'.

All the same, he persuaded Night Nurse Gerda to have our beds moved further apart, and I agreed. Now a spell has been cast over this enlarged space between us. A cursed zone in which neither of us dares to set foot. Thus the Hippy always gets out of the left side of his left-hand bed, and I always get out of the right side of my right-hand bed, and we keep strictly to these sides when getting back into bed, too, so that we will never meet in the cursed space, which is so precisely and consistently delimited that it has a kind of glassy quality to it – which of course seems mad to the uninitiated.

When Donald Day came to visit me – old now, white-haired and doddery but with the same booming voice – he couldn't understand why he mustn't put the bottle of good single malt on the chair between our two beds, a chair that had been left there by accident after the ward rounds. But the Hippy says he needs this exact distance between us, a neutral nirvana in which no object is to be placed that has been in contact with me (a comb, for instance, a toothbrush, a testimony) or that will be in contact with me (like a single malt, which is now trickling through half my body and, although it may trickle out again, will leave some residue behind).

But, having established this condition, the Hippy then took an interest in Donald Day, asking him if he really met me in Riga and if he had really been such a terrible scourge to the communists as I claimed. 'Oh my goodness,' Donald laughed. 'You should have seen me and this old dog here during the Cuban Missile Crisis. We were too anti-communist even for Senator McCarthy. We'd have eaten people like you for breakfast.'

That sort of thing.

The Hippy refuses to believe that a former member of the SS-Einsatzgruppen can end up in the CIA.

But it's the most natural thing in the world.

6

You may regret the errors made by National Socialism, but you may not misuse those errors to call National Socialism itself into question.

Hub neither blushed nor trembled as he said that.

Nor was it sarcasm.

For three days, I called in sick. My brother indulged me. But on the fourth day he came to find me in my apartment, the furnishings of which I had hacked to pieces in order to prove to someone, probably myself, that I didn't want any of this – for the apartment was a Jewish *trouvaille*, along with everything in it. Almost all the senior SS officers I knew at that time lived in lovingly hand-pillaged interiors. They had complete sets of bedroom furniture in Galilean oak, and it was a joy to slumber through the night in them. Many a Sturmbannführer said that, after these invigorating experiences, he could never again live in rooms where the furniture belonged to him.

Hub took the vodka away from me and poured it down the sink. 'Drinking is God's way of telling you that you have too much time on your hands,' he said. Astonishing to hear him speak of God – a relic from his theology days.

Then he flung the empty bottle to the floor with the other empty bottles and gave me a piece of news he called 'fabulous'. Reichsführer Heinrich Himmler was coming to visit. In just a few days' time. Travelling through newly conquered colonies had become a favourite routine of his, and so he was planning to spend several days in the Baltic states, beginning in beautiful Riga. And since there was no other SS officer in the whole Einsatzgruppe with such a profound knowledge of the culture, art and intellectual history of our homeland, Brigadeführer Stahlecker had agreed to confer on me the role of local adjutant and guide.

'I don't think I should meet Herr Himmler,' I said.

'But, Koja, this is your chance to rehabilitate yourself! Himmler lives and breathes education and culture! You'll have him eating out of your hand, and you'll be out of this miserable business here before you know it.'

'I don't think I should meet Herr Himmler.'

But three days later, I did meet Herr Himmler. He was admiring the medieval city from an open-topped Mercedes coupé, which was parked to the south of the feudal Ritterhaus and surrounded by a retinue of illustrious, uniformed SS men. Stahlecker was with him. And so was my brother.

When Hub saw me approaching the group, he came to meet me and hissed, 'Look friendlier!' He led me past the Wehrmacht generals (to whom he might have said the same thing), made straight for Himmler and introduced me. I gave the proper greeting. Himmler looked me up and down with a self-satisfied expression.

'Your brother tells me that you draw exceptionally well.'

I couldn't answer; I just stood there, looking at this unusually short-sighted man who placed so much value on his executioners' *esprit de corps*. Hub responded for me, saying that in fact I did draw exceptionally well.

'Well then, Obersturmführer, why don't you do a caricature of me?'

'Now, Herr Reichsführer?'

'You've got five minutes.'

I obediently pulled my sketchbook out of my jacket pocket, took my pencil and began with the eyes. You always have to begin with the eyes – a lot of people who can't draw falsely believe you can start with the outline of the face or even the nose, but that's the beginning of the end. I drew the eyes of a hyena, because that was how Himmler laughed, letting out a loud bark and then suddenly falling silent again. He had tiny teeth, but they would have to wait. Below the eyes I put a snout, a beautiful pig's snout, and below the pig's snout his moustache, and below the moustache an open, bovine mouth, very lopsided, with a little hay poking out. Himmler did not get a chin, because he didn't have one, and his ears became the ears of a common marmoset. The last thing I had to do was choose the shape of the head, and was wavering between carp and hippo, but finally plumped for a good old hog, partly because of its hanging jowls.

'I've finished, Herr Reichsführer.'

'Let's see it, then.'

Himmler looked expectantly at Hub, who took three brisk paces towards me. I handed him the caricature. Hub stared at it uncertainly for a long time.

'Well, what's the matter?' Himmler asked impatiently. The whole of Riga's SS top brass was staring at my brother, waiting to see what he would do.

Hub folded the paper, tore it into tiny pieces and put it in the pocket of his leather coat.

'I don't believe the Obersturmführer has quite captured you, Herr Reichsführer.'

'Can he do better?'

'He can do much better. I believe the Obersturmführer is a little nervous.'

'There's no need to be nervous. We don't bite.'

I came to my senses and made a second drawing that portrayed Herr Himmler as Lancelot, in shining armour, with the features and moustache of Douglas Fairbanks.

Then we drove right across the Baltics together, Herr Himmler and I. Throughout the trip, the Reichsführer kept up a running lecture in his light Bavarian accent, which was actually rather like yours, Swami – and whether you believe me or not, he was extraordinarily well versed in those spiritual teachings of Asia that you, too, have explained to me with such great knowledge and conviction. Yes, in essence Himmler was the first hippy I'd ever met – at least, in respect of being an independent spirit. And he was capable of leaving all his cares behind, too. Like all Buddhists, he loved animals, and one afternoon we had to stop for two hours on one of Estonia's country roads, which were afflicted with long toad migrations, and switch off the engine in order to let all twenty thousand toads cross in safety.

Of course, Herr Himmler was also a committed vegetarian; he was always taking homeopathic remedies; he believed that the Teutons had come to earth from space, in an ice comet that landed somewhere near Bad Wimpfen; and he asked me what my star sign was. People born under the sign of Scorpio, I learned at once, are typically sensuous and will feel at home in the cities of Münster, Osnabrück and Lisbon.

And Himmler delighted in waxing lyrical about his beloved SS.

Once, he explained to me that this holy order required men with Nordic blood, intelligent and intolerant. That was the most important thing. Was I intelligent and intolerant enough, that was the question.

I could say nothing about my intelligence, I replied, since that lay entirely in the eye of the beholder. But when it came to intolerance, I had made considerable progress in recent weeks. Himmler gave a satisfied grunt.

I visited Reval in Estonia with him and we strolled incognito through the medieval streets in the Old Town of the Teutonic knights ('What an everlasting monument to German methods of town planning!'), finally stopping outside the Russian Orthodox Alexander Nevsky Cathedral, up on the cathedral hill. Himmler didn't like it: he thought the onion domes too surprising an intrusion into the cityscape; they looked terribly out of place among Reval's Gothic architecture. Nor could he stand all the gold on the roof ('Womanish, my dear Solm, a womanish frippery!'). He gave the order to start immediate preparations for the building's demolition, and his two adjutants departed at once to set the necessary wheels in motion. As the Reichsführer walked away quite calmly, lost in his own thoughts, I stumbled after him in shock, meaning to ask him to reconsider the matter. But before I could say anything, he grabbed my arm and cried out:

'Obersturmführer, did you see that couple who just passed us?'

'I'm afraid not. Respectfully, sir, I am still thinking about the Herr Reichsführer's true words regarding the cathedral.'

'A whippersnapper of a German sea cadet! And just look at the girl he's with!'

He pointed out a couple who had overtaken us, an eighteen-year-old recruit with a blonde Estonian girl on his arm, making sheep's eyes at him.

'A Mongol girl! The shape of her face is entirely Mongol. Just extraordinarily Mongol. Incredible!'

Himmler ordered me to stop the sea cadet and bring him over at once. The boy was extremely surprised, but he followed me, stood to attention and saluted the Reichsführer-SS in the prescribed manner. The latter's outburst had subsided, and he said in an indulgent tone:

'My dear boy, would I be right in thinking that you were in the Hitler Youth?'

'Yes, sir, Herr General!'

'And did you learn any race science there?'

The boy looked blankly at Himmler.

'I mean, do you know what the different races of mankind look like?'

'Yes, sir, Herr General!'

'Have you not noticed that the girl you have on your arm there is a pure Mongol?'

The boy hesitated for a moment and looked at his girlfriend, who although she understood not a word of the conversation could see very well that they were talking about her, which brought a flattered grin to her lips. The sea cadet drew himself up to his full height.

'Herr General! I specifically asked her about that! She told me she is not a Mongol! She's a teacher!'

Himmler looked perplexed. He was so perplexed that he even forgot to have the Alexander Nevsky Cathedral demolished the following day, though the SS had already piled all of the dynamite available in the city into the nave, and assigned three explosives experts from a Wehrmacht engineering division to oversee the complex task.

After five sunny days, we took Herr Himmler to Spilve Airport (he was tanned and very cheerful), and my Reichsführer presented me with a parting gift: the large SS 'children's frieze' candlestick, with the motif of children all the way around it, in finest Allach porcelain – although this gift was really reserved for the birth of an SS family's fourth child.

'Take it as an incentive, my dear Solm. Your rich talents should not be allowed to dry up. Scatter your seed in a nice fat furrow!'

'I will, Herr Reichsführer!'

'And don't forget: you are just a member!'

He pointed to the inscription on the worldly-wise children's frieze candlestick: 'In our eternal clan, I am just a member!' I thanked him politely for thinking me such a valuable member, and I'm sure I looked moved. I raised my right arm in a dutiful salute as the Reichsführer lifted a hand in parting from inside the plane. And I shouted 'Heil Hitler' amid the engine noise, for I had been told that he was an excellent lip reader, this fellow, from a distance of forty metres it would be child's play for him, yes, I might even have shouted 'Heil Himmler'. I felt a little as I had done in those long-ago wartime days when the Bolsheviks marched into Riga, and the cavalry soldier on the pony waved to the small boy that I was then, and some impulse made me return the greeting. You would probably call it a survival instinct.

This time, by contrast, Hub's reaction was effusive. He told me that Himmler had been quite taken with me.

And it wasn't long before this liking bore fruit.

Just two days later I was instructed to take on another special mission. I was being transferred to the front in Leningrad. I became an adjutant to Walter Stahlecker, the commander of Einsatzgruppe A, which was now hunting down spies, terrorists, assassins, Gypsies, Jews and, last but not least, a large number of oil paintings that been unable to flee from the Tsars' palaces, a stone's throw from the enemy lines. My job was to check the accuracy of Stahlecker's reports to Berlin, since hardly anyone there trusted him. I was to keep the Brigadeführer under observation day and night: Himmler loved to have his generals watched, especially when they were men like Stahlecker, a psychopath who craved validation.

I never forgot that this strutting muscle-man, who hardly ever laughed (though when he did, his laughter was loud and long), had ordered me to shoot at an exposed brain. Nor did I forget how amused he'd been by the way in which I did it. My reports reflected these things.

I reported that Stahlecker scorned cover and self-preservation in battle, and that every hail of bullets was like a tonic to him.

I reported that this was because he claimed to be invincible and would never be hit; the bullets had to get out of his way.

I reported that he took every opportunity to impress people, and to this end drove around the outskirts of Leningrad in a car full of bullet holes, a triumphal wreck with broken side windows that had sheets of metal riveted over them.

I reported that Stahlecker had ordered his officers to masturbate thoroughly every morning and evening.

I reported that the reason for this lay in his concern for our self-discipline.

I reported that Brigadeführer Stahlecker's nickname in the 18th Army was 'Arselecker'. In the 4th Tank Division it was 'Stahlfucker', and within his own Einsatzgruppe, 'The Sicko'.

I reported that Stahlecker would go on exterminating Jews in his jurisdiction even when there were no Jews left; at that point, he would just put the most Jewish-looking Russians in front of a firing squad and keep sending high execution figures back to Berlin.

I reported that on the twenty-second of March nineteen forty-two, during a partisan battle, a part of Stahlecker's body was perforated by a projectile flying randomly through the air, despite his invincibility.

I reported that this body part had been the Brigadeführer's behind, or to be more precise, both buttocks, which were shot clean through.

I reported that Stahlecker died on the twenty-third of March, not as a result of this minor injury, but (according to the doctors) of a complete circulatory collapse caused by shock at the realization that he did not have supernatural powers.

All these reports had the effect of restoring the Reich Main Security Office's trust in me. In late summer, however, I still had to survive a partisan mission in Belarus. My unit was stationed to the west of Minsk, between Uzda and Slutsk near the Naliboki Forest, where we fired mortars into the swamps and slaughtered a great many birches and alders, but not a single partisan.

Our commanders were so bitter at this that they marched us out to surrounding homesteads and villages, peaceful communities where the villagers smiled and waved to us, and we shot them all dead. And when we had shot them, we shot their dogs and cats, pillaged, destroyed, burned houses to the ground, and within a few hours these thriving settlements were transformed into realms of the mineral, vegetable and anthropomorphic.

One of these villages was called Vishneva. It was only many years later that I would recall that name in the presence of an Israeli minister; my memory was aided by a barn on which we had written: 'Vishneva glows' in large Cyrillic letters before setting it alight.

I thought Vishneva was the gates of hell, the maw. But it seems just to have been one final, perverse test.

Because now, Herr Himmler was starting work on a new project and, since he liked me, I was to be a part of it.

7

I met Schellenberg, the only SS general without a handshake, for the second time in my life, and once again he was a polite guppy, this time even more polite than the first. 'I rather suspect someone has fallen for your charms,' was the only barbed comment he made. I was then permitted to take a seat on his brothel-red velour sofa. From behind his machine-gun desk he read me a quote from Lawrence of Arabia, and then asked if I had any inclination to conquer the seven pillars of wisdom in the service of the SS. Why not, I thought – we're already quite familiar with the seven pillars of stupidity, madness and criminal perversion.

There were millions of Russians wasting away in the prison camps – Schellenberg said, launching into his speech – and the only way these people could survive was by putting themselves in our service. And so the Reich Main Security Office had begun to consider what services the Russians might actually render. Then they recalled the pharaohs, who turned their Hittite prisoners into spies, tools of Egyptian strategy with no will of their own. And that was exactly what the SS now planned to do with the Russians.

Rameses shaved the heads of his slaves, tattooed secret messages on their scalps and then waited for the hair to grow back over the hieroglyphs so that they might be dispatched unnoticed through the enemy lines and shaved bald again at distant outposts, where their subversive heads would reveal the ruler's important messages – and in the same way, our Russians were to become the scalps we wrote on, the legs that carried us, the arms and hands that held our sub-machine guns.

Schellenberg's Ancient Egyptian analogies culminated in the assertion that our new operation would eat the larva of communism from the inside out.

Its name, he told me, was Operation Zeppelin.

Operation Zeppelin would train thousands of Russian volunteers as guerrilla fighters, saboteurs and scouts, and drop them into the Soviet hinterland where they could foment uprisings and defeat the Red Army, which in recent times, unfortunately, the German divisions had been finding it increasingly difficult to do.

'Of course, Operation Zeppelin requires capable and sensitive German leaders. And someone who values your artistic sensibilities has put in a good word for you.'

'I'm pleased to hear that, Herr Brigadeführer.'

'Everyone deserves a second chance.'

'Thank you, Herr Brigadeführer.'

'But there won't be a third.'

Until we left Riga, a copy of Arnold Böcklin's *Pan in the Reeds* had hung in Papa's studio.

As a child, I had this composition before my eyes every day: it looked so peaceful, full of croaking frogs and burgeoning nature. The picture told the story of the nymph-hunter Pan, a lecherous buck who has set his sights on the chaste wood nymph Syrinx. Rather than give in to him and his huge, hairy prick, Syrinx escapes her pursuer by getting her sisters the river nymphs to change her into a reed. The lustful Pan, cheated of his roll in the hay, cuts some reeds and makes them into a set of pipes. In Böcklin's painting, he sits surrounded by the warm, damp reeds, playing mournful melodies on the remains of his beloved; Papa told me that nymphs are mortal.

I was deeply shaken by this idea. The pan pipes were nothing but a corpse; they were made out of a dismembered female body, of whatever variety, and their husky tones, which Papa was able to mimic by whistling very softly, went right through you. 'That is the terror of Pan,' he once told me in a soft voice. 'Or *panic*, as we say. Panic and terror are very close to the idyll from which they suddenly erupt. Fear is quite different, Koja. Fear is always terrible, but it prepares us for the horrors to come, like the night does. Terror, though, my darling boy, terror lives in broad daylight, it comes suddenly, out of the blue.'

And so I had always thought of Pan as the god of terror.

I sold Papa's copy of the Böcklin painting after his stroke. I didn't want the constant reminder that war reigns supreme, even in love.

But the longer I stayed with Operation Zeppelin (and I stayed a long time), the more frequently I was reminded of Papa's picture, that elegy of somnolent violence, the god of bombing raids and assassinations in a state of advanced dreaminess.

The start of November nineteen forty-two was as arcadian as Papa's painting (although it was wet and cold rather than humid). My new area of work altered my daily life. And it altered me. I had nothing more to do with the SS-Einsatzgruppen. I became an intelligence officer again. A specialist in reconnaissance and defence.

I had learned my lesson. As much as I had come to detest the constellation of mendacious secret-service men after Maya's death, it was a relief to stagger away from the killing squadrons. Yes, that's the word for it: Operation Zeppelin began with a great sense of relief.

Initially, my transfer took me to Silesia, and a site near Breslau where Guppy Schellenberg had had an enormous camp complex hastily erected for the Russian volunteers. I became head of the central spy school.

My predecessor, a glassy-eyed dervish, explained at our handover meeting that the Russians needed animal tamers rather than commanding officers. 'They're hungry tigers! Feed them vodka! Whip them senseless! Never turn your back on them!'

I gave an inaugural address to the four hundred Russians in the training camp using my best Anna Ivanovna Russian, full of diminutives, silly jokes, flattery, ribaldry and open warnings. The tigers licked my face like kittens. They were mostly awkward young men with open expressions, often funny and boisterous and glad to have escaped the hell of the prison camps, just as I thanked fate every day for allowing me to teach in a kind of story-book boarding school. There were swots and class clowns, there was cramming and homework, there were language lessons; there was a playground, there were pranks and even a real school bell.

After a while, however, I realized that many of these conscientious schoolboys, who of course were also being trained to use radio equipment, guns and explosives, to forge official documents and develop other subversive skills, were not entirely suited to the work. The cohort also included a large number of Soviet spies and SMERSH double agents, mostly at the top of their classes. And more than a few were simply waiting for their first chance to get home.

I needed a right-hand man.

I needed someone like Uncas or Chingachgook, a friendly, brave, loyal Mohican who would worship me with all his heart.

One Sunday morning, as I sat drinking coffee on the veranda of my quarters and looking out at the cloud-draped autumn day, I noticed a young lad some distance off drawing figures in the damp sand with a stick: a crowd of faces, as it seemed to me. I called out to the boy and asked what he was doing. And he stood to attention and respectfully reported that he was drawing a dream he'd had the previous night, in which some of his family had ascended into the sky as birds, to look for him, but they hadn't found a bird like him anywhere, for he was living in a giant egg with other unborn birds, and then the egg started to sway and they were at sea, and the lower part of the egg, which was suddenly a ship, sprang a leak, and a lot of sharks swam into the ship and ate the birds, but he had a medicine he could take that allowed him to spit out all his organs, and he spat them into a pot, and then he was so light that he could suddenly fly, and he flew up into the sky with this pot under his arm, but his babushka wasn't there, and nor were Valery or Piotr or dear Anoushka.

I had never heard such a status report from a soldier – particularly as, having saluted, the lad started drawing another face in the sand, a woman's face, in the centre of which I planted my SS boot, my coffee cup still in my hand. I looked at the unique engravings on the ground beneath my feet, spreading like a carpet of scars ten metres in every direction, trailing ornamental flourishes. I asked the boy who he was, and as he walked around me he said that if he ate the organs out of the pot he could land back on the ground, and then he would be Grishan from Uzbekistan.

Ten minutes later, when I had snapped him out of his trance and roared at him to do a hundred press-ups for failing to give the prescribed greeting (he did two hundred, by way of penance), I decided to make Grishan from Uzbekistan my Mohican.

There are better methods of finding a useful agent than a dream. But ultimately it doesn't matter, because you can't trust anyone, not a single human soul. I already knew that. And I know it still.

Grishan's unswerving loyalty to me, right up to his terrible death, is something that I cannot understand to this day.

And then my telephone rang.

'Heil Hitler.'

'Hello, Hub.'

'Do you remember Arnold Böcklin?'

'What?'

'*Pan in the Reeds*?'

'Yes, of course.'

'He had fourteen children. Eight of them died before him, three went insane.'

I straightened up: 'insane' was our code word for things that no one must know, especially not an inquisitive telephone-exchange girl.

'Yes, right – and what about Arnold Böcklin?'

'I hear there's an exhibition of his paintings near Auschwitz.'

'Near Auschwitz?'

'In Krakow.'

I said nothing.

'Do you fancy going to see it?'

I said nothing, waiting to hear what he would say next.

'Ev hasn't been yet, either.'

'I'm pretty busy here, Hub.'

'Ev hasn't been, even though Krakow is so close to where she works.'

How is it that I never managed to put myself in his shoes? Although he had been at the centre of my life for so many years? His voice sounded strained and urgent.

'You'd like me to go and visit Ev?' I asked. 'Is that what you're trying to tell me?'

'It's not too far from where you are. And I gather you have a feeder camp there?'

'Are you coming, too?'

'I can't. I'm stuck in Riga. Though I would so love to see the *Isle of the Dead*.'

'Auschwitz?'

'Böcklin's *Isle of the Dead*. The famous painting. That's in the exhibition as well.'

'I'll keep an eye out for it.'

'Look up a man named Dressler while you're there.'

After we had ended this fanciful telephone call, I told Grishan he was coming on an official trip with me for a few days. He was to pack me some clean underwear.

I arranged the marching order, which was relatively straightforward, because I was able to issue it myself. I simply had to call Berlin and give notice that I was going on a tour of inspection. Operation Zeppelin really did have a feeder camp in Auschwitz. A feeder camp that I had not yet inspected. It was now high time.

There was, of course, no Böcklin exhibition in Krakow. No *Isle of the Dead*. No *Pan in the Reeds*. The Krakow Cloth Hall had only one art exhibition to admire, which had been praised to the skies in the press: 'The Jewish World Plague'. It was quite clear that I was supposed to be checking on my sister, not looking at metaphysical enigmas. The conspiratorial call from my brother had been prompted by some kind of threat. I had to set off as soon as possible.

It was just two hours by train from Breslau.

But I decided to take the car.

8

'And what then?'

'I picked Ev up.'

'What did she do?'

'She refused.'

'She refused to be picked up?'

'She refused to pour splinters of wood and glass into her patients' open wounds.'

'Oh my God.'

'Or inject them with bacteria to promote decomposition.'

'Oh my God.'

'One of her colleagues shattered the patients' limbs with a hammer to create the most perfect injuries possible. The sort of injuries you see in war. And he asked Ev to do the same.'

'And she refused?'

'No, she did not refuse.'

'Oh my God.'

'She took the hammer and, using all her strength, she hit the doctor's hand with it. Twice. Bang, bang. Well, you know how she can be.'

'That's not right either, though.'

'No, it isn't right.'

'She must have been crazily pale.'

'Like snow-white driftwood.'

'And?'

'Solitary confinement.'

'In Auschwitz?'

'When I arrived, yes.'

'And then?'

'Then I picked her up.'

The Hippy switches the light on and decides to read a comic, although it's already past midnight. He has an astonishing number of comics. I haven't mentioned that yet. *Asterix and Obelix. Gaston. The Marsupilami.* I don't read that kind of thing. But what I like about *Tintin* is that this Tintin character looks like the cartoons I used to draw of Hub. That's just what Hub looked like as a young man: Tintin, the boy reporter. Cheeky, dynamic, still boyish, somehow, and with the same blond quiff, later eaten away by baldness.

Tintin in Auschwitz, that's what it looks like to me, when you just bury your nose in that pappy comic. There I was, expecting you to slit your wrists. After that whole circus you put on before. You are a false saint. And now you just turn to page fourteen and carry on reading where you left off. Thomson and Thompson have purple hair. Does it distract you? Or are you integrating everything? Thomson and Thompson watching human experiments that Professor Calculus regrets? Do you have no decency? No respect? Don't you know that one doesn't just read a comic when someone is telling you this kind of story? How do you think it all makes me feel? Please be so good as to listen to me. Put that away!

Thank you.

And please turn the light off again.

Thank you.

You see, picking Ev up was no easy matter. It was difficult. It also required a bit of luck. Dressler, for one thing! A friend of Hub's who worked in the political department at Auschwitz, Department II, an Obersturmführer. Pure luck!

And other relationships, too. Money.

And the fact that she wasn't in the SS! Incredible luck. Women couldn't be members of the SS, even if they were SS doctors. She would otherwise have been dealt with more harshly. Himmler knew no mercy.

There was no talking our way out of the fact that the hand was pulp. Bang, bang. But the swine had tried to molest Ev several times. There were witnesses. Dressler and I spoke to this pervert, who was afraid for his surgeon's mitt, and explained to him that if there was an official investigation, we would make it out to be attempted rape. We'd say that Ev was only defending herself against his molestations. This was a thoroughly effective strategy on our part. Do you follow me?

In any case, after three days of tough negotiation, Ev was finally sitting beside me like a salted slug in the back seat of the car, as Grishan drove us home. But what did home mean. She refused to come to the Zeppelin camp with me. She would never again go anywhere that was run by the SS. She said practically nothing, but she said it over and over again. And Grishan listened.

I had to take her to Breslau. To a hotel. We booked into the Excelsior on the market square. It was easy and inconspicuous enough to get a double room, despite my uniform, for I was Herr Solm and she was Frau Solm. That's what it said in our passports.

That night, the Solms slept together for the first time. They did not sleep together out of sadness, or because they hadn't seen one another for two years and had each thought about the other constantly all that time.

They slept together because it was the only way of saving Ev from dying. Something had died in her already, and in the night it came out of her ears and nose and mouth like black flies, as she said herself. I sensed it rising through her, and then I pressed my lips to hers and held her nose and ears closed, but I had only two hands, and so she took over the ears herself, and I caught the flies on my tongue and crushed them. But there were so many. I can't explain why everything suddenly became so straightforward. When people are in very great pain, they all feel a heaviness inside, but when the pain gets even greater, when it bursts, then some people feel as though they are inside a helium balloon.

That is certainly a dangerous thing, and even at the time I knew that none of what happened then was right. But it was also absolutely not wrong; it was the only thing possible, and so we slept together, my flesh in your flesh, your flesh in my flesh, over and over, and so we spoke to one another as though we were meeting for the first time. We were incredibly tentative, caressing the skin we found like a breeze. We stayed in that hotel for three days and perhaps we hoped to reach a conclusion. I don't know if we really felt anything like hope; perhaps a prospect is a better word. A horizon. You know, it is sad that a horizon doesn't mark the end of the world, but it is a prospect nonetheless.

And perhaps everything would have reached a conclusion, if Ev hadn't got pregnant on one of those nights, I think it was the third – the ninth of November, my birthday. And just as Hub's birth and Grandpaping's death fell on the same day, perhaps Anna's conception and my birthday fell together, too, and Ev's death, of course. For something in Ev had died that day, there were too many corpse flies, she *died and became* as Goethe says, and was renewed. Nothing ever comes to an end. Nothing reaches a conclusion. Every solution is a problem.

When I took Ev to the station in Breslau, from where she would catch a train home to Mama in Posen, we still hadn't mentioned Hub, even once.

But after Grishan, as obliging as a Chinaman, had fetched her suitcase from the boot and we were walking to the waiting room together, she told me that from now on, she would do everything in her power to fight the Nazis. From now on, she would only listen to enemy radio stations. She wouldn't donate a penny more to the winter aid charity. She would say 'Hello' and never 'Heil Hitler'. She wouldn't wash or iron or sew silver buttons onto any more SS uniforms. She would tell everyone what she had seen in Auschwitz. She would tell them what was happening to the Jews. She would tell Hub, too. And that was when she finally spoke Hub's name. The old station clock above our heads informed us that we didn't have much time left.

I implored her.

'No, Koja,' she said. 'Be quiet. I'm going to talk to Hub. He needs to get out of there.'

'He can't get out. And neither can I. We can't just leave the SS. You have to understand that.'

'Have you ever done anything unjust?'

'No, Ev.'

'Swear to me that you've never hurt another person.'

'I swear.'

We deceive people in all kinds of situations, don't we? But the question is always what effect the deception will have on the person being deceived. I think the effect on Ev was extremely positive. Reassuring, Hub would have said. And so I then assured her at once that her husband had never done anything to be ashamed of, either.

But she just retorted that Hub had got someone to write fake letters to her from Krakow for a whole year, to prove that the previous tenants of their villa in Posen had found a nice apartment. But as Krakow was only fifty kilometres from Auschwitz, she had of course gone to 24 Huttenstraße and had not found any Brusila family there, just a lot of surprised Reich-German faces peering out of stolen apartments, none of whom had ever heard of the Brusilas. There are no secrets that time does not reveal, Koja, she said quietly. All lies get out in the end. And Auschwitz will get out, too, I will make sure of it.

I explained to her that she couldn't do that: part of the extremely accommodating agreement with Dressler and the nice garrison doctor was that no hint of what had happened must reach the outside world. I had given my word of honour as an SS man (she let out a scornful laugh, but only one, and it sounded like a dry cough). All her papers had been changed, I added, and she now appeared in the files only as a student observer and not as a camp doctor. Several people were relying on this interpretation of the facts being maintained.

'Interpretation of the facts!'

She turned pale with hatred. And although I begged her and tried to call her demons home, she closed herself off from me, and I grew increasingly desperate; the train would soon be here and then her life would be in danger. She had to stick to what had been agreed. She mustn't say anything to Hub, and she absolutely mustn't let him know that her views had changed: it might be no more than a passing raincloud, nothing serious. She was dependent on Hub, I told her. She absolutely could not risk him breaking with her; and he would be capable of breaking with anyone who didn't have the same enemies as he did. Enemies were the most important things in his life, not friends, not love – quite unlike you, Ev, you don't need enemies at all.

'No, Koja,' she declared. 'In this case there is only one truth. And you and Hub, you have to get out of the SS.'

Resign.

We were standing by her Reichsbahn-green carriage. The locomotive's boiler was fully stoked, and an unwelcome gust of wind whirled the steam about our faces. Then something glittered below her throat, the silver chain with the silver Jesus on it, which had come to the Solm family along with her, and which would soon be just an old lump of metal. Because I had to tell her how much I loved her, and I had to tell her that only my uniform could protect her, just as Hub's uniform protected her, and so I also had to tell her why she needed protection. She was already sitting in the compartment, reaching her hand out to me through the open window, more the sketch of a hand, a first draft made of cold, glassy little chicken bones, and I told her about the Meyer and Murmelstein business, as much as I could manage in forty seconds.

And then I said, '*Vos, du host gornisht nisht gevust? Vi iz dus meglekh?*'

How *was* it possible that she didn't know?

I watched for a long time as the train departed, and her half-hand was the last thing I saw, for she didn't even shut the window.

9

Hub was the one who sent me fresh photos of my daughter every week.

His daughter, as he believed.

Her name was Anna. She wasn't named for Anna Ivanovna, however, but for Anna, Baroness von Schilling, Mama's grandmother, my great-grandmother, Anna's great-great-grandmother and Opapabaron's wife, who went to Alaska with her husband when he became governor and was made a queen by the Tlingit Indians. In Tlingit culture women were regarded as clever and men as strong. And that meant no man could lead a tribe; only a woman. No man was permitted to say a prayer. Only a woman. Everyone was given their mother's surname, and when they married, the Tlingit warriors had to take the name of their squaw. Although in any case, all Tlingits were called Eagle or Wolf or Buffalo.

It was a great honour for Anna, Baroness von Schilling to be crowned a Tlingit queen, and the reason for her coronation was that she had managed to cure an Indian child of smallpox just by singing a lovely song in his presence, so the Tlingits believed. For they had a great belief in the power of song, and sang their creation myths together around the totem pole every evening.

But the family stories had to be sung in private, and only the eldest woman in the family had the right to sing to her offspring about things that had gone before. All Anna, Baroness von Schilling had to offer was 'Es ist ein Ros entsprungen', but she had to repeat the performance to the delighted Tlingits many times, for she was a queen. A few years ago at a CIA conference in Oregon, I met an American colleague who came from Alaska and whose grandmother had been an Alaskan Indian, and he claimed that this melody had often been sung to him as a little boy; he'd thought it was an old Indian song.

In any case, the Tlingits had wanted to put a peg through Anna, Baroness von Schilling's lips, as is the custom for queens, and she had actually considered going through with this torture just to ensure there would finally be peace in the Russian colony. But her husband, the governor of Russian America, Opapabaron von Schilling, had treasured the flawless and fleshy fullness of his wife's lips and wondered what kind of figure one would cut at the Tsar's annual ball in St Petersburg with a piece of wood in front of one's teeth. And so after a while wars did break out again, and the great majority of the Tlingits eventually died of the diseases brought in by the Russians and the Balts.

I thought Anna an excellent name. The baby looked so sweet that a lip-peg would hardly have disfigured her. She was a determined, fearless little princess who very much took after her mother. Hub was mad about her. Ev wrote to tell me that he had brought her and little Anna to Riga, where they occupied the only SS officer's villa in the city on which rent was paid every month. Hub took great care of the family, she added, and spent every spare second with our Anna. Ev liked to speak of 'our' Anna, of 'our' worries about her, of 'our' sweet little sparrow, because everyone could feel included in that 'our'.

Although Hub was an exemplary father in so many respects, he had little free time. He'd been withdrawn from the SD and promoted to Obersturmbannführer, and was now a frontline commander for

Operation Zeppelin. He was responsible for all the operations carried out by Hauptkommando North. And he was therefore my immediate superior, based in Riga.

Perhaps this is tedious.

But I still think at this point that it might be worth learning a little more about Operation Zeppelin. For you, I mean. Please don't grow impatient, I listened when you gave me a lecture about Kundalini meditation, the only part of which I've retained was about alpha and theta brainwaves – but still, I know it aims to break down emotional tension.

Operation Zeppelin, by contrast, positively encouraged emotional tension. The universe had changed, you see. By which I mean the war.

Following their victory at Stalingrad, the Soviets managed to put more than six million people into the field. A complete ghost army, moulded from the mud of the battlefields, for that was the precise number of soldiers they had lost since the start of the war. And so, although we had killed them all, they now had twice as many troops as we did. It was a magical and mysterious thing.

We, on the other hand, were bleeding to death, like a living animal whose throat has been cut. Arms manufacturing was mushrooming in the USSR, and the huge scale of the American deployment left us in no doubt that in the long term our fire had gone out. Hitler knew that. His generals knew that. Even Hub and I knew it, because we were the ones who acquired that knowledge for the people higher up.

Time was against us.

People therefore began to work on alternative strategies. They tried everything. Miracle weapons. The atomic bomb. Fresh meat for the SS from half of Europe, even Moslems from Turkestan, Yakuts, Swiss, French and Flemish men, and a handful of Brits from the island of Jersey.

But the strategy to end all strategies was Guppy Schellenberg's idea of getting the Russians themselves to fight against Stalin. An absurd notion to anyone who had so much as leafed through Hitler's *Mein Kampf*. Especially since my horoscope-obsessed Reichsführer was only half-heartedly prepared to arm these people. He had once produced a small, meticulously put-together brochure about them entitled *The Subhuman*, and had it distributed to our fighting forces.

But the universe had changed.

After Stalingrad, everything was different.

Schellenberg told my brother, and my brother told me, that my tranquil existence as a headmaster in Breslau was now over. It was time to move Operation Zeppelin into its operational phase. I had to relocate our alliance of SS men and Russian pariahs to Russian soil, in order to quickly improve the quality of intelligence-service reconnaissance, and to start forming the first guerrilla movements in the Soviet hinterland.

For that reason, I was transferred from Breslau to Pleskau, a pretty, fortified Russian cathedral city, to which one of my ancestors, Hermann von Schilling, had laid siege for four months in the Middle Ages. He lined up his catapults on the bank of the dark green Velikaya River – which was rather like the Mississippi at this part of its course – and fired horse cadavers in lovely high arcs over the city walls, which must have created a magnificent image of stallions galloping across the heavens, but also brought a strain of anthrax into the city that carried off almost all its children.

Pleskau has been Central Russia's most westerly point since time immemorial. It lies no more than a few versts from the Estonian border. Lake Peipus is close by. And Ev (to come back to her, and to me, for a moment) was of course also close by.

From Pleskau, Grishan and I could reach Riga in four hours at most, via sandy roads that were cut straight as a die through light birch woods. Hub was usually away on tours of inspection when I arrived. He had to coordinate all of Operation Zeppelin's bases in Northern Russia. My brother was glad to have me there so often, taking such special care of his family. Ev's nerves were shot to pieces. She often complained of headaches and joint pain, and suffered periods of deep despondency. My brother had given me strict instructions about the medication that Ev should be taking every day, and I had promised to make sure she took it. He was relying on me. And so I seldom went into his bedroom with Ev; we made love in the guest room, with Anna beside us in her Moses basket.

As with any betrayal, it felt muted at first, cushioned by the certainty that we could stop at any time. We had friendship and kinship to keep us immune from the terrible shame, and above all, our love was in no way physical; the physical act was just an incidental addition that purified or perhaps grounded it. Sometimes she would tell me to hold her wrists, and I would hear the crack and scrape of her cartilage as she writhed and turned this way and that, trying to find a position just for me. Sometimes tears spilled from her hand-blown opaque glass eyes, and I had an inkling of the well of anxiety down which she was falling and where she would remain trapped for what seemed like eternities, although she never revealed a single detail about Auschwitz. We often imitated the things we'd done in childhood: she would bend low over me and observe my erect penis at close quarters, and the smell of our old apartment would come back to me, the floor polish, my father's paints, and the chamber pot under our bed.

Ev had a maid called Olga, a Russian girl; once, we didn't hear her ringing the bell, and when the sound finally reached us, Ev tore herself away and rushed to the door. And I saw that the window had been wide open, allowing Ev's little cries to fly out into the hot, dry, breathlessly listening midsummer's day and settle in the trees, on the grass, and on Olga waiting at the door – so I feared.

At such moments of immediate danger, I hoped that my heart would rot away. I despised the pair of us for the triviality of what we were doing, and for all the cunning with which we armed ourselves against surprise visitors (at night, before we went to bed, Ev always placed little tin cans on the flagstones of the path, pling, pling, pling). I resolved to punish myself with a kind of inner absence, but that would last two hours at most, for then Ev fell into a shattered state that I could only repair by being fully present. I liked to watch her nursing our little Anna, loved the tiny smacking sounds of the baby's suckling lips. It was the sound of completely innocent hunger; our own hunger sounded so different.

I never asked what rituals Ev and my brother performed. I simply had no desire to know, though Ev wanted to know everything about me.

I told her about Maya, and after she had wept with me for my beautiful sweetheart, I managed to pick up charcoal and paper once more. I'd never thought I would be able to draw a woman's body again without imagining decomposition, but that, too, I managed. I used a different technique from my drawings of Maya, different pencils, different colours. Ev's flawlessly sad, almost bony body was better suited to muted, light colours, and I left a lot more lines out, a little like the Frenchmen I'd seen in Paris.

I always asked Ev to look at me.

Anna's birth had already convinced her to do exactly what was expected of her. She might have wished fire and brimstone upon the Nazis, and always made me feel that my work put a distance between us (I was never allowed to wear my uniform in the house, never allowed to tell her the smallest thing about the front) – but for the outside world, she disguised herself as someone who toed the line and stayed loyal to the swastika. She had told Hub only what she couldn't avoid saying about Auschwitz, because of course, Dressler had reported back to him. She spent two months in a sanatorium in Bad Pyrmont, trying to forget.

But then her belly began to swell.

When I came to Riga from Pleskau, she would sometimes be waiting for me at the door, and would cry out with glee and hug me because the BBC had reported the Royal Air Force blowing up a dam or reducing a whole city to rubble. I couldn't share her enthusiasm, and nor did I hope that our troops would soon be defeated. I might not have been fighting for my country, and certainly not for the Nazis, but I was fighting for the people close to me – not with tremendous courage, perhaps, and not with the degree of fervour that Hub displayed, but fighting all the same. I was fighting like a person who would much rather be sitting in the Tuileries and pressing an autumn leaf into a morbid memory between the pages of a book.

I have never been a hero.

Ev and Hub, on the other hand, were both heroes in their own way. For me, shining heroism is embodied in someone who remains unfailingly loyal. And they both stayed loyal, though their loyalties were entirely different. Hub Solm was only ever Hub Solm, and Ev Solm was only ever Ev Solm, but whether I was ever or never Koja Solm – except in those brief, bewitching moments in Ev's house – that is something I will never know.

10

I usually arrived back at my command in Pleskau in the dawn light, just before the start of the working day. The frequent partisan attacks meant that we were not supposed to travel in the dark without a convoy. But

Grishan didn't care, because I didn't care. He switched off the head-lights and raced through the treacherous night for the sake of his sinful Obersturmführer, who sat behind him waiting for God's vengeful fist to strike. There was never any fear to be seen in the back of Grishan's neck, the only part of him I could see in the darkness. He believed in fate and often told me about his peculiar dreams.

His artistic talent had been evident from our very first meeting, when he'd inscribed his family's faces into the sand.

Whenever I stopped on a daytime journey and took out my sketch-book, he would fall into a reverent catalepsy.

I once gave him a watercolour of a little birch wood, and when he died, I found the picture in his breast pocket, flecked with blood. I still have it today. Since he was bubbling over with envy and eagerness, I let him have one of my sketchbooks. Weeks later, when I had long since forgotten this casual gift, he shyly showed me what a few fragments of charcoal had achieved in the meantime. I saw wild, expressive convul-sions, I saw his comrades depicted as gnomes and his superiors as trees, drawings naive as a child's, but made with a passion I have never once achieved. Grishan had hardly any technique, but this scrawny, dreamy shepherd boy, who would kill anyone I pointed at without so much as blinking, was surely the greatest artist I have ever met.

Later, we often went out into the countryside together, which, as my father had always said, longed to be seen. Papa had taught me plein-air drawing, and in turn I now became Grishan's teacher. Gazing out at endless plains of feathery grass or sitting amid carpets of violet flowers, I repeated all Papa's lessons about cross-hatching, vanishing points and washes, which made me mourn his death all over again. Grishan learned quickly, without losing his potency. He only gained.

The Zeppelin unit under my command was stationed in a little village eight kilometres from the centre of Pleskau, right on the banks of the Velikaya. The base was therefore known as 'the river camp'. This was where the guard company was quartered, a team of fifty Cossacks. The Russian spy recruits lived there, too: green boys, pale and frightened, newly arrived from the Breslau preparation camp.

My spy school proper was a few kilometres further east. It was housed in a requisitioned primary school, where the volunteers, who were officially called 'activists' and had undergone demanding aptitude tests at the river camp, were trained and prepared for their missions. The staff of Pleskau Command, as the unit was officially known, were also relocated there.

It was not a place I liked to be. It had the atmosphere of a slave galley, and on the opposite bank of the river, in the glare of what were usually magnificent sunsets, lay the wounded city, depopulated, exhausted, raped, bombed, and ruled over by a huge Wehrmacht garrison. Hatred blossomed everywhere. And not just on the streets of Pleskau; in the open countryside, too. Partisan brigades attacked German bases, police stations and local administrative buildings. The few staff in these outposts were often butchered to a man. At least once a day, explosives would be detonated on the railway line to Narva that passed three kilometres north of the river camp.

Over the summer and autumn months, I myself was quartered in the most picturesque location you can imagine. The Khalakhalnya estate lay twenty kilometres to the west of Pleskau, a long way from any reminder of the war. Here we built stables, kept chickens and cows, raised pigs, and from time to time, in a fit of colonial grandeur, bestowed a few piglets on the local population.

I loved everything in Khalakhalnya: the gas lamps in the evening, the bats in my room, the constant smiling of the sun god as he warmed this place that was almost entirely cut off from the hostile world outside.

Surrounded by meadows and shimmering woods, the estate was staffed only by a ten-strong guard unit of musical Caucasians, Grishan, and my two closest colleagues: Untersturmführer Möllenhauer (the melancholy Pierrot from my Bessarabia days), and the Drinker, my old chauffeur, who had now grown so corpulent that he could barely fit behind the steering wheel. I had requested both these gentlemen from the Reich Main Security Office, and been given them.

In addition to providing my Pleskau unit with bread, meat, milk and eggs, the estate's most important function was as the final stop for teams of spies who were fully trained and ready for deployment behind the Russian lines. Each group consisted of four activists, and they were accompanied on their mission by a Russian instructor with an officer's ranking.

Möllenhauer was the general staff officer responsible for the precise planning of the operations. He distributed equipment, provisions, weapons, clothes and all other materials to the volunteers, and was in sole charge of inducting them into their missions and destinations. He would bring each unit over to the main house, pursued by a swarm of flies, and before me they would repeat their pledge of allegiance to the Führer and Holy Russia with a tot of vodka in their hands – and from that moment on there was no going back, no escape from the journey they had to make.

Those dead men walking were then accommodated in small log cabins, observed for a few more days and put through one final series of psychological tests.

After about a week, a vehicle would appear in the distance, throwing up clouds of dust. It was always the same armoured box van with no side windows that collected the team of spies from their isolation and took them straight to Pleskau airfield. Then all that remained for the men was the noise of the Heinkel's engines, and the leap out over the tundra.

On three or four occasions, agents who had been inducted into all the top-secret details of their mission then revealed themselves to be insufficiently reliable during the final security checks. At that point, they knew too much, and their knowledge had to be extinguished.

There was nothing I hated more at Khalakhalnya than the times when Grishan came to see me in the main house, knocked politely on the glass door of the veranda and told me with a gloomy look on his face that we had 'a fire'. No one wanted 'a fire'. But I couldn't send 'the fire' back to the main unit in the river camp; that was impossible.

It was always Grishan who took on the job of putting out these fires. I don't know how he did it. Nor did I want to know. He took the man in question into the stables, arm in arm and chatting in a friendly manner. Whatever happened after that made no noise and left no blood behind. I never saw the corpses, either.

Two decades later, these events were the subject of a state prosecutor's investigation against me. I was suspected of disposing of an agent who had become inconvenient, without any legitimation or cause. Just like that.

The BND made these investigations go away, and the matter never came to trial. But I must say that I thought it was a bit rich. The accusations weren't true. In Khalakhalnya, Grishan only ever reported a fire when the fire was real. Afterwards, his dreams would burst out of their magma chamber, his gnomes and trees changed and, for a week or two, became Rorschach blots on the paper I gave him. He was no cold-blooded killer; he was a loyal man. A soldier.

I can still remember one such case.

The day before the order was given for this particular unit to fly out, Grishan had checked all the agents' knapsacks, trunks and gun bags, which by then were packed and ready to go – and this was something that never usually happened, because the packing was such an elaborate process. He was as generous as ever, allowing the men to take with them photos of their girlfriends and parents, as well as condoms or Tolstoy, although both were forbidden. All personal items were forbidden in the wilderness.

But just when it looked like the inspection was over, Grishan turned back and took one last look at the Russians' things, discovering in the process that the overstuffed pack belonging to the keenest of them all, a handsome and very popular balalaika player, did not contain the expected balalaika, but a full Soviet uniform, forged papers and a genuine NKVD identity card. The musician would have killed everyone the minute they landed. His agent handler. His fellow combatants. He even had clearance to hunt down his compatriots' girls, and the brothers and sisters, mothers and fathers who could be identified from the photos in their wallets. That was his mission. And our mission was to stop our boys from suffering that fate.

On Grishan's recommendation, the balalaika player was turned over to his bunk-mates an hour later. They took their time, stripping the living flesh from his bones with our corn scythes and – since he had given up his right to a grave – finally turning him into smoke that rose from the chimney of our little estate bakery.

That may sound barbaric, my dear Swami, and it *was* barbaric, and for some weeks afterwards I could not bear to eat home-made bread.

But it is in the nature of every intelligence service to protect itself quite rigorously from betrayal. Compared with what I saw later in the CIA, where torture, elimination and cover-ups were the American way if ever there was the slightest suspicion, what happened at Khalakhalnya was nothing. When I visited Indonesia as a diplomat a few years ago, the CIA's military advisers were teaching General

Suharto's anti-communist death squadrons 'happy killing'. Killing to rock music. It may sound fanciful, but how melodious do you think the interrogations of the Vietcong in Saigon are right now?

Hub and Ev also came to see me in Khalakhalnya, right after Anna's birth.

Hub had been granted two weeks' special leave for his wife's confinement. It was August, an August that glowed with heat, as hot as two Augusts added together.

When I stepped out onto the first-floor balcony, I could see dusty woods to the left and right, and between them a sallow field of weeds and burned sunflowers, through which the plumb line of the field track led up to our gate. The evening wind blew thousands of dead wild flowers through the open windows. They speckled the sleeping Anna and the waking Anna, and we wondered whether a blossom-covered baby might already be storing away her first sensory impressions, which would cling to the folds of her brain until she was an old lady.

We blew the petals from little Anna's skin, carried her outside and pointed up at the Russian clouds rolling above her, at which she gurgled happily. We pulled faces and played the fool for her until she fell asleep again, smiling. Then we put her back in her room on the first floor of the main house and each inhaled the scent from the hands that had held her.

Some of the activists had made a wooden cot, a little canopy bed *en bleu*, to pass the time as they waited for the death to which I had to send them.

I recall only fragmentary images from this visit. A door with stained-glass panels that Ev flung open with a ringing sound. The large living room with the crystal chandelier, beneath which we sang 'Es ist en Ros entsprungen', the old Indian song. And of course, the day when Grishan showed us the picture he had painted of Ev: her green, sweat-damp face in the style of Van Gogh, which was in bad taste, according to a disgruntled Hub, but was perfect in its form of bad taste.

I had just one moment alone with Ev, and she told me that she loved Hub immensely, immensely, and we kissed.

Just a few months after that, everything changed.

For when the first snow had fallen and Grishan was tying the wolf that he had shot and skinned to a fence post – the naked, yellowish-white body head down, an old Russian custom meant to ward off the other wolves – I saw a convoy of Wehrmacht vehicles appear behind him, approaching our estate. In each of the open cars there huddled a freezing private with a sub-machine gun in the firing position, because the partisans were everywhere now.

The two open-topped Kubelwagens and the truck pulled up outside my door. Grishan left the cadaver hanging, wiped his hands on his trousers (how often had I told him not to do that?) and hurried towards them. He was going to ask the drivers to park somewhere else: the honourable commander, recently promoted from Obersturmführer to Hauptsturmführer, didn't like it when someone blocked his uninterrupted view of the snow. But by then I had stepped outside to give the necessary instructions myself, and the unexpected guests were already alighting.

I recognized Maya before she recognized me, because she was looking at the skinned wolf, repelled by it in a way that wasn't like her at all.

11

Perhaps I should first say a few words about Jan Vermeer; he will allow me to describe the outward circumstances that made Maya's sudden reappearance not only shocking but also entirely plausible – as you, too, will see in the end. Jan Vermeer will help you to see my time in Khalakhalnya in quite a different way: behind what I have already told you lay a set of dynamics completely invisible to me, which led quite logically to Maya's arrival just as a river always flows to the sea.

The name Jan Vermeer may not mean anything to you, Swami. He was a painter of the Baroque period, from the Dutch city of Delft. The city was founded by Godfrey the Hunchback, and that's exactly what its skyline looks like, too. Jan Vermeer didn't paint a huge number of pictures during his lifetime. Perhaps he was lazy, perhaps he was just careful; in any case, he wasn't trying to break any records. I believe that is also one reason why he never painted anything momentous, no saints, no Virgin Mary, and certainly no Rubenesque allegory of the blessings of peace. His called his paintings *Study of a Young Woman* or *Woman with a Water Pitcher* or *The Milkmaid*.

For that reason, and because his quiet, well-balanced compositions always place figures directly in the light, I followed his stylistic example when I came to paint the staff of my Pleskau Command, a collection of highly insignificant men.

In Pleskau and Khalakhalnya they learned deception, disguise and killing. But they didn't learn it from me. I myself still had a lot to learn when I arrived. Above all, I had to learn to treat my men in a way that inspired fear and respect, as well as the sense that they were dependent on me. They therefore all appeared in front of my easel.

As much as they accepted the Flemish art of portraiture – educated and sensitive as they were, across the board – they were still reluctant to sit for their commanding officer. For one thing, he was no Jan Vermeer (he wasn't even a Chardin). For another, they sensed that the act of concentrating on a person's facial features also captures elements of his inner being.

The old myth that possessing a person's likeness gives you power over him is still present in all of us. I was doing a pastel portrait of my deputy Girgensohn in half-profile; he had been sitting for a while when his eyelids began to flutter and his cheeks reddened – and at the end of the sitting he made a confession, stammering that he had taken four jars of caviar from the stores and sent them to his family in the Warthegau. I called the picture *The Glutton*, since Girgensohn was Pleskau Command's quartermaster and had a weakness for delicacies from the Auvergne.

After the war, staying true to his culinary preferences, he joined the French foreign intelligence service – almost all my colleagues, in fact, sought some professional continuity. You have no idea how quickly the subversive skills they had learnt in my employ were snapped up by democratic governments once Hitler had gone up in flames.

My enemy intelligence officer, Obersturmführer Dr rer. pol. Dr phil. hal. Hans von Handrack, also managed to land on his feet. At the Zero Hour, he took refuge first with the CIA, and then in Herr Gehlen's organization (about which I will say more later), and spent decades serving the German intelligence service as a section head and *Nature morte* of himself. I drew him as the epitome of the weary, Baltic slowcoach, measuring the distance to the stars in a vast number of coffee spoons.

His deputy, Untersturmführer Dr Gerhard Teich, was a geographer and ethnographer from Leipzig who specialized in Eastern

Europe – though by profession, he was actually a dwarf. He later became an academic adviser to the Kiel Institute for the World Economy. As I learned, the Dwarf told the British everything, literally everything he knew about me, and in the interrogation transcripts I discovered that he had even made some wild speculations about the relationship between me and my 'beautiful sister-in-law' as he called Ev. Years before in Khalakhalnya, when he arrived at my makeshift studio as instructed ('Respectfully, sir, Untersturmführer Teich reporting for a portrait, sir!') his face was a mask of resistance and defiance, and I asked him if that was how he wanted to be immortalized in my planned heroes' gallery.

'What heroes' gallery, Herr Obersturmführer?'

'The heroes' gallery of our staff officers, downstairs in the salon.'

'I haven't seen any pictures down there at all.'

'Well, they will only be hung when the staff officers fall in battle, Untersturmführer,' I explained indulgently, after which the Dwarf tried to look a little more friendly and less dwarfish.

Unfortunately, it was the Russians and not my German staff who found themselves in the heroes' gallery at the end of the war. There was Major Lashkov, a former Imperial Guards officer who was responsible for the activists' basic military training, and whom I immortalized with his Cossack beard and his gold lorgnette, just because it was the only lorgnette in the entire SS. And then there was the Russian SD man Pavel Delle (who taught marksmanship) and Captain Palbyzin, difficult to draw because of his partially paralysed facial muscles, who was in charge of the vital counterfeiting workshop. There were others whose names won't mean anything to you, but who, as we will see, sadly did not fare so well against the Soviet need for retribution as our own men did.

Of all my officers, whether German or Russian, the dutiful Möllenhauer was my favourite by far (I allowed him to take on the handsomest Russian farmhand as a manservant, though he was too loud during sex, which almost got him brought up before the SS court). Möllenhauer's pale face was rather feminine: small, with a snub nose, and larger eyes and a rounder chin than Slowcoach Handrack, Glutton Girgensohn or the professional dwarf. At Möllenhauer's request I did him the favour of painting him, Pierrot-like, in an elegant white shirt and not in uniform like all the others.

He returned the favour in nineteen forty-nine, when he wrote an eight hundred-page report for the CIA on Operation Zeppelin that verged on the fantastical. It contained the note that: 'Following a legendary manoeuvre during the Bessarabian resettlement, Hauptsturmführer Solm was without doubt regarded as one of the SD's best Romeo agents.'

He wrote nothing of my penchant for making portraits of colleagues; he possibly thought them a mere eccentricity and did not recognize their value in leadership terms. But it was his kindly remarks about my anti-Soviet attitude and my imaginative (if not overly spirited) leadership style that really stood me in good stead with the Americans.

To recapitulate, my sceptical Swami (and I say this in all modesty): my Pleskau Command, led by banal characters and captured in Vermeer's Flemish colours, managed to become the most effective German spy unit on Russian soil during the summer and autumn months of nineteen forty-three. Over that period, my people dropped twenty sabotage and killing squads far behind the Russian lines – a fact that always elicited gasps of astonishment during job interviews with the CIA, years later.

The activists mostly came from the areas in which we were operating. Within a radius of fifty kilometres, they could make contact with family and friends who could help them to form an underground network.

But more important was the fact that Möllenhauer and I wanted our agents to have first-class equipment, and Glutton Girgensohn turned out to be a master of procurement. That was the key to our success.

A standard group of five men received a lavish arsenal consisting of five Soviet carbines, five sub-machine guns, twenty-five hand grenades, four German and two Soviet pistols, five daggers made in Solingen, a Soviet machine gun with fifty thousand rounds of ammunition, two hunting rifles, thirty kilos of plastic explosives, fifty kilos of mining explosives and a hundredweight of dynamite. Essentially (and if they were not quite in their right minds) they had enough munitions to attack a whole garrison – at least, one that was deeply asleep.

On top of this, there were a hundred thousand roubles in cash, half a pig in tins, several hundredweight of millet and pasta, a hundred kilos of salt for salting down the game they would hunt, and a mass of tools for constructing their earth bunker. We even provided Dextro Energy cubes, ten tins of high-caffeine Scho-Ka-Kola chocolate, a hundred lemons, a thousand Prontosil tablets, diarrhoea tablets, aspirin, quinine and two thousand cigarettes, and to be on the safe side five suicide capsules (inscribed with the typically German instruction 'Take only if situation is hopeless').

But the most important item was the communications umbilical cord linking them to Germany, a very small and effective radio developed specially for Operation Zeppelin, along with the requisite batteries and tools.

I suppose that listing all these things might be giving me a little flush of sentimental pride, an old spy's ailment, forgive me. But of the twenty sabotage groups we deployed, seventeen lines reported back. That in itself was quite an achievement. Unfortunately, after reaching their destinations, sooner or later a large number of our Zeppelin agents were arrested and turned by the NKVD, and towards the end of the war we had only three or four loyal teams of spies left in the Soviet Union. But at least we were able to sell them to the Americans later – though unfortunately, the latter just caused chaos with their utter stupidity.

But there were bull's-eyes, too. We managed to build up anti-Soviet resistance groups in the South Caucasus, for instance, since the activists there had close family ties with the local population.

Operation Ulm, which aimed to disable the industrial energy supply in the Urals, reported an early success. The proud radio operator, speaking from five thousand kilometres away, told us that his team had managed to fell three electricity masts in Novosibirsk. We were so delighted by this news that I had vodka distributed to the whole command staff, until my intoxicated lorry drivers jumped, screeching, into the Velikaya, where three of them drowned, one driver per electricity mast, as the grieving Möllenhauer rightly remarked.

A triumph that was bitter in another way, namely the planting of a small Zeppelin army in Moscow, brought me a promotion to Hauptsturmführer. Operation Joseph, under which SS activists were stationed just a few hundred metres from Red Square, went not only dramatically but tragically wrong – though more of that later. In any case, it cannot surprise you to learn that luck was only hesitantly on our side.

For of course there is no denying that, in the end, almost all the activists we dropped behind enemy lines fell victim to cold, hunger, brown bears, poisonous mushrooms, the NKVD, SMERSH, defective parachutes, their own despair, the People's Court, bacilli, viruses and flesh wounds, loneliness, the abysmally stupid Yanks who couldn't operate the radios and, last but not least, Germany losing the war. No one came rushing in to rescue our Robinson Crusoes, who had held out for years in the ancient forests of the Urals, although of course that rescue had been the most important promise of all.

And don't go thinking that the Nazis were the only ones who went in for such madness. Each of the warring nations sent out suicide squads of this kind, and I know that from a Buddhist-Hindu point of view (forgive me, I can barely tell them apart) warring nations themselves are unacceptable, so what on earth can one say about suicide squads?

The Soviets, for instance, lost thousands of their agents when they were dropped, or rather shoved out, without a parachute. Admittedly these – well, let's call them jumps – were made from planes flying low and slow over swampy, marshy areas. But all the same, no one wants to hit the ground at full speed from a height of thirty metres, however wet it is, and nor does that feel especially 'low'. Our defence corps would comb the swamps in long lines, picking up all the badly injured human May bugs, who could only lie there on their backs, kicking helplessly.

Even the British, who to this day have far and away the world's most effective secret services, had very little luck. Just look at Ian Fleming, the James Bond author! His special troop with the licence to kill – the Red Indians of the British naval intelligence service – operated behind enemy lines with so little to show for it that he was denied promotion three times. Two years ago, in the Imperial War Museum in London, I saw the jacket that Commander Fleming wore on his escape from Dieppe in nineteen forty-two. So, just let me say: the stories that this underachiever sucked out of his fingers somewhere in Jamaica are a lot less authentic than the Tintin ones.

The Americans were spectacularly unsuccessful, too – on all of God's green earth, they really are the nation with the least talent for secret-service work. The head of the military intelligence service, Bill Donovan (Wild Bill Donovan, they called him) was trying to drop his agents into enemy territory at the same time as me, and he did it right over the Odenwald forests. He did it, and it killed them. Wild Bill never heard from any of the twenty-one two-man teams who landed in Germany.

And when it comes to fantastical, positively insane operations, the USA leads the international table of excellence by a country mile. Donald Day himself told me that the whole planning department under his command had to spend months figuring out whether it was possible to burn down Tokyo with the help of bats, which they planned to gather en masse from their roosts in the caves of the Rocky Mountains. They thought they might strap incendiary bombs to their backs and release them into the air (Wild Bill Donovan believed that Tokyo was made of paper).

The reason I am telling you all this is to do with an event that is gradually appearing over the horizon. The break with my brother – begun by Mary-Lou's birthday Monopoly, encouraged by the high-stakes poker of the SS and culminating in the Russian roulette that Ev and I were blithely playing (and you can really lose your head, playing Russian roulette) – this break was just waiting to be made complete.

And it was no less a person than Joseph Stalin who would take this task in hand.

A few weeks after his August visit to Khalakhalnya, Hub received me in Riga. He was looking restless behind his office desk; restless, but buoyant. He was just showing me a brand-new photo of our daughter (Ev in a headscarf and apron, feeding apple purée to little Anna, apple purée!) when he could finally contain himself no longer, and blurted out the news that the Soviet head of state was to be killed.

The Soviet head of state, I repeated in a whisper, handing the photo back.

Killed, exactly, said Hub. He added some stronger terms for clarity ('snuffed out', 'wiped off the face of the earth', 'at any price').

Hub's feverish excitement was accompanied by a level of cigarette consumption that took your breath away. I opened the window, though there was already an autumnal chill in the air. Distracted, I turned and looked out over the buildings of Riga, thinking of the Petersburger Hof where Ev was already waiting for me in room two-one-five, beneath the reproachful roof that I could see from Hub's office, a shame-red copper.

As I prepared myself inwardly to do the deed with Ev in a few minutes' time, *vis a tergo*, she growling on all fours, I more quiet and modest as I knelt behind her, Hub blazed away at my back in a mixture of hubris and desperate revenge fantasy, telling me that in the power centres of Berlin they were hatching a murder plot that would turn the tables again in the final minutes of the war.

I closed the window and showed some interest.

Dispensing with Joseph Stalin, my brother explained solemnly, was a matter very close to Heinrich Himmler's heart. The SD's head of foreign intelligence (that same Guppy Schellenberg who had bored me with the details of his office armaments) was insisting that Hub take personal charge and assume overall responsibility for the operation. It had been decided that the operational side, meanwhile – the preparing, conducting and debriefing – would fall to my Pleskau Command. And the reason for this was that my unit contained the only agent in the Third Reich they trusted to crack such a hard nut.

'The only agent?' I heard myself asking.

As I penetrated Ev's vagina and looked down at her undulating back just a quarter of an hour later – I had actually run the final few metres – I was breathing heavily for several reasons, of which Piotr Politov was certainly the most earthly.

12

Piotr Politov was a remarkable man.

He arrived at the Pleskau river camp a few weeks before Himmler's decision to have Stalin killed, on one of the usual transports from Breslau. The Reich Main Security Office had ordered me to train him as 'a terrorism expert' for unspecified 'special missions'.

Major Lashkov (the one with the lorgnette) and Captain Delle (marksmanship) were delighted; they talked about him as though he were a beautiful racehorse. The first time I saw Politov (I remember it like it was yesterday: he was standing outside the barn in Khalakhalnya, beside Grishan, who was brimming with envy, while behind the pair of them a hawk spiralled up into the sky), I was struck by his similarity to Max Schmeling, the boxer, whose legendary modesty he did not share.

'I quick, I strong, you Hauptsturm,' he said to me with a grin, giving a salute that was both spirited and perfectly executed.

Grishan hated him from the off, probably because the robust

Politov was his opposite in every way. He had an intimate knowledge of the corrupt Soviet economy of favours they call 'Blat', which I don't understand at all. He was quick to grasp things and make decisions, and had a great gift for adapting himself to his situation. All the same, he was no bootlicker; he made sure he mouthed off, acted up and clowned around just enough for his colleagues to respect him. He had a stupendous political education, knew practically all the Soviet laws and decrees off by heart, and was completely unscrupulous.

The strongest bond between us was the death of his father, whom the Bolsheviks had shot in front of him when he was still a child. I once dropped a hint to him about Grandpaping's tragic end in the parsonage pond, and Politov leaned forward and patted my hand as a tear welled up in his weaselly eye.

'Herr Hauptsturm,' he whispered. 'No need worry about Politov. That never happen to Politov. Politov is veery good swimmer.'

His personal history was a mixture of primitive and salon art, an ice-age cave painting, only decadent, like someone dressing the Bison of Altamira in silk suits: a model of fakery.

Shortly before the war, Politov had defrauded his employer of a dizzying sum of money while managing an oil depot, absconded with it and evaded a nationwide manhunt. Then, by means of forged documents, deception, misuse of titles and usurpation of authority, he managed to worm his way into a job as an examining judge at the Voronezh state prosecutor's office.

A few months later this self-proclaimed, charismatic and surprisingly youthful judge was drafted into the Red Army. There, under his false name, he pretended to have been trained as an officer, rose through the ranks, was awarded several medals and ended up as a company commander. At the start of nineteen forty-two his identity was discovered to be a complete fabrication, and he deserted the same evening to avoid arrest by the NKVD.

After coming over to the Germans, he asked the very first interrogator he encountered for permission to kiss him. I could see from his personnel file that he denounced his fellow Soviet prisoners to the Gestapo shortly thereafter. The Gestapo classed him as only partly reliable, but with a great talent for subversion. The qualities attributed to him by his assessors were 'natural leadership', 'cunning', 'quick thinking', 'anti-Bolshevik sentiment', 'avarice', 'ambition' and 'lack of principles'.

This man was the perfect weapon.

On the day that Hub tasked me with training Politov as Stalin's assassin, there began a phase of my work that no longer followed the conventional principles of National Socialist officialdom. I now became SS-Hauptsturmführer Siegfried, with Politov as my good sword Balmung.

Together, we set off up the mountain to slay the dragon.

We wanted to start bathing in Stalin's blood, rather than his shit.

In the months that followed, academics, diligent researchers, brilliant analysts and gifted painters threw themselves into an assassination mission that contravened the Geneva, Hague and assorted other conventions.

The only conventions it did not contravene were those of the Nibelungen legend.

And they were the only ones on our minds.

I call this state the Gordian phenomenon. Because a man who slices through the Gordian knot rather than untangling it always feels fantastic, until he has to answer for the hacked-up rope. The Gordian phenomenon is something I encountered many times later in life – during the Cuban Missile Crisis, for example. But the execution of our Russian traitors, which Grishan literally took in hand without any trial or possibility of appeal, also had a Gordian sheen to it.

One of my first steps was to extricate Politov from the official camp and put him up in Pleskau itself, under a false name. Glutton Girgensohn found suitable accommodation for him in the Old Town, secured him a position as an engineer with a building company, and prohibited him from spending more than one hour a week at his workplace.

Instead, Piotr spent a lot of time with me. Before we could tell him anything about the Herculean mission for which he had been selected, I had to get to know him inside out. And the best way of getting to know someone inside out (as I always say) is by painting their portrait.

None of my men longed to become part of the heroes' gallery like Piotr Politov did. He brought a comb to our sitting for his marvellous Max Schmeling hair, and a second comb, a small one, I swear, to style his bushy eyebrows. He could not stop ferricking about, as Mama would have said; he sniffed my pastels, and for a moment I was slightly worried he was going to eat them.

It took some work to find a suitable pose for him, one that would also bring Jan Vermeer's calm into my picture. Papa always said that one line was always more important than the others at any given time. But with Politov, all movements and therefore all lines were of equal importance. With him, all I could see were details (details are all mouth and no trousers, my father said). I simply couldn't penetrate Politov's spirit. And failed to capture his shape.

And while I daubed helplessly, arranging and rearranging his nose, mouth and chin, shaken by how unlike my portrait was to the man, each failed line helped me to see more clearly that this project would never work unless Politov was given a female companion. Not for sexual reasons, he didn't need a companion for that. But for reasons of self-aggrandizement. All men need constant affirmation, but the degree of affirmation that Politov was already demanding from me was so great (asking was he sitting well enough, was he sitting still enough, was he sitting in the right light, should he unbutton his shirt, did I really think his teeth were a rare shade of pure white or was that just my good German manners, could he have a look) that it was clear: only a genuine, long-term female companion could give him the level of uninterrupted appreciation he needed if he was going to blow Stalin up.

'There's no need to look so gloomy, Herr Politov,' I therefore told him a few days after the disastrous portrait session. 'Everything is ter-rific. Berlin is pleased with you. You should start looking around for a woman.'

'Forr woman?'

'For a woman.'

'What kaind of woman?'

'A good woman.'

'A woman that do for Politov wash and clean?'

'No, not a cleaning lady. A woman you like.'

'Oh – whore?'

'You know what a wife is, don't you?'

'Children?'

'Exactly. The mother of your children.'

'Politov no want children. Politov want die for Chitler.'

'No one wants to die for Hitler. Not even I want to die for Hitler.'

An expression of chasm-deep surprise came into Piotr's eyes, as he listened to the thoughts whirring around his head. I could see him doing it.

'No die for Chitler?' he whispered, horrified.

I switched languages, though I could tell he didn't want me to, and used my Anna Ivanovna Russian in an attempt to form the crumbs of our conversation into some kind of nourishment.

'Man is not meant to live alone, it goes against nature,' I said, starting with philosophy. 'Why should you, Activist Politov, not lead a normal family life?'

Of course, from Activist Politov's point of view there was much that spoke against leading a normal family life: his daily routine consisted of instruction in shooting and close-combat techniques, advanced driving and motorbike courses, boxing, and lessons in poison-mixing and various other methods of killing. But since I insisted on it, Politov did begin to look around for a bride in Pleskau, and since he looked not only like Max Schmeling, but like Max Schmeling playing John the Baptist (I'm thinking of a picture by Dürer that now hangs in the German National Museum in Nuremberg), it took him less than a week to make the acquaintance of the seamstress Shilova, who had a job in a mending workshop ironing uniform jackets for the German officers.

I didn't have the slightest objection to the girl: Shilova was pretty in a self-contained way, twelve years younger than the thirty-two-year-old Politov, and her father was languishing in a Siberian prison camp, where he had spent many years, for anti-Soviet activities. She was a perfect fit.

'I hope,' I said, 'that you won't have anything against us training your future wife as a special agent?'

'Chail Chitler!' he said, briskly. He had nothing against it at all.

I discussed it with my staff officers. While Glutton Girgensohn thought it would be a great coup to marry two agents to one another and then send them off on a suicidal assassination mission – it reminded him of Abelard and Héloïse's doomed love, which was so good for the Church – the professional dwarf was sceptical. It might well be, he argued, that on account of her life-receiving juices, the woman would want to keep the man's life-giving juices for herself and would hamper him in his deadly mission, not truly appreciating the abstract principle of heroism. Möllenhauer was glum, pointing out that we would be – he wouldn't say malevolently, but still – sending a young girl to her death.

This outburst of emotion met with blank looks from all sides; I even heard the professional dwarf mutter into his poison beard that this was a homosexual opinion. Slowcoach Handrack declared that he really had no views on the matter and was therefore with me, whatever I decided to do.

That same afternoon we telegraphed to Berlin that Politov was, in our view, ideally suited to this great mission for our fatherland. He should, however, be sent to Moscow with a female activist, who must be fully trained in a very short space of time. As we had only male instructors on the base, we requested that the Reich Main Security Office send us a female instructor, Russian if possible, with sufficient intelligence-service experience.

I am sure that if we had not sent this message, I would never have seen Maya again.

13

It was around five kilometres on foot from Khalakhalnya along the edge of the woods to the little knoll that the farmers called 'Broschnij': the giant, or rather the giantess. It was the only hill in the area, and although it had nothing whatever in common with the Carpathian massif that centuries ago had offered Maya and me a refuge from the world, with most of a roof over our heads, it was still the only place I could think of with a view. A single tree stood on its crest, a maple. The Russians believe that the maple protects against witches, and I took that as a good sign. I leaned against the trunk and ten minutes later saw someone emerge from the shadow of the woods and walk towards me. A wolf howled in the distance (searching dolefully for his mate, who was hanging on our fence), at which the figure paused for a moment. She looked like an ink blot against the snow. Like a raven's wing.

And then she was standing beside me.

It wasn't very dark.

I learned that she had not faced the firing squad, but I could see that for myself. I learned that my voice contained a lot more nails than it used to and was full of orders. The Russian language is given to images, and I think she was trying to say that I didn't sound friendly, warm, the way I sounded in her memory. I learned that she had been tortured, but only in two sentences; the rest she showed me. I learned what her arms and her back looked like by stroking them, and feeling all the lumps and scars. Her physical beauty was gone. I learned that she was afraid of wolves and glad that I was carrying a Luger (she knew all about hand guns). I learned that she had gone over to the Germans because she'd thought that all Germans were like me. I also learned that that wasn't true. I learned that Major Uralov was dead. I learned that she couldn't have children now. And that she had fallen in love with a guard in the reformatory, who had kept her alive and was sent to Siberia for it. She said that I still had a sadness in me, and that now she had one too. It was something that developed over time, it was nothing special. I learned that she had been very fond of me back then, but that all my drawings had been taken from her and Uralov had wiped his arse on them. I learned once more, and again later, that Major Uralov was dead. And I learned that the view here was quite different from that view over the steppe, and of course she remembered how I loved a sweeping view, and incidentally I learned that it was cold, but we learned that together. And finally, we joined hands under the maple and Maya promised to treat the activist Shilova well and always to call me Herr Hauptsturm-führer and never Koja.

I spent many nights shut away in my room, as you can perhaps imagine.

I didn't want to hear a knock at the door.

When it was light I saw that they had cut both of Maya's cheeks as well, and the corners of her mouth had been ripped open with a jigsaw blade. She could no longer smile, only grin; she would be forced to grin even in her coffin, or in the depths of grief.

Because there was a war on, and because we intended to kill Stalin, we had no time, and I didn't want to think too hard about anything.

And I really didn't want to hear a knock on the door.

But the next time I went to Riga, I didn't sleep with Ev. It wasn't that I consciously decided not to; the decision was made much deeper within me, in the place that controls breathing and grief. It would not have been right, not even right in the wrong way that we needed at that time.

And I had no desire to.

And it is perhaps a measure of how much I loved Ev that I was able to tell her how little desire I had.

And she cut off the shining dark hair that hung in front of her face in order to see me better, and then she took me in her arms, although she wasn't very good at taking someone in her arms, because she believed that her arms were either for clinging on, or for swinging freely. She took my temperature and placed our baby on my stomach, and I searched for Ev's eyes in Anna's face and for a moment saw the beloved elephantine eyes of my own father. One trait I had inherited from him was never making any firm resolutions, and if you did, then not sticking to them, especially when you had resolved to shoot dead your own sons, and I recalled that day, nineteen-nineteen, when Hub had said to Papa that I was still so little.

I didn't feel I had grown any bigger since that day; only Anna gave me the sense of being bigger, and I put her fingers between my lips like all fathers do, and she liked my warm, wet mouth.

When I have to speak of these outward events, then you must not forget, Swami, that my soul was sick at that time and all outward events, however terrible they may have been, eased the pressure on my soul, though of course they didn't take the burden.

I sensed how much Ev needed me. I sensed that she was worried about Hub. She said as much, too, but she could say all kinds of things, given the time. I preferred to believe the muscles in her neck, which tensed when we talked about him.

He hadn't told her anything about Stalin; I was the only one who gave away all our secrets to her, like a gossiping fishwife.

She claimed that Hub had changed, that he was becoming increasingly hard, taut, glittering. And in order to get ahead in the SS, he was pressing her for a second child, although it was only six months since she had given birth. That was the disconnected way she spoke. Just one thing after another. And she said she dreaded the day he would find out about her parentage. '*Er vet mikh teytn*, I am certain of it: he will kill me.' I reassured her. Hub couldn't kill anyone (well . . .), he would never do anything to her (personally). He loves you (true). And you love him (don't you?).

'*Ikh veys nisht*, Koja. I really don't know.'

*

We only ever called her Shilova, although her first name was Natasha, my favourite Russian name. Major Lashkov set down his lorgnette in protest and refused to impart any military know-how to Shilova, no matter how modest (in his view, there was no place for women in war, and that was one of the reasons he was anti-communist, because the Red Army had invented the 'gun woman'). But the marksmanship instructor and serial rapist Captain Delle took great care of the new recruit.

For this reason, I was glad that Maya was always with Shilova. She taught her how to use a combat knife. She taught her not to stand staring like a mule when someone throws a hand grenade, but to pay attention (she would have got on well with Papa, who regarded paying attention as the most important thing in both art and life). And that you should never leave a briefcase in an enemy's car – Maya taught her that, too.

All the other things a member of the Soviet secret service has to know – Shilova was to be restyled as a capable NKVD official – she learned during long and tearful mock interrogations. Every evening, Maya reported back to me. I listened to her and looked at her scars. We were very polite, like two complete strangers who just happen to be travelling the same road. Afterwards, I always drank my vodka alone.

In November, Politov married Shilova. She was one of the prettiest girls in Pleskau, no doubt about it, and there was only one reason she allowed the horror into her life, first in its drowsy forms, but soon as a stark reality: she was in love.

I acted as witness at the spy-wedding I had inspired. As we stood outside Pleskau's old cathedral and all the guests cheered for the happy couple, I was cheering for two corpses on call (at least they were two corpses kissing). When I stood to the right of the cathedral altar, amid all the candles and incense and bleeding icons, and the four and a half generations of pastors in my family looked over my shoulder and discovered that their descendant and heir was sending a happily squeaking mouse off to the gallows accompanied by the sound of bells, I felt the urgent need for vodka once again. But no one could have drunk that much vodka.

The Gordian glow, which my purely professional efforts had refracted into a perfidious idea, was now extinguished. Regret was all that remained. But this regret did not rise up, did not take the measure of my brain; it merely tied my guts in knots, corroded my vegetal nervous system, altered my pulse, my blood pressure, my muscle tone. And the bread, the salt, the stealing of the bride's shoe, a white dress in front of a wrought-gold pope – these were the images of a wedding party that contained a funeral within it, a beautiful, yes even a joyful funeral.

I, at least, knew that. And I and all my colleagues also knew that Politov was already married. He had left his wife behind in Ekaterinburg. And that was something Shilova never found out, never, at least not from us.

Before we could reveal our plans to the newlyweds, there was one final set of points to switch. Synchronicity was essential for the attack on Joseph Stalin. And chronology. Whether it was possible for us to travel from the origin (the invigorating idea of an assassination) to the final destination (*exitus letalis*) depended on the sequence of stops in between.

Our Joseph Commando in Moscow (I introduced them earlier) was just such an in-between stop. This commando was a secret Zeppelin cell of two activists based in the city centre, whose job (*nomen est omen*) was to observe Stalin. The two Josephists had been dropped into Russia and had seeped into its capital city six months previously – their success was largely down to our excellent passport-forging department. Reaching Moscow with their forged papers, getting through the city's endless checkpoints (erected in a fit of paranoia about spies), finding a place to stay, creating a front for their clandestine existence – in chronological terms, all this was an a priori achievement by these men, a foundation on which to build everything that followed. But the pair (we called them Over and Out) could do little more than wait for what was to come. Twice a week, Over and Out made radio contact with us, right under the eyes and ears of the Lubyanka. That alone could have turned this in-between stop into the final destination (with the *exitus letalis* befalling our own side, naturally).

When, after a long gap in communications, we heard that Joseph Commando's apartment was covered by an official rental contract, and our two knights of the sad countenance (former tsarist guard officers) had official work permits and were labouring in a road-building gang, the synchronicity of the coming events seemed manageable. The Moscow hideout was in place. Politov and Shilova could be initiated.

And our most senior commanding officer, Brigadeführer Schellenberg, wanted to take care of that in person and in his guppy-like manner, with the right degree of pompousness and paternalism.

The six of us flew to see him in Berlin. A fierce winter storm shook the decrepit Ju 52, the inside of which smelled of diesel, turpentine and Shilova's vomit. There was a general whining noise emanating from both metal and people, especially our air-sick special agent in the back row, who kept throwing up into her paper bag. Maya was holding her hand. Möllenhauer and Politov stared out at the pounding storm. I was sitting right at the front, separated from Hub only by the aisle. He twiddled his fingers, looking pale and utterly flat.

The air is for sparrows, Opapabaron once told the Tsar in eighteen eighty-something. His Serene Majesty, as technology-obsessed as the whole century was, wanted to invest in the building of airships (the Lenoir gas engine). The Schillings were perfectly happy to sink in the Atlantic, as they had often done, with the loss of all hands, and their own hands on the tiller. But to fall out of the sky, from which ordinarily only rain or seagull shit fell (Opapabaron could know nothing of phosphorus and benzene, sea mines and bombs), and smash like a hen's egg on the ground? That was unworthy of a Baltic seafaring dynasty. Viewed through this lens, there was a kernel of family history to Hub's fear of flying – but all the same, it didn't fit his self-image.

His handsome SS nose began to bleed. I passed him my handkerchief, and he took it and pressed it to his face. As it turned into a monochrome Emil Nolde watercolour, a crushed tulip in the snow, he tilted his head back, smiled absently and told me that Ev was cheating on him.

'Is that some kind of joke?' I said, husky-voiced.

The co-pilot stepped into the cabin and shouted words that we could barely hear over the hurricane. He seemed taken aback by Hub's bloody handkerchief; he crossed himself and left again.

Hub said he didn't make jokes. Ev was cheating on him, he just didn't know why, how, when and with whom. He would really like to hire a private detective. Like Erhard had once done. But there weren't any private detectives any more. Could I send one of my Russians to Riga for him? A Russian who could tail her, take some decent photographs and document the whole disgraceful business, that would be perfect.

Horrified, I exclaimed that it wouldn't be easy to find someone discreet. Hub said he didn't have to be discreet; he could be shot afterwards.

'Are you serious?'

'About what?'

The plane suddenly dropped a hundred metres.

'What you just said?'

'Do you know how I'm feeling? Do you have any idea?'

'Hub,' I heard myself say sympathetically. 'You can't shoot one of our Russians.'

He lowered the handkerchief, studied it like an unwelcome gift (which it was, of course) and pressed it back into my hand.

'I know,' he said, nodding. 'But they're going to die anyway.'

Then I got a headache.

When the turbulence subsided, Politov went and sat beside his exhausted Shilova and sang a Cossack song to her in a soft voice. 'Monotonously rings the little bell', poison in a minor key for betrayed husbands. Beside me, Hub brooded dully over his suspicion (but what suspicion?). The cut of his uniform was flawless, a flawlessly fitting uniform made of putrid foliage. It stank, or he stank. Ev certainly hadn't washed and ironed it for more than a year. What had Hub discovered? I stole sideways glances at him, but all I could see was resistance. His fingers danced over the windowpane, on the outside of which a sheet of ice had formed. From time to time he slammed his fist against it, making everyone look at us.

After landing at Tempelhof, we were picked up by two luxury Gestapo sedans. In thin rain, we glided through a badly mutilated city. Ruined buildings and smoking rubble everywhere. A library on Lützowplatz must have been hit not long before. Thousands of smoke-blackened shreds of paper whirled through the air; a few pages of Lessing plastered themselves to our windscreen. Hub sat beside me like a puppet.

We dropped off the women (among whom Möllenhauer must certainly be counted) at Café Josty. From there, we drove on to tranquil, unmutilated Schmargendorf, where SD Office VI, our headquarters, had requisitioned a former Jewish retirement home. It was a long brick building striped like a zebra, with a Bolshevist flat roof. The canteen was a Bavarian-style pine-panelled parlour, which had been created in the prayer room. We waited there for several hours on sturdy wooden benches, two thirds of us drinking ersatz coffee out of swastika porcelain, while the remainder chose beer (above us, the Stars of David on the ceiling had been skilfully pasted over so as not to spoil anyone's appetite). Hub eventually shouted at an orderly for some trivial reason. I asked him to pull himself together and he went off to the lavatory, I think he was crying.

Guppy Schellenberg met us in his office, which had none of the grandeur of the pre-bombing Prinz-Albrecht-Palais, apart from the enormous Renaissance desk, which the Brigadeführer couldn't bear to part with, not least because of the reassuring machine guns it contained. 'What can I say,' he huffed indignantly, rapping on the wall with a bent forefinger, 'racially speaking, a degenerate building through and through. At least we sent the architect to Theresienstadt, a gentle protest against his cretinism.'

Schellenberg had not lost his permanent arrogant smile. Perhaps it looked a touch more frozen than in the good old days of German triumph. He received the cheerful Politov and the pale Solm brothers, both approaching collapse in their own way, with perfect affability, though he had only twenty minutes to spare. Hub got to his feet for a moment, stopped where he was, shook his head and sat down again. Schellenberg showered Activist Politov with compliments regarding his undeniable similarity to Max Schmeling. And then, abruptly changing the subject, he asked the Russian whether he had the heart for a mission to eliminate the Soviet head of state. Over sparkling German wine and fruit, Politov explained a few fundamental things that we should know about his heart. I knew them all already. Hub wasn't listening.

That same night, following a discussion with Heinrich Himmler, Brigadeführer Schellenberg approved the operation that would be carried out by Pleskau Command.

It was given the name Finest Hour.

14

The next day, Hub called in sick.

The rest of the Riga delegation, in the company of two polite Standartenführers and a relentless drizzle that was gradually turning into snow, drove to a firing range that lay far outside Berlin's city gates. We were met by a snappish major who led us into a long, single-storey building with bricked-up windows. There, ten metres underground, Politov was shown the special equipment that had been developed for him over the past few months, under conditions of strictest secrecy, of course. But then, what secrecy is not strict, I thought, and at once my mind turned to Ev and our rather pliable, fragile, battered secret, and it took a while until I was fully back in the room.

At that moment, the major was saying 'a tank-breaker', in almost tender tones as he held a small device in front of my face. It consisted of a short steel tube around sixty millimetres in diameter, a grenade attachment, several leather straps, wires in different colours, and a button switch. A mini rocket-launcher, slim enough that Politov could strap it to his bare forearm and pull a coat sleeve over it, and you wouldn't see the slightest bulge underneath. Politov laughed and turned this way and that as if standing in front of a wardrobe mirror. He really did need a lot of affirmation.

The presentation included other secret weapons: electronic limpet mines; special parabellum pistols made to shoot poison ampules; newly developed silencers; a motorbike with a reverse gear. Later, Politov and I even went to an aeroplane assembly plant in Brandenburg to inspect the special plane that was needed to transport the commando, a four-engine Arado 232. The whole state-of-the-art display was put on for the benefit of our fascinating, promising, top-quality collaborator, who was bursting with spirit and confidence; the aim was to make a lasting impression and convince him of the superiority of German military technology.

And that was a dire necessity.

During our stay, Berlin was visited by several devastating air raids. Houses in flames, people fleeing, the bombed-out population cowering in bunkers. None of this suggested that a final victory was on its way.

The morning after one of these night-time raids, during which I had almost been driven mad with despondent worry – about Hub, Ev, myself – I could no longer bear Politov's relentless cheerfulness. In exasperation, I sent him off to buy stockings for Shilova. She had her heart set on transparent nylons, which the Femina-Palast would sell you at an eyewatering price and without the need for coupons, if you had SS contacts.

On his way to buy stockings, Politov observed some drifting sparks setting light to a large apartment block. The fire was just getting started; it was nothing more than a little cloud of smoke in the roof space, and it awakened his ambition. In no time at all he had raced up the stairs, grabbing two buckets of water from a landing on his way, and was heading for the attic, the source of the fire. But before he could reach the hatch, he heard a woman's voice screeching from downstairs, 'My buckets, my buckets! What are you doing with my buckets?'

Politov turned at once, ran back down the stairs, put the buckets down at the woman's feet – 'Hhere two bucket!' – and walked out onto the street at a measured pace, where he sat down in an armchair rescued from the block next door and watched impassively as the fire that he would so have liked to put out burned the building to the ground.

I believe that was the moment when Herr Politov began to have second thoughts, Möllenhauer later told me (he had gone with Politov, intending to buy some nylons himself, of course).

Shortly afterwards, Hub rang me at the hotel. He explained in a flat voice that he was already on his way back to Riga. He had joined a Wehrmacht transport. There were a few things he needed to find out. He was leaving me in charge of the delegation. Written confirmation of this was to follow by telegraph. I was to stick to the pre-agreed schedule for the rest of the trip.

I heard a crackle on the line. The conversation was over.

I hung up.

The luxury guesthouse on the Kurfürstendamm where we all stayed is still intact. The building survived all the air raids. When I was in West Berlin a few years ago, I went back to look at the entrance. The luxury was no more, but the revolving doors were still there. So was the dark splendour of the old leather wall-coverings in the stairwell. It's impossible to imagine now, the colours of the old Reich capital, the way they glowed, a bombast that shone as if Tintoretto had painted it, free of all earthly heaviness. I went up to the third floor and stood outside the room I had stayed in back then, put my ear to the door and listened to the hours I'd spent running back and forth in there thirty years before. Striking my forehead against the wall (bong, bong). Biting my knuckles. I couldn't call Ev in Riga: it was far too likely that the line was already tapped.

Later, I lay in bed. And I was still lying in bed much later than that, numb with worry. Like lead falling into water.

There was no possibility of sleep, so I dragged myself down to the breakfast room, where I found Maya. She had taken down the black-out blind, and through the window shone what light a few stars and the moon could manage from behind the clouds, without the aid of gas lamps, neon signs and headlights. It wasn't much, a silvery-grey light, as if she were sitting in ashes, that's what it looked like. A grisaille.

The clock chimed half past two. Its hand was the only thing moving in the room. The figure at the window, by contrast, might have been made of plaster. I sat down with her. We were silent for a long time.

'It's nice when it's dark.'

'Yes,' I said.

'Then you can't see how ugly I am.'

'You aren't ugly.'

'I disgust you.'

'No.'

'You feel sorry for me.'

'No.'

'You don't feel sorry for me?'

'I'm sorry for what's been done to you. Not for what you've become.'

'If you were blind . . . that would be the worst thing for you, wouldn't it?'

'Why?'

'Because you're a painter.'

'You might be right, yes.'

Outside we heard giggling, a drunk couple out breaking the curfew. Otherwise the night was completely silent, it was like being in the countryside. No cars. No people. No air raids. Just the clock in the corner.

'It wouldn't be the worst thing for me if you were blind.'

I looked at her. It had always been difficult to read her, even when she was still an open book and not a mosaic of fragments.

'It's a long time since anyone has said something so nice to me,' I said.

'Do you have someone?' she asked, just as quietly.

'No.'

'But your heart belongs to someone else. I can see that.'

Now there came a gruff voice from outside, some distance off. The drunk couple had obviously run into a patrol.

'If you lose the war – and I believe you will lose the war – so, if you lose the war, we will both die, one way or another. But I think that, in a few years, everything will be beautiful again for all the people we have known.'

'Yes, perhaps,' I said.

'What did you do to your forehead?'

'I ran into the wall, up in my room.'

'Oh, that was you.'

'Yes.'

'Bong-bong.'

'Yes.'

'Quite a few times.'

'I bit myself, too,' I said, sliding my hand across the table towards her. She felt it, lingering on the sloughed-off shreds of skin. Her fingers were cool.

'Shall we pray together?'

'I'm so very sorry, Maya.'

'Why not?'

'I used to pray with someone when I was a child. I can't pray with anyone else.'

'It's best when you're a child.'

'Maya?'

'What?'

Tentatively, I pulled my hand back, leaving hers lying quite forlorn on the table.

'I'm going back up to my room.'

She cast her eyes down, but there was a hint of colour in her cheeks.

'Yes, let's go back up to our rooms.'

Two days later, I received a telegram from Riga.

DEAR KOJA STOP PLEASE COME STOP DISASTER STOP EV

15

My sister had always been concerned about her health. Even as a ten-year-old, Ev had the most incredible ideas. Sometimes she would come rushing into the kitchen and shout, 'My ears are rotting off!' She thought her ears were as soft as old peaches, and no one was permitted to stroke her head, not even Mama, because the slightest shock might make her ears fall off and then they would have to be buried and she wouldn't be able to hear anything.

She thought about cancer a lot. And sometimes she would crawl into bed with me and cry because she was imagining an ailment she had read about in Charles Dickens. Starvation, for instance. Or Pickwickian syndrome. When she was studying medicine, she told me that Pickwickian syndrome was now called Obesity-hypoventilation syndrome. But you could only get it if you were very fat and constantly full. So you could never have starvation and Obesity-hypoventilation syndrome at the same time. The only good thing about these two ailments was that they were mutually exclusive.

Please. Ev was serious about that. Her obsessions were a real burden to her. Sometimes she found the strength to laugh at herself. But often she didn't. Once, when there was a wave of flu spreading through the Belgian Congo, and we had Congolese bananas – which were still a delicacy in those days – she refused to enter the kitchen. For three days. She was fourteen then. She spent a great deal of time thinking about death. The hereafter had a kind of fascination for her, and that was why she liked to pray so much. Both her parents had died and she had landed on an entirely unknown planet at the age of eight – while the old planet, her original mother earth, floated through the galaxies stripped of all life – and so she was driven by the fear that she, too, the last of her kind, an outmoded life form, possibly damned by the Almighty, might perish at any moment from the most unimaginable infection or ridiculous organic disorder, which would threaten no one on this new star but her, the alien from the old earth. It wouldn't take a storm to sweep her away, nor a wind, not even a breeze. A mere breath would suffice.

The months that Ev spent in Auschwitz must, for this reason alone, have cemented her belief that anything is possible at any time, even the unthinkable, the unimaginable and the incomprehensible. And the trigger for these things might be something even less than a breath – a dark brown iris, for example.

Compared with that, the injuries that Ev received from my brother were reassuringly unmysterious. Nothing more than bruises, oedemas – and a crush wound above her left eyebrow, which had been sutured half successfully with a simple interrupted stitch. But all the same, an asteroid storm had broken through Ev's stratosphere. That was what her husband's blows had been for her.

Rocks from outer space.

I went to see her at home. Little Anna was asleep behind the nursery door that I had painted in bright colours weeks before. I could see furniture lying on the floor or standing lost and dreaming in the middle of the room, washed by waves of books that had been pulled off the shelves and rippled across the floor. All the colours were present in Ev's face. She had taken care of all the medical treatment herself. Hub had had to help her stitch the wound, racked by explosive sobs that made the needle dance every which way. Now each of them had given the other a smite scar, she joked bitterly, or: 'we're both smitten now'. And it took me a while to recall that she had stitched his lip after his first duel, so that each of his kisses reminded her of that time.

She couldn't leave the house, couldn't even go out into the garden, probably for weeks to come, except when it was dark. Even sunglasses and a scarf pulled up to her ears didn't disguise it completely. Olga wasn't allowed to come, either; she mustn't see the Herr Obersturmbannführer's wife in this state, or the wrecked house. Ev refused to tidy up or touch anything. She just looked after little Anna, who cried incessantly.

Hub had been completely beside himself, had fallen to his knees, begged her to forgive him, my red patch, my red patch, he screamed – so she told me. He was talking about his retina, which turned red when he was angry, had done even when he was a child, and he just kept screaming and screaming.

'We have to stop this,' Ev whispered.

'Of course,' I said.

'He'll kill us. He will kill all three of us, I know it.'

'We'll stop.'

'I didn't recognize him. His face was gone, he was just a pair of eyes.'

She told me that he had beaten her in a wild frenzy when she refused to tell him what had happened.

He had found one single clue. A page from her diary. It must have come loose at some point and slipped down behind the headboard. And a week ago, when a grape had fallen off his plate in the bedroom and rolled away under the marital bed and he didn't want the grape to fester away beneath him or even just dry up, he pushed the bed to one side, and there was the grape lying on the lost page, like a magnet on steel. He picked the paper up and read the few lines written on it, which described a sexual encounter in which he had not been involved. It featured words that Ev and I used. And a date. And a reference to a beautiful drawing of Ev, naked. It did not feature me. Not by name. But Hub wanted to know who it was about. Ev said nothing. He wanted the rest of the diary. She lied. She told him she'd burned it, that the affair was over, over and done with, and she was ashamed. She was ashamed.

Minutes later he had to leave for the airport, to board a plane to Berlin, and he was soon speeding with me and the others towards our Finest Hour.

Ev was beside herself with nausea and jitters, self-hatred and guilt, but she hoped she might still be able to make everything all right. Then suddenly, he was at the door, three days before he was due back. 'Who is it?' he asked as he crossed the threshold; she was still drying dish soap from her hands in the hallway when he started hitting her. He shook out every drawer in the apartment and moved all the tables and cupboards and bookcases and found a few grapes, a piece of bread, a great quantity of insects, and two dead and decaying mice covered in mould.

But he did not find the diary: she had hidden it well.

Still, he didn't give up; he checked the date marked on the page, combined it with other appointments, combined it with speculations about the drawing she had mentioned, combined it with the choice of words on the corpus deliciti, and finally came to the conclusion that there was only one person who could have gone behind his back in such an opprobrious manner. And he shook her again and again and asked if it was true, if it was this person, he couldn't imagine it was anyone else – please, Koja, I'm so desperately sorry, she wept, but in the end I had to say: yes, it's true.

'You told him it was me?'

'No. Not you. He would never believe that.'

'Who, then?'

'The driver.

'My driver?'

'Yes.'

'Grishan?'

'He was here that day.'

'You told him you slept with Grishan?'

'Well, he was always here when you were. And he's so handsome. And you know, I went out walking with Grishan a few times when Hub and I came to see you in Khalakhalnya. And he painted me. You said it reminded you of Van Gogh?'

'Your green face, yes.'

'And Hub was so jealous when he saw that green face; he told me I shouldn't allow a Russian to paint me.'

'Ev.'

'I'm sorry. I'm sorry.'

'Ev, this is very bad indeed.'

'I know. But he's the only person who draws, apart from you.'

'I need to speak to Grishan right away.'

'I've spoken to him already.'

I can imagine that someone like you, who didn't live through this time and sees the world as a kind of Woodstock, would find it almost impossible to gauge what these words meant. These words meant that my sister had managed to make contact with Grishan more quickly than her husband had. This was thanks to considerable good fortune, or perhaps a combination of fortune and necessity, and ultimately it was thanks to Joseph Stalin himself.

Precisely two days earlier, on the twelfth of January nineteen forty-four, the man of steel had instructed the Red Army to begin a major offensive along the whole length of the northern front. As my brother was laying into his sister, two million obedient Reds overwhelmed our winter positions at Luga and Novgorod, and raced towards Leningrad and Pleskau, forcing Hub to let Ev go – though he was already in a state of sobbing contrition. The black telephone was ringing on the upstairs landing, because on his rampage he had neglected to rip the phone cable out of the wall. An enervated Hub whimpered into the receiver: yes,

Solm, what do you want. And he was given a code number. A code number means an emergency call. And an emergency call means that you have to hurry to your office without first dealing with your wife's lover.

Two hours and four minutes after this emergency call, the conscientious Grishan parked my official car, a spotless Opel Olympia, neatly outside Hub's snowed-in driveway, just as I had instructed him the previous week before getting on the Ju 52 to Berlin. He was to collect Ev and her daughter and drive them to the airfield, so that baby Anna could be waiting there to welcome us – her loving father, and her loving father disguised as her uncle – laughing and babbling. It was meant as a surprise for Hub, a nice surprise of course. That was the plan. A plan that had been thwarted by various decisions, first and foremost Hub's fateful decision to return to Riga early.

Amid the hurricane of calamities, I had forgotten to let Grishan know about the change to our arrival. No one had told him that his services were no longer required. He knew nothing.

My lad therefore rang the Solm family doorbell in error, but as per his instructions (a terrible combination) at the agreed time. He stood to attention and straightened his very clean uniform, and then waited, admiring the attractive mix of red and pale-coloured bricks from which the villa was built. And as a few snowflakes drifted past his admiring eyes, Ev opened the door, and he saw the lady of the house, beaten, bleeding, with four tremulous stitches above her eyebrow, and a face that looked like nothing he had ever painted. He was invited into a house that had been turned upside down, where he learned all about Ev and me: things he never should have learned and certainly never wanted to learn. He was also informed that he, Grishan, had had an intimate relationship with the lady of the house, which he, Grishan, was to confirm to anyone who asked, at all costs and in all circumstances, even though he, Grishan, was entirely ignorant of this sensational state of affairs.

These were Ev's instructions, which she could only mumble because her face was so swollen.

I'm certain that Grishan listened wide-eyed and very respectfully to these instructions and took them in without passing any judgement. He didn't say much, and managed to hide a touch of consternation behind his natural dignity.

Going against my original order, he then drove as fast as he could back to Pleskau. The lady of the house had told him to, wishing to prevent him and her husband, the Obersturmbannführer, from laying eyes on one another too soon.

When I heard this, it was clear to me that Ev had now created a chief witness. Grishan could blackmail us however he saw fit. He could make any demands he wanted. Or he could be big-hearted, loyal, forgetful. If he chose, he could simply enrich his dreams, enjoy his power and imagine Ev stark naked.

Whatever he decided, we were in his hands.

I bade farewell to Ev, the first time we had parted for years without my touching her. In the hall, idiotically, I picked up two books and left eight hundred where they were, just as I also left my daughter and Politov and Shilova in Riga. Just as I left Riga itself.

Möllenhauer (dumbfounded) was the only person I (dazed) took with me on a medical transport to Pleskau, towards the two million Red Army soldiers who were approaching at speed from the other direction. The officers' car allocated to me was left at the prefecture. I was in no condition to risk encountering my brother there.

When we arrived at the Pleskau Zeppelin Command in the middle of a snowstorm, shivering for many reasons and several hours late, the place was in uproar. Glutton Girgensohn came over, flapping his arms, and cried out three times in succession, 'Our good Lashkov!' Then his red, hypnotized-rabbit eyes looked into mine, and he fell into a quaking silence. It took me a quarter of an hour to get the story out of my deputy, who was highly competent in epicurean matters but overwhelmed by everything else. The evening after I had left, he said, a plain horse-drawn sleigh carrying four men in sheepskins armed with sub-machine guns and hand grenades had drawn up outside Major Lashkov's private quarters, a small farmhouse not far from the river camp. The sheepskin men had knocked politely on the door, waited patiently until it was opened, and then gagged and bound the landlady and sat her beside the stove, where she could get a good view of everything, before asking our good Lashkov to put on some warm clothes. They bundled him onto the sleigh and whisked him off like a captive

Santa Claus with his beard fluttering in the wind, right under the nose of a Zeppelin guard post three hundred metres away.

After telling this story, Glutton led me to a tin bathtub in the provisions store. He pulled a cover from the tub, and by the light of the dancing oil lamps I suddenly realized that my Jan Vermeer gallery of heroes was now open. Glutton tapped his riding crop on a block of ice that had been hacked out of the almost entirely frozen Velikaya a few hours previously. The naked corpse, curled up, shimmering violet and encased in a layer of ice five to ten centimetres thick, was missing its left foot. The scalp had been completely removed down to the back of the neck. But I was most taken aback by Lashkov's beardless chin, which had also been scalped. The gold lorgnette had been rammed through his right eye socket, so far into the brain that the stem had disappeared completely and only the two lenses were sticking out, like a painting by Georges Braque.

I ordered my men to pour petrol into the bathtub up to the rim and set this expressionist artwork alight: the only form of funeral possible when the ground is frozen. As we saluted and stared into the flames, Glutton said he feared that Lashkov, whose body was now crackling and shattering, might have given away the real names of our Russian agents. No one who was being flayed alive could be blamed for that, our sympathetic Möllenhauer put in. But the cover names of our activists, who were wanted by Stalin for high treason, were their families' life insurance policies.

If we were going to avoid unrest, we had to give up the spy school, the river camp and Khalakhalnya at once. The front was advancing towards us, and Möllenhauer reported that Soviet artillery fire was chewing up the German divisions like a monstrous combine harvester, turning them to pulp.

I ordered an emergency evacuation and retreat to Riga, preparations for which were not even interrupted during an overnight bombing raid by the Soviet air force. A munitions depot was hit on the far bank of the river, and burned for two days.

All the pandemonium only added to my inner turmoil: I had not found Grishan. He wasn't in Pleskau or Khalakhalnya, when I went there to collect my personal possessions. But at the river camp I came across the professional dwarf, Teich, who was just about to have a set of fireproof metal boxes containing the staff archive loaded onto a Magirus Deutz. Around us, everything that wasn't nailed down – straw mattresses, blankets, barbed wire, school desks, even two little puppies – was being piled up for transportation. As the men worked, he told me that Grishan had driven back to Riga with all his things not long after arriving here, following a special order from Obersturmbannführer Solm. He'd taken his Opel Olympia. My Opel Olympia. With spiteful generosity, the Dwarf added that in the absence of my own vehicle, I was welcome to flee with him in his official car. But much to his astonishment, that was not necessary. I informed him that his car and driver were being requisitioned to serve his commanding officer's needs with immediate effect, and he could travel in the back of the lorry with his fireproof metal boxes; that was where he belonged, and nowhere else.

When I called Hub on the open long-distance line, we discussed only official business. There was no mention of where Grishan was, nor of my visit to Ev, and certainly not of his calamitous behaviour relating to either.

His voice explained in a metallic tone that there was currently no suitable garrison compound in Riga that could be freed up for my unit. We would have to move into Riga Zoo, along with all our horses, our cows and even the Khalakhalnya pigs. That was all that could be done for us at the moment. Over and out.

Our convoy set off the next night, along the snow-covered road that glimmered beneath a hostile full moon. From the air, it must have seemed a tempting, narrow, milk-white river with small and even smaller black specks travelling along it, like rafts bound together, drifting helplessly towards the Baltic Sea – that was us: lorries, sedans, an armoured car, horses. After a predictable strafing attack by a low-flying Soviet plane, which sent the cattle transporter up in flames with our beloved pigs aboard (for days afterwards the driver, who managed to escape, smelled of frying bacon), we reached the safety of Latvia and finally the city of my birth, which was slumbering as if deeply at peace.

Our two hundred Russians set up their camp as instructed in the city zoo. It was idyllically situated in the Kaiserwald villa quarter, not far from the concentration camp of the same name. Camp staff had a pleasant walk morning and evening between their workplace and the requisitioned Jewish villas, and could take a short zoological detour at lunchtime to unwind, which was probably the main reason for the occupying forces keeping the zoo open despite the war. Camp Commandant Sauer, who was woken at the weekends by the cheerful trumpeting of Siam, the cow elephant (his property lay directly opposite the main entrance), had on occasion fed an entire day's rations for the inmates to the starving animals, simply out of love for them. He gave the meagre supplies of fat to the polar bears, to make their dull coats shinier. And so we found the zoo's animal inhabitants surprisingly well fed.

The tropical houses were home to numerous exotic species, and they now became our bedfellows. Most of the soldiers quite understandably wanted to camp in the more than pleasantly warm terrariums. The fat Mississippi alligator, whom the Latvians had christened 'honey chops', needed heat and humidity, as did all the anacondas, boas, iguanas and geckos, who cheered everyone up. And they were quieter than the chimpanzees, who also sometimes threw shit at us. A whole contingent of Russians camped in the elephant house. Some men even slept as close as possible to the big-cat cages, to benefit from the tigers' body heat. Our commando's numerous horses were put out into a large enclosure with the fallow deer. They were shaggy little Koniks, who could weather the icy January temperatures.

The eight cows we had loaded into the lorries in Khalakhalnya with their legs tied together did not emerge unscathed at the other end. Because of course, despite being told not to, some of the Russians had sat on the bellowing animals during the journey; they had no desire to stand up for hours at a time. One of the cows died under the weight of half a dozen swaying Crimean Tatars. But at least there were schnitzels and steaks for a whole week, which raised the troop's spirits a little despite the demoralizing retreat.

I didn't see Hub until two days later. He sent someone to fetch me from the conference room that we had set up in the aviary. It was dotted with blue and red parrots, some of whom learned to say 'Heil' and 'Hitler' (one even said 'All over for Hitler', after which political questions were asked of the officers' cadre, and the unpatriotic parrot ended up in the cooking pot). As I walked past them now, the birds all looked at me, presenting their beaks like rifles, mute as fishes.

He was waiting outside the door, wreathed in cigarette smoke. It was still early. We didn't exchange any greeting. Without a word he turned, pulled up the collar of his coat and marched off, leaving me no choice but to follow him. We crossed the wintry zoo in silence, skirted the ice-covered swan pond and climbed a wooded hill, at which point I realized that Hub was heading for the wolf house, which was situated some distance from the main buildings. No soldiers were quartered here, since the wolf house was nothing more than a large, windowless log cabin into which the pack could withdraw when their enclosure got too cold or too windy for them.

My official car, the much-missed Opel Olympia, was parked outside the fence. Containing Grishan, in one form or another, so I thought. But as we approached, it was two SS men who leapt out of it and saluted. Hub nodded to them, spat his dog-end into the snow and said that he and I would go in alone. They were to wait outside the door. They would rather have waited in the car, you could tell.

The slight trembling in my hands told me that my assessment of what was going on here was correct.

One of the men fumbled with the gate to the enclosure, opened it, and let Hub in. In two strides he reached the wolf house, where he threw open the door and turned slightly towards me with a cool gesture of invitation. I went in first.

The darkness that surrounded us and the astringent smell of wolf urine took my breath away. Hub pressed the light switch and a bare bulb flickered into life above our heads. On the far side of the cabin, Grishan was cowering on the dirt floor, squeezing himself into a corner. He was tied up, his ankles bound with a belt and his hands fettered in front of his stomach. His index and middle fingers were missing their nails.

' "Now the bird is on the lime",' Hub grunted.

'What's going on?'

'The bird who's been laughing at us.'

At that moment, I knew the torture had done no good.

The things Grishan knew about me were still ensconced behind his swollen left eye, which looked like it had been painted on linden wood by the anonymous Meister der Erasmusmarter, and through which he could barely see me. All that remained of his right eye was pulp and scurf.

'He laughed at us,' Hub said. 'When you were taking care of Ev, he was laughing. Whenever you were out of the house, he went to her, and he laughed and laughed.'

'Let him go,' I said in a flat voice.

'A husband's friend says to him, "Hey, I hear your wife is really good in bed!" "Well," he replies, "some say she is, some say she isn't." '

His laugh was throaty and bitter, it wasn't a laugh at all.

'This isn't you, Hub. You're not in your right mind.'

'The bird confessed it all.'

I told Hub what I thought of him torturing my defender, my shield, my faithful squire, and beating our unfaithful sister. He apologized, said how ashamed he was of what he'd done to Ev. Then he took three paces over to Grishan and drove the heel of his boot into his face. My driver spat a tooth out onto the floor, swung his upper body back to a vertical position, and radiated dignity. Even in Khalakhalnya, when he had strangled or garrotted or suffocated traitors with one of the chamois leather cloths in the stables, I am sure he accomplished it with the greatest decency and dignity that an executioner can have.

I told my brother to leave off. He'd had his fun. I would deal with Grishan.

'No, Koja, wait for the lime.'

'You wanted to be a pastor once, Hub. Let's stop this.'

But Hub merely gave me a smile that I had never seen before, and walked over to the opposite side of the log cabin. He unbarred the heavy, creaking wooden door and opened it slowly, revealing the snow-covered enclosure, the brown paths that the wolves had trodden through it and the wolves themselves, unmoving, like carved bluegrey granite sculptures in this fenced-off world that they didn't quite understand. That uncertainty was the only thing you could see in their motionless, staring eyes. Hub went over to a little table, picked up an enamel bowl that I hadn't noticed before, squatted down with it in front of Grishan and began to declaim softly:

' "Now the bird is on the lime; he flaps and flaps but cannot fly." '

'What is that?' I asked.

' "A black tomcat comes creeping slow, his claws are sharp, his eyes aglow. Up and up the tree he climbs . . ." '

He paused, holding the bowl aloft in his right hand as if about to tip the contents over Grishan's head.

' ". . . towards the birdy on the lime." '

I watched the fingers of his left hand reach into the bowl and take out a sirloin from a Khalakhalnya cow, dripping with blood.

'Don't do this,' I said through gritted teeth.

' "The birdy thinks: Alack the day, the cat will eat me anyway. And though I cannot use my wings, I still have time to sit and sing." '

He dropped the steak into Grishan's lap.

' "And twitter as I used to do." '

'Wake up, will you? This is sick!'

' I like that birdy's attitude, ' Hub whispered. Then he got up and put the bowl down in a corner, quietly, so as not to frighten the wolves.

Grishan leant to one side and drew a face in the dust with one of his injured fingers, a circle with a line for a nose, an upturned curve of a mouth and finally two little commas to represent closed eyelids. The face of someone sleeping, dreaming, the dream of a life or a death.

'Are you coming?' Hub asked, one hand on the door handle; the first wolf had already lowered its head and taken a tentative, lurking step towards us.

'I'm coming,' I said, and only swung my fist back at the very last moment, just as I'd been taught. Hub slid down the door with an expression of immense surprise on his face. The second blow broke something, his nose I think, and he began to fight back. Then we both went at each other with our fists.

At some point I realized that the SS men were standing over us. And then there was a wolf looking on at very close quarters. Hub shouted at them all to fuck off, which the SS men obediently did, while the wolf left only after snapping up the steak from Grishan's lap. Then my brother was straddling me and hitting me in the face again and again with the flat of his hand, and I couldn't go on, and I wished he was dead. And then I screamed at him that I loved Ev and that it was all my fault and that I was the one who had dishonoured him, but never, never Grishan, who had nothing but honour in his heart. I screamed all this out, and Hub left off hitting me, like a man completely saturated with pain. It was only Meyer and Murmelstein that I did not scream about, and of course my daughter Anna, my little point of light at the end of the tunnel that was this life.

And then I fell silent, and by now all the wolves had come into their house and were standing around us, a mesmerized audience, quiet and reserved, and one of them licked some blood off the floor that might have come from Grishan or me or possibly Hub.

Hub nodded pensively.

'So, that's it, then,' he said in a mild tone, and I could no longer see any trace of madness in his eyes.

Then my brother unbuttoned his holster, drew his Walther PPK and put a single bullet in Grishan's forehead. First, his body was catapulted back against the wooden wall, and then it slumped forward into the dust, his head landing right in the middle of the dreaming face.

16

Mama arrived by train in April. It was almost two years since I'd last seen her. She looked more hawk-like than ever, and her face also seemed to be turning into Papa's: she had developed the cleft lip that was really his, and his yawn as well.

She had stopped weeping, regarding it as a bad habit. And perhaps all these outward reminiscences of Papa (she was also growing the exact same two liver spots by her left cheekbone – simply, I think, because she wanted to) gave her the sense that he was back with her. She would never have thought of leaving Posen herself, for she had always drawn strength from her daily walks to his grave. She spent at least half an hour chatting to him every day, for preference in the French they had once spoken at the Tsar's court, or in Russian, for she missed Russian things. By contrast, Mama did not like the Latvians at all, and never had: she thought them proles and curs, horny-handed peasants, and that was one more reason not to come back to Riga.

But Hub had asked her. Telepathically. Telephonically. And in letters that were at first signed 'Hubsi' and then, later, 'Hubsikin'. Mama was needed. Ev had gone back to work, this time at the Wehrmacht hospital. Which meant that for one thing, someone had to take care of Anna. And for another, someone had to take care of Ev.

All contact between my siblings and me was broken off. Hubsikin now addressed me with the formal 'Sie'. When we attended meetings together, he would give everyone his hand, including me. But he never actually shook my hand. He extended a slack, seal-like flipper, as if challenging me to crush it, just as I had crushed everything else that was his.

I grew accustomed to not moving a muscle in my hand, either, and we greeted one another like two drowned men washed together by a heavy swell. Afterwards, I always cleaned the corpse-poison from my fingers.

The only evidence that our colleagues saw of this broken relationship was my compulsive washing, and the curious indulgence with which Hub treated me, a lenient and perfectly correct attitude beneath which there lay no tension, just as there was no tension in his hand.

Glutton Girgensohn, Teich the professional dwarf, and Slowcoach Handrack retuned the antennae of their loyalty once news of our fight in the wolf house got out. And of course, it was also peculiar for two brothers to be on such formal terms. Though admittedly, Hub required everyone to use that form of address with him. You know yourself, my dear Swami, what happened here when you called my brother '*du*': he stood over there by the door and called you a pansy, in case you'd forgotten.

Möllenhauer was the only one who backed me to the hilt, in part because I was the only one who would overlook the Saturnalias with barmen or limber rent boys that might otherwise have cost him his head. All the others showed me a friendly face, but then carefully hid themselves away in the small, dark cracks in the walls, nothing but lizards.

Of course, Mama quickly noticed that something fundamental was wrong. No red autumn Calville, no delicious apple cake, no games evening could disguise it. With bottomless dismay, she came to realize that Ev and Hub and Hub and I and Ev and I were ourselves the dark clouds that she wanted to drive away from us. She even threatened to leave Riga again and go back to Papa in Posen, who never argued with her, or with anyone else (she was very glad that Jeremias von Otten-klonk and Peter Johannson were lying either side of him, no ladies were buried there, thank goodness, and both these gentlemen were highly educated and companionable). To encourage her to stay, Hub gave her the best room in his villa, namely the former master bedroom, now entirely refurbished: the defiled bed hacked to pieces, the horrified walls painted and covered in Papa's pictures and sketches – the patriotic ones, that is (Teutonic knights on their black steeds, galloping across the ice of Lake Peipus, that sort of thing).

But Mama was still suffering from Papa-sickness, and in late spring my brother therefore started organizing spectral family Sundays, when we sometimes went to Jugla as we had done in ancient times, and stayed in the old dacha (now rented by Hub) that Papa had loved so dearly. Perhaps Hub also chose it because there was not a single room there in which Ev and I had ever had intercourse.

Of course, Hub could not address me as '*Sie*' in Jugla. Instead, he fastidiously avoided addressing me at all. At the dinner table it wasn't too obvious, since he could just say, 'Might I have the salt, please?' It was more difficult when Mama played *Skat* with the three of us, but he navigated the problem with a form of politesse used by Fredrick the Great: 'May *he* lay the first card!'

It was striking how considerate and tender he was with Ev; something you could tell just from the fact that he never wore his uniform in her presence. And she was working hard to create an intimacy with him that never seemed false to me, only strained, though it was also needy. They were both wonderfully kind to little Anna, and once, when she was bitten by a gander, Hub was the first to rush over and blow on the graze.

I did everything I could not to send Ev any kind of signal, not even a signal of my concern. I actually tried to think of Anna as my brother's child, and to convince myself that Ev had lied to me. I was certain she hadn't, but I tried to convince myself all the same. Nothing is more dependable than doubt. In the face of the catastrophe that hung over us all, I tried to bury everything I had ever felt for her in a deep pit, as the Romans buried their treasure when the Teutons were advancing on them.

On one of these Sundays at the start of June I brought Maya with me, just for Mama's sake.

For weeks, Maya had tried to honour my wishes and keep a respectful distance, but that arrangement fell apart the evening she arrived at my Kaiserwald villa to give her usual report, rang the bell for five minutes, spent another five hammering on the locked door, and finally climbed in through the open kitchen window to find me not sitting behind my desk but lying on the living-room floor in a puddle of urine that contained at least three parts of alcohol per thousand, and a quantity of my own blood. When I woke up the next morning, I had been washed and rubbed with ointment, and was lying in bed. Maya was lying next to me, and we talked and cried until, two hours later, she tentatively climbed on top of me, slid slowly down, took my penis in one hand and guided it to the place where, four years earlier, it had been exactly right.

Oh, Mama was delighted to meet my 'little girlfriend'," as she called her. Russian conversation always cheered her up. She took Maya to her bosom at once, in part because of the Turgenev poems, of which Maya knew so many.

It was strange to be in Jugla with her. I sat under the yew tree at the knock-kneed table, watching the budding branches cast a shadow that had once fallen on Mary-Lou. And now it fell on Maya. The whole garden was still full of that old Mary-Lou summer. I wouldn't have been too surprised if Monopoly dollars had dropped out of the sky and Papa, tethered to the apple tree, had made a grab for them, to the sound of angry yelling from my brother and sister. All summers are alike. When it's warm, you don't miss those who are lost or dead. You just don't want to die yourself.

Despite the sunshine and no matter how hot it got, Maya wore a high-necked dress with long sleeves that came down over her wrists. A scarf hid the scars on her neck. Only her slashed face with its clown grin was bare and visor-less, and wanted my face or my hand or something of mine to use as a shield between my family and her torment. I failed to shield her from my mother, however, who thought herself a good apothecary and spoke to Maya a great deal about inner beauty.

But I loved her scars, every one of them. I could have looked at them all day, those imprints of the human cruelty and malice that my beloved had survived, just as my beloved had survived me. In this garden that blossomed with memories, that was exactly how she seemed: she was a survivor, who clothed herself in the fabrics of a normal person so that she wouldn't be recognized as such – but she was so beautiful. The beauties of the mind, as extolled by Mama, were only to be seen in Maya. Unlike Ev, she didn't have much that would be found interesting at an opera ball or a literary salon, and yes, perhaps even in that proud garden. But when I lay beside her at night and looked at the river delta that had been flogged into her white back, and the lines on her cheeks where no downy hair grew for me to lick – then she was my Queequeg, my harpooner and cannibal from *Moby-Dick*, whose cheeks had also frightened a fair few people. And I became her Ishmael, a name that she invoked after I had read the book aloud to her, for Ishmael was the only survivor of the *Pequod*'s encounter with the whale, and she prayed every evening that I would be her sole survivor, for then there would be two of us.

In Riga, Maya had become my closest colleague.

I couldn't see it clearly at the time, but she effectively replaced Grishan and became the bridge between me and the Russian activists, just as he had been, the bridge to their cosmology in any case (in metaphysical terms), for it is important that Russians regard a superior as a human being.

Nobody mentioned Grishan's disappearance. It was *not mentioned* in such a way that it became obvious the disappearance had been noticed and was making everyone fearful. But they accepted it, in the way you accept an avalanche when you're in the mountains; it was only to be expected. Even Möllenhauer pretended there had been no predecessor to my new driver, who was not a new driver at all but an old one: the Drinker. And the Drinker behaved as though we were still in Bessarabia. A human life didn't count for much, and the life of a Russian was a Russian life, and therefore nothing at all.

Maya knew that. It might have been why she was so conscientious, so efficient and so very standoffish at work – dismissive, even – always giving off an air of hardness and unapproachability, just like a harpooner.

It was only in the unfamiliar waters of Jugla that she was the one harpooned, a miraculous whale. Hub treated her with a hostile courtesy; his contempt was barely noticeable. Like Mary-Lou, she was not exactly perfect, racially speaking, though of course nor was Ev, and little Anna certainly wasn't, either: she wasn't even Hub's Aryan daughter, but the Aryan daughter of his sister, who wasn't even his Aryan sister.

My brother, of course, didn't have the slightest idea about any of that.

This is the strange thing about the paranoid secret-service life: having useful knowledge that other people don't have – and the power that you feel this knowledge gives you – drives you into the cold. At that time, I wanted to retain this pleasant chill forever, at least with Hub. I never wanted him to discover the whole truth – and if he hadn't, it would have saved a lot of people's lives.

*

Our commando moved out of the zoological gardens a few weeks later (taking one of the delicious tapirs with us, a rare treat), and was relocated to Riga-Strand. Here, we resurrected the spy school in two former spa hotels, and transformed a Jugendstil villa into our staff building. And every third day, at the start of the mission briefing, when Hub had thrust his dead flipper into mine and listened to the reports from subordinates in ominous silence, he would ask why Joseph Stalin still wasn't dead.

His venom was directed at me.

In fact, I had been hard at work, pressing ahead towards our 'Finest Hour'. Nothing else provided more of a lasting distraction from Grishan's shattered skull (and the dark dreams he seemed to have bequeathed to me, which I was now dreaming in his place) than the pure and inspiring preparation for an assassination. I imagined its perfect composition, artistic in the best sense; ideas lit up in me like stained-glass church windows, and in my imagination a stream of colours and explosions shaped itself into a Sistine Chapel of terror, as Michelangelo might have seen it before he ever picked up a brush. I had not only goodwill but a sum of four million Reichsmarks at my disposal, approved by Himmler himself – a fortune, enough to equip half a tank brigade.

But of course, creativity has nothing to do with money. Creativity is first and foremost the joy of association, of changing perspectives, overstepping boundaries – in other words, it has to do with the plasticity of the brain, and my brain (not yet hindered by a bullet, of course, but you know that) stretched a surprising distance to come up with the perfect legend for our saviour, super-activist Piotr Politov. His legend was the creative core of the whole operation, a core that I and only I could create, just as Dalí created Surrealist art from his mad dreams.

In the end, I decided to go all-in. After weighing up the options, it seemed best to transform Politov into a gold-plated artillery major. He should be a hero of the Soviet Union, a comrade whose heroic deeds had got him injured on several occasions, and who was now assigned to a front-line army corps and tasked with the procurement of lorries and canon. This mission gave him the ability to travel all over the interior of the Soviet Union, to use accommodation set aside for visiting officers and – for as long as his poor state of health allowed – to stop off in Moscow without arousing more than the usual level of suspicion.

Politov and his Shilova would reach the Soviet capital by motor-bike following a secret parachute drop (unnoticed and under cover of night – I had already conjured up a detailed image of it all on my canvas, I was a Canaletto of conspiracy). They would then proceed to the apartment occupied by our Joseph Commando. From there, with the support of activists Over and Out, Politov would spend the weeks that followed assessing the situation, finding out the times at which Stalin appeared in public and working out how to get as close as possible to the dictator's vital organs.

So much for my rose period.

To facilitate Politov's own creative response to the situation, Glutton Girgensohn equipped him with all kinds of artistic tools. He was given poison darts, a sub-machine gun, an army pistol, two hand grenades, a limpet mine with a remote detonator, and the 'tank breaker' we had seen in Berlin, for getting through the official armoured car that took Stalin to the Kremlin every morning, as the Josephists had informed us.

The painting was very colourful, but it would only make an impact on the course of art history if the reality could match up to my imagination. The Achilles heel was the long period of time, potentially several days, between our agents being set down in Soviet territory and reaching the apartment in Moscow.

To keep the risk as small as humanly possible, everyone else in my artist's studio had to work with absolute precision.

It was Möllenhauer's task to get hold of all the uniform items, medals, weapons and transportation for the spy to end all spies, and – most importantly – enough cash to last him for several years: one million, two hundred thousand roubles (in five and ten chervonets notes), fifteen thousand roubles painted into a savings book, a thousand US dollars, and five hundred English pounds.

Captain Palbyzin's speciality was making genuine-looking documents and stamps, which he produced to an impressive standard in our workshop. The masterful hand of Palbyzin (a true da Vinci of personal identity papers) created Politov's pay book, his marching orders to Moscow, thirty blank sets of marching orders, food stamps, leave passes, his party membership card, an NKVD-SMERSH ID, three field-hospital discharge sheets (filled in), various bits of certification relating to his injuries, and one hundred and eight rubber stamps covering all the relevant military units, field hospitals and authorities.

Captain Palbyzin also taught Politov to write in different styles, so that, graphically, he became five different Politovs. He taught him the quirks of various administrative procedures and above all, the bureaucratic details of producing identity papers.

And finally Captain Pavel Delle, our reliable rapist, trained Politov in all classes of weaponry, as well as close combat and the use of the complicated 'tank breaker', which seemed the most realistic option for transforming Joseph Stalin into, as you might say, the image of him I most longed to see.

Since the chosen colour palette of Politov's legend – the one I had dreamed up – called for him to be a badly wounded war hero, I needed forgery in this respect, too, or rather: mimicry.

I therefore went to Politov, with whom I had developed an excellent relationship since acting as witness to his marriage, and explained the principle to him. Just as defenceless hoverflies (I began) are very convincing mimics of the European honeybee, in their flight, their buzzing and their warning livery (I went on), and in this way avoid being eaten by birds (I added for the sake of clarity), so he, my dear friend Activist Politov, must adopt an insect's camouflage in respect of his alter ego's crucial war wounds. Politov gave me an earnest and manly nod, but he didn't have a clue what I was getting at. I sometimes express myself in a rather complicated way, dear Swami. People who are not well-disposed towards me call it inflated. And so I tried again with Politov, using a different kind of clarity. I explained that the Führer and Reich Chancellor had decided to send him – the Russian who was to save Europe from the Bolshevik menace – into enemy territory disguised as a cripple.

'Wery good, sir!' Politov said obediently.

And in order to make this disguise as convincing as possible, I went on, the best surgeons in Riga's military hospital were going to break one of his thigh bones under anaesthetic and pin it back together incorrectly to make a convincing cripple of him.

'Wery good, sir!'

I was pleased that he took it so well. And so I immediately added that they were also contemplating a club foot, because a club foot generally looked very effective.

'Wery good, sir! And how Agent Politov quick dash again, after?'

'Dash?' I asked.

'Dash,' he reaffirmed. 'Quick, quick. Dash.'

He ran very fast down the corridor and back up, to show me what he meant, and I recalled that as a young man he had been a local athletics champion.

I could hardly tell him that there would be no more dashing once his mission was accomplished. It seemed self-evident that he would die a Russian martyr for the SS and Adolf Hitler – or to my mind, let's say, for humanity. Politov was the only one who seemed oblivious to the notion. And no one told him.

The principal drawback to my beautiful painting was that, for the crucial moment after the attack, the paints ran out. There was not even the beginning of a rescue strategy, an escape route, no plan of action whatever for Herr and Frau Politov, however fanciful (apart from shooting or poisoning themselves, or blowing themselves up, something along those lines). And to me, such a thing would have seemed ridiculous. Because whether the mission failed or hit the bull's-eye, the operation itself would inevitably end with the capture of the brave secret-agent duo – and ultimately, therefore, with torture and death.

So when Politov asked about his post-operative dashing prospects, I didn't explain to him that his chances of survival as an assassin were zero – though perhaps I should have done, given that he had said himself he didn't want children, just to die for Adolf Hitler. But he was still panting so handsomely from his short sprint, and he was such a vital, attractive athlete, a man in the rudest of health, that I couldn't bring myself to do it. And so I merely spoke in ominous tones of the animal kingdom, where the species that has no or insufficient camouflage is doomed to extinction.

But Politov resisted the idea of becoming an insect with all his might.

'It puts that death-defying courage in a rather different light,' Möllenhauer sighed sheepishly at our crisis meeting.

'Yes,' the professional dwarf snapped back, 'Activist Politov will never, ever be prepared to sacrifice his life if he finds it so difficult to sacrifice his leg.'

But there was no going back now. The Red Army had already regained control of all former Soviet territory, had invaded Estonia and the former Poland, and was threatening the borders of Latvia.

On our nights together, which all the drudgery and the approach of midsummer were combining to shorten, Maya told me that the mood had changed in Operation Zeppelin. Many of her countrymen were trying to get themselves recruited as double agents by the Soviet underground, which was all-powerful even in Riga – it was the only way to escape certain death if the Allies triumphed. Everyone could feel the dusk descending, the coming *finis*. But we all pretended we were standing in bright sunlight. By day, Maya and I managed to evade the choking sensation by concentrating on our mission. And in the evenings, we focused on each other's arms, hands and fingers (especially the fingers!), our sounds, scents and tongues, and on every last spark of strength, with an immense tenderness that was both impossible to escape and much too soft to give us anything to cling to.

Sometimes Maya would cry out in the night or talk in her sleep, and her Ishmael would lie beside her, overflowing with her pain, while the vast sea whispered outside.

Following protracted negotiations and substantial persuasion on my part, Politov reluctantly agreed to some cosmetic procedures on his flesh, if not his bones. The plastic surgeons performed several operations to give him deep wounds in the kidney area, and a few scars on his face and the backs of his hands. His legend (shrapnel entry and exit wounds in the hypogastric region) would seem plausible under a superficial medical examination. An X-ray, however, would be the end of him.

The final element of his medical preparation was performed by the dentist, who fitted a screw-in metal cap with the obligatory cyanide capsule hidden inside. On no account was Politov to be taken alive by the NKVD. He understood this, and asked the dentist to put a gold crown on his incisor while he was there. He thought it looked rather swish.

Six weeks later, Politov's training was complete. His artificial scars had healed. He was capable of driving any Russian motor vehicle, had mastered the motorbike (a custom-built model), could lay booby traps and knew, in the words of Captain Delle, 'everything there is to know about poisoning and hanging a person, and throwing them off a moving train'.

Natasha Shilova's basic, special and radio training was also at an end. But Maya seemed dissatisfied. Her student was unstable, she told me, with no willpower and little resilience. Shilova had been sick on the plane to Berlin, Maya said, and she would be sick on the plane to Moscow, and she would be sick every single day she was there; if Stalin were to appear in front of her, she would be sick all over him rather than shoot him.

'Are you saying she's a dead loss?'

'Well, she's in love.'

'That's no excuse.'

'Being in love is no excuse?'

'No, it's a serious character flaw.'

She turned to me, her bare chest rising and falling, and her eyes sprang into mine, which was always how it felt when she looked at me, as if her eyes were bouncing into me like rubber balls, and I had no defence against them.

'What we are doing to her frightens me,' she said gently, laying her head on my chest. I stroked her hair.

'We shouldn't think too much about it.'

'I know.'

'This is war.'

'Maybe we could go to America,' she said after a little while.

'What makes you think that?'

'America is taking a lot of people in. Pavel Delle says Roosevelt wants every Russian who is against Stalin.'

'So, Pavel Delle says that, does he?'

She raised her head.

'Yes, but you won't punish him for it, will you?'

'Why should I?'

'He also said that, if we lose, Stalin will force Churchill to hand us all over. I'm very curious.'

'If you weren't so sweet, I could quite easily have you shot. You mustn't say these things, my love.'

'You don't think about what will happen later, do you?'

'What do you mean by later? When Stalin is dead?'

'Oh darling. Let's make love.'

The first attempt to drop Politov and his wife into Russia was made in mid-June nineteen forty-four, but it was unsuccessful. The plane encountered heavy flak, was forced to turn round and had trouble with its landing gear on the way back, a problem that looked like the result of sabotage. On the turbulent flight, Shilova's stomach filled two bread bags (right to the top).

Preparations for the next attempt required several days, which meant that most of the officers were able to take leave. Mama invited us all to the summer estate of Baron Otto Grotthus, one of her former admirers. He turned out to be a merry widower; feeling homesick, he was one of the few old Livonians who had managed to get special permission to return to Latvia and his ancestral seat of Spahren.

From the moment the Baron met us outside his country house, he made practically every noun he uttered into a diminutive, asking the men-*chen* to please walk this way to the guest room-*chen* and leave their suitcase-*chen* there and then just relax and take a break from the war-*chen*. And so we had a final summer holiday, though the freshness we expected in the countryside vanished by mid-morning, as the temperature reached North African levels. Five years after the nineteen thirty-nine 'summer of the century', you could once again see the forests burning on the horizon at night, and when you stepped outside, your feet would send up a cloud of dust that smelled of bitter almonds, from the jasmine that had just finished flowering.

My family assembled, internally shattered but otherwise convivial, in the shade on the two verandas. Hands or seal-flippers were shaken, and Hub's lurking eyes followed my every move.

I saw Ev unsupervised just once, in the only place where we could meet alone: the latrine out in the picturesque setting of the estate woods.

She was just opening the wooden door and stepping out, still smoothing her dress down over her thighs, when I stopped abruptly three metres in front of her. For one shocked moment, we both froze. A thread of bashfulness spun out between our pupils. She seemed embarrassed that I was about to set eyes on her excrement, and I was embarrassed that she knew I was all too willing to do so. She was wearing light-coloured cotton, and there was a film of perspiration on her face. She had never liked the heat, since it made her eyes seem to protrude more, and her breathing was shallower, too, though perhaps there was another reason for that now. Making an uncertain gesture, she said that it was very hot – probably just for the sake of saying something. Yes, I replied, that's true. Some of those strawberries with soured milk would be perfect right now, she said hastily, they were the best strawberries you could imagine (that was true, too), and Baron Grotthus was so nice.

'Yes,' I said. 'You look good.'

For a while she said nothing more, and the space between us grew until it felt like distance, and then she said, in a changed voice, 'Do take care, Koja. He means to destroy you.'

She walked away quickly.

Later, she handed me a dish of those fabulous strawberries (I counted each one of them, and I still believe she gave me more than Hub).

That evening, Maya asked vaguely how I felt about my sister. I didn't reply, because I had never told her anything. She just nodded. I think Maya was one of those people who know that the essential thing is not what you say, but what you don't.

I was allowed to play with little Anna to my heart's content. And from this, I knew that my brother didn't suspect a thing. She was almost a year old now, and was admired for every tiny step she took. She could say three words: 'Mama', 'Anna' and 'dan'; 'dan' meant tank. I rolled around with Anna on the lakeshore, put snails on her little belly, wrapped her in my bathing robe (she shouted with glee) and taught her the fourth word she ever learned: 'Papa'.

When she was sleeping in her cot in the garden, beneath a turquoise parasol, I drew her eyes.

And later, when I showed the drawings to my mother, she took her glasses, held them in front of her hawkish face, brought the paper up close and cried, 'So, little Anna looks like you, my poppet!'

Hub didn't hear that.

Before darkness fell, I liked to take a walk along the whole length of Spahren Lake, to the south side. Like most Russians, Maya hated taking walks and regarded hiking as an indignity. I therefore mostly went alone.

One evening, with the Saharan heat still humming in the ground (I could feel it smouldering through the thin soles of my canvas shoes), I sat down on the bank despite all the midges and watched the sun setting behind the reeds, and just then a strange noise started up all around the lake. Squinting, I discerned a kind of movement, as if the air were trembling, and then I saw that thousands upon thousands of dragonflies were shedding their larva skins, almost all at once. As they broke through the skin they made a noise that sounded like a crowd whispering, and in my mind's eye there appeared the image of the insect that has to camouflage itself to avoid being eaten – and then hundreds of shimmering green, translucent, well-camouflaged insects flew up to surround a man who almost disappeared in their midst, although he fancied that in a few days' time he was going to change the course of world history.

17

My mother is exactly as the Hippy imagined her.

The first thing she does is to find out whether he is related to any of the great European royal dynasties, because then he would, so to speak, automatically be related to her. But of course, that isn't the case.

The Hippy tells her at once that he is from lower-middle-class stock, and from Upper Bavaria on top of that, and that his father killed himself. No one ever lacks for a good reason to do away with himself, Mama says drily; and that reminds her of her nephew twice removed, Nicholas de Staël, who was a few years younger than me, and whom I don't think she ever met, and whose paintings she also thought dreadful, like everything else about him apart from his none-too-close familial relationship to her. But she does respect the fact that he threw himself off the terrace of his studio in Antibes, because Antibes is one of Mama's favourite towns.

She tells me how Hub is doing, that he is comfortable and has a nice cellmate, and she asks me if the Hippy is a murderer or a rapist or just a good-for-nothing.

Curiously, she doesn't address this question to the Hippy himself, though he is lying a metre away behind her, and is now indignant for a variety of reasons. She has completely ignored the distance and the no-go zone that the Hippy has deliberately created between our beds, and is sitting quite comfortably exactly halfway between us.

No, I say, Herr Basti wouldn't hurt a fly, he is a swami and has a highly spiritual disposition.

Ah, well then, he's probably a common fraud, Mama says with a friendly smile. I suspect she no longer quite understands the difference between prison and hospital. She forgets which of her sons is accommodated where, for what reason and for how long. But for a ninety-five-year-old, Mama is still impressively virile. She looks like Sitting Bull, her back ramrod straight when she sits down; she does use a walking stick, but she can move quite nimbly with it, even on soft ground. She doesn't live in a nursing home; she is still in her little flat in Nuremberg, which is stuffed full of everything she was able to rescue from the Baltics. She is sure she will live to be at least a hundred, because all her female ancestors who died a natural death (which admittedly wasn't many of them) reached biblical ages.

My mother asks me how I am.

'We were just talking about Spahren.'

'Pardon me?'

I lean over and switch her hearing aid on.

'WE WERE JUST TALKING ABOUT SPAHREN. SPAHREN, NINETEEN FORTY-FOUR. DO YOU REMEMBER?'

'Ah, Grotthus, the old rascal. Those were splendid strawberries.'

'IT WAS INCREDIBLY HOT THAT SUMMER.'

'It was incredibly hot that summer. Goodness me, it was hot. And little Anna was such a tiny thing. The two of you played so nicely together by the lake. I still have the drawings you did of her then. You learned a lot from Papa, but you were never too good at children. But then they are so difficult, because they don't have any angles. It was incredibly hot that summer.'

I can't speak.

'What a shame,' says Mama then, 'that little Anna died so young.'

The Hippy leaves me in peace. It is hours since Mama left, and he is still leaving me in peace. When Mama comes to visit, she almost always talks about Anna. How often have I asked her not to.

I want her to stop visiting.

How often have I asked her.

She left a scarf here. By accident. And as usual, a tin of home-made almond biscuits.

I'm sure Hub has one, too.

Manna from heaven.

How small your fingers were, smaller than the rain.

Not a day passes.

My little, little girl.

18

To commemorate the third anniversary of our invasion of the Soviet Union, Baron Grotthus loaded champagne-*chen*, glass-*chens* and the Solm-*chens* in festive mood into his horse-drawn carriage, and drove us out to Lake Usma, a large lake fed by the Courland swamps, which turn it a peaty brown. We swam in the murky water to cool off and escape from the flies, and towards midday we saw a lone motorcyclist rattling out of the pine forest towards our lakeside dune. Just before he reached us, his wheels got stuck in a sandy hollow; the bike threatened to topple sideways, and in order to prevent this he was forced to jump off while keeping both hands on the monster's handlebars, like a helpless torero taking a bull by the horns. His steel helmet fell to the ground.

Hub trudged over to him, annoyed at the intrusion and wearing nothing but dark blue swimming trunks held up with braces. Faced with the task of picking up his helmet, giving the prescribed salute, stopping his motorcycle from falling over and handing Hub the urgent telegram all at the same time, the motorcyclist froze, and my brother retrieved the telegram himself (left-hand breast pocket, it took a little while).

This was how the news reached us that the Red Army – who loved timing their operations to coincide with jubilees – also intended to commemorate the third anniversary of our invasion of the Soviet Union. Early that morning, they had mounted an ostentatious memorial offensive along the whole length of the front line, overrunning our positions and crushing everything that stood in their way. They had 3.7 times the personnel we did, 9.4 times the artillery, 23 times the tanks, 3.6 times the assault rifles and 10.5 times the planes, and with every elegant stroke that Ev swam far out in the lake, fifty German soldiers died.

Before we set off for Riga and our units, we drank a toast to the hospitable Baron (three months later, the Soviets burned his house down with him inside). And then we listened as Hub proposed a toast to this momentous day, marking its significance with the fanatical radiance of his face, but also, unfortunately, with his ridiculous bathing trunks. At my side, Maya let out one small giggle. She was only giggling, I am certain, because something had tickled her at that sulphur-coloured moment, probably one of my secret fingers – but I can't remember. The only thing I can recall now is the look Hub shot her: it came back to me later, after everything that followed. Only then did it seem to acquire a meaning, and to be black as pitch.

Twelve weeks passed between that twenty-second of June and the final assault on Riga. Twelve weeks that even a Buddhist like yourself with no interest in world history and temporal dimensions – a man filled with empathy for all creatures that are born into suffering – would describe as a radical act of creation: at the end of those twelve weeks, one million German soldiers had to be reborn.

Meanwhile, Operation Zeppelin was at a standstill. All flights were banned until further notice. Politov couldn't fly to Moscow now. He had to watch his target sitting in the Kremlin, in the best of health, while the German supermen he so loved fled like rabbits. Shilova saw him trembling on the couch in the mornings, racked by sobs. Every day Stalin's troops advanced another twenty kilometres towards Riga. There was no panic yet; you could just feel a dull, silent despair brewing in the streets.

Hub got Mama and Anna Ivanovna onto one of the evacuation ships as soon as he could. They took little Anna with them, and she waved from the upper deck like a good girl while her mother and father (I don't mean myself, of course, I stayed out of sight, far back amid the bustling crowds) stood on the quayside respectively giving free rein to their tears, or hiding them (Hub of course).

Ev had to stay behind. All the Red Cross staff had to stay behind. The sense of immediate danger was nothing new for Ev, who had been in danger all her life, but she had never been so happy about it.

She could hardly wait for the fall of the Third Reich.

Soon we could hear a distant, whispering rumble, barely perceptible at first but coming steadily closer: the front. Since my Russians and I were the only unit still stationed at Riga Strand, I was made Kampfkommandant, in charge of defending the area.

I most certainly did not want to be a Kampfkommandant. The day after my nonsensical promotion, the Red Army's 1st Baltic Front broke through to the coast south of us, cutting off the route back to the Reich for thirty German divisions. We were sitting in a mousetrap. In the fragile, faded surroundings of my sleeping-beauty spa hotel I had to gee up two hundred Russian traitors (all of them horrified and in fear of their lives) by providing them with guns, ammunition and cyanide capsules. Only the deserted Tuckumer Woods, twenty kilometres wide and composed of unreliable pines with little undergrowth for cover, separated our high-class bathing resort from the Soviet lines.

Glutton Girgensohn suddenly began grovelling to God Almighty in his room every morning, while Möllenhauer was fucked every night by a little brown-haired Turkmen chap, to which no one could have remained oblivious: during the act, my life-loving adjutant appealed loudly to the exact same deity. Slowcoach Handrack even asked me to put an immediate stop to these undignified bacchanals, but he could go to hell. I claimed that Möllenhauer, a morally impeccable officer, was just having Teutonic nightmares.

Our nerves were stretched to breaking point.

If we were taken prisoner, the Russians would send us straight to the eternal hunting grounds.

Hub summoned me to the prefecture.

When I stepped into his office, he was examining his new epaulettes, holding them up to the light like precious artefacts. He had been promoted to Standartenführer with immediate effect, he explained, as if in passing. All of the SS police units in the city were under his command: the Gestapo, the SD and the local police force. I congratulated him politely. In a less dire situation it would have sounded very much like becoming Jesus Christ and Alexander the Great.

He asked me how Politov and Shilova were holding up.

Politov was tense and Shilova did not make a good female agent, I told him.

'What does a good female agent look like, then, Hauptsturmführer?'

'Maya Dzerzhinskaya is a good instructor, at least, and an example to Activist Shilova in every respect, Herr Obersturmbannführer.'

Hub thought about this for a while before recalling that (as of a few minutes ago) he was a Standartenführer, and should be addressed as such. And then he instructed me to assist an SS unit that had flown in from Berlin a few days previously. Their task was to dig up the fifty thousand Jewish corpses we had created in the Bikernieki Forest, to burn them, grind the bones to unrecognizable powder and boil them into jelly, with assistance from the inmates of the Kaiserwald concentration camp, who, when their work was done, were also to go the way of all flesh.

'I'm sorry, Herr Standartenführer, I don't understand.'

'Exhumation.'

'We're digging up the Jews and burning them?'

'You understand me perfectly.'

'And why are we doing that?'

'So that the enemy doesn't find them.'

'I respectfully request to be excused from this operation.'

'Negative. Fall out and get to work.'

For a moment, the image of a woman with no top to her skull and a little baby in her arms flashed before my mind's eye, skeletal briquettes now, which I was supposed to set alight in the Bikernieki Forest and grind to dust, and I told my brother to go and fuck himself.

Hub blinked once, but otherwise I saw no movement in his afternoon-tea face. He stood still for a long while. Then he pressed a button on his desk. A secretary and his adjutant promptly appeared.

'Hauptsturmführer,' Hub said to me solemnly. 'I am now issuing you with a formal warning, in front of witnesses. In light of your achievements with the ongoing special operation against Moscow, I will refrain from repeating the order I've just given.'

'Thank you, Herr Standartenführer.'

'I strongly advise you never to refuse an order again.'

'Very good, sir.'

'If you did, you would have to bear the consequences, including the ultimate punishment. I will tell you this only once, and for one reason only: because I am your brother.'

'Thank you, Herr Standartenführer,' I said, 'for being my brother.'

In the days that followed, an oily ash began to fall from the sky, and I realized that the wind from the east was bringing with it an abominable stench. Along with the smell of the Jewish corpses, which some Hauptsturmführer not burdened with being related to Hub was now dutifully burning, tens of thousands of refugees streamed into the city. Endless queues of people formed outside the offices that were allocating the final berths on ships bound for Germany. In their faces you could see all the colours of desperation (scarlet and begging-red, bile-green and yearning yellow, the fluctuating rosé blush of high blood pressure and, for so many, chalk white, the international colour of surrender).

In our commando, too, there was unrest. A radio operator killed first one of the activists and then herself, we didn't know why. And when Glutton ordered two Ukrainians to investigate a suspicious burrow in our section of the front, they retorted, 'After you!' He and Möllenhauer were struggling to maintain discipline.

In the face of all this, Maya found a courage that I did not see in any of my German colleagues, or among the Russian men. She refused to let anything put her off her stroke; she swam cheerfully out although no land was in sight, that's what I mean by courage. Everyone she encountered was buoyed by her slashed little fox face, just from the way she looked at them. I have never met anyone, not even a swami, who harboured so little hatred. And one evening, as we were sitting side by side on my balcony, kept awake by the distant thunder of the artillery and watching the summer lightning fork and flash on the horizon, I asked her if she could imagine becoming my wife.

She actually clapped her hand to her mouth in a child-like expression of shock. Then she got up, still pressing her hand to her face, went over to the bed, flopped onto it, crept under the covers and pulled them up over her head. I nestled up against her, thinking I might have angered her, because it wasn't a real proposal, no rose, no going down on one knee, nothing really, just a question. But the question made her so happy that she bit my arm, hard. The pain made me groan, and then we had a pillow fight, and because she could well imagine becoming my wife, I let her win.

By the end of August, the battle for Riga seemed imminent. The Army Group Command ordered us to evacuate the majority of German civilians from the city within two weeks, as well as all the female Wehrmacht medical staff.

Some unsettling news reached me, and although it violated the pact of fraternal neutrality, I hurried to the Düna Central Wehrmacht hospital. When I entered the foyer, I saw that it had been transformed into a busy dressing station. Before me lay a red, white and army-grey rag rug of wounded men, who had been transported there straight from the front lines. The place stank of iodine and excrement, and when I finally found my sister outside the operating theatres on the second floor, beside a sack of amputated limbs, she was wearing a blood-stained gown, and I could see she hadn't slept for days. She saw me, but she was turned inward, inside a hard shell of determination that I could not pierce.

'You shouldn't have come, Koja.'

She walked away, and I followed her.

'I hear you've taken yourself off the evacuation lists.'

'He's having the hospital watched.' She stepped into the central admissions area, which, like the foyer, was filled with rows of new arrivals, lying close together and almost all still wearing battle dress. She stopped by the boy who was groaning loudest; a bullet had hit him in the groin and his canvas trousers were saturated with blood. She poured a glass of water from a large carafe and gave him a drink.

'Please reconsider. Please, Ev. You can't imagine what things are going to be like here in a few days. Think of little Anna.'

'The agreement was that we wouldn't meet alone.'

'I know.'

'I'm not leaving. You can see what things are like here.' She put the glass down and dabbed the boy's mouth dry. 'And I have plenty to atone for, you can believe me when I say that.'

She left the injured man and went out. He couldn't speak; he just lay there with his back arched in pain, turned his head to watch her go. I gave him some water too, I have no idea why, perhaps I just wanted to do a good deed for once. But who knows if he even wanted water.

I found Ev in the stairwell. She was leaning against one of the large windows, looking out.

'Why is Hub allowing it?' I asked, moving to stand beside her.

'What?'

'Why is he allowing you to remain in such danger?'

'He can keep an eye on me here.'

She said it without any sarcasm, jutting her chin towards the street. I followed her gaze. In the doorway of the building opposite there stood a Gestapo officer in civilian clothes. He was looking up at us. I had a passing acquaintance with him.

'You have to leave, Ev.'

'No. *You* have to leave. Use the back entrance. He might not have seen you.'

When the attack began, the Soviets unleashed one thousand three hundred tanks on Riga, more than Hitler had scraped together for the whole of France three years earlier. Within a few days, our defence was on the point of collapse. The human and material losses were so devastating that all the music corps were disbanded and the baffled trombonists and horn-blowers (to say nothing of the army bakers) were equipped with hunting rifles, for which there wasn't even any ammunition.

My Riga-Strand division was lucky. The Soviets didn't want to attack through the Tuckumer Woods. The rapidly deteriorating weather – a series of downpours, each following hard on the heels of the last – washed our makeshift defence positions into the sea. Prolonged rainfall turned the trenches into mud baths. Later, mortar rounds landed in our section of the beach, and Captain Palbyzin was cut clean in half like butter (widthways, not lengthways) by shrapnel. That was the end of our forgery workshop. Pleskau Command was pulled out of the front lines and moved to the city centre as an operational reserve unit, stationed in what had once been Horaz High School.

The enemy's might was breathtaking, and it was killing the city. The transport system was paralysed. Offices and shops were barricaded. No one cleared away the huge piles of autumn leaves, and the streets began to rot. From my window, I could see a stream of people fleeing across the great bridge over the Düna, out into nowhere. Old horse-drawn carts and vans, men, women, children and bellowing livestock. Streaming rain; the wind ripping the sky wide open.

This was the end.

The telephone rang in the middle of the night. Emergency call. All officers were to report at once to the prefecture. In battle dress but not ready to march. I let Maya sleep and called my chauffeur, the ever-wakeful Drinker.

As they arrived, everyone looked pale and uneasy.

Hub received us in his fifth-floor office, where all the blackout blinds had been raised. We could see out of the windows, and, standing packed together in the dark room, we had a view over the whole city. I could feel the warmth of the bodies around me, see their silhouettes and hear their breathing. Their faces remained invisible; they smelled of sleep, fear, aftershave, chewing tobacco and musty cotton. Hub had drawn himself up to his full height behind his desk, hands on hips, looking at our shadows. Strangely, by way of greeting, he said, 'Very humid in here, gentlemen!' He turned and opened the window behind him, letting cool autumn air and the background thunder of the artillery into the room. Outside, and not too far off, was a panorama of all the pyrotechnic efforts that precede the taking of a city: explosions, shell strikes, blue threads of smoke, the muzzle flashes from the tanks, the suburbs in flames. And above all that, cherry-blossom clusters of exploding illuminants. Spectacular, it must be said.

Tonight, my brother announced, and then cleared his throat as if he had begun speaking too hastily (a red flare drew an inquisitive arc around his head, looking like it was listening), tonight, given that our city is about to fall, Berlin has decided to make the move on which everything depends. The Führer has just given permission for us to carry out the final attack on Joseph Stalin. The commando will fly to Moscow. As soon as possible. Spilve airfield can only be held for a few more days. All men to battle stations.

I would love to have a word for 'shock mixed with entirely hollow delight'. A word for 'euphoria at avenging Grandpaping, dampened by the prospect of sending a married couple to their certain death' would be welcome, too. But there are no simple words for what I felt in the breathless silence that followed Hub's short speech. All I can tell you is that for a moment I was flooded with pure happiness, pure *at-long-last* happiness, but at the same time it felt stale and tainted.

An author's pride. Or a painter's pride. An artist's pride, in any case. Perhaps that was what won through when I returned to Maya in the early morning. We made love exhaustively, Rembrandt always did the same with his wife before revealing a new painting. Nervous, expectant, pre-exhibition sex. We didn't know what 'ooh's and 'aah's this exhibition would attract.

We had just two days to make the necessary preparations. Palbyzin was keenly missed. The professional dwarf took over the final updates to Politov's papers, but he didn't come close to replacing our halved master forger. Pavel Delle checked over all the weapons, and Möllenhauer managed the logistics. I took Politov to Ulei Cinema, to show him freshly obtained enemy newsreels before he flew out. Politov watched Soviet officers standing on deck, Soviet officers giving artillery orders, Soviet officers reporting to Stalin, Soviet officers horsing about in occupied Kiev, and the peasants and workers of the Soviet

Union blowing kisses to the camera (the female peasants and workers, that is). After absorbing these images for ten minutes, he turned to me and asked if he could watch *Gone With The Wind* while we were there.

'Pleease, Herr Hauptsturm, Politov love Clark Gable, because Clark Gable look like Politov. Because Clark Gable do things like Politov. Because Clark Gable kiss like Politov kiss Shilova.'

I liked Politov as Clark Gable much more than I liked my brother as Clark Gable, I must say (though Hub was much too bald now for such a comparison to enter anyone's mind). And in any case, I needed to ease my conscience a little. I sent Glutton Girgensohn off, and in the space of two hours, in embattled Riga, he managed to turn up the only Latvian copy of that Southern epic with its well-treated slaves. That evening, Politov and his wife sat arm in arm in the cinema stalls. They wept and wept, and so did I, my arms wrapped around Maya in the box. The Tara plantation tormented me; it made me think of Opapabaron's plantations, of Grandpaping's fruit trees, of the red autumn Calville – but still I kept looking over, tear-blind, at the couple I had mortised together.

Slowcoach Handrack took over the job of liaising with Hub, who reported back to Berlin. Perhaps I should have asked myself why my brother accepted a slimy egg-white like Slowcoach (who was really only good for beating) as a liaison officer. Every day he entered the prefecture with the same vacant, bored expression, slouched across the floor in the boots his boy had spent two hours polishing (although Hub regarded marching or striding as the only acceptable methods of conveyance for an SS officer in SS boots) and awaited instruction, never showing any initiative or contributing any ideas of his own – all of which would have been a red rag to Hub. I didn't think too much about this aberration, though; I was glad to be rid of Slowcoach, and downright happy to avoid any direct contact with my brother.

Hub insisted on making Slowcoach my official deputy (his liaison role with my brother suggested greater seniority), but I reassured Glutton that this hierarchy was only for the purposes of the Finest Hour, and not for all the time afterwards.

19

When the day came, it was cool and cloudy. Drizzle was forecast for the evening.

Maya woke me early and brought me ersatz coffee in bed. While I was shaving, she came up behind me and kissed my bare shoulder, without catching my eye in the mirror. As she left the bathroom, I thought I detected a determination in the way she moved, a very slight strangeness in how she held her head. It was confusing, because in the morning there is seldom anything strange between lovers (nor in the evening, just the hours in between). But I was so preoccupied that I forgot it again at once. After we'd breakfasted together, hardly speaking a word, we went to find our agents.

Politov seemed composed. He was sitting in the uniform store in a set of Soviet underwear, eating vast quantities of cherries and spitting the stones across the room into the wastebasket. He never missed. Five of my colleagues were bustling around him, ticking off all the items of equipment, all the medals, guns, stamps, papers, uniforms, photographs and bits of radio apparatus one last time, and packing it all up.

In the next room, Maya was taking care of Shilova, who sounded like she was having a panic attack. Slowcoach Handrack was with them. Now and again you could hear loud sobs.

In the afternoon, I drove to the airfield with Slowcoach, to go over the final details with the Luftwaffe. He had brought a green ammunition case, which was also to be taken on board at the behest of Standartenführer Solm. It was sealed. Slowcoach said he hadn't the slightest idea what was inside the sealed ammunition case, but his guess was ammunition (he had less imagination than a squirrel, and the latter would be less surprised by a nutshell without a nut in it).

After our meeting with the Luftwaffe officers, I intended to drive back to headquarters, but was stopped by a telephone call from my brother. He ordered Slowcoach and me to oversee the installation of our radio unit in one of the hangars. The most important task here seemed to be laying out a buffet table with sparkling German wine, fruit and Laima chocolate.

*

In the early evening, just after sunset and within a second of the time Berlin had given us, the Arado-232 landed. It broke through the low cloud like a gigantic flying dinosaur and swooped towards us: a miracle on the verge of extinction (only seven of them in the world). Later, I stood on the rain-damp runway and laid my hand reverently on the dinosaur's hide. Eight built-in machine guns. A cargo bay that could hold a car. Hydraulic cargo doors. Night navigation equipment. And twenty rubber wheels under its fuselage, which would allow the plane to roll over trenches after landing as if they were made of cotton wool. It took a six-man crew to tame this miracle of modern aviation technology. The pilot looked like Hemingway; he greeted me and then asked casually, 'Where are the passengers?'

The passengers were missing. There wasn't much time. The airfield was situated to the north of Riga, still well out of range of the Russian artillery. But enemy night-fighters might turn up at any minute. Luftwaffe assistants rolled out the special Soviet M-72 motorbike, prepped and ready to go, and left it by the Arado's cargo doors. The rest of the commando's equipment was swiftly unloaded from our lorry and secured inside the dragon's mighty belly with ropes and straps.

As a thin rain set in, I spotted a long, grey, humming worm of unlit vehicles crawling through the darkness towards our airfield. In front was the general's car belonging to my brother, which pulled up close to the Arado. The other luxury sedans parked in a line behind it. Glutton Girgensohn, Möllenhauer, Pavel Delle, the professional dwarf and a dozen other senior officers and NCOs climbed hastily out and gathered in the open hangar, from which the plane would be monitored by radio during its flight. Maya had come as well. Of course. She didn't get too close to me; that was how we always kept things at work.

Politov was the last to get out of his car. He came striding over just as Mr Armstrong, the moon man, came striding towards the Apollo rocket in his space suit a few years ago in Cape Canaveral. He stood to attention in front of me, smoothed his black leather coat and asked with uncharacteristic seriousness where his wife had got to. I asked Slowcoach the same question. He made puppy-dog eyes at me and said she was on her way.

While we were waiting and in order to distract him, I asked Politov to perform a few loading and unloading manoeuvres on his motorbike for the assembled officers. The bike and sidecar were pushed

backwards into the plane's open fuselage. The doors closed hydraul-
ically. Everyone marvelled as the cargo flap, big as a barn door, which
also functioned as a ramp, moved as if by a ghostly hand and locked
itself automatically: I had never seen anything like it, and nor had
anyone else there. After a while the flap opened again, and Politov rode
his motorbike out. The SS officers clapped enthusiastically. The motorbike was finally loaded back into the plane and carefully secured. The
final preparations for take-off began.

But Shilova still wasn't there.

Now Politov started to get nervous. I tried to reassure him. Hub, who
by this point had looked around the hangar, spoken to the radio oper-
ators, ruffled the Luftwaffe's feathers with his arrogance and helped
himself from the buffet table several times, approached the Russian
agent. Slowcoach Handrack was at his side, looking as if they were
made for one another. An alkali feeling crept over me (a feeling of flesh
in caustic soda) as I spotted the green ammunition case in Slowcoach's
hands, the one he had brought with him that morning. Something
didn't seem right, and at the second or third glance I realized it was
the seal, which had been broken. Why hadn't Slowcoach said anything
about it? Whatever was in the case, it clearly wasn't ammunition, or my
colleague's thin arms would have dropped off by now.

Hub coughed. The people in the hangar fell silent and I thought my
brother was about to give a speech. But that wasn't at all what he was
planning. He just locked eyes with our Soviet colonel, who was decked
out according to all the rules of fine art, and said:

'Activist Politov! Good luck and blessings and Heil Hitler!' He
paused for a moment, gave another little cough and went on, 'Since
Activist Shilova cannot be here, her place will be taken by Instructor
Dzerzhinskaya.'

He looked at Maya. Boulders came loose in my throat and caused
a rockfall, I don't know how far down, and then he addressed my harpooner Queequeg directly.

'Instructor Dzerzhinskaya! Good luck and blessings to you too,
and Heil Hitler!'

Maya returned his salute with a look of confusion. I saw Slowcoach
slouch over to her. He pulled Shilova's NKVD uniform out of the case
he was carrying and handed it over. He took no pleasure in the act.

Then he extended a hand to show Maya where she could get changed, and will you look at that, it was the small, seemingly pointless wooden screen beside the radio unit, which he'd asked one of the carpenters to put up that afternoon, evidently already aware of what was going to happen. I clenched my sensitive artist's fingers into a fist that I swore to myself would knock the last remnants of vitality out of his face.

But he was the only one who seemed to be in on this plan. Everyone else looked thunderstruck. Surprisingly, the professional dwarf was the first to pull himself together.

'Forgive me, Herr Standartenführer,' said the Dwarf. 'We've been training Activist Shilova for almost a whole year. All the identity papers, all the service records, all the credentials have photographs of Activist Shilova attached to them.'

Trembling, he opened his briefcase and started searching for proof of this, but Standartenführer Solm didn't even look. 'That isn't important, Untersturmführer,' he snapped. 'The important thing is that the take-off is punctual to the minute.'

And with a smile, he received a salute from the newly dressed Comrade Maya Dzerzhinskaya, who had giggled at him three months earlier on the shores of Lake Usma.

'I don't see,' he said contentedly, 'what else could stand in the way of permission for take-off.'

His officers gaped at him as he took an apple from a fruit platter on the small buffet table, obviously intent on devouring it in front of me.

'Herr Standartenführer,' I said in a flat voice, 'you cannot send the instructor to Moscow in the activist's place.'

'Well, Frau Shilova has suffered a nervous collapse.'

He polished the apple on his sleeve.

'She often does.'

'And you told me that Instructor Dzerzhinskaya was an example to Activist Shilova in all things. You did say that.'

I reached into a pocket of my uniform and took out the slip of paper that Guppy Schellenberg had handed to me in Berlin.

'The mission order I have here is only for Shilova.'

He glanced at the paper. It bore the signature of our superior officer and expressly assigned Politov and his wife to Operation Finest Hour; no one else.

Hub thought for a moment and then declared in an off-hand

manner, 'In view of the situation that has arisen, it no longer applies only to Frau Shilova.'

'Forgive me, Standartenführer,' I said quietly, 'but that's a betrayal of the Führer.'

Standartenführer Solm held the apple up, his mouth already open to take a bite.

'Allowing the plane to take off without the trained activist,' I went on hurriedly, 'and without the protection of properly forged papers, means putting the whole undertaking at risk. How many minutes will it take for Activist Shilova to get here?' I asked Möllenhauer.

'If she's still in her quarters, then about sixty, Herr Hauptsturm-führer.'

'Sixty minutes, Standartenführer! We should allow ourselves that time!'

Standartenführer Solm, still holding up the apple, looked at my people, who turned their heads away in embarrassment. Then he opened up the full arsenal of his rank.

'Hand over your weapon!' he ordered.

I saluted, took my pistol from its holster and passed it to the befuddled Möllenhauer.

'Report to headquarters,' Standartenführer Solm ordered. 'And await the court martial there.'

He placed the apple back in the fruit bowl and gave the order for take-off.

Maya Dzerzhinskaya, my sad angel, the rich, earthy glitter from a mine of unhappiness, looked over at me from inside a much-too-large uniform. She had been forced into this, I was sure of it, for I saw no surprise in her eyes. No horror. Not even a hint. She had not been permitted to speak to me. And she wasn't permitted now, either. Politov led her out into the rain, towards the Arado, shaken at having to leave his wife behind.

The last that Ishmael saw of Queequeg was the silhouette of her hand pressed against the dimly lit bull's-eye window of the plane as it glided slowly onto the runway and off into the night.

III

The Golden Calf

I

Shortly before the city fell, I was up before a flying SS court martial, accused of serious insubordination and high treason.

It took them twenty-two minutes to sentence me to death.

The three-man tribunal was headed by my three-headed brother (all the heads were his; the other two judges were only themselves from the neck down).

The verdict was not legally binding, since it had to be approved by Heinrich Himmler.

I was confined to a cell in the prefecture. A windowless, stinking cellar room, from which I could hear whimpering through the heating pipes just as I once had sitting in my office at night, years before, three storeys above the rats that now kept me company. I could hear them streaming out of the holes, but couldn't see them: the light bulb hanging from the ceiling above me only flickered on when someone looked in through the peephole in the door, which happened once an hour. Otherwise, it was as though Maya's old wish had been granted, as if someone had gently scooped my eyes out of their sockets like blancmange and laid me in a warm bed of blindness, in a black that belonged to the hereafter, though I was still alive.

Shells were falling all around me.

Much, much later I would learn that, two evenings before the execution was due to take place, Ev had come to find my brother in the prefecture. He hadn't come home to her for a week, choosing to sleep in his office instead. And so he was lying on his leather couch when she appeared before him. The white of her hospital uniform extended the white of her face into the room, at least, that's how I imagine it: I see Ev's cold glow in my mind's eye and I cannot believe that, in the following sixty seconds of that encounter, she blinked even once.

'Everyone's talking about what you're going to do to Koja,' she said quietly, looking down at him. 'No one can believe it, and no one can do anything to stop it. But there's one thing you should know: the day that I stand at his grave, you will have to start running, because if I should ever find you – and I'm certain I will find you – then I will strike you dead, or poison you, or inject you with anthrax bacilli, just like I learned at Auschwitz, I swear that to you on our daughter's life.'

'You won't stand at his grave,' my brother said, and made sure that Ev was put on the last boat the following morning.

I learned of this because Heinrich Himmler did not like flying court martials. It's possible he had fond memories of the walks we had once taken around lovely Reval, or perhaps he had my flattering carica-ture of him as Lancelot on his desk. In any case, the Reichsführer-SS decided that I should not face a firing squad without the prescribed hearing. A telegram arrived from Berlin, insisting that I be shipped off to Germany. I was to be brought up before a proper SS court there. Without delay.

My brother entered my cell as he used to enter our childhood bed-room when he wanted to know if I'd been playing with his tin soldiers. I blinked at him as he stood in a rectangle of electric light. I could hear the doors of the other cells being opened out in the corridor. One after another. There were no voices to be heard, just one or two gunshots as the contents of each cell were permanently disposed of. I flinched at every bang, my body resisting the violence that was eating its way towards me.

My brother sat down on a footstool he had brought with him, handed me Himmler's telegram and said flatly, 'Congratulations.'

Then we had to leave.

My fellow prisoners, glimpsed from the central corridor as we passed by, seemed to be asleep in their own blood, while their execu-tioners and Standartenführer Hubert Solm, trailing my lowly person in his wake, hastened out into the courtyard.

The noise out there was hellish. Our eyes began to stream at once. The smoke from the burning gatehouse almost completely enveloped a truck and two saloons, which were waiting with their engines running. We jumped into the cars beneath a vaulted ceiling of sound: the high whistle of falling shells, and the crash of a four-storey facade collapsing right behind us.

Four or five minutes later, the prefecture was fully evacuated. A

conscientious Scharführer even stopped to lock the front doors, causing an officer to scream at him – and since he couldn't bring himself to
throw the keys away, he laid them carefully beside the doormat.

I was not handcuffed. I sat there in my filthy SS uniform in the back
of the Opel Olympia (it might even have been my own), surrounded
by Hub's people, none of whom I knew. We drove out of the courtyard
in a convoy of three vehicles and sped west through the bursting city,
towards the only escape route: a gap in the Soviet encirclement that the
Wehrmacht had pooled their efforts to blow open. Missiles dropped
like cobblestones out of the sky. The streets were deserted. Here and
there along the avenues, a tree was in flames. The Wehrmacht seemed
to have withdrawn from the city entirely. We didn't even come across
any rear-guard units.

'With any luck, Ivan won't have reached the bridges yet,' the
Scharführer croaked from the driver's seat, flooring the accelerator.

The SS convoy turned onto Elisabethstraße. For a moment it was
silent, cathedral-silent, it seemed to me. I listened, and so did everyone
else in the car, our heads slightly raised or tilted back, trying to pick up
the scent of the future.

Then a lightning flash came from somewhere and we were flying
weightlessly through the air. As I floated head first towards the asphalt,
my eardrum burst, and although I was still fully conscious, all objects,
all certainties and expectations melted together into a monstrous mushroom of silence. It was dark, and since it was dark and quiet, I calmly
considered certain movements. Moving my arm, for instance, was
something I wanted to do, and couldn't. I was lying wedged in what
felt like cotton wool but was actually twisted metal; something sharp
had pierced my groin, but it didn't hurt.

There was warm blood flowing into my mouth; it wasn't my own,
but that of the man above me, who by the time I opened my eyes had
no face left.

I struggled queasily onto all fours and crawled out from under the
body and through the window of the smoking wreck.

When I emerged, it looked like the whole winding street ahead of
us had been torn up by a kind of meteorite a few seconds before. A
massive crater yawned in front of me. The truck with a dozen of our

SS people aboard no longer existed. There was just a mess of flattened, melted steel, wood, flesh and bubbling rubber.

A direct hit.

A piece of bomb shrapnel that two men could not have lifted – a huge, serrated chunk of metal – had cut a senior SS officer in two lengthways, a variation on the way Captain Palbyzin had been halved. Smoke was rising from both man and shrapnel. The force of the explosion had hammered another man's skull down into his ribcage. Where his neck used to be were just a pair of astonished, protruding eyes. Ten metres away, an SS man, no more than a boy really, sat squealing incessantly. His sphincter had failed. He seemed otherwise unharmed, and had probably just been thrown from the open bed of the truck.

Hub's car lay on the far side of the crater. The blast had acted like a giant fist, slamming it into a wall, where it looked like it was glued. From a distance I could see lumps of flesh or entrails hanging out of the chassis. And Hub's arm.

I yelled at the shit-covered SS man, and the two of us crawled on our bellies over to the burning car. We pulled at the arm and my brother slithered out in one piece, after which the car exploded. That brought him round, and he was amazed that I had saved his life. Not that he said so, but he was amazed. And while he was still marvelling at this fact, we saw a T-34 two streets over, rolling sedately towards the Düna. Just then, my hearing returned.

'Fuck!' Hub shouted. 'We have to get out of here!'

He was completely covered in burn blisters, but still managed to gather the stinking SS boy and two other survivors around him and explain to them that all the vehicles had been destroyed by the shell. This came as no surprise to any of us, since we represented the least destroyed of these destroyed vehicles. Then he ordered us to carry on and fight our way through to our own lines, on foot, quick march. It was only when I went to stand up that I realized the explosion had got me, too. I fell to the ground with a piercing pain in both feet that I had not been conscious of before.

'His trotters are fucked,' the older SS man said.

'We'll carry him,' Hub decided.

'If we're carrying him anywhere, Standartenführer,' the other man retorted, showing us the raw flesh peeling from the wounds on his back, 'then it'll only be to the other side of the road.'

Something inside me was thinking, but it wasn't me.

Something was thinking about the children we once were. About my desperate father's bullet, from which my fourteen-year-old brother had protected me. And that other bullet, towards which, a quarter of a century later, he was proposing to carry me carefully across the sea to Berlin, this time protecting not me, but the stumps of my legs. He was my shield and my destruction and the reason I was what I was, became what I became. Something thought all of these things without my active participation – without the thoughts shaking me, making me roar and rage and tear open my gangrenous heart. And as I watched all these thoughts from a great distance away, rising up like clouds and raining down over me without wetting my innermost being, I myself was also thinking. I was thinking about Maya, who had or had not reached Moscow, who had or had not killed Stalin. Had not, if the situation here was anything to go by.

Why does a person love people? Why does a person love people even though every love perishes? Why is the desert that is our souls populated with little green olive trees, which almost all get annihilated by sandstorms, and yet always sprout again? Yes, why does a person love people? Why did I love Maya? Why, on our last night together, had I seen her eyes fixing on a horizon that was entirely boundless, the promise of a place where I would be loved boundlessly, where everything I was and everything I was not would be gratefully accepted? Why did I miss her so much, when we had always known that we were impossible, and when for so long we had loved only our own desire? And why had I loved Mary-Lou? Was it chance? Or did everything follow some trivial pattern? Why in heaven's name did I only love women whose names began with 'M'? Maya. Mary-Lou. Mumu from Riga. They all began with 'M'; even Ev, whose real names were Meyer and Murmelstein, began with 'M', and the image of this 'M' shot through my head as a second T-34 rolled across Elisabethstraße, one block closer than the first.

'I'm staying here,' I said to Hub. 'You can either shoot me, or you can give me something to bring some meaning to the situation.'

'What do you mean?'

'How can I stop them?'

Hub looked at me the way he looked at everyone, arms flat against his sides, one foot resting on a fallen street lamp. A hippy would say he was *cool*. Then he nodded to the SS man who was bleeding the least. The man hobbled around the shredded bodies gathering up their weapons, and finally laid three pistols, a sub-machine gun with a wet gleam to it, two rifles and several hand grenades at my feet. He explained how to use the MP 40, which I was not familiar with, while the shit-covered boy vomited and Hub and the other fellow secured the area. The artillery fire had ceased. I knew the Soviet reconnaissance troops must be close by.

I was expecting that anything might happen next. But I never expected Hub to pick up a rifle, order his men to move off at once, and then position himself beside me and my sub-machine gun. No, no one could have expected that.

They left us lying in the bomb crater and disappeared.

For ten minutes, Hub, not saying a word, was a fraternal presence at my side, his gun aimed and ready. I could smell his aftershave, and couldn't fathom why he had put on aftershave on a day like this. I heard him breathing, and from time to time there was a groan, because he could now feel his burned skin.

'What are you doing?' I asked.

'I'm not going to leave you here to die alone.'

'You are such an arsehole.'

He didn't say anything; he didn't move, or even groan again.

'Get out of here and take care of your family!'

'You are my family.'

I turned to one side and shot the sub-machine gun into his right hand at a range of fifty centimetres. He rolled backwards. I could have comfortably held the gun to his head.

'I don't want to be in bad company at such a vital moment,' I said. 'If I die here, you'll know I thought you were an arsehole until my dying breath.'

He held up his bleeding hand and looked at me, looked at me through his bleeding hand, through the hole in it, I mean, and nodded. Then he got up, and all the madness of the last days, weeks, months seemed to have been wiped from his eyes; they were the eyes of a small, serious boy.

The last I saw of Hub was the vein pulsing on the singed back of his uninjured hand, as he placed a pack of five cigarettes beside the hand grenades. I saw that this hand, stained black and violet, wanted to touch me in farewell – I could see it, but it didn't happen.

It was a wonderful feeling to be left there without him.

The first thing I did was light one of the cigarettes.

I don't recall being downcast. Feverish, at most. I didn't even feel lonely when he'd gone: I was submerged in all the thoughts in my head, my own and the ones I was watching, and it was a strangely companionable sensation. I flicked the cigarette away, picked up my gun and set my sights on the street in front of me. I would shoot at the first forehead that came round the corner. I thought that was all right. Vice versa, too. Being torn apart, hacked to pieces, squashed to pulp is a prospect that affrights the flesh much more than one little bullet. Today, now that one of those bullets lives inside me, now that I've been shot in the head myself, I take a different view of things, Swami, but at the time it seemed like an acceptable solution.

It was an hour or perhaps a day – several showers of rain had fallen, in any case – before the Russians found me.

I awoke, soaked to the skin, from a poisonous sleep. I could see four shadows looming above me, human silhouettes, with not only their sub-machine guns, but my own MP 40 pointing at me. I froze. So this is the second to end all seconds, something inside me thought. The little second of death.

But that is not what happened next. The shadows took hold of me. Grasped my arms and legs, dragged me up out of the ashy mud and ran to the commissar with me hanging between them like a suspension bridge.

He interrogated me briefly and considered shooting me, but he liked my Anna Ivanovna Russian. He knew a poem by Heine. He reached into his pocket and took out a tuning fork that he evidently always carried with him, struck it on the edge of a table, held it to his ear, hummed an A and declaimed in German, holding that note: '"On earth we fain would happy be, nor starve for the sake of the stronger."' Then he switched his declamation down a gear and whispered, '"The idle stomach shall gorge itself with the fruit of hard labour no longer."'

He grinned, put the tuning fork away and had me transferred to a stretcher, because of my legs.

*

Five months later, one day in March, as the snow turned to slush and the ice floes on the Düna clanged and cracked beneath the constant grey of a low northern sky, I was taken to Moscow and delivered to the Lubyanka, where they mocked, humiliated and tortured me for many months.

And it became clear to me why a person loves people: because he *has* to love, because for every individual it is the only hope of staying human in spite of it all.

2

'There, that's the transformation,' the Hippy says.

'Sorry?' I say.

'The transformation: that was when you became a wonderful person. That's why you've been talking about these things for so long – to hide your feelings. But you won't say anything more now. Now it's all going to be fine.'

'No, no, I'm going to tell you everything. This is still just the start.'

'Yes, the start of something new.'

'The start of my life.'

'A person loves people. You're right about that. A swami couldn't have put it better.'

'But a person doesn't love all people. I didn't love anyone in the Lubyanka.'

'Don't tell me about that. Concentrate on your feelings.'

'Is it not a feeling, when you don't love someone?'

'Not one that you can say Yes to, with a capital "Y".'

'You wanted me to tell you everything. And I *am* telling you everything.'

'But everything you tell me is just talk. Now you're talking about the Lubyanka and all the horrible things that happened there. You're just talking to distract yourself from what you felt, and maybe still feel now – it's one of the easiest things you can do.'

'I'm talking so I don't have to talk? And I'm talking for the first time about something I've never spoken about before, so that I don't have to talk about it?'

'Yes, why not, that's exactly it.'

'But that's completely barmy! What would I do that for?'

'It takes your mind off your feelings.'

'And how can you tell that?'

'You haven't cried once.'

'Aha.'

'Not once.'

'What are you trying to say?'

'Come on, man, what kind of question is that? Why don't you cry? Hasn't it become clear to you that – and look, don't take this the wrong way, but that you're sickening human scum?'

My eyes turn away from the frosted-glass panes they have been staring at, my back tenses slightly and I look over at him. Curled into a ball, clinging to the bedpost, sandwiched between the white-painted iron bedside table and my unhappiness, he watches me, forcing one of his vague pothead smiles.

Slowly, in order to get the meaning of the words clear in my mind, I get up, cross the ridiculous metre of speckled tiles that he has declared a demilitarized zone, and perch lightly on his bed. His eyes are almost popping out of their sockets with fear.

'You think that I'm scum?' I ask, gently.

'No, for heaven's sake, I think you're a wonderful person, how many more times do I have to say that? But I've been waiting for the transformation for a while now. For the moment of metamorphosis. Because honestly: all this time, you've been talking about yourself as if you're scum, and not turning the corner towards the pure feeling that needs to flow out of you.'

'You want me to start blubbering in front of you?'

'Look, the problem is – if you just keep talking and talking, then the repressed emotions get stored up in your body. Either right there in your physical body. Or in one of the ethereal bodies, your spiritual, mental, emotional bodies. Clear so far?'

All of his bodies are trembling, and I try to reassure him by assuming an expression that is at once sympathetic, indifferent and imperious.

'Completely clear. So we should skip the Lubyanka.'

'Yeah, maybe don't describe all the horror and just get straight to the feeling, man, then it won't inhibit your energy flow. And could you maybe go back to your own bed? Please?'

'What feeling would you like me to get to, then?'

'Guilt maybe, or fear,' he says, when I am back under my covers.

'But,' he adds after some hesitation, 'tell me yourself, *compañero*: what was your overriding feeling back then?'

3

When I think back to my time in the Lubyanka, to the months and years amid the arches of its basement jail, which circled around me like carousels and which I am not allowed to describe to you, my ever-more-incomprehensible Swami – when I think, then, of the perpetual winter temperatures and the perpetual summer clothing (insofar as those clammy cotton rags may be called clothing at all), when I think of the damp and the vermin and the hunger, then it is not feelings of guilt or fear that are uppermost in my mind. It's the feelings of weakness and pain, that very specific pain, for instance, that the extraction of fingernails leaves behind in the memory's cabinet of curiosities, but especially in the fingers themselves, of course, the tips of which are numb to this day.

And even if I disregard these for a moment, even if I ignore the needs of my physical body and let my spiritual, emotional or whatever-else body speak to me, manifestations of myself that are clearly responsible for whining, trembling and fear – even then, it isn't feelings of guilt and fear to which I would say Yes with a capital 'Y', to skim off the scum inside me.

An overwhelming loneliness was the feeling that dominated me during those years.

When I speak of this loneliness, I get a nutty aftertaste in my mouth: old, rancid nuts, you understand? And even then, you can wait for the tears to come until you're blue in the face. Loneliness was my horror. And yet it became my sweetheart. My horrific sweetheart. That was the only reason I survived the Lubyanka. I know that now. Loneliness never forces you to do anything, there is no forcing with her, no misunderstanding. She is simply bad for you. She makes you suffer. But she is beautiful. Have you never seen her? Mine was tall and very thin, she had black hair, deep green eyes, a face that followed you everywhere. Into every filthy hole. And into every interrogation room. When you love loneliness, you are never alone. That's the crazy thing about it.

And it's important that you don't let the interrogation officers prise her from you when you talk to them. They try to become your partners, your nearest and dearest. But if you confide in them, if you give yourself over to them even for a second, you are lost. Once you've tasted that intimacy, you can't bear it to be withdrawn, and the loneliness will come back all the stronger, but she won't be your friend again. You have to stay loyal to her, unconditionally.

The only NKVD officer who ever led me into temptation was Comrade Nikitin.

Nikitin was a reticent satyr of almost fifty years old, who had fallen ill with Graves' disease during the battle for Moscow due to the shortage of iodine. Nikitin's bulging eyes gave him an amphibian appearance; you could never drown him, because he could breathe underwater, that much was immediately obvious.

Despite his power, his suffering and his Jewish heritage, he was astonishingly polite to me. He had a goitre the size of a terrapin, and his frame was wasted and skeletal, but he always struggled to his feet when the guard brought me into his office. He would offer me his hand, bony and soft at once, a little moist and as cold as a corpse, and even as I was shaking it he would begin to talk about art. Comrade Nikitin knew a great deal about the Russian avant-garde; he'd studied painting at the Vitebsk Academy under Marc Chagall in nineteen twenty, and a triptych of blue-bearded violinists with several flying goats and angels in attendance hung on the wall behind him, probably to entice his victims into commenting on it.

Aesthetically speaking, our tastes were similar. He applauded when I confessed to him how much I despised suprematism. He opened a drawer and pulled out a thick photo album of all the suprematists he had personally interrogated and tortured in the very chair where I was now sitting.

I also saw police photos of Meyerhold and his wife ('a very beautiful actress, such a shame'), a photo of Kandinsky from the year nineteen twenty-one ('That's when I was just getting started here'), a private picture of Nikitin, arm in arm with Lion Feuchtwanger outside the Lubyanka's front entrance ('He just came to visit, and thought the building so splendid he wanted to move in at once') or Isaac Babel ('Ah, his death was very unpleasant, but he spent two months in the cell you are in now, I'm sure he must have scratched some poems into the walls, have a look!').

In short, Nikitin went hell for leather at my loneliness, trying to tear her away from me, using our talk of artists to build a sly bridge into my dust-mote of a heart, using the collective, Homeric 'WE', and what we had in common, to finish me off. To begin with, he didn't even bring up the subject of my secret-service work.

I had written hundreds of pages for the Soviets, telling them what they wanted to know. Names, places, operations, Zeppelin. The names and addresses of our Russian and Latvian spies. I had to give them all up. Most of all, they wanted to know every last detail about my brother. About Heydrich. About Guppy Schellenberg. And I told them.

But I only talked up to the edge of the abyss.

I said nothing about the abyss itself.

I left a few things out.

I left out the massacres. I left out the Bikernieki Forest. I left out the Moshe Jacobsohns. They were lying beneath the pack ice of my silence, which Nikitin tried to melt rather than hack away. Not to blow it to pieces with torture, like the others did. But to thaw it with well-tempered compliments about the drawings I was now permitted to do.

He granted me a pencil (although I could easily have rammed it through my eye and into my brain to escape this earthly monotony forever). He had the guards give me paper, two sheets per week. And I drew my scurfy bones, my badly healing feet, my penis, flaking like soft pastry, it was nothing more than a piss hose, and I shook my face out like an old penis, too, on the occasions when I looked at it in the mirror and drew it with disgust.

Nikitin was delighted with this evidence of my decline; he hung some of the drawings alongside his blue-bearded violinists and congratulated me on my great talent.

The end of the war passed me by.

A noisy street party being held over my own grave.

On the ninth of May, I could hear the crowds cheering through the thick walls. Trumpets. Happy tanks. No more Hitler. Peace among the nations.

The summer came. The autumn. The winter.

The following spring, Nikitin started taking iodine tablets and the terrapin in his throat shrank, which you could hear rather than see. His voice gained volume and lost warmth.

I became Four-Four-Three.

In the summer of nineteen forty-six, I caught typhus.

When it began to snow again, Nikitin withdrew my pencil and paper, both my drawing paper and my lavatory paper, and I had to start wiping my arse with my fingers again. I sank into a snowdrift of time, everything gradually going white before my eyes. There was no poem by Babel on my walls. The only word written there was 'shit'.

Nikitin was waiting for something specific. He even told me he was waiting for something specific from me, and was disappointed that I wasn't giving it to him voluntarily.

It was clear to me that I wasn't going to live much longer.

'Now then, Four-Four-Three,' he whispered to me one day, 'we've talked a lot about the visual arts. But never once about the art of photography.'

'I'm not interested in photography.'

'That's a great shame,' Nikitin said.

He placed a packet of black-and-white snapshots on the table. I picked up the photos and saw myself. I am wearing an SS uniform. I have a pistol in my hand. I am standing under a canopy of black trees, aiming the pistol at people who are lying in a pit.

'I find photos fascinating,' Nikitin added.

I saw that baby again, the baby I only used to see in my dreams from time to time. Now he was staring out of the photo, babbling cheerfully, so it seemed, straight at me, while I fired at his little head, and I remembered the photographer who had positioned himself beside me, and in the background I could see Brigadeführer Stahlecker and Hub watching as I emptied the whole magazine into that tiny body.

'Fascinating, yes. An interesting word. From the Latin. *Fascinum*,' Nikitin went on. 'It comes from the same root, incidentally, as the word 'fascism'.

'I was forced to do it.'

'Of course you were. I merely wanted to draw your attention to the composition. The interplay of man and nature.'

I couldn't say anything more.

'He was a great artist, this photographer. He starved to death in

Stalingrad. And that's when we found this striking evidence of his talent, in his pack.'

I turned aside and vomited into the wastepaper basket. Nikitin was sympathetic, waddling out from behind his desk and laying a hand lightly on the back of my neck, and his secretary brought in a new wastepaper basket at once, a metal one from which nothing could seep out.

'What do you want from me?'

'Splendid,' he said with a satisfied grunt. 'Now we're on the right track. What I want from you is a little reflection, please: what else might you have forgotten to mention, in addition to this afternoon in the forest?'

But I didn't want to reflect on it. I had been in this line of work long enough to know I didn't want that.

And so there began a phase that I am not allowed to describe, I know, my highly sensitive Swami. But there was a classic change of coach. The thugs took over the daily timetable. And they focused on my fitness for months using dumb-bells, skipping ropes and leather whips. I marvelled at all the things they could do. But I marvelled silently. And some time at the start of nineteen forty-eight, having survived my third mock execution down in the firing-squad cellar, doubtless on Nikitin's orders, I was brought back to him.

Unlike me, he looked healthier now; even his goitre bobbed up and down with a livelier air. He didn't get up or shake my hand, and he didn't let me sit down. A lamp was aimed directly at my face. I was weak with hunger. My bones had been beaten to a pulp, leaving me on the point of collapse. For the first time in our long acquaintance, Nikitin did not start the conversation with remarks about European art history. Instead, he asked if I had ever heard the name Politov.

'No,' I said.

He laughed congenially, held up a warning finger and gave me the kind of look you would give a cheeky little boy.

'No, I haven't,' I repeated.

'So, you never had any dealings with a Mr Piotr Politov?'

'No.'

'He was planning to murder our great Vozhd.'

'That's terrible.'

'Yes, our dear father Stalin loves his people. He cares for them just as he cares for the roses and the apple trees he has planted at his little dacha.'

'I expect he also plants beautiful lemon groves and grows melons.'

'You could say that, yes.'

'And has put up nests for the birds and the squirrels in his garden.'

'I'm sure you aren't intending to make fun of anyone?'

I shook my head.

'That's good.'

'Forgive me if it might have sounded that way.'

'I will overlook it just this once.'

'What was this assassin's name, again?'

'It doesn't matter what he was called. If you don't know him.'

'Of course.'

Nikitin looked me up and down. His bulging toad eyes, whose lids no longer fitted over them in sleep, were as inexpressive as glass marbles sitting in porridge.

'Our information,' he said softly, stroking his goitre, 'is that this criminal Politov was trained in Riga by an SD officer and sent out to kill Stalin. The SD officer fits your description.'

'But we SD officers all look alike,' I said with a rusty laugh.

'Please be so good as to confirm once more for me that you do not know this man.'

He opened his green photo album and took his time searching for a particular page. Then he showed me the photo of Piotr Politov. Clean-shaven, but with tangled, wet hair, bruises below his left cheekbone and a vacant expression, he was staring into the distance through the lens of the NKVD camera. In his hair, which was a mass of filth and blood, I saw a huge quantity of white feathers. They had wiped his face, but white down still clung to his eyelashes, as if he'd just had a pillow fight. An ashy feeling of horror rose through me: the photo quite clearly showed Politov's corpse lying on marshy ground, his eyes wide with surprise. That was why they couldn't play the two of us off against each other, I suddenly realized. His death was my only chance to wriggle out of this. I said, 'No, I've never seen this man before.'

Nikitin nodded sadly, slammed the photo album shut, leaned back in his chair, swayed once to the left and once to the right, and announced, 'I really thought, prisoner Four-Four-Three, that there was something like a bond of mutual respect between us.'

He pressed a red button on his desk, looked me up and down again, and a pained tone entered his voice as he sighed, 'Yes, I would go so far as to say you had become a real friend.'

The door opened and two guards came in.

'But where is it written,' Nikitin added, 'that we have to forgive our friends?'

I am not talking. I am feeling my feelings, dear Swami, as my mind walks once more along the corridor down which Four-Four-Three was then led, flanked by guards whose black eye sockets became bottomless wells beneath the dim passageway lamps. Their faces were a pincer, such focus in them, and I could feel my luck running out with every step I took. Nikitin hobbled along behind us like the devil himself. He had never accompanied me anywhere before, never so much as left his office with me. I had never seen him so angry.

We entered the Lubyanka's stairwell, an operetta of stone in which large film-set lanterns made the marble glitter. Nets were strung between the balustrades across every storey so that no one could throw themselves to their death. We descended all the way to the cellar without speaking a single word, past the guard posts, through the system of two barred gates, into the confusion of the jail.

As we passed my cell and walked on down death row, I realized that this was not a place of mock executions. In a special room down here, there was a table. Syringes filled with syrupy yellow liquid rolled off it and razor blades slid down it, since the floor sloped steeply to help the blood drain away.

Another guard came out to meet me and put a blindfold over my eyes. Now I was really nothing but an emotional body. The word 'fear' doesn't even come close to describing the whistling cold that swept through my blood and turned it to ice. This feeling. This feeling of only being able to breathe through your teeth, in which tiny little lungs have been blown open.

We went down a few more stairs. I heard deep voices. Murmuring. Then two pairs of strong hands gripped me from the left and right, and I felt Comrade Nikitin very close to me.

'The reason you are going in there now is that I can no longer believe you,' he panted, his voice suffering from all the steps and the damp air.

My hands were cuffed behind my back, a door was opened, and I was led into a cell that stank of excrement and sulphur. The blindfold was removed and I landed, like jettisoned ballast, in front of the grey shadow that three years previously had been Maya Dzerzhinskaya.

4

This is what had happened: the Arado had flown east and crossed the front lines. The night was black as pitch. Low clouds were gathering far below. It was raining. Maya Dzerzhinskaya couldn't see any of this. But the radio operator, the back of whose sweaty neck she was staring at, kept relaying the flight details to the passengers, including the meteorological conditions.

They were half an hour from the landing site when the beam of a searchlight sliced through the darkness and yellow balls of flame flashed up to their left. Flak fire, the bass notes of which reverberated in the plane's outer skin and shook Maya's back. She pressed her spine more firmly against the metal, as if trying to absorb every wave of pressure, and deep in her bones she felt the plane pick up speed and start to climb. But the shells were already exploding so close by that there was a booming in her skull. And the sword of the searchlight's beam was coming closer and closer.

The pilot made a sharp turn and changed course. A second searchlight appeared, and then a third. Soon the Arado was unable to outrun them. The cabin was suddenly lit up as brightly as if it were on fire.

Maya was not afraid any longer.

She had been crying all through the flight, without anyone seeing, not even Politov, who was cursing without pause into the motorcycle cap he was holding over his face. Her mouth was pressed to the back of her hand. She smelled her skin, its familiar scent. Recalled kissing her own forearm for the first time as a thirteen-year-old, to practise kissing. And she kissed the back of her hand now, making it easier to think of me, hundreds of kilometres away, of the look I had given her from the airfield, and she gave a comforting kiss to that final look, amid a hail of explosions. She always feared destruction, but not her own, and as she kissed one hand, she pressed the other against her eyes to stop the tears from coming again.

Several small pieces of shrapnel hit the fuselage, but none pierced it. The pilot changed course once more, and finally managed to leave the danger zone.

There could be no thought now of landing at the planned location, a remote patch of heathland outside Smolensk. The pilot, whom Hub had forbidden from aborting the mission, had to improvise and seek out an alternative, unreconnoitred landing site. In enemy territory. Under fire. At night, in the rain. Possibly while being pursued by fighter planes.

The three landing lights mounted on the nose were all he had to see by.

To see rocks or trees.

At around one o'clock in the morning, the plane reached a landing site a hundred and fifty kilometres north-west of Moscow, without being spotted again by the enemy air force. Potato fields as far as the eye could see, the on-board radio operator said.

No rocks. No trees.

The plane circled and began its descent towards what they hoped rather than knew was a treeless farmer's field.

But that wasn't the case, as Maya realized when she looked out of her round window a few metres above the ground and saw, by the plane's landing lights, a meadow with jagged, four-metre-wide tank traps dug into it. There was a loud crack as they touched down. All the windows shattered. Someone screamed. The plane was flung around its own axis, skidded into a copse of young fir trees and stopped abruptly, pierced by splintered branches. Passengers and crew crawled from the wreckage. Some were bleeding. The gunner's hand had been ripped off by a branch. Apart from his groans, there was absolute silence. And darkness. And endless, pouring rain.

Maya looked around.

It had been the right idea, she thought, to land the plane in this area. In the middle of the former front line. Almost all the surrounding villages had been burned down. No one was still living in the ruins. And the field was a long way from any roads. That was good.

All the same, someone might have seen the crash-landing. Every minute counted.

The Germans hurriedly lowered the cargo flap and helped Politov and Maya to haul their motorcycle and sidecar out of the wreck. Maya watched Politov crumple onto the churned-up grass. He chewed on a blade of it, sheep-like, as the shock spread through him in concentric waves. And as she watched him, she fell into a kind of hypnotic state. In these seconds of hypnosis, Maya decided she wanted to see me once more. She decided it just as she had once decided to survive Uralov, to survive being taken prisoner by the Germans, to survive Operation Zeppelin; just as she had even survived her father, a dirty old man who had called her to him day and night when she was still no more than a child.

She opened her eyes again, straightened up, spat out the fear and took the initiative, checking her gun and loading it, drawing courage from the sound. She was already putting on her motorcycle helmet when, behind her, the pilot flicked a burning match into the lake of fuel that had formed beneath the plane. The whole thing was ablaze in a matter of seconds, and it was bright as day.

'Are you insane?' Maya hissed at the pilot. 'That's a beacon! It can be seen from ten kilometres away!'

The man looked at her contemptuously, said those were his orders, and turned on his heel. He and his crew laid the gunner, who had now lost consciousness, under a tree, where he slowly bled to death. Then they took their weapons and vanished into the night.

They spent seven weeks working their way back to the front, getting caught up in several battles along the way, and were finally taken captive by a SMERSH commando following an hours-long gunfight on the Polish border. Stalin had them all charged, convicted and executed as war criminals for their planned attack on him.

But of course, as they left the crash site and were swallowed up by a wall of rain, they didn't yet know what was to become of them. And I, too, only learned years later that the captain had been held in the Lubyanka, one floor above me, until his execution. Nikitin told me that the farewell letters he wrote to his wife before his death were very beautiful and of some literary interest.

Maya went over to Politov. He didn't react.

She tipped a bottle of water over his head, which did no good, since it was pouring with rain anyway. So she slapped his face with the flat of her hand, once, twice, and that perked him up a little. It sounded like she was talking to a child. They were on their own now.

If we don't get away, we're going to die.

Dear Piotr. Come on, come to me.

Politov got onto the motorbike as if in a trance, started the engine and drove away, with Maya in the sidecar.

When they were out of sight of the plane, she ordered him to stop. She got out, unstrapped the radio and threw it into the bushes. The heavy set had been mounted on the front of the motorbike, where it obstructed their view. Politov said nothing. Maya had decided unilaterally to call off Operation Finest Hour. Getting rid of the radio that was supposed to keep them in contact with Germany and enable them to request supplies meant that Maya had no intention of killing, or being killed. Her only intention was to support me. To get back to me, against all flags, as grey geese do, and yes, you're right, I do see myself as scum when I think about this woman and see what humans are capable of.

First, Maya had to save herself. She had to save herself and Politov, who was a rock of sadness bound inside his wedding ring, which he was rubbing nervously. Maya shook him. She wept with him. She shouted at him, telling him that the stupid plan to blow Stalin up with a rocket only existed in the heads of decadent Nazis. Not in her head. Not in his. They weren't idiots, were they?

And gradually, Politov's hope of not being an idiot returned. His self-preservation instinct began to stir. His strength. His dashing. After all, they had more than a million roubles in cash. And a perfect disguise. All they had to do was survive the next few hours, when thousands of people would be hunting for them.

Politov leapt onto his motorbike. He looked like a changed man. But this sudden energy that was flaring up and revving too hard inside him was no replacement for a compass, and in the darkness, in the lashing rain, he found it almost impossible to get his bearings. First he roared along a field path that ended in a ravine. Then they found themselves on the shore of a lake that stank of petrol and was filled with wrecked and partly submerged tanks.

After driving around aimlessly for a while, they saw a village that had been reduced to rubble and headed towards it. In the village they came across a drunk young woman walking her little dog, the only male survivor in her family, and Politov asked her to show him – his name was Tavrin now, and he was a hero of the Soviet Union – the way to Rzhev. She got on the back of the motorcycle with the dog, laughed hysterically, threw the dog in the air and caught him again while they were moving, and sang out the directions. But where they ended up was just another village, every bit as ruined as the first. The girl disappeared into it. And then came another village. And another.

Politov sped blindly eastwards, growing ever more paranoid.

At around six in the morning, when it was getting light, they came to a road block outside a hamlet called Karmanovo. Politov fumbled with his pistol case. Maya held her nerve and asked one of the three armed officials in very friendly tones for directions to Rzhev. The guard had a Cossack moustache and pointed the way.

A little miracle, Mama would have said.

It was still raining, but the rain was lighter now, and in this illuminating dawn, now that Politov had survived his first checkpoint, a plan for him and his companion suddenly took shape. A real, obvious plan: Maya had spent some of her life in Rzhev, staying with her mamushka's sister, a cook, as I knew. She would be certain to find somewhere to hide there. The main cross-country roads were clear – so long as the NKVD and SMERSH didn't suspect that the saboteurs from the burnt-out plane, which had presumably now been discovered, were in possession of a motorcycle.

Politov stepped on the gas and overtook some kolkhoz farmers in their horse-drawn carts, who were heading for their fields despite the storm and the early hour. His understanding of the directions to Rzhev that the Cossack at the road block had given them was different from Maya's. Instead of turning left, as she yelled at him to do, he turned right. And instead of turning back when the road reached a dead end and dirt tracks forked in two directions, both of which were wrong, he took a short cut down a forest trail, despite all Maya's protestations.

Maya was getting nervous; precious time was running out. Minute by minute. And minute by minute it was getting lighter and drier. Finally, after Politov had sped straight through the woods, they came unexpectedly back onto a paved road.

Politov whooped and, as Maya began to hate him, drove much too fast towards another road block. As they pulled up, however, they realized it was not another road block at all but the old one in Karmanovo, where they had been so cheerfully received hours before.

This time, though – perhaps because it was now daylight, the rain had stopped and the recently discovered wreck of the Arado had triggered a large-scale manhunt for German spies – this time, the moustachioed and no longer friendly Cossack took a much closer look at the appearance of this highly decorated major. All of Politov's papers were in order. But it was clear that the passport photo of Shilova glued into Maya's identity card bore only a distant resemblance to Maya's scarred clown face. She lied that the photo had been taken before her accident, a car crash that had torn her face and half her body to shreds.

The official was prepared to accept this explanation, but then he was struck by another detail: Politov had pinned his Order of Lenin to the wrong side of his uniform. Every Russian child knew where the medal was supposed to go: pictures and articles glorifying the 'Heroes of the Soviet Union' appeared in the papers all the time. Growing suspicious, the official asked where the comrades had come from. Maya was about to reply as Pavel Delle had taught her, and as she had taught Shilova. But Politov cut her off, taking a harsh tone as he ordered the comrade to stop hassling a senior officer who had been decorated with the Order of Lenin, and to let them through that instant. The man was shocked: a few weeks earlier, NKVD directive J 1423 had given strict instructions to all troops that no Soviet officer was to bypass a routine check by pulling rank. Ever. Under any circumstances.

And so the official saluted, obediently but thoughtfully, let Politov drive on past him and past a small flock of chickens, and then opened fire with his sub-machine gun. The bullets hit the tyres, Politov's left arm and the right chamber of his heart, as well as a snow-white Poule de Caux hen. The bike and sidecar skidded into the ditch and overturned, and the couple were pulled out of the mud by the Red Army soldiers who had come running. All that could be done for Politov was to confirm his death. He had fallen face down on the dead chicken, explaining the blood and the white feathers in his hair captured in the NKVD photo, which would puzzle me years later.

Maya got away with just a few bruises. She was taken prisoner, searched and handed over within a matter of seconds.

It was half past eight.

*

My operation to snuff out Joseph Stalin, more than a year in the planning and costing many millions of Reichsmarks, had lasted seven and a half hours. Its failure meant that the course of history was not changed, and my candidacy for worldwide fame was forever revoked.

Just a few hours after Politov's demise and the capture of Agent Dzerzhinskaya, Comrade Nikitin arrived on the scene. He pulled up in an elegant, black Moskvich, in which he'd installed not only a daybed but an oxygen canister, which he used periodically to refresh his voice box.

Maya hated him from the very first interrogation, since, as with me, he would never just plunge into the maelstrom of the problem. At first he merely spoke of her delicate profile, which reminded him of Akhmatova. It was lucky for Maya that after the interrogation and a little cup of tea, he did not order her immediate execution, but suggested to his superior in Moscow that they play the long game via the radio with Maya's fascist handler in Riga. With me.

And for that, they had to keep her alive.

The radio operator at the German command in Riga could recognize her rather jerky hand, the nuances of her manual Morse code transmission. And Hauptsturmführer Solm (who by then, unbeknownst to Moscow, was confined to his Gestapo cell in the Riga prefecture) was familiar with Piotr's way of writing, which Maya also knew and was able to imitate.

And so Comrade Nikitin sent his people out to find the German radio equipment that Maya had flung into the bushes, bring it back and give it a thorough clean-up.

Twenty-four hours after her arrest, he took a seat beside the spy, told her that her profile was actually rather more like Marlene Dietrich's, and dictated the first radio message she was to send me. It never reached me, of course (I was busy awaiting my execution), but it will have sent my brother into a paroxysm of delight: 'Solm. Drop successful. Wing damaged on landing. Crew destroyed plane, went west on foot. We on way to Moscow. HH. Piotr.'

This major deceptive manoeuvre was signed off by Lavrentiy Beria himself, the Schellenberg of the Kremlin, whose nickname was 'Malignant Tumour'. The same nickname had once been given to Brigade-führer Stahlecker, and it was an entirely justified *nom de guerre* for every secret-service boss I have ever encountered.

Beria's commitment to this cause was rooted in the fact that Stalin had threatened him with serious consequences if any other German murder commando should succeed in getting within a hundred kilometres of him. And so, until the end of the war, Maya kept up Nikitin's charade and sent my brother messages that looked as genuine as possible, so that the Russians could spot and intercept any subsequent threat early on. A transmission from the thirty-first of January nineteen forty-five reads: 'Solm. In this testing hour we promise utmost dedication. Situation serious. We need telescopes and German songs. No matter what, we will pursue completion of stalled mission. Live in hope of victory. HH. Piotr. Maya.'

Hub replied in my name: 'Piotr and Maya, heartfelt greetings. Victory will ultimately be ours. It may even be closer than we think. Help us and do not forget your oath. New team will bring good folk song collection soon. Solm.'

In order to capture the members of this new team, the NKVD set up a dummy apartment for Maya on Lesnaya Ulitsa in Moscow, hoping that one of the German spies would turn up there. It was a handsome apartment furnished entirely in German Bauhaus style, in a block built at the turn of the century. Maya was a baited hook, dangling for years on Marcel Breuer furniture to lure in the advertised commando. They kept waiting long after Germany capitulated. But no one came. Not in nineteen forty-five. Not in nineteen forty-six. And not in nineteen forty-seven.

At the end of the year, the NKVD shut up the apartment and stuck Maya in a Lubyanka cell.

We stood silently, facing one another.

Maya didn't move. She was like the walls. Only further off. Peripheral, in relation to the walls. That's how I felt, too. Negligible. Absent. Temporary. And with all this petrified violence surrounding us, I felt all the more that when we saw each other it was for no longer than a breath of air. Maya's fragments – cheeks and beauty and suffering and the recognition that hit me like a ray of sunlight – flew around my ears, although she was just standing there, her eyes two dusty black chips of wall, flying towards me.

If you were to ask me whether I had forgotten her shape in those three years of imprisonment, I would have to say no, not at all, I could still draw her from memory. But this breath-of-air moment was something I could never reproduce later, though I tried a hundred times. I couldn't draw the way she froze there, three metres in front of me, her fingers like wing tips against her collarbone, her feet parallel on the stone floor, her face dirty and pale, a landscape with ravines cut into it. Although years earlier I had begun to love her a little, I don't know whether that prologue might have ended up as the whole play, were it not for this cursed century forcing us into this moment. Into this eternal cell.

Nikitin's hoarse voice gave me mere splinters of what I have told you here about Maya's fate, my dear Swami. Most of it I learned only later. Much later.

But what I sensed then was this goal she had, the goal she reached the moment I stepped over the threshold. She had found me. I had found her. The hypnosis had worked. And of course, you are right to say that I am one giant human flaw, but she was not, and now I will have to weep. I will have to snivel, to blubber, howl and whine, the tears running down like those of a little Bavarian girl. Running down like pee. Because back then, I couldn't cry. I was all periphery, do you see? I was the edges of a person. I was hollowed-out and lonely. But I've already told you what loneliness means.

My emptiness. Maya's silence.

And Nikitin talked and talked.

He said what a liar I was. He listed my crimes. He listed her crimes. He said that the time was up now, and there was nothing more he could do. The war was over. Even the aftermath of the war was over. Soon he would have to shoot my colleague, my agent, my beloved, a traitor to her country – and that profile of Akhmatova, of Marlene Dietrich, yes, of the majestic Cleopatra, would be gone. He would have to shoot me too, of course. We were of no further use. His hands were tied. He held me entirely responsible for everything. I and I alone held all three of our fates in my hands.

'What can I do?' I said, and it was odd to hear my own voice, because at once I felt a longing for Maya's voice, for her soft, rolling consonants, and at the same time I feared it might no longer exist. They might have cut out her tongue, a house speciality in those years.

'You must cooperate, Four-Four-Three. We already know everything about you.'

'I *am* cooperating.'

Still, she didn't speak a word. She didn't breathe. Didn't even blink.

'No, this is not cooperation. You must tell the whole truth, leaving nothing out. Do you know what Karl Marx said?'

'I'll cooperate.'

'Karl Marx said that we are products of our environment. People change. People can improve themselves if they only want to.'

'I want to.'

'We will work together on your self-criticism.'

'I'll work.'

'Do you really want to cooperate?'

'I'll cooperate.'

'Do you want to become a useful member of socialist society, freely and from the bottom of your heart?'

'I do.'

'Then we shall turn you into a spy for the Soviet Union.'

'Maya,' I said.

And at last, she said my name.

5

It was spring again, almost summer. A Wednesday in May nineteen forty-eight. The wind drove me along the broad valley. I was a mere speck creeping along the valley floor, slow and anonymous, a beetle. The mountains, elephant-grey, rose to my left and right.

The moving air was still harsh and cold. A Föhn wind was on its way, I could feel it, though I didn't yet know the word 'Föhn'. The Föhn changes the blood, its composition. It makes you numb and cross and dims your thoughts, so that I sensed a kind of malice in everything around me. Perhaps the mountains are merely indifferent. But it felt as though they were about to spit rockfalls down on me.

On the spy.

The road I was taking forked into a forest track and an avenue of elms, just as I'd been told. The little river's eddying water was a milky jade green. I sat down once again on one of the great boulders along its bank, lowering myself into the smell of the wet moss. I saw the cruelty and hardness of the world in the burgeoning meadow grass, the rich red of the nearby roofs, the violet mountainsides, the azure blue of the sky, even in the light brown dots of cows that the dot – no, the speck – of a farmer was driving across a pasture some distance off. No one who has come straight from Hades can see anything in all this beauty but God's utter scorn. I felt excluded from earthly creation, mocked; I was not part of things, just capturing them for a second, like a camera. For I knew all this could be taken from me at any moment, and so I regarded it as deceitful and not to be trusted.

I didn't even trust the black trunk of the elm as I leaned against it; I saw the cracks and splits in it with exaggerated clarity. The grain of the bark. An ant.

It had taken me seven hours to get here from Munich. First by train to Garmisch-Partenkirchen. That was where the Mittenwald service had terminated early, when there was yet another power cut. I finally got a lift to Klais with a lumber merchant. Then continued on foot. He told me to turn off at Erderlinger Hof. And now I was on the road to the Spital Pattendorf nursing home, and the little church tower two kilometres off was already in sight.

I got to my feet again, wished the ant luck, and made for the buildings, which looked nothing like Munich's grimacing, bombed-out ruins. A man in a nightshirt came towards me, windmilling his arms and crying, 'Blaisi, Blaisi!' A nun followed in hot pursuit.

I passed through the main gates and into a large inner courtyard. Along its four sides were three accommodation wings and a stable block, and at its centre stood a well, a pair of chestnut trees, a weeping willow and several mental patients, who were arguing over which of them was allowed to sit on the only bench, and whether it was green or infected. I approached a nun who was hurrying anxiously towards this group, and told her who I was and that I was looking for my mother and sister. She just shook her head and pointed towards a pergola, in the shade of which a little girl was sitting on a stone step.

She was perhaps five years old. She had a sketchpad on her lap and was drawing the Lord God. The Lord God had glasses and a beard, of course. He could see people naked through his glasses. He could see through clothes. Even through your skin. And the angels have wings so they can fly him everywhere. They're trying to make me Catholic. But Amama says over her dead body they will.

The girl said all of this as I stood before her, the words pouring out of her like a waterfall. She was wearing a red, white and black dress with little red hearts sewn onto it, clearly made from a large Nazi flag: a black strip dog-legged down its skirt against a white background. Her face might have been drawn by Hans Holbein, so pale and English was it. My sense of exclusion lessened at the sight of her, and I marvelled at how like Ev she looked. I couldn't imagine having brought something so beautiful into the world, and had to resist the urge to give her a paternal pat on the head.

'Are you new here?' she asked.

'Yes.'

'Are you a cripple?'

'No.'

'That's what I thought, when you was standing over there. Or is it "were standing"? Oh, bother!' she smiled.

'And what was it you thought?'

'I thought, he's definitely not a cripple, he's a less able person.'

'And what's a less able person?'

'Someone who lives here and doesn't have a limp or anything.'

'An idiot?'

'Mami says you mustn't say idiot.'

'She's right.'

'You say less able person. Except Amama. She always says idiot, and sometimes she even says loony, but that's Bavarian, and I'm not allowed to talk Bavarian.'

'But you shouldn't say cripple, either.'

'I know. My papi is one.'

I stared at her.

'So you're just a normal man?'

I nodded.

'But if you're a normal man, I should call you "sir".'

'You don't have to do that – and you know why? Because I'm your uncle. Your normal uncle Koja. And you're normal little Anna, am I right?'

She looked at me, now with a changed curiosity and an inspiring intensity.

'Gosh, Uncle Koja, you're very thin.'

'Yes, because I was a prisoner of war. They've just let me go.'

'If you like, I can steal an apple for you.'

'Oh, but I'm sure your mami wouldn't like that.'

'Well, she's at the hospital. And Amama is out in the fields. And you did only just stop being a prisoner of war.'

She disappeared inside the building and came skipping back five minutes later with two apples and a hard-boiled egg. She looked over my shoulder, because I had picked up her sketchbook, the worst paper I've ever held in my hands, and was using children's coloured pencils to sketch the old woman with dementia who had now laid claim to the green bench under the weeping willow.

'Gosh, that's really lovely, Uncle Koja,' she said, both polite and appreciative, and I knew I wanted her to become much prouder of me.

Then we ate the apples and shared the egg.

I stayed with Anna until dusk fell, letting her show me all around the nursing home and learning that she wanted to become a nun when she grew up, because then you could be called Sister Elegiana, Sister Ambrosilla, Sister Violentia, Sister Ditberga, Sister Nemesia, Sister Waldeburga or, last but not least, Sister Aldemarana. Or even Mother Superior. But she didn't want to be called Sister Anna, not in a million years, and she didn't want to be a Catholic, either, for fear of upsetting her amama, of whom she was extremely fond.

To show me what kind of place she was living in, Anna introduced me to the nursing home's inmates. There was Fluttermonkey, who ran everywhere waving his outstretched arms as he went. Crab Man, whose wooden leg was screwed on wrongly. The fat Bellringer, who used to be a ship's cook in Hamburg. Liesl-with-the-Voice. Pastor Sepp, so called because his brother was a man of the cloth. Oxen Sepp. Sepp the Chemist. The Chin-ninny, who was a cap fetishist and had a chin like a chest of drawers, and who delighted Anna by making dog and cat noises. And finally, One-Leg-on-Crutches, who secretly read tarot cards – ungodly, heretical magic though that was. One-Leg-on-Crutches was a former prisoner of war, like me. He told me that a hard fate lay in store for me, but if I happened to have a cigarette for him, he could check the cards again.

When evening came and a mist rose off the Isar and the sun sprayed the courtyard and the mist with light, Mama appeared out of the glittering vapour. She came trudging in through the gate, and I saw her before she saw me. A small, golden woman in a grey headscarf, wiry and energetic and wearing a skirt that looked to be made of old Wehrmacht trousers. She finally spotted me, stopped and shook her head. The spade literally fell from her hand. But she picked it up again at once, because weakness had always seemed suspect to Mama, in herself and everyone else, and then came towards me chuckling with weakness all the same. I ran to her and she embraced me and held me tight, hitting the small of my back tenderly with the spade, and I could smell earth and weeds and strawberries and age and that scent I had known ever since I could smell.

We wept and wept and said how much we had missed one another, and she kept looking at me, her eyes swimming with tears, shaking her head and lamenting, what a skinny rake of a man I had become, and weak as a kitten.

We went up to Mama's lodgings and into the roomy parlour, as she called it, while Anna got ready for bed in 'the little room', which was not a room at all, not even a little one, but a cupboard. The whole apartment consisted of just that spacious parlour, which contained three beds, a table, several tabourets (as Mama called chairs that were not to be trusted), a washstand and a huge old painted wardrobe. The walls were hung with pictures I had painted and given to Ev more than a decade before. There was nothing there to suggest Hub's existence. I could see a bloom of greenish mould on the ceiling.

'Well, it's a roof over our heads, at least,' Mama declared. 'We were quite on our beam ends when we arrived, with our clothes in rags, but we were given a few things, mostly old, and Anna is especially well taken care of by the district commissioner and the nuns.' She took a couple of chopping boards, some cutlery and a loaf of bread from a small cupboard. 'The Americans handed out clothes as well, in Mittenwald. But only to Poles, Ukrainians and so forth, who hadn't already got what they needed by attacking and robbing people. But not, of course, to such second-class outlaws as German refugees!'

Her talent for indignation, her arrogance, the quickness to judge that made her seem harsh had not been dented one bit by the years of humiliation. And those years were quite clearly not yet over.

We said a prayer before supper; there were radishes and celery to go with the bread, along with a little schmaltz, and water from the well. The bunch of meadow flowers I had brought with me stood in a tin can.

Mama took care to avoid certain topics, I noticed. I didn't want to ask directly how Hub had become a cripple. And she didn't volunteer any information, either, didn't mention my brother and sister at all. Instead, she told me all about the difficulties of being a Protestant family in Catholic enemy territory – a part of the country which, to cap it all, spoke an impossible dialect that threatened little Anna's future prospects. 'The nuns have been dispatched here from their convent. Dragons, the lot of them, and all that excessive churchgoing and jabbering prayers does nothing to change their bad character,' she complained. 'Have you heard the monotonous way they intone litanies? A synagogue is nothing in comparison.'

'What's a synagogue, Amama?' Anna asked.

'It's a church for Jews. There, now, be a good girl and eat up your radish.'

'And what are Jews?'

'They are people of faith who aren't Protestants.'

'Catholics, you mean?'

'Not quite.'

'Brilliant!' Anna cried in delight. 'In that case, when I grow up, I'm going to be a nun with the Jews!'

We put Anna to bed, left the room, and went out to sit in the Alpine-foothills evening, the cool, damp air from the nearby river seeping into our bodies. A lot of birds were still singing, even though it was already pitch dark. It sounded as though myriad nightingales lived here. But in truth it was the nursing home manager's blind budgerigars, whose eyes had been chemically burned by leaking gas in a Munich air-raid shelter three years previously. They were now oblivious to the great Karwendel range, or at least the view of it, from their cage by the open window ten metres above us.

'I won't ask, my darling.'

'Thank you, Mama.'

'The situation is clear, in any case.'

'Do you think so?'

'Behind immeasurable suffering, at the true root of it, lies sin. But there is a remedy.'

'I'm sure there is.'

'When sadness issues forth from sin, then gladness is a child of redemption. And today I am glad. So glad!'

'I'm glad too, Mama.'

'You are alive, and that means God is protecting you and showing you his love. He protects Hub and Ev, too.'

'Are they well?'

She hesitated, didn't answer, which was not her way at all. Eventually, she laid her birdlike hand on my knee, gave me a resigned look and said quietly, 'I am so very glad.'

By the time we returned to the roomy parlour, Anna was asleep. Mama said that Ev often spent the night in her hospital accommodation in Mittenwald during the week. She only came back up here every few days. 'You can sleep in her bed tonight. We're not expecting her until tomorrow.'

And so I slept in Ev's bed. I burrowed my nose into her pillow, burrowing for her scent, burrowed and burrowed but smelled only soap. I searched for her hairs and found them; one had wound itself around a button on the pillow, and between my thumb and forefinger I could even feel its torn-out root, like a tiny onion.

I woke in the middle of the night.

'Uncle Koja, you have to get up.'

'Hmm?'

'You have to get up. I need a wee. Really badly.'

For a second I didn't understand, confused by the wisp of a dream and ancient memories of a night thousands of years ago, when little Ev relieved herself in front of me, the start of everything, the start of Anna, too, in a way.

Anna shook me and showed me her chamber pot, insisting that I stand outside the door while she produced her little puddle of shame. She sent me out and even carefully locked the door (twice). Then she forgot about me and went back to sleep, while I stood in the darkness, staring at the double-locked door.

I didn't want to wake her or Mama, so I didn't knock; I just settled down with a sigh on the huge flagstones, wrapped in one of the red gingham curtains that I had painstakingly unhooked from the curtain pole. And as I lay there, listening to the muffled groaning and snoring of the lunatics asleep behind the rows of doors, I felt a sense of gratification that Anna had inherited my modesty, my great fear of nudity, my dread of my own excrement, my own sweat and blood.

No, she would never become a doctor, at least not a good one.

And, filled with a boundless love for my daughter, a love that had only just hatched on that malicious, scornful day but was already giving me something to cling to, I fell asleep.

<h1 style="text-align:center">6</h1>

The great chamber-pot parade began early the next morning. All the fairy-tale characters came shuffling, stumbling, scuttling and hopping over me, carefully carrying their full enamel pots, greeting one another in friendly tones with 'Morning' or 'All right, there' or 'How do' on their way to the only lavatory, beside the feed store and the washrooms on the other side of the courtyard.

Fluttermonkey spilled a few drops, and everyone got out of his way as he came rushing and flapping past bearing a huge pot; I, too, wriggled over to the wall and sat upright.

Anna was very sorry that I'd had to sleep on the hard floor, and she promised to draw me a picture in which I would be lying on a bed of white clouds in heaven, because they were so soft, and she promised never to lock the door again. Never.

Then she had to fetch her ancient satchel and leave for the village primary school (Catholic, but neither Mama nor Ev was able to look after her themselves). Her pigtails whisked away, and she was gone.

Mama took up her spade again and disappeared off to do work about which I learned nothing more.

I remained in the nursing home. Ev had been on the night shift and would return in the afternoon. I took myself off to the home's church, a Gothic chapel dressed in a patchy baroque costume, a suitable place in which to love life from death, just as Ev must be loved from death, I was sure of that.

But then Ev was not who I met at all.

A grey, pre-war DKW pulled up in the courtyard and an amputee climbed out. I marvelled at his athleticism, and only recognized my brother when a nun greeted him with 'Good day, Herr Solm'. It was only later I learned that the bullet I'd put through his hand had caused splintered fractures and blood poisoning, and the Wehrmacht doctors had been forced to amputate first his hand and then his forearm – and finally, due to inadequate post-operative care, his upper arm as well.

After the war, he made the best of the loss and wrote a manual entitled, *Not a Cripple – A Victor!*. An almanac well worth reading, with the medical aspects edited by Ev. It was inspired by the madhouse where his wife and daughter lived and contained a wealth of useful tips for the daily life of a man mutilated in war. He had even worked out how to cut his own fingernails and tie his shoelaces one-handed. There were photographs showing how to operate scissors with a bent knee, or make a skilful loop in the lace using your thumb and little finger. And of course, how to drive a car with one arm. An instant best-seller, which no one has heard of these days. Hub now has flesh-coloured prostheses made of weatherproof PVC – though of course, he wasn't wearing one (and indeed had no need of one) when he hit you on the head, my dear Swami. Medicine really has come on in leaps and bounds.

But back then, there was merely an empty jacket sleeve dangling from Hub's shoulder as he hurried across the courtyard with the nun at his side and a small doll in his remaining hand, evidently a present for Anna, to whom he was making a surprise visit.

I called his name.

Ten minutes later he was on his knees in front of me, sobbing. It was impossible not to notice that he had turned to God, since he asked me whether I had turned to God, too. And he said that where sin had become mighty, mercy had become mighty, too. And it was only odd phrases like 'what a dunderhead' or 'that's just pissing in the snow' that told me this truly was my brother.

After another ten minutes he drove off again, having assured me that I had his blessing, and he hoped I would be happy with Ev.

I was monstrously confused, as you can imagine: my desire for revenge was waiting somewhere between the cruel Standartenführer and the snivelling servant of God, and it was just too strong to remain there, unfulfilled.

When my sister finally arrived, the flowers that we sat among seemed to have an inner glow, like the mountains, and above all like Ev herself. She was wearing a wasp-waisted light-blue skirt with a slit up the side; I had never seen anything like it. She must have bought it in a real shop. There was so much material that it spread out around her feet like a river delta. She wore it with a plain, light blouse, cut down from a man's shirt, which emphasized her boyish figure.

She did her best to be light-hearted, which felt rather put on, especially as we had greeted one another with just a brief hug. As we each felt the nearness of the other's body, she suddenly got hiccups, but still she tried to tell me – interrupted by regular hiccuping – that after fleeing to Germany she had stayed here at Pattendorf first and foremost to be closer to God, whom she had begged day after day to keep me from harm. And she had sworn that if I should ever come back from prison, she would convert to Catholicism. Now that I had, she would therefore have to become a papist.

I wondered what was going on with my siblings and their religious fervour. Even during the most horrific months in the Lubyanka, I'd never had a conversation with Jesus Christ, only with my sweetheart loneliness.

'Mama won't like that, you know,' I said, just for the sake of saying something.

'No, but in some ways it will make things a lot easier for Anna here.'

'She has grown into such a sweet, pretty girl.'

'And she's inherited your talent. And your way of overcomplicating things most of the time.'

'Does Hub know?'

Ev hiccuped, which made her fingers hop off her knee, beautiful doctor's fingers, one of them wearing a full set of marriage jewellery, all of them a little nervous. She put a hand to her throat, stroked the skin over her voice-box (where my lips had sucked so often many years before) and shook her head.

'He still thinks she's his daughter.'

Then she started ripping up tufts of grass as if they were hair.

'We separated after the war, as soon as we arrived here.'

'Why?'

'What he did to you . . .' She trailed off and wound the blades of grass around her fingers in silence.

'He was here earlier,' I said.

The blades of grass were torn into tiny pieces and fluttered down into the light-blue river delta.

'We spoke,' I said.

'That's good.'

I nodded, with a sense that the wind gathering in the valley was warmer, milder than the day before.

'He often comes over from Munich to see Anna. Sometimes he sleeps here, too.'

'In your bed?'

'Yes, in my bed. We're still married.'

'Of course. That's a very good thing.'

'And we're careful with each other. We're friends.'

'Really?'

'He's stopped drinking,' she replied evasively. 'And he has a real faith now.'

'He's not the only one, it would seem.'

'And he's very sweet to little Anna.'

'How is he doing professionally?'

'Are you just trying to make conversation?'

'What? Why? No. I just want to know what he's doing.'

'I don't really know,' she said listlessly. 'But he has a car. And who has a car? Only racketeers and black-market traders. But officially he works for a haulier in Pullach.'

'A haulier?'

'In Pullach, out near Munich.'

'A haulier? With one arm?'

'Do you still love me, Koja?'

'Ev.'

'What?'

'Of course I still love you.'

'I just mean, because you didn't bring me a present.'

'You will never change,' I smiled.

'I waited all this time, you know. I believe that you're my fate. And even if it was terrible, what we did, it was still right. And *I* would have brought you a present after all these years, even if it was a stupid pebble from down there.'

She pointed out at the Isar with a disgruntled look on her face.

'Ev, I don't know anyone in the world but you who would say such a thing.'

'Are you saying you think I'm peculiar?'

'Unusual, I would say.'

'Anything else?'

'What do you mean?'

'Attractive?'

'Yes, I think you're attractive.'

'Desirable?'

'Desirable.'

'Desirable despite all the lines on my face and the bags under my eyes and even though my hair is going grey?'

'In that skirt, even if you were bald you'd still be the most desirable woman I've ever met.'

'Is that so?'

'As truly as I'm sitting here.'

It was only now that she looked at me. The expression that came into her eyes was one I knew of old; it told me her mind had raced far ahead, her life was already playing out somewhere else, and she just had to catch up with it to make this great promise come true, and it would be easy for her to catch up – that was written in her eyes, too, and it reminded me of something.

'We've still got two hours before Mama and Anna get back,' she said tentatively.

'That's good.'

'We can stay out here in the fresh air, observed by half the religious community of the Alpine foothills . . .' The sentence faltered, though there was more of it to come, and I thought she was going to start hiccuping again, but then the rest spilled out in a rapid torrent. 'Or . . . we could go up to the parlour.'

You know, I really couldn't imagine her ever becoming a papist.

And I knew then what her eyes reminded me of. It was the picture of a snowy owl that Papa had drawn when I was five. He'd told me that snowy owls won't blink even once until they've got what they want: a mouse.

'Don't you want to?' she asked uncertainly, sounding almost hoarse.

'Well, the fresh air is nice,' I said helplessly.

She hiccuped just once. In disbelief.

Then she started ripping up the grass again. After a while she said, in a changed tone, 'I'm sorry for being so childish. But I would like to live with you.'

'I'd like that too, Ev.'

'I'm serious.'

'But we can't.'

'Is there someone else?'

'Yes, there's someone else.'

We sat there, both of us looking up at the mountains. She shrugged twice and eventually said, 'Really?'

'Really.'

'That's all right.'

'Ev . . .'

'I'll always love you. And I don't regret a single day of all these years I spent waiting for you.'

'Ev . . .'

'Please go now. I'd like to be alone for a while.'

That evening, when I had returned to the Schwabing North reception camp, I wrote a long letter to Maya Dzerzhinskaya. I enclosed it with a dispatch that I sent to Moscow the following day, via the agreed cover address.

I was letting Comrade Nikitin know that I had succeeded in contacting my family.

7

Four months later, Hub picked me up in his chugging two-cylinder DKW at the Stachus square in Munich. He had Anna in the back, and she wrapped her spider arms around my neck from behind. She drew out the vowels in both 'Uncle' and 'Koja', which were breathed onto the back of my neck. 'Uuuncle Koooja.'

Children were playing on the heaps of rubble opposite the Karlstor. Hide and seek, I think. They didn't play executions as much now. So Anna told me.

We drove through the ruined city, past numerous construction sites and even some freshly rendered buildings, though for the most part the streets were lined with hell-black reminders and remains, dumps of sooty terracotta and rubble, roofs like exposed ribcages and windows with nothing but bluish-white clouds behind them. We passed the lively black market at Sendlinger Tor and reached the large bone depot to its south. I handed in a basket containing five kilos of foraged bones, which I'd dug out of bomb craters, mostly the skeletons of cats and dogs. Anna had even brought leftover bones all the way from the nursing home's kitchen in Pattendorf. They didn't accept human bones. In payment, we received two large pieces of hard soap. We got back into Hub's car with a sense of pride.

'You won't have to do this kind of thing for much longer, Koja. You'll have plenty of dough soon enough,' he said with a grin, the cigarette in the corner of his mouth dancing as if glued to his lips.

'But, Papi,' Anna said, 'the nuns always say you don't need dough to be rich.'

'And they are quite right, little one. "Serve one another with the particular gifts God has given each of you."'

We drove out of the city through the Isarvorstadt, Sendling, Thalkirchen and the well-to-do village of Solln, heading south on Wolfsrathausener Straße, to the occasional whipcrack of the ancient engine backfiring. Every metre we travelled brought fewer traces of the war, and we sang Lutheran hymns all the way. Hub took this a little too far, and so a few swashbuckling Landsknecht songs were added to the repertoire.

We passed through the city limits, overtook a few farm carts, and just outside Pullach we turned down a narrow gravel road towards the Isar.

After four hundred metres, we stopped at a barbed-wire fence and a makeshift gate. A coloured GI wanted to see Hub's papers. The only person I knew in that skin was Mary-Lou; I'd never seen a black male hand so close up before, at least one that wasn't proffering drinks or pastries. My brother took care not to touch it as his identification was passed back through the open window. The GI then snapped the hand up to his forehead and said in English, 'Welcome home, Mr Ulm, sir.'

Then he saw Anna and me.

'This is my brother,' Hub explained.

'Mr Neu-Ulm, sir?' grinned the soldier, who had obviously been getting to know his way around the picturesque Alpine foothills.

'He's been announced,' Hub replied in a sour tone.

The soldier checked his guard book, and then raised the barrier quite unhurriedly. We rolled into the huge compound where Hub had been – how shall I put it – working for more than a year.

From the moment we arrived, it seemed a perfect parody to me. A parody of Weimar classicism through the medium of absurd architecture. There were neatly trimmed lawns as far as the eye could see, and two dozen Nazi copies of Goethe's famous summer house (on the Ilm, you know the one I mean). They had steep-hipped roofs and stood at ease, spaced regularly around a rectangular green the size of several football pitches. A blood-and-soil idyll, just waiting for Goethe's Erl-King to arrive.

'Who built this?' I asked Hub as we got out of the car. 'And who was he trying to spite?'

'But, Koja, isn't this beautiful? A whole village, surrounded by all this green space! Far away from the hubbub of the city. Look, Anna, there's the swing, just over there.'

My daughter bounded over to the swing, the centrepiece of a neat playground with a little slide, a sandpit and monkey bars. We strolled after her, and I noticed a flagpole the height of a tree on the other side of the playground, with a Stars and Stripes flag vibrating in the light breeze.

'I'll give you three guesses as to who used to live here,' said Hub.

'Snow White and the seven hundred dwarves?'

'Martin Bormann. With his whole entourage. SS-Brigadeführers upwards. And over there, on the other side of the path, is the Führer bunker. Want to go and take a look?'

'Just tell me one thing, Hub: why did the Yanks choose to set up here, of all places?'

We had reached Anna, who was begging for someone to give her a push, and he was more than happy to oblige, was Uuuncle Koooja.

'Oh, it isn't the Yanks. No, this is an entirely German project. And a godly project, too. I wouldn't be here otherwise.'

He spat out his dog-end, and before I could react, he gave our daughter a very unamputated push.

'The Doctor hates the Yanks. They're just our useful idiots.'

'Papi means our useful less able people,' I explained to Anna as she flew past.

'They're trying to set up their own secret service now. The Tsay-Ee-Ah, it's called.'

He sounded like a braying donkey. It was only years later that we would start calling it the See-Eye-Ay, pronouncing it the American way, which we were all still avoiding back in the late forties.

'A few of them have come here to learn from us.'

'To learn what? How to lose?'

'There's no need for that.' Hub's face grew serious; he looked at his watch. 'It's time. I'm going to introduce you to the Doctor. Think about what I've said.'

Think about what I've said.

Things between us were almost like they used to be. Big brother, little brother. Grandpaping's legacy. A duality of saying things and thinking about what's been said, caretaking and rebellion, Hubert and Konstantin. And hadn't Hub's way of routinely taking decisions away from me – something I had suffered and tolerated since we were children – been exemplified with my death sentence? And hadn't I acquiesced to this death sentence he had passed on me, in the same way I had acquiesced to him eating my dessert, to being born in the wrong month, to wearing his hand-me-downs? Or to thinking about what he'd said?

He could always look after me, he could always govern me. Even now, after everything that had happened. He wanted to find a place for me, just as Comrade Nikitin had suspected. If he had shot me dead in the war, he would, in a certain sense, just have been finding a place for me. And now he had become godly again, just as he had been godly before. Of course: he'd studied theology; of course: he knew all the psalms and Bible verses. But he had known them when he convicted me of insubordination, too. They just hadn't been at the front of his mind back then.

Serve one another with the particular gifts God has given each of you.

And I would. I would serve him now with the particular gift he had given me. I felt nothing but coldness as that thought went through my mind.

But he seemed guileless. He seemed to regard it as only natural that I would still be dependent on him, on his connections, his secrets and the decisions he made.

The fact that I was no longer sleeping with Ev, which neither he nor she understood, at least restored a little of my self-esteem – or rather, my independence. Although I wished him the worst that this world had to offer, I was still trying to bring the two of them back together. The idea pierced the hard, squalid little parlour of my heart, it's true.

But Anna needed a father. And I was prepared to do anything for Anna, and that was the root of this new intimacy between us all, which I intended to abuse as considerately as possible.

We left Anna squealing with delight in the playground. Hub set off towards the compound's main building, a long, two-storey affair, and I followed him. To my surprise, the closer we got, the clearer it became that Bormann's villa had largely ignored the demise of its former master. The haughty, claws-out Nazi eagle, carved in stone above the front door, was still clinging on, albeit to thin air where the swastika beneath had been chiselled away. The garden was home to abandoned, slender bronze Teutons by Thorak and Breker. And on the end wall of the large ground-floor dining room, ladies with heaving bosoms were binding stalks of wheat into yellow sheaves.

We waited there. My head resting on a blue frescoed apron.

From time to time, a white-liveried orderly brought us a cup of ersatz tea.

When the Doctor finally appeared, accompanied by an adjutant who never left his side, the first thing that struck me was his sunglasses. An umbrella unfurled above his head could not have surprised me more. These days you see them in every bad spy thriller, but at that time I thought he must have eye trouble.

We got up, and he called himself Dr Schneider.

Until that point, I'd only had dealings with one of the three prominent Nazi secret-service bosses: the always well-coiffed SS guppy Walter Schellenberg, head of the SD foreign intelligence service, who that very day – it was the fourteenth of September, nineteen forty-eight – was fighting the death penalty before the Nuremberg court.

The second Nazi secret-service boss, Admiral Canaris, head of the military intelligence service and an extremely surprising would-be Hitler assassin (in the end, his small stature and the concentration-camp rations made him such a flyweight that, when they hanged him, he had to be hauled back up and dropped again five times before his neck broke), was someone I never met.

And the third Nazi secret-service boss was now standing before me, with his bald head and his bat ears and his sunglasses, calling himself Dr Schneider for the same reasons that Hub was known as Herr Ulm.

I knew his real name. As the head of the FHO, the army's military intelligence unit on the Eastern Front, General Reinhard Gehlen had worked closely with Hub's Operation Zeppelin. It was a miracle the general was still alive. And was permitted to go on living quite blithely, as far as the US Army was concerned; for some inexplicable reason, they would rather see Guppy Schellenberg hang than Gehlen or Hub.

'Terrific,' said the Doctor. 'You don't look anything alike.'

'My brother only returned from the Soviet Union a few weeks ago,' Hub explained.

'What's your point?'

The point was that I was still a half-starved skeleton, while my brother had begun to gain weight and his features were becoming doughy. It was impossible to say that to the general, and so I tried making a joke: 'Well, they performed an operation on my face. May I introduce myself? Solm. I'm honoured to meet you, Dr Schneider.'

I stood to attention and very nearly gave a Hitler salute.

Gehlen came right up to me and took off his glasses. I could smell pipe tobacco, see his cerulean eyes, and a little moustache with a pair of pursed, dwarfish lips beneath it. He's going to kiss me, I thought. But then, ten centimetres from my face, he just said, 'He doesn't have any scars at all.'

It had been a mistake, I realized, to try making a joke. Jokes vanished in his mind like raindrops in the sea.

'Just goes to show,' the Doctor said, turning to both his adjutant and my brother, 'that the enemy is already streets ahead of us in facial surgery. First he pounds his victims to a pulp, and then he sews them back together as if by magic. You must have your brother photographed for the archive after this, Ulm. Good for propaganda, too: human experiments in the East!'

'Very good, Herr Doctor.'

I would never get the opportunity to correct that error. Years later, Gehlen would come up to me in the middle of international negotiations and introduce me to some Filipino or Jordanian military officer, to impress them with the words, 'Isn't that an incredibly straight nose?'

When Gehlen had dismissed his adjutant and invited us to accompany him to his office, we found ourselves in a room that was furnished like a well-to-do funeral parlour. White tulips on the table, a crucifix on the wall, a death mask of Frederick the Great beside it. A hodgepodge of

Protestant and Catholic devotional objects, surrounded by every shade of brown in the world.

Nothing could have been in greater contrast to the many-mirrored, plush, red-velvet brothel into which Guppy Schellenberg had transformed his Berlin office. There was no machine gun hidden in the desk here, no false wall panel revealing a drinks cabinet filled with brandy and Scotch, no built-in microphones. Even the secretary looked like a Salvation Army tambourine major. While Schellenberg had been suave, urbane, perfectly proportioned and an expert in the many uses of charm, the most charming thing about Gehlen was his complete absence of humour, for which he tried to compensate with condescension and arrogance.

'So, you want to come and work for us?' he asked me rather brusquely.

'It would be a great—'

'Just yes or no, please, that's what the short words in our beautiful language are there for.'

'Yes, Herr Doctor.'

'Lubyanka?'

'Yes, three years.'

'Recruited?'

'By the NKVD. My handler's name is Nikitin.'

'A nasty fellow. Keep the line open. We'll give you information to feed him.'

'Very good.'

'SS?'

'Yes, my final rank was Hauptsturmführer. Operation Zeppelin.'

'Expelled from the SS?'

'Yes, by my brother. It was the only way to get me out of Himmler's firing line.'

The lie is a tender lover. Such soft hands.

'What I really value in SS men,' the general growled with some satisfaction, 'is their reliable opposition to the world view against which we are working. And I think I sense this opposition in you, too.'

'Thank you, Herr Doctor.'

'Good. Then let me tell you what you see here. Or do you already know what you see here?'

He gestured towards the window, almost dismissively.

'A good deal of sunshine and green space, for one thing,' I said, trying to remain vague and following his gaze out of the window, even putting on the same expression of basic mistrust.

'Western Europe.'

'Western Europe, excellent.'

'Western Europe, which is in danger of going under, amid the chaos of economic disruption and the communist thirst for power.'

'That's exactly what I see,' I agreed, narrowing my eyes.

'And since there is a Russian steamroller rumbling towards us, my closest colleagues and I have made our information, our files and our know-how available to the LE.'

He said 'Ellee'.

'The Ellee, Herr Doctor?'

My brother cleared his throat.

'The Lesser Evil, Koja.'

'The lesser evil?'

'The gum-chewers.'

'I see.'

'I would like to make it clear,' the Doctor added, 'that we reject the Americans' degenerate lifestyle.'

'Of course, Herr Doctor.'

'Democracy is for proles.'

'Very good, sir.'

'Social democracy is to be resisted.'

'Naturally.'

'The Twentieth of July plotters are all flops and traitors. None of *them* is coming to work for me.'

'Good.'

'There won't be any anti-Semitism here. But of course, there won't be any Jews, either.'

'Understood.'

'We don't need Nazis here. But Hitler was an interesting person, and he knew what he was doing.'

'An outstanding dictator, Herr Doctor.'

'I was with him often enough to be able to confirm that.'

'Every word you say gladdens my heart. It would be a great honour to serve—'

Gehlen interrupted me by raising his right index finger like a conductor's baton. Then he propped his hands on the small of his back, stepped closer to the window and looked out with even greater determination in his eyes. Before the panorama of the distant Alps, Bormann's pastiche Goethe-houses squatted around the large lawn, where my, my, my Anna was swinging all alone, beneath the flag of the United States of America.

'Your daughter?'

'Mine,' Hub said, erroneously. 'You've met little Anna, haven't you?'

Gehlen nodded, lost in thought, and then turned to me.

'Do you have a family, too?'

'No.'

'That's a shame. But perhaps we'll get you down here anyway. Herr Ulm will tell you how things work around here.'

Two hours later we reached the Flaucher, an old beer garden around a forester's lodge in the city's southern Isar meadows. We sat down in a secluded spot on the pebbly bank. The river was shallow here, and the water clear with a greenish tinge; a very faint fishy smell rose from the stones.

'There isn't much water coming down from the Alps at the moment,' Hub said. He had rolled up his trouser legs and put his feet ('trotters', he called them) in the water. 'Pale as new cheese,' he said when he saw my calves, all the colour gone from them after years in the Lubyanka – he had picked up other Bavarian expressions, too, dropping the odd one here and there into his Baltic German. To Anna, he called out, 'Happy wallowing, piggy-whidden!' She was splashing a few metres away in a dammed-up pool, and after Hub had got us two glasses of *Weissbier* from the bar (his hat pulled low over his face), I found out how things worked in Herr Gehlen's compound.

'From now on, your name is Dürer.'

'I've always wanted to be called Dürer.'

'Heinrich Dürer.'

'All right.'

'Our organization is the Org. Nothing more. That's what it's called.'

'I work for an org?'

'For the Org. The. Not a. The Org at Camp Nikolaus.'

'A little joke?'

'No. We moved in on St Nicholas' Day, the sixth of December.'

'Right. It's a good job you didn't move in on the twenty-fourth.'

'Everyone who works for the Org lives in the compound. Their wives. Their children. Everyone.'

'Me, too?'

'You. Me. Everyone.' He sighed. 'It's just Ev who is adamant she wants to stay in Pattendorf, in that miserable place. She would have a good life in the Org. And so would little Anna.'

I said nothing; I was watching Anna tiptoe her way across the riverbed, her feet bare, her arms outstretched like a tightrope-walker. 'Look at me! Paaaapi! Uuuncle Koooja, my balances! I'm not losing my balances!'

Hub smiled at her, took a sip of beer and went on, 'Camp Nikolaus is a fully independent entity. There's a kindergarten for the little ones. The older children attend the camp school. The men work in the various departments, and almost all the wives are secretaries.'

'A paradise.'

'There's a market garden, a library, cinema, swimming pool, two playing fields. The Doctor has even had a golf course put in. We've got our own bakery, our own laundry, our own petrol station and our own hairdresser.'

'So all you need now is a cotton plantation and a deep-sea fishery.'

'For that we use the Yanks' PX stores. They have steaks this big there. This big!'

He showed me with his one hand. I looked at my piece of hard soap, which was lying next to the beer, and thought of all the cat skeletons I'd had to scrape out of Munich's bomb craters to obtain it.

'There's one other important thing,' he said quietly, taking one foot out of the water and pulling his knee up. 'Munich is out of bounds.'

It was the first thing that had really surprised me.

'What do you mean?'

'It's a forbidden city. Like Peking. Or Lhasa.'

'I don't understand.'

'No entry. You can get our bus once a week to shop at the McGraw Barracks. And once a year, the whole Org goes to the Oktoberfest together.'

What I heard was 'Orgtoberfest' – my confusion possibly caused by Hub repeating several times that Munich was otherwise completely out of bounds.

'I'm not allowed into the city at all?'

'If Gehlen catches you in the Englischer Garten without permission, you're for the chop. Life in society is taboo from now on. We're ghosts. We live in a ghost town. No one can know we're there. That's the price.'

'And these people here?' I asked, looking first at a couple of fat anglers who were dozing dully away on the bank, and then behind me at the beer garden, which was packed with war profiteers, Yank-lovers, black-market traders and a lot of Bavarians in lederhosen, clutching blond beers.

'We're sitting on stones by the Isar here, Koja. This is fine. But we're not allowed into the beer garden.' He pulled his hat down over his face again, as if to emphasize his words. 'If you want to visit a beer garden, there's a minimum safe distance of forty kilometres.'

He drew a circle in the air with his finger.

'The same goes for family outings: at least forty kilometres away. Holidays: at least a hundred kilometres. And we don't have any contact with the surrounding villages. None. You can't even buy a newspaper there. Parents keep an eye on their children. They're forbidden from making friends with the village kids.'

'Are you not taking things a bit far?'

'Who are you?'

'Who am I?'

'What's your name?'

'Koja.'

'Your name is not Koja.'

I said nothing.

'Your name is Dürer. And you've always wanted to be called Dürer. Heinrich Dürer. And Munich is swarming with KGB assassins. And you don't want them asking you who you are and what your name is.'

'You've tricked me into this.'

'Welcome to the Org.'

'What am I to do?'

'I put you forward for Department 1, acquisition of foreign intelligence. But the Doctor went over your file, and your training.'

'And?'

He stood up and rolled his trouser legs back down. He called for

Anna, who made a fuss because the water was so lovely and cold and she was looking for mermaids, and when he had told her off – as you used to tell children off back then, when they weren't out of the water on the count of three – he looked at me and said, 'You studied architecture. We need a reliable architect.'

In the autumn of nineteen forty-eight, I became a reliable architect for a doctor with no face and no name, the man who was using the winning side's millions and the losing side's personnel to distil an arcanum of promising relationships into an intelligence service that also had no face and no name. And no place where it was permitted to exist.

And it was in this place that didn't exist, because it had no permission to, that I began my aesthetic programme – my alchemical programme, you might say – with a three-metre-high and four-kilometre-long brick wall around the compound, which had previously been secured only by a barbed-wire fence. And while the compound itself did not exist, the wall most certainly did, which was a contradiction that could not always be resolved when subjected to questioning (from Ev, of course, but also from baffled walkers).

All the same, I created permanence in the midst of the amorphous and the ghostly, and it might well be said that the site's structural transformation from sealed to hermetically sealed proceeded from my drafting table alone.

I had beehives installed along the outside of this wall, and fake greenhouses on the inside, so that the population (i.e., the baffled walkers) would imagine hundreds of gardeners, botanists and beekeepers inside these fortifications, who just wanted to be left in peace to rake, sow and cultivate.

I turned the Führer bunker, hidden away in a dark grove and known to everyone as 'Haus Hagen', into a counterfeiting workshop.

One floor below the workshop, I created the world's largest stamp store. In what had once been the private rooms of the Greatest Field Commander of All Time – a suite of ice-cold concrete caves – I installed tightly spaced walls of shelves that held a hundred thousand rubber stamps. You could find everything there from the official seal of major Brazilian cities to the stamp of a small hospital in Turkistan.

I had all reminders of the Thousand Year Reich ('Entry permitted only when air-raid siren sounds!') painted over in white, and ripped the Führer's bathtub, the Führer's shower and the Führer's bidet (strictly speaking, the Führer's lady-friend's bidet) out of the Führer's bathroom. I allowed only the Führer's lavatory to remain, though it was then walled in with fittings *made in the USA*, and I took great pleasure in relieving myself in this silent place.

I also worked on the Doctor's official villa. New carpets had to be purchased (without a swastika pattern); I had the hallways painted and the lamps replaced. For Gehlen's office, I designed a mighty trophy cabinet, the inner doors of which could be opened and folded out into a map of the world done in inlay work. The Soviet capital was the only metropolis to be given an initial letter, a limewood 'M', which the Doctor mistakenly believed stood for Moscow, though of course it was really Maya.

Beneath the Org's kindergarten, a nuclear bunker was dug out for the little ones; the Reich Labour Service barracks next to Haus Hagen were transformed into tiny offices, and Anna got a second swing, right outside my office window.

Is there anything more lovely than watching your small child on a swing?

I myself moved into a Goethe-esque gingerbread house in the far reaches of the compound – though I did have to share it with an informant handler, a planning specialist and a fat, jellyfish-like outlaw from Upper Lusatia, about whom to this day I know little more than his name, which was Hortensius Vierzig. At least, that was his exotic alias.

We never talked about our identities or our jobs. And when men cannot talk about themselves or their work, they lose all desire for communication, and so we didn't really speak, though it was never silent, either – we played cards (*Skat* or *Doppelkopf*) and studied our Erdinger *Weissbiers*.

The most difficult element in Camp Nikolaus was, as always, the human one.

Many of Hub's new colleagues were already known to him from the Reich Main Security Office.

Sometimes he would call me over to his rooms, to help him welcome these gentlemen. It was not always a party.

Two former SS-Standartenführers, for example, burst into ringing laughter when Hub said 'Good morning' to them. They gave him an emphatically German greeting in return and put their arms around his shoulders, their way of trying to express comradeship and joy at this reunion.

Another, who had once set fire to seven Parisian synagogues, made a little bow and enquired how, in such an independent, self-sufficient set-up, they could have forgotten the camp brothel.

They all had their fitted kitchens measured up and their offices furnished by me and my construction unit, most choosing stained oak.

Very soon, I encountered some of my former SD colleagues, including Möllenhauer, gayer than ever, who had entered into a solid marriage of convenience with a lesbian concentration-camp guard (in contrast to his Pierrot pallor, she blushed very prettily and had a voice as tender as a Sappho poem).

They lived just two cottages down from me, and their names were Herr and Frau Pichelstein. I spent many evenings at their house. Möllenhauer seemed genuinely pleased to see me alive. He was certainly surprised to see me on good terms with Hub. But he asked no questions. He had always been clever, clever and cunning. And he was therefore also the only person with whom I could slip out from time to time and secretly drive into Munich for the evening.

While he took the opportunity to flit around the city's homosexual bars until the following morning, I met with Nikitin's contact man in a changing series of beer halls.

I always sat alone, preferring a table near the window. The agent would position himself at the bar. We wore hats as a sign that we could be approached, and took them off if we felt someone was watching us.

We exchanged our secret messages in the lavatories. He received all my architectural plans, staff profiles (so far as they were known to me), important memoranda and summaries of my conversations with Hub.

I received letters from Maya, which could only ever be read there and then, in a shithouse that stank of urine, under a naked bulb. I read them at least ten times before they were consumed by the flame of my cigarette lighter. The filmy ashes crumbled to dust between my fingers and I carried them around with me for as long as I could. I learned these short letters off by heart, like the one from the ninth of November nineteen forty-eight:

My love! A thousand kisses everywhere. How I miss you. I miss you endlessly. I have the feeling that you miss me, although I am with you. I am lost dust in all your pockets. I am as invisible as it is. I read a lot. They let me. I thank them. I will always miss you. Your boom-boom-boom. I go through my time without you. And what I did and am, everything, everything, in the end only your name. Dearest Koja. No bong-bong now! I wish you a very happy thirty-ninth birthday.
    Maya

I sobbed, and whole panoramas passed before my eyes as I read her words. Confused words that didn't sound like her at all. Words that were nothing more than proof it was her writing to me, and not a censor. I tried to hold back the tears, and squeaked in my cubicle. The sound of a mouse being trodden on. I'm sure the men who were pissing into the metal gutter on the other side of the lavatory door thought that someone was masturbating behind the bolt with the red 'occupied' sign. What could I do, beyond studying the loops of the handwriting like a graphologist? Beyond trying to discern Maya's mood from the length of the tails on her 'g's and 'p's?

I couldn't learn long letters off by heart; I only remembered a word here and there, peculiar phrases like 'sugar conversations', which appeared in her letter at Christmas nineteen forty-eight:

How often I dream of our afternoons in the mountains, back in Bessarabia. My love, do you remember? The rain on the tin roof? How young I was. How simple happiness was. And now I am an old woman of twenty-seven. I have lost three teeth. Since your last letter, I have had time to improve myself. You are doing everything you can to save me and [the name that followed was blacked out by the censor] *from the punishment that is really only our due, and so we have the pleasure of sugar conversations.*

I didn't know what was meant by that. Was 'sugar conversations' another way of saying torture? Or interrogation? Was it another way of saying anything, or did it simply mean conversations about sugar? Could I ask about it in my next letter? Or would she lose another three teeth if I did?

While I often sank into depression, my letters to Maya were optimistic and had comical little drawings in the margins. I wanted to make her smile.

I wrote to her that I was achieving great things for socialism on the invisible front. I told her that in view of my successes, she might be released in as little as five years, and then we could have children, one happy child for every Lubyanka year. That made five, if you started counting now. I drew five portraits of little Anna, including her plait bobbing as she didn't lose her balances, which Maya thought wonderful.

I always came back from these evenings completely exhausted, but also emotionally unburdened; back to Camp Nikolaus, the ghost archipelago. I blew in, unnoticed, through the doctor-door that the far-sighted architect Konstantin Solm had built into the perimeter wall. The door was intended for the sole use of the Doctor (who had the only key), and his traitorous architect (who had the only other key).

Despite what I was doing (the moral implications of it, I mean), I felt as calm as a grazing sheep. Keeping Maya alive was worth any price. And it is just as desirable to keep oneself alive, where possible. My goodness, I was calm. I really would not counsel anyone towards lies and treason. Except in certain circumstances. Lying is often the only shield for the selfish and the yearning. It keeps all the important things functioning. No family would survive if its members were not permitted to lie. Nor would any nation state. There is no world without lies, and a world in which lying is accepted is just as impossible.

Unfortunately, lying tends to make us think ourselves all-powerful. When it came to Hub, for instance, I had the exhilaration of forgiving him for Maya's fate, because he was now in my hands. Because I could be affectionate towards him. Because he was like a pet to me, a rabbit.

But I was cut off from the rabbit, which is a rather unfortunate turn of phrase, so let me say: I was cut off from my own hand, which was stroking it. And please, revered Swami, you mustn't think that the truth meant nothing to me at that time. The truth remained my highest commandment, but it conflicted with my other highest commandment: self preservation.

*

And so I revealed to Comrade Nikitin in as much detail as possible how perfectly Dr Schneider and his two hundred adepts were continuing what they had learned under Hitler and done for Hitler, in the service of Washington. Discovering the size of troops and military movements, calculating potential economic advantages and production figures, keeping records of staff and redeployments in the top ranks of the East's armed forces. I also revealed that some of them believed Nikitin to be a woman, and a good-looking one, at that.

However, they hadn't the faintest idea of political nuances, or even the enemy's mentality. Reinhard Gehlen had followed the general staff's rule of thumb never to bother oneself with learning foreign languages. And so he knew only one Russian phrase: '*na zdorovie*', although that didn't stop him from launching into occasional monologues about the Slavic disposition. He was capable of the same very basic interaction in English ('cheers'), French ('*à la vôtre*'), Italian ('*cincin*'), Japanese ('*kanpai*') and later Hebrew ('*mazel tov*'), when dealing with Mossad. But since he harboured a mistrust of all other languages based on their fundamentally foreign character, that was all. In Spanish, even this rudimentary vocabulary broke down: he believed there was a Spanish equivalent of the German '*Prost*', which there famously isn't, and so, much to the Falangists' surprise, the Doctor always raised a glass to the prostate, '*a la próstata*', very politely, very cluelessly. And then down the hatch.

All the same, his agents had mastered the ABC of enemy surveillance.

His hive of secret-service bees, on a high plain by the Isar, was busy making a delicious marsh-blossom honey. The swarm buzzed and hummed. Absolutely true.

In March nineteen forty-nine, when Gehlen's private house was to be renovated, much greater demands were placed on my architectural skill.

The LE had given the Doctor a villa on the shores of the Starnberger See. It was in Berg, a picturesque fishing village which prides itself to this day on the fact that King Ludwig II succumbed to madness there and drowned first his physician and then himself in the lake. You Bavarians really are peculiar people.

The Doctor's two-storey property was primarily composed of bays and little turrets in the classic rural style, and before the family moved in, it had to be adapted to the needs of the paranoid import-export entrepreneur that Dr Schneider claimed to be.

First, I tackled the three-metre height that was required of the perimeter wall: my speciality. Then I turned the tool cellar into accommodation for the Doctor's bodyguards. I had the doors and window shutters of the timber-framed house reinforced with steel plates, and saw to the installation of an alarm system.

The real challenge, however, was to place small electronic listening devices all over the house for the KGB; Comrade Nikitin had been very insistent on this point. The renovation work allowed the walls themselves to be comprehensively bugged, using plastic containers the size of hen's eggs, powered by highly concentrated alkaline batteries (manganese electroplating, a brand-new innovation), which sat very nicely in the cement and could transmit radio signals for up to two years. They were a world first, much like the KGB itself (the Kremlin's Good Boy, a favourite taunt of Reinhard Gehlen's). The KGB was still a playful puppy in those days, and went by an entirely different name, but it was gradually becoming the organization we know today: a monstrous guard-dog with a metallic-sounding bark, deadly breath, a hundred heads and a snake's tail, and the last of those was me.

One day, when I was alone on the building site after work had finished for the day, hacking into a freshly plastered wall in order to place one of these plastic eggs, I heard the key turning in the front door downstairs.

In a panic, I threw wet cement at the wall and just managed to smooth it down over the microphone-egg with a trowel before the door opened and Frau Dr Schneider, alias Frau General Gehlen, alias Herta von Seydlitz walked into the room. She was a carefully dressed lady in her early forties, thin and angular, with scaly-looking skin on her face and hands. She had a portrait of her distant ancestor, Friedrich Wilhelm von Seydlitz, under her arm, I really don't know why. Perhaps she was looking for a good spot to hang it.

In any case, we fell into conversation: her forebear, the famous syphilitic cavalry general (pacifists like yourself won't have heard of him) had recently been pulled out of his two-hundred-year-old baroque mausoleum on the other side of the Iron Curtain by vengeful Soviets, and scattered in the woods of Silesia – his bones had, I mean.

Within five minutes it emerged that some great-great-great-aunt of

Frau Gehlen's, who came from a long line of Silesian aristocrats, had emigrated to Courland in the times of Peter the Great, and had been liberated there by a Schilling, a man of whom I had never heard, but then Mama's family is a large one.

Anyway, the Doctor's wife decided that we were related, so to speak, or at least might be, and she let out a delighted peal of laughter when she learned that I was actually an artist.

'I'm afraid the need for aesthetics is rather absent from Reini's life,' she sighed. 'To him, the visual arts are a stage magician at Circus Krone, turning yellow blots into green blots.'

The Doctor's wife insisted that I call her Herta, though of course decorously retaining the 'Frau'. Frau Herta. Herta with no 'h' in the middle (and without an 'M' at the beginning, which I found reassuring). She was sociable, clingy, and completely starved of company. She had also immediately introduced herself to her new neighbour, the actress Ruth Leuwerik ('Frau Ruth'), bringing over home-made apple cake (home-made by the cook, naturally). She hated her husband's reclusive life. He, who would have preferred to maintain all the presence of an amoeba, must have found his jolly wife a terrible imposition. I never saw him smile when she was there. I think he was always afraid.

For his birthday, on the third of April nineteen forty-nine, Frau Herta gave her husband a three-quarter-profile portrait by me, or rather, a three-quarter profile as yet to be commissioned from me. A kind of art voucher. All her Seydlitz ancestors had been depicted in the same three-quarter profile: looking sideways at the viewer always gives a subject an air of profundity.

I think that the general's first impulse was to fire me, not least because his wife had referred to him as Reini in my presence. But Frau Herta was very stubborn, and after three weeks of the silent treatment (he was silent, not I), he muttered to me one lunchtime in the Camp Nikolaus canteen that his wife thought it would be a good idea to have me paint his portrait. But he would only tolerate this under the condition that I didn't force him into an asinine three-quarter profile.

I agreed to that.

The second condition was that I could only paint him from behind.

'From behind, Herr Doctor?'

'The back of my head, and my back.'

'The essence of a portrait, Herr Doctor, lies in capturing a person's features.'

'Then just capture the back of my head as best you can. And please make the ears a little flatter against the head. And a little smaller.'

'But the essence of a man, of his personality, shouldn't a portrait express that, too?'

'I'll think about whether to wear a hat.'

'I'm afraid a hat doesn't provide a great deal of mimic expression, Herr Doctor.'

'You know what? Paint my wife, instead – then you'll have mimic expression.'

'Is there no part of you I could paint from the front that might please you even a little?'

If you are condemning my hypocrisy, my dear Swami, then please never forget Maya. Please don't forget that I was tormented by letters and memories. How often I woke in the night with a start, seeing that figure dissolving and floating towards me in the Lubyanka's death-row cells. Don't forget that. The sugar conversations. The lost dust in my pockets. The limewood 'M' in the Doctor's cabinet. I certainly never forgot it.

The Doctor thought for a while, his lips folded in on themselves. Then he asked me sullenly, 'Can you do lodges?'

'Lodges?'

'Yes?'

'What do you mean, exactly?'

'Can you paint an Alpine lodge?'

'A log cabin, you mean? Yes, I think so.'

'Then paint my beloved Elend-Alm lodge. I would like that.'

I learned that, when the Doctor was still a general, he had spent the final days of the Second World War in a cabin by this name, on the Elendsattel above Schliersee, just this side of the Austrian border. It was a place very close to his heart, and hadn't the slightest thing to do with *Elend* – misery – in the ordinary sense.

In April nineteen forty-five, the deserting general had awaited the German capitulation high up in the glorious Bavarian mountains, along with six of his most loyal staff officers. Around him, the Alpine flora blossomed above the millions of microfilms he had buried in watertight aluminium containers. They held all the information about the USSR that his staff had managed to gather over the preceding years, ready to be sold to the solvent and eager Lesser Evil.

And this historic moment – the deer-shading lodge, the tangy nard-grass meadow and the humus-rich soil, spiked with metal film cases, all waiting tensely for the Americans' arrival – this was what I was to capture. With him, Reinhard Gehlen, and his cherished staff officers inside the building.

'Shall I paint you looking out of the window?'

'No, no, I want a picture without any people in it at all.'

'Then how do I make you apparent in it, Herr Doctor?'

'Well, *I'll* know that I'm in the lodge.'

The Doctor gave me a few photos of the Elend-Alm (it really was just a plain log cabin) and tasked me with creating a fresco, four metres wide and two metres high, in his living room. Genre painting. Lots of brown and green, the worst colours in the world. Frau Herta was not thrilled at the prospect, particularly as she liked more modern art: the great Impressionists, Manet, Degas and Monet.

'Frenchmen and communists – no thank you, Herta,' Dr Schneider scoffed. 'I'd like a beautiful wooden lodge and plenty of nature, painted so that you can tell what it is. That is what I'd like. That's what I'd like. That's what I'd like!'

Fresco painting is not at all easy: everything has to be painted in one sweep onto damp plaster, so that the pigments seep into it like an infection, inflaming it with blue, red and yellow. And so every day I applied a fresh layer of lime plaster and painted the Elend-Alm in the usual *giornate*, one small section at a time, from bottom left to top right in the manner of Tiepolo (from whom I needed to take nothing but patience).

One morning in early May, the bus was late. I half ran up to the Doctor's house (spurred on by the hope that I might finish the whole thing that evening). As I rang the doorbell, I noticed a black saloon parked in the driveway. Dusty. Cologne number plates. The British-occupied zone.

Frau Herta opened the door with a mildly perturbed expression on her face.

'Good Lord – do you hear that, Herr Dürer?'

The first thing that sprang to mind was a woodpecker. Then I realized that someone was hammering the house to pieces, at least, that was what it sounded like.

As I raced up the stairs to the first floor, I prepared myself for the worst.

I threw open the door. Light plaster dust hung in the air. Before me, in two comfortable leather armchairs, sat the Doctor and his visitor, their hands gripping the chair arms. The visitor was a haggard, ancient tortoise of a man with tiny slits for eyes. Their black suits, their bald heads, even their eyelashes were coated in snow-white powder.

'What's he doing?' I asked, stupidly, referring to a chauffeur whom I had never seen before. The chauffeur blinked at me with large sheep's eyes, and slowly lowered the pickaxe that he seemed to have smashed into the poor Elend-Alm several dozen times already. My fresco was half shattered and the carpet was covered in multicoloured rubble and well-proportioned fragments.

'Good morning, Herr Dürer,' the Doctor said politely – but I had no desire to be polite, and cried out in a fury, 'You've ruined the whole picture!'

The Doctor turned solemnly to his guest.

'May I introduce the artist, Herr Dürer.' Then to me: 'And this is Herr Adenauer from the CDU.'

The tortoise merely nodded.

'Herr Adenauer was keen to see the house,' the Doctor said, making no sense.

'Nice lake, that,' the old man said in an unmistakable Cologne accent, squinting out at the Starnberger See and adding, 'Oh, aye, very nice.'

'Unfortunately, Herr Adenauer . . .' The Doctor sighed, before taking a breath, coughing from all the dust particles that had danced into his lungs, and starting his sentence again. 'Unfortunately, Herr Adenauer saw another house yesterday, belonging to Major Heinz, that old no-hoper.'

'Oh, now, Major Heinz is a good man.'

'I tell you, Heinz is an imposter!' the Doctor shot back. 'An imposter, and a Twentieth of July man, don't forget.'

The tortoise reached into his trouser pocket, took out an egg-sized container, unscrewed it and presented its guts to me (though really to the Doctor): a microphone, a transmitter, a battery.

'Listening device,' Adenauer summarized.

'Ridiculous,' Gehlen said.

'Very sophisticated methods.'

'Heinz is just inventing things to make himself look important.'

'Found it in his house, he did. Soviets put it there. Cemented into his wall, it was.'

'Oh, please!'

'Was a foreman Heinz had known since before the war. Bought off by the enemy, just like that.'

'Couldn't even handle—' The Doctor was racked by another coughing fit, which sent little white clouds up from his clothes in rhythmic bursts. 'Couldn't even handle a master bricklayer, old Heinz.'

'But you, my dear General, aren't seeing the quantum of geopolitics.'

'You don't seriously believe I would allow bugs to be placed inside my own four walls.'

'Well, we'll see about that, won't we?' the old man said pensively, his eyes on the disfigured wall. 'Let's see what all comes plopping out of there.'

'You're hacking my picture to pieces,' I said, quivering, 'to check whether there's one of these things hidden behind two weeks of hard work?'

'You see the trouble this has caused, Herr Adenauer. Now the artist is getting upset as well.'

'Ah, well then,' said the guest, putting on a placatory expression, 'let's stop this silly business, after all, eh?'

'No.'

The tortoise man laughed, and you could tell he didn't laugh often.

'You're an eccentric, Herr Doctor, right enough.'

'Because I won't tolerate being compared with that dimwit Major Heinz? His intelligence service is about as trustworthy as his walls.'

'No need to be jealous now, my dear General. We'll come to an agreement, you and I. If I should become chancellor, naturally.'

'Of course you will become chancellor.'

'Aye, well, it'll be a close-run thing. What I wouldn't give to know what all else the Social Democrats are cooking up.'

'Shall we find out?'

'Now, then – I didn't hear that question.'

'That's because I never asked it.'

'Herr Müllerstein, you can leave off now.'

The chauffeur nodded deferentially and leaned the pickaxe against the wall, right next to the tiny piece of very modern surveillance technology that was just peeking out of the plaster. It had been shredding my nerves ever since I set foot in the room.

But the chauffeur didn't see it, and nor did anyone else. He picked up his floury uniform jacket, put on his chauffeur's cap and left the room. I picked up a chunk of plaster to conceal the treacherous plastic egg.

'Herr Dürer,' the Doctor said, stopping me in my tracks. I turned to him, on the point of passing out with fear. He and the tortoise man were wiping the white dust from their faces with their pocket handkerchiefs.

'How would you like,' Herr Gehlen asked, 'to become a member of the Social Democratic Party?'

8

The Hippy can't eat solids any longer. He survives on soup and porridge. Night Nurse Gerda cares for him in a very touching way. It occurs to me that he has stopped complaining. But he seems much more tense than usual. That's worse than the complaining.

He had a visitor recently.

Someone he called 'Pilgrim'.

She was a thin streak of a woman in Jesus sandals and a green and brown batik garment that drooped from her bony shoulders like the leaves of a recently felled tropical rainforest. She sat on the Hippy's bed for an hour and asked about the frequency of his occasional erections. Then he got one.

Later, she placed her hand gently over his skull-screw. It didn't seem to bother him, and so, as if it were the most natural thing in the world, she began to scratch and fiddle about with the screw. It took a little while, but eventually she turned it as if were a common or garden tap. She had this strange grin on her face, of course, that all these people have. Do they constantly see Jesus, or what? I really don't know what she was expecting, but eventually there was a noise like a bus opening its pneumatic doors. I said do take care, both of you, that's a brain, not a toy. But the Hippy hissed at me to mind my own business. That in itself was odd: as a swami, he always claims that none of us has our own business, and that this so-called business suppresses our cosmic consciousness and blocks the energy flow for everyone.

'Wow, that guy's a real square,' the Pilgrim murmured critically.

Then suddenly, she was holding the skull plate in her hand. Some small metal thing fell off and rolled across the floor. The woman looked sleepily at Swami Basti's exposed brain, said it was really beautiful, and asked the Swami if she should stick a candle in it.

And that was when I realized, unfortunately much too late, the irreversibly life-threatening nature of the situation. I shouted, although I am not allowed to shout, because the bullet in me doesn't like it, and while shouting I pressed – no, hammered on – the emergency call button for the nurse, or the call button for the emergency nurse, one or the other, and then of course all hell broke loose.

They wheeled the Hippy into theatre at once and tried to save his life. And since then he hasn't been able to eat solids. And is constantly nauseous. That's how it is.

He won't hear a word against the Pilgrim. He claims she has natural healing powers, and unlike me she is sensitive. And she would certainly never hide bugs in the walls and eavesdrop on people.

I ask if it's better to stick candles in people's heads and light them. But he shrouds himself in an icy silence – this man who can talk until the cows come home. It's a long time since he has called me by my first name. He is approaching a state of boiling rage that I am familiar with from Hub. And in that state you only open your mouth to spit fire and brimstone, not to talk about trivialities or to praise the Lord.

'Basti?'

'Uh huh?'

'We can't go on like this.'

'What?'

'You're in a terribly bad mood.'

'I'm dying.'

'Shall we smoke some grass?'

'I don't have any grass.'

'Of course you do. I'd like to go up on the roof and smoke with you again.'

'You never smoked with me before. You watched me smoke.'

'I'll pay for it.'

'You just want me to go mad like your colleague that time and fly away over the rooftops of Munich and then be dashed to pieces.'

'Maybe I *should* have a smoke myself.'

'You?'

'You and me.'

'You said you're not taking marijuana again, ever.'

'Yes, but I feel like breaking the mould.'

The Swami gives me a shocked look. Then he fixes his eyes on the wall opposite, raises his voice and announces, 'I don't have a clue what this man is talking about! I don't take illegal drugs! I don't violate any laws! I don't know this man! He's a complete stranger to me!'

He gets up and starts investigating every corner of the room. He looks in the bulb sockets of the table lamps, unscrews the cover from the intercom. A glance under the bedstead.

'What's all this in aid of?' I ask.

'Hang on, I'll have it in a minute.'

'I haven't installed any listening devices in here, if that's what you're getting at.'

'Sure about that?'

'How on earth would I?'

'And cameras?'

'Of course, I have a nobody like you watched around the clock by a team of specialists. Why would I do that?'

'You're trying to provoke me. You want me to have a joint. To document my drug-taking, *which I don't do*. You want to get me locked up.'

'You *are* locked up, Basti.'

'You want to do something bad to me.'

'You're at death's door, Basti. There's nothing worse anyone can do to you.'

'Thank you!' he says, all fire and brimstone.

'I wish you well. You wish me well.'

'I'm not sure if you do wish me well.'

'That scum business is starting to get old now.'

'But where's the transformation? When does the conversion begin? When do you become wonderful?'

'I don't! I am not a wonderful person! I never claimed to be. You say I am, because of that rosy swami shit welling out of your brain that stops you from seeing people as they truly are.'

'I don't have to listen to that from someone who kills Jews and Russians and shoots his brother's hand off and betrays everyone he meets.'

'No one gets to choose when he is born, and where, and in what circumstances. You grow into the age in which you find yourself, and God knows, not everyone can grow up in an age when hippies are left alive.'

'I can't deal with aggression.'

'But you're the one being aggressive!'

'I'm not aggressive. I'm in a bad mood.'

'You *are* aggressive, with all your messianic balderdash, saying the world is one particular way and not another.'

'There are truths of being.'

'That makes me want to vomit.'

'There are.'

'All truths of being are nothing but God-awful opinions. You grow into these God-awful opinions, all of which belong to a particular age. All of which are the product of a particular age. All God-awful opinions present themselves as valid and lasting. And they are anything but valid and lasting.'

'But the world is getting better.'

'The world is getting *better*?'

'You surely can't believe that the patriarchal principle is still going to exist forty years from now?'

'What on earth is that?'

'You know, the dominance of men over women. The suppression of sexuality. Bourgeois marriage. All that is going to vanish. I mean, that's totally obvious.'

'In the year twenty fourteen, the whole world is going to be an ashram?'

'Of course. And there'll be no more people like you.'

I don't say anything more. We have reached a point where there is nothing more to say. There isn't even anything to keep quiet about. All we can do is transcend; in this respect, the Buddha-Vishnu-Hare-Krishna circus has done a service to mankind, I won't dispute that. I know that some people can travel from one place to another without moving. But anyone can do that in a dream, and that's why I've always liked dreaming so much. And sleep, without which there are no dreams. For that reason I do not fear death, the longest sleep that mankind is granted.

And so I sink back into my pillow and wait for the virginal temple dancers, skipping towards me on little yellow clouds.

'I'm sorry, *compañero*,' the Hippy says twenty minutes later, his voice altered. 'I overreacted. Of course there will be people like you. I didn't mean to offend you.'

'You didn't offend me. I offended you. And I meant to.'

'I don't understand how you can work for the Nazis and for the communists and for the reactionaries – and then end up joining the Social Democrats.'

'But I haven't told you yet whether I actually joined the SPD. And we're still a very long way from the end.'

'Did you join the SPD?'

'Yes.'

'I don't know whether I'd be glad if you went and converted to Hinduism now.'

'Politics is a ship of fools, my friend.'

'And why didn't you just stay on as an architect in Camp Nikolaus?'

'Because the world wasn't getting better. Nothing ever gets better. Ever.'

9

The occupying powers' secret services regarded the Org as a cesspit, a pool of warm, bubbling slurry into which anyone might relieve himself at will, and the Doctor swam in a sea of disdain and piss.

Major Lewis Maxwell from the British MI6 referred to him merely as 'the turncoat'.

The French (SDECE) called him 'Fantômas' among themselves and made fun of his eyes and ears: he had the best guarded eyes in the West (*lunettes de soleil!*) and his ears stuck out like Charles de Gaulle's, and were even the same size and shape.

The Munich representative of the US military secret service (CIC), Colonel van Halen, discovered that he was known in Pullach as the

Lesser Evil, and from then on refused even to shake hands with the Doctor.

Instead, he invited the competing CIG to take over the Org.

The CIG, however, politely declined, saying that you shouldn't let anyone who'd kissed Adolf Hitler's ass kiss your own, and please, dear Basti, spare me from having to explain the work or even the abbreviation of the wretched CIG, and allow me to come to the point: the British, French and US counter-espionage organizations were openly hostile towards us.

The newly founded CIA, which everyone had now stopped calling the Tsay-Ee-Ah, was the only pleasing exception.

They loved us as every mother loves her child, however wayward it might be.

We were suckled and swaddled, we were well-nannied and given plenty of things to play with. The Best Mom Ever ensured our quality of life in every respect. She sent a dozen babysitters to the camp every day to pat people on the back, ask if their shoes pinched, and see that everything was all right. All the things that altruistic liaison officers do.

Many of them had brains; they had studied at prestigious universities, and were scientists, writers, journalists. On Sundays we went out to the playing field with them and played an absurd game with an egg-shaped ball.

During the week, we exchanged information.

It was no surprise, then, that opposite Haus Hagen one May morning – the day was rather overcast, and still almost cool – I bumped into Donald Day, the old swashbuckler from Riga. He had packed in his job as the *Chicago Tribune*'s Russia correspondent, grown fat as a Buddha, and become an analyst for the Agency, as he called the CIA. He instantly invited me to join him for a Latvia memorial beer.

You can't say no to that.

'The British faggots and those syphilitic Marie Antoinettes sit up there on their high horses and say why are you using the fucking Nazis?' he ranted, smacking his lips, as we sat in the Flaucher before our tankards and *Weißwurst*, casting all the Org's beer-garden-visiting rules into the last May wind. 'What kind of a dumb question is that? It's completely impossible for us to operate in southern Germany without you guys.'

'I'm not a Nazi, Donald.'

'Of course not. But I am a Yank. And the minute I order a bratwurst here, everyone can tell I'm a Yank. But when you order a bratwurst, no one can tell you're a Nazi.'

'I'm not a Nazi.'

'Of course not. But what I mean is: who can disguise themselves in this country better than the Nazis? Who knows Germany better than they do? Who's the most organized? Who are the best anti-communists? I'll tell you: people like you.'

'You're making me really cross here, Donald. I'm the opposite of a Nazi. I'm in the SPD!'

'Not using Nazis would be like castrating ourselves. So we use them. And shall I tell you something else?' He patted my knee and turned his little-lamb eyes on me. 'Those stuck-up Tommies use them too, when no one's looking. The Frogs use them, when no one's looking. Even the commies use them.'

'The communists? I find that hard to believe.'

'I'm telling you: there are KGB men in Moscow who organized the morning roll-call in Auschwitz.'

'Incredible.'

'Those cocksuckers in the state department don't think gaining an advantage is a good argument for it. But one thing is clear: there's no way to avoid World War Three. And if it's going to happen, we should at least win it.'

It was Donald Day's influence that brought my work as the Camp Nikolaus architect to an end and plunged me, overnight, into a labyrinth of old scars and new wounds.

The CIA had moved on to squandering American citizens' tax dollars on large covert operations against Stalin, the most covert of which was the finance and training of a secret Ukrainian guerrilla army. And for this, they needed the Org. The paramilitary units were to be formed in the Bavarian state capital, for the simple reason that this was where the Ukrainians in exile had gathered.

Donald asked me to seek out Ukrainian Zeppelin survivors and other counter-revolutionaries who were eager to see some action.

The first advantage to this was that it finally gave me official permission to go into the city. The second was that the task turned out to be child's play. Munich was overflowing with malnourished and malcontent Ukrainians.

At the Ukrainian University (in Pienzenauerstraße, not far from here, on the other side of the Englischer Garten), all I had to do was put up a single discreet notice. Thirty young patriots were soon swapping the lecture theatre for a new war. Several exiled senior members of the Bandera Group, fascists to their marrow, were recruited via the US consulate. And then there were my old, battle-hardened Zeppelin veterans, whom I found in the barrack settlements in the north, or in the foreigners' assembly camp at Zirndorf.

A few of them recognized me. One even still wore the canine tooth of a tapir that we had slaughtered in Riga Zoo around his neck, as a talisman.

These former warriors were now being fed by the Caritas soup kitchens, scraping a living as day labourers and longing for danger and adventure. They clutched at my grandiloquent promises; they were as inquisitive as capuchin monkeys, and I lured them into perdition with chocolate, cigarettes and whisky.

The volunteers were put up in three former pilots' barracks at Schleißheim Airport. I was given an American MP uniform with no insignia and became the troop's operational leader. Since I needed some kind of rank, they called me 'Chief'. I took Möllenhauer with me as my deputy. We looked like two Yankees from Wisconsin. The Doctor got a fright when we reported to him in full US gear for our special mission, and he ordered us to show the gum-chewers how to get Eastern Europe back under control.

Our commander, however, was indifferent towards Eastern Europe. He was a narrow-minded man from the Deep South by the name of Dana Durand, who had reached his position through a combination of accident, negligence and error.

Instead of 'Operation Zeppelin' the project was named 'Red Cap'. The name was taken from the headgear of American railroad porters, a helpful but not very heroic occupation, and in Ukrainian it was also a synonym for 'lickspittle' – a fact that Washington had sadly overlooked.

As if that were not enough, we presented the rebels with velvet berets, which were supposed to be red, but had more of a rosy-pink shimmer to them, and no self-respecting Ukrainian puts on a pink jester's hat unless someone is holding a gun to his head.

The guerrilla units were to be flown across the Iron Curtain in a Douglas C-54, parachute into the Ukraine and work their way forward to join the rebel Bandera separatists in the forests near Kiev. They were promised unlimited financial and military support, and everything under the sun for the post-war period. Their orders were to hold out in the swamps, killing as many Soviets as possible, until American troops marched into the USSR.

The planning, preparation, equipping and execution of the operations lay in my hands. My deputy and I went about all of this just as we had during Operation Zeppelin: ultimately, the whole song and dance was merely a da capo under a new flag.

The Americans gave as much of a damn about the activists' fate as we Germans once had. But they didn't even have the decency to feign concern, or interest.

The commander gave speeches in which he blustered about how great it was to kill communists, because that brought with it the privilege of being killed by communists, which was a much more desirable fate than being killed by him, Major Durand.

Although I functioned as interpreter for his speeches, I never translated this nonsense, which was intended to be humorous, but would have caused significant irritation among the troops. Instead, I slipped little Russian sayings into my simultaneous translations, which were entirely meaningless, but gladdened the Slavic soul. For example, instead of: 'You sons of bitches better learn to disguise yourself as well as the homos do,' I gave them Tolstoy's little maxim: 'If you want to hide a tree, you need to take it into the forest.' And the watchword: 'Die bravely, not pitifully!' was exchanged for something like: 'There's only one letter's difference between fabled and failed.'

It was thanks to my artistic interpretation that during his speeches, which were the speeches of a dangerous lunatic, Major Durand found himself looking at faces that were open, credulous, and expressed full agreement. This sent him into ever more insane tirades.

By the end, he only ever addressed the soldiers as 'my plutonium'.

Möllenhauer and I clapped our hands to our foreheads when it became clear that the US training staff, which consisted of seven or eight ignoramuses, believed all members of the Ukrainian nation to be Martians, who were useful on planet earth for picking cotton, at most. The former students of the Ukrainian University were even denied the English-language course they had requested, on the grounds that no teaching capacity was to be wasted on illiterates. Every mistake that we Germans had made in Pleskau and Khalakhalnya, the Yanks repeated, only worse. I felt as though I were in a picture by William Blake, who once painted the soul of a flea, and the souls of all the Ukrainian fleas hopping around us seemed to rise up and envelop us like a dark cloud.

The only significant difference between Zeppelin and Red Cap was the far more impressive array of equipment we now had. In the SD, we'd had to make do and make up for things that were in short supply, but the Red Cap camp was stuffed to the gunnels with black-market weapons and munitions, helicopters, Jeeps, hand grenades, uniforms, frozen T-bone steaks, cornflakes, Bibles and everything else one needs for political overthrows.

I suffered an attack of abdominal colic each time I had to accompany a commando to the take-off runway at the Schleißheim airfield. The procedures and orders were familiar, because we had retained the good old Zeppelin rituals from Pleskau and Riga – apart from the parting 'Heil Hitler' of course. I heard the engines and smelled the jet fuel and the rain-soaked grass and was overcome by memories of Maya's hand, the two fingers I had seen scratching at the window of the Arado, half an eternity ago.

And as I saluted and watched the fleas hopping onto the planes, one after another, with the same composure and suppressed desperation that Politov and Maya had taken with them on their flight, it was clear to me that we would never see them again.

In fact, they disappeared within a few minutes in the night sky; they were dropped over the Carpathians and sent to slaughter, every last one of them. They received neither reinforcements nor any other kind of support. Just the coded messages on Radio Free Europe, broadcast into the ancient forests of the Ukraine, telling them to chin up. And since Möllenhauer had given the friends of the free world high quality receiver terminals for their journey, they set off towards imprisonment, interrogation, torture and death to the sound of Glenn Miller's 'In The Mood' or George Gershwin's 'Rhapsody in Blue'.

On top of this, I was forced to accelerate their downfall. I had to report all the Red Cap deployments and target coordinates to Comrade Nikitin. And in so doing, I escorted these men (some of whom I knew from Khalakhalnya, lads with whom I'd shared a tapir, sung 'Katyusha' and cursed our pink berets) off this planet of pain.

To speak plainly: I sent them to their deaths.

I killed them, my sad Swami.

There's no other way to say it.

You will understand that this was a completely untenable situation. You will understand that I was half-cracked and mazed, as Mama would have said. I'm no hero, but I have never felt I was an amoral person. I may have been a traitor, but I was not a cowardly traitor. I felt no courage in me. But I could be brave. At least, on occasion.

And in one way, my concern for Maya was also a concern for the state of my own soul: this concern gave me the illusion that my every disgraceful action was performed to serve a higher purpose – and what higher purpose can there be than the protection of a female agent's life, once forfeited according to all the rules of art?

But to sacrifice others for her sake, and in the way that I did, was akin to what Pieter Brueghel painted in *Mad Meg*, or the pillaging of hell. The painting uses only shades of black, red, yellow and brown, and in it, Meg strikes out at demons and hordes of fantastic beasts, only to then march into a wide-open maw herself.

I tried to preserve a shred of decency by providing Moscow with the wrong coordinates for the landing sites. But the risk was incalculable. The KGB might have infiltrated Red Cap and learned the correct coordinates from other sources. A precipice over which Maya and I might fall, should my inaccuracies ever be exposed.

I had to find a way to escape the impending doom.

You may have gathered this from my tone of voice, from the long pauses, but I find it difficult to speak of this time. I would rather strike it out of my life altogether, particularly as it was brief and featured no notable characters: everyone I encountered in Schleißheim, with the exception of the ignorance made flesh that was Major Durand, passed by me like mist.

Fresh reservations or even maledictions may well be taking shape in your mind, my dear Swami. And yet: I cannot leave out those weeks, so inglorious, so drunken and tangled, filled with scruples that pounced like two million mosquitoes on my stupid blood.

When there was not a single drop left in my veins, I drove out to see Ev in her Pattendorf madhouse. She sent Anna out of the room and cooled my forehead with a wet cloth. She didn't want to know any details. My disjointed stammering and the fact that she was my sister and my unfulfilled love was enough for her. She injected me with a serum that triggered a severe reaction, an acute infection that allowed me to report in sick just three days later.

While I was in hospital, I implored Hub and Donald to release me from this operation against our Soviet arch enemy. I told them the Americans' incompetence had completely demoralized me, perfectionist that I was.

Although neither of them understood my request, they accepted it. They called the Chief and his deputy home to the blessed Org after just three months of wandering in the Red Cap desert, at the end of August nineteen forty-nine.

Not long after, Möllenhauer returned to his home town and took over the Org's Hamburg branch, and I lost my closest colleague, which saddened me. I had always liked him, though his forename had never crossed my lips. It was Günther. We wrote to each other every Christmas, until a few years later, when a rent boy cut his throat.

The Doctor transferred me to the domestic division, and when Comrade Nikitin found out, he was apoplectic with rage.

For weeks, I received no message from Maya. I was given to understand that I must do everything in my power to get back into Red Cap. And I pretended to try my best, forging official requests and sending the carbon copies to Nikitin, with assurances of my devotion.

I don't know what would have happened if the KGB had sent me one of Maya's ear lobes by way of encouragement. I would probably just have done as I was told. But no ear lobe arrived, and nor did any other part of her body. Nothing was severed from Maya, nothing forced into her, no injury caused.

Nikitin seemed to trust me.

It really was within my power to escape from Operation Red Cap.

I almost believed that myself, it was laughable.

By the time Konrad Adenauer was elected by a majority of one – his own vote – as the first chancellor of West Germany, on the fifteenth of September nineteen forty-nine, I had brought the murky Red Cap chapter to an end and moved into a new office in Pullach, in Barrack E.

I was in charge of domestic enemy surveillance for Section III. My task was to keep dossiers on a list of targets. First and foremost, this work saw me collating information on the Social Democrats.

Now and again I was assigned to special operations, though they were hardly worthy of the name. Since I was the Org's only portraitist, I occasionally had to produce composite sketches of enemy agents – a rather tedious and taxing exercise, artistically speaking. Even painting little blue flowers on Delft porcelain is an easier task.

And because no one but me in the whole of Pullach understood or spoke Yiddish, I had to spend weeks listening in on the bugged hotel rooms of Israeli commission members during the negotiations over German reparations.

Since these represented the high points of my job, I can quite justifiably claim that the work I did for Section III was the most boring, trivial and harmless work one could do anywhere in the Org.

And so I was happy as a clam.

My efforts to organize a real flow of information for the KGB were also bearing plentiful fruit.

I had taken up the position of treasurer in the Munich-Schwabing branch of the SPD, using my real name. My visits to Munich were thereby finally legitimized, and the meetings with Nikitin's living letter boxes seemed less risky and acquired a nice rhythm.

One of my KGB tasks was to keep a record of all Adenauer's attempts to have the Doctor, who was loathed by a broad sweep of French and British allies, appointed head of the German secret service, in the face of considerable opposition.

He made a great many attempts, Swami. You see, there was fierce debate about whether the Federal Republic of Germany – occupied by the victorious powers, controlled by military governors, sovereign only on paper – was actually permitted to have a secret service at all.

The negotiations, on which my informants reported to me, went on for a year.

I presented the latest updates at the large Monday meetings in Camp Nikolaus, which were still being held in the summer of nineteen fifty, and I could see how anxious they made the Doctor. He rocked back and forth in his armchair, getting worked up over every new detail.

'What kind of stupid name is that?' he barked.

'I'm sorry, but I gather that's what the office is called,' I said apologetically.

'Office for the Protection of the Constitution?'

'I'm afraid so.'

'It must have been a socialist who came up with that miserable title.'

'It was a cross-party commission, which voted unanimously in favour of it.'

'But the country doesn't even have a constitution to protect. All we have is a provisional Basic Law!'

'Yes, one suggestion was "Federal Service for Guarding the Basic Law".'

'Guarding the Basic Law?'

'That's right.'

'Am I to become a guard of the Basic Law? Is it behind bars? *Guarding the Basic Law?*'

'There was no majority for that suggestion, Herr Doctor.'

'And what else was on the table?'

'"Federal Office for Germany-wide Investigations".'

'And?'

'That wasn't an option because of the acronym.'

'Acronym?'

'FOGI.'

'FOGI?' he asked.

I said nothing.

'For heaven's sake.'

I said nothing.

'President of the old FOGI?'

He heaved himself out of his chair and began to pace up and down, red-faced, in front of all the heads of department.

'I understand! To hell with their old FOGI! Why don't they just go back to calling us the Abwehr? Or the security service?'

'Security service, Herr Doctor? Sicherheitsdienst? SD?'

'Well then, federal security service for all I care.'

'Because unfortunately, the other members of the commission thought the best name would be "Office for the Protection of the Constitution".'

'What's it called again, when it matters what other people think?'

'Democracy, Herr Doctor?'

'No, decadence.'

'I see.'

'I don't know why, but my wife has taken a shine to you, Dürer. I am to invite you and your brother to our garden party next weekend.'

'It would be an honour, Herr Doctor.'

'Anything else?'

'Well, if you become president of the Office for the Protection of the Constitution, we may well have to move our headquarters to Cologne. Herr Adenauer wants to have us close by.'

'Then I'm counting on you, Dürer. You must find a nice house on the Rhine for my wife.'

While each department began trying to generate enthusiasm for the upcoming move among the employees who were to be transferred to North Rhine-Westphalia, I travelled to Cologne at Frau Herta's behest, to find a tasteful home for the Gehlens, alias Schneiders.

On Kastanienallee in the Marienburg suburb of Cologne, a long way from the centre of the cathedral city (which was still an ash-covered Pompeii, five years after the bombing had ceased), an estate agent showed me around a dream property, in which Schinkel's severity had been updated with neo-baroque cherubs. It had a large garden, a swimming pool and a tennis court.

Unfortunately, it had one disadvantage: no one wanted to let it go for a song to a decorated Nazi general, as they had done with the house in Berg on the Starnberger See. When I telephoned Frau Herta and spoke with enthusiasm about this gem of a house, and with regret about the other interested party who might be putting in an offer that very day, she told me excitedly to take care of the purchase at once and pay the asking price.

I asked if she was sure about making such a major decision without seeing the place, solely on my advice. Yes, yes, she laughed brightly. I had such fabulous taste. And anyway, Reini didn't care about such things. Reini could happily live out his days in a rain barrel.

Unfortunately, Reini did care about such things. He cared very much. Because Reini did not become president of the Office for the Protection of the Constitution.

He therefore did not have to move to Cologne, and above all did not require a palatial house in a city that was now on a par with Stalingrad in his estimation.

The occupying powers of Great Britain and France had won out after a long struggle against Adenauer and the disunited Lesser Evil. They lifted the Doctor's keenest competitors, namely the conspirators against Hitler from Admiral Canaris' circle, into a place in the sun.

As one of our moles in the chancellor's office later told me, the British governor Sir Robertson himself had marched up to Adenauer after the decision, shaken him heartily by the hand and said how proud he was that this spelled the end for that Nazi scoundrel in Pullach.

It seemed to be the end for all of us.

A paralysing heaviness descended on Camp Nikolaus. We submerged ourselves in the silence of our now unprotected castle, and went about our work as if performing dull piano exercises.

At the end of nineteen fifty the Org was on the point of folding. The CIA had sunk millions of dollars into a secret organization that had now been ditched and was slumbering its way towards oblivion.

Just five days after the decision against Reinhard Gehlen, twenty-four colleagues in the technical department handed in their notice. They had been recruited by Cologne.

Hub called them rats.

The mood had hit rock bottom when, one winter evening with snow already on the ground, my brother and I walked across the Bormann villa's paved courtyard and in through the front door.

The rooms lay in twilight, insufficiently illuminated by two standard lamps. An adjutant waved us through the large ballroom and into a smaller, wood-panelled room, the former music salon. With the exception of a small cocktail bar in one corner and a Louis XIV table and four chairs in the other, a Bechstein grand piano was the only furniture.

It stood directly in front of the window. The room was lit by a cluster of candles on the table and a reading lamp above the music stand.

The Doctor was sitting at the piano, his back ramrod straight, playing Bach. The adjutant motioned us over to the table. We sat down and spent five minutes listening reverently to the prelude and fugue in A-flat major from *The Well-Tempered Clavier*, until the bright final chord rang out.

'Now then, Herr Dürer,' the Doctor said without turning to me as the last notes faded away, 'you have purchased this luxury villa on the Rhine.'

'Your wife asked me to, sir.'

'I'm sure you don't want to thrust this transaction onto my wife.'

'Of course not.'

'Naturally, you will pull out of the purchase.'

'It's already done.'

'Good.'

He began a little prelude, but before it could progress into the fugue, I cleared my throat and said, 'The estate agent merely wants to keep the brokerage fee.'

The Doctor turned away from Bach and towards us.

'How much?'

'Five thousand marks.'

'Fine. You should be able to afford that.'

A moment of silence as he got up and crossed the creaking floorboards to our table, took his seat and opened the file that was lying ready there for him.

'Is it your opinion, Herr Doctor, that I should pay this sum myself?' I asked in subdued tones.

'Of course. Is it not yours?'

'Well, that's a whole year's salary.'

'You bought a house without consulting me.'

'As you wish.'

'I'm sure Herr Ulm will be able to help you out. That's why we pay such high salaries, so that one can help one's relatives in an emergency.'

'Certainly, Herr Doctor,' Hub replied dully.

'I also expect you, Herr Dürer, to serve me this FOGI president by Britain's grace on a silver platter.'

'I'm already working on that.'

'Then let's begin.'

The skin was taut over his cheekbones, his face expressionless as he looked at me. I opened my file and scanned through my notes.

'The gentleman's name is Otto John.'

'I know his name is Otto John. I didn't know he was a gentleman.'

'Well, he's a president, at least.'

'Smart Alec. Carry on.'

'Otto John, president of the Office for the Protection of the Constitution,' I therefore went on, feeling cowed and keeping my eyes on my papers, 'is a member of the liberal left, married to a Jew. He managed to shirk war service. He was active in the resistance against Hitler and acted as a courier for the Twentieth of July plot. His brother was executed by the SS for high treason.'

'Forgive me, I completely forgot: would you gents like a biscuit?'

He slid a plate of biscuits towards us, which we politely declined, while he began to nibble.

'After the plot was defeated,' I continued, 'Otto John himself fled to England via Spain, and worked against Germany with the British radio station Soldatensender Calais. After the war, he offered himself to the Allies as a witness for the prosecution. He testified against several Wehrmacht generals. There was a lot of bad blood there.'

'You really should try them. Especially the macaroons.'

'Otto John hasn't the first idea about secret-service work,' I said impassively. 'He is said to have an excellent legal mind, and spent many years working as a legal counsel for Lufthansa. Politically, he is aligned with the Social Democrats, and describes himself as an anti-fascist and philo-Semite. His wife is Jewish, as I mentioned. She's almost ten years older than him, supposedly a lesbian. No children together.'

'And that's all?' the Doctor asked with his mouth full.

'He is said to be a skirt-chaser. And there's another rumour that he's a homosexual and hires rent boys several times a month. His hobby is alcohol. He is also addicted to pills and often in debt, because he invests a lot of money in his art collection. He once said he could kill for art.'

'Our country's security seems to be in excellent hands.'

'Adenauer is against him, and is trying to remove as many areas of jurisdiction from him as possible. He will never take over foreign intelligence, that much is certain. The operational side of the organization is run entirely by his deputy, Albert Radke.'

The Doctor nodded and chewed his biscuit slowly as he poured himself one of his incredible 10 p.m. cups of coffee. I had never before seen anyone sink three spoons of sugar into a small cup of coffee without creating a single wave.

'I know Radke,' he said eventually. 'Radke will be helpful to us.'

'Really?' I was surprised, though not as surprised as I was years later, when I learned that Albert Radke was an old friend of the general's, whom the latter had planted in the Office for the Protection of the Constitution himself.

But at the time I said, obliviously, 'Radke has been trying very hard to recruit our people for days.'

'As far as the Org's situation goes,' the Doctor grunted, stirring his coffee, 'you may leave that to me.'

'Very good, sir.'

'When it comes to the Greater Evil, this crisis shaking all of us' – he tapped the spoon gently on the rim of the cup – 'well, I think the Lesser Evil will help us to rid ourselves of it.'

He sighed almost contentedly, closed the folder, leaned back and slurped his coffee, as though he were sitting outside the picturesque Elend-Alm cabin.

After a while he said, 'And with regard to Otto John, I expect you to finish him.'

'I'll pull together all the available information.'

'I said finish him, not pull together information. It's in the national interest that a leftist traitor to the fatherland, a man with perverse sexual proclivities and serious psychological problems, does not take over the German intelligence service. That decision must be reversed.'

I didn't know what to say to that, so I just bowed my head, snapped my file shut and clasped my hands together. All gestures that might express silent agreement. I sensed an air of pedantic ceremony settling around the walnut table, perhaps called forth by the closing of both folders, perhaps enhanced by all the shadows that the candles were casting onto the walls. And beneath the silence that suddenly seemed monkish, like the silence of an abbey, I heard Hub's shallow breathing tail off, as if he were literally holding his breath.

Then he said, 'Liquidation?'

The Doctor didn't laugh, as I thought he might. He didn't laugh at all, he didn't look up; he just waited for Hub's word, a word spoken by a God-fearing Christian, to evaporate.

'We should consider every option,' he said earnestly, and I had a sudden, egregious urge to eat the last biscuit that was sitting in front of me, and I took it and finished it.

'But let's put that on the back burner for the time being. There are other ways and means. And my instinct tells me that Herr Dürer will find those ways and means.'

11

Three days before I first met Otto John, a man whom I will describe to my dying breath as a gentleman, the entire Solm family celebrated Christmas together in Pattendorf.

Mama had wanted a typical Baltic Christmas Eve. It was not the golden nuts, the mistletoe bough, the sealing wax or the spiced oat broth that bothered me. It was the bright red apples, which would inevitably become *Schmalunz*, an apple purée whipped with sweet milk, but before that were to be used for the fraternal ritual that had not been performed for years.

Little Anna insisted on hearing the story that lay behind it, but really, she knew already.

'Please, please,' she begged. 'Please, Amama, tell me how the communists held Grandpaping under the water until he ran out of air.'

'It's Christmas Eve, darling,' Ev chided her. 'We only want to think about nice things today.'

'That's quite right, sweetheart,' Hub added. 'Enough now, or you'll be off to bed lickety-split. And your amama shouldn't be telling you all these horror stories.'

'In any case, Grandpaping got plenty of air again very soon,' my mother explained in her inimitable fashion, 'when he was up in heaven.'

We went to the Catholic Christmas mass with all the lunatics and cripples – there was no Lutheran service – which was held in the nursing home's cold, incense-saturated baroque church. All the monstrances and candelabras quivered as the patients tried to sing 'Silent Night', striking up a wild, holy howl, accompanied by a roaring organ and the last of the blind budgerigars. The home's manager had placed them at the front, up on the gallery, where they sang for all they were worth in their soiled cage. The nuns' cheeks turned red as they said the 'Our Father' and intercepted escaping idiots. The Chin-ninny started licking a large Christmas candle, perhaps because it was made of real beeswax and tasted of honey.

When you stand in a church with your daughter for the first time and see her wide eyes, and the gleam in those eyes tells you that she is listening carefully to the big words dripping from the pulpit, then this Bavarian Latin stops sounding so phoney. And all the pain and humil-iation and breakdowns the people around us had suffered made little Anna's radiant future stand out with tremendous clarity. She could not become anything but a good and helpful person, who would never sink under the weight of her own existence as her two fathers had; she would raise herself up above everything that makes us small and ugly and mean.

'Why are you crying, Uncle Koja?' she asked, in the slightly hoarse, head-cold voice she had inherited from Ev. Her hand rubbed mine comfortingly, and I told her that I was happy, not sad – as tremen-dously happy as she was herself.

'Yes,' she chirruped, 'because the Lord Jesus was born today.'

And I registered my sister's fluttering eyelashes, heard her heart leap, and at her side was my brother's empty sleeve, which trembled constantly, and I belted out 'Oh, how joyfully, oh, how merrily' with the rest of them, and I hoped for a time of truth bringing grace divine, and so instead of 'Christmastide' I sang 'Christmas-truth', over and over again, because it is terrible being in a church with your daughter when she doesn't know it.

When we had trudged back through the deep snow to Mama's par-lour, when we had admired the decorations on the red Baltic Christmas tree, a pilfered pine felled by Hub's remaining arm, when Mama had woven 'the silver hair yarn', as she called lametta, into her delighted granddaughter's plait to make her more *Christkind*-like – after all the fuss had been made – the presents were given out.

Anna found the legend of the Nibelungen under her gift cloth, one hundred and twenty-four pages, hand-written by me over thirty-three nights and illustrated in Indian ink, with Hagen as a drab knight and Siegfried shimmering heroically. Not only did he have my brother's features; he also had just one arm, the left one, in which he held his good sword Balmung (ah, it made me think of Politov). I permitted myself some artistic licence and improved the old tale by having the evil dragon bite off the knight's hand – that was also the best of my illustrations. Little Anna chuckled and Hub's breathing told me how moved he was. They leafed through my book, fascinated left-handers the pair of them. Like many men in their mid-forties, Hub had started to breathe rather loudly, and he flung his remaining Siegfried's-sword-holding arm around me as he used to do and recited a psalm.

I thought I saw a trace of mockery in Ev's eyes. She had a holiday mouth, as Anna called lipstick, and how I would have loved to see her normal mouth, her everyday mouth, but it was only her childhood mouth that I could see, for its pale lips were spreading a laugh over little Anna's whole face.

'Thank you, Koja, for doing something so lovely for my little girl,' Hub whispered very softly. 'It must have taken you weeks.'

Mama finally brought us the blasted apple, a little board and a knife, and we solemnly did what was expected of us. Shared the thing. Put pieces in our mouths. Hosanna in the highest.

Mama, whom everyone now called Amama, recounted the old stories in the guttering light from the Christmas tree as we chewed mystically. She told of an apple flung at the bridge of a nose half a century before, of the frog on Grandpaping's corpse, of the holy martyrdom of Hubert Konstantin Solm and the fathomless evil of the Bolsheviks.

Nor would Amama be dissuaded from mentioning the water under which Grandpaping was held until he ran out of air. Little Anna's features twisted in rage, and she exclaimed that all Bolsheviks should be turned to stone, and I knew that she must on no account learn who her real father was, and above all, *what* he was and for whom he was secretly working.

Then came the first roast goose since the end of the war, we nibbled on sweet liver sausage and jellied fruits, Anna was given her little sip of Madeira, and Hub raised his glass and announced that, after years of separation, his beloved wife and his beautiful daughter were going to move in with him again in Haidhausen.

Yes, they would all be living together again, he repeated in the silence that had fallen.

He told us that his company, Hubermaier Haulage in Pullach (Hub and Hubermaier, he hadn't stretched his imagination terribly far) had given him notice on his little apartment in the company compound. Ev quickly added that she had been offered a good job at the Munich Children's Hospital. It was rather different from an Alpine infirmary.

Amama was the first to pull herself together, and said how 'awfully, awfully' glad she was at this incredible surprise. 'Mercy,' she said, and trembled a little.

I trembled a little, too. I joined everyone else in drinking a toast to a happy resumption of married life. We all promised Amama that we would come and visit her in the madhouse as often as we possibly could. And then a mood of abeyance spread through everyone. Apart from me: I felt as though I'd been gutted. I was suddenly uneasy, dejected – envious, even – with a sense of impending calamity, although actually I always had that, apart from the moments or the years when the calamity was quite inarguably upon us.

'You've gone all funny again, like you were in church,' little Anna said later. She was already in her nightshirt and I was standing beside her in the corridor, looking out of the window. You could sense the moon glowing faintly on the far side of the mountains.

'I'm not sad, I promise you that.'

'It's wrong to lie.'

'You're right, Anna, it's wrong to lie.'

Fluttermonkey and Liesl-with-the-Voice strolled past and blew kisses to us.

'Is it true that Siegfried only had one arm?'

'Yes, that's true.'

'Didn't you just draw him like that to make Papi think you like him?'

'I love your father very much.'

'Do you love Mami, too?'

'Yes, of course.'

'She says she loves you as well, even though you lie such an awful lot.'

'Oh really, does she say that?'

'Siegfried *can't* have had only one arm, or he would never have been able to defeat Brunhild.'

'Well, maybe Brunhild only had one arm, too; we've no real way of knowing.'

'Then how did she manage to tie up King Gunther on their wedding night?'

'Well, maybe King Gunther didn't have any arms at all. Or legs.'

'You really are a terrific liar.'

'No, Anna. The truth is the most precious thing there is between people.'

'Is that why you sang "hail the joyful Christmas-truth" at mass?'

'I think you must have misheard.'

'I did not mishear. I was watching you very closely. You sang "Christmas-truth".'

I couldn't say anything.

'I want to be a painter when I grow up, like you.'

I couldn't say anything.

'Would you like that?'

I still couldn't speak. But I managed to nod.

'Christmas-truth is an awfully beautiful word.'

'Merry Christmas, Anna.'

I kissed her on the forehead.

'Merry Christmas truth?' she asked.

'No, sweetheart, Merry Christmas.'

'Merry Christmas, Uncle Koja.'

The Cold War was at its height that winter of nineteen-fifty. The papers were bristling with psychoses and rumours that bore no resemblance to serious news, and usually ended with a question mark. Korea? Iraq? Greece? Berlin?

This war was everywhere, or as Mama called it, the Not Peace Not War. And the Not Peace Not War climbed into every 'hello' that people uttered to one another. Anything might be an attack. Even the daily weather forecast in the newspaper was reminiscent of war-reporting. Sometimes there was talk of Siberian cold fronts, a broad line of them pushing west, crossing the Elbe in V-formations. Heavy storm damage was to be expected, and the lows would be treacherous. You couldn't even trust common-or-garden hail (it broke through roofs and Mama's umbrella).

In this atmosphere of paranoia, spying was a dangerous business, and it cost a huge number of real and suspected secret-service employees their lives.

For that reason, my visit to Otto John in Berlin was planned in minute detail.

At six in the morning, the day after Christmas, I had to report to the American military logistics officer in Munich's Central Station. He assigned me a seat on an American troop train to Berlin. It was the usual military procedure since the Berlin blockade had been lifted. I was practically impossible to tell apart from the Americans. I wore a thick scarf, a light-coloured trench coat, dark trousers and a beret (a gift from Ev, which she had pulled down over my forehead two days previously, on Christmas Eve, with a small, wistful smile).

In Helmstadt, Soviet soldiers boarded the train and checked all the civilians' papers. My meticulously forged documents did not arouse their suspicion.

I stood at the window as we passed through the Eastern Zone. Of course, there was nothing in particular to see. Snow, primarily. The streets were deserted, the station platforms empty, and as the train reached Berlin and pulled slowly into Bahnhof Zoo, I was presented with the image of a Carthaginian wasteland.

The American station officer stood on the platform, shouting orders for the ceremonial disembarkation. The first was, 'All ranks from general to colonel!'

These gentlemen alighted from the first-class carriage.

There was a pause, and then, 'All ranks from colonel to captain!'

The staff officers followed.

'All ranks from captain to sergeant.'

A cloud of every uniform imaginable.

And then: 'Germans.'

The GIs laughed at us as we Germans crept out past them, a procession of nervous, restless lemurs. I took a taxi the short distance through the ruins and rubble of Kurfürstendamm to Bleibtreustraße. Looking at the new buildings rising up to my right and left, I felt relief at no longer having to work as an architect. I would rather have erected Org walls for the rest of my life than perpetrate these pitiful structures, like a toddler's building blocks.

Anna Ivanovna opened the door to me. She was approaching eighty now, and her eyesight was all but gone; she could only see silhouettes.

'Oh, Kojashka, my treasure, is that really you?'

She felt my face, and my trench coat; she was steady on her feet despite her age, and lived all alone in a surprisingly large ground-floor flat, ice-cold due to the coal shortages. There were tears in our eyes as we embraced. I was visiting her because the Org considered private accommodation much less conspicuous than a hotel. My name could not be Dürer here, of course – but in any case, my mission called for me to use my real name. The risk was entirely my own.

Anna Ivanovna heated water for tea in her battered samovar, and kept patting my cheeks as we talked about the Baltics and all the Baltic mortalities, which did not interest me.

'Ah, my dear Koja,' she sighed later, 'such a shame you did not turn out a girl!'

I spent the whole night thinking about these mysterious words.

The next day, I was collected by the head of the Org's Berlin outpost, more hosepipe than man, who cleared his throat continually. He took me to meet Wolfgang Wohlgemuth at a café on Lietzenburger Straße – and I know, I know, there are too many names in this story already, you're right. But one of the things about conspirators is that there must be a great many of them, a whole gang, in order for the conspiracy to function, and so I'm afraid there is no getting around all the names, my highly focused Swami.

If I were to take your suggestion and name people after their most prominent characteristic, then I would have to call Wolfgang Wohlgemuth 'The Whole Width of the Street'. His was a sunny, here-I-come disposition; he regarded himself as the honeypot and the rest of humanity as bees, though only the female of the species, of course.

I, meanwhile (who was not a honey bee on account of my sex) was a kind of ichneumon wasp in his eyes. The ichneumon was completely unprepared for such a brilliant honeypot, had no idea what to do with it, and its heart felt quite choked. Though of course as a member of the arthropod family (and the Org) it did not *have* a heart to beat wildly with joy at Wolfgang Wohlgemuth's fabulous presence. And so I merely said that my name was Solm, Konstantin Solm, for the purposes of our work here Koja was best, and Herr Wohlgemuth generously declared that I could call him Wowo.

And as the Org's man in Berlin walked away, clearing his throat, firmly convinced that he was leaving two loyal Western agents to their clandestine conversations, in reality two loyal Eastern agents were sharing cherry slices in an entirely socialist manner.

After his third bite, Wowo asked me what kind of shape the Org was in. He considered the Stasi to be an 'allotment club'. Ulbricht was 'the lad with the petty cash'. Wowo certainly didn't mince his words. And in some ways, I enjoyed meeting another mercenary, a double agent whom I could study for any obvious psychological defects.

But there was nothing.

Wowo came across as neither contrite nor despondent. He didn't seem to be a morphine addict, either; he was a full and cheerful member of the Berlin café society that had evidently been quick to re-emerge. He looked like a UFA Studios film star, like O. W. Fischer on an Old Heidelberg set, even as he sat there with cream spilling out of his mouth. His leather shoes were a gleaming white; his complexion suggested the island of Sylt.

Comrade Nikitin had passed Wowo's file on to me, so I knew that the successful gynaecologist was also a Don Juan, or rather a womanizer. He was also a jazz trumpeter, a bohemian and a close confidant of Otto John's. He had spent some time in a concentration camp, and had been a secret communist since the thirties. Wowo had also been involved in the resistance against Hitler, stitching John's brother back together when he was very seriously injured. That was why he was so close to my target. Theirs was a special kind of trench friendship.

I would never have gained access to Wowo if he hadn't happened to be spying for the KGB as well. Nikitin had orchestrated our meeting. He was doing everything he could to ensure that I fulfilled Gehlen's wish and finished Otto John.

Nikitin wanted to see Gehlen at the head of a German secret service. There, he would have me as his cheerful mole, but with John he had no one but Wowo. And Wowo was a mere informant, with little influence and an overly high opinion of himself.

'Otto will be there at about eight tonight,' he purred. 'I've invited a few friends over, all of them Sartreans. I hope you speak *un peu* French.'

Feeling an urge to puncture his pompousness, I said, 'Primarily I speak *un peu* Russian, and I like to speak it with *un peu* Russians.'

He clearly took the hint. His complexion lost a little of its freshness.

'Later on,' he said hastily, lowering his voice, 'I will steer the conversation in such a way that you'll have a chance to draw some quick portraits of the guests. Otto loves that sort of thing. The rest is up to you.'

'*Honi soit qui mal y pense*,' I declared.

Does the name Otto John mean anything to you?

It might not mean anything to you at all.

Otto John went down in history as one of the most refined traitors ever to set foot on German soil. To this day, others describe him as the victim of an abduction. And more than a few believe that he met his end back then and was replaced with a doppelgänger who strolled into prison in his place. The whole thing was a mess. He nearly caused the government to collapse, as well, which I'm sure is something young people like you don't know. And without his downfall, the West German secret service as we know it – the Bundesnachrichtendienst – would never have existed, which is something that no one at all knows.

The role I was forced to play in this affair is not one I am proud of. For despite his capriciousness, his dissolute lifestyle and naive passions, Otto John also had a razor-sharp mind, wit, courage and an incredible wealth of winning human qualities, of which his fundamental decency was certainly the one that differed most starkly from the picture that is still painted of him even now. He was one of those people who do not grow a single centimetre taller than they truly are by virtue of the offices conferred on them, which of course made him the very opposite of all those tadpoles of politics, who never could separate their sense of historic responsibility from the short-lived froghood they attained through their personal advancement.

Amphibians think air and water are one and the same.

Otto John never did.

That was something I realized the evening I first met him at Wowo's villa. As president of the Office for the Protection of the Constitution, he was one of the most influential men in the new Federal Republic. He was wearing a white suit with a bright blue pocket square, and you could tell from the nonchalant way he was sitting on the grand staircase that he really just wanted to have a nice evening.

He was the same age as me, but much more boyish. The youngest man to hold public office in the Federal Republic of Germany. He looked not dissimilar to John F. Kennedy. He was vain about his hair (thick, dark and combed back from his face), his skier's tan, his mental virility – but not about power. That seemed evident at once. He had a contrary, unequivocal aspect that could lead a person to become a revolutionary or a depressive, but not a sunglasses-wearing spook. Although his majestic beauty filled the whole room, he always seemed to be standing on the sidelines – even later on. A contradiction, like the rest of him.

Wowo embraced me – even kissed me – and cried out: good grief, good grief, how many years has it been? I shook hands with various people, and then we arrived at the staircase.

'Look here, Otto,' Wowo said excitedly. 'I must introduce you to a very great friend of mine from the old days: Koja Solm. Phenomenal artist!'

John blinked. He was already drunk.

'What short of art, if I may ashk?'

His tone was friendly, and he spoke in a soft, tipsy, apple-wine Hesse accent that he kept in check only with difficulty.

'Oh, Wowo,' I said bashfully, reminding myself of all the information I'd received, before explaining with an effective combination of shame and modesty, 'compared with giants like Dalí or Picasso, I'm a mere dwarf, I just daub a little.'

'You admire Picasso?'

'Oh, you've heard of him?'

'*Heard* of him?'

He laughed incredulously, gave me a look of mock dismay and then switched back into his Frankfurt sing-song. 'Oh, geddon with you, ashking me a thing like that.'

'Well, not everyone has.'

'I love Picasso!'

I knew, of course, how much Otto John loved Picasso. But because it was my job, I said I didn't.

Then I added, with a good dose of irony, 'Well that is a rare thing indeed: statesmen and modern art!'

'Truth be told, I am actually a bit of a collector. We have a little sketch from the Blue Period, Lucie and I, from when Picasso was twenty, incredibly beautiful, isn't it, Lucie (ishn it, Looshie)?'

He turned to his wife, who was sitting three steps above him, and she nodded, and in the nod I saw a hint of reproach, which might mean 'Stop showing off!', or possibly 'You shouldn't drink so much!' or 'Please leave off speaking in that provincial dialect!' Herr John positively revelled in his dialect, though he could switch it off almost entirely when the situation called for it.

He took a large swig of cognac, smiled at me and told me that his heart belonged to the Fauvists, the Expressionists and Käthe Kollwitz.

'Well now, that really is a coincidence,' I exclaimed in astonishment, taking my fishing rod and casting out into the river, towards the beautiful, unlucky trout. 'Because, you know, I also dabble a little in art dealing.'

Now John gave me his full attention. He rubbed his eyes and merely said, 'Oh yesh?'

'And just now I have a very nice wartime self-portrait by Kollwitz.'

'Oh, geddon with you,' he cried suddenly in the thickest, coarsest Hesse dialect. And then, with a laugh, 'You're just pulling my leg now, you are.'

He called Lucie down to him in a state of great excitement; she was an austere beauty with a soft voice, who last year (or was it this year?) brought out a book in London with the programmatic title *The Art of Singing*. You really must read it before you die, if I may say so, my dear Swami. She asked me at once in English whether I could sing, since I had a typical tenor voice box. Within a short space of time our conversation covered *Guernica*, the Condor Legion's bombardments, Jerusalem, the Bauhaus, existentialism and, of course, my work as an art dealer.

'Well, we all have to make a living,' I said bluntly. 'At the moment I'm looking for gallery space in Schwabing. So far it's all been via personal contacts. So please, do come and pay me a visit. I have a small but excellent stock of degenerate art.'

'Degenerate!' John cried indignantly. 'All that talk of "tortured canvas, spiritual rot, incompetent lunatics". It was perverse, the way those Nazi devils pounced on the great artists. Criminals, the lot of 'em!'

'You don't have to tell me that.'

'Oh, don't I?'

'The Gestapo put our sort behind bars in forty-four.'

'No!'

'I'm afraid so.'

'You were in the resistance?'

I nodded gloomily.

'Sentenced to death. In Riga,' I added. 'For high treason. It was a miracle the sentence was never carried out.'

'The SS shot my brother in Moabit.'

I was nearly shot by my brother and the SS, but I couldn't say that. Instead, I said, 'That's terrible, Herr John. It was a terrible time.' And as that terrible time rippled for a moment through our old resistance-fighter hearts, I added, 'I was assigned to the SS as an interpreter. Helped the Jews where I could. They caught me at it, and I was court-martialled.'

'You have my full respect, Herr Solm. The fullest respect. I really am ekshtraordinarily pleased to have met you.'

'I'm pleased to have met you, too.'

He drained his glass with great elegance, hiccuped trustingly and poured himself another at once.

'It's rare to meet an avowed anti-fascist, these days. The old Nazi goons are crawling back out of their holes everywhere you look.'

'Honey!' his wife said.

'What? It's true,' John muttered.

'I very much share your opinion,' I said rather primly. 'I joined the SPD two years ago; it's the only party doing anything to oppose this backsliding into barbarism.'

'Oh, I am glad,' said John. 'I really am glad.'

The trout was on the hook.

'Now tell me, what do you think of someone like Klee? Or Kirchner and Franz Marc?' I asked, slowly reeling in the line.

'Ah – looking at them, I feel quite stupid and insignificant.'

'Then I'd like to show you a purple horse with a yellow mane by Marc. If you should happen to be in Munich, I mean . . .'

'Unbelievable,' John said in English. 'You really are unbelievable, old boy.'

'Might I do a quick drawing of you? Now? The two of you sitting like that, you and your beautiful wife?'

My little sketchbook appeared from my jacket pocket as if by magic, my pencil was sharp, my eye too, my mind lively, my conscience numb.

'Oh, that's a very touching image. If you wouldn't mind keeping still just for a moment. And do smile!'

12

That was the start of my acquaintance with the Johns. The paintings I had been bragging about were in a CIA depot on Königsplatz, in Munich. They were what was left of the art looted by the Nazis, the property of Jews who had been dispossessed and murdered. The collection, insofar as one could refer to organized theft as collecting, had been found in nineteen forty-five in a salt mine at Altaussee. Hitler's Rosenberg Office had stored it there to be flogged off later. For some reason, after the American Central Collecting Point was closed, these pictures had not been restored to their rightful owners, as so many other artworks were, and they were now the agency's responsibility.

I'd heard about the paintings from Hub, been to visit them, and received the Doctor's assurance that if I was successful in making contact with Otto John, I would have free access to them.

But getting my hands on these valuable paintings in practice, following my lightning rise to prominence as an art dealer, was another challenge entirely. And I needed them at once.

'No,' the Doctor said. 'The Americans are fighting tooth and nail for them.'

'Why?'

'They're hanging this stuff in their own offices. I've been told that the US motor pool has submitted an application: they want something for their walls.'

'The truckers want a Max Liebermann to hang in the lavatory? Wouldn't a couple of pin-ups do?'

'It's a difficult situation, Dürer.'

More difficult still was my need to obtain business premises in the space of a few days – a fully equipped gallery, really. Plus a reliable assistant, a forged denazification certificate, records, credentials from the Latvian Academy of Art, relationships with other art dealers in Munich – and all of this with the highest level of secrecy. The Office for the Protection of the Constitution was sure to put me and my business under the microscope as soon as my contact with its president became more regular.

The Doctor almost passed out when I told him what the monthly rent was on a small shop in Salvatorstraße. It lay at the midpoint between the Jewish-run Palais Bernheimer on Lenbachplatz (where Göring had so liked to buy his oriental rugs, with the legendary words to Otto Bernheimer: 'You've a fine Jewish nose for these!') and Adolf Hitler's favourite art dealer, Adolf Weinmüller, on Brienner Straße. The coffered ceilings were painted with chinoiserie and for a pretentious, intact nineteenth-century townhouse, the rent was fair to generous.

Thank God Comrade Nikitin also helped out: he couriered me a packing crate of oil paintings belonging to deceased enemies of the workers.

In what I assumed was a piece of KGB humour, the consignment included my drawings from the Lubyanka. My cracked body. My penis, dying like a squashed slug. My cell, inherited from Isaac Babel. And I even unpacked the dancing-blue Marc Chagall triptych that had hung in Nikitin's office.

If Otto John had known that it wasn't just the CIA, the German government and the predatory Doctor's Org who were sawing away at his trunk, but the KGB, too – and if he had realized that all these dark forces were united in me and my supposed integrity – then he would most certainly not have come to visit my gallery in such jaunty good spirits, and with increasing frequency.

He turned up four or five times a year, usually without Lucie, so that I could take him out 'on the razzle', as he put it, to the Glockenbach quarter's gay bars.

Otto loved the kind of transom windows and bull's-eye panes you find in the Deutsche Eiche; he usually retreated to the darkest corners there to talk about the symbiosis of art and Eros, which often came together in the bar staff. He usually left his two bodyguards at the hotel, and as soon as we were away from prying eyes and he had a bottle of wine in him, he would grow voluble and familiar, and talk about himself in the third person.

'Not the dashing Otto's favourite place!'

'Where?' I asked in surprise.

'Why, here, the city of the Movement.'

'Oh, that's all water under the bridge.'

'Who knows, who knows.'

'Come on, I'll order another round.'

'Koja, do you know that numbskull Reinhard Gehlen?'

That came entirely out of the blue. He would sometimes drop the customary formality and call me Koja when he was in his cups, at least until daybreak. I glanced over at the waiter, made a two-more-beers sign, and the camp young man nodded condescendingly.

'No,' I said.

'Numbskull isn't nearly strong enough, mind.'

'Who's that?'

'Nazi general. The crème de la crème of them. Supports more damned spooks here in Munich than my whole organization can afford. And his rabble are snooping on me as well.'

I suddenly grew very warm under the arms, and laid my jacket down on the bar stool beside me.

'He wants my head. And America is keeping him alive,' he added, 'because actually, America wants my head.'

'You haven't told me yet whether you liked the green Paul Klee.'

'Don't you have any interest in this, Koja?'

'Not especially.'

'But you go out to Pullach quite often, so I've been told.'

I might have blinked a little, but that was all.

'Yes, my brother works there. For a large haulage company.'

'A large haulage company, eh?'

I nodded.

'Is this your esteemed brother?'

He pulled a thin file out of his coat pocket and showed it to me. It was Hub's SS staff file.

I nodded again.

'Says here he was the SS-Standartenführer in Riga.'

I couldn't stop nodding.

Herr John reached into his coat again ('Where the devil are my glasses?'), bent over the file ('No man alive can read this scrawl!'), found what he was looking for and said, 'He sentenced you to death, your esteemed brother.'

'Where did you get that from?'

'Part of my job, isn't it, getting my hands on this kind of thing.'

I was probably showing signs of anguish. In any case, he leaned forward and placed a hand on my shoulder.

'Be vigilant always, Solm.'

That hand gave my shoulder a good, hard squeeze, while his other slid the open file right under my groaning eyes.

'Believe me, this here,' he said, his index finger tapping Hub's youthful SS features, 'this here stays between us. It's a sign of greatness, that you still keep in touch with this beast of a man. Greatness and tragedy.'

He had now switched back into his professional high German, in which there was only the merest hint of the usual dialect. His brain was working overtime. Mine too. Another customer's hyena laugh sloshed over to the cage in which I felt I had been trapped.

Finally, he let go of my shoulder, and I sensed him loosening up.

'I understand. He's your brother. Once a brother, always a brother.'

The laughter ebbed away into an enigmatic giggle. The bar was full of young, perfumed, greedy men. Many of them kept looking over at John, who seemed wealthy, fragrant and generous. The perfect prey.

'Perhaps you should know that your brother is not working for a haulage firm.'

'He isn't, Herr John?'

Otto John shook his head sadly.

'He's one of Gehlen's senior staff. Calls himself Heribert Ulm. He'll try to question you about me. You've told him that we're acquainted, I take it?'

Tears welled up in my eyes.

'Oh, don't fret about it, Solm!' he cried, with an indulgent wave of his hand. 'Just tell him we discuss art. And otherwise, keep your distance from him.'

He put the file back in his coat, turned his big eyes on me and said, 'How on earth could he do such a thing to you?'

Then he called out to the waiter, radiating that generous guilelessness that made him so entirely unsuited to his job.

'Hub was badly injured in the war, you know,' I said eventually. 'I love him. And I hate him. I understand him. And I don't understand him at all.'

A tear splashed onto the tabletop, to great effect.

'Your soul is too gentle. You're like Van Gogh, Solm, from a purely psychological point of view. Lucie loves the drawing you did of us.'

'You mean to tell me that my brother . . . that he's gone back to the secret . . .'

I was so shaken that I couldn't finish my sentence, and the head of the OPC actually began to dab my nose and eyes with his pocket handkerchief.

'I hope this won't cause you to change your relationship with him abruptly. That would . . . well, it might be rather conspicuous.'

'No, no,' I said, sadly. 'You're absolutely right. Once a brother, always a brother.'

'And, you know,' Otto John sighed, 'once a secret-service man, always a secret-service man.'

For five minutes, we hung our heads over our empty beer glasses in silence. I kneaded Herr John's handkerchief in my hand, still not knowing whether the evening was going to end in my arrest.

'Don't take it too hard,' John said at last. 'Gehlen is recruiting an army for Adenauer using old Nazi goons. And I'm very glad you're not among them. That you found your way out of the Nazi trap. That is a precious thing indeed. Do call me Otto.'

'Please, call me Koja.'

'Your good health, Koja.'

He took the beer that the camp waiter had just plonked down in front of him, clinked glasses with me and drank in long, deep draughts as he watched the waiter's waggling arse move away from us.

'I can't trust anyone in my own office now. We poached a few people from Gehlen. But some of them are servants of two masters. If that bastard catches me here, it's going to be used against me.'

'Why? We're having a beer, that's all.'

'I need a chauffeur,' he said. 'He must be absolutely loyal and discreet. I've no use for blabbermouths.'

He cast a meaningful glance at two farmhands sitting at the bar, who were quite openly sticking their tongues in each other's mouths. I knew exactly what he meant.

'Do you know anyone?'

'Me?'

'Yes.'

'In Cologne, Herr John?'

'Otto.'

'In Cologne, Otto?'

'Someone close to you here might be better. I need to know there's nothing fishy about 'em.'

'You mustn't put your trust in people like this, Otto. You . . . you barely know me.'

'No, I do know you a little, now. I know you're not crooked. And Wowo has told me the same.'

Then he got up, shook my hand, went over to the two farmhands, exchanged a few words with them, flashed his charming smile, paid for all the drinks, and the three of them left together. I didn't see him again that night.

13

The art gallery, or rather the whole idea behind it, functioned right up to the moment that Otto John and Lucie blew in entirely unannounced one day, both of them determined to buy my Kollwitz portrait.

As usual, I ran through my arsenal of excuses: it had been reserved by someone else, there wasn't the expertise to authenticate it, there was still an ongoing legal dispute.

But it was no good.

'You're doing your damnedest not to make any money here, aren't you?' Otto laughed, ruffling my thinning hair.

Lucie took out a fat bundle of hundred-mark notes and pressed it into my hand. Her warm eyes and Otto's open, keen face told me that they meant to do the poor, unsuccessful art dealer Solm a favour, saddled as he was with a Nazi swine for a brother. Kollwitz wasn't so expensive in those days. You have no idea how the prices skyrocketed a few years later.

In any case, Lucie quite simply took the picture off the wall, tucked it under her arm without having it packed up, and trilled, 'Come along then, Otto,' as she left my jangling shop.

Otto embraced me and was gone.

It was a catastrophe.

I was not allowed to sell the artworks. That was part of the deal. The paintings were merely on loan to us from the CIA for the purposes of my secret mission, to give the appearance of an art dealership for as long as necessary. But it was necessary for longer than we had ever anticipated. And the crazy thing is that I would still have been the owner of that gallery today, if the vagaries of world politics had not forced me to sell it (though I've had another gallery for some time now, while world politics have remained fundamentally the same – but we'll come back to that).

Hub, the Doctor and I considered all our options.

Finally, we instructed the chauffeur whom Otto had hired on my recommendation to stage a break-in and steal back the Kollwitz. I'll give you three guesses as to who that chauffeur was: the Drinker, of course, my valiant driver from the old days in Bessarabia. We had tracked him down in Hamburg, where he was working on the shipyards. He was a constant janissary, who looked on me as his sultan and would have conquered Constantinople for me if I had only asked him.

So of course, getting old Frau Kollwitz (actually, she was still young in the portrait) off Otto's wall and spiriting her away was a piece of cake. Though it would have been conspicuous and therefore not very clever to remove only the picture that was on loan from the CIA. To avoid laying a trail back to me, then, we also stole a couple of beautiful landscapes by Kandinsky and, naturally, the most valuable piece: Picasso's sketch for *La Vie*. The blue man, talking to his wife while his naked lover clings to him. Wonderful.

The robbery was carried out in a very leisurely fashion, one mild spring evening while Otto John was out. All the pictures were delivered to the Americans at once and disappeared into the depot. The Org wanted to keep the ten thousand-deutschmark sale price. But I protested, and managed to get half the money, at least, back to the inconsolable Otto, which further cemented our friendship.

Our loyal Drinker had enough presence of mind to prepare himself convincingly for the subsequent investigation (he plunged a knife covered in someone else's fingerprints into his left shoulder, and left it sticking there at a picturesque angle). This gave credence to his story about having disturbed the burglars and given chase. Otto John, who was an unlucky man to his marrow, only put his internal security service onto the case, rather than calling the police.

'What would it look like, eh?' he muttered. 'The head of the secret service can't even guard his own house? How is he supposed to guard his country, the muttonhead?'

Nor could Otto bring himself to fire his driver, who was bleeding and whimpering most effectively; he drove the Drinker to the hospital himself. Although he was suspicious of the Drinker, as I learned later, he left him in his position. The idea of treating any living creature unjustly, be it a mere fruit fly, put him in a moral quandary.

When he read my report, the Doctor just shook his head. He regarded squeamishness as not merely weak, but criminal.

The numerous casualties among his informants and secret troops behind the Iron Curtain never elicited a single word of regret from him. He saw them as people who, in return for first-class remuneration, were willing to a) serve a good cause and b) take the consequences.

In the early fifties, when the head secretary to the East German prime minister Otto Grotewohl, one of the Org's top agents with the ingenious alias 'Daisy', was exposed, and was guillotined in a particularly cruel way (the Stasi spread the rumour that the girl had been placed on the block face up, so she could see the blade plummeting towards her), Gehlen simply shrugged.

'You need a few martyrs,' he said drily. 'Some people have to cop it.'

Despite his leatheriness, even the Doctor had to concede that there could be no second art robbery at Herr John's house, no matter how successful the first had been.

Otto was beside himself.

The worst thing from our point of view was that he was finding it so hard to get over the loss of the Picasso. He was a hair's breadth away from giving up collecting altogether. That would have been the end of my contact with him, but more importantly the end of his financial commitment to art, a commitment that made his life (not just any life, you understand, but the life of the OPC president) appear so wonderfully misguided and decadent.

Another problem was that my establishment also attracted passing trade: splendid Bavarian hunting jackets, first-rate loden coats, shimmering Rieger furs, all of them profiting from the burgeoning economy. How could I go on showing them these pictures when none could be sold?

And most importantly, what was I to tell my new assistant, Monika, who kept the business running when I (while always wary of potential surveillance) went out to Pullach? I had to instruct her never to sell a picture, under any circumstances.

Nor could I afford to alienate my colleagues: the art dealers, the gallerists, the museum directors with whom, over time, I necessarily had to acquaint myself.

One day, while I was out of town, the great Bernheimer came into my gallery. Otto Bernheimer, good day to you, he boomed at my assistant, that beautiful drawing there in your window, I'd like to buy it. I'm sorry, the girl said. I'm afraid that isn't possible. Oh my, is it sold already, the little picture, the great Bernheimer asked. No, sir, it isn't for sale. At that, the art dealer laid everything that was in his pockets on the table, which was a great deal of money, because he was in the habit of rolling his banknotes into thick bundles, like a pimp. And he said my dear girl, might you be so good as to see whether it could be sold after all. I have around three thousand marks here. Perhaps four. And this artist, he isn't very well known. What's his name? Solm? Never heard of him.

Well, Swami, the city's greatest art dealer had fallen in love with the portrait of my Lubyanka penis, which I had priced at two hundred marks and hung in the window, never guessing that my Monika wouldn't have parted with it for the British Crown Jewels.

That might have been what tipped the balance.

In any case, I began to change my strategy.

All the works were now for sale.

And when Otto John came to visit me again and wanted to buy an egg woman with an egg child by Oskar Schlemmer, I said it was a very fine choice, withdrew to my new apartment on Kaiserstraße for a few days and simply copied the picture.

My training with Papa, decades earlier, had been so thorough that I was still a master of all the usual and the unusual techniques, even after all that time. It took a little practice. But from the chalk gesso and tempera all the way to the varnish, I could carry out every step of the work myself. And Oskar Schlemmer, with all due respect, was a dauber whom even little Anna could have copied.

I sent Otto my version of the egg woman with the egg child (having permitted myself to correct a few intolerable errors in the blue glaze – no one notices these things anyway). There was no complaint of any kind. The original went to the US depot. And I suddenly had a lot of money.

I needed to find a way of avoiding the troublesome test, customary at that time, to establish the authenticity of older paintings. And so, on some of my copies, I had no option but to create a craquelure, a network of hairline cracks in the canvas that makes any oil painting look like the wrinkled skin of an old man, but only decades after it has been painted.

As a short cut to this effect, I used Papa's Copenhagen process (named for one of the jobs he took after the Great War in the Danish capital, where a mansion was to be filled with artificially aged smut – I don't know the precise details). I bought myself a drying oven, which I heated to a hundred degrees Celsius. Before slowly warming up the painting in the oven and thereby drying it out, I drew it over the edge of a table, once lengthways and once widthways, which achieved an extraordinarily genuine-looking pattern of cracks. Finally, I applied a dirt glaze of house-dust, waste-water residue and egg yolk, which I wiped off before the final drying session so that the dirt remained in even the finest cracks. The effect was uncanny.

Older oil paintings that Nikitin had sent me often served as the base for my pictures. I treated them with a scouring paste, then scraped off the surface with a razor blade or coarse sandpaper down to the primer, and created the most splendid Lovis Corinths on them.

The Johns invited me to their house in Cologne several times. Our bond grew strong enough for me to learn of almost all Otto's plans and projects. And so I saw quite clearly that the Office for the Protection of the Constitution that this president was trying to build was an organization where crucial decisions were made under the primacy of the Holy Naivety.

The guiding principles of all Otto John's actions might very easily have been your own, my dear Swami: first, legality and loyalty to the constitution; second, democratic responsibility, and an occasional intoxicating substance (third).

But there is one thing you must know: the less a secret service understands about democratic responsibility, the better it works. And legality and loyalty to the constitution aren't much help when you have to kill Soviet spies (intoxicating substances, on the other hand, are).

And so it was no surprise that Otto John's colleagues were up in arms. Firstly, their boss was jettisoning all the former Gestapo people he could rumble, excellent specialists whom his head of operations, Herr Radke, had sweet-talked away from the Org. Herr John relied on by-the-book surveillance to combat communist infiltration. He even introduced the term 'surveillance warning'.

'When you say "surveillance warning", Herr President,' Albert Radke once asked him icily, 'do you mean that we are warning the target that they are under surveillance?'

'That's right.'

'But if we warn them, Herr President, then there will be no point in having them under surveillance.'

'Exactly. And if we no longer have them under surveillance, then eventually we will no longer need the OPC. Isn't that splendid?'

Radke stared at his boss as if he was deranged. John wasn't an anarchist, though; he was far-sighted politically, and had a ready sense of humour. Both of these things went down like a lead balloon with his senior staff.

Unlike the Doctor, Otto did not take the least pleasure in plotting. He did nothing to neutralize his adversaries. Even when the Doctor, following his failed bid for the OPC presidency, had several tons of penicillin stolen from German hospitals and flogged it to the Soviets to compensate the CIA for their financial outlay, John didn't report it to the government.

He still regarded Gehlen as 'a numbskull', but not himself. He wanted to remain upright and was determined to fashion the German secret service strictly according to his instructions from parliament.

Even the former Canaris forces in his office were up in arms, because John would not permit them to form a foreign intelligence service in secret.

'If we don't,' Radke warned him, 'then sooner or later you are going to get slaughtered by Gehlen.'

'Oh Radke,' John said amiably, 'you know, as we say in dear old Frankfurt, there'll always be some bastard trying to screw you over . . .'

You might regard it as arrogance.

But Otto John was certain that he was holding all the trump cards. He was a lifelong civil servant and had another twenty-five years until he was pensioned off. Plenty of time in which to shape his organization as he saw fit. Chancellor Adenauer didn't have twenty-five years at his disposal; he would have been a hundred by then. He didn't even have fifteen years, because that would have made him ninety. And in five years he would be eighty, and would have enough to do controlling his own bowels. So what could possibly happen?

I should have known it at the time, and perhaps on some terrace of my consciousness I did know it: one day, this unbridgeable political divide, on the other side of which stood Chancellor Adenauer, the Americans and the plotting Doctor, would be the end of Otto John.

He himself said that his future was limited by his dreams. Night after night he saw his little brother, murdered by the Nazis, calling up to him out of his grave, telling him there was enough room for them both down there. And as when they were boys, Otto would then slip into Hans's roomy coffin and snuggle up to him, quelling Hans's fears with the warmth of his body and his Hesse babble.

You can perhaps imagine how horrified I was to be told that I, of all people, had been earmarked to eliminate Otto John.

14

The last thing I see is his wide-open mouth, and I marvel at just how wide open it is: I truly believe I can see all the way through his head, up to the screw in his skull.

Then everything goes dark.

When I wake up, I am in a room made of peace and quiet.

Night Nurse Gerda is with me, sitting on my left, and she is not a night nurse at all.

She quite often has a day shift, and this is one of those days. She is ensconced in a hazy late afternoon. She's pleased that I have woken up, and fetches the Greek doctor.

Now he is standing on my right and asking me what happened.

I say I can't remember.

'But you have a bruise on your right cheek. How did that get there?'

'I can't remember anything,' I say.

'Did you fall? You were lying on the floor when we found you.'

Well, then I must have fallen, I say, but I really can't remember.

'You were very lucky,' the Greek doctor says. 'Were you attacked?'

'What would make you think I was attacked?'

'Well, Herr Bastian says he attacked you.'

'No, that can't be right,' Afternoon Nurse Gerda puts in (I really don't know what to call her now). 'Basti would never do such a thing,' she stammers, getting quite agitated. 'Never, never, he couldn't hurt a fly, and he's so terribly sad . . . he's been grieving over Herr Solm for days now.'

'That's true,' I say, meaning that the Hippy could never hurt a fly. But grieving? For days? Over me? I don't understand.

'You've been in a coma,' says Day-and-Night Nurse Gerda. 'For a long time. Hours and hours.'

And the Greek doctor asks, 'Can you tell me how many fingers I'm holding up? Good. Now say after me: oxypicotosins. Good. And what plant is that in Nurse Gerda's photo? No, it isn't cannabis. And how do you know what cannabis looks like?'

'I think he's feeling a lot better already,' All-Weather Nurse Gerda says with a hint of urgency.

'You still need to keep a close eye on him,' the doctor tells her.

He turns to me.

'We had to open your head up briefly. Keep as still as you can for the next few days.'

I promise him I will.

He says I shouldn't look in the mirror for the time being, and I repeat that I really can't remember anything.

Later, Nurse Gerda (to be neutral about it) wheels me back into my old room. The Hippy is lying in his bed. He has a hand-towel over his face, a white one. He has been laid like a table, so to speak.

'He does that all the time, the thing with the towel,' Nurse Gerda sighs.

'I'm sorry,' the Hippy whines from under his towel. 'I'm so sorry.'

'Oh Basti,' Nurse Gerda says. 'You've been given the all-clear. Herr Solm says you didn't attack him at all.'

'He's lying,' the Hippy says, 'he's a really, really good liar – he's a secret agent, you know.'

Nurse Gerda helps me get from the trolley to the bed.

'Poor Basti is a bit confused, Herr Solm. His mind is confused, you know,' she whispers, so quietly that I can barely hear her. 'If you want another room, just say. Though the two of you do get along so well. And you've both had such severe setbacks now. That creates a bond between people, doesn't it?'

'I don't want to change rooms,' I say.

'Oh, you're so nice,' Night-Again Nurse Gerda sighs, with some relief. 'A real gentleman.'

Then we are alone, the towel with the Hippy under it and me, and the first thing I ask him is, 'Why did you attack me?'

Grandpaping was a pastor, a Lutheran martyr, and even so I've never had a real sense of spirituality – as you know, Ev. This is a fundamental difference between me and our brother. Even when I was allowed to commemorate Hubert Konstantin Solm's death in church in front of everyone, I didn't find God, though I was twelve at the time, the best age for such things.

The Catholic Christmas we had in Pattendorf was bizarre enough, with all the budgerigars and lunatics, who taken together could easily pass as angels. But I can't let that experience pass as genuine transcendence.

My only contact with Islam came in the shape of a Bosnian imam in the Waffen SS, who had been assigned to Operation Zeppelin by mistake and was always wanting to roll out his prayer mat in the orderly room.

In recent years, I have turned my attention to Judaism, first and foremost because I wanted to understand you, little sister, but not least for reasons that I will have to explain to the Hippy later.

And so I have had brushes with a few of the great world religions in my life, to no effect.

But Buddhism only entered my consciousness, along with all the Hinduistic, Bastianic, magical elements embedded in it, when I met the Hippy. He talked incessantly, in his swami way (and his swami way really has nothing to do with Buddhism), about how all unenlightened beings are subject to an endless cycle of birth and rebirth, and so on and so on. If you die unenlightened you become a snail, and then a goat, and so on.

The goal of Buddhist practice is to break out of this eternal snail-goat-man cycle of suffering. And the only way to do that is through ethical behaviour, following the five precepts, practising meditation, and avoiding all violence.

In this hospital, for the first time in my life, I have felt something like spirituality. Although I really can't take religion seriously, the genuinely childlike quality that is particular to Buddhism has made an impression on me. Or perhaps it is only particular to the Swami, that's possible. In any case, I was programmed for reception, but not for receiving a beating, and certainly not from the non-violent Swami himself.

So why did he get out of bed, come bounding over and hit me on my damaged head – something that might have killed me?

Let's try a more sensitive approach.

I hear sobbing from under the towel, and since there is no sense in being harsh or shouting, I sigh and ask again, quite sympathetically, why he did what he did.

'That poor Herr John,' comes a whisper from beneath the fabric, 'and you killed him.'

'Killed him? I was supposed to kill him. But I never said I did kill him.'

'You said "eliminate".'

'Why don't you just listen to me? All I want is for you to listen.'

'I can't take it any more!' he sniffs. Then he pulls off the towel to reveal an anguished Jesus Christ face, puffy with weeping, and there is another faint, 'I'm sorry.'

I try to nod, but it's impossible. My head feels like an elephant is sitting on it.

'I lose my chakra if I allow my emotions to rule me. I've been trying to meditate for days. But I can't control my anger any more. Why didn't you warn Herr John?'

'That wasn't my job.'

'Everything we hear shapes us. We hear leaves rustling and it makes us calm. I thought I was hearing the rustle of a forest when you were talking. But all I can hear is the trees burning.'

'I'm sorry, too.'

'Words change us. We shouldn't use bad words. I think we should talk about love most of all.'

'I *am* talking about love, believe me.'

'That isn't love.'

'It isn't love, to sink to such depths that you set aside everything binding and truthful for someone else?'

'For someone else? But you only ever do things for yourself!'

'That isn't true.'

'Oh really?'

'Just keep listening until I've finished my story. When we first met, you said everyone just wants to hear endings, not beginnings. But you've only heard the beginning, and not the end.'

'You want to talk about love?'

'I *am* talking about love. I'm telling you a love story. Two, in fact. Aren't you hearing them?'

'I'm not hearing them, no. I'm not.'

15

Then listen closely.

Because there is something missing from my account. One life is never a complete picture, certainly not a life as incomplete as mine. I haven't told you everything, and I can't, because you keep interrupting me with your emotions. So do me a favour and prick up your ears.

On the twenty-seventh of December nineteen fifty, when I first met the unfortunate Herr John in Berlin, at Wowo's house on Lietzenburger Straße, I was driven by a single desire: to fulfil my mission and do everything the Doctor had asked of me. I was also determined to fulfil all of Comrade Nikitin's expectations. And why? Why, my dear, horribly mistrustful Swami?

So that I would see Maya again.

All the letters we wrote, all the hopes we expressed to one another, were just messages in bottles from the hereafter. They were washed ashore, they dulled the pain, they stoked the need, but they gave me no coordinates to sail by.

Can you imagine, my hard-of-hearing, my practically deaf Swami, what it meant when Comrade Nikitin told me that, on my visit to Berlin, I would have the chance to see Maya? Shall I shout it into your ear? She was coming to Berlin. I was going to Berlin. Do you understand those two simple sentences? Can you relate them to one another?

Of course you can, you're not stupid.

I had become a vital informant for the KGB, and in order to keep me permanently dependent, to transform me into wax, sand, foam, into black shoe-polish that they could use to grease their system and make it shine, they held out this prospect to me. I had demanded it. A prospect. A high perch from which to spot an island when it appeared on the horizon.

Are you listening?

I won't ask again, I really just want to make sure you're listening to me.

When I was on the troop train to Berlin, when I was drinking Russian tea (and a little tot of vodka) with Anna Ivanovna, when I met Wowo over cherry slices and piqued Otto John's interest with Käthe Kollwitz, I was thinking of nothing (beneath all the insignificant thoughts that allowed me to survive and function) but that possible, impossible moment. If I did as I was told and lured the poor trout Otto John into my net, then that possible, impossible moment was something I would get to experience.

It was Christmas.

She was in Berlin. I was in Berlin.

Just to reiterate.

Do you hear?

I was prepared to dissemble, to betray and to lie. I would not have hesitated to play any role, to use any piece of cunning or trickery, to clear anyone out of the way in order to trap the president of the OPC – or an elk, or a whale, or whomsoever the trophy was to be.

This trophy was the only thing that could persuade Nikitin to grant Maya and me an hour, perhaps even several hours together – in one message, he mentioned a whole day.

I lived for that day. That day in Berlin, that possible, impossible moment, was what spawned the grotesque idea of the art dealer Solm cosying up to the art collector John.

When I staggered out of Wowo's villa in the early morning, with Otto John's visiting card in my pocket and cognac in my heart, I took the S-Bahn into the Soviet sector.

I got off at Friedrichstraße, walked to Oranienburger Straße and found the black car as described, in a rear courtyard. The driver said nothing as I climbed into the back. Our eyes met for a second. Then he started the engine.

We drove through a Berlin that I felt I was seeing from inside an aquarium, a Berlin that differed markedly from the three Western sectors. More broken. Shabbier. Poorer. Headscarves. Workers' caps. Not a trace of Christmas anywhere. I didn't care.

We reached a housing estate in the north of the city.

'Karlshorst,' the driver said, and it was the only word he had spoken during the whole journey. An equivalent to the Org's estate, only larger. A whole town of suburban houses, surrounded by a wall that, God knows, I would have done a much, much better job of designing.

Comrade Nikitin received me in the KGB building, a former German army pioneer school.

His goitre had all but disappeared, but his Graves'-diseased eyes now looked like two ping-pong balls onto which someone had painted a dark dot. Unfathomable pupils.

The first thing that Comrade Nikitin asked me, quite genuinely, was whether I had found time for a visit to the Pergamon Museum. I had not the slightest need for our former patterns of conversation. I slammed Otto John's visiting card down in front of him – Otto had written his private phone number on the back.

Then I asked if she was there.

Nikitin gave me a friendly smile and recited some love poem by a Russian poet, whom he had shot personally a few weeks before. No, I'm exaggerating, I don't know – and I didn't know then, either – what he'd been doing in Moscow. My anger and my impatience had taken possession of me. In any case, he took his coat off the hook, put on his fur hat and, limping along on his walking stick, escorted me to the small villa himself.

I saw her silhouette at the window up on the first floor. She didn't dare raise her hand, but even from thirty metres away I could tell that she was weeping, though her mouth was not twisted. That, too, I read in her silhouette. Contours are everything, in painting as in life.

'This villa was designed by the architect Seuberlich in 1907 for a man called von Raspe, the owner of a coffee plantation. You'll see some caryatids in the foyer with Negro heads, a reference to the coffee. And then there's a fresco from the twenties. You should really take a look at the fresco.'

'Can I go in now?'

'I'll come back to collect you in forty-eight hours. From this spot. Don't be late.'

He turned round and disappeared.

I couldn't see a guard anywhere – there was no one at all, apart from a few crows perched on the ridge of the roof. I rushed in, and although I had thought we would both turn into pillars of salt at the sight of the other, we simply flew into one another. Halfway up the stairs. Molten metal.

We bathed naked together in an opulent bathroom tiled in lapis-lazuli blue, washing each other and melting together again and again: I, dripping old iron, she like quicksilver.

We helped soap one another, each massaged the other's hair. We compared our bodies, our skin, our backsides, even our eyesight, trying to measure how cruel the time had been to us.

Maya's scars were better healed now, and there were no new ones. Although she was thin, she no longer seemed undernourished. Her breasts drooped a little, and she was ashamed of them. But I liked to lift them slightly and then let them drop. Her skin was not just pale but snow white, or even greenish. I suspect she seemed more perfect to me than she was, and I scarcely saw the scars on her face, preferring to lose myself in her eyes.

She had grey hair now, stone-grey, entirely grey hair with white strands mixed in, although she was only twenty-nine. She had lost five teeth. You could hardly tell: of her front teeth, only one incisor was missing. I put my tongue into the gap. We took our time with every-thing, though I had an erection from the very outset, which, in view of how momentous and how desperately sad our meeting was, I found inappropriate. She was also afraid that her sexual organs might be des-erted. Lifeless. That was how she phrased it. She never said 'pussy' like Ev did, but after a while she took my penis in her mouth. And then everything was all right.

We lay, holding hands, in a bed with sheets that smelled of elder-flower. Although the walls were bugged, we talked uninhibitedly, just as we had done in the mountains of Bessarabia. She wanted to know if I had a partner. I confessed a few alleyway affairs, visits to by-the-hour hotels that had made me unhappy, for I no longer loved to fuck with-out hope, as I once had.

'You mustn't give any consideration to me, Koja. I owe you my life.'

'We'll move in together, when you're released. Then I'll come to Moscow and be a prison guard.'

She giggled, and it was such an improbably beautiful thing to hear.

'You'd make a terrible prison guard. You're much too polite.'

'Would you be so good as to stop struggling while I'm flaying you?'

She laughed and asked me, with a cautionary glance at the listening walls, not to go too far.

A little later she said that she didn't like me being lonely and waiting for her. Because in the end she would be shot – that much was clear.

'Nothing is going to happen to you, Maya. I will succeed. I'm going to become a hero of the Soviet Union. And then they'll let you out.'

'Of course, my darling. Let's say no more about it.'

'Hasn't Stalin abolished the death penalty?'

'Be quiet and listen to the earth quaking.'

I listened.

I certainly listened better than you, dear Swami, deafened by your honour as you are.

I heard the earth quake beneath us, as we lay there quietly, and sometimes not so quietly. And then, my eyes turned upwards, I sud-denly saw a bacchanal – the fresco of which Comrade Nikitin had spoken. It was painted on the ceiling and depicted an obscene union, spurred on by cymbals and drums, between two naked Roman consuls and a limber Grace, who looked so like Ev that I sat up. It really was one of my father's paintings, evidently a product of his wide-ranging erotic painting trips. I recognized his brushstrokes, his colours, the striking absence of green, and the nipples that were mother-of-pearl white.

But how had Nikitin recognized it? There was no signature, no ini-tial or *fecit*. What kind of monster would debone our souls like this, and select this particular house for me and Maya, this house and this room and perhaps even this bed where my father had been, thirty years before, imagining Ev of all people as his model, his own daughter.

Maya asked me what was wrong, and that might have been the time to tell her all about Ev, about Ev and me and little Anna. But I didn't. I couldn't bring myself to wrap anyone else up inside the gauze-thin mantle of time that remained to us, and so this opportunity passed me by like a missed train, and not even with Maya did I explore the whole country of truth.

Only with Ev had that been possible, with Ev, who was being penetrated above our heads, in her anus and her mouth, with one white phallus and one brown, while we embraced and caressed one another beneath her.

Ev, whom I wanted to forget.

And I held Maya as tight as my own life.

The villa was well heated, clean, and fitted out like a luxury hotel. There was a cupboard full of food in the kitchen. Ham, bread and even oranges, in the middle of winter. Whatever Comrade Nikitin had been thinking when he arranged all this, it seemed to me very close to what a swami would call enlightened mercy.

Sometimes we curled up together in a large armchair that we had moved over to the balcony window, so that Maya could fill up on as much sky as possible. Her eyes followed the drifting clouds; she was gladdened by every bird she spotted, and hoped that next time we might meet in summer. We talked nonsense until dawn, with the lights out. She smoked like a chimney. She could smoke with the glowing tip in her mouth, like the Red Army soldiers on wartime nights, so that the glimmer of their cigarettes wouldn't give them away.

Nikitin had even thought to provide a sketchbook. But I didn't want to waste a single minute. Unfortunately, I drew nothing. I merely wrote a letter at the end, while she was sleeping after we'd made love, a letter full of kisses and vows, and I illustrated it with her ear, one foot and her left hand, which was resting against her cheek.

How soft, how tremendously soft her breathing was.

16

My return to Munich was the start of a wonderful new life. Nikitin promised to invite me and Maya to the Karlshorst villa twice a year. His letter sounded exceedingly friendly. It really did say 'invite'.

He also held out the prospect of obtaining a pardon for Maya, if I was loyal and did my duty for the Soviet Union.

He left no room for doubt: the annihilation of Otto John and the salvation of Maya Dzerzhinskaya depended on one another; they went together like good deeds and gratitude, or man and wife.

The Kremlin would benefit from the infected Doctor (infected with me, if you would like to regard me for a moment as a Soviet bacillus) being raised onto the throne.

And I would benefit from Maya.

I didn't hesitate to do what was necessary for a second.

Can you comprehend that, uncomprehending Swami?

My art gallery on Salvatorstraße in Munich, financed by two enemy secret services, was probably the best business idea I've ever had. In no time at all, my eager copying of all those Klees, Kandinskys, Münters etcetera brought me considerable financial gains (I went to visit Gabi Münter in Murnau the following summer, and later showed genuine paintings by her on commission, but they hung on the walls like lead, which no one would believe these days).

I moved into a bright three-room apartment on Kaiserstraße in Schwabing.

Hub, Ev and little Anna lived quite close by.

I saw Anna as often as possible. I gave her drawing lessons, just as my father had once done with me (always with an apple juice close at hand, a sanctified one). Lines, shape, perspective, light, shade, building up the layers of a picture, and a whole host of horses. Horses from the front, horses from behind, horses with riders, smiling horses ('Horses don't smile, sweetheart'), all right then, happy horses, less happy horses – you could tell by the tongues lolling out of their mouths – horses standing, horses galloping, never horses trotting, because trotting is stupid, large horses, never small horses, because ponies are for scaredy-cats, apart from Shetland ponies, they're cute.

I had set up a small studio in the Kaiserstraße flat, and there I showed my daughter how to compose a picture and what a vanishing point is, and had her draw her own fingers, fingers in the rain, I still have those fingers, but I have locked them away, they churn me up inside even now, those small rainy fingers.

The Academy of Art was nearby, and they were more than a little surprised in nineteen fifty-one when I enrolled the eight-year-old Anna on a life-drawing course. It required special permission, because strictly speaking a child was not permitted to look at naked adults.

But it was easy enough for a gallerist to befriend the professors there, all of whom needed a gallerist. And so the grumpy Professor Grobl finally accepted my Anna, for she was, one can quite justifiably claim, extraordinarily talented. She also took the course very seriously and got into the habit of sticking the tip of her tongue out when she was concentrating on drawing, or listening to the professor. Once, in front of all the other students, she asked the life model if she wouldn't mind adopting a different pose for once.

'Goodness me – what pose?' the rather sturdy odalisque asked, taken aback.

Anna said very politely, 'Like a horse, please.'

The whole room laughed and all of them loved Anna, because she was pure poetry, even when she was doing badly. But she wasn't doing badly.

Hub and Ev seemed to be growing closer. They had left Haidhausen and now lived a stone's throw from the Englischer Garten, a paradise for conventional husbands and wives because of the good air, and the street they lived on was called Biedersteiner Straße, and they lived a perfect petit-bourgeois life there.

But I could sense my brother's fear. And I, too, was afraid, for I could scarcely resist the pull of Ev; it was a physical attraction, an iron-filings-to-a-magnet attraction.

Papa's fresco in Karlshorst, which my eyes would always light on when I met with Maya there, caused me such anguish that one day, I chipped off the dark penis with a spoon. The young Ev's face, too, sucking on a consul.

Sometimes, when we saw one another, all Ev would have to do was buy a loaf from the baker with a particular attitude, and the way she took hold of the bread, or perhaps the way she squeezed it, perhaps the sound of the crust cracking, would remind me of a coital moment from years before. And although it did not arouse me, it pierced me to the quick like a bullet, the pain of which you only feel later.

And worse still was one summer's day that comes back to me now. On that day, she stepped on a shard of glass at the Nordbad swimming pool, and her face contorted. It exposed tiny fissures in her cheeks which you could barely see otherwise, similar to the artificial craquelures that I was creating on canvases in my drying oven at that time, and for a second all the destruction that Hub had once slashed into her face flickered into view.

There were only two options for ensuring temperance.

The first was to emulate my brother's bigoted faith, which was expressed with a kind of desperation in his churchgoing, his Bible study circles, the practised humility that was supposed to let him entrust his fate to the Almighty and His wisdom. It was something I seriously considered.

The second option was to find a woman.

Of course, my relationship with this woman had to be as unattractive as possible while still being bearable, and it had to be one that I could terminate at any time. A relationship that would pose absolutely no threat to Maya, but might finally convince Hub that I no longer presented any danger to him. I decided firstly on the second option, and secondly on the first woman who sprang to mind: Monika, though the only thing I had ever liked about her was the 'M' in her name.

Monika was my gallery assistant, a thin, colourless streak of a woman, a bespectacled weed with a tiny but rather wide nose, whose sense of humour was even worse than the Doctor's, but who really loved to laugh – an extremely trying combination. She had started at the Org as a typist. She was the daughter of a Wehrmacht major, who wouldn't have her in the house any longer on account of Bertolt Brecht, whose books she would read while laughing uproariously (you see what I mean).

She loved her work in the gallery, because she loved art. Unfortunately Monika, whom everyone called Mokka, had no eye for it at all. She was probably the least artistically talented person I have ever met, which fascinated me in a way: it didn't dampen her enthusiasm for art, although she couldn't see what was beautiful even if you showed her. Her enthusiasm for me was probably rooted in my being the one who showed her. She loved me for my art, the art that I sweated out and of course also owned, so she thought (wowee, all those famous paintings by classical modernists!).

In a way, the large age gap between us was another attraction for her.

In the first few months that she worked for me, she had two admirers who often picked her up from the gallery by turns, one almost Adonis-like, both of them dashing at the very least. She threw them over right before my aged eyes, watched them through the gallery window as they walked away, and sighed precociously in my direction that they were too young and green for her, those nice boys. What a shame.

One of them even turned up again after that, and she behaved like the Queen of Sheba.

I wondered how this was possible. She was neither strikingly pretty nor inspiring, she wasn't entertaining or especially clever, and the fact that she was educated and well-read was the only remarkable thing about her – although everything she thought sounded rather second-hand. It was easy to be quiet with Mokka. And when you work together in a gallery for hours at a time and have nothing to say to one another, it's very important to maintain a pleasant atmosphere in which to say nothing.

Sometimes, however, she would have an attack of the monologues, especially when she had encountered supposedly interesting people on the tram, whom she could spend hours describing. There was a miner from the Ruhr Valley, for instance, who had told her tales of deep shafts and his silicosis, and whom she actually brought with her to the gallery (afterwards, she had to fan the fine soot off all the pictures).

One evening, after selling a very difficult von Jawlensky forgery for a tidy sum, I invited her out to the Bayerische Hof to mark the occasion with a celebratory dinner. I had no ulterior motive. I take no pleasure in sleeping with employees; it's like sleeping with a pet.

But it turned out that this was where her talent lay. She drew my attention to her hands, which toyed gracefully with her red-wine glass. She laughed a great deal, always with one Cranach-esque hand covering her mouth, because she didn't like the way her teeth looked.

Well, she should have seen Maya's teeth.

We ended up in a third-floor hotel room. I'm sure it was her first hotel room, but she undressed quite naturally, and didn't seem embarrassed by her protruding pigeon chest, her flat feet, her small but astonishingly firm arse, or her tiny breasts. To my surprise, she smelled a lot better than she looked. With the first thrust, I actually heard her little joints crack, which made me feel sorry for her. But then she threw me onto my back and sat astride me, and I very quickly realized why her two handsome admirers had been so fond of her. She was a true virtuoso in the sack. Her secretions allowed her to do all kinds of things, her voice could imitate whole storm fronts, and she could dole out the sort of punishment that made you practically beg her never, ever to stop. Sexually speaking, that slip of a girl was certainly the best thing that has ever happened to me, including the lavish Mary-Lou, and after the 'M' in her name it was the second thing I liked about her very much.

The third thing I liked was her shyness, which overcame her again the minute we left the bedroom. She made it very easy for a person to dominate her, sometimes gently, sometimes less gently.

And fourth: I would never be able to love her, which tipped the balance firmly in her favour.

'So that was your girlfriend yesterday?' Ev asked me when I came to collect little Anna and take her to Professor Grobl's life-drawing class at the academy.

'Mokka, yes. What did you think of her?'

'She's nice.'

'That bad, hmm?'

'When you came out of prison, you said there was someone else.'

'Let's not dig all that up.'

'I just thought that one day . . .' She paused, waggled her open hand and gave an impish cry of 'Hoo-hoo'. 'You'd bring this great, mysterious woman to meet us. Not some Cinderella.'

'The handsome prince was very happy with Cinderella, wasn't he?'

'Now I'm starting to feel sorry for her.'

'And aren't you very happy with Hub?'

Before Ev could say anything, Anna pushed past her with her drawing things under her arm.

'Shall we go, then, Uncle Koja?' she said sternly.

'Yes, let's go.'

'I painted three more horses yesterday evening.'

'You shouldn't paint so many horses.'

'She does what she wants, Koja,' Ev said, kneeling down and running her forefinger down Anna's nose. 'She gets that from me. But isn't it lovely to see what she gets from you?'

It was extremely dangerous for Ev to say such a thing. Anna was clever, and at an age when she could look beneath words, and she therefore fixed indignant and slightly narrowed eyes on me, and a splinter of her attention remained on the curve of my nose. She would never learn (and nor would I) whether a few years later her own nose might develop that curve.

I didn't speak to my sister for many weeks after that.

All that is mutable is but reflected.

17

While things were getting better and better for me, they were getting worse and worse for Hub.

At first, the only indication was that he had started laughing again.

Anna told me that she hadn't been able to sleep, because Papi had spent the whole night laughing with Mami, or rather without Mami, because Mami never laughed, only him. But his laughter was no longer the full, ringing laugh that burst out of his whole body, which I had so loved when we were children. It had taken on a shrill, scornful tone.

That was how I learned that Hub had also started drinking again. It was only when he had some booze inside him that he could laugh; only then could he bear the fact that, when he laughed, his empty shirtsleeve hopped about, and so we all dreaded this sound, because we knew that the laughter had nothing to do with fearlessness, as it once had, but the opposite: fathomless fear and anxiety, but above all, alcohol.

I think that from the moment Ev arrived at Hub's door with all her bags and baggage, and little Anna, and laid her body and mind down beside his – something he had been longing for since the end of the war, and even during the war, even when he was made of nothing but hatred – from that moment on, then, he had been filled with an uncontrollable fear that he would have to face another loss. The coldness and hardness he had shown towards me and Ev in those deranged years seemed to have been shot away along with his arm, had transformed into regret when he turned back to the Church, and had finally gone up in smoke when Ev returned – but poisonous, fearful smoke. And now tender blossoms of bitterness were growing inside him, which he complicated further with profundity and godliness.

And thus he was practically asking for Ev and me to meet without him, as we did on those afternoons when he was at his Bbible study group, for instance, and I was sitting in the drawing hall with Anna when Ev arrived, and we interpreted the lines our daughter had drawn together.

Or sometimes he would telephone me at the gallery, and ask whether I could take 'the little one', as he called her, to the paediatrician. And then Ev always came too, because she never left Anna alone when she was ill. And she never called her 'the little one', either (perhaps because she really was so small), but 'my treasure', and sometimes 'chield' (Bavarian), and sometimes 'rebbelus' (Baltic), which means vine louse. We would sit side by side in a waiting room with typical children's drawings pinned all over the walls, scribbles that Anna disdained on account of her artistic majesty, and she would sometimes tug them off the wall in order, as she put it, to 'make them right'.

I think Hub was constantly putting us to the test. Maybe he did it unconsciously; maybe he was testing us in the same way he felt God was testing him. He grilled Mokka about our relationship, was satisfied to hear that we were thinking about having children (I never thought about having children, at least not with Mokka – I already had a child) and would now and again make supposedly humorous remarks about the sexual fidelity of those present.

Once, Ev got up from the table where we were having coffee and left in a rage, I can't remember why.

We never once spoke of what could not be discussed, of what had happened years before, I mean, and yet it hung in the air like the smell of decomposition.

Hub let me look into his heart just once, as we were driving out to Pullach together one morning. Out of nowhere, he asked me if I was ever going to go behind his back again.

'Because next time, I won't want you to die, Koja; I will die myself.'

He let out that horrible laugh again. Homeric.

I swore to him that he didn't need to worry about that.

Most importantly, I swore it to myself.

Interestingly, I didn't regard it as betraying my brother when I secretly rummaged through his desk, photographed his files, copied his lists of agents and transcribed our conversations. And when in the end all the material, fresh as dew, was sent off to Comrade Nikitin and thereby to Moscow, I saw it merely as the price Hub had to pay for my having to save Maya, whom he had destroyed.

This often went through my mind when I saw him at lunchtime, sitting on his bench in the middle of the Pullach green, chewing the sausage sandwich that Ev had made for him. As he squinted in the sunlight I composed sentences for my letters to Maya, and I became conscious of the fact that, when she read those sentences, Maya would not be squinting in any sunlight. At most, she would squint in the glare of light bulbs as she vegetated in her cell, because at a particular historic moment, Hub had been living in a version of himself where it was impossible to sleep well for very long. And so he had simply swapped it for another version. I call it 'the memory-free evangelical version'.

Hub never mentioned Maya; her fate was not the subject of a single conversation. He thought Maya was dead, insofar as he thought about her at all. She had slipped the mind of 'the memory-free evangelical version', just as Politov and Grishan had, and Mortimer MacLeach, and perhaps even me – my earlier, unevangelical self.

You know.

Hub prayed a lot, concentrated on his work, and as his jaws ground together his thoughts were always on new Org operations.

And when I observed this grinding from thirty metres away, I was gripped by a sudden wild urge to rob him of his idiotic secret secrets – as Anna called the things you tell nobody but your favourite doll. And it felt entirely right and proper that I was repaying Hub's intercession on my behalf with Reinhard Gehlen, and his support in finding me a career, by dashing every one of his efforts without his knowledge.

From my perspective, that wasn't betrayal: it was punishment.

Every slip of paper and every piece of information that I got out of him represented a tiny contribution towards the reparations he didn't know he was paying.

I swore that I would stop this trade as soon as Maya was free and we could explain everything to him. And if Hub should have a problem with it in some far-off future, I would press into his hand the five teeth and ten years that Maya Dzerzhinskaya had lost, and he would only be able to stammer indistinctly, flooded by a tide of guilt and embarrassment.

*

When I look back on how I justified all this to myself at the time, I am astonished. What illusions man creates for himself! How willing he is to keep a kind of moral debit and credit record, though it exists nowhere outside his own perception! How easy it is to bask in the warmth of truth, to switch it on like a sunlamp, even when one is not only living in the coldest of all deceptions, but is oneself the cause of it!

To this day, almost everyone I have met (and I count you in this total, too, revered Swami), follows a reality compass that always points in a direction favourable to him, and wrongly regards this as north, even when his compass points south, or to hell. Do we not all tremble our way along this needle, even at the considerable risk that we will have to twist facts to fit them into our reality? Is there not 'a memory-free evangelical version' in all of us? And isn't it therefore understandable that Hub would suddenly take up his bleating laugh again, even though he was in immense pain?

It was only with the Doctor that this laughter left him, though he felt immense pain in the Doctor's presence, too.

But with the best will in the world, there could be no laughing at the Monday meetings in Pullach, nor any weeping, shouting, lamenting or begging. The only emotion permissible on these occasions was cynicism, and that was reserved for the Doctor himself.

Hub had to suffer the deployment of this emotion against him a great many times, first and foremost regarding his interest in hard liquor and church services. Beneath the mockery there lay a powerful disdain, which was swelling all the time. Reinhard Gehlen might have placed an almost blind confidence in my brother at the start of their professional relationship, even putting him in charge of the vital Department VII (Soviet Union), but this benevolence was now shrivelling as various failures and slip-ups came to light.

Hub had been Gehlen's man for all seasons. He had helped the CIA to sink gold bars into lakes all over the mountains and forests of Bavaria, Hesse, Baden-Württemberg and Lower Saxony, and to bury stores of weapons for the battles that lay ahead – but quite a few of these secret bunkers had been broken into and cleared out, and the perpetrators could not be found.

Many of the agents who had passed through Hub's sinister department were also exposed. Informants in Russia were arrested by the dozen. Numerous materials forged in our workshops (such as two million counter-revolutionary stamps, on which the SED's general secretary Walter Ulbricht was depicted with a hangman's noose around his neck) went up in flames as they were being transported covertly to East Germany.

One mishap followed another. Hub couldn't understand it. He could understand it so little that one morning he punched the bathroom mirror in a rage and broke his middle finger. He even came to believe that there must be a leak somewhere in the Org, a suspicion that the Doctor waved away with a disdainful gesture: 'There are no rotten eggs here.'

I put my arm around Hub's shoulders and appealed to his conscience. He mustn't talk such rubbish. Who in the Org could be a potential traitor? Could he name anyone he thought capable of such heinous acts?

Hub began to weep, thanked me for my concern and resolved to pray even more in future, and to go to church more often.

Of course, his star was falling because Moscow had begun to act on the information I was giving them. I'm quite sure of that. But I didn't allow that thought to enter my mind; instead, I chose to believe that Hub's whisky-breath wafting down the Org's corridors, his bitterness and the fact that he was so 'fucking cagy' (Donald Day) were principally to blame for losing him the handsome VIP armchair in the conference room, to Gehlen's immediate right.

A new face soon appeared in that seat. Heinz Felfe, a sycophant who was as slippery as an eel; Hub had been up in arms about his recruitment.

'I know Felfe,' Hub had told the Doctor. 'He's a pig in pinstripes.'

'He was in the SS, like you. He worked on Operation Zeppelin, like you. He ran Soviet informants, like you. He just doesn't drink as much as you do.'

'Felfe was under my command. He's unreliable. We should really give him a thorough vetting, see what he's made of.'

And that is what the Doctor did, but in his own unique way, namely using the fluorescent X-ray eyes that lay behind his sunglasses – and that would have to suffice. It had sufficed for me, too. And I was glad of it, just as Felfe must have been, because after me he was the second Soviet mole that Nikitin had set on the Doctor.

Of course, I didn't know that at the time.

In the space of a few months, Heinz Felfe managed to sideline Hub in his own department. He followed Gehlen's thinking like a shadow every step of the way, and was so conscientious and so quietly obedient that it began to seem intrusive. There was something cat-like about him; he produced initial results very quickly, like an eager black pussy-cat who leaves three dead mice at your door every evening in the hope of praise. I hate cats.

But no one, not even I, would have guessed that everything Felfe dragged in was dressed-up material that the Soviets had given him. One of his greatest coups was a detailed site map of the KGB headquarters in Karlshorst, which he produced with a flourish one day (scale: 1:1000). I spotted our beloved villa on it, the refuge and sacrament of the holy Maya-Koja invocation. And one vertical projection even showed which lavatory was used by which KGB officer.

In his childish delight, the Doctor asked me, his former architect, if I would be a good chap and use this document to construct an architectural model of the enemy secret-service HQ (though of course the architect *was* the enemy, and not a good chap at all).

For weeks, I spent my evenings in my studio, cutting obedient balsa wood into the correct cubage. I placed a little house filled with longing at the centre of the model, with a sugar-glass window and a balcony made of split matchsticks. I had a God's-eye view of this balcony, looking in through the window from which we would look out into the universe, Maya and me, without ever seeing HIM. Oh, my Swami. The Doctor put the model in the trophy cabinet with the fold-out doors (where the limewood 'M' blazed) and was sorely tempted to run a model railway through it.

Nominally, Hub remained the head of Department VII, but Felfe's triumph was enough to put him in a position where he could later give away the most important secrets of the West German military, the federal government and NATO.

Before he was arrested, the damage and humiliation that Heinz Felfe managed to cause to the German intelligence service was only exceeded by the damage that I inflicted on it myself.

But back then, I was riding a wave of success.

Whatever the Doctor might have intended when he tasked me with finishing Otto John, the war between the two secret-service bosses was now in full swing, with conspicuous advantages for the away team, FC Pullach.

'Very nice,' the Doctor often said approvingly as he read my surveillance reports: the information about President John's visits to gay establishments ('dens of iniquity'); the lists of Otto's confidants who could be bribed and persuaded to work for the Org; all the notes on disparaging things Otto John had said about the chancellor, the foreign minister, the US president (whom he called a Nazi, although Mr Truman, of course, had thrashed the Nazis); a police report of John being drunk in charge of a vehicle, which the Office for the Protection of the Constitution ensured was never taken any further. But most importantly, my old chauffeur (the Drinker, as you will recall) provided solid-gold information about his employer's breakdowns, panic attacks and addiction to pills.

Gehlen made good use of this information.

He fed it into political circles, sent a dossier to Adenauer himself.

He used the material that I brought him to deconstruct Otto John, transforming him into a caricature that was then put through the political shredder.

And how could I have tried to undo any of this? Nikitin had always led me to believe that toppling Otto John was the only way to free Maya.

Otto looked increasingly defeated when I went to visit him and Lucie in Cologne. 'Ah, Koja,' he sighed then, 'these are infamoush timesh. Infamoush timesh, old boy. And if I'm not careful, they'll be the death of me.'

I can safely skip over the months leading up to this, in which the OPC dwindled to become the instrument it is today: an office that gathers information about hippies like you, entirely harmless oddballs and idealists – and I really do say that with the greatest respect.

But an intelligence service with no police authority, no double-entry bookkeeping, no operational base, no foreign division and no weapons depot is an intelligence service with no power, or you might say: with no nobility. Originally, this office was supposed to become the nucleus of a brilliant and all-encompassing institution. That was General Gehlen's vision, at least, when he was angling to become its president.

But now he was doing everything he could to deny his rival all the powers essential to creating a secret service that could operate both at home and abroad.

'Gehlen has thrown in his lot with the Yanks and is giving up the whole of our country's east,' John complained. 'At bottom he is a traitor, there's no nicer way to say it, not even in dialect.'

He was comfort-eating and gaining weight. By lunchtime his alcohol barometer indicated an approaching storm front. In the evening there was a smorgasbord of drugs as well, and at night he couldn't sleep. The invisible snare was pulling tighter around him with every passing day, and he sensed he was dealing with an enemy to whom nothing was sacred. 'He doesn't want my job now,' Otto moaned. 'He's just creating a second service. A shadow service, which Adenauer will eventually endorse. They don't want to protect this nation. They want to wage war.'

But until the occupation statute was lifted, Otto could be sure that he had the Brits' full support. They still viewed the Doctor as a revenant of the Führer, partly due to his grey Hitler moustache (a risqué feature that no one in Pullach who valued his job dared so much as mention).

Mokka and I were invited to Lucie's birthday party in Cologne (I gave her a small, exquisitely forged Ernst Ludwig Kirchner, which I called *Hamburg Harbour*, and which looked not only deceptively like Hamburg, but also like Ernst Ludwig Kirchner, though he had never set foot in Hamburg, and neither had I).

Unfortunately, Mokka drank a little more than her fill that evening, which had an effect on her natural shyness. She also had some bones to pick with me (my lack of enthusiasm about us getting engaged, for one thing), and laughed like a madwoman when Lucie introduced us to her godfather, Theodor Heuss. Her laughter turned first into screeching and then into sobs, for sadly Mokka was always tense and jealous at parties, and Theodor Heuss, the great comforter among the presidents of West Germany, put his arm around her and listened as she told him what a scoundrel I was, and how many ladies I was making eyes at, and Theodor Heuss kept saying, 'Oh, but you're still so young.'

Later I drifted around the party with Mokka, now adequately placated by the head of state. The theme for the evening was 'Rule Britannia'. Mokka kept pursing her lips at me for a kiss, and between these annoying kisses I had to explain to her why she could see so many Englishmen.

This was due not least to Lucie John, the birthday girl (I told her), in whose life there were many Englishmen (as Mokka knew), because as a German Jew she had been offered a safe haven by the British. And now she was offering the British a safe haven in return, on her birthday, in the form of rum punch, roast beef, Yorkshire pudding and mince pies.

Mokka was more than a little surprised when we finally spotted Otto John in a cluster of jolly Brits; he'd had a Union Jack specially tailored for the occasion, and turned into a double-breasted jacket that made him look like Admiral Hornblower. The expressions on the faces of all the non-Brits (undersecretaries in the Bonn government, members of the Bundestag, people whose houses had been bombed in the war) ranged from embarrassed to stony, but the president of the OPC had no interest in non-Brits.

'Miss Mokka, you're looking tip-top,' he called out to us in his Hesse-accented upper-class English. 'Bring your boyfriend to join us, there are some very fine *Wichtigtuer* over here.'

The gentlemen we went to join conformed to every single Oscar Wilde cliché. The one who stood out especially was a fat, sarcastic gnome of a man with Groucho Marx glasses, who introduced himself as, 'Sefton Delmer, pleasure to make your acquaintance.' He was Britain's best-known political journalist, and had once been Otto's ultimate superior at the forces radio station Soldatensender Calais. He kept calling his host 'Patriotto': 'Now then, Patriotto, stop playing the fool and let's have some of those peculiar German drinks!'

Otto invited Mokka to touch his Union Jacket (it was made of silk!) and then introduced us to Delmer's companion, an ageing professor visiting from London for a few days and dripping with distinction.

'*Pedo mellon a minno*,' the gentleman said in a soft voice, his head inclined towards Mokka. She smiled uncomprehendingly, while Delmer groaned, 'Oh my goodness, *linguists* – what on earth does that mean?'

'Speak friend and enter,' the professor explained. He told us he was speaking Sindarin, an elvish tongue. He was far and away the most eccentric Englishman I met that evening. In addition to Sindarin, he was fluent in German and claimed that his name should have been Johann Tollkühn, before telling us with a lofty gesture about his ancestors who had come over from Saxony. He was an Oxford don, of course, and like all scholars in that beautiful city, had a spot of egg yolk on his white collar. When, at the high point of the festivities and extremely merry, Otto began to complain bitterly to us about the Org, the professor's interest was piqued. 'Orc?' he said. 'What are you talking about?'

And Otto explained what he was talking about. The professor listened and told us that years ago he had written a little children's book with a great many Orcs in it, and then he said that he saw the short-statured Mr Delmer as a typical dwarf from Moria, and that nice 'Miss Mokka-Bokka' as a cunning, marriage-mad elf, and Otto John as a hobbit.

But it was impossible for him to explain what a hobbit was, he said: that would break up the whole party and take the focus off 'the marvellous Lucie'. He did, however, give a very vivid description of an Orc's appearance. And from that evening on, it was the name that Otto, Mokka and I gave to Gehlen's humanoid, sharp-toothed, wolf-haired and grey-skinned colleagues – except, of course, on the odd occasions when I was one myself.

The professor dubbed me Sauron – a kind of sorcerer, I think – and I learned that long ago, his family's German name had been reshaped into 'Tolkien': regrettably, he said, a diphthong like the German 'ü' was impossible to pronounce in England.

Sefton Delmer, the dwarf from Moria, was very interested in the Orcs.

Otto had told him how successful they'd been in gaining a foothold in the Bonn government, and establishing the forces of evil in the British Sector. Delmer subsequently mounted an offensive that had serious consequences. On the seventeenth of March nineteen fifty-two, the *Daily Express* in London printed an article by him with the headline: 'Hitler's general now spies for dollars'.

I don't wish to bore you, I really don't, but I recall the opening lines of that article to this day, for the same reasons that some people memorize Goethe poems.

Watch out for a name which is going to spell trouble with a capital T. It covers what in my view is some of the most dangerous political high explosive in Western Europe today. The name is spelt Gehlen and is pronounced Gale-enn. Ten years ago this was the name of one of Hitler's ablest staff officers. Today Gehlen is the name of a secret organization of immense and ever-growing power. As he expanded, plenty of former Nazis, SS men and SD men (Himmler's secret service organization) crept into his staff where they enjoyed full protection. Today Gehlen is the head of an espionage organization which has agents in all parts of the world. The Americans supply the funds. The danger of the organization lies in the future.

The article hit Camp Nikolaus like a bomb.

Nothing about the Doctor had ever appeared in the media before. There were no photos of him, no descriptions, no articles. He gave no interviews, made no comments, he removed his sunglasses only rarely and reluctantly, and the same went for his hat. Until that moment, the Doctor had regarded himself as so secret that even he could almost believe he didn't really exist.

At a stroke, that changed.

18

While Anna was getting older, but no taller; while Hub was fighting desperately to keep his job, which was clearly slipping away from him despite his efforts; while Ev turned to paediatrics to distract herself from the second chance that she was giving my brother for the third, fourth and fifth time without him realizing it; while Mama was organizing little Protestant reading groups in Catholic Pattendorf by way of resistance, and the Chin-ninny was getting ready to convert; while once every six months in Karlshorst, Maya and I looked forward to a life, and Mokka descended slowly into a depression that she tried to puncture with her laughter; while Hub's laughter sugared his rage and Anna's laughter exploded and Ev seldom laughed – while all this was happening, the undeclared war on Otto John entered its final phase.

Ultimately, it was his breakdown that set the wheels in motion.

One evening, the Drinker found Herr John delirious and floating in his swimming pool. Lucie had gone to visit her daughter in London for a few days, and her husband had evidently taken a cocktail of barbiturates, antipsychotics, tryptamine and twelve-year-old Scotch, which had subsequently managed to escape his stomach and was turning the lovely blue swimming pool a shade less blue. Otto was in a state of complete physical and mental collapse. Wowo had to be flown in from Berlin specially, since his patient refused to be treated by any other doctor.

Wowo then called me from Cologne.

'I think it's time,' he whispered.

'Sure?'

'Terrible persecution complex. Paranoid reactions. You should come.'

'Is Lucie all right with that?'

'His friends need to do everything they can to get him better now,' he sighed duplicitously. 'I'm sure he will come to realize that this job is just ruining his health.'

'Yes, Herr Wohlgemuth,' I said despicably, 'we must think of his health.'

'He sets great store by your judgement. Can we count on you?'

I knew that the KGB had offered Wowo the prospect of becoming head surgeon at the Charité Hospital in East Berlin. He would be the successor to Professor Sauerbruch, whose assistant he had once been: that was the trophy he could win with his betrayal.

'I won't let Otto down,' I said, a touch too unctuously, before hanging up.

In the Bormann villa, the corks popped and the Orcs cheered, now that it was all over for the Anglophile Protector of the Constitution.

That evening, I wrote another long letter to Maya, explaining that she just needed to have a little more patience now. I laid my black heart at her feet.

The victory was so close.

Unfortunately, Mokka came into my room, saw that I was writing a letter and watched my tear-stained face grow instantly hard. Her lips began to quiver in a way that always infuriated me, but she said nothing and left again at once.

Now I really had to come up with some scheme to rid myself of her in a way that was both elegant and irrevocable. Because however badly I treated Mokka, she didn't or couldn't read the signs. She was genuinely still hoping that one day we would get married. I was being vile to her, and my anxiety about it and my inability to hurt her properly and draw a line under the whole thing made me viler still.

When I reached Cologne the following afternoon, equipped with best wishes for my fishing trip from the Doctor, Nikitin and even little Anna (who, like Ev, thought I was going to an art auction), I soon realized that it wouldn't be hard to tip Otto over the edge. His face was bloated, his pupils had a dull sheen, and in some ways his mental state was not so different from my brother's. Neither of them understood the world any longer, both doubted themselves, and both were completely blind in the eye that looked at me.

'It'sh all over,' Otto said in a monotone as I came through the door. 'All over for the dashing Otto, Koja!'

A remarkable statement, full of self-pity, spoken with closed eyes from a crooked mouth, crooked like the mouth of a newly poisoned Roman senator. He was lying on his living-room couch like a dead man, in a white nightshirt smeared with jam. Lucie was sitting beside him, pressing a damp blue flannel to his head, while Wowo stood behind them, filling a syringe. He even managed to squeeze a tear from his eye.

'What on earth has happened?' I asked, my voice overflowing with concern as I set my suitcase down.

'Well, it's a bit rich, you coming to visit me. What's this then? Come in sackcloth and ashes, have you?'

He took the flannel from his forehead and looked at me. And in his eyes I saw something I had not reckoned with: a determination to defend himself, a determination that was well hidden beneath his frailty and did not seep into it.

'What do you mean, sackcloth and ashes?'

'I'll show you,' he said, his voice almost gentle, as he slowly righted himself.

'Honey, please don't!' Lucie said in English, urging him to lie back down.

'We're just taking a quick trip to the office. Won't be long.'

'Please don't put yourself under too much strain,' Wowo implored him.

'I actually think it might be more of a strain for Koja.'

He stood still to let Wowo give him the injection. Then he went and got dressed.

I was feeling unsettled as we glided across Cologne in Otto's official car. The Drinker was at the wheel, giving me warning glances in the rear-view mirror, so I thought. Otto himself remained cold and forbidding. He toyed with the blue flannel, pressing it against his throbbing forehead from time to time.

His organization's home was a new eight-storey building, an unadorned lump of a thing on Ludwigstraße, which had been thrown up overnight using cardboard, breeze blocks and the worst possible taste.

The hallways still smelled of paint and fresh plaster. The floors had been covered with a soupy red paste, magnesite, the cheap version of linoleum. The contrast with the ostentation of Pullach's Bormann salons could not have been greater. There was no Goethe-house pastiche here, just plain humility. Nothing overblown; underblown, if anything. Even the choice of ceiling lights – bare bulbs surrounded by brass wire – seemed to suggest disdain for an organization that was both self-reliant and powerless.

Otto led me into his office, through an anteroom so tiny it looked as though it had been cut in half. His secretary seemed quite startled to see us. She had her hat and coat on, ready to go home for the day. Her boss nodded vaguely to her from under his flannel as he held the office door open for me. I went in, and before he could say anything I felt a sudden draught, perhaps from the half-open window, perhaps from the door, which was not yet closed, or perhaps because I was in freefall, back down the eight storeys I had just climbed up, and hadn't yet hit the ground. I was staring at the municipal-green wall behind Otto's desk, on which hung the blue man talking to his wife, with his naked lover in his arms.

The picture.

The drawing, remember?

The Picasso I had stolen.

And right beside it I could see Käthe Kollwitz, her hooded eyes staring out into the grass-coloured room with its Thonet furniture and the two Zulu spears in the far corner (a gift from the British colonial office).

'Do take a seat,' Otto said, and so an armchair made of chrome tubing took my weight, checked woollen upholstery, brand new, into which I am certain such a level of panic never descended before or since. Herr John told his secretary that she could go home now, toodle-pip, and closed the door. He went over to a wall cupboard and took out two cups, then fetched the teapot from his glass-topped desk and poured me a cup of violet-black tea, which must have been incredibly cold. Then he sat down opposite me and I watched him pour himself a cup as well, holding the flannel over his eyes. His hand trembled.

'You remember these two pictures, Koja?'

'Yes,' I said.

I don't know which of our faces was greyer, more unhealthy-looking.

'I was at Ivone's two weeks ago.'

He was referring to the British high commissioner.

'They were hanging in his drawing room. Just like that.'

He snapped his fingers.

'A gift from the American administration.'

'It's unbelievable, them turning up again like that.'

'Yes, it's *unbelievable*,' he said in English.

He spoke using those lovely, mumbled vowels that give the Hesse dialect its homely character, and even help sarcastic remarks to retain a trace of human warmth.

'Koja, is there anything you would like to tell me?'

There wasn't the slightest thing I wanted to tell him.

In a similar situation, Gehlen would first have picked up his teacup, added his three spoonfuls of sugar and stirred it for hours, stretching my nerves to breaking point, but Otto was much too nervous and bewildered to use deceleration as a weapon. He knocked back his cold tea like medicine and shuffled forward to the edge of his seat.

'Then you should know that these artworks which once belonged to me, which some bastard stole from my living room, and which I have missed like a puma misses its cub' – he had to pause for breath as he looked up at the Picasso – 'that these artworks came from the US Army's store of art looted by the Nazis.'

'What?'

'They were being kept in a cellar owned by the CIA in Munich, full of pictures that were not restored to their rightful owners. Those owners are apparently unknown.'

'How remarkable.'

'Not really.'

'So, do you believe that the CIA . . . the CIA stole those pictures from your house?'

'Not really.'

'No?'

'If it had been the CIA, the Americans wouldn't have given the damn things away, and certainly not to Ivone. But Gehlen's people work for the agency, too . . .' Another pause for his poor lungs, and then, in autosuggestive dialect, '. . . Gehlen's people, shotten souls the lot of 'em.'

'I see.'

'No, I don't think you do see. These pictures resurfaced four weeks ago – and of course, I had the matter investigated.'

His teeth gleamed in a slightly twisted, unnatural smile. He put the flannel down, got up and hobbled over to a filing cabinet, and I realized he had forgotten to put socks on – his left shoe encased an obviously inflamed ankle. He opened a cupboard door and pulled out a thick lever-arch file. He placed it on the table in front of me and began to pace around the room, dragging his left foot a little.

'The Orcs are everywhere, Koja. They've been shadowing your dear Otto for years.'

'You need to be careful about voicing these suspicions. Wowo says the same.'

'Who recommended the chauffeur to me?'

'He's completely trustworthy.'

'He might have been trustworthy in the war, killing Russians. That's probably where you know him from.'

'What makes you think that? You really are acting very strangely, Otto. Can you give me a clue as to what this is all about?'

'One thing at a time, same as eating dumplings! Right?'

'What are you accusing the Drinker of?'

'I don't believe he really disturbed the burglars.'

'He got a knife stuck in him!'

'Yes, his own knife.'

'Really, Otto, this is absurd.'

'Who recommended the chauffeur to me?'

'We've been through that.'

'You recommended him!'

'Otto, where are you going with this?'

'He works for Reinhard Gehlen.'

'Impossible.'

He pointed at the lever-arch file.

'Page 324.'

I looked. 'Good Lord,' I said.

'And now to you!'

The blood suddenly rushed up my neck and into my face. I could hear my heart beating wildly. I was swimming in blood.

'Page 325,' he said. And then, 'There you are, cat's out of the bag.'

He fell grimly silent as I read the report about me, which gave me a chance to marshal my thoughts.

Amid all the explosions set off by each line in that report, I was able to establish that the Office for the Protection of the Constitution had only discovered my early work as an architect in Pullach. They had no knowledge of my later participation in the CIA's Red Cap programme, or my operation for the Org's main domestic division. I tried to flush the blood back down my neck and clutch at this straw.

I turned my attention to the open book that was my aggrieved, migraine-afflicted companion, and began to leaf through it. The most important thing in these situations is to provide an immediate explanation. A secret agent's basic metallurgical training tells him that silence is always silver and speech is always golden. I talked for my life, and more importantly for Maya's life ('Leave off, Koja, no use now'). In any case, I managed to find the words, and although every word that passed my lips was a lie, I lied with a passion that convinced me I was saying nothing but the pure truth ('Oh, stop feeding me your bullshit'). I explained to Otto that I had never worked for the Org, except for that one year when I was contracted as an architect, with the humiliating job of building a wall ('I can't listen to this dog-dancing any longer').

'My brother got me that job,' I cried. 'What was I supposed to do, starve? You know he was a hair's breadth from sending me to the gallows. And that was his way of making amends. I started dealing art straight after that contract finished. I never worked for Gehlen. Never. I have nothing to do with the Nazis!' I yelled. 'I'm an anti-fascist!'

'You deceived me.'

'No, I told you who I am. And what I said is true.'

'I was so fond of you, Koja. So incredibly fond.'

He was breathless.

'The only thing I didn't tell you, Otto, was what my brother did for a living. But you found that out yourself.'

'I don't believe you!' he shouted, bright red in the face.

'I'm an artist, Otto!' I shouted back in my defence. 'An artist and an art lover and yes, I'm an architect, too! My goodness, I built a children's playground in Pullach! With two little swings! Does that make me a criminal?'

He took the blue flannel and hurled it full force at my head. Perhaps that gives you the best indication of his character. He could have flung his teacup, or – as the Doctor would have done – one of the two Zulu spears behind him. But he was just a flannel-flinger. I looked at him and saw an indecision that was both angry and – the longer I looked – beset by doubt, and I had an inkling that one last chance was creeping towards me.

He turned away, clenched his fists and wrestled with himself.

'Swear to me,' he said when half an eternity had passed, as he massaged his scalp with his fists, 'swear to me that you have never worked against me.'

'I swear it.'

'Swear by your love for Mokka.'

Since I didn't love Mokka, I found that I could swear without hesitation.

After my repellent, cowardly, desperate oath, which would torment me into insomnia only years later, Otto flopped into his chair and crumpled in on himself. Rationality posed no threat to the innocence of his child-like soul. With a bit of analytic effort, he could have taken me apart. But it wasn't in his nature. He was a sentimental old romantic through and through, as fragile as all romantics are, incapable of believing that the people he trusted could be cunning and mean. He was the most unsuitable person you can imagine for the secret service. Winnie-the-Pooh would have acted more shrewdly.

He was highly intelligent, of course; he sat there and did not believe me. But he didn't refuse to believe me, either. I sounded convincing, and Otto John was a man of sounds. The beauty of a voice was more important to him than what it was saying. That was probably why he'd married a singer.

'Gehlen thinksh he can take me out of the picture,' he muttered indistinctly, kicking off the shoe that was hurting him and firing it into the corner. 'But he'll be the one taken out of the picture.'

It was time now to be quiet, to park my speech and save the beauty of my voice.

'Do you know how many members of the SS Gehlen's organization employs?'

I didn't.

'Did you have any idea that two thirds of the top officials in the federal criminal police are former SS officers?'

I hadn't any idea.

'Has anyone ever told you that half the ministry of the interior is made up of Nazi Party members?'

No.

'And you say you're an anti-fascist?'

'What are you getting at?'

He pointed to the file.

'We've got a hundred and forty of those. Full to the brim with everything you need to know about the hydra.'

'Research?'

He shook his head.

'SS files.'

'SS files?'

'Personnel files from the Berlin Document Center. And from other sources.'

'You're intending to use these SS files against Gehlen?'

'Gehlen. Adenauer. Schröder, the minister of the interior. The whole damn lot of 'em.'

'Are you insane?'

'It's all getting sent to the press.'

'Are you completely insane?' I repeated.

'I don't know if I can still trust you, Koja. You may well inform them about this. I don't care. It can't be stopped. There are things in there . . .'

He laughed softly and began to massage his raw ankle.

'Your brother was in Riga. Took part in the massacres of the Jews there. He was front and centre. It's in there. And Lucie's family was deported to Riga.'

'You're making a mistake.'

'And they tortured my brother to death in a concentration camp. Cut off his eyelids so he couldn't sleep. Do you know what happens to an eyeball when its lid is cut off?'

'You mustn't pass incriminating material to the press.'

'The same as happens to an apple once you've peeled it. It rots.'

'You're not listening to me, Otto.'

'They all need to prepare themselves for the worst. Your brother is going down for murder. You can tell him, if you like. And we're going to pull Gehlen's war criminals out from under him and have them shot.'

I turned my eyes away, looking to the blue man on the wall for comfort, wondering how he came to love these two women, and recalled Picasso's wonderful statement: 'Painting is not made to decorate apartments. It's an offensive and defensive weapon against the enemy.'

This heroic thought – a direct contradiction of Papa's opinion, since all his life my father's painting had only ever decorated apartments, bacchantes, ceremonial erections and all – almost made me forget that Otto John was a dead man.

19

I woke with a start. But it was only Maya, wrapping herself around me. She had just come back from the lavatory; I could hear the cistern. We usually tried to stay awake for the two days that were granted to us. But the more time passed, the more often we nodded off. Like grenadier guards on duty whom someone has forgotten to relieve.

I looked at the clock as she burrowed her head into my arm. Fifty minutes left.

'Germany are world champions,' Maya whispered.

'What?'

'You're world champions.'

She had been listening at the bathroom wall, as we always did when sitting on the lavatory. We knew that the guard was sitting behind the thin wall, following our every move via the bugs that lurked behind the villa's wallpaper, and inside its plugs and stair rods. He often listened to the radio, an offence that carried a severe penalty, but it was better than him listening to us.

'It was just on the news. Three–two against Hungary.'

'Then we can talk.'

'Yes, we can talk. He's not listening.'

And what could he have heard, apart from the transparent sounds that come with love, particularly the smacking physical sounds, but also the others. All the Petals, Snufflekins, Little Mice, Poppets, Honeys, all the Kisskayas, Tsayushkas, Dorogos, Slatkayas cooing at one another in the villa must have been wretchedly boring for the half a dozen KGB ears we used up in the course of a weekend.

'What are you thinking, my Kisskaya?' she asked.

'Only fifty minutes left.'

'Don't think that.'

'All right, I won't think it.'

'This has been wonderful again.'

'Yes, it has.'

'But you're gloomy.'

'My darling.'

'I don't want you ever to be gloomy again. I will always sing songs to you. Afterwards.'

'What kind of songs?'

'Songs to make you happy. Like the song about the bank of the Kazanka River.'

'How does that go?'

'We'll sing it when he's listening again.'

'Do you want to sing it to him, too?'

'Well, you said we should talk now.'

'My darling.'

'But what is making you so gloomy? What is in your boom-boom-boom?'

She meant my heart, and tapped the knuckle of her index finger against the relevant place. We had a lot of words now for the things that were important in those hours. I looked up at my father's painting on the ceiling, hoping this would be the last time I set eyes on it.

'I have to do something very difficult.'

'What?'

'I can't tell you.'

'That's a shame.'

'But you mustn't think I'm a bad person.'

'You're the best person I know.'

'But I'm bad, too: I don't love many people.'

'You love only me.'

'Come, now – I'm not quite that bad.'

'I've only ever loved scoundrels, because they're such good kissers.'

'My darling.'

When we said our goodbyes, I told her that next time I would be coming to fetch her. That was as certain as an Amen in church.

At the time, I thought she was more cheerful than she'd ever been that day because now she had the prospect of future happiness.

Was she attractive? Her hair had grown thin, and the gaps in her teeth and her shashlik face, as she called it, lessened her physical appeal. But though they had ploughed up her beauty, it blossomed still in every corner of her smile, her throat, the pride that was undented by her imprisonment, her two shoulder blades that rolled like fields, the white of her remaining teeth, which were not so few in number (twenty-three), the little hairs on her arms, her birch-and-beech body, her amber-coloured eyes. It is such a cliché to speak of amber eyes, a best-loved-poems way to avoid just saying light brown. But her eyes really did contain a kind of resinous, fossilized – by which I mean ancient – wisdom, a wisdom expressed in the blood of trees that I searched for so often on Riga's beaches as a child. And now I found it in the last look she gave me.

That shine.

After that, I had to go and see Comrade Nikitin. He looked terrible. Sick and old like never before. His eyes were in much greater need of sunglasses than the Doctor's. He came here from Moscow just once a year to instruct me. I was surprised to find him sitting in a very small, shabby office rather than the magnificent room that was usually reserved for him in Karlshorst. He read my mind and almost apologized for the cramped conditions.

'It's being renovated, Comrade Four-Four-Three. Everything will be made new.'

'It's nice when everything's new.'

'Isn't it? But by next time, everything will be old again.'

I asked him straight out if our agreement still held. He told me it did. I asked him to give me his word. Ridiculous, really, when I no longer set any store by my own word, and had already betrayed Mokka and Otto John and my own brother and a juicy chunk of my fatherland.

He looked at me. There wasn't the slightest hint of mockery in that look.

'I give you my word that after your mission, you and Comrade Three-One-Three will be deployed in West Germany together. Though only on condition that you call your first-born Nikitin. Nikitin the Second.'

Although he was as keen to joke as ever, I sensed a new concentration, or maybe even a sadness beneath that joke. Perhaps it was the difficult circumstances of the past year – I need only mention the seventeenth of June nineteen fifty-three. A million workers on the streets, volcanic eruptions of strike action and mass protest, dozens of deaths. That put the KGB under pressure; they hadn't seen an uprising in the GDR coming, not a hint of it, and the magnitude of those events took them completely by surprise.

I asked Nikitin whether there might not be some other way of resolving the situation with Otto John. But regrettably not. I was already at the door when he called my agent number one last time, and I turned round.

'I meant to say: congratulations,' he said, scratching the scraggy remnants of his goitre. 'That was a great goal by Rahn.'

A few days later, my brother explained to me how it was going to play out.

We were in the Hotel Kempinski.

We were in the Hotel Kempinski because we couldn't be at Anna Ivanovna's: she had died of flu three months earlier. She'd left us an old bed, several photos of Grandpaping, an amulet, five icons, two ostrich feather hats, her beloved samovar, a book of handwritten Russian recipes, and Ev's birth certificate and other papers.

After Anna Ivanovna's funeral, once Ev had taken possession of the papers and read her parents' names, the names Meyer and Murmelstein,

I was off the hook. The documents existed now. Ev didn't have to reveal that she had known about her Jewish roots for years, because Hub's treacherous brother, the former SS-Hauptsturmführer Koja Solm, had told her about them after two days of uninterrupted and melancholy sexual intercourse in Breslau.

That very day, Ev took her documents and went out to Pullach, meeting Hub at the gates of the Org. He was pleased to see her at first, but not for long, because she soon showed him the birth certificate and explained that she was a Jew and his daughter was half Jewish. That was quite clear from Anna Ivanovna's papers. And she wanted to join Munich's Jewish community at once, at least what was left of it, with body and soul.

At the flea market, she bought a few Jewish ritual objects, a Hanukkah menorah, Havdalah candles and several Star of David amulets (even one for Hub, just imagine that). She also bought a kosher cookbook. Little Anna thought Ev's ma'amouls and hamantaschen so delicious that she told Hub how happy she was to be 'a sweet little Jew-face'. She drew her first self-portrait around that time, choosing to pose as Queen Esther, with moonlight eyes and an oriental crown on her head.

What I really want to talk about is Hub and me, at the Hotel Kempinski.

But you also need to understand how troubled my brother was at that time.

He, or at least 'the memory-free evangelical' version of him, had at first just seemed stupefied in the face of all these developments (like an elephant shot with a tranquillizer dart, in the moments before it collapses). After various phases of paralysis, however, he began to throw fits of rage that prompted Ev to call me on several occasions. And every time, I came rushing over to Biedersteinerstraße, and little Anna wept a great deal and told me that Mami and Papi had been screaming at each other awfully, and she mimicked what she'd heard.

Hub's laugher and Hub's screaming came one after the other, and it was hard to know which to fear more.

And now, weeks later, I was sitting with him in the brand-new Hotel Kempinski, in a spacious, tastefully furnished suite, and he was showing me the gun I was to use to eliminate the president of the OPC.

In Hub's best-seller *Not a Cripple – A Victor!*, the sophisticated self-help manual for people who had lost an arm, he had included instructions on how to clean and load a gun, engage and release the safety catch, cock and fire it with only one hand. The chapter had the rather baroque title: 'Handless Handling'. Now Hub held the Walther PPK to the floor with his right foot as he demonstrated all the pistol's features with his left hand – which was strange, in that I already knew these features inside out.

'Why are you doing this, Hub?'

'It's an official briefing.'

'I know how it works.'

'Don't mess this up, do you hear me? Don't mess it up!'

Magazine release button.

Safety de-cocking lever.

Manual cocking.

Firing pin.

Trigger guard.

I had to repeat all the terms after him.

He was nervous. This operation was Hub's last chance to remain a part of the innermost circle. The Doctor had left him in no doubt about that.

Three weeks previously, I had delivered the news that Otto John was not thinking of stepping down from his position. At first, it caused some loud muttering in Camp Nikolaus and then, when I had given more details, dismay. But hearing about those hundred and forty files of material in his possession, which meant that the most senior members of the Org could distribute several dozen years in prison evenly among themselves, led to naked hysteria.

Heinz Herre, for instance, the spindle-thin CIA liaison officer, stood up at the end of the briefing, bared his teeth and suggested simply setting the whole of the Cologne Office for the Protection of the Constitution on fire one night, with all the bloody files inside, and with any luck a few eager fucking lefty analysts as well. That ridiculous new building was a blot on the landscape in any case, he shouted.

Heinz Felfe liked the aesthetic aspect of this solution, but worried that all the information about enemies of the West German constitution would go up in smoke as well. Herre blustered that that didn't matter a jot, the Org could put enough enemies of the West German constitution behind bars on its own, goddammit, we didn't need those dilettantes in Cologne for that.

Someone else whispered tentatively that the CIA laboratories were researching little tropical insects that ate paper, and could devour whole archives in a matter of hours, like piranhas demolishing a herd of cows. You could just smuggle the insects into Herr John's office and let them loose. Twenty thousand would surely be enough.

Someone laughed, and a fist fight nearly broke out.

Only the Doctor remained icy, listening to the tumult. Eventually he said, 'The files are not the problem.'

The room fell silent at once.

'That's true,' Hub replied. 'The files aren't the problem. Herr John's right-hand man, Albert Radke, has been on our side for years. He could easily make those files disappear as soon as John left his position.'

'But he isn't going to leave,' I said.

'No,' Herre roared, 'he wants to kill us!'

'Which means that Herr John is the problem,' the Doctor said.

Then he sent everyone out of the room apart from Hub, Felfe and me.

Three former SS officers and one former Hitler general remained, to defend Western democracy from a dangerous madman, who had the absurd idea that former SS officers and Hitler generals were lurking around every corner.

'So, gentlemen, what do you suggest?' Gehlen asked, almost casually. As was his way in dramatic situations, he offered us coffee, biscuits and cold drinks.

'We need to increase the pressure on that Brit-lover even further,' Felfe said, trying his luck with a platitude.

'And how are we going to do that, Friesen?' Hub asked, sucking at his cola bottle. He used Felfe's alias in conversation as often as possible, because he thought it sounded splendidly repellent. 'My brother has made sure he's getting it in the neck from all sides. He couldn't be any more unpopular.'

'Yes,' I confirmed, gesturing towards a newspaper article I'd brought with me. 'The minister of the interior, Schröder, actually expresses his mistrust of him on the record here.'

'Read it out!' the Doctor ordered.

I picked up the paper and read: ' "With regard to domestic security:

when Germany achieves full independence, as we believe will be the case in a few months' time, we will have completely free rein . . ."' I paused, looked up, explained that this was the crucial part coming up, now, listen to this, and went on: '". . . completely free rein to entrust the protection of the constitution to personalities who are truly beyond all doubt."'

'The minister says that?' Felfe marvelled.

'Exactly,' I said. 'He wants someone in that post who is *truly beyond all doubt.*'

'Boy oh boy,' Felfe said, whistling through his teeth.

'So when the British leave, it'll be curtains for John?' Hub asked.

'Well, he won't get any more work protecting the constitution, at least, it says so here in black and white. It also says he's a lame duck.'

'That's the point at which you put a bullet in your head, isn't it?' Hub muttered. 'When your own boss humiliates you like that.'

'I fear that bullet will not be fired by Herr John himself,' Gehlen said airily.

We all counted the spoons of sugar that went into his coffee. It was five.

'In this fine spring weather, I should like to take my coffee outside, with Herr Friesen.' The Doctor stood up, and so did Felfe, the purring mouser. 'Perhaps Herren Ulm and Dürer can stay here and ponder the situation a little further?'

That was a liquidation order.

Have you ever received a liquidation order, Swami?

Such a thing comes as a shock to anyone – not just hippies who regard picking flowers as an act of terrorism. I was so dumbfounded that I suddenly recalled my bio-negative energy. A technical term that Papa had borrowed from his favourite book, *Genius, Madness and Fame*, and to his chagrin was forced to apply to his children, when the thirteen-year-old Ev climbed into someone else's garden in Jugla, scrambled up a fruit tree and pinched three kilograms of pears from a great height (while I kept a useless lookout down below, standing by the trunk with a basket in my trembling fingers).

According to Papa, bio-negative energy was what turned Michel-angelo, Benvenuto Cellini, Leone Leoni, Giuseppe Cesari, Caravaggio and even Bernini into thieves, conmen, forgers, accidental killers or murderers. It was an abnormal affinity with crime that lurked deep within the Italian art world in particular, and which also drove Ev and me to the forbidden pears. Papa was certain of it.

That was the only time in my life I ever received a beating from my usually so good-natured father. It was particularly painful because that beating had to atone for Ev's sins as well (a girl could not be chastised in this manner, and certainly not with a riding crop). I also needed to learn that even an artist – for that was what Papa hoped I would be – must be measured against earthly and therefore legal norms. 'You are at risk, my darling boy,' Papa said, close to tears as he applied salve to my whipped back, 'at great risk.'

It may be that psychologically speaking I am a thoroughly bio-negative, quasi-Italian personality – as you believe, too, my biased Swami.

Even so, a liquidation order was such an unimaginable thing for me that, having received it, all I could do was leave Pullach without another word, not even goodbye, in the hope that it hadn't been meant that way.

But it had been meant that way.

Hub actually blossomed.

He felt nothing but pure joy at being permitted to take on, plan and oversee the Doctor's mission. He even laid off the drink and doubled his churchgoing, perhaps because he already knew that what he was planning would count heavily against him at the final judgement.

At weekends he knelt and prayed at various altars, but during the working week, with the assistance of the Org's operational department and Donald Day, he came up with a top-secret and completely insane assassination plan.

Berlin was to be the locus of this operation. A ceremony would take place there on the twentieth of July nineteen fifty-four, to mark the tenth anniversary of a very different assassination attempt on Hitler. Some of the conspirators in that plot had been shot dead, strangled or beheaded; others had died by their own hand, and only a few survivors had lived to see this anniversary – among them, the OPC president, Otto John.

He was therefore cordially invited.

The president of West Germany, important government representatives and high-ranking Allied ambassadors would not be the only ones giving him their full attention at this event: two Ukrainian sharp-shooters, remnants of my Red Cap troop, would have their eyes on him as well. Their Springfield M1903-A4 precision rifles could fire two shots each, at least if they remained relatively undisturbed.

But as the grounds of the Bendlerblock complex would be sealed off by the police, the assassins had to position themselves in the adjoining Tiergarten, an area that was still cratered from wartime air raids. And unfortunately, the route of the memorial procession did not pass by there.

That was why they needed me.

My job was to secure an invitation to the event from Otto John and, during the ceremony, to get him into a good position for the Orc snipers. If they should miss their target, I would have to draw my weapon and shoot back very inexpertly at them. And as I did so, a regrettable accident would occur. A stray bullet would enter the brain stem of the president of the Office for the Protection of the Constitution, bringing silence with it.

In the ensuing general chaos, the assassins could leap into a US Army vehicle that would be standing ready, and be taken to safety. A letter had been prepared from a German Communist Party cell claiming responsibility, so I was told. Nothing could happen to me; the Org would protect me, and I was Otto John's friend and art dealer, a man known to have been in lively contact with him for years, who had now caused a tragic accident. No court in the world would convict me.

That was the theory.

This absolutely brilliant, perfect and recherché plan had just one flaw, and that was me.

I did not want any part in this plan.

Not under any circumstances.

The reason I found it so troubling was that it would have been a much more brilliant and perfect and recherché plan if I was meant to be eliminated, too. That would take out one of the most important witnesses against the Doctor. And in any case: why did we need two snipers? I couldn't see the reasoning behind it. When two toreadors enter the ring, there must be two bulls, as well. Was I not practically offering myself up as a second bull? By extending the scope of the operation just a little, would Hub not be able to rid himself of his brother, whose loyalty he was never sure of, and who had already ruined his life once?

Our relationship deteriorated day by day. It was not just the different levels of empathy we showed in our dealings with the Orcs. I was also talking more often and more deeply with Ev, something that Hub himself had provoked. My relationship with his daughter was closer than his own, and the same might have been true of my relationship with Ev, although no boundaries were ever crossed there.

He could see that things were coming to an end between Mokka and me, and that put him under pressure. Made him anxious, let's just say. And my commitment to the SPD, the sudden wealth generated by the art gallery, the rise in social status that my friendship with Otto had brought me, my growing prestige with Gehlen – all of this must have contributed to my brother slowly losing himself in alcohol, mawk-ishness, laughing and screaming. I could imagine – and I had a good imagination – that in this state of mind Hub might slide a pair of cross hairs between himself and me.

I didn't trust him.

And I didn't trust his crazed piety, either.

Once, he told me that, in the Bible, it was always the eldest son who came off worst, had I ever noticed. The eldest was always left out in the cold. It started with Cain and Abel. Cain was the eldest, and what did he do? Exactly. Then look at Esau and Jacob. Then all of Jacob's sons: the eldest are bad, the youngest are good. And when the Israelites flee from Egypt, God kills all the firstborn sons. What does God have against firstborn sons? What does God have against me? And why does he prefer you? Hub asked me all of these questions, and I really didn't know what to tell him, and he said, just look at the parable of the prodigal son. He's the youngest, too. They slaughter the fatted calf for him. It's bullshit, Koja.

No, I really didn't believe in his piety. He may have been no artist, but he had a great deal of bio-negative energy, and he spread it around so generously that it frightened me. Have you ever seen a one-armed man praying? He can't put his hands together. He makes a fist.

All the same, I had to do what I had to do.

It was Comrade Nikitin's will, too.

Without my categorical obedience, I couldn't keep my categorial promise to Maya.

And so in the Hotel Kempinski, with a heavy heart, I signed the three forms (one green, one yellow, one red) and Hub handed over the Walther PPK.

In the days that followed, I often carried the pistol with me, in a halter slung from my left shoulder. It's a myth from the cheapest pulp magazines that you can tell when someone has a gun under their jacket. Someone with your posture, for instance, could walk around all day carrying a pistol and no one would see a bulge. Not even if you were wearing nothing more than pyjamas. You just have to look a little ill and hunched over whenever you walk anywhere, pull your shoulders forward as if your back hurts, and no one will notice you're armed to the teeth.

20

By the time I collected Otto and Lucie John from the Tempelhof Airport in Berlin on the fifteenth of July nineteen fifty-four, I had got used to that hunched posture.

Otto greeted me cheerily. He had decided to take me at my word. All his reservations seemed to have been swept aside, and in his face, which was marked by the struggles of recent months, I saw the old, familiar warmth, which shook me to the core. 'Good of you to pick us up, old boy. No Wowo? Where is the bugger?'

'No Wowo' was a favourite phrase of Otto's when he was missing Wolfgang Wohlgemuth. I hadn't brought him to the airport. He was not in on the operation. And no one needs to double the number of friends they are lying to.

All the same, the doctor turned up at the Kempinski that evening. He found me in the hotel bar, took the bar stool beside mine and ordered a bloody Mary. The yellow light bulbs above the bar shone on his creamy white hair, making it look almost blond.

'What's up with you?' he asked, with a hint of venom. 'Good God, you look terrible! Have you just got back from some typhoid region of East Asia?'

'The music is terrible, that's the only terrible thing here,' I said.

He looked over at the jazz combo, which was jamming away beneath a pink plastic seashell.

'You're not wrong there: the trumpet, in particular.'

The bar was quite busy, but not packed. I let my eyes roam over all the guests, but couldn't see anyone who looked familiar or suspicious.

'And what might you be doing here, Herr Wohlgemuth?'

'There's something afoot, I can tell.'

'Not that I know of.'

'Is he planning to defect?'

'What?'

'I could drive him.'

He took it in good spirits when I gave him the bird. It actually amused him. Known all over West Berlin from the Memorial Church to Clayallee, on first-name terms with actors like Gert Frobe, he might already have been recognized by a number of the other guests, and that alone prevented me from grabbing him by the scruff of the neck and dragging him out of the bar.

'Don't look so disgusted,' he said in friendly tones. 'I just wanted to let you know that I'm on hand if you need me.'

Wowo smiled at me, and I did not smile back.

'You're talking absolute nonsense,' I said with exaggerated equanimity. 'Otto would never defect. Has the head of a secret service anywhere in the world ever defected?'

'Apart from Reinhard Gehlen, you mean?'

'Apart from Reinhard Gehlen, I mean.'

'Don't treat me like an idiot. Even the newspapers are saying that Minister Schröder wants shot of our patient. That means the chancellor wants shot of him, too. And what are you doing here, bowing and scraping around him all day?'

'I'm taking a holiday with some dear friends, that's all.'

'How touching, it brings a tear to my eye,' he said.

'It's very incautious of you to turn up here like this.'

I straightened my hunched back, unbuttoned my jacket a little further and let him get a good look at my bulging pistol holster.

He curled his lip, knocked back his Bloody Mary and slammed the empty glass back down on the bar in front of him.

'Okay, then. Whatever you say. I'm going to meet with him and advise him to switch sides. And I'm willing to bet you will do the same, Herr Solm.'

He got up, strolled over to the band and made the baffled trumpeter hand over his instrument. The guests began to applaud as Wowo, swaying like a Caribbean palm, mounted a sustained assault on Louis Armstrong, playing 'Heebie Jeebies' and other Hot Five songs. And although I had no desire to, I was forced to stay sitting there for a few more minutes.

I know all this sounds like a cock-and-bull story. Not just to you, revered Swami, but to me, too. And not just now; it did even at the time.

I left the bar and went up to my room to escape the jazz. The suite was on the top floor. I couldn't sleep; I opened the window and looked over at the Tiergarten, at all the trees with their lush crowns of leaves, and I thought about their sedentary life and the summer that was reaching its zenith in them. The night was not a dark one, and in its grey half-light I could vaguely make out the trees, patches of quivering green, and above them the pinkish-purple glimmer on the horizon as the morning arrived, accompanied by the twittering of the first birds.

I stood there at the window for three hours, maybe four, and listened to each blackbird waking, unable to imagine that just a few days later on the other side of the Tiergarten, two kilometres away, I would shoot a man dead. No, I couldn't imagine it. I would not do it.

And at the same time, I knew that I would do it, no matter what.

Because never, not for a second, did Maya's barbed-wire face leave me. And when I didn't sleep at all in the nights that followed and spent until six in the morning searching for the evening star in the firmament, I then lay down and took comfort in the fact that, in the not-too-distant future, I would be only half a bed, half a table, half a house and half a war-and-prison love. How I looked forward to being united with the other half, who was so much better than me and would heal my pitiful half, reform it, beautify it, paper over it with guaranteed cheques for my longed-for happiness.

And with these thoughts I always fell asleep, not giving a moment's thought to Mokka, who believed me to be her better half.

The Johns were staying in another hotel, the only place in Berlin that had a homely south German sound to its name: Hotel Schaetzle.

Her husband had appointments to attend to, and so Lucie asked me to explore the city of her birth with her. It was twenty years since she'd last been there. The weather was a dream, the people seemed dreamy too, still trembling with joy over the sensational event that had taken place a couple of weeks earlier at Wankdorf Stadium in Bern. The words *world champions* were on many people's lips that summer.

Lucie wanted to go walking in the Tiergarten, of all places. She was interested in borders and trellises, fountains and urns, and was dumbfounded to discover that large areas of the park were nothing but tree stumps and grassed-over bomb craters. The Berliners had felled the old trees after the war and turned them into firewood. Hundreds of saplings had been planted, but they still looked like little scarecrows, and in fact the sparrows were too frightened to go anywhere near them. Lucie's horror made it easier for me to vomit without her seeing. The walk felt like a pre-examination of the crime scene. An inspection of the madness to come.

I dragged us both into a café on Kurfürstendamm, it may have been Café Kranzler. There, over raspberry ice cream, we talked about the Johns' loyal friends, among whom, despite all the friction, I was still counted. Right at the top of the list, however, was Theodor Heuss, Lucie's godfather and her father's best friend when they were young. She told me that she had spoken to 'Theo' about me. My fate, the sad fate of an unbending resistance fighter who had defied the Nazi dictatorship, had made a deep impression on him, she said. She would introduce me to him.

The raspberry ice cream melted in the sun.

Lucie's godfather was re-elected as president of West Germany on the seventeenth of July nineteen fifty-four, in the half burned-out Reichstag.

But I didn't see him until two days later, at the senate reception in the Schöneberg town hall. I sat with the Johns and their old, trusted, very British-looking friends at a table on one side of the long Brandenburg Hall, washed by waves of tinkling glasses and shreds of conversation from the knots of people at neighbouring tables, all hoping to be graced with the guest of honour's presence.

But, following his brief after-dinner speech, the president didn't look left or right as he headed straight towards us, and greeted everyone at our table heartily. He shook my hand, too, and once Lucie had introduced me as 'the unbending you-know-what' and 'a wonderful artist', he gave me a rather unpresidential slap on my ribcage.

Unfortunately, he hit the Walther PPK that was slumbering under my left arm.

'What's this then, are you armed?'

'Naturally, Herr President,' I said, because what else was I supposed to say.

Heuss blinked for a moment, said, 'Jolly good, jolly good,' giving an impressive demonstration of his thoroughly liberal mindset, and probably thinking that artists were always doing peculiar things. Then he left.

It was of course completely nonsensical for me to be carrying the pistol everywhere I went. Perhaps I was hoping to be arrested. I don't know.

Apart from this incident, however, the evening proceeded entirely according to protocol. It was only when the hour had grown late that Otto John was to be heard saying, 'Even here, it's wall-to-wall Nazi scum! Even here!'

He was standing at one of the neighbouring tables, three sheets to the wind, steadying himself on a heating pipe and directing his sallies with a champagne bottle, which was cheerfully sloshing out its contents just as he was. Lucie leapt to her feet at once to calm him down. But he was completely calm, he yelled. 'I'm completely calm! But you lot – you won't be calm for much longer, oh no!'

That was where Otto was wrong, however: the four hundred guests at the senate reception, and the forty-four waiters, and even President Heuss, grinning and motionless as Mao, were a picture of calm. They were as quiet as mice as they watched this secret-service chief with his boyish good looks run off, his wife in hot pursuit. As he went, beside himself with fury, panting and red in the face, he yelled into the huge ceremonial hall, 'You've got another thing coming, all of you! You've all got another thing coming, you fascists!'

Then he stopped suddenly, threw his arms wide like an operatic tenor and sang with great fervour: 'Heija bobbaja, kill the hen dead, it lays me no eggs and eats up my bread.'

We took him back to his hotel and undressed him, but he hardly registered what was happening; he just chuckled blissfully, 'Schaetzle, Schaetzle, Schaetzle, ah, Hotel Schaetzle.'

Lucie thanked me with tears in her eyes, and told me it was the upcoming memorial event that had got her husband so worked up.

'You're a true friend, Koja. A wonderful, wonderful person.'

Yes, that's what she said, just as you always do, my Swami. And then she added, 'You will still pick us up tomorrow, won't you?'

I went back to the Kempinski and didn't throw myself out of the window.

21

The next day was a mixture of permanent and transient feelings. *My* permanent and transient feelings I mean, of course: on that day, the twentieth of July nineteen fifty-four, I was the only one with feelings; what everyone else involved in the assassination had were not feelings but clear objectives. They wanted these objectives to be realized, and if they were, that would lead to feelings – positive ones. Or if they weren't, then to less positive ones.

But I had a monstrous number of objectives, all of which contradicted one another. And strong, contradictory objectives always lead to strong, contradictory feelings.

I didn't want Otto to die.

I didn't want Maya to die.

These two things could not be reconciled.

I didn't want to shoot anyone.

I especially didn't want to shoot Otto.

I didn't want to be shot.

I didn't want to be a secret agent.

I didn't want to be a liar.

I wanted to hail the joyful Christmas-truth.

How, if you please, was all this supposed to happen?

One permanent feeling that day was a painful need to urinate. Another was fear.

The transient feelings depended on which objectives were thrusting themselves to the fore at any given time.

An assassin should not have feelings. I had impressed that upon Politov again and again. But impressing doesn't do any good.

Hub had given me my final instructions early that morning, when I went for an innocuous walk in the Tiergarten despite the drizzle. He pulled me into a bush. Beneath dripping branches of mistletoe, I learned that the Ukrainians were already lying in their positions, disguised as forestry workers. How can you dress up as a forestry worker in the centre of Berlin and call it a disguise? Especially when you barely speak any German? And then lie down in the mud, when it's raining?

I shouted at Hub. But I was just trying to compensate.

After breakfast, which consisted of a long look into my coffee cup, I collected the Johns in a taxi, as arranged. They were already waiting outside their Schaetzle, like black mushroom stalks beneath their dark umbrella. Otto was feeling better. But he seemed delicate and permeable, a man wrapped in tissue paper. He began to weep silently in the taxi, and I sweated like a pig and felt the sweat drenching the pistol in my armpit. There was a rumble of thunder outside. A storm seemed to be gathering.

'I'm going to see Wowo after this,' Otto said out of nowhere. 'He wants to speak to me.'

'You do that, Otto,' Lucie nodded. 'Wowo is always so good for you.'

'I hope I don't fall.'

'No one is going to fall.'

The Bendlerblock, the former seat of the Wehrmacht high command, is situated on the Reichpietschufer, by the canal to the south of the Tiergarten. It is a forbidding hulk of shell limestone, into which at that time a few public bodies had crept back. Transport authorities. That kind of thing.

Unrelenting rain was pounding against the taxi's windows as we pulled up at the gates, behind dozens of other taxis and black government sedans, from which people were hurrying towards the inside of the building. We got out, but were instantly overwhelmed by water and crowds: Otto greeted a stream of people whose hanged and shot husbands, siblings and friends he had outlived, a fact for which he seemed to be apologizing with every handshake, every embrace, and even the odd salute.

Mama would have fitted in perfectly here. A distinguished mixture of grief and *gloire* was gradually filling the courtyard where von Stauffenberg and the other aristocratic would-be assassins had been hanged. It would have sated her need to mourn in a way that befitted her status, the kind of thing that just seemed inappropriate for deceased Sepp the Chemists and Chin-ninnys.

Otto showed Lucie and me the window where he had smoked a final cigarette with Count von Stauffenberg following the failed uprising. His fingers then walked down the stairs (fled, rather) and pointed to the escape route he had taken, across that courtyard, stumbling over the loose cobble that was still sticking as far out of the ground as it had then. 'Someone needs to flatten that,' he said. He fell silent then, caught his breath and said, 'Tempelhof.' And then again, 'Tempelhof Airport.'

Then his hand simulated a plane taking off, a gesture meant to explain to us how he managed to be the last person to escape from the Bendlerblock. He'd raced to the airport and, as a Lufthansa legal counsel, got himself on a flight to Spain, a few minutes after the SS launched its search for him.

The large, square internal courtyard was enclosed on all four sides by five-storey facades. At its centre stood a naked bronze figure with its hands bound. No one had thought to protect the rows of chairs from the storm, and so Countess Moltke was one of the first to sit down, bolt upright in her black velvet dress, in a puddle of water, meaning that everyone else had to do likewise, without wiping the seat dry, out of respect.

When Philipp Boeselager started to speak – he was a former explosives supplier who still looked incredibly young, like a student – Otto whispered that he, Otto John, had not even been an explosives supplier, just a courier to Madrid, but his brother, Hans . . . And then his voice cracked, and Lucie took his left hand, and I was on the point of taking his right, and he was sobbing so loudly that everyone turned to look at him, and I had to fight back the tears myself.

Then it was time, the pre-agreed time, I couldn't believe it.

The rain washed our faces blank, all except Otto's. I tugged at his coat, told him something very important had just occurred to me, could he come with me. Please. I had to get him over to Bendlerstraße, because that was where the foresters were waiting, the Ukrainian foresters and their rifles, two hundred metres down the street. It really was as easy as Hub had said it would be, a barrier you had to walk past, a handful of police officers. That was all.

But Otto refused to go.

He showed no signs of moving at all.

Instead, he buried his head in Lucie's embrace, and the only word he would say was 'Hans', as all the papers later reported. Hans, Hans, Hans. 'My brother.'

I broke out in a sweat that soaked the rust-proof Walther PPK, for now Maya was on my mind again, her amber eyes. *There along the bank of the Kazanka River.*

Permanent and transient feelings.

Then an awful lot of transient feelings fell away at once, and slowly, very slowly, I got a grip on my objectives.

'Otto!' I whispered. 'It's about Gehlen. There's something I need to tell you about Gehlen.'

But Otto howled louder and louder, and I wondered what would happen if, in front of all these people, I drew my gun and shot down not only a survivor of the Bendlerblock (a weeping survivor, at that), but the last, the very last survivor – no one but Otto had escaped the sealed-off building ten years before. I'd be setting off that ultimate fire-work on the twentieth of July, as well! My God, all the Nazis on earth would sing hosannahs.

My reluctant heart was flooded with outrage that someone could dare to kill a resistance fighter in this sacred place – and what made me even more furious was that I was supposed to be the bastard who did it. Then an idea suddenly sprouted in my mind, shooting up like a fly agaric, and I wondered why this bright red idea with its white spots hadn't occurred to me before. Why I hadn't thought of Wowo.

Suddenly, everything seemed simple and logical, and the surprising new thing was that even my permanent feelings changed. The need to urinate disappeared. The new fear was the opposite of the old one.

And when a white-clad children's choir came out of the dry, with a forest of black umbrellas above their little heads (expressing a mystical affinity with the harmony and disharmony of this place), and when they raised their childish voices in an almost sweet sound, and even Lucie John, the classical singer, began to sigh at 'Ave Maria', Otto could take it no longer.

He tore himself away from his wife, leapt up and ran across the courtyard, straight towards Bendlerstraße.

I was surprised – perhaps in part at how incredibly fast Otto could run. But he was exactly the same age as me and far fitter; he loved sailing, skiing, mountaineering and Eintracht Frankfurt. You could see all that as his feet drummed on the cobbles, straight through the gates, past the guards and into the assassins' sights.

I was hard on his heels, I can tell you, but then he ran into the road and a shot rang out. A clap of thunder sounded at the same time. Otto fell onto the asphalt.

Then I was with him and threw myself over him, so that they would have to kill me to get to him. I helped him up, though I was still half on the ground myself.

'That was a gunshot,' he stammered.

'Nonsense! It was thunder.'

I pushed him behind a parked car.

'That was a shot! I heard it!'

'No one heard a shot. It was just the thunder.'

He was unharmed. The police officers were eyeing us with interest, but none of them moved from where they were standing.

'They tried to kill me! They're going to kill me!'

'No one's going to kill you, Otto! What are you doing out here? What made you run off like that? Come away from the road.'

Shielding him with my body, my arm around him, I drew him out from behind the car. We crossed the pavement and took cover behind a pillar. And then, flanked by the stares of policemen, who thought we were barking mad, I escorted him back into the Bendlerblock complex.

There, underneath an entrance arch, we both started to cry. Or rather, I did – he had been crying for some time already, and we wept together over the final bars of 'Ave Maria', and I told him that he must go and see Wowo. He must.

'Ah, I tell you, that was a gunshot, old boy, but once again no one believes me.'

And those were the last words that Otto John spoke to me in this life.

22

GREATLY HONOURED HOSPITAL ADMINISTRATORS

WHAT IS THE POINT OF ME TELLING YOU THAT THERE IS A CRIMINAL IN THIS HOSPITAL ACTUALLY IN MY ROOM?

WELL? WHAT HAPPENS? WHY DOES NO ONE CARE?

THE FOURTH PATH OF THE WISE HAS A LOT TO SAY ABOUT THIS. SAMMA KAMMANTA.

PLEASE COME AND GET ME OUT OF HERE. BUT NOT NURSE GERDA. SHE BELIEVES THE CRIMINAL. SHE BELIEVES I AM CONFUSED IN MY MIND. MY MIND IS TOTALLY FINE, THAT IS WHY I AM WRITING TO YOU.

UNCONFUSED.

I WAS NEVER GOOD AT GERMAN BUT I ALWAYS GOT BS IN MATHS.

ALWAYS.

I CAN PROVE IT.

A CRIMINAL. HONESTLY. HIS NAME IS SOLM.

GET ME OUT OF HERE. IT IS LIKE MY WHOLE JOB TO BE INTERESTED IN PEOPLE. A PRIEST, I MEAN. IF YOU BELIEVE ME THEN SEND IN THE DOCTOR (GREEK) AND TELL HIM TO SAY BLESS YOU THREE TIMES (NOT IN GREEK) ALTHOUGH I WILL ONLY SNEEZE TWICE. THEN I WILL KNOW.

VERY RESPECTFULLY YOURS

BASTI

P.S. YOU NEED TO GET ME OUT OF HERE.

23

Wolfgang Wohlgemuth had to choose between: twenty-four suits, four apartments, five mistresses, two ex-wives and one current wife who was not at home; and one Walther PPK, which I held to his forehead at the end of the evening.

But at the start of that evening, our relationship had still been excellent.

'Really?' he'd asked me then. 'Otto's coming?'

'I'm sure he will come.'

'That's good.'

'He's going to defect.'

'Didn't I say so?'

'Yes, but he doesn't know it yet.'

Wowo made his trumpet mouth, realized that no note was coming out, smiled and said with that incredible condescension of his, 'Goodness me, what a lark.'

Ever since I'd leaned the tear-stained Otto John up against a pilaster in the Bendlerblock four hours previously, I had been on the move, or, to put it in terms typical of my profession for once, on the run. I had taken to my heels and run out of the main entrance, past two flabbergasted Orcs who had come to intercept me. One of them stood in my way, shaking his head regretfully, but I rammed into him and he fell over like a child. I leapt into the nearest taxi, and no one followed me.

When I reached the eastern sector, I found a phone box and dialled the number I was not allowed to dial.

I met Comrade Nikitin an hour later on Karl Marx Allee. His Graves'-disease face was a mask of fury. I told him what had happened and what, in my view, needed to happen next, and searched his eyes for the danger this put Maya in, but found nothing; he just nodded. Everything would be arranged, he said tersely. I should make Informant XT Zero-Three-Three an offer, an extremely generous offer.

'I'm making you an offer,' I therefore told Dr Wolfgang Wohlgemuth two hours later, once he had smuggled me up the back stairs of his gynaecology practice and past his receptionist. 'It's the job of chief physician at the Charité.'

I don't know if, in his place, I would have abandoned twenty-four suits, four apartments, five mistresses, two ex-wives and one current wife for an elevation in medical rank. But his eyes lit up, and he told me he was ready to convince Otto to do what was without doubt the right thing for him.

I waited in an expressive side room overflowing with drugs, which Mama would doubtless have described as 'a glory hole'. At eight o'clock the doorbell rang. I couldn't see Otto, but I heard him. He seemed to have calmed down, judging by his voice, which blended with the rain that was still pattering against the window. It meant that I could hear very little of what was being said as I listened at the closed door; nothing, in fact.

Eventually the final patient left, followed by the receptionist. Time trickled away. I ate a few amphetamine compounds out of the dark little tubes on the shelves, which, according to the leaflet in the pack, promised everything from increased alertness, concentration, self-confidence and focus, all the way to tunnel vision, ventricular fibrillation, euphoria, increased sexual prowess, eye tremors and teeth-grinding.

After about an hour, Wowo slipped into my room and whispered that Otto was in the lavatory and he had the feeling things were not going well.

'What do you mean by that?' I asked.

'He doesn't want me to drive him over there.'

'Not even for two hours?'

'Not even for two hours.'

'Have you told him he'll be given files on Globke and Oberländer?'

'He says he has enough SS files.'

'Give him an injection.'

'What?'

'A sedative.'

'Have you gone mad?'

'Or put something in his drink.'

'Otto is my friend.'

'Then do something for him, for once!'

'Only if he comes voluntarily.'

'Your friend came within a whisker of being killed today. You don't have the slightest idea what I'm risking here for all of us.'

'I'm not going to bloody kidnap the man, you lunatic.'

And that was the moment at which the amphetamines took their pleasing effect, especially with regard to increased self-confidence and teeth-grinding. Herr Wohlgemuth got to know my Walther PPK quite intimately. And believe me, after everything that had happened in the previous few days, I had a strange urge to try the thing out. A gun that you soak with your armpit sweat but never use makes the person carrying it ridiculous, especially to himself: it makes him feel worthless and unnecessary, and that was what I told Informant XT Zero-Three-Three, and you cannot imagine the speed with which he produced that sedative.

A mere ten minutes after the future chief physician of the Charité had sidled out of the glory hole, the door opened again, and he beckoned me over into his sitting room. Otto was lying in a leather armchair, beside a skeleton painted in various colours. His head rested on the chair back, his eyes were closed, he was snoring softly. His arms were limp and there was a cognac glass lying on the floor in an orange puddle.

'Let's go,' I said.

'But, Koja, my dear Herr Solm,' Wowo whined, 'we absolutely *cannot* do this.'

Of course we can do this, I thought, and said out loud that we had no choice. He needed to make sure Otto came round quite soon, I told him, but he should also give him something longer-lasting to render him more amenable and less inclined to make senseless objections.

I also advised the doctor, who was looking completely over-whelmed, to think of himself and pack a few personal items, underwear for instance, and not just his trumpet. He must destroy anything that could connect him to the GDR or senior members of the Org. He would not be coming back to the house.

'Am I to give everything up? My practice? My apartment? My wife?'

'Yes, but the order you put those things in is your own business, of course.'

I dictated a letter that he would leave for his receptionist (the pride and justification of a KGB agent on the run). Then he packed a bag, and I called the Charité from his telephone – at that time, East and West Berlin still had a common phone network. When our contact at the other end answered, I handed Wowo the receiver. He listened for a moment, then stood up straight and whispered into the phone, 'Yes indeed, my good friend and I are coming now.'

After that, he injected Otto with a dose of chlorpromazine, but I didn't care what it was called, the important thing was that it worked.

'He will follow my suggestions as if under hypnosis. This has a sedative effect, caused by reversible blocking of two sub-types of dopa-mine receptors.'

'I didn't understand a word of that.'

'Otto will do what we tell him.'

'Good.'

'But not for long. If we're stopped at the checkpoints, I can't make any guarantees.'

'Do you have a second car?'

'My wife's.'

'You go in front, in your car, with Otto. I'll follow you.'

'He's going to wake up any minute now.'

'*Tempus fugit.*'

He gave me the key to a pale pink ladies' Fiat. I drove it out of the rear courtyard and waited in front of the building. There was such a strong smell of perfume inside the car that I had to wind the window down. The heavy rain hit my left cheek, my left hand and left thigh. I kept a watch on the flooded, deserted Uhlandstraße as the dusk turned slowly into night. The parked cars, shimmering dully beneath two flickering street lamps, seemed to be empty. No one had Wohlgemuth's practice under surveillance, apart from me of course.

The lights in the sitting room went on shining and shining. It was taking much too long.

I was just about to pick up my gun and go stalking back between the grey marble pillars and into this obnoxious parody of a Renaissance building, when the gate to the rear courtyard opened again. A pair of headlights appeared, and Wowo's American Ford rolled out past me. Otto was sitting in the passenger seat, seemingly in good spirits.

I started the car and followed the Ford. The Walther was lying on the seat beside me. And I didn't fling it out of the window as we approached the sector border, either.

Back then, seven years before the Wall went up, it was still easy to get into East Berlin: all you had to do was show some deference, a passport, and a nice face to the police on both capitalist and socialist sides.

To this day, I don't know which crossing point we headed for. But I do remember Wowo driving faster and faster, racing through the night. Meanwhile, all I could see were streaky red tail lights.

The Fiat's windscreen wipers were worse than useless.

As we approached a barrier, I caught sight of two men in uniform. They were armed with British sub-machine guns, but they weren't pointing them. The rain sprayed off their coats as they stepped forward, evidently ordering the half-sedated and entirely kidnapped Protector of the Constitution to wind his window down. They were given two hopefully well-forged passports, and held them under a tarpaper awning to examine them by the light of a torch.

I could certainly have taken out the first guard with a salvo fired straight through the windscreen. But after that, the second guard would have fired off a hundred and twenty shots in the space of seven seconds with his sub-machine gun, in whatever direction.

A more sensible plan, I decided, was simply to drive around both guards.

They had retreated under the rickety tar-paper shelter and were taking their time with the passports. I would have to drive around the tar paper, too, I thought. I would have to drive my flimsy ladies' Fiat around the whole guard house. And then there was the lowered barrier, please let it not be made of any kind of metal.

I thought all this, put the car into first gear and readied myself.

But nothing happened.

The passports were returned to Wowo's Ford, and it was waved through. They didn't bother too much with me, either. The guard just pulled the hood of his dripping oilskin lower over his face, and I am sure that our luck was thanks to the rain.

Many years later, Otto himself would testify that his best friend – or rather, his former best friend – Wolfgang Wohlgemuth had lured him into his practice, drugged him with a sedative and later hypnotized him. He never went to the East of his own volition, he said; he was abducted and taken there. He could remember nothing more, apart from the fact that they had set off from Wowo's practice at a crazy speed. Then he lost consciousness and after a wholly narcotic twenty-four hours (Otto sometimes had a funny way of expressing himself), he awoke at the Soviet headquarters in Karlshorst. He saw three guards and a woman in a doctor's coat in front of him, he said – the injection commando. He also saw and spoke to an ancient and severely disfigured KGB officer.

Otto did not see or speak to me, but I saw and heard him through the mirrored glass behind which he came round, to find himself lying on an operating table. Nikitin greeted him like his own brother. I mean, with kisses on the cheek and forehead.

Amid Otto's protests and imprecations, our comrade produced a West Berlin morning paper (the *Mopo*, perhaps), which already carried the front-page headline: 'WEST GERMAN SECRET-SERVICE BOSS DESERTS'. Then he offered Otto John, who was frozen in shock, an anti-fascist partnership on equal terms, so that together they might lead the Federal Republic of Germany away from the henchmen of Hitler who had infiltrated it, and back onto the road of democracy.

Or something like that.

After a little back-and-forth ('pen-pusher', 'shit-spouter', 'filthy communist devil') Otto declared that he was willing to cooperate.

Faced with the bridges he was coming to realize had been burned for him with the West, and the gentle hints about imprisonment, torture and the KGB's psychopharmaceutical arsenal, it was a smart decision.

He began to tell the patiently listening Nikitin of the evil that was rearing its head in the West. First and foremost, he told him about the one hundred and forty enlightening lever-arch files that were sitting in his office in Cologne – though that was no longer true. I would learn soon afterwards that his deputy, Albert Radke, had already taken possession of the files and handed them over to Gehlen, meaning that they were ultimately dumped into the sea.

Otto also mentioned a few exemplary democrats, including (not in first place, but still) the loyal Konstantin Solm: 'An upright man and an artist. He's had a hard life. At the Twentieth of July memorial event he was trying to tell me something about Gehlen. I don't know what it was, but it seemed urgent.'

Otto paused for a moment, closed his eyes. They had seen too much already, and in some ways also too little, and now they were thinking about what had happened two days previously, and they recalled nothing, for when they opened again, all I saw was depopulated spaces.

'Perhaps someone could ask him what he wanted to tell me,' Otto began tentatively. 'But I'm sure Koja Solm would never collaborate with a secret service, not one from the West and certainly not a shit-spouting secret service from the East. It's not in his nature.'

I saw Nikitin steal a glance in my direction. He put one thumb up.

Maya was going to be all right.

24

You might think that now an undisturbed and lasting peace and happiness would have settled over the house. My family's house, I mean, which of course consisted of several houses. The Pattendorf nursing home, for instance, which we visited often for my sprightly mother's sake, and because little Anna was so fond of the mountains and all the horses too, of course. There, she was able to draw, stroke, feed and ride them; Munich still had very few, and even the dray horses were gradually being retired.

Then there was my own home, where I was working on a kind of distancing project with Mokka: a very gentle, kind separation, which she might not even notice until she was content to be far away and have nothing more to do with me, but to think of me and my sweet wife with friendship and affection.

I counted the Lubyanka in Moscow as one of my family's houses, too, for that was where my future bride lived, under straitened, but relatively comfortable conditions, as she wrote. She told me how much she was looking forward to moving house.

And finally, there was the apartment on Biedersteiner Straße where Ev, Anna and Hub lived. Its rooms were the setting for most of the disturbances that now followed, which were both childish and unavoidable.

The bright, tidy kitchen was where Hub hit me.

When I returned from East Berlin, I rang his doorbell and, standing in front of his oven, claimed to have spent two days in the brothels of Kreuzberg following the botched operation in the Bendlerblock. He hit me with his one arm. He hit me right in the face. He hit me as hard as he could.

It hurt, and I told him that it was all right to strike me once, but the second time he should use his other arm. He hurled himself at me in a rage, but I just clung to him. He was monstrously angry and frustrated. The failure of the assassination attempt on Otto John had sealed his fate.

A few weeks later, he was demoted. Instead of a whole division, he was now merely head of an Org sub-department: domestic counter-espionage, Upper Bavaria region. With that, he lost access to the meetings of the department heads; the Doctor didn't want to see him any longer.

He did, however, want to see me. The fiasco in Berlin was not laid at my door, especially because the whole affair had ultimately been concluded in the best possible way for General Gehlen.

Otto John would bear the stigma of defection for all time. The uproar it caused in Germany, capturing the attention of millions and keeping the political establishment in suspense, is something you can't imagine today.

Otto held an international press conference in East Berlin, at which, under pressure from the KGB and the Stasi, he was forced to present his defection to the GDR as a voluntary one. Like the majority of the population, the Solms were glued to their radios, and heard Otto trying to explain his motives to the world:

'In the Federal Republic, the foundation for political activity has been withdrawn from me.'

His voice, indignant and with no trace of that self-soothing Hesse dialect, boomed out of the ether.

There was a pause, during which you could hear the listening mass of journalists: breathing, rustling, the noises cameras make when you operate them. As they clicked away in an increasingly rapid staccato, Otto went on, sounding strangled now:

'My work has been continually undermined by the Nazis who are once again on the ascendent in political and public life, and the minister for the interior has now made it impossible for me to continue this work, by announcing to the press that, after gaining independence, he would have free rein to entrust protection of the constitution to personalities who . . . who are truly beyond all doubt.'

Every sentence he uttered contained so many clauses that it was almost impossible to follow. But the essence of his announcement was that he wanted to stay in the GDR and fight for the reunification of Germany from there.

When a journalist from the dogged British contingent at the press conference asked what Herr John, whom she called 'Mr John' with an English 'J', made of the situation for the West German secret service, he said, 'As everyone knows, the American-financed Gehlen Organization has been working against my office for years as it tried to protect the Federal Republic, through democratic means, from enemies both on the left and on the right.'

A whisper ran through the crowd of two hundred and fifty journalists: in East Berlin, someone speaking of 'enemies on the left', when the historical fact was that there could be no enemies on the left, only friends, was worth a whisper, at least.

'The large team of senior staff,' Mr John went on, 'employed by this Gehlen Organization includes countless SD and SS officers who committed abominable war crimes and sat in judgement over German resistance fighters or simply killed them. This Gehlen Organization gives a safe harbour to all those who fought for Hitler to the bitter end. Resistance fighters are ostracized as turncoats in Gehlen's ranks.'

The Doctor rejoiced.

Any patriot regards a verbal attack from a deserter and officially certified traitor as proof that he has done pretty much everything right.

No one in West Germany took Otto John's accusations seriously.

As far as they were concerned, it might just as well have been Stalin or Ivan the Terrible commenting on Gehlen's character flaws.

The one hundred and forty files, which Otto never did more than hint at in official interviews, did not re-emerge. But who would have taken an interest in them, anyway?

Otto's deputy, Albert Radke, certainly didn't. And – despite what he had done with those papers – he was eventually appointed commissarial head of the Office for the Protection of the Constitution.

All doors were therefore now open for the Doctor in Cologne, as well as in all the regional seats of government, and that finally enabled him to reach for the stars.

Essentially, then, the abduction of Otto John to East Berlin, and his decision to save his own skin and let Ulbricht parade him in public like a dancing bear, was also the birth of the Bundesnachrichtendienst – the BND – out of the spirit of total conspiracy. The effect on John was more deadly than physical liquidation could ever have been.

'Now the worm is in the apple,' the Doctor gloated, casting himself as the worm.

Comrade Nikitin said the same thing, though he regarded the Doctor as the apple and me as the worm.

He was tremendously happy that now, with my help, he could skim information off an intelligence service that was completely infiltrated by the Soviets. In late summer, he sent me a congratulatory dispatch, telling me that I was to receive the Red Banner Order Third Class, and from now on would also be getting substantial monthly bonuses. Agent Three-One-Three would be prepared for handover in the autumn.

Handover. What a word.

My joy was so great that I simply didn't see the threat Hub's frailty posed to my family.

Although I had plumbed the depths of the blackness that could darken Hub's soul once before, the good news accumulated inside me into a sum total that did not exist. There is no sum of good news. All pieces of good news stand alone and can be annihilated individually or together by the slightest folly. The arithmetic of good news lies in its nilpotence. But I had the wind in my sails and was focusing on myself, as a painter should. Today, I could slap myself for not spotting the signs. Instead, I overestimated my triumph.

In addition to Nikitin's Red Banner Order (they actually sent it to me through the German postal system, it really was a shame I couldn't show it to anyone), I was also given the Doctor's medal of honour, specially instituted for this occasion, the 'Organization Service Order' (Orgsorder for short, and I couldn't show that, either, though I could take it to my grave).

The design of this medal, which to this day is still recast and placed around the necks of deserving secret agents, spies and traitors, was left to me. I suggested an image of the Elend-Alm lodge (Ah, I liked the name) – but Gehlen preferred St George, his favourite dragon-slayer. For the material, I chose brass. He, however, insisted on solid bronze, and, for me personally, gold. After all, he gushed, I did manage to finish Otto John in the best possible way, just as Iago once finished the naive Othello in the best possible way, with false sympathy, pretend loyalty and feigned friendship.

The Doctor presented me with the eight-carat Orgsorder at a ceremony in the Org's canteen. All the firm's division heads, and the heads of sub-divisions and sub-sub-divisions, came to applaud and hope for an Orgsorder of their own. In honour of the occasion, even the demoted Hub was given permission to attend. I don't know why I was so convinced that he would soon get over all this: I saw his hate-hardened eyes, but I didn't believe them.

That afternoon, Gehlen gave a speech, announcing that ten days after Otto John fled the country – and thus ten days after the moral destruction of the Office for the Protection of the Constitution – Federal Chancellor Konrad Adenauer had given him a personal guarantee. As he spoke, the Doctor stood like Hannibal in front of his elephants. He let them trumpet and stamp their feet on the Bavarian ground, and then he told them the chancellor had assured him that, over the next two years, all of the Org's warriors would be transferred into the official service of the Federal Republic of Germany.

'The Org is dead!' he cried. 'Long live the BND!'

A Carthaginian cheer washed over the Doctor, and in the midst of the cheering he put an arm around my shoulders, and Hub saw it.

I remained in close contact with Lucie John. The loss of her husband – who she believed was buried under a mass of lies like the victim of an avalanche, many hundreds of kilometres away on the other side of the

Iron Curtain – left her stunned, but it broke neither her heart nor her beautiful backbone. She and her British friends were convinced that Otto had been kidnapped from West Berlin and brainwashed.

Lucie was outraged at the coldness with which Adenauer and the government had dropped her husband, even though the evidence suggested Otto had not fled to the East. First and foremost, he would never have abandoned his wife without saying anything, leaving her defenceless and exposed to all that mockery and scorn. Everyone who knew Otto and Lucie knew that the pair were Philemon and Baucis to one another. All those heterosexual, homoerotic and polymorphously perverse indiscretions were not what Otto longed for, body and soul – even if he never passed up an opportunity for them, because he was also an overgrown child.

All through her husband's Babylonian imprisonment, Lucie John, née Manén, never doubted him and his love for her. She was glad of my loyalty, and when she heard that my sister was Jewish, like herself, she came to visit us in Munich.

Hub avoided this visit, not wanting to sit around a table with 'three Jewesses', by which he meant his wife, his daughter, and the wife of a man he had wanted to kill just a few months earlier.

Like the idiot I am, however, I didn't pay this much heed. I don't understand myself. I simply don't understand myself.

Unfortunately, my separation from Mokka was not as kind and gentle as I had hoped when I began our ambitious distancing project. But it wouldn't be long now until I picked Maya up from Karlshorst, brought her across the border and had to introduce her to my circle of friends and relatives as a former prisoner of war.

'Don't you like me any more?'

'Of course I like you, Mokka. I like you very much.'

'Well then, why do you want me to move out?'

'Perhaps we just need a break.'

'A break? I don't need a break. I do everything for you, don't I?'

'You do, my Mokka.'

'I do your washing and your ironing, and I cook for you and I learn all the periods of art history off by heart for you, and I . . .' She paused for a moment to wipe a drop from the end of her nose. 'And I . . . I sell all those forged pictures for you.'

'What forged pictures?'

'The pictures that you forge.'

'I don't forge pictures.'

'Oh, and I'm the Pope.'

'You're joking, aren't you?'

'I'm not stupid. I can tell when paint is fresh, you know. I do paint a little myself.'

I groaned, for there could be no disharmonies more horrible than Mokka's. Roses and tulips in the style of Renoir, who Papa said could only paint hats – just horrible.

'I know I don't paint well, not even as well as little Anna. But even *that* I do for you, to earn a little of your respect and love. I am a *person*, Koja.'

'You are a very, very lovely person, Mokka. Even so, all good things must come to an end.'

'I'll never tell anyone you forge those pictures. Because you're very good at it. I admire you for it, really. And if I could paint as well as you do, I would forge pictures, too, and I'd earn so much money, and I wouldn't care, because I'd be earning money for you and for our children.'

'I don't forge pictures, Monika.'

'Oh, so you're not even going to call me Mokka now?'

'Dearest Mokka,' I replied gently, 'it's slander, what you're saying about the pictures, I could report you to the police for that, you know.'

'Oh stop it. I'm not going to blacken your name. I still love you, even though I know that you go behind a lot of people's backs, and that little Anna is your daughter.'

'Anna is *not* my daughter.'

'Come on, a blind man could see that she's your daughter. Your brother is the only one who doesn't see it, and I really don't know why. You think I'm slow. But I have eyes in my head.'

'I just wanted to give you some time to find a nice place to live. I thought you could stay here until you'd got somewhere.'

'All you do is use everyone. Everyone.'

'But yes,' I sighed. 'Perhaps it's best if we just put it behind us right away.'

'You treat me so badly, and you're always so good to your sister, and I know you've slept with her at some point. I notice all of this, and I just accept it, and I'd even be understanding if you were still sleeping with her, because she's very beautiful, and because I love you.'

'I'll go and get a suitcase.'

'Is that the only thing you liked about me, that I was good in bed?' She was crying.

'Don't say you *were* good in bed, Monika. You *are*. You are good in bed.'

'Oh how mean. You're so mean.'

She walked out of the house, sobbing and tender and ugly as a raven chick fallen from the nest, dragging the suitcase behind her, her whole body suddenly racked by a mighty shudder of horror. I watched her go. I watched for a long time, relishing the sensation of complete weightlessness that had come over me.

Ev was the first person I told.

She was not pleased to hear I had jilted Mokka. That surprised me.

And the news that Maya would be coming back from Russia was too much for her powers of imagination and recall. That surprised me, too.

Two women beginning with 'M', she said slowly. And the vowels are so similar. How is one supposed to tell them apart?

I reminded her of Riga's final days, and our summer with Baron Grotthus, when Anna was still so little. There was the girl with the cuts on her face, remember?

And because no one forgets a slashed face, I was able to watch my sister remembering, and see the expression of disbelief that was inextricably linked with that memory.

It was just before sunset. We were sitting beneath scattered, fat autumn clouds in the autumn grass of a riding stables near Pattendorf, watching Anna ride her first pony, which I had bought her. It was an Icelandic pony financed by the KGB – it actually had a red sheen to it – and was cheerful and rather devoid of character.

'Look what I can do!' Anna cried out, letting go of the reins and riding around the paddock hands-free, while the Alps cheered her on.

'Stop that!' Ev shouted, rather shrilly, I thought.

Anna obeyed, but you could tell she wouldn't obey for much longer. She was eleven, but small for her age, and was often still taken for a nine-year-old. And so pain was gradually breaking into her life, as it does into every human existence, pain and humiliation and feelings of inadequacy – but never when she was on her mare, Parvenue.

'So, Koja, do you believe you and this Maya will get back together?'

'Yes, I believe so.'

'Is that the woman you spoke of, years ago? We were sitting over there, do you remember?'

She pointed.

'You had just come back from being a prisoner of war yourself and you looked terrible, thin as a rake. And I told you I had waited for you. And you said there was someone else.'

'We've been in touch for a while, yes.'

'But how is that possible, being in touch with someone in Russia?'

'Aren't you pleased?'

'Oh, of course I'm pleased for you, Koja. But I'm very unhappy.'

Anna and Parvenue accelerated from a walk to a gallop without passing through a trot. As in drawing, she hated the trot. You got awfully shaken up without any reward in the form of speed. And when she learned that trotting was a fundamentally unnatural way of moving for a horse, a gait thought up by humans to keep harness-racing tracks in business, she decided that, when she grew up, she would abolish that nonsense once and for all, and liberate all the horses of the world.

But she had not reached that point yet, for it would mean having to liberate Parvenue as well.

I could see Ev's whole body tensing. It always did when Anna started to gallop. Ev was imagining all the possible injuries she might sustain. She had even brought a book home from her practice containing illustrations of especially nasty head wounds – caused by cavalry battles, not galloping, as I ventured to point out. And little girls didn't fall onto heavy cuirassier sabres, either.

'Slow down, Anna! That's enough, now!' Ev cried all the same, leaping to her feet.

I took her by the hand and pulled her back down to me. She twisted free of the hand warily, but stayed sitting.

'Why are you so unhappy?'

'You shouldn't have given her that pony. If only because of Hub.'

'Why not?'

'It's something he can't do. He doesn't have as much money as you. It's humiliating for him.'

'But I'm only doing it for Anna.'

'Hub is very unhappy, too.'

Anna was now riding slowly out of the paddock. Ev had always allowed her to gallop across the open meadow to finish, even though it made her knuckles white with anxiety.

'Things are going so well for me at the moment, and I don't want things to be bad for the two of you.'

'Maybe we shouldn't have tried again, Hub and me. He won't watch Anna ride. He won't watch Anna draw. He doesn't want to take Anna to Israel.'

'You're going to Israel?'

'I don't know. Germans aren't allowed to go there. I don't know what our future looks like.'

She turned to me. The wind coming up from the river ran its fingers through her hair.

'We're still betraying Hub. Maybe we should tell him the truth. The whole truth, I mean.'

'You mustn't even contemplate that, Ev.'

But she was contemplating it. Her lips were pressed together with that air of defiance she often had when asserting her will. She looked over at our daughter, who was flying across the grass like a Cossack, shouting and happy.

'It's making us all sick, Koja,' she said after a while. 'I wouldn't tell him if I was going to live my life with someone who wasn't him. But now that we're together, I have to tell him.'

'No.'

'Koja, I live with him, I see him every day.'

'I don't want to hear any more about it.'

'But you know, he's like a good uncle to Anna. And you're like a good father to her. You're both already behaving as if you knew what you really were.'

'And I do know. But that knowledge would destroy him.'

'I'm really frightened, Koja. I'm really frightened that something will happen.'

'Like what?'

'It isn't right. It's the last big lie.'

It was the last big lie for Ev, but not for me. And I think that was why I couldn't understand her. The last big lie is something that will drive anyone mad. A thing you have to be rid of. A thing that torments you. But I only know that now, as an old man. I didn't know it then, not yet.

'Listen, Ev,' I said. 'When Maya is here and when she has a baby, then we can tell him, as far as I'm concerned. If I am living with Maya and she has a baby, he won't leave you – but only then. Because then, he'll feel safe.'

'Why should he feel safe?'

'Because it means we won't get back together.'

'I would never get back together with you, Koja. Not for anything in the world. You've grown so incredibly cold.'

Her tone was friendly and yes, thoroughly warm. Tender. I turned to look at her in surprise.

'What makes you say that?'

'How could you treat Mokka that way? I didn't like her. But she would have done anything for you. She would have gone to the moon for you. How can you just . . .' she searched for the right word '. . . replace her?'

'She's too nice.'

'Too nice?'

'You called her that yourself. Nice. And a bit ordinary.'

'I didn't know then that she would go to the moon for you. You'll never find someone like that again. People who would go to the moon for you are not just nice. And they certainly aren't ordinary. I would never go that far for anyone. Not even you. I only do things for my own sake. Just like you do.'

'The thing that still shocks me about you,' I smiled faintly, 'is that you always say precisely what one mustn't say.'

A sharp shaft of light struck her as the evening sun rolled out like a gold coin from under a moving wall of cloud. She shielded her eyes and looked for Anna. But all we could see as we squinted into the sun was Parvenue's silhouette trotting along the horizon, without her rider.

Ev scrambled to her feet. She started running. I ran after her. We shouted Anna's name. There is nothing worse for any parent on earth than having to shout their child's name. And nothing separates them from one another like such a torment.

After five terrifying minutes (tingling fingers, a high ringing sound in my ears, the fermented meatloaf rising back up my gullet), Anna came out from behind a bush. She gave us a lopsided smile and said she'd been playing a trick. We had stopped watching her. So she hid and waited to see what would happen.

I saw Ev's lips begin to tremble. Then she slapped Anna in the face, began to sob, and threw her arms around the girl, who was now also sobbing.

And I threw my arms around them both. And sobbed with them.

25

On the ninth of November nineteen fifty-four, my forty-fifth birthday, I picked Maya up in Berlin.

I don't imagine hippies enjoy shopping, and certainly not with a view to making themselves look chic. So you probably can't imagine, my dear Swami, how many Munich gentlemen's outfitters I drove mad. At Blösdorfer, the shirt specialist, I had them show me cutaway collars, pin collars and tab collars. At Lodenfrey I bought a coat, exchanged it, bought another coat, took that one back as well and eventually went to Rieger for a fur. When it came to the suit, I couldn't decide between cashmere, silk, mohair or cotton.

When I had arrived at a decision (cashmere), I spent a long time choosing the right tailor. Eventually I opted for a wonderful Italian on Lererstraße. His name was Pietro Cifonelli. Pietro Cifonelli said he would do everything he could to bring out my unique qualities, *sì*, but with elegance, *signore*, not extravagance. He asked me if I preferred baroque (*barocco*) or renaissance (*rinascimento*). I decided on classical (*stupido classico*). But Pietro told me that *stupido classico* was not his area; for *stupido classico* I would have to go to an English tailor, one who wasn't interested in elegance, merely in dressing boring people correctly.

And so I took the renaissance option and received some rather overbearing pinstripes on a grey background, lightly padded at the shoulders, with a beautiful line. A high waist and soft, majestic coat tails. To go with it, a pair of Budapest shoes of finest cowhide leather, and a new hat, which looked simply wonderful.

For Maya, I bought several ladies' outfits in rather muted colours. I had not dared to enquire about her size. Depending on the food situation in the Soviet prison system, it could vary considerably. My two large welcome suitcases also contained pralines, a bottle of Bordeaux, perfume, Mereschkowski's *Leonardo da Vinci* (a book that she wanted, though I had made her want it), a pearl necklace, two first-class tickets on a Lufthansa flight from Berlin Tempelhof to Munich Riem, and a map of Italy I had drawn, showing all the cities we would visit in December, marked with little caricatures of our broken visages (she with her goulash face; me showing my age, puffy and almost bald).

It was splendid to land in Berlin, in the most dreadful November weather.

Outside Tempelhof Airport I gave a stick of chewing gum to a maimed veteran who was begging there, something I had never done before. I took a taxi and went to Friedrichstraße with all my luggage.

The usual KGB driver was waiting at the usual meeting place, and was more than a little surprised at the number of leather suitcases one could fit into the boot of a decrepit Pobeda. Comrade Nikitin had written to tell me that I was welcome to spend another night at the Karlshorst villa with my future bride. But the closer we got to the Soviet headquarters, the more urgently I wanted to snatch Maya up and drive away with her at once. They could send our deployment orders to us later.

When we pulled up outside the KGB building, I took all the suitcases out of the car, although the driver offered to look after them for me. I could tell what he meant by 'look after'.

Nikitin had been right: the large office in the KGB block already looked old again. I couldn't detect the slightest trace of renovation. Typical, I thought. The adjutant who had come out to meet me set my cases down and saluted, probably because of the Red Banner Order, which I had taken out and pinned to my fine cashmere in the car. He told me someone would be with me in just a minute, and withdrew with a snappy farewell.

I had been in this room several times, but never without Stalin and the KGB chief, Beria. Both portraits had been taken down and exchanged for those of their successors, Khrushchev and Ivan Serov. I wondered if that was what had really been meant by 'renovation'.

Then the door opened. My heart leapt with joy, because it thought my eyes had seen Maya when they spotted grey hair approaching. But it wasn't her; it was a woman in uniform I had never met before, fifty years old, short and spherical. She gave me a very formal greeting, and when I asked, ingratiatingly, whether she was Comrade Nikitin's charming adjutant, she said coldly that she had never been an adjutant, at least not since the war. Then she looked me up and down, eyeing my suitcases, my fur coat, the suit, the hat I was carrying, even my shoes.

'And what might your title be, comrade? His Royal Highness?'

I sensed that something here was very different from what I'd expected. Comrade Nikitin had sent me a secret message just two days before, giving a friendly and precise explanation of how what he called 'the handover' would proceed.

'Well then, Comrade Four-Four-Three, do have a seat.'

I sat down, and as I was taking my seat, she took hers, too, and that surprised me, for the seat she took was Nikitin's.

'My name is Pertia, General Pertia,' she explained. She also explained that she was my new agent handler with immediate effect. She had the job of carrying out the handover as instructed. General Nikitin was deceased.

'Deceased?' I repeated, in shock. 'But he wrote to me just the day before yesterday.'

No: over the past few months the comrade general's correspondence had been taken over by capable colleagues, who had imitated the general's own, less than socialist phrasing. From now on, that would cease.

A reddish veil descended in front of my eyes from all the blood that was rising into my head, and General Pertia was transformed into a reddish strawberry, and her uniform was red as well, and I had to take care not to answer any questions that hadn't been asked. I put my hat on, I don't know why, like a soldier donning his helmet under fire, perhaps.

The woman cast a keen eye over my headgear. We would surely both have been surprised if I had stood up.

But that didn't happen.

General Pertia cleared her throat and picked up a small cardboard box, which I had not noticed before, though it had been on the desk the whole time.

'Now, Comrade Four-Four-Three, let us turn to the handover of Comrade Three-One-Three.'

Yes, a strawberry, soft and getting redder all the time, on the verge of rotting; perhaps it had been sweet once, perhaps.

'I am empowered to give you this.'

She slid the box towards me. I couldn't get up, I was pinned to my chair, gargling with my innards. She raised the box slightly, showing it to me, then put it back down and made a casual gesture indicating that I had the right to take it at any time. She put on a pair of glasses, reading glasses. And then, her eyes now large, she read: '"In Case H/314 lm-1951 against Maya Dzerzhinskaya, the defendant was found guilty of voluntarily defecting to the German side while serving as an NCO in the II Penal Infantry Regiment of the 359th Infantry Division of the 30th Army on the Kalinin front, on 31 May 1942 in the city of Rzhev. This was an act of high treason."'

I needed something to focus on, and chose her glasses, which she adjusted after each sentence.

'"The defendant was sentenced to death by the military tribunal of the Supreme Court of the USSR on 1 February 1952."'

She sighed, scratched her double chin, straightened her glasses.

'"The sentence was carried out on 31 October 1954 at Butyrka Prison by a gunshot to the back of the neck. The execution took one minute and thirty seconds."'

She laid the glasses aside and looked at me without them. I couldn't tell exactly what she was seeing, but I had the sense that she was now looking at Pietro Cifonelli's tailoring with a new interest, the fit of my tap collar, the Prince Albert tie knot I had learned specially for Maya, the Budapest shoes and, of course, the two calfskin welcome suitcases.

'Comrade Four-Four-Three. You have rendered outstanding service to the Soviet Union. For that you deserve our thanks and recognition. I am very sorry that the handover has to take place in this form. I would now ask you to take possession of the remains of Comrade Maya Dzerzhinskaya.'

I just stared at her.

'This box, I mean.'

I know.

'You need to take it now.'

I managed to take it.

'Then, on behalf of the KGB, I am empowered to extend very warm wishes for your birthday.'

26

It rained for six years, nine months and six days. There were periods of drizzle, when you could step outside and put on a convalescent face. There was the usual heavy rain. There were flood-like downpours that submerged whole roofs. There was freezing rain, warm rain, monsoon rain. There were even times when it cleared up; a few breaks in the clouds.

From another temporal perspective, I would say that the rain was predominantly a misty drizzle, but by that definition the rain lasted eleven years, two months and five days.

From where I am today, it actually seems to me that the rain never stopped; ever since my forty-fifth birthday the air around me has been condensing, one misty day after another.

Wherever I stood, wherever I went, it was never dry.

And on those rare occasions when it was, ash would start falling from the sky, or snow, which seemed less damp and sometimes brought peace.

I learned a great deal during those years of rain. For instance, I never underestimated anyone again, just because they were too nice or a little too ordinary.

I might have wished General Pertia was nice or ordinary.

I might have wished Maya nice and ordinary and completely toothless, her skin cut into strips like leather. I would have loved her all the same, I know that now.

I've thought of Mokka often in my life, and hoped she was doing well, and a few years later I even searched for her. But by then she had emigrated to Australia. She disappeared somewhere in the bush. Perhaps she is farming Australian camels there now, or prospecting for diamonds in Kimberley, or has a dozen ugly, art-obsessed outback children. Wherever she might be, I hope and pray that she can forgive my arrogant and unbearable self.

The little box contained Maya's five teeth. I looked at each of them again and again. Once I gave them to a dentist to check their condition, and he told me all the teeth were very decayed, soft as paste. I painted the teeth – this was in the early sixties – I painted each of her teeth on giant canvases, canvases that were a greyish white like the teeth, so that they looked like thick fog in November. It was my psychiatrist who recommended I do that, and I fell in love with her, because I had confessed almost everything to her, though not as much as I've told you.

General Pertia also gave me the death certificate, where I read over and over again that Maya was executed on *31 October 1954*. But she had been handed her death sentence on *1 February 1952*, shortly after we met in Karlshorst for the first time.

There were exactly one thousand and three days between the first of February nineteen fifty-two and the thirty-first of October nineteen fifty-four.

One thousand and three days of last meals.

One thousand and three days of last thoughts.

One thousand and three days for mad, desperate longings to erupt, or would that have been the one thousand and three nights?

Take time every day to sit still and listen. Pay attention to the melody of life that plays in you. Isn't it your Buddha who says that? Every life has its measure of pain. But over all those one thousand and three days between her sentence being passed and carried out, Maya knew that eventually she would get a bullet through the back of her neck – at the very moment, in fact, when my task was accomplished. That is pain without measure. Unimaginable pain. When she laughed and dreamed and smoked cigarettes with me, Maya had been a living corpse, even in her ecstasy, in its fading, perhaps especially then.

And yet there had been moments during those one thousand and three days when she was happy, when her happiness was not a disguise. That moment when we were taking a bath together in the lapis lazuli bathroom, and I washed her condemned legs. Or when we looked up at the sky as if with a single eye. And all the letters.

She wrote that she wanted me to wear my best clothes when I collected her.

And so I wore my best clothes to collect her teeth.

I never unpacked the two calfskin suitcases. I would have found it impossible to take her outfits in my hands. They were made of chiffon, fabric that falls slowly to the floor when you throw it in the air. Oh, Maya would definitely have thrown them in the air, I can see her doing it now, as her smile explodes and she catches the cloth on her face, her lovely shashlik face.

And that is why the calfskin suitcases are still in my attic, untouched, just as they were when I brought them back from Berlin, stuffed with old summer fashions, my gorgeous map of Italy and the bottle of Bordeaux that must be worth a fortune now. In nineteen fifty-four, I slept with them in my bed, clinging to them at night, because I had nothing else to cling to. I shut myself up in my apartment for weeks, thinking that the rain would soon stop.

I underestimated that rain.

I intended to cut myself off from General Pertia, but my declaration of commitment meant that they had me in their grip.

All the same, I shat on the whole world, Swami.

I didn't invite anyone into my ark.

The gallery stood empty.

I took leave from the Org. My phone didn't stop ringing. But I never once answered it.

Ev wanted to know what had happened. She surprised me as I was waiting outside the Academy of Art for Anna with Maya's teeth in my mouth, tasting the teeth, wet with tears. I was so startled I swallowed two of them (they re-emerged later), but I revealed the three larger ones, dropping them into my pocket handkerchief, much to her amazement.

But I couldn't be honest with her, you understand?

Instead I said to Ev: Maya's plane crashed. It fell out of the sky an hour after taking off in Moscow and exploded when it hit the ground. And these teeth are all they found of her in the Taiga (so I said several times).

Ev wrapped her arms around me. Then she advised me to throw the teeth away. They couldn't possibly belong to the love of my life, they were KGB fakes, teeth the KGB had pulled out of a dolphin's jaw, they didn't look human. You've been conned, Koja. Maybe you've been taken in by a spy. Maybe she's living her life now out in the Taiga and they were lying to you all along.

It sounded so straightforward, my dear Swami. And so splendid.

Oh, if only it had been true. Then she would still be alive.

And one evening, a few days before Christmas, I got the telephone call.

It was my brother, and I could hear in his voice that I had to come.

The shouting was so loud that I wondered why the police hadn't turned up at the house already. I hurried up the stairs and saw little Anna outside the open door to the apartment.

She was crying.

My darling. What's wrong?

And through her tears she told me that Mami said Papi wasn't her papi. Uncle Koja was her papi. You.

Me.

The impenetrability of the human gaze is almost always dissolved when we are surprised. But only for a brief moment, then the shock comes rattling down like blinds.

My darling. Stay out here and don't move.

Papi's got a pistol, and Mami's very quiet, Uncle Koja.

It didn't sound quiet; all I could hear was yelling. But the yelling was my brother's.

I ran into the apartment and down the hall, a little bend to the left, and then I was standing in their bedroom. Ev actually looked the same as ever. She was leaning against the window, not crying, just slowly shaking her head, horrified that I had come.

Hub was standing there with his pistol, looking like a clown. A one-armed man with a pistol does look like a clown, you know, a figure of fun. You laugh at him.

'A Jewess and my filthy brother,' this drunk man shouted. 'The pair of you have destroyed my life! Why does God hate firstborns? Why does he love second sons and Jews?'

'Calm down, Hub, please calm down!'

We heard police sirens in the distance, a long way off, still, but at least they were there.

'How could the two of you put me at its mercy again! Destruction! At its mercy! What did I do to you? I never did anything to you! I was so forgiving! I gave you your life, Koja! I trusted you again! You're sleeping together!'

'No, Hubsi,' Ev shouted, but he didn't want to be called Hubsi. Not now.

He pointed the gun at her head. A Walther PPK. The gun from Berlin. 'You stole my daughter from me. You're worthless, Ev. *Omnium bipedum nequissimus. OMNIUM BIPEDUM NEQUISSIMUS!*'

'Calm down, Hub!'

'THE MOST WORTHLESS OF ALL THE BIPEDS!'

'Hub!'

'That's the fatted calf, that child out there. That's what you're getting now, Koja! The fatted calf! You've taken everything from me! My wife! My honour! Even my job! Maybe *you're* the spy they're all talking about! Are you the pig grunting in our sty?'

'Calm down, Hub.'

'Are you the mole?'

'No, Hub. Goddammit, put that gun down!'

'I'll tell you both what I'm going to do now. I'm going to put a bullet in my head in front of you. Right here. That's what I'm going to do.'

Ev screamed so loudly it even drowned out the police sirens that were just turning into the road. 'Papi, what are you doing?' said a tiny voice, and I spun round, and so did Hub, both papis spun round, and the movement brought his finger down onto the trigger. The bullet left the barrel, and I swear I saw it leaving the barrel and scratching Hub's temple as it passed, because he had turned his face, and I knew what was going to happen. My daughter's eyes were wide. What beautiful skin she had, pale as she was. Then she fell down, as if she'd been pushed, and very quickly her little belly turned entirely red. And in the commotion that surrounded us I was at her side, raising her eyes with my own, and she wanted to ask me something, there was something on her tongue, and she couldn't, and then she just said again, 'Papi, what are you doing?'

My darling.

And she was gone.

It rained for six years, nine months and six days.

IV

Black Red Gold

I

The Hippy has reduced his future expectations of me to a minimum. I have filled him – at length, and at his insistence – with my lived time, which is collecting in him like rubbish in a skip (so the Hippy says), and he has no desire to continue being filled in this way. The effect that he expects it to have on him is not a positive one.

He has written a letter. To the hospital administration. A hurtful letter, regarding me.

He wants to tip the rubbish away. He wants to get out of here.

'I'm becoming so desolate,' he complains. 'So oppressed and troubled and, like, grief-stricken. So much dukkha everywhere. I'm getting these really bad pains in my kidneys. I have to read cheap comics all the time. Loads of *Asterix* and *Tintin*, to stop me thinking about the babies and that poor little girl. I don't want to go on lying here, the room is full of evil. I don't want to stare at my door and know the police are sitting on the other side. I don't want to despise any *compañero*. And I don't want to take back a single "wonderful". No, I need to leave you, Herr Solm.'

He has stopped calling me Koja altogether, and has never left anyone in his life, I'm sure of that.

I gave Night Nurse Gerda five hundred hopeful deutschmarks, and she tried to talk the Hippy round. She mistook his intention for willingness, but he was not only willing to be transferred out of our room; it was his firm intent, and he expressed it more urgently than ever.

'Out!' he said. 'Out, out, out!'

'But none of the other rooms are as good, my dear Basti,' Night Nurse Gerda pointed out. 'One with a caretaker from Erding, who has just had an operation, where you won't get a wink of sleep. Rooms full of the outside world like number three up at the front, with a homosexual florist in a sea of hyacinths. Or the terrible room with the army

469

officer. I won't be able to bring you your cannabis anywhere, and there'll be no one to talk to about your flaws.'

'I don't want to talk about my flaws,' Basti said. 'Then I might as well talk about the dukkha-dukkha.'

'The dukkha-dukkha?'

'Death.'

I won't talk about death. I promise him that.

Quite honestly, I won't even talk about life after death, resurrection or reincarnation, although there is no one better for that than a swami. And no richer focus for such a conversation than my own daughter, turned to dust.

But I won't talk about death and, as the Hippy should realize, I am currently talking first and foremost about life – about *his* life, which he is so desperate to change. He is not doing well, and so someone should be with him. They have shaved his head, casually shearing off the remaining half of his Botticelli quiff, because he needs to have a second screw drilled into his skull. His pain is getting worse all the time, though I don't know the details of that, either. And the Greek doctor has told the Hippy – I was lying in the next bed, listening – that he won't be going home any time soon. It sounded like never.

So the Swami's future is not boundless, either; its possibilities are slowly transforming themselves into fixed, uninfluenceable components of his past, into a medical history, which is perhaps the most interesting thing about him.

Not that anyone but me would tell him such a thing.

He wants to leave, all the same. He is desperate to get away from me, doesn't want to see or hear anything.

And so they transfer him, one autumn-gold Friday morning, and put him in with the army officer, a pilot who managed to escape from a crashing starfighter.

And that's supposed to be no dukkha, is it?

Now that the story's beginnings are long since told, and we are slowly approaching the end, I regret being left on my own in the room.

I do get a new roommate, a motorcyclist, but it isn't the same. The motorcyclist isn't there. He left his face on the asphalt, along with his teeth, spread over a fifty-metre stretch between where he slipped on the rain-wet road and the nearest tree trunk. I don't think he will ever speak again. And what might he say about the purpose and value of human misery, when he already embodies it in an almost ideal manner?

Grandpaping, for instance, a pastor of the old school, would have been convinced that the death of my beautiful, talented, and entirely innocent Anna was an expression of meaningful intent by a divine authority, for Grandpaping's own life was extinguished by divine decree. At least, that is what he surely believed to the very last gulp of his parsonage pond.

Papa, on the other hand, who broke off his theology degree because he felt tormented by Grandpaping, and understood the natural world with an artist's precise eye, was convinced that the only existential threats to us are the meaningless whims of fate – and that is exactly what he would have read in Anna's abrupt mortality, nothing more.

But what about the third and final possibility, which is attested by none of my ancestors, but seems so obvious: How could anyone not see the whole catastrophe of a person's life as the consequence of his own mistakes? Why blame it on God or fate? A man who shoulders the blame for what happens to him also has the power to improve his lot.

A father who shoulders the blame for the bullet that smashes through his daughter does not have the power to improve his lot. But if he knows that this supposed twist of fate was the result of his own mistakes, then at least he can avoid those mistakes in future.

He can avoid murder.

He can avoid deception and betrayal.

He can avoid all crime.

He can avoid vice.

He can avoid the SS.

He can avoid the Org, the KGB and the CIA.

All right, perhaps he can't avoid the Org, the KGB and the CIA. But he can improve himself, that's what I'm saying.

So why won't Basti listen to me? Why won't he listen to how I became a better person? He was waiting for the transformation, wasn't he? Now we've nearly reached it, and what does he do? He packs his suitcase and moves into the worst room, with a pilot whose karma evidently stopped him from deploying his ejector seat properly.

*

I'm being unfair.

I'm being unfair to the Hippy.

I don't want to oppress him. I spend a lot of time looking out of the window, watching the autumn that now lies on the lawn down below, the carpet of yellow, red and rust-brown leaves; I see them as a million torn-off butterfly wings, from which an occasional sparrow rises up and flies off into the grey sky.

'Oh, my dear Herr Solm, what a sad face you're making,' Night Nurse Gerda sighs.

She is standing behind me, by the motorcyclist, changing the bandages on his face. Like a potter she stands there, her nimble fingers shaping a lump of clay.

'The summer is over,' I say.

'Yes, the summer is over.'

'How is Basti?'

'I put him in the worst room, just as you wished. But I don't feel good about it.'

I nod. She received another five hundred hopeful deutschmarks from me for that room, with its view of a highly unsavoury army pilot. Perhaps we don't become better people, any of us.

'I know you want him back,' Gerda says. 'I want him back, too. Over there in the worst room, they don't have anything to say to one another.'

'I only have his best interests at heart.'

'Of course. Well, at least he's getting a little pipe again from time to time.'

I sit up and take notice.

'A little pipe – how?'

'Oh, well, the pilot doesn't realize.'

'You're bringing Herr Basti hard drugs, is that what you're saying?'

'But, Herr Solm!'

'What?'

'Hard drugs! Really! That's a mean way of putting it.'

'In his condition? I thought they had to trepan his skull again?'

'It helps to take his mind off it. And the pilot honestly doesn't realize. The pilot is almost always unconscious. And when he isn't unconscious, he's yelling in pain.'

The motorcyclist's head is packed a little too hastily into the white gauze bandages, meaning that he has to draw air in through gums that are clamped together (and of course also through the bandages that Gerda quickly tugs away from his lips). Just because he can't speak, doesn't mean he can't hear and understand.

'Nurse Gerda,' I say, with a note of charm in my voice, 'would you mind covering the motorcyclist's ears for a minute?'

She does it without hesitation, though he only has one ear left.

Two days later, we meet on the bench directly below our windows. We are only allowed outside for a short while (the freshness of the fresh air here is always regarded as a danger to life and limb).

We are both carrying unfurled black umbrellas, to prevent anything from falling out of the sky onto our sick heads, be it raindrops or bird droppings.

The Hippy approaches, passing between the two elms, lopsided and wrapped in a dressing gown, his already sheltered skull hidden inside a plastic bag from Edeka, I wonder why. His gait is overly cautious and stupid, a product of his condition, which is growing increasingly similar to my own. He sits down beside me, keeping as much distance between us as possible, and in his pinched features I see signs of obduracy.

I say, 'What's the plastic bag for?'

'They've been drawing on my head.'

'Really?'

'They're deciding on the best place to put the new hole.'

'Can I see?'

'No.'

We sit there, both twirling our umbrellas above our ruined heads, I very slowly, he far more nervously. We are gazing out at the hospital's little fountain, which will not be splashing for much longer. They always turn it off at the end of October, so I have heard.

I say, 'Well, anyway, thank you for finding your way here.'

'You gave Nurse Gerda money,' he bursts out, not looking at me. 'You paid her to stop giving me grass.'

'Is that what she said?'

'You paid her for the awful room! And for information about me! And you paid her so I would come and meet you here as well!'

'I'm surprised Gerda would tell you something like that.'

'Why are you doing this? Why do you want things to be bad for me?'

'But I don't want things to be bad for you,' I say. 'I want to give you money, too. So that things will be good for you.'

He turns his head towards me jerkily, like a flock of watchful seagulls.

'Oh yeah? So you think you can buy me, do you?'

'I only want to buy your time.'

'I don't have a lot of time left, and you know that.'

'No one can know that.'

He lowers his umbrella, exhales slowly, bends down and picks a handful of elm leaves up from the ground. I'm sure he would rather chat with the elm leaves than with me, and he could do, he often talks to plants. They must surely have a lot on their minds, too, especially those dying leaves in his hand. He regards them with great sympathy. He's going to burst into tears if I don't hurry.

'Let me make a suggestion,' I say quickly. 'We'll meet here once a day, and finish what we started out in the fresh air.'

Mutely, he shows me the elm leaves. Or perhaps it's the other way round and he is showing them what kind of a man I am.

'My dear Basti, what do you say to that?'

He remains stubbornly silent, just shakes his head slowly, and the Edeka bag wafts briefly to the left like an extended Edeka brain.

'And what I will give you in return is not those herbs Gerda grows on her balcony. We're talking about Marrakesh Gold here!' I say enticingly. 'Straight from the dealers at the Hauptbahnhof – top quality!'

I pull a golden ingot of hash from my coat pocket. It was not the easiest thing for Gerda to procure.

The elm leaves fall to the ground. The Swami hesitates, takes the cube, and for a moment I worry that he might swallow it straight down. His eyes fix themselves on mine. In the left, dove-grey iris there is a glimmer of desire; in the right, slightly greener one, a trickle of resignation.

Then he says quietly, 'So, you actually do think you can buy me.'

'It makes me sad that you see it that way.'

'I'm scared of you!'

'You really have no reason to be afraid of me.'

I remove the plastic bag from his head quite gently and let it go. A gust of wind takes it, exposing a shaved Maori scalp covered in blue lines and symbols. I can see exactly where the second hole is to be drilled, and tap the spot wistfully with my finger.

'I'm really scared of you!' he says.

2

Ev lay in Anna's bed.

From morning till night.

She didn't get up, didn't wash, ate nothing, and drank a lot of water and the camomile tea that I made for her morning and evening and put outside Anna's room.

When the sweat on her skin grew thick and sour, she crept out to the bathroom at night and cleaned herself up quietly and carefully, so that her smell wouldn't mix with the smell of Anna that clung to the bedsheets, in which she buried her teeth, her fists and her mind.

She always locked the door behind her. After many days I was forced to kick it down, when I could no longer hear any wailing from inside, or breathing, either – not even with the stethoscope that I took from Ev's medical bag and pressed against the closed window, balancing with some effort on the narrow ledge that separated the third floor from the fourth.

Ev had always breathed a little too loudly, even as a child when we played hide and seek, with a rattle in her throat that sounded almost like giggling and made her easy to find behind beds and curtains. But now she had become inaudible, and I had no idea how she was still getting air. All her survival reflexes were exhausted. In the end she lost so much weight that she was nearly as thin as during that starving winter in Riga, when her ribs had stuck out like wire under her nightshirt. Three days after Anna's death she had tried to drink thirty nails in a glass of milk. They stuck sideways before they entered her gullet and she spat them all out, but they had done such lasting damage to her throat that after that Mama and I didn't leave her alone for a second.

Hub was still in custody.

I moved into his and Ev's abandoned bedroom. The sound of the gunshot still echoed there when sleep refused to come.

I spent two nights staring at Hub's bedcovers and his pillow, where you could still see the impression of his head, if you had sufficient powers of imagination. And yes, imagination had always been my greatest power.

And so I took the whole lot down to the courtyard, hung it over the carpet hanger, soaked it with Hub's entire stock of vodka and set light to it. Burning feathers drifted all the way up to Ev's window, but of course she didn't see them.

I had the coffin brought into the sitting room. It had a pleasant smell, but was an ugly brown that Anna would never have liked, and so I painted it blue, with a golden moon and silver stars. Afterwards, Mama lined it in white satin and laid a little pillow from Opapabaron's crib at one end, to cushion her head.

The pallbearers were to be Erhard Sneiper, Anna's second cousins Fieps and Flops, Papa's almost blind brother (a journalist who hadn't written a word for the past thirty years), Anna's class teacher Herr Delaroix (a Huguenot with early-stage gastrointestinal cancer) and a Jakobus Solm whom I did not recognize from any family anecdotes.

In any case, Ev slid the list of names that I had placed beside her morning tea back under the door, three minutes after receiving it.

It had 'NO BALTS' written on it in capital letters, and only Herr Delaroix, on account of his French background, was so assuredly not Baltic that his name was allowed to remain on the list. Anna's non-Baltic art teacher (deep roots in Bad Tölz), her two riding teachers (who didn't even know where Riga was), the stern Professor Grobl (born in Nuremberg and uninterested in any landscape that wasn't Mediterranean), Boehringer, the former head of the Pattendorf nursing home (a Catholic, which meant he couldn't be a Balt), and Dr Julius Spanier, an entirely surprising Jew, were also permitted to shoulder the blue coffin, and both the colour of the coffin and the choice of pallbearers caused uproar among the other mourners.

Mama had seen this uproar coming days before, when Ev had begun to talk a little again, though only through the closed and now patched-up door. It went something like:

Mama: Are we sure we want a Jew and a Catholic as pallbearers?

Ev: Yes.

Mama: You do know what Grandpaping thought of Catholics, don't you?

Ev: Yes.

Mama: But . . .

Ev: I can't do this now, Mama. Please.

Mama: Of course.

Mama leaned her arm on the door jamb and counted slowly and noiselessly to ten, because decisions had to be made, and overwhelming sensitivity had never been in Mama's *vision générale*. She didn't understand why people couldn't just pull themselves together a little; in the end, blows of fate were a purifying storm through which the Good Lord made us walk.

Mama: Eva, child?

Her daughter did not respond.

Mama: I'm sorry, Ev, but there's one thing I'm pondering.

Ev: What?

Mama: It might sound *étrange*, but we don't have a single relative among the pallbearers, not a single Baltic German and not even a baron, and I do think it would be improper and a touch repudious if there were a Jewish person carrying Anna's coffin instead.

Ev: There's a Jewish person *in* Anna's coffin, Mama.

You mustn't misunderstand my mother. Her heart has always been bright, but never warm. Within five minutes she had packed her things and left the apartment, and I couldn't be angry with her for it. She would have dearly loved to slam the door behind her, but of course her upbringing was too aristocratic for that.

'Why are you being like this?' I asked later, sadly, sitting outside Ev's battered door, my chin resting on my knees.

'I'm Jewish,' she said. 'And so Anna is Jewish. Mama should be glad it isn't a Jewish funeral. Then there would have been a lot more Jews carrying the coffin.'

'Are Jews even allowed to carry a coffin with a cross on it?'

'He took Anna's appendix out.'

'I know.'

'Have you heard of the Society for Christian–Jewish Cooperation?'

'No.'

'He founded it.'

'Ev— . . .'

'Dr Spanier survived two years in a concentration camp, and still founded the Society for Christian–Jewish Cooperation. Of course he's allowed to carry a coffin with a bloody cross on it.'

'I'm sorry if I upset you.'

'The appendix nearly ruptured.'

'I know.'

'And it doesn't matter which God didn't save Anna.'

'Of course.'

'It doesn't matter which God is the heavenly father who took his child to him. What kind of fucking father does that?'

'You're right.'

'Protestant funeral! Catholic funeral! Jewish funeral! I don't care!'

'All right.'

'I don't want it! I don't want any of it! I want Anna to be alive!'

'That's what I want, too, Ev.'

'Maybe we could just leave it.'

'Yes, that would be nice. But we can't leave it. Anna *isn't* alive.'

Ev wept.

'So what shall we do, Ev?'

Ev wept.

Then I wept, too.

'Can't we bury her like the Tlingits?'

'No, we can't, Ev.'

'But Anna loved the Tlingits so much. And when you told her stories about the Tlingits, she loved that.'

And then a slightly yellowed watercolour came under the door. I picked it up, blew my nose, dried my eyes and saw my daughter's elegant brushwork, the Indians she had painted in red onto damp blue, the same blue as her coffin, and at the centre of the picture there was a benevolent white lady in an elegant sea-otter fur, blessing a child on the shores of Alaska, and this lady was my great-grandmother Anna, Baroness von Schilling, or rather my daughter's idea of her – my daughter, who was named after that temporary Tlingit queen. Above the watercolour, in beautiful cursive letters, was written: 'Anna I, 1845', and the picture was signed: 'Anna II, 1954', and then I did think it would be a good idea to attempt a Tlingit funeral.

Since Anna II could not be burned beneath the night sky with music and dancing, I decided on the Munich Waldfriedhof, the woodland cemetery, and a sensible North American-Indian burial. I rented a burial plot beneath a lovely grove of spruces whose green could not have been more sub-Arctic if they had grown in Alaska itself, and insisted, much to the wonderment of the Munich cemetery board, on having the grave dug with the head end facing north, the direction from which the great white bear would come to check on my daughter.

We had the countenance of a protective bear engraved on the head-stone as well, which unfortunately came out as a teddy, and the whole funeral party sang 'Es ist ein Ros entsprungen' with us, my great-grandmother's shamanic song.

Ev was still no more than a shadow in those ice-cold January days, in touch with nothing and no one but the hereafter. In this mood, she came up with the mad idea of inviting Anna's pony Parvenue to the funeral (the Tlingit creation myth sees in animals a hidden god, who wants to mourn just as we do, and Anna had loved nothing more than her little horse).

The pony came swaying all the long way there from his stable in Holzkirchen, accompanied by Anna's friend Erna Müllerlein, but of course an irate cemetery attendant prevented the animal from going all the way to the grave; it had already eaten a wreath of flowers at the front gates.

In all honesty, even without the pony everyone believed that Ev had completely lost her mind. Mama was ashamed, and the Balts clapped their hands to their heads. Ev could not completely hide the monstrous force of her pain under the numbing formal duties that were required of us both, which included bearing unbearable burdens. One of these was the burden of my brother's presence; he stood on the right-hand side of the grave, accompanied by two policemen, in the sunlit west. The blue coffin, the pony, the Jewish and Catholic pall-bearers and the absence of a Protestant blessing seemed to trouble him more than the cause of the event itself. At least, that is what I thought I read in the flashing eyes of the Unspeakable, as Ev called him. The Unspeakable himself did not speak a word, and Mama was the only one who embraced him.

On the fifth of January nineteen fifty-five, we buried our daughter on a shady, snow-covered hill beneath a spruce tree. It would grow into Anna as the years passed, I was sure of that as they lowered the little body into the earth. I bent down, and the soil being slowly shov-elled over a golden moon on a blue background sharpened my sense of empathy. That empathy would spread out to cover so much – and it might be the only thing that renders the decisions I was to make over the coming months comprehensible.

Because a few weeks later, when I was still staying in Ev's apartment overnight to keep an eye on her; when, despite all the despairing overnights, we still had no idea how life was supposed to go on; when we laid three places at the table first by mistake, and then deliberately (but never a fourth for Hub); when neither of us wanted to deal with Anna's things and therefore turned her room into a shrine, from which we did not dare dispel a single molecule of her smile; when Hub was released from custody and the police investigation was suppressed; when even I had leaned on Ev not to press charges against her cursed husband-brother, who cursed us in return; when we both decided to call the accident an accident, and – with a little imagination (my imagination more than hers) – even an accident for which no one was to blame; when all this had completely overwhelmed our existence, Ev crept quietly into the bedroom one night, where I was lying awake, unable to sleep, unable even to rest.

She sat on the end of the bed and asked if I was asleep, and why I had the window wide open in February.

As she spoke, her meagre breath came back to her in soft clouds. The moonlight was bright enough to see it, and I was relieved to be watching her breathe again and hearing her lungs. I took that as a good sign. And in a white cloud of breath, illuminated by the uncertain but manic gleam in her eyes, she informed me that she'd decided to emigrate to Israel.

I got up at once, closed the window, turned the heating on, fetched my coat and laid my eiderdown around her shoulders. She didn't seem to feel the cold at all, though she was wearing just a nightshirt and didn't even have socks on.

'You can't emigrate to Israel.'

'But why not? What life is left for me here? I hate it all. Last month they founded the West German Army. It's madness. The country is full of lunatics and idiots!'

'Yes, but you can't emigrate to Israel.'

'They're looking for medics there. They're crying out for them. There's a whole new hospital in Haifa, and no one to staff it.'

'Ev, forget it! There is no way you can emigrate to Israel!'

'Give me one sensible reason why that shouldn't be possible.'

'Israel is where Jews live!'

'But I am a Jew.'

'You're not a Jew, Ev. You worked in a concentration camp.'

In the darkness I saw her eyebrows form round arches.

'What do you mean, Koja? What are you talking about?' she asked quietly, her voice unguarded, almost astonished.

'Don't tempt fate. You're not a Jew.'

'My parents were Jews.'

'Your parents were Jews who converted to Christianity! They were Christians! Jewish Christians! Your adoptive parents were Christians! Your brothers were Christians, Christians and Nazis! Nazi Christians! Your heritage is Nazi Christian and Jewish Christian, your country, your name, your whole culture, all of it Nazi Jewish Christian! Even your papers are Nazi Jewish Christian, because I forged them myself! Your whole history is good Nazi Jewish Christian history!'

'You can change history, though. You're always changing yours.'

'Israel is a joke, Ev. The Orcs think the country will have been invaded by nineteen sixty. The Arabs will raze it to the ground and cut every throat they can lay their hands on.'

'What is it, Koja? Why are you so angry?'

'I can't lose you, too.'

'Koja.'

'I won't survive it. I just won't survive it.'

She took my hand, lay down by my side, spread my eiderdown over us both, over our heads. She laid her nose against my throat, a nose that grew wet, and her eyelashes, which also grew wet, fluttered like tiny lengths of barbed wire against my skin. I felt Ev's fierce desires beneath her despair, which I could not ease with my own despair. No despair can ease another, just as no inferno can extinguish another.

'All I see are caves,' she whispered, and her fingers scuttled, comfortless, across my forehead. 'Caves are all I see at night, tunnels, pipes, caves, like our cover here is a cave. When I leave the cave, I feel sick. I feel a pressure here in my throat, pain in my stomach, I get cramps in my belly, my arms feel paralysed, my legs, this finger here, can you feel?'

She meant the finger that was still scratching at my forehead, cold and soft like a mortally ill caterpillar.

'I don't want to leave the cave, because I know you're always here in it with me. If I happen to see a landscape, a few trees, a stream in the fog, then I take my cave with me, in a little bag or in my hand, and I know when I open it up you will be in there; it's like a tent made of stone.'

'You're not well. This is severe depression you're suffering from. We should go and see a doctor.'

'I am a doctor. Let's go to Israel, please.'

'Both of us?'

'I want to go there with you. All we have left in the world is each other.'

'Ev – I'm *really* not Jewish.'

'You're in the secret service, Koja. Can't the secret service make a Jew of you?'

'You're sick. You really are very sick.'

'I can help you to become one.'

'No one can do that!'

'I'm a doctor. I can remove your foreskin if you want.'

This is what I mean by empathy, honoured Swami. After everything that had happened, how could I respond to my mad sister's grief with anything but maternal care? That was what I felt most for her then, after Mama had gone.

We didn't sleep together, we didn't even desire one another, the physical attraction was that of stuffed animals. Maya's elemental absence had filled me with so much longing that all I could do now, faced with her even more elemental absence, was feel an even greater longing. It was a hole that the elemental presence of Ev could not fill. We drifted through the apartment where our daughter was shot as if lying side by side on an ice floe. And I understand, of course, that Ev wanted to spy a sliver of land on the horizon of this seemingly endless polar sea – but what made her think of Israel?

At that time, Israel was not a country; it was moon rock in the possession of moon people. The idea that the Jews could have their own state after two thousand years of wandering lay beyond all imagination.

Three years after Hitler's corpse was burned in a tin bath in the garden of the Führer's bunker, a handful of Zionists incensed his ashes by proclaiming the establishment of the Israeli state in a distant port town on the Levant. And as soon as the state had been founded, they placed the *herem* on Germany, a rabbinical condemnation that encompassed the entire population from babies to the elderly. All transport, all trade, all relations with Germany were prohibited. The German language, German music, the import of German newspapers, German magazines and German books, the staging of German plays, the breeding of German shepherd dogs, and even the baking of German cakes, were forbidden in Israel. (Back in the Golden Twenties, the Zionist WIZO cookbook had included a recipe for apple strudel – but in those days, no one knew how much the Führer would love his Linzer Torte).

Everything German was exorcised, without exception. No German foot must profane the ground between Haifa, Tel Aviv, Eilat and Jerusalem. And no Israeli citizen was permitted to travel to the outlawed country, to attend funerals or bar mitzvahs, to visit sick relatives or even to reclaim the real estate of which they had been robbed. Every passport was stamped with the words: 'Valid to any country except Germany'.

Even letters and parcels from Germany were sent back; the West German Bundespost had lost its marbles and started proudly featuring the faces of Germanic 'helpers of humanity' on its stamps, philanthropic Bodelschwinghs, Sonnenscheins, Pestalozzis and Kneipps, all shining with benevolence, a terrible provocation to Israeli postal workers whose families had been gassed.

In nineteen fifty, when the Western powers declared an end to the state of war with Germany, the Knesset protested and debated whether to set a warning example and formally declare war on Germany itself. The motion only failed to win a majority because prime minister Ben-Gurion pointed out that twenty thousand obscene Jews had, despite the *herem*, returned to the land of the goyim. In any Israeli war with West Germany, they would be the ones who suffered.

A good two years before Anna's death, in the spring of nineteen fifty-two, I myself had spent several weeks on a special mission stationed in The Hague. And there I experienced the *herem* for myself, quite a unique experience, I must say.

The Oud-Wassenaar country house hotel, with its Burgundian pomp, was the setting for negotiations between Germany and Israel over the payment of reparations. Adenauer had asked his old friend Gehlen to assign a couple of reliable Orcs to these negotiations. They were to form the secret-service protection detail for the German side, but they and I would also be tapping the Israeli delegation's telephone lines.

And let me tell you, sceptical master: telephone lines had never been tapped with such devoted precision, though admittedly it was not a difficult job. A listening post had already been set up in the cellar during the German occupation, supposedly by the Gestapo, and forgotten there in the retreat (the well-stocked wine cellar, by contrast, had been neither set up nor forgotten by the Gestapo). Since the Allies and probably also the Dutch hotel owner had never considered removing it (who would disassemble a first-class listening post? It would be like ripping out a first-class parquet floor), it was still functioning flawlessly several years later, and we rented it for a princely sum. This way we could be all ears, with practically no risk of discovery, a *sine qua non* when sitting on such a powder keg.

Weeks earlier, an Israeli terror cell had carried out a bombing aimed at Chancellor Adenauer – here in Munich, incidentally, one dead (yes, I can see you're surprised by that, Menachem Begin was behind it, and he's another one destined for greatness, let me tell you). In Israel, angry crowds had tried to storm the Knesset at Begin's instigation and lynch all the members of parliament who had agreed to starting reparation talks with wicked Germany.

The negotiations in Wassenaar, then, were as untidy as expected. The Israelis were not allowed to shake hands with any of the Germans. They were even banned from smoking, so that none of the damned could offer them a light. And although all the Jews and all the goyim could speak German, they insisted that the negotiations be held in French, the beautiful lingua franca of diplomacy, though barely anyone present had mastered it.

The situation was made more difficult still by the Israeli commission splitting into factions, which were bent respectively on vengeance and forgiveness. I myself heard an intransigent vengeance-seeker shouting down the telephone at his delegation leader, Felix Schneebalg, calling him a fascist-lover and forgiveness-Yid. This ear-bashing had been triggered by Schneebalg, not long before, secretly slipping a note to his German counterpart Otto Küster, asking the latter about his Swabian accent, which could not be suppressed even in French. When it emerged that Schneebalg and Küster had attended the same secondary school in Stuttgart, and even made fun of the same Latin teacher there, the two of them sent this teacher a postcard that said:

Dearest Dr Schlehmil, sending greetings and our best wishes from The Hague, where we are jointly seeking – as you know – the Aurea medi-ocritas. With fond regards, Snowy and OK.

This transgression would cost Snowy Schneebalg dear. Israel came very close to stripping him of his position. And even when that was off the cards, the head of the Israeli delegation found himself subjected to all kinds of animosity and a torrent of Yiddish curses, which I, as the Org's only Yiddish expert, dutifully transcribed.

But otherwise, little Yiddish was spoken in Wassenaar. The Israelis preferred Hebrew, and the only person in the Firm who spoke Hebrew was the head of our Palestine department. He was a lightning-blond religious-studies scholar from Cologne whose cover name was Hach, first name Friedrich, though he was known to all as Palestine Fritz.

Palestine Fritz was of the same build as me and had a thin moustache. He often sat next to me in that April-cold wine cellar in Holland, concentrating as he murmured along with the words coming from the headphones. Like many natives of Cologne, he was always trying to make people laugh. Wine put him in a good mood, and caused him to consume flowers – tulips for preference, including the stem and leaves. And on one of these occasions, with his mouth still full of petals, he bragged loudly that he could get any spy to Israel who wanted to go.

Any spy.

It was the fourteenth of February nineteen fifty-five. Ev was in the kitchen, six weeks after the Indian burial, preparing for Anna's eleventh-and-a-half birthday – she didn't want to wait for her twelfth.

She was cooking little Anna's favourite Baltic dish, *Klimpen* with blueberry sauce, and I laid Anna's small spoon in front of me, the silver one inherited from Amama. It had once fed me, too, before I had ever been stretched on the rack of human memory. And, like thorns pressing into my flesh, I recalled little's Anna's fingers dexterously guiding that little spoon in a never-changing ritual, sticking it into the dumpling and quartering it cleanly, with a nice sense of symmetry. *Quarkknödel* they call them here in Munich, *Quarkknödel* and compote. They smelled so good.

We had bought brightly coloured balloons, which I blew up. When I reached the red one, I told Ev that I might have found a way to get us to Israel, but it was only after two more blue balloons and a yellow one that she turned to me and said that, in that case, I would need to strike Maya out of my heart.

'But it's done, Ev.'

'I found her teeth. In a cigar box. You've still got her teeth?'

'They might not even be hers. You said so yourself. They could be teeth the KGB picked up from somewhere.'

'Throw them away.'

'What?'

'Or can't you do it?'

'I . . . I don't know . . .'

'Do you put those teeth in your mouth and suck them?'

'What makes you think that?'

'You're a romantic, that's what makes me think it.'

I went over to her at the stove, surprised by her fit of misplaced despair. I took the little quark ball from her spoon and slid it into the gently bubbling water.

'Maya was on her way to me when her plane crashed,' I lied, staying as close as I could to the truth. 'Why must I strike her from my heart when she went to her death for me? You won't strike me from your heart when I go to my death for you.'

'Why should you do that?'

'In Israel, Ev? What else would I do there?'

The next day, we celebrated Anna's half-birthday, surrounded by eleven-and-a-half birthday candles, balloons, all her drawings and her death mask (a plaster cast that I had made in the coroner's office twelve hours after her death; one of Gehlen's contacts had got me in there). Ev opened the window and threw all the dumplings, and the porcelain bowl they were in, out into the snow. Perhaps some starving birds were pleased to see them. How Anna had once loved to feed swans, ducks and sparrows, which she used to call 'parrows' when she was very small.

Ah, my parrow, a happy birthday to you, from behind my tears, a very happy birthday.

3

Palestine Fritz's Pullach office was a tiny attic room in one of the Goethe-esque summer houses, where only a cardboard partition wall separated him from the Panama desk (a plan that was alphabetical rather than pragmatic). He knew much of what there was to know about Judea, the Talmud and the Kabbalah, and he knew it from Adolf Eichmann.

In Wassenaar, he had once hinted at having planned the most marvellous trips to Palestine in the thirties with this knowledge-hungry Hebraist, though unfortunately those trips could not then be made (reluctance from the British on the matter of visas). And his superior, so he claimed, had never said a bad word about the Jews. Herr Eichmann had passed his respect for foreign and above all destructive cultures on to his young apprentices, not least Dr Hach himself. He had left that office and returned to the university, his mind greatly enriched, long before the regrettable corollaries of Eichmann's office came to pass. But everyone in the Org knew that Friedrich Hach, alias Palestine Fritz, still corresponded with his former boss, who called himself Klement and was living in Argentina.

'He *looks* like a Jew now, as well,' Hach often sighed, which sounded descriptive – perhaps he'd been sent photographs?

A large map of Palestine hung on the wall behind Dr Hach's desk, from the time of the British Mandate, with a plaque alongside it showing the most important information about Jewish dietary rules. Did you know, for instance, that a Jew is not permitted to eat a hawk, because he will then start to hunt mice himself, which of course he is also not permitted to eat?

In any case, Palestine Fritz looked completely nonplussed when I walked into his office and smiled at him politely. He got up, shook my hand and expressed his deepest sympathy.

I didn't want sympathy; I wanted to know if he remembered Wassenaar.

'What times they were, Herr Dürer!'

'That little café by the canal?'

'Oh, the *poffertjes*!'

'You told me in Wassenaar that you could get anyone into Israel who wanted to go.'

Palestine Fritz removed his hand from my shoulder, where it had been providing a brief spell of warmth, and then didn't know what to do with it. Eventually he put it on his hip, but only for a moment, then to the back of his head, where some short hairs were waiting to be scratched, and I think after that he forgot about it, and so did I.

We sat down at his desk, and he asked tentatively – mistrustfully, in fact, his voice lowered because of Panama – if I was planning to do damage to anything in Israel, people, property, anything.

'No, nothing like that. My brother's wife would like to emigrate to Israel.'

'Oh – is she a Jew?'

'Yes.'

'Your brother's wife is Jewish?'

'Yes.'

'Really?'

'Yes.'

'So, she – and we're talking about your brother, whom all of us here . . .'

'Was I not clear in what I said?'

'So . . . is she certified as Jewish?' he asked after a pause.

'How do you mean?'

'Does she have papers to prove her heritage?'

'Papers?'

'It isn't a tragedy if the papers don't exist. Plenty of papers no longer exist, because of the' – he shook himself as if he had water in his ears – 'because of the heat, of course.'

'Er, what heat do you mean?'

'Just the usual heat of war.'

'Aha.'

'Flames, for instance. Archives going up in flames, passports in flames, residents' registration offices – all a sea of flames. But a person's identity can also be attested by witnesses, or affidavits from two—'

'No, no, of course there are papers,' I said briskly, meaning the Anna Ivanovna papers, and those that the master forger Solm would now have to produce.

'Oh, well then, there may not be any serious problems. The Law of Return grants the right of citizenship to any Jewish person who settles in Israel. And a Jewish person is anyone who has a Jewish mother.'

'Good. How would someone like me get to Israel?'

'You want to go to Israel, too?'

'No, it's a purely theoretical question. Someone *like* me.'

'Someone like you is a German. Germans can't go to Israel.'

'I know.'

'Unless they have a Jewish mother.'

'I see.'

'Otherwise, you would have to convert – I mean, someone like you would.'

'How does one go about that?'

'It isn't easy, not to say very complicated.'

'And what does very complicated mean?'

'Someone like you would have to know and observe all six hundred and thirteen mitzvot. He would have to find a rabbi who would take him on, and then spend a year attending synagogue. Someone like you would have to be accepted by the community. And that's a matter of his appearance, his demeanour, how he smells, how he greets people . . .'

'I can only become a Jew if I smell nice?'

'Sympathetic appeal is part of it, yes. But actions are the most important thing.'

'Go on.'

'If your actions are agreeable, you enter the second year with your chosen rabbi, the liturgical year. Then you learn thousands of Torah commandments and appendices off by heart, and if you manage that, well, that's wonderful, then you can build a sukkah for your family or blow the shofar, but if it isn't one of the universal Noachian principles, like zedakah, for example, then it isn't really a mitzvah. And then the examining rabbis of the Beit Din will fail you without a second thought, and you'll have to move to another town and spend another two years trying to become a proper Jew – that is what you need to do if you want to go to Israel. Someone like you, that is.'

Interesting how much you could learn from Adolf Eichmann, I thought.

But what I said was, 'That certainly does sound complicated.'

'Well, yes, and you do have a job to do at the Org.'

'So how do you get anyone into Israel who wants to go?'

'So far, no one has wanted to.'

'Why not?'

'Because no one is that stupid, Herr Dürer. Any German caught spying there would be hanged.'

As if to clarify this, he slung an imaginary rope of air around his neck, knotted it at the back and fastened it to a branch with his right hand, while sticking his tongue out of the corner of his mouth, what larks.

Two days later came the meeting that had been creeping towards us for weeks, which the Doctor called 'the talk'.

Reinhard Gehlen sat in the drawing room of the Bormann villa, wearing a new pair of sunglasses and shovelling mountains of sugar into his tea. He was flanked by his two most important colleagues. The man on the left had survived a bullet passing through his face and neck on the Eastern Front. His name was Wolfgang Sangkehl. And on Gehlen's right, Heinz Danko Herre, who was known to everyone as Pinocchio, for several reasons that included his physiognomy. They and their boss were smoking for all they were worth. It was like sitting in front of a three-vent volcano.

The Unspeakable was waiting opposite them. He was pale, thin, but not quite ready for the earth to swallow him up. I had been placed a long way from the table, in a soft brown armchair against the wall.

Gehlen offered Hub his condolences, in a voice that sounded the way a blank sheet of paper looks.

'Thank you,' my brother said, almost inaudibly.

'However, today we need to have a very urgent discussion about your future, Herr Ulm.'

'Naturally, Herr Doctor.'

'Your daughter's tragic accident has placed the Org in a difficult position. We had to give up some of our cover in order to get you off the hook.'

'I am aware of that.'

'Your brother and your wife made statements that were as favourable to you as they could be.'

'Indeed.'

'And yet, Herr Ulm, you have filed for divorce.'

'Yes.'

'Could you reveal to me why that is?'

'No, Herr Doctor.'

Gehlen nodded and tapped a little ash into his saucer.

'I don't like it when my employees get divorced.'

There was no mention of whether he liked it when his employees shot and killed their children.

Hub thought for a moment before clearing his throat and declaring that he would accept all the Doctor's decisions regarding his future at the Org with meek humility. His only request was that his work bring him into no further contact with his brother, Herr Dürer.

I picked up my teacup and drank: a stupid, second-son reflex.

'What a shame,' Gehlen said. 'Herr Dürer has only good things to say about you.'

'That's nice. The question is whether I have only good things to say about him.'

'Well, I shall take that as read. First and foremost because I only want to hear good things about him. A most excellent man, your brother.'

Gehlen plucked a crumb of tobacco from his lip and turned to me with a friendly smile.

'Herr Dürer, I hear you are toying with the idea of moving to the land of the Crusaders?'

It was a miracle that the cup didn't slip from my hand, believe me. But I pretended to have scalded myself and puckered my scalded lips, playing for time as I tried to work out where this was heading. What lay behind Gehlen's question? Was he contemplating a crusade?

'The truth is,' I began cautiously, 'I was making purely hypothetical enquiries to the Palestine desk, as to whether it was possible for someone like me – and that is the precise phrase we used – for someone like me, then, to travel to Israel.'

'With Frau Ulm?'

'It was really just a hypothetical question.'

'There you are, then, Herr Ulm,' Gehlen beamed at the Unspeakable, 'we will send your brother and your ex-wife to Palestine. You will no longer have even the merest hint of professional contact with one another. That will reassure you, won't it?'

You could see Hub turning even paler than he already was. But he managed to nod all the same. 'And as to your future with the Org – well, I think we can work something out.'

'Thank you,' Hub croaked.

'Herr Sangkehl, remind me what we were thinking of in that regard.'

The adjutant, red-cheeked and wearing a permanent expression of surprise thanks to the bullet that had ripped through his face, clamped his cigarette between his lips at the point where his long, rubbery scar formed a second mouth at right-angles to the real one, from chin to nose, though of course that mouth didn't open. Sangkehl leant forward, puffing on his cigarette and pretending to check something in his documents, which could not possibly be the case with all the smoke he was producing.

'Canteen, Doctor,' he finally said half-heartedly.

'Ah, yes. You'll take over the service canteen.'

I know my brother in all his guises, and I am sure that – little Anna or no little Anna – he would have drawn a gun, held it to Reinhard Gehlen and Herr Sangkehl's heads and made new bullet holes in their faces, if he'd had one to hand just then.

But he didn't. All he could do was exude a dangerous calm.

'You want me to cook and bake?'

'Good Lord, no,' the Doctor said with a snide laugh. 'I eat here every day. No, you will oversee the running of the canteen; it's a vital role. Sangkehl, tell us what's involved.'

'Purchasing, managing staff, scheduling, general business management tasks. It's a huge responsibility: over a thousand meals a day!'

'Doctor, in all modesty,' my brother hissed, 'I was this service's head of operations. I was responsible for the Soviet Union. I ran the whole show for you.'

'That's right,' Gehlen replied in friendly tones. 'And when the BND is officially up and running in the next year, it could be more than two thousand meals a day.'

When I got home that evening, I could hear her panting from the front door.

Ev was kneeling in her former bedroom, which was now mine, sawing frantically. She had taken a jigsaw to the bed and split it into kindling.

She'd hacked up the living room sofa as well, and an armchair the Unspeakable had been especially fond of. The kitchen table's legs had been amputated. She must have been sawing all day; there were blisters on her fingers, and the palm of her right hand was red raw. She seemed disorientated as I took the saw from her hand.

'Ev, what are you doing?' I asked senselessly.

'Did you see him?'

'I saw him, yes. It wasn't too bad.'

'I don't believe that.'

'Gehlen took the stuffing out of him and, do you know what? Israel might actually happen.'

She didn't seem to be listening.

'The Doctor made a remark about it. A really very promising one.'

'Right, right, the Doctor made a really promising remark.'

She smiled so bitterly that it wasn't really a smile, and for the rest of the evening she fell into a disdainful, accusatory tone, only the top notes of which sounded vaguely nice (though she couldn't twitter as she used to in any case; her robin-redbreast tongue had been cut out, and in its place was something reptilian, deeply forked, which could poison you with vicious words). She spat on her hands, and, when the saw was not returned to her, looked around for some other occupation. I could do nothing for her. She was a mortally wounded animal that has to stay upright on its own, because anyone who rushes to its aid gets bitten.

And so I watched as, full of buried, aimless anger, she finally began to scratch at the wallpaper with a cake slice. Of course, as she did so her eyes took on that difficult look I had always loved in her. But she was also approaching the limits of her sanity.

When she was worn out, filthy and sitting before a pile of debris, I urged her to come back to my functioning flat on Kaiserstraße and stay the night there. But she refused. She couldn't vacate Anna's room, even for one night.

I was uncertain what to do. I couldn't leave her alone in that state. But there was nowhere for me to sleep in the ravaged apartment, apart from Anna's bed.

The fact that Ev eventually allowed me to get into Anna's bed with her should have been warning enough. She curled up wearily against the wall, telling me I had bad breath. I was to leave her in peace and not say another word.

And I didn't say anything. I was silent. Silently hoping that she wasn't taking my cursory erections against her back too personally. To me, they seemed to be a series of purely physiological occurrences that were easy enough to explain, and they probably were. But all the same, when she had fallen fast asleep, I moved my lower half very cautiously towards her and parked my you-know-what against her warm, grieving behind, for she insisted (something I should have mentioned) that we get into bed naked. Anything else would have made a mockery of our familial relationship – those were her words, believe it or not.

Eventually I got so hard it was beyond unpleasant, and while I couldn't impose on her, I was also spellbound by her billowing breath, which had reached almost normal volume. I felt at first a twitching and trembling inside me, and then the start of a volcanic eruption, at which I arched away from her and pressed myself firmly into the sheets just in time, into my own body heat in a manner of speaking, where I came, gushing silently into bedlinen that was roughened by a layer of fine sawdust.

Ev woke with a start, saw what had happened and hit me in the face.

'What the hell?' I cried out in confusion.

'You're ejaculating in Anna's bed?'

'I'm sorry.'

'What were you thinking?'

'There was nothing else I could do.'

'You're destroying her smell!'

'I'm really sorry, I was dreaming.'

'I want to smell Anna! I don't want to smell your sperm! Here, go on, smell your sperm!'

She pushed my face into the wet patch.

'Can you smell that?'

'Stop it, will you? What am I supposed to do?'

'You were lying against my back. Can't you just do it on my back? Or just open my arse cheeks when you feel it coming and do it in there, like a fucking pocket! At least then it can be washed off.'

'I hate it when you're this vulgar!'

'Oh, I'm the vulgar one? Am I urinating in my daughter's bed, then?'

'Sperm doesn't have the least thing to do with urine!'

'You don't have to explain that to me! You don't have to explain that to a doctor, young man! God, I have to wash it out, right away.'

She rushed to the bathroom and I could hear her running water into a bucket.

'Have you gone mad?' I called after her. 'You've been lying in this unwashed bed for weeks. Nothing smells of Anna any more! All it smells of is your hysteria!'

'This room is Anna! Nothing is going to change in this room!'

She came back with the full bucket, rubbed at my wet patch with a damp cloth and made it bigger.

'Nothing's going to change? But you've changed the whole apartment! Take a look around, it looks like a battlefield out there! And if we ever get away, then this room will change, too! Everything will be thrown out! Everything that reminds us of Anna will be thrown out! There'll be nothing left!'

'I don't want to share a bed with you if you can't control yourself!'

'Fine, then I won't stay here. I'm only here because you asked. You asked me to get into bed naked with you.'

'Because of your body heat. Because I find your body heat comforting. But it doesn't comfort me when you lie here with your stinking mouth and ejaculate in Anna's bed!'

Now the rage was swelling inside me. I could have burst at her legendary rudeness, a rudeness that flooded over me in warm waves, and I emerged from it and took hold of her hand with the stupid cloth in it.

'Let go of me this instant!' she shrieked.

'You're mean and heartless! I do everything for you, I bear every burden for you, I'm even going to Israel for you!'

'Let go of me!'

'Do you know how dangerous that is? Do you know what might happen to me in Israel? Have you even the slightest idea what I am letting myself in for if we emigrate?'

She tore herself away, screamed, 'Carbuncle!' at the top of her voice and tipped the whole bucket of water over the bed – probably to cleanse it of me and my disgrace, I don't know, she didn't give any explanation, just stood there holding the dripping bucket and surveying her handiwork in consternation.

There was a knock at the apartment door. I flung it open as a guard flings open the door of a prison cell. A startled neighbour in a Wee Willie Winkie nightshirt told me he would call the police if we didn't quiet down, and then he caught a glimpse of the furniture, sawed into kindling and glinting in the light from the hallway. He quickly left again.

When I came back, Ev was still standing by the sodden bed, outwardly unchanged but suddenly sober, looking as though she was chewing up all the nastiness and insults that were in her mouth.

And with this bitterness still on her tongue, her strength suddenly failed her. She sat down on the floor, on the half-armchair, leaned against Anna's easel, and said, more to the easel than to me, that she was probably a bit mad at the moment and she was very sorry. It was hard for her to go to the end, to the end of the world, but she had to hang on, and she was going to start preparing to emigrate now, with or without me, she had already given her notice to Dr Spanier, at least told him she was going to give her notice, notice of notice, all right, that meant nothing, but she would do what needed to be done. And she hadn't been asleep and had very much wanted me to lie behind her, though the word 'penetrate' didn't fit with what she was feeling at that moment, and certainly not 'ejaculate'. She wanted me to protect her, as I had the power to do, and she couldn't believe that I didn't have the power to go with her wherever she had to go, where she had to go so that she wouldn't die.

'Do you love me, Ev?' I asked.

She moved away from the easel and met my eye. I heard her snuffling smile crawling away from me.

'I'm so tired, Koja. I can't love anyone. I'm afraid I just can't.'

'That's all right.'

'Come on, everything is wet. Let's lie down on the carpet and put our arms around each other.'

'Even though we don't love each other?'

'You love me though, don't you?'

'Yes.'

'That's enough.'

You will understand, revered Swami, why over those difficult weeks and months I seriously considered sending Ev to a psychiatrist or at least a health spa. She didn't belong in Israel, but in Bad Pyrmont, Baden-Baden, Bad Ischgl, or a Baltic spa town with a pier and a park full of sea-salted roses and old people in huge, high-ceilinged breakfast rooms, but most importantly no adorable children to trigger terrible memories. Ev's nerves had extended themselves out of her brain and into her hair, all the way to the ends, that was how she put it, and once, she cut off a lock just to see whether it would be like cutting off a finger.

<h1 style="text-align:center">4</h1>

I needed to prepare myself for Israel. So Palestine Fritz said. I had to be forearmed – mentally, spiritually, culturally and above all linguistically. The Org needs an outpost in Israel (he told me). Things are happening there (the head of department added mysteriously) that bear no resemblance to the official story. The Doctor requires an eye in Tel Aviv. An ear. Perhaps even a full set-up.

Organs. Senses. Everything.

It might be a while before they figure out how to make this work, Hach whispered. In the meantime, I should get on the right track.

Be prepared, he said in English.

Palestine Fritz loved English.

I was introduced to a language teacher: Jeremias Himmelreich, a friendly man of my own age who moved slowly, his body hunched as if in fear or sullenness.

I met him for the first time at the start of March nineteen fifty-five, in Café Burger on Luitpoldstraße. He was sitting at a little table wearing a crumpled suit, lips akimbo, engrossed in Friedell's *A Cultural History of the Modern Age*. A huge comb made of ten trembling fingers was stuck into his overly long, prematurely white hair, making it stick up in all directions and giving him the appearance of a dandelion clock. And he wafted through life like a dandelion clock, too. He seemed to react to everything around him, even the slightest breath of air, as if it were a hurricane. I was afraid he might break apart and float off if the waiter hurried past us too quickly. The only thing holding him together was the wiry pair of Trotsky spectacles wrapped around his head.

As soon as he returned my greeting, I heard his Baltic accent. He was an Estonian, a rather awkward 'lummox', as Mama would have called him. His father, an eye doctor who had once come second in the city bridge tournament in Tartu, had passed on his gentleness to Jeremias, and his mother had given him her Czernowitz panic, as he called it, a latent state of alarm that had saved his life during the years of persecution. He didn't go into detail. He taught me Hebrew via his soft Baltic dialect, with the philological pedantry that sees something a touch anachronistic in Judaism.

'I can't do Modern Hebrew,' Dandelion said pensively, 'much too modern. So we'll talk the way Moses did, all right, Herr Dürer?'

Learning the script was an arduous business. That took almost half the spring. Reading from right to left, and writing from right to left, is not my forte. But for each new letter I mastered, Dandelion rewarded me with a Jewish joke.

The *aleph* joke, a beginner's joke that was therefore assigned to my personal C-class, went: The woman next door asks, 'How old are your two little ones?' The Jewish mama points proudly to the contents of her pram: 'The doctor is six months old, and the lawyer is two.'

The *dalet* joke, a solid B-class, was one of Dandelion's favourites, but the punchline was one I found emotionally challenging: An ancient couple, the husband ninety-six, the wife ninety-five, come to the rabbi and say, 'Rabbi, we want to get divorced.' 'Oh dear God – why, after seventy years of marriage?' 'We wanted to wait until the children were dead.'

It's a good joke, I'm sure. But tears welled up in my eyes all the same. It is so completely unnatural, it contradicts the necessary course of things so fundamentally, for a child to die before their parents, that it goes beyond your understanding and your powers of imagination, and that's why it can be funny, as I said to Dandelion. He was moved to see me weeping at one of his jokes and passed me a napkin; he was a good man.

Ultimately, it was this *dalet* joke that created a special bond between us, and after that, Dandelion expanded the jokes to encompass all areas of life, luxurious A-class jokes such as the *tav*. This was a lindworm of a joke, which must always be told with an air of joylessness, something that Jeremias Himmelreich wore from morning to night in any case, underpinned by a whole arsenal of dour facial expressions:

On the morning of his wedding, the bridegroom comes to see the strict rabbi. 'Rabbi, this evening, after we are married, may I finally dance with my wife?'

'But you know that the law does not permit that. Men dance with men; women dance with women. There are no exceptions when it comes to dancing, not even on your wedding day.'

'But afterwards, I am allowed to sleep with my wife, aren't I?'

'Of course, as it says in the holy book: be fruitful and multiply.'

'And what is permitted?' the bridegroom asks. 'Only lying down, or can we do it sitting up?'

'Sitting up is no problem.'

'Her on top, me underneath?'

'That's fine.'

'On the kitchen table?'

'Uncomfortable, but permitted.'

'Oral sex?'

'That's quite all right, as long as it doesn't replace the act of procreation that is pleasing to God.'

'What about standing up?'

The rabbi, beside himself with rage, slams his fist down on the table and yells, 'Are you meshuga? Absolutely not!'

'But why not?'

'That could lead to dancing!'

Dandelion required me to tell all the jokes in Hebrew, with as close an approximation of his detached, listless delivery as I could manage, for that would open all kinds of doors to me in Jewish society.

Over time it became clear that Jeremias Himmelreich was carrying a secret around with him. A secret he wanted to keep to himself, though hints of it rippled the surface; it had to do with a long-past love for a woman with the most un-Jewish of all names: Christiane. He kept talking about her as if her spirit were standing beside him, visible to all.

He might tell me what Christiane would think of this or that, or whether she would have liked me. She was the one who suggested which restaurant we should go to (we often went to restaurants, since Christiane thought that Hebrew was best learned among strangers, over a nice glass of wine, although of course Christiane had never learned Hebrew herself).

Dandelion had met his Christiane at the Charité Hospital in Berlin – that much I had worked out for myself. It seemed that they had both been young doctors, working in the surgical department, when they fell in love. Later, during the Thousand Year Reich, something dramatic or tragic or (as so often with Balts) grotesque had clearly happened. I

CHRIS KRAUS — 499

thought I heard a distant echo of racial defilement, but I never got any further than that. Himmelreich remained guarded.

Otherwise, he spent his life in almost complete isolation, like one of the early hermits. It was a long time before I learned exactly where he lived. He seemed to have hardly any friends or even acquaintances in Munich. And nor could I understand why he, a qualified surgeon, was not working in a hospital, but taking odd jobs on the murky fringes of the German secret service (it was only later that I learned Dandelion simply couldn't stand the sight of blood).

He was a very refined, unusually cultivated person, not dissimilar to you in his guilelessness, and as fond of his jokes as if they were small living things.

I was unprepared for his sudden disappearance. I waited for him in the Osterwaldgarten, eating my *Weißwurst*. After a long, cold winter, the spring was as lively as a newly hatched chick. I sat in the beer garden under the sparse shade of a budding tree – Himmelreich avoided direct sunlight. We were planning to continue with conjugations, *ani kotev*, *ata kotev*, *hu kotev*. But he never arrived.

Palestine Fritz was very perturbed when I called and told him. We took an official car to Radio Free Europe on Oettingenstraße, where Himmelreich edited the Czech programme for the CIA. But no one in the studio had seen him.

Nor was there any trace of him in his one-room apartment near the Englischer Garten, though the ironing board was set up and a red-hot electric iron was lying on its back, heating the whole apartment, it was so small.

Twenty-four hours later, after a moderately heavy shower of rain, a Forst Kasten forester stumbled upon a rope tied round a branch, with a noose at its end in which my Hebrew teacher was hanging, three metres above a carpet of bluebells. There was a ladder leaning up against the trunk, its feet pressed deep into the wet forest floor. But there were no footprints at the bottom of the ladder, and I am almost certain that Herr Himmelreich had jumped over the bluebells onto the first rung, to avoid crushing any of the lavender-coloured flowers. He was dangling peacefully from his branch, admiring the surrounding trees with their green shoots and their zest for life from behind his Trotsky glasses. The sullen, melancholy look on his face made him seem about to tell a joke. A Jew goes and hangs himself in a German wood, something like that. The overnight rain had plastered his unruly garland of hair flat against his head, as if he had never been a dandelion.

I looked at the police photo for a long time, and read through the suicide note, which left me perplexed, because it had been written by the friendliest, most likeable and courteous recluse I have ever met.

'You fucking apes,' this remarkable document began:

You fucking apes, you false madmen, I was never in this world for you. Are you secret policemen moved by anything but lies? Do you still lower your bastard faces before God? Kiss my arse, you bastards, no, that's too good for you. Dürer is a lying swine, too. He who lives in longing will grow into a giant. If only the heart were not so faint, you stupid oxen!

Just a few days later, I received a telephone call from Gehlen's secretary, who said that the Doctor would like to invite me to a tea evening at his villa on the Starnberger See, that coming weekend, if it suited.

It was years since I had been to the Doctor's house in Berg, and never to one of his famous tea evenings. Only country squires and former flying aces were usually summoned to these occasions, mostly members of the Silesian nobility who might one day marry Gehlen's charmless daughters.

One of these daughters opened the front door to me, clad in a parliamentary-democracy vision of a cocktail dress – shockingly progressive, that is, and violet to boot. But her manner was no different to Mama's half a century before at the Tsar's palace, as she escorted this late arrival, stricken by all manner of tragedies, to her father. We walked to the rhythm of Tchaikovsky's *Swan Lake*, which was fizzing around the whole house from a record player.

The house was brightly lit. We had to pass by various jolly potential sons-in-law, who were standing with their teacups before the darkly shimmering panorama of the Starnberger See. If they had turned round, they would have noticed a last smudge of greenish brown paint on the large wall opposite, the remains of the Elend-Alm that I had once brought to life there.

But then, why would they have turned round.

The violet daughter knocked on a door (two short knocks, one long, two short: a perfect secret-service family down to the smallest detail), then opened it quietly and led me into the small smoking room.

Gehlen was sitting at his bureau, a table lamp behind him. I stood for a few seconds in the light from the party. Then the daughter nudged me forward, said, 'Herr Dürer, Father,' and shut the door behind me, sweeping the beam of light from the carpet and, with it, the shadow I was casting. The sound of *Swan Lake* ceased abruptly, and I was enveloped in a dark grey that was illuminated only by the small, dull lamp.

Gehlen's silhouette motioned me closer with a desultory wave of his hand. As I approached, I almost stepped on a huge, dopey-looking Labrador, which was lying next to a large wood stove. It took a moment to grow accustomed to the dark and see that, a little distance from the wood stove, Palestine Fritz was sitting on an overstuffed oriental leather cushion, as if skewered to it.

He was wearing a black suit, and his patent leather shoes were placed neatly beside his feet in their checked socks. As his smirking eyes met mine, I knew that something was very, very wrong.

'Would you like a cup of tea, or something else?' the master of the house asked me.

I said I would very much like a cup of tea. Then, taking his slender, pointing finger as an invitation, I lowered myself onto a second overstuffed cushion beside Palestine Fritz's.

'A gift from the Jordanian royal family,' Gehlen said airily, as he poured me some tea from a silver pot. 'In the Jordanian royal palace, one takes one's shoes off to sit on them. Here, too.'

Our seats were not uncomfortable, but much lower than Gehlen's, who looked down on us like a Bedouin sheikh and poured the hot tea quite calmly above my head. I obediently untied my laces and slipped out of my shoes, placing them next to my feet as I listened to a short lecture on the advantages of going barefoot, from spiritual, orthopaedic and secret-service perspectives (the barefoot Comanche is always at an advantage). And I also learned how keen the Doctor was to cross the Alps barefoot the following summer, because of his back, of course, which would benefit greatly from the trip.

'But we're not here to talk about my back,' Gehlen said, having done precisely that at some length. He handed me the cup.

I slurped the tea, which tasted of nothing at all, with great reverence, and the Labrador snored, or perhaps it was the grinning Palestine Fritz, I couldn't have sworn either way.

'What a tragic incident, that business with your teacher,' Gehlen said when he had sat down again. He could say such things without making a tragic-incident face; that was left to me and me alone, for Palestine Fritz was still grinning like a Cheshire cat. 'But we should leave these perfectly understandable human emotions out of it for the moment, Dürer, and address the larger context.'

'Very good, Herr Doctor.'

'You are familiar with Israel's attitude towards our country?'

'Naturally.'

'And any *Homo politicus* who still has all his marbles can see that things are not going to get any easier over the coming years.'

The Doctor leaned back in his bureau chair, and it was only now that I noticed he, too, had taken his shoes off and was rubbing his heels together contentedly.

'But I personally have come to believe,' he went on, his two big toes revelling in their freedom to move, 'that Israel will not permit anyone to wipe it off the map. And therefore, sooner or later, the game will be afoot.'

'What game, Doctor?'

'Your game, Dürer. No one is forcing you into it. It's your game. We're agreed on that, are we not?'

I sat up straight and told the nimble feet of West Germany's top secret-service boss (for I could not look into his eyes) that I would take the job, voluntarily and very gladly, but that with the greatest respect I would appreciate some details.

'There is a high-stakes undercover mission to be carried out in Israel.'

'How high are the stakes, exactly?'

'They could not be higher.'

Palestine Fritz had not moved a muscle until this point, but now he responded as though to a code word. After quickly reaching down for something at his side, he thrust a slim, pre-prepared folder at me.

I took it, got up and walked in my stockinged feet over to the table lamp, where I put down my cup of tea (a wise decision) and pulled my reading glasses from their case. I saw the words 'classified material' on the front of the folder and, beneath them, 'Himmelreich'. I opened the folder and took three minutes to work through it, then another three to regain my composure. After that, I returned the documents to Palestine Fritz and sat back down on the cushion from the Jordanian royal family, though it now seemed to be filled with fragmentation grenades and plastic explosives.

'I'm to be a double?'

'A perfect double, to be quite honest,' Palestine Fritz put in excitedly. 'The simple fact of his Jewishness means you could get a long way with Himmelreich's identity.'

'This man hangs himself, the whole thing is all over the newspapers here, and I'm supposed to pick up where he left off?'

'There hasn't been anything in the papers,' Palestine Fritz assured me. 'At our request, the police made the incident disappear. There is no Himmelreich corpse. There is just a live-and-kicking Himmelreich, and he is sitting in front of me.'

'Alive and kicking for how long?'

'As long as you want. No one is going to miss your teacher, he doesn't have any offspring, and his mortal remains have already been turned to ash.'

'Someone is going to miss him.'

'Not in Munich, they won't. No social contacts at all. His family never left Auschwitz. And professionally – well, he worked for the Org and the CIA, which is to say, no one. His colleagues at Radio Free Europe are sworn to secrecy. They won't say anything about him, or about knowing him. And really, no one does know him. You're a lucky chap, Herr Dürer.'

'Am I?'

'Himmelreich will be your ticket to Israel.'

Just so that you understand, my possibly hopelessly confused Swami: Herr Gehlen and the optimistic Palestine Fritz were planning to take advantage of Himmelreich's suicide. They were planning to take his name, his characteristics, his interests and his loneliness – to peel his whole Jewish skin from his flesh, in fact, and drape it over me like a blood-soaked cloak of invisibility.

From outside, we could hear bright laughter accelerating into a gallop, even startling the Labrador out of his slumber. Gehlen, too, looked towards the door, on the other side of which a new record was playing, 'Moonlight Serenade', poison for the ears.

'There is one tiny thing, though,' Palestine Fritz said then, turning to me – and for the first time, I thought I could see a shadow at the corners of his mouth and in the clearing of his throat. 'A tiny thing about Herr Himmelreich, but there's no need to make a drama out of it.'

My Swami, I . . . I said I would tell you everything, and I will, although the chamber of dukkha we are now entering is a particularly unexpected one – unexpected for me, but perhaps also for you, since you too will have built up a picture of good, helpful, bluebell-loving Herr Himmelreich, through my eyes, so to speak. But those eyes were closed, and you saw only what I wanted to see. My eyes were barricaded and Palestine Fritz broke down those barricades for me, though he started by telling me what I already knew: that Herr Himmelreich had begun his degree as a *Studiosus medicinae* at the University of Tartu in the early thirties, but finished it in Berlin.

In his first job as a junior doctor at the Charité, Dandelion met and fell in love with a young colleague, Christiane of course, who espoused the popular ideas about race at that time. And she conjugated Himmelreich's round blue eyes into a splendidly Teutonic form, an impression that he initially did nothing to dispel, because he was crazy about this girl. In an effort to keep her, he summoned up his Baltic and Jewish chutzpah and passed himself off as an Aryan for quite some time. But eventually, just before the Nazis took power, he came clean with her, though he knew full well that he was liable to be abandoned at the speed of light.

That is not what happened, however.

Christiane chose him and not the German people (at least, that is how the chief physician put it when he sacked them both). Christiane's choice was so emphatic that they even got married. The bride's parents, quite unlike the bride herself, had been firm opponents of Hitler. Her father had heaped blame on himself by representing the Social Democrats as a town councillor in Potsdam (the Social Democrats were blamed for everything), and her severely disabled brother was always at risk of euthanasia. The more oppressive the situation became for Himmelreich, the more steadfast his wife grew.

During the war, he and his wife had to move into a Berlin Jewish building. In order to protect her, to save her socialist father from the camps, to prevent Christiane's brother being taken to a killing facility, and of course to escape deportation himself, he began to work for the SD – at her request.

He did so with a heavy heart. He hesitated for a long time. But when Christiane's father was picked up by the Gestapo and beaten until he suffered a heart attack, Himmelreich stepped up and became a first-class informant, sniffing out Jews in hiding from the Scheunenviertel to Kurfürstendamm, befriending them and finally delivering them up to the Gestapo.

'Himmelreich was a police dog?' I asked in disbelief.

'Police dog, denouncer, collaborator. The whole nine yards.'

'And you think that's a tiny thing there's no need to make a drama out of?'

'Hardly anyone knows. At the start of nineteen forty-five, Frau Himmelreich was killed in an air raid.' (Because she and her husband weren't allowed down into the air-raid shelters. Jews and their relatives were banned from them, which you may not know, Basti, being so young.) 'Himmelreich survived. In the post-war chaos he went into hiding, avoided all his old friends for fear of being recognized. He attached himself to the SD men he'd served in the war and started serving them – or rather, us – again after the collapse.'

'You don't seriously believe I'm going to let you send me to Israel as a former police dog?'

'Oh, Herr Himmelreich was always very careful. There aren't many Jews who know about him. The ones he betrayed were almost all gassed.'

We truly are stunted apes, climbing stunted palm trees for the very last rotten coconuts, only to sacrifice them to the little longing in which we live, the longing that – Himmelreich's cryptic suicide note was correct on this point – makes us giants. He may have thought that I was a lying swine and so was he, but I liked him a lot. He was a sensitive, educated, poetic lying swine, and I said as much to Palestine Fritz.

'You see,' Fritz grunted cheerfully, 'all of that applies to you as well. You'll make a better Jeremias Himmelreich than he ever could have been himself.'

All you need for betrayal is a handful of pain and anguish, and a single shining star in the sky, so that from time to time there is a little light amid all the horror.

Dandelion's shining star was Frau Himmelreich, and now mine would have the very same name. What madness.

'Well, Herr Dürer, are you man enough for it?' Gehlen asked, finally putting his shoes back on. 'Then I can explain your mission to you.'

5

After the war, the Möhlstraße area of Munich-Bogenhausen was the country's largest Eastern European shtetl, full of kaftans, noise, silverware merchants, and home to a huge black market. But when Ev and I arrived there one cool, rainy September day, it lay before us like a ghost town. The last remaining kosher restaurant, the Astoria, was shut. The market with its wooden sheds, stalls and makeshift kiosks was long gone. The synagogue, too, had moved out of the nursing college; the Jewish kindergarten and even the Jewish primary school had closed down.

Only a few of the villas that rose up to our left and right along Möhlstraße were still occupied by Jewish institutions. They had helped tens of thousands of eastern Hassidic Jews who'd been snatched from the jaws of the Holocaust and had settled in Munich for a year or two, a way-station on their escape route out of Poland or Russia. They were bound ultimately for Palestine or America, by legal or illegal means. The offices of the Jewish Agency, the American Jewish Joint Distribution Committee and the UNRRA were now standing empty. All that remained was the Hebrew Immigrant Aid Society (HIAS), at number thirty-seven, an elaborate wedding cake of a house, waiting for any latecomers.

People like us.

We rang the doorbell.

A lady named Rosensaft, short, old and wiry, opened the door. She greeted us with a friendly 'Shalom' and showed us where to leave our coats and umbrella – there had been a cloudburst shortly before our arrival. Then, taking small ballerina steps, she led us up to her office on the first floor. We sat down at her wobbly little table and looked at the wall opposite. There was a poster there with an image of two tractors, ploughing green furrows in the shape of a Star of David between two gigantic, tanned breasts, which on closer inspection might have been desert dunes. The writing beneath the picture said: 'Welcome to Israel – Keren Hayesod – United Israel Campaign'. Outside, it started raining again.

Frau Rosensaft placed a bowl of ancient, hard biscuits in the middle of the table and listened with the patience of angels as Ev told her that her parents were Latvian Jews, and that she intended to move to Israel (she really did say 'move') with the help of the HIAS. But she didn't speak any Hebrew, didn't practise the Jewish faith, wasn't too familiar with the rabbinical writings, had no idea about Passover or Yom Kippur, had never been an active member of a Zionist association, never been in a concentration camp, at least not as an inmate (at this point I gave Ev a sharp look), was not persecuted under the Nuremberg Laws, and had in fact survived the Third Reich in concealment, thanks in part to her work in various National Socialist organizations (Frau Rosenhaft bit noisily into an aniseed biscuit just at that moment, thank God), and also to the name Solm, which she had acquired through adoption, and then again through marriage.

'You married your own brother?' Frau Rosensaft asked, intrigued.

'He's not my real brother.'

'Do you have children?'

'Had.'

'Oh my goodness.'

'One.'

The startled Frau Rosensaft nodded, interrupted her consumption of the all-too-worldly biscuit, finished chewing liturgically with her hand in front of her mouth, and then said, crumblessly, 'Your husband stuck by you in the days of persecution?'

'I wasn't persecuted.'

'Was your husband persecuted?'

'No, neither of us was persecuted.'

'Why not?'

'He was an SS-Standartenführer.'

'Oh,' said Frau Rosensaft. With a slow hand she took another biscuit from the bowl and crumbled the whole thing pensively between her fingers. Before the meeting, I had told Ev she should introduce herself using her birth name, or better still her mother's maiden name, Murmelstein, an admirable name in every respect – but no, Ev insisted on honesty. Why does everyone (apart from secret agents, of course) believe that honesty is the best policy? Honesty is a doomed policy, unless it can be used to serve some cunning end.

'Frau Solm is now divorced from Herr Solm. It was a quick divorce,'

I therefore explained rather eagerly, almost adding, 'a blitzkrieg divorce, really,' but how would that have sounded on German soil?

'Oh,' Frau Rosensaft said again. Then she said nothing more for a while, sorting her papers and running her tongue over her dry lips. Finally she turned to Ev, her face already a different colour, and hissed, 'And who is this gentleman, if I might ask?'

Just imagine if I had said, 'My name is Solm as well, and I was not persecuted, either.' We would both have been thrown out at once.

But I was Jeremias Himmelreich now, and that was what I told Frau Rosensaft, in a firm voice. I was able to cite numerous instances of persecution. Himelreich (which is to say: I) could also provide proof of a small pension given to victims of persecution. Himmelreich (I) had had a concentration-camp inmate number tattooed on his (my) arm three weeks previously, and to cap it all, Himmelreich (I) had been circumcised (without Ev's involvement; I didn't want that. I still couldn't walk properly, though – it's a painful procedure, and slow to heal).

As I was revealing some parts of my new identity and not others, I could sense Ev, at my side, inwardly pulling away from me. She couldn't bear these – well, let's call them less-than-half-truths. When I then said that Frau Solm and Herr Himmelreich (we) had met outside the Munich Reichenbach Synagogue and got engaged the same afternoon, still sitting on the steps of that house of God (the blitzkrieg approach again), she catapulted all traces of devotion out of her face. This more or less anticipated the conflict that raged between us over the coming weeks: from then on, Ev began to reproach me for my supposed double life, on which, of course, she was basing her whole existence.

Honesty became her mantra.

On the tenth of October nineteen fifty-five, we said our marriage vows at Munich Register Office III (without Mama's blessing, unfortunately; she found it difficult to get over the fact that her children were becoming Jews. If they had at least become Alaskan Tlingits, then they could have taken Indian names as well and all been allowed to marry one another, but Jews? There had never been such a thing among the Barons von Schilling). As we said our vows, then, solemnizing the marriage arranged in secret-service heaven, and Ev Solm, born Meyer-Murmelstein, was asked did she take this man, Jeremias Himmelreich, to be her lawful wedded husband, until death did us part, she replied yes, I take you, Koja Solm. It was an answer that made the bride-groom's blood run cold, and the registrar hastily flick forward and back through his papers a few times.

The wedding was entirely unglamorous; Mama could never have endured it. Our witnesses were not Palestine Fritz or any of the other Orcs who were trying to impose their service on us (as Ev believed), but two tramps from Saxony whom we had engaged at the train station for the price of two bratwursts each (one before, one after).

Ev didn't touch me once during the ceremony, not on the arm, not on the hand, and not on the face, which you can also touch by looking. She withheld all the intimacy she had given me for a lifetime before that day.

When I put the ring on her finger, I in turn tried not to touch her, a vengeful reflex that didn't trouble her in the slightest, but distressed me deeply. I wished for Maya's finger, which would have leapt through this ring like a dolphin's snout, frisky and happy, yes, I would have liked to stroke that finger, even if were nothing but a worm-gnawed bone.

When the registrar saw my tears, he took them for tears of joy. Secretly, I was squeezing Maya's teeth between my fingers. That was wrong, I know, especially because Ev's relationship with these lucky charms was so difficult, and she had asked me on no account to bring them to the wedding. I had therefore sewn them into the hem of my jacket. She didn't find them, though she had patted me down quite thoroughly in the gents' toilet beforehand, much to the surprise of a transcriber urinating next to us. I swore to Ev that I would not think of Maya, or wish her teeth back in her beautiful mouth (but of course, that is precisely what I did).

Ev thought me a liar, but it was she who was forcing me into this deception. Without her, I never would have become Dandelion (the barber on Kaufingerstraße shook his head: regrettably, my few remain-ing hairs could not be shaped into a Himmelreich garland).

In the Föhrenwald displaced persons camp, south of Munich, we spent a few autumnal weeks in the company of other Jewish strag-glers, attending all manner of compulsory courses in preparation for Israel (Hebrew, Zionism, agronomy with a focus on the plantation economy). We were supposed to study Herzl, Tagore, Stefan Zweig, Rosa Luxemburg and Martin Buber's *Ich und Du* together, and to give useful, edifying literature to one another, and do you know which book Ev slipped under my pillow? Gandhi's *The Story of My Experiments with Truth*.

When we arrived at the port of Marseilles just after new year nineteen fifty-six, and the French border authority demanded an explanation for the two-metre-tall crates we wanted to take to Israel, I told them these contained Herr Himmelreich's (my) highly necessary painting equipment.

Ev suffered even from this small experiment with truth.

On the other side of the Mediterranean, the Israeli customs officials in Jaffa marvelled at this enormous quantity of materials, and wanted to know why I was bringing seven hundred and fifty watercolour paint-boxes with me. Ev said (though no one had asked her) that these were 'first-class German art supplies' for the shop we were planning to open in Tel Aviv, which could take 'the quality of Israeli painting to a whole new stage of development'.

The customs officials looked at us without expression.

Before I could say anything, Ev had already started enthusing, with the best of intentions, about how German art materials led the world in terms of quality and thickness of pigment. We had come, she said, to help advance Israeli culture in this unusual way, and had they never heard of Hermann Schmincke's finest artists' paints, Horadam's patent watercolours, Mussini resin-oil paints from Nuremberg, Lyra's huge range of gouache colours, Faber-Castell's famous eight-sided pencils, Staedler's cedarwood and red-chalk empire, or even the legendary Lukas paints from Düsseldorf, with which Van Gogh himself had fallen in love (not forgetting Schoenfeld's sublime mineral blue).

A deal of persuasion was necessary on my part to prevent the enraged customs officials from setting fire to all my perverse fascist paints right there on the quayside. It took me weeks and a proportion of the smuggled Org wealth to release the confiscated wares, in order to set up the shop that was my cover story.

I remember, as we stumbled out of the customs shed afterwards, that Ev kept calling out, 'Sixth of the first, fifty-six!' which was that day's jubilant date. I had to pick her up off the ground, which she was fervently kissing in true pilgrim style, and tell her that it couldn't go on like this.

'I can only protect you if you protect me, too,' I insisted. 'I can only be here with you because I'm in disguise. If you go over now and tell those people who I really am, they'll hang me. They'll hang me, Ev.'

She laid her head on my shoulder and nodded weakly. 'It makes me sick.'

'What does?'

'Your motive for being here makes me sick.'

'You're my motive for being here.'

'You've come here to spy on this country, Koja.'

'Please don't call me Koja.'

'It makes me sick that I'm not allowed to call you Koja.'

I took her in my arms, and although we had only arrived a few minutes before, everything felt wrong: the decision, the mission, my skinned penis, the logical pain, the far from tropical, almost cool air, everything.

'For God's sake!'

'What?'

'Just look at this wonderful country!'

She tore herself away from me and gestured, seemingly spellbound, towards a few mangy dogs and the dust-stained palm trees that fringed Jaffa's port. Flayed animal cadavers and evil-smelling fish were hanging in the January sun; it was market day for the city's last remaining Arabs. I could not see any wonderful country beyond the swarms of flies that buzzed in front of my face; there was nothing wonderful at all. Tiny grains of dust collected on my lips and gave the flies more purchase there.

The bus from Jaffa took us first along the coast, then into the derelict former Arab neighbourhood of Manshiyya, and finally past a few orange groves, from where it was a short drive into neighbouring Tel Aviv. We rattled all the way down Dizengoff Street, past its white Bauhaus cubes to the bus station, where Ev and I were spat out, she with shining eyes, I full of doubt and unhappiness.

Carrying our suitcases, we turned the corner into nearby Ben Yehuda Street, where we intended to look for temporary accommodation in one of the immigrant bed and breakfasts – and found ourselves back in Germany. Between the mobile snack bars, which stood on every corner and cul-de-sac, everyone was speaking German. There was no sign of the *herem* here. Despite all the official bans, there were German cafés and German bookshops; all the butchers were German, and there was a Bavarian bakery and a master confectioner from Königsberg. But no German art supplies shop, which came as a relief to me.

An old gentleman who looked like Gerhard Hauptmann approached us with a hawker's tray of books around his neck. 'Hello there, Mr and Mrs,' he said in a soft, Otto John Frankfurt sing-song, 'I can shniff out a Yekke from a hundred metres off.'

He tried to sell us Goethe's *Elective Affinities*, and when I didn't immediately take the bait he started declaiming it to us, in a stentorian voice and a broad Hesse dialect, Goethe's own language.

That evening we went to bed in a tiny chamber lit only by a green light bulb. In the room next door, other hotel guests were attempting to slaughter a chattering goose, and I finally managed to shake off my fearfulness and my crippling disorientation.

I told Ev in simple words that I was feeling great misery, but not because of her, and that I was in love, but not with her, though my great and overflowing brotherly love was hers for all time. This was the only truth I had to give her. It was something I had never been capable of deceiving her about, and never would be in future, either.

I therefore asked her to think of me as an honest person, at least as far as she herself was concerned – she whose honesty was a torment to others (me) – and she must not hold my longing for a dead person against me, since we both longed for one and the same dead person, and for me there was another as well.

Is it not always the dead who drive us?

We were sitting side by side on a British camp bed that squeaked quietly. Ev put her hand on my leg and left it there until I grasped it.

'It's good that you aren't in love with me,' she said a little hoarsely.

It was not in my power to do anything. She took the initiative and began to undress me. She unbuttoned my shirt, stripped it off me, pulled my vest over my head, undid my belt buckle, relieved me of my trousers, and – carefully, so as not to dishearten my still-sore member – my underpants as well, and asked me to do the same to her.

Then she whispered, 'Sixth of the first, fifty-six.'

We slept together as the goose died in the next room, the goose and I both screaming in pain. It was like sleeping with a scorpion.

Later, I realized how quietly we could both cry.

Afterwards, we prayed as we used to do, and it suddenly occurred to me that there must be only one reason we had instituted this ancient religious ritual when we were children: to avoid any unsettling kissing.

And to avoid any unsettling kissing, we called on God together again.

First, we tried in Hebrew.

But the old sense of solidarity refused to come.

And so eventually we blessed our new life as Jews in a rather unorthodox manner, with the Christian evening prayer that Grandpaping Huko had planted in our family, seeding each word so that it would go on growing in and through us.

I thank you, my Heavenly Father, through Jesus Christ your dear son, that you have kept me this day in your mercy, and I ask that you forgive me all my sins where I have done wrong, and keep me in your mercy this first night in the Holy Land, too. For into your hands I commend myself, my body and soul, my beloved sister and the many who have died and all things. Let your holy angel be with me, that the evil foe may have no power over me.

Amen.

6

The first weeks in Tel Aviv were taxing.

We registered with the German-Jewish aid organization, the name of which was quite genuinely Olej Germania. And the hazelnut-brown women who worked there insisted that people call them 'the ole Germans'. Fine. My intention to douse Israel with German paints met with amusement there, in any case.

All the same, they helped me to find a recently bankrupted florist's on Ben Yehuda Street where I could set up a fragrant shop. There was enough space for a small gallery as well.

We rented an apartment very close by, at the quiet, Shir-Street end of Graets Street, and moved into a stick of chalk that seemed to have been designed by my old Professor Krastins, so crooked and modern was it. I really had not made much effort with my architectural studies in Riga, but I still could have managed a box like this with a flat roof, a curved oriel window and a little balcony, even in my first semester.

We lived on the second floor, in a tiny two-room flat that Ev furnished in steel and light wood, and decorated with our daughter's pictures. That might have been a mistake, subjecting ourselves to all those cheerful ponies, reminding us every day of what we had lost.

There were five other households in our building, all from Europe. Most were married couples who had managed to escape the death camps. Their children played dodgeball outside on the newly tar-macked street, where they were a constant source of dismay for Ev.

Sometimes she invited Shoshana Kohn to lunch, the little girl who lived next door, nine years old; her parents both worked at the power station and were grateful for Ev's help. Shoshana taught us Hebrew over dessert. She was tremendously likeable and spirited, a little black-haired moppet who shone in everything she did: history, maths, sport, guitar and above all, scouting. In her blue skirt and white girl-scout blouse, she was the Kohns' personal Israeli flag, hoisted above Auschwitz day after day.

Everyone in the building felt sorry for us: we were already in our mid-forties and, once Shoshana had told the neighbours about all the beautiful children's pictures in our living room, they drew the obvious conclusion. The unfathomable, devastating conclusion.

No one ever asked us.

They thought we were like them.

A lot of people had lost offspring to the gas. All the children in our street had been born after the war. And they all missed relatives: grandfathers, grandmothers, aunts, uncles, cousins, just as we missed our daughter. Families had only one child, or two if they were lucky. And behind each of these small families was a larger family who hadn't made it.

Herr Krausz from the upper ground floor had lost his first wife in Kaunas. Madame Anton (first floor) had two sons ripped from her arms in a camp and thrown onto a lorry, which played marching music as it drove first to somewhere else and then to the cremator-ium. Shoshana's grandmother was in a psychiatric hospital outside Tel Aviv – she'd been forced to watch as they burned her husband alive in a Minsk street. The minuscule caretaker's apartment on the ground floor, consisting only of a lean-to and a water closet, was home to the old caretaker Levy, whose thirty-four close and extended family members were 'over there', which was Levy's term for dead. He suffered from constant migraines, for which reason he was always holding a flannel to his forehead – morning, afternoon, evening, even while he swept the street. When he began sweeping, he could only hold the broom with his left hand, while his right pressed the flannel against the direction of travel, and against his memories.

The demons slept everywhere in that building, and not just in our bedroom.

Perhaps that was what gave Ev some small relief, and made her realize that a life in the shadow of death was still a life.

And life was not dismal. Tel Aviv could never be dismal. Optimism was a civic duty there. As arduous as the working week might be, and as heavily as our daughter's dust weighed on us, our evenings were often spent on the beach. Ev and I sometimes swam out as far as the fishing boats.

At the weekend, people filled their sinks with water and placed a carp in them, because gefilte fish was as much a part of the sabbath as a kiddush was. Shoshana's parents always rang our doorbell on Sundays, so they could come and read the newspaper on our balcony, the only one in the building – *Rosenthals Neueste Nachrichten* and *Yiddish Velt*.

When the days grew warmer, the children danced around the brightly coloured ice-cream van, begging for ice water, which the ice-cream man splashed over their screeching heads. On the roof opposite, the Eisenstejn family played cards half-naked, drinking vodka or kosher wine and raising their glasses to us. Everyone poked fun at them, calling them 'the battleships'.

Ev let herself fall into this colourful crowd. Perhaps she sensed that the absence of large families always leads to the formation of new large families that aren't based on blood, but sometimes just on neighbourliness, and then on blood after all, when neighbours share a loss that craves compensation. We had not been there long before even I felt a transfusion of Jewish blood entering my veins, though Ev immediately condemned this idea as a relic of racist attitudes.

'Will you stop thinking about everything in terms of blood and race?' she admonished me. 'These are just good people who have been through bad things, and feel a sense of kinship because of it.'

'Yes, and I feel that kinship, too, which is absurd.'

'Why should it be absurd? You feel kinship with me, and I feel kinship with them. The only absurd thing here is that you're working against them.'

'I'm not working against them, Ev.'

'What is it that you're doing, exactly, apart from sitting in your shop, waiting for customers?'

That was difficult to say.

My subversive activities boiled down to one weekly meeting in a changing series of cafés, where the CIA 'station agent' would buy me a sensible cup of coffee. It was my old friend Donald Day, whom the Americans had shipped over so they could share in my valuable information. But all I had to report was that, in the course of the year, my strenuous efforts of salesmanship had managed to reduce the seven hundred and fifty watercolour paintboxes to seven hundred and forty watercolour paintboxes, and my wife had found work at the Assuta Hospital, not far from our apartment.

'Don't worry,' Donald told me, handing me the telegram the Org had sent me via the American Embassy. In those first few months, the telegrams were my only porthole to Pullach. And the downside to this arrangement was that the Yanks could read them and see the same thing I saw.

General Gehlen wanted to avoid collusion. Just as a matter of principle. And so Palestine Fritz didn't wire me specific directives or details that might give the CIA clues about what was going to happen.

Unfortunately, that meant those clues didn't reach me, either.

'But this is idiotic,' I told Donald in frustration. 'What's the point of this whole operation? First they catapult me over here, and then they leave me in the dark about what exactly I am supposed to be doing.'

Donald, too, was angry in his gruff way. He believed the Org was double-dealing, and he wasn't wrong about that. He sweated continually, and complained about the heat even when it wasn't actually hot. When we took our leave, he wished me all the best and said he was sorry it was all going to kick off soon.

I waited as the weeks passed, nervously anticipating the starting gun that would set me off on my mission.

It might surprise you that I said nothing to Ev, when the fact that I was doing what I had to do and what I had come here for troubled her so greatly. But she would have found the scope of my job alarming. And crushing the little signs of recuperation that I saw in my sister was the last thing I wanted to do.

For I did see her as my sister at that time, though since the greenish night of our arrival we had begun to be more than brother and sister to one another. But the high degree of care that my scalped, converted *schmok* craved (the reddening beneath the glans made Ev compare it to a kind of coral you could see when diving off the coast of Tel Aviv), meant that both the radius and (most importantly) the intensity of our sexual favours was very limited. At most it was possible – and sometimes also bitterly necessary – to blow gently on it.

Ev's periods of depression also prevented her from unfurling her body with her usual generosity. On the contrary, she often curled into a ball next to me, like a woodlouse and for the same reason.

When someone ages in close proximity to you, they age imperceptibly – and so it was only the distance that little Anna's non-resurrection blasted into our relationship (a distance that lay before us anew every morning when we woke up, and which I saw approaching every night with the same fear, until the gap was closed again by a loving glance or the sound of the toothbrush on Ev's teeth), that made me realize my sister was now forty-six years old. Her hands still danced in the same beautiful, imperious way, but her hair had gone grey almost overnight. Her thin frame made it seem even greyer and duller, or perhaps it was the pitiless sun turning it to ashes. Her knees hurt, and had to be protected from steep steps and falls, as if they were twice as old as the rest of her complicated bones. Her face, fragile and faded in half-profile, was covered in a network of fine lines. It looked like one of my baroque paintings with its craquelure, or like a sheet of ice that someone had struck with a hammer.

But even so, beneath this coat of time was still hidden the pretty little girl who had once burrowed so jubilantly into my life. It would not have surprised me if she'd thrown off this coat with her typical aplomb – tadaaah! – and stepped out in front of me, young, naked and reckless, with no perverse divine plan in her ovaries for a daughter who would die before her.

We often went out: by night, Tel Aviv smelled even more intoxicating than it did by day. At the start of April, the *sharav* began to waft the sea up into the streets. The warm air lingered beneath the almond trees on the boulevards. There were wonderful performances at the Habimah Theatre, not a word of which we understood – but we saw Yiddish plays, too, during which I whispered one comment after another into Ev's right ear, although she raised one shoulder (the left) as I did so. It was a gesture of complete rejection that I knew of old, but ignored from behind a smile that remained unrequited.

There were a lot of parties on Graets Street, and we spent our first public holiday with the Kohns, caretaker Levy and our other neighbours in a small park nearby. It was the May Day Lag BaOmer holiday, though in nineteen fifty-six it fell on the twenty-ninth of April.

The children from our building and the buildings next door carried bows and arrows and gathered kindling and scraps of plywood for their bonfire in honour of the brave Bar Kokhba, who had seen off the Romans two thousand years before in good Battle of Teutoburg Forest style. All the street's residents crowded round the pile of wood, someone lit the fire, and the children cheered and fetched a straw man they had made at school.

For the first time in years, it was not an effigy of Adolf Hitler; they had burned him so often before. Instead, it was modelled on the Egyptian president Nasser – by me, incidentally, since Shoshana knew I could draw funny caricatures. Mr Nasser's bulbous nose and sorcerer's mouth went up in flames to great applause. Ev and I wrapped our arms around one another, clapped by small children and overwhelmed by our daughter's dust as it danced around and on us.

Two days later, everything changed. I met Donald Day in Café Mersand. He was carrying a briefcase that he slid over to me with one foot, to make it look a little less dramatic.

'It's party time, buddy.'

Was this some kind of joke, I asked him. Nothing was prepared, no one had told me anything, and the telegram from Palestine Fritz that Donald handed to me said: 'Himmelreich: please proceed as arranged. Handover as arranged. Await further instructions pending other side's reaction. Hach.'

They might as well have sent me a recipe.

'When?'

'Tomorrow. Eight o'clock.'

'Where?'

'You know where.'

I learned when he would pick me up (half past seven), what I should take particular care over (clothing) and that he was suffering in the heat (thirty-two degrees Celsius in the shade, too hot for early May). The identity papers I would need were in the briefcase. I looked at them. I had another new name, though what it was isn't relevant here. In my job, you change names like you change tyres: there are winter names, summer names, spare names, patched-up and cracked names, and of course punctured names, which can be fatal.

At home, I went over all the important things, the important encrypted things, the important things I'd memorized, the important unimportant things. Finally, I laid my hands on the documents I needed, and I will say how in just a moment.

That night, I couldn't sleep. I went out into the street barefoot, crossed it and walked down to the deserted beach. First, tar beneath my feet. Then something softer. Warm, coarse sand. I sat down and put my hands into it. It was like wool. Warm, silver wool beneath the half-moon. The salt water had deposited small mementoes there: shells, shards of coral, the odd crab. And a little seaweed.

I looked out at the ocean, considered wading into it and sinking down to join the seaweed, to be washed back up in a few days just as it was.

But I didn't do it. I lacked the strength, and the motivation.

7

'And what about the teeth?'

'The teeth?'

'The *compañera*'s teeth?'

'What about them?'

'Did you have them with you, on the beach?'

'I always have them with me.'

'Even now?'

Rather than answering, I fold my umbrella, put it down on the bench and lift my head to check that there really is no rain falling. Then I reach into my dressing gown, pull out the silver cigarette case and open it.

'I've never shown this to anyone but Ev.'

Curiosity is his greatest weakness. He doesn't want to look, but he looks anyway. He has fished the Edeka bag out of the fountain where it landed. He is holding it in his fingers like an accusation, rustling it. He is annoyed.

At the same time, he is not annoyed, because nothing good comes of annoyance, no emotion leads to anything good, and so he folds the bag up carefully, lays it down beside him on the wet bench and looks eagerly into my cigarette case. Five small yellow human teeth on red velvet.

He asks if he can touch them. But I don't want him to.

'Then give me the Marrakesh, and that's your lot,' he says sullenly. 'I've listened for long enough.'

'But this is where it gets exciting.'

'I've listened for long enough,' he repeats. 'Anyway, we've been sitting here way too long as it is.'

'Why did you ask me about the teeth?'

For the first time, and completely unexpectedly, I see hatred in his eyes, just for a moment: a dark veil.

Then the veil is gone again, and all that is left is shock. He is shocked at himself.

'Go on, tell me. What's on your mind?'

'You have no idea about death, man. Not the slightest idea,' he bursts out, before sucking his lips in defiantly.

'You think so?'

'Yeah. You can kill. I mean, you have killed. And of course, you can die. We're both going to die soon. But you should know that she's a long way from being gone.'

He points to my cigarette case, which I shut almost reflexively.

'See, I believe that was your *compañera*. Your *compañera* stopped you walking into the ocean and becoming seaweed. She was in your pocket and she stopped you.'

'Oh yes? How so?'

'If you knew about death, then you'd know how, man.'

'So, you know about death, do you?'

'There you go again, sounding all sceptical and disbelieving. I could easily go back to my room now, you know. It's cold out here, just in a dressing gown like this.'

'Forgive me. What do you know about Maya's death, honoured Swami?'

'That's easy. When the *compañera* was shot by the communists, then the communists, of course, believed that was an end to her. But that's bullshit. You can't shoot a person dead.'

'Can't you?'

'No. A death sentence is a joke. Let me tell you what happened to your girlfriend after the bullet went into her and flew through her.'

'Please do.'

'Within ten minutes, a white, masculine energy – at least, a lot of swamis describe it as white – went from her head,' he says, pointing to a spot on his bald scalp that the doctors have already marked with a small whorl, 'so, from her head towards her heart. And then the *compañera* experienced a great clarity, and thirty-three different kinds of rage vanished.'

'Maya didn't know thirty-three different kinds of rage. She was never angry.'

'Then a red, feminine energy rose up from the middle of her body . . .' he goes on, still blithely spinning his thread. He opens his dressing gown, lifts his pyjama top and points to a spot below his navel. '. . . Up towards the heart. And forty different kinds of attachment vanished.'

'Attachment?'

'Yeah, man, bonds. Like, being fused together with the world. Don't you know what attachment is?'

'Go on.'

'When the red and the white light came together in the *compañera*'s heart, then a – how shall I put it – a deep blackness came into being, and seven kinds of ignorance dissolved.'

'Goodness gracious me.'

'Then a blazing white light appeared to your girlfriend, which the swamis call "tudam". Tudam means the spirit is in the heart. The tudam was the moment when body and spirit were separated. About half an hour after she was supposedly shot dead, then, her body really was dead. The body stayed behind. The spirit fell into a swoon. What's funny about that?'

'Nothing. Nothing is funny.'

'Then why are you laughing?'

'I'm not laughing. But it sounds so implausible. What kind of swoon?'

'We call it the seventy-two-hour swoon.'

'Aha.'

'After seventy-two hours, the consciousness reawakens, and because it still has old habitual tendencies, it seeks out familiar people and places. And if we're talking about *compañera* Maya's consciousness, then it will have sought out her five teeth as well, of course. And I believe it liked it there. It's quite likely that Miss Dzerzhinskaya's consciousness is there even now.'

He points to the silver case that I am still holding.

'Are you trying to tell me that Maya is living in my cigarette case?'

'That would be too simple. Your girlfriend doesn't have a body, and of course that caused her great confusion. Panic, even. The way phenomena are perceived changes when you're in that state: things seem muffled, like in a fog, and then they vanish again. Do you see what I mean?'

'Mmhmm.'

'And that just increases the confusion. Around ten days after she was shot, your girlfriend's spirit finally became certain that she really was dead. And of course, that leads to another brief swoon.'

'And has Maya awoken from . . . from this swoon now?'

'Of course. And after that, she either sought out new parents, by going into an egg and a spiritually related spermatic cord, in which case she'd be a little girl again now, right? Or she's still clinging to you, not leaving you, you and these teeth. Which I'd say is the more likely option, *compañero*.'

I give him his cube of hash and don't see him again for two days.

It is a while before we meet on the bench again.

I have decided not to talk about Maya any more.

What I feel or don't feel about her, what I remember or don't remember of her, expands like an explosion when I feel or remember it.

It doesn't fit into her five teeth.

It is simply too great.

8

I was there before half past seven, but not by much.

I waited down at the harbour, at the agreed spot, where the bus turns round on the yellow painted forecourt. Behind me, a ship's horn sounded in the distance. The note was like a solid, deep axe blow, parting the complacent air. I tried to pat the nervousness out of my first-rate evening suit, and took a few steps in my new Walker shoes, pacing up and down in order to feel my strength despite all the trembling.

Then Donald pulled up in a clapped-out Ford without any diplomatic plates. I got in, we roared away and, although it was a short journey, Donald managed to tell me how *fucking hot* it was three times.

Even at that time of day, half an hour before the sun had fully set, it still burned your skin.

The American Embassy had a frontage of dark brick, probably the only dark brick building in the whole of Tel Aviv. Three storeys. The lowest windows were on a level with the small front garden, and had been bricked up.

Donald led me up the steps and in through the front door. I showed my new, false passport with the new, false name in it. The GI, a short-statured Comanche, glanced at it and saluted his approval. Donald took me up to the first floor and headed for a door with a ribbed glass pane in it. He opened it, trudged up another three brass-edged stairs, and, wheezing, reached a second door made of heavy oak.

He knocked nonchalantly and entered a room filled with American presidents in oils, staring down at an oval conference table. And at four men, who turned to face us.

None of them seemed especially pleased to see me.

Donald pointed at the vacant seat nearest the door. I went over, said, 'Shalom,' sat down and pretended not to notice that none of them returned the greeting. I placed my briefcase on the table, anxious to see what would happen next.

The man at the head of the table gave the impression he knew. He was the youngest there, but had the look of a wise Druid as he nodded to Donald, who was clearly on edge. Donald sat down in a corner by the door just behind me, where I could only sense him in my peripheral vision. The young gentleman opposite me folded his arms on the tabletop and sized me up. There was derision in the slightly repulsed corners of his mouth, which formed an isosceles triangle with the handsome dimple in his chin. Seldom had anyone reminded me so much of Humphrey Bogart.

'So, you're the German ambassador?' Mr Bogart said eventually, in German.

It might have been his unexpected eloquence that threw me off, or his majestic youth, or simply the proximity of danger – whatever it was, I instinctively raised my arms before answering, a gesture of pure embarrassment. In doing so, my elbow caught the briefcase, which fell and hit the parquet floor with a crash, spilling all my papers, a sandwich, and a lipstick that Donald must have left in there by accident, and which therefore rolled loyally towards him and came to rest beside his shoes.

No one laughed. No one even grinned as my face turned red and I gathered up the documents. Had a blushing spy ever been beheaded, something inside me wondered, and as I sat back down I said, in my bad Hebrew, 'My name is Jeremias Himmelreich. I'm very pleased to be able to be here with you.'

It seemed an eternity before an ugly, bald-headed dumpling of a man, who did as little to introduce himself as Bogart had, interrupted the icy silence. *'Der shoyte ken afile redn vi a mentsh.'*

'Shoyte' means 'idiot', and you can imagine the rest, Swami. I wondered what Herr Himmelreich (the real one, not me) would say to such an insult; whether he'd pull the *tav* joke out of his sleeve, for instance. I considered that for a second, but had to quickly dismiss the idea due to the unforeseeable consequences.

'Brider, es shlogt mir tsu der gal,' I said instead. *'Ikh veys nit tsi dos iz klor: Ikh bin a yid!'*

Don't worry, Swami: I will give you a faithful translation of everything that was said in that room. I know how difficult you find Yiddish – and no wonder, coming from Chiemgau as you do. (Though on the other hand: don't swamis know all the languages of the world, including those of the birds and the marmots?)

In any case, Bogart congratulated me on being a Jew, and went on in friendly tones, switching to Yiddish: 'The CIA tells us you have an excellent pedigree?'

'I've known this guy for a long time,' Donald confirmed from behind me, putting his lipstick away. 'Himmelreich is one of the German intelligence service's best agents.'

'All right,' said Bogart. 'This matter being as confidential as it is, we accept that Germany wants to negotiate using an emissary. We ourselves will send Colonel Tal' – he indicated the man to my left – 'over there in the next few days, straight to the Israel Mission in Cologne.'

Colonel Tal had the forearms of a wrestler and all manner of nose-breaking skills, one could see that at first glance. There was a pair of sunglasses pushed up onto his buzz-cut hair. He was wearing a green Hawaiian shirt in place of a uniform.

'Colonel Tal will then play the same role in your country as you are playing here. Also incognito. Would you please pass that on?'

I nodded and tried to put on the most in-the-know face I could, though I had no real idea what was going on. I hated Palestine Fritz, who had not briefed me about any of these people.

'And I'm sure you'll understand that, as a foreigner, you will be placed under observation. You'll remain a citizen of Israel for the time being. You won't be stripped of your citizen's rights, but this gentleman here . . . ' – he gave a cover name, I could tell just from the sound of it – '. . . this gentleman will be your contact in Tel Aviv.'

He indicated the man next to him, a dwarf with an enormous head and even larger ears that – I swear to you, worthy Swami – were the exact same shape and size as those of Reinhard Gehlen.

If I had known that this man was really Isser Harel, and if I had also known what role Isser Harel would go on to play in my life, I would surely have taken a closer look.

It was not him I tried to penetrate with my mind, however, but the dumpling man, who was the last to be introduced and stared at me with undisguised hostility. His name was Goldenhirsh, apparently, and he had something to do with failed foreign policy, as I would later learn.

Once everyone knew what everyone was called or wanted to be called, Bogart turned to me again.

'Shimon Peres, director general of defence,' he said simply, running a hand through his coal-black hair. 'I represent the prime minister and defence minister Mr Ben-Gurion.'

He gave me a winning smile. His self-confidence seemed very natural and not consciously polished. He looked more dazzling than Bogie, the way Bogie might have looked if he had also been a very good tennis player. But in the way he moved, there was also a shimmer of the rough grace of Bogart's wife, Lauren Bacall, and that's no wonder, either.

When I met Bacall many years later at a dinner in New York, she told me that Shimon was her cousin, her father's nephew, an asshole of a father who had left her when she was six years old to go off and fuck some shiksa from Brooklyn instead of her mother, yes, that was the way The Look talked after too much bourbon. She despised her father, for which reason her name was not Peres like Shimon, but Weinstein like her mom. Why she became Bacall is another story entirely, a tale from anti-Semitic Hollywood, as you can imagine – but forgive me, my dear Swami, I digress. Let's return, then, to the badly painted American presidents looking down on this table, at which the cousin of this century's greatest style icon sat opposite me, on tenterhooks, tense hands clasped in front of him.

'Go on then, Herr Himmelreich, shoot,' he said. 'What's the status of our anti-tank guns?'

I must have stared at him quite stupidly.

'The status of your anti-tank guns?'

'Yes. And the patrol boats?'

'The patrol boats?' I repeated, sounding like the Chin-ninny in Pattendorf and probably looking like him, too.

'The . . . patrol boats that you are currently building for us, my friend?'

'He's completely clueless,' Dumpling said crossly.

'Be quiet, Benji.'

'But if he's clueless.'

'You're clueless, too.'

'Me? I'm clueless?'

'It's just that the two of you are clueless about different things.' And to me: 'What information do you currently have?'

'Well,' I said, 'my authority has instructed me only to discuss this on Israeli soil.'

'You *are* on Israeli soil.'

'Are we not all to some extent on American soil here?'

Donald looked up in surprise, as if he'd missed something – which he had, since he couldn't speak Yiddish.

'Well, then,' Peres said gently, in English, 'perhaps our host will kindly leave us alone for a moment.'

Donald couldn't grasp what was going on; the shock even made him stop sweating, so it seemed to me.

'You want me to leave the room?'

He glowered angrily at Peres, shook his head like a bull who has no appetite for the torero, and then left abruptly without saying another word.

I reached into my briefcase and pulled out the grey envelope that I had smuggled all the way here, three thousand kilometres on trains, buses and a passenger steamer, glued to my grandpaping, to the back of the portrait that Papa had given to me years before.

Peres broke the seal, pulled a slim folder from the envelope and scanned the first few pages. After two minutes, he closed the folder again and ran his fingers over the red sealing wax in amazement.

'You are not familiar with the content of these documents?'

'I am to deliver it to you. But I don't know the details, no.'

'But you do know why you're in Israel?'

'We are to finalize arrangements for the delivery of the arms that Germany is making available to you.'

'Correct. That's what we are all very much hoping for. It isn't an easy business.'

'No,' I said. 'I was almost arrested for bringing German watercolours into Israel.'

'Yes, and watercolours don't even require you to break trade laws. Mausers do.'

'The Germans,' Dumpling hissed indignantly, 'the Germans used Mausers to shoot thousands of our brothers and sisters dead.'

'Benji, that really isn't going to get us anywhere.'

'And why don't we arrest this would-be Jew, this man who knows as much as a new-born? The Germans haven't told him anything. Because Germans never tell a Jew anything. Because Germans are what they are!'

'And that is why they will know exactly who they are sending here.'

'It's a disgrace (*a shande*!) that we're letting someone into Eretz Israel, to move around freely, take a good look at the military complexes and bunkers, and pass their positions on to the Arabs.'

'Mr Himmelreich is a Jew. He won't do that.'

'Well, he'll certainly pass everything on to the Germans!'

'You are speaking disparagingly of our guest. That isn't fair. Mr Himmelreich can't help it if certain directives exclude him from the information he is to transmit to us.'

'A fine transmitter he is, with nothing but air in his head.'

'My superiors believe it is right,' I said, 'not to overburden me with secret information.'

'Yes, you're working entirely unburdened by secret information,' Dumpling scoffed, 'so entirely unburdened that you don't even know you're here!'

'It says here that we can transfer everything via him,' Peres said, looking at the file again.

'I don't trust any Jew who works for the Germans. And the fact that you would trust someone like that, and are speaking so openly in front of a stranger, Shimon, shows once again that you would make a pact with the devil himself.'

'We need weapons, you know that as well as I do. And the Germans have the best weapons – here, have a read of this!' He threw the folder to Dumpling. 'It says that they'll deliver the patrol boats in two months! We just need to give him the details of the handover.'

'I'm sorely tempted to tell Sharett about the whole fucking thing. It's unforgivable that all this is going on behind his back, it's a real disgrace (*a shande, a shande, a geherike shande*)!'

'You know where Sharett can go?'

'Where can our foreign minister go, then, hmm? Where can he go?' Dumpling barked.

Shimon Peres told him.

That sent Dumpling into a fit of rage, and he screamed that Peres was a spineless careerist, fawning on the Germans and betraying his whole nation and his own relatives.

'You're upset, Benji. You can apologize later.'

'I will not apologize! Not to Ben-Gurion's bootlicker! Not to a green boy who has no regard for history!'

'I know they killed your mother. But what do you know about me?'

'I don't want to know anything about you!'

'You're dishonouring me, Benji. You're dishonouring me in front of our friends. You're dishonouring me with our guest listening. And you're turning us into a laughing stock with the Americans.'

Dumpling looked at him, his eyes steaming, small capillaries bursting in their cloudy white. He was leaning on the table, his arms straight and his chubby little hands clenched into walnut-brown fists. We could all hear his lungs rattling. Eventually he lowered his eyes and sat slowly down again. No one moved, no one blinked. Even the American presidents seemed to be holding their breath. Somewhere on the floor above, a secretary stalked across the parquet floor in high-heeled shoes, and it occurred to me that no one had turned the light on, even though it was getting dark outside and we were now nothing but contours and shadows.

Peres waited a whole minute before reaching for the water carafe. He poured two glasses, slid one over to Dumpling, who ignored it, and drank the other in great gulps.

'Rabbi Zvi Meltzer was my grandfather,' he began quite calmly, 'and as he taught me the Torah, he also taught me to respect history, Benji.' He set the empty glass down. 'I see him clearly before me, with his white beard, wrapped in a prayer shawl. A magnificent figure he cut in the Vishneva synagogue in those days, believe me.'

For God's sake, I thought, please let that not be true. Please not Vishneva.

'I liked to hide under my grandfather's prayer shawl. And I listened to his lovely voice. That voice still echoes in my ear to this day, saying the Kol Nidre prayer.'

I went to Vishneva once. Do you remember, Swami? It was after Stahlecker's death. Belarus. Vishneva. 'Vishneva glows'.

'I recall him standing on the station platform, waiting for the train that was to take me away. To take me, his eleven-year-old grandson, away forever. I remember his tight embrace. And I remember his words, when I saw him there at the station for the last time: "My boy, always remain a Jew!"'

I reached for the carafe and poured myself some water.

'When the Nazis marched into Vishneva ten years later, they ordered everyone to gather in the synagogue.'

I held the glass and saw the water in it trembling.

'My grandfather was the first to enter, wearing the same prayer shawl in which I enveloped myself as a child.'

I drank.

'His family followed him.'

I drank.

'The doors were barred from the outside. The Germans wrote "Vishneva glows" across the whole width of the wooden building. Then it was set alight.'

I drank.

'All that remained of the community was embers. Embers and smoke. There were no survivors.'

'I'm sorry, could I have a little more water?' I asked.

'Of course,' said Isser Harel, the short man with the Gehlen ears, getting up from his seat.

'So I would ask you for a little respect, Benji. It is precisely because I am thinking of my grandfather that I will do whatever it takes to obtain arms for our country. Wherever those arms come from, no one will ever trap us in a synagogue and burn us alive again. Not your people. Not mine. Mr Himmelreich,' Peres cried out in surprise. 'Why, you're quite pale. Is something wrong?'

'No, no, everything's fine.'

I realized I was slowly sliding off the chair.

'I expect his people were burned, too,' I heard a voice call out, and the last thing I saw was George Washington, bending over me with a worried look on his face.

9

It was nineteen forty-seven when the Jewish underground movement Hagana started using hundreds of handguns from General Rommel's stores, which had swayed across the Sinai Desert to Palestine on the backs of camels.

A year later, shortly before the War of Independence broke out, the Israelis bought twenty-five Messerschmitt planes from the Avia works in Prague, where they had been manufactured for the Luftwaffe. They painted over the swastikas with Stars of David and, in the old Messerschmitt tradition, shot down enemy Spitfires (wearing Egyptian paint).

During the bitter battles with Jordan, Syria, the Lebanon and the kingdoms of Iraq and Egypt, MG42s, known as 'Hitler's buzz saws', were smuggled to Israel from the South of France.

Substantial numbers of family-owned Heckler and Koch pistols came from the Sicilian Mafia.

Greek gunrunners were able to supply considerable quantities of MP40s.

In short: German weapons prevented the downfall of the Israeli armed forces.

In nineteen fifty-two, following the negotiations in Wassenaar and West Germany's commitment to paying reparations, new prospects opened up. Once, a team of experts from the Israeli defence ministry even travelled to Germany disguised as a delegation of top Italian chefs, but didn't make much progress on the arms-trade front, not least because no one from the delegation could speak Italian, or even cook (they also refused to hold an Italian flag; the leader of the delegation took it to be an Iraqi one and therefore burned it in public outside the only trattoria in Munich, much to the surprise of everyone inside).

From nineteen fifty-three, the Israel Mission in Cologne coordinated Germany's supply of goods to Israel (it was an institution that Menachem Begin's Herut Party hated with a passion). It, too, tried to buy armaments covertly, disguised as 'fuel-burning equipment for the baking of Alsace bread'. The two patrol boats that Peres asked me about had also been declared as bakers' ovens.

But all these efforts ceased when, following the Paris treaties and the re-armament agreement with the NATO allies, West Germany set its sights on creating its own army: the Bundeswehr.

No Israeli politician was prepared to begin negotiations with the newly appointed Bundeswehr generals, all of whom were Wehrmacht veterans with blood on their hands – possibly Jewish blood. This refusal was triggered not so much by moral reservations as by naked fear. If news had got out that they were dining with the devil, there would have been uprisings in Israel, and anyone involved would have been compromised for all time.

It was this reason and this reason only that prompted Reinhard Gehlen to exchange my foreskin for the opportunity to smuggle me into Israel as a Jew. Only via a Jewish agent such as Jeremias Himmelreich – emotionally unstable, ignorant of the facts, and liable to faint – did this top-secret arms deal, which was also in Germany's national interest, seem possible.

That is what I was doing in Tel Aviv, revered Swami.

That is why I found myself in the American Embassy.

That is why I came to on a leather sofa, beneath a rattling ceiling fan, in a small, dusky office where Donald Day was sitting with the window open and the blinds closed. He had a beard like a woolly mammoth; his jacket was off and his shirt drenched with sweat. For once, the gun in his shoulder holster didn't appear to be of German origin (it was a Browning).

He was smoking.

I sat up, feeling woozy. There were no American presidents on the wall, just Niagara Falls, which I would very much have liked to see crashing down on Donald, and I told him as much.

'Shut up,' Donald muttered grouchily, before explaining a few complicated states of affairs that I would much rather have learned about a few weeks, days or even just hours earlier.

'Bullshit. It's a good thing you knew so little,' he growled.

'What's good about it? I was led around by the nose like a dancing bear.'

'What if they'd caught you earlier, and tortured you?'

'Why would anyone want to torture Jeremias Himmelreich?'

'They wouldn't want to torture Jeremias Himmelreich! They'd want to torture *you*! You are not Jeremias fucking Himmelreich!'

'And what would I have told them?'

'Exactly: nothing. If you don't know anything, you can't say anything.'

It had been a precautionary measure, he told me bluntly, just as it had been a precautionary measure to arrange the meeting in his embassy instead of somewhere out there, where I would not have been a lodger in the most powerful country on earth, but a mere defenceless organism.

'I collapsed like a debutante,' I complained.

'That was a great bit of acting, buddy. But it didn't do any good.'

He pulled out a pocket handkerchief and wiped his face, without taking the cigarette butt from his lips.

'What do you mean?' I asked.

'They're not going for it.'

I sat up, feeling the draught from the fan on my scalp, or perhaps it was something else that was turning every hair on my body into a needle.

'I think Peres would have accepted you,' Donald murmured. 'But that Goldenhirsh . . .' He didn't finish his sentence, just left it hanging in the steaming air and watched with a melancholy expression as it was hacked to pieces by the ceiling fan.

Then, after a little while: 'It's a shame, but Ben-Gurion has been weakened. He was tripped up by a couple of Jewish agents in Cairo who were caught and hanged, the jackasses.'

His mouth twisted into a disdainful sneer that made his cigarette drop its ash.

'Sharett may not be in the top job any longer, but he's still the foreign minister,' he went on, reaching for an ashtray. 'He hates secret agents. He hates the war. He wants peace with Nasser's goat-fuckers at any price. It's pitiful.'

'If the Jews want weapons, why get them from Germany, of all places?'

'Where else would they get them?'

'What I mean is: why don't they *buy* them elsewhere?'

'How? Global arms embargo! Global sanctions! And why? Because the Palestinians don't have enough rose petals under their asses here!'

'What about America?'

'My homo government?'?

'America supports Israel.'

'You're the only one who believes that. The homo foreign ministry is shitting its pants with fright. The homo defence ministry is shitting itself, too. All the homo politicians are shitting themselves, and even Eisenhower is sticking to the United Homo Nations' embargo. The CIA is the only one not shitting its pants, because it doesn't have any. I'm a naked station agent. I'm sitting here just as God made the CIA. This meeting here is all on me. Why do you think your name is George Springsteen?'

He jabbed a fat, furious, reactionary Yankee forefinger at my fake passport.

'Well, what now?' I asked.

He proffered the cigarette packet. I took one and lit it with his lighter.

'Now, you go on over to our telecommunications room and let Pullach know you're coming back.'

I took two drags and blew some lovely smoke rings into the half-dark, before saying, 'Donald, I live here. I'm not leaving.'

'Are you kidding?'

'I'm quite serious.'

'They won't accept you as a negotiator. Goldenhirsh is against it, because he thinks Sharett is against it. And Peres doesn't dare go it alone. So farewell, my lovely.'

'That's my home now, out there,' I said, blowing another puff of smoke towards Tel Aviv.

'Do you think that just because you got your cock docked and had a damned number branded into your flesh, this can ever be your home?'

'I'm a Jew now. And that's what I'm going to stay.'

Donald stared at me. Then he stubbed out his cigarette, got up, went over to the window and looked out through the blinds.

'There's a green Simca down there that I think I've seen before,' he said in a different voice. 'But then, maybe not. There's a lot that look like that.'

He sat back down. I said nothing.

'Believe me, buddy, the boys here are really good. During the British Mandate, they called themselves "Shai". The Shai had Jewish spies, Arab spies and British spies. They even had the sheep and the goats spying for them. There was nothing they didn't know. Now they call themselves the Shin Bet.'

'Never heard of them.'

'And the Mossad.'

'Never heard of them.'

He thrust a business card at me with a picture of a severed lion's head on it. No name. No number. It didn't mean anything to me, but he told me to keep it somewhere safe. The gnome with the elephant ears had left it for me. Isser Harel. That was the first time I heard his name.

'They will take three months at most to crack your identity. They'll unscrew the sewage pipes under your house and rummage through your stools. They'll search your trash cans. They'll break into your apartment and inspect every square inch of your drawers. And when they know who you are, WHO YOU REALLY ARE, they'll take one of your precious Faber-Castell pencils and draw a line through your name with it.'

10

After that peculiar evening at the American Embassy, people were always standing on the street.

There was a fellow with a floppy hat who would sit on a flower crate outside my shop on Ben Yehuda Street for hours, as if wanting me to paint him in the melancholy style of Edward Hopper.

Opposite Graets Street, an eternal-student type patrolled with a walking stick, occasionally leaning against a tree to recover from the effort of patrolling.

Even when I went to meet Donald in cafés, men with coal-black sunglasses sat nearby. They often ordered the same drinks as us, and wrote down what we were all drinking in their little notebooks.

On our evening swims, Ev and I were always followed by an eighteen-year-old boy, as handsome as Thomas Mann's fatal Tadzio, who sat on the beach at a reverent distance and did not take his eyes off us for a moment. Once, I blew my top, stormed over to him with remnants of sea dripping from my skin and hair, and declared that I enjoyed being followed by him tremendously, but he could have the decency not to use his eyes so much, to cast them on us so shamelessly; that was the most rudimentary principle of surveillance, and I did know what I was talking about.

Starting the next day, there were two of them.

They didn't even leave Ev alone. Someone was always waiting outside the hospital, and he followed her home in the evening on a bicycle, keeping a steady distance as she walked.

When Shoshana Kohn came to visit us one day, to go through our Hebrew exercises, she seemed unusually quiet and evasive. When we asked if there was anything troubling her, she opened her eyes wide and shook her head vigorously, then closed her eyes very slowly and gave us an even slower nod. She confessed that she had been summoned to the headmaster's office at school. Two men were waiting for her there; they apprised her of this and that, and finally pressed a camera into her hand.

'Here,' she said, showing us a Leica rangefinder. Well, fancy that: you could get hold of a German camera in the land of the import-export ban. 'I'm supposed to take photos of your apartment,' she murmured under her breath, but she shouldn't have breathed a word to us, even under her breath.

We allowed Shoshana to carry out her task (to be honest, it was I who photographed my apartment for her, wanting it at least to be recognizable and in focus), but two weeks later she lost her position as scout troop leader all the same. Not long afterwards, she was thrown out of the scouts altogether and had to give her uniform back. Her family's fluttering blue and white was lowered for good.

After that, we only saw her when we happened to bump into her in the hallway. She always lowered her eyes and squeezed past us. Her parents' Sunday visits to read the paper on the balcony ceased, as well.

'What is happening to us, Koja?'

   'How often have I told you not to call me that?'

   'Why are you being so aggressive? We're in our flat. No one's going to hear us here.'

   'Are you really so sure about that?'

   'There's no one here, is there?'

   'There are microphones you can seal into walls.'

   'Yes, and little green men live on Mars.'

   'Ev.'

   'What?'

   'Would you go back to Germany with me?'

   'Why?'

   'Would you?'

   'No, Koja, and you know—'

   'Don't *call* me that!'

   'There's no need to shout.'

   'Goddammit!'

But there was a need to shout.

She left the room and came back five minutes later, when I sounded like a sand timer again.

   'Why are you so dejected, my darling?'

   'I'm not. Not at all.'

   'Why are these people following us? Is it something to do with your work?'

   'You don't have to put on a sympathetic act now.'

   'I've been awful to you.'

I said nothing.

   'All these months.'

I said nothing.

   'You didn't deserve it. I'll try to do better.'

   'Then go back with me.'

   'I can't.'

   'They'll kill me, Ev.'

   'What is going on?'

I told her everything.

At least, everything that could be told.

Afterwards, we lay in bed, each giving the other something to cling to in this maw through which everything was devoured and quaffed and breathed and choked and spat out and swallowed back down, because it is the world, this maw, nothing but the world.

'But, look,' Ev whispered tenderly, three centimetres from my face, despite the heat of three thick blankets piled on top of us so that no microphone could pick us up, 'when you lie down there on the beach trying to get a tan, I always wish for you not to get skin cancer. And when you're in the water, I hope you don't drown – because ninety per cent of all people who drown are men, and a lot of people drown off Tel Aviv, I've pumped salt water out of lungs before, you'd be amazed. Then I hope a shark doesn't come across you and that there isn't a lightning storm, when you swim as far out as you always swim. When you lie beside me afterwards, then I wish for you not to have caught anything in the last few days; I hope you won't get any of the diseases I see at the hospital every day, smallpox, typhus, deadly infections. And when I've wished all that, I suddenly get the feeling that one of my fears or perhaps all of them together are about to come true, that you will drown and burn and die of skin cancer and be carried off by a virus, all at once. And then my only wish is for that to happen to me at the same instant. So, if they're going to kill you, I want them to kill me, too.'

She kissed me under the bedclothes in a way she had not kissed me since Anna's death. We would pray together that evening, it was a certainty.

'When we were little,' she whispered, 'I could never imagine that one day I would meet a prince with whom I'd want to die a good death. I might have thought I'd want to live a good life with him. But living is so terribly hard, Koja. It's hard enough to meet a prince in the first place, even if he lies and manipulates people and never tells the truth, which means he can never become my king.'

'I know, Ev.'

'Can't you become my honest king, Koja?'

She lay beside me, and although she was trying to sound as light as a trilling bird, she felt worthless and shattered, ashamed and guilty. She would never come back to Germany with me, she said so over and over.

'What do we do in Germany,' she whispered. 'Bake cakes, go and hear the robins, walk in the Bayerische Wald, buy a grave, live apart, deceive our brother, not tell the truth, lose our child because we haven't told the truth.'

'The truth,' I replied tentatively, 'is what cost little Anna her life.'

'It was the lie,' Ev breathed. 'It was the lie. Don't we need a birth? Don't we have to birth ourselves, if we don't birth a child? Tabula rasa? A kind of purification? We've never been able to be ourselves. When I first came to you, I wasn't myself, either. Perhaps that's why my life has no meaning. It sounds banal, but it's true. The banal evil, the banal good, the banal truth. I invested in outward things, Koja. Often very stupid things. Mostly I invested in other people's affirmation, really expecting them to think me quite mysterious, without having to achieve anything worthy of recognition myself.'

'You were a good doctor. You are a good doctor, Ev.'

'I feel shame and regret for what I've done with my life,' she said. But it can't go on like this. If you go back to Germany, that for me will be like you dying. You'll be gone. And then I will die, too.'

'You're pressuring me. You're coercing me,' I complained.

'No,' she said. 'All my life, I just wanted other people to reflect and reassure me. I never loved anyone but Anna. I think I love you, but I don't know if I can trust myself. There is one thing I know, though: this is the whole truth, here, for the first time in my life. There's no false bottom to Israel. I can't leave here. And if they kill you, they'll kill me, too.'

'Ev,' I said, but she had stopped listening. She turned her head away and started asking questions, largely to herself, which I later wrote down because they sounded so mad.

Why do you feel more alive when you're unhappy?

Why isn't it possible to fly high in a sky that madmen are driving nails into?

Why are there German words you can't translate into Hebrew, words like *Feierabend*? How would you say it? 'The end of the working day'?

Why isn't my shadow a problem for me, when it is for so many others?

Why do we know so little?

Why don't I like to fuck any more, when I used to enjoy it so much, and why don't I want to feel your healed cock inside me, in my womb or in my mouth, though it tastes so good and does me so much good, too?

Why am I asking all these questions, Koja?

Why can't we stay here, and you become my honest king?

I I

It was no longer possible to meet Donald Day by covert means. Surveillance had turned them all into overt means.

And so I called time on the whole business of concealment and took a taxi straight to the American Embassy, like a tourist whose passport has been pinched.

There, I was given the telegrams from Pullach. Station agent Day personally handed me the written order from Palestine Fritz to get myself on the next plane to Paris and take the train back to Germany from there.

My mission was over.

'Sorry, buddy,' Donald said. 'I can't stand by and watch you dive headlong into unhappiness here. Mossad has officially asked whether we have files on you. The air is getting thin.'

'My wife doesn't want to come with me.'

'She's in no danger. She can stay here until God thinks up an eleventh commandment.'

'She's my wife. She can't stay here. Somehow, we have to get her out.'

'Against her will?'

'Once she's out, she will want to be.'

'What do you want to do? Sedate her with a blowpipe like a rhino, and fly her out on a Convair plane?'

'Is that possible?'

'You really have seen too many spy films.'

Midway upon the journey of our life, I found myself within a forest dark, for the straightforward pathway had been lost. Ah me! how hard a thing it is to say what was this forest savage, rough and stern, which in the very thought renews the fear. So bitter is it, death is little more.

And so Dante ran through my mind. How Papa had liked to quote him, as he was painting his small round arses that Mama wasn't supposed to see. I was being scourged in my own Inferno. I was a head frozen blue in the Ninth Circle of Hell. But what, my learned Swami, what can a cursed man in a dark forest do?

I got back in the taxi.

I went to see Ev at the hospital.

I went over to the bastard. He was already waiting for her by the entrance, and was honestly astounded to find his bicycle snatched from him (by me). I held it high above my head, flung it to the granite paving slabs with all my might and trampled on it.

Then I strode in through the double doors, jostling a doctor and knocking his glasses awry as I went, and almost ran into the operating theatre where Ev had just amputated someone's lower leg.

When she came out to see me in the corridor, I knelt before her and told her it was impossible for me to become her honest king. The power of deception had me in its grip, and only if she let herself be grasped by it as well could our life go on. She had to be willing to become my cunning queen. Even if it was the most repellent thing she could think of, it was also the most truthful way forward for us. It might cost us everything, it might demand everything of us.

Then I took her hand, to which small spatters of blood still adhered, and laid it against my cheek, and she came down to me like a saint. She enveloped me in her long, thin arms; arms that would never leave me in the lurch, I sensed that.

We went out to the front of the hospital together, where the bastard was trying to fix the bicycle I had trampled. You cannot imagine how taken aback he was when I pressed the small business card Donald had given me into his hand, the one with no name or number on it, just a lion's head, and told him that my wife and I wanted a meeting, as soon as humanly possible.

12

To this day, no one knows exactly where the Mossad headquarters are located.

Back then, in any case, we were invited to a rather dilapidated Arab villa in the Moorish style. Its proportions were that of a small palace, and it stood on what used to be King George V Boulevard in Jaffa, but was renamed Jerusalem Boulevard in nineteen forty-eight.

A Packard sedan had picked us up that morning, and drove us in through a gate guarded only by two palm trees. I was struck by their complete absence of palm fronds; they suppurated like two large yellowish-brown boils against the lush green of the circular lawn.

The chauffeur took us to the main entrance, where he had to knock on the wooden door and whisper something (presumably a password) through a small hatch to someone inside. The door opened as if by magic, and we were led into a vestibule with bare walls that still bore the mottled outlines of things that used to hang there. Only a decades-old, one-eyed lion's head remained, badly stuffed and mounted high above our heads, where a swallow nested in its moth-eaten mane. Below it, an Israeli flag hung a little crookedly.

We were taken into a side room, where fussy oriental wood panelling protested against the brutal emptiness that surrounded us. Someone who despised all comfort had exchanged what had presumably been magnificent furniture for tubular steel and metal twine. There was also a wooden table with nothing on it save a black telephone and an intercom.

After quite some time, a door flew open and the small, careworn Isser Harel came in. In the American Embassy, his ears had been marginal-ized by President Jefferson hanging behind him (the president with the smallest ears ever to have occupied the White House). But there was no painting here in his office, not so much as a dab of colour to compete with those bright red rabbit lugs.

Mr Harel was wearing a crumpled, sand-coloured safari shirt, crum-pled, sand-coloured trousers – in fact, even his sandals looked crumpled and sand-coloured, though they were just old and scuffed, and must have been dark brown years before. I could hardly take my eyes off his azure socks, from which midnight-blue veins snaked up his calves. He greeted Ev with a kind of puritanical bashfulness, while he regarded me without any expression at all. I couldn't even discern spiteful conde-scension in his features; and they remained opaque when I told him that my wife and I were here because we wanted to work with the Mossad.

'And do you believe,' he asked, in his sullen castrato voice, 'that the Mossad would like to work with *you*, Mr Himmelreich?'

My queen, who had become cunning overnight, couldn't help herself (that was typical of her): she explained to Mr Harel in her best Yiddish that, as a faithful Jew, I had just been waiting to place all my strength in the service of Israel.

'If your husband has so much strength to give,' Mr Harel said, pulling on his large left jug-ear, 'why doesn't he try the Tel Aviv refuse-collection service first?'

It was only years later that I realized there was no irony in sentences like this; you can scarcely imagine a more irony-free creature than Mr Harel. In reality, he had developed a tactic that I had observed decades before in my old governess, Anna Ivanovna. Some people hide their real thoughts in a thicket of entirely unconnected words, which are nothing but a smokescreen and have no meaning whatsoever. As they are talking, quite incompatible synapses in their brains connect to one another, and I was almost sure that, while Mr Harel's mouth was still saying these grotesque things, an invisible firing squad was lining up behind his retinas and taking aim at me.

'There are a few things I would like to explain to you, if I may,' I therefore said, with some haste – and since Mr Harel was not demanding any explanations at all, I embarked on an entirely unsolicited description of Mr Himmelreich's personal advantages, as I imagined them in keeping with my own self. This was quite a challenge: first, I had to reveal Mr H's surprising survival in the Third Reich, and then I had to turn the collaboration with government agencies that had facilitated his survival into a laurel wreath – which, thank God, Ev placed on my head.

'We are aware,' she explained, with precisely the right combination of humility and feminine warmth, 'how confusing our visit must seem to you. But during the years of oppression, my husband never harmed a fellow Jew. He could never have done such a thing, it isn't in his nature. He ran errands, that was all. Passed on deportation orders. Nothing more.'

I heard how these inglorious deeds had plunged Mr Himmelreich into a great inner turmoil, a turmoil that might explain his desire to serve the Israeli state from now on, for all time. And at my side, Ev wanted the very same thing.

Mr Harel's small eyes narrowed to slits.

'Name?' he snarled.

Ev gave her false name, which was mine, and then her real name, which was also mine.

'Solm?' Isser asked, taken aback.

'I was adopted by a Baltic German family when I was nine.'

'Do you know Standartenführer Hubert Solm?'

'Yes. My brother,' said Ev.

'Your brother is one of the people we're looking for.'

'I know where he is.'

'We both,' I added, 'know where he is.'

He stared at us, but didn't ask how Jeremias Himmelreich came to know the whereabouts of his wife's brother.

Ev said, 'I heard about what Hubert did in Riga. Appalling things.' She sat up straight. 'But I was a child of Jewish parents, and his family saved my life. And that's why I find it hard to simply damn my brother.'

Particularly as she had been married to him – a detail that, had it been mentioned, certainly wouldn't have made the atmosphere in the room any less tense.

It was remarkable how quickly Ev adapted her vision of absolute honesty to fit absolute necessity.

I'm afraid that being honest is never absolutely necessary.

Mr Harel sat down behind the bare desk, pressed a button on the clunky intercom and asked in Hebrew, were cells Zero-Four and Zero-Five in the house jail still occupied, or had they come free. A rasping voice replied that someone would see about it right away and report back to him. The colonel took his finger off the button and crossed one knee over the other, flashes of azure and midnight-blue beneath them.

'Mr Himmelreich, what else did you want to tell me?'

'I was sent here by my government,' I began (and to this day I am amazed that in the circumstances I managed an obliging smile), 'to convince your defence ministry that the German government departments are absolutely reliable. Germany is currently building its own army, as you know. The government is interested in long-term, unofficial cooperation with Israel, independently of the fact that Germany's foreign policy supports the Arab states. The German defence minister – Strauß is his name – guarantees that any kind of agreement will be kept completely quiet.'

'There is a Defence Minister Blank in Germany. There is no Defence Minister Strauß.'

'There will be one. Very soon. And I have been assured that his ministry will provide you with arms faster than you can say "knife".'

'At what price?'

'In return, the German government expects a substantial relaxation of the import and export restrictions on bilateral trade. All transactions relating to the Luxembourg Agreement' – now, I would have to go back quite a long way to explain the Luxembourg Agreement to you; please don't make me, my knowledge-hungry Swami, please don't – 'all transactions relating to the Luxembourg Agreement will in future be made only via the provision of goods, and not the transfer of cash. And the consultations with your defence ministry will take place initially via me.'

'You want Defence Minister Ben-Gurion to negotiate with a former SS snitch?'

'You see, Colonel, it was the fear of this question that made me hesitate so long before asking to see you,' I sighed. 'In the Third Reich, I lived in a privileged mixed-race marriage. Do you think it right to spurn me as an SS snitch for that reason? My first wife died in a hail of bombs because, being the wife of a Jew, she wasn't allowed into the air-raid shelters. But Kurt Himmelreich, Hannah Himmelreich, David Himmelreich, all the Himmelreichs I loved, were murdered. So do you really think it's right to show me your contempt?'

I noticed that, beside me, Ev was projecting the word 'contempt' onto me, then onto herself, onto us both, and this disapproval gave her a noble quality, even a kind of contrite dignity, and I prayed that my devious queen would not give in to her urge to open a pressure valve somewhere in our enormous lie (a harried gesture perhaps, a sigh, something that might give us away).

'I don't believe you do think it right,' Her Majesty said graciously, after a silence that was a little too long. Mr Harel had used that silence to fall into a kind of lethargic stupor, casting tired eyes down to look at his broad dwarf hands with their bitten fingernails.

'Neither of *us* thinks it right, in any case,' I reasserted nervously, wagging a finger back and forth between me and Ev. 'We came here to be absolutely honest with you.'

I caught sight of a very unqueenly twitch; she really had to stop doing that.

'And as a sign of our honest intentions,' I went on, 'I am offering to report on everything my side says and does relating to issues in the Middle East, from now on.'

Now Mr Harel yawned.

'My husband is not doing this from a lack of loyalty,' Ev hastened to say.

'No, of course not.' I let out a nervous laugh. 'I believe that Germany and Israel must become good friends. It's our responsibility, after all the terrible things that have happened.'

I saw a second yawn; this time he didn't even put a hand in front of his mouth.

'I . . . I' – a stutter slipped out – 'I for my part would like to be the first good friend to you. But I have to offer that friendship entirely on my own initiative. Because naturally, my employer . . . well, he does not yet support a friendship of this kind.'

'We don't want any kind of salary, or any service in return,' Ev stammered. She was on the brink of hysteria, while Mr Harel looked like he was about to take a little nap. 'We love Israel. All we want is to live in this country, and to serve it. And my husband is exceptionally well placed to do that.'

'If you . . .' I began, but then my voice failed me. I cleared my throat and tried again. 'If you could perhaps contact Mr Peres again and tell him what we're offering?' I paused for effect, long and noisily, reaching into the breast pocket of my shirt and pulling out a folded sheet of paper, which I laid on Mr Harel's desk. 'Well, it could be the start of a friendship between nations.'

'What is that?' my gruff interlocutor asked.

'The personnel record for Friedrich Hach, the head of my service's Israel desk. My superior.'

Harel unfolded the paper and looked at it.

'He's an alcoholic?'

'I'm afraid so,' I said.

'Marital difficulties,' I said.

'Serious ones,' I said.

There was a knock at the door. An adjutant came in, saluted and announced that cells Zero-Four and Zero-Five were both vacant, though Zero-Five still had to be cleaned out. He was carrying a half-full bucket.

Mr Harel nodded hesitantly and laid the sheet of paper down on the desk in front of him. Then he stared into the distance, lost in thought, as though searching for a spark of inspiration.

'You're from Latvia, then,' he said. 'So am I.'

He got up and walked over to us. He stopped in front of Ev, as he probably once stood before his orange trees on the kibbutz when harvest time was approaching. He saw as little necessity in kissing a woman's hand as he had in kissing an orange, that much was obvious, but he nevertheless made a half-hearted attempt at it. It looked like he was checking the time on Ev's watch.

'I am Colonel Harel,' he told her solemnly. 'Your brother shot a lot of people. Including a lot of people from my family. Good people.'

He was still holding her hand in his.

'Perhaps one day you might introduce me to him.'

She nodded.

'If you want to work for me, you should call me Isser. Not sir. Not Harel. Not Colonel. Just Isser.'

Now we both nodded.

'Welcome, Ev. Welcome, Jeremias.'

Behind him, the adjutant clicked his heels together, causing him to spill a little water, which I thought had a reddish tinge. Then he turned round and closed the door behind him. Colonel Harel: one metre fifty-eight tall; ears like Dumbo; head of the Shin Bet, Mossad, Aman and soon Lekem, too; a state secret on crooked, waddling alligator legs. He opened the door again and led the freshly minted Mossad agents back past the lion's head and out of the building. Releasing them into the sweltering heat of a neuralgic day, he remarked that they made a handsome couple.

I was trembling all over, and so was Ev, but we really were a handsome couple.

13

The first snow is falling early this year. Really, all you need to do to achieve wisdom is to watch the snow falling and silently covering everything beneath it, the undergrowth and the excrement and the horrific memories. The Hippy, too, looks like he's been scattered with salt. He is sitting on the snow-covered bench before me, wrapped in a dark fur that I gave him, which loses a little more vitality with every white flake.

'Shouldn't we go inside?' I ask, shifting from one foot to the other. His fur is warmer than my own.

'I'm glad I'm not in your room any more, *compañero*.'

'Then everything's fine, isn't it?'

'I'm getting a single room after the op. When your head is this broken, you get a single room.'

'Come now, your head isn't all that broken.'

'It's wandering.'

'Your head?'

'Kind of like tectonic plates, the doctor says.'

'I'll bring a nice new lump of Marrakesh for you tomorrow.'

'Nurse Gerda says I'm not allowed any more.'

'Because . . .'

'Because of the drugs, that's why. The drugs are lit matches, and the hash is the fuse, and when the matches light the fuse, then eventually it'll go boom in there.'

Over his hippy skull – soon to be held together with two screws, and invisible now beneath the fur hat pulled down over it – his hands mime a bomb exploding, fingers flying away and all the rest of it.

'You don't want any more hash?'

'No, man, of course I do. But if something happens, then you'll know it's your fault.'

'Nothing's going to happen.'

I beat my arms across my body to get the blood into my fingertips.

'So why did you betray that poor man to Colonel Harel?'

'What poor man?'

'That Herr Palestine Fritz. He was so nice to you.'

'Dr Hach was not nice to me. And I didn't betray him. They couldn't do anything to him.'

'You told them he had marital problems. And alcohol problems.'

'I only said that to make him seem a little more vulnerable.'

'What do you mean, vulnerable?'

'Easily damaged. Secret services like other secret services when they are as vulnerable as possible.'

'Am I vulnerable?'

'My dear Swami, the word was invented for you.'

'And you betrayed your brother, too.'

'It was a bit more complicated than that.'

'You bring dukkha on people. Everyone who meets you is marked by dukkha.'

'Could you leave off the dukkha-nonsense for a minute?'

'Would you have betrayed me, too, if it was useful to you?'

'Why are you so furious again? You're like this all the time, now.'

'So, would you?'

'You really should get up now, Basti. If Nurse Gerda catches us out here in the snow, we'll be for it.'

'You would, I know it!'

He doesn't get up. His thumbs flit across the tips of his fingers. They're red, but he seems not to feel it. A new brain dysfunction, perhaps. He could freeze to death and still feel warm, at least in his outer extremities.

'I thought you might at least be slightly pleased that I was doing everything in my power to support Israel against its enemies. Without me, there would have been no arms trade with Germany, you know.'

'I don't like talking about arms. Arms are dukkha, too. Everything that brings death is massive dukkha.'

I sit down beside him, despite the drifting cold, put my tongue out, catch the snowflakes and taste them. They don't taste of anything – either because of my bullet upstairs, or because snow has always tasted of nothing, just as windowpanes taste of nothing when you lick them, or Delft ceramics (you'd be amazed at all the things I've licked in the course of my life).

But now there is a numbness on my tongue as well, as if one were shaving off the papillae with a razor blade. I wonder why I place so much value on this feeble wretch – who was once cheerful and annoying and chattered away without pause, but now hums with sadness – why, then, I place so much value on him listening to me. *Well, because a little edification can't hurt him*, I answer myself at once.

And I say, 'Colonel Harel sent several Israeli agents to Cologne. And in autumn nineteen fifty-six, ten days before the Sinai War, the first delivery of aid arrived in Israel: American half-tracks.'

The Swami interrupts the flitting of his thumbs, takes a little snow in his hand and rubs it into his face.

'Later, the deliveries became more substantial. They included Noratlas and Dornier aircraft, Fouga Magister jets, helicopters and self-propelled gun mounts, ambulances, anti-aircraft guns and remote-controlled anti-tank guns. And of course, submarines.'

The Swami puts his hands over his ears, to which a little snow is still clinging.

'Oh man, I said I didn't like talking about arms!'

'But with the arms came peace. And you do like talking about peace.'

'So, you brought peace to Israel?'

I must tell you that, recently, I've observed something in the Swami that never came to light in the first moments of our acquaintance. Let's call it a self-encouraging hostility. He shovels a second load of snow onto his hand and rubs it into his face, but what he really wants to do is rub it into my face. And since that doesn't sit well with his religion and his temperament (or my own), he sublimates this impulse into words, and asks me, with that same scorn in his voice that he so detests in me, whether I brought peace to Israel.

Of course I brought peace to Israel.

Peace with Germany, at least.

14

Ev and I stayed in Israel.

No one called us back to Pullach: the BND was proud of me. The CIA profited from my knowledge. The KGB left me alone. And the Mossad grew fond of me.

I could invite Shimon Peres out for a lemon sorbet in one of my favourite cafés on the Tel Aviv seafront promenade, and quietly agree a deal on Uzi machine guns. Peres knew that the invitation came from the German secret service, and in this knowledge, he ate his lemon sorbet with such a shudder of ecstatic enjoyment that the ice rapidly melting between his Lauren Bacall red lips seemed a metaphor for every kind of political rapprochement.

The time was ripe for change.

The Soviet Union had started arming the Arab military, cheerfully driving forward the most radical of all changes for Israel, namely its obliteration.

Faced with this threat, Ben-Gurion had hatched a plot to replace Moshe Sharett as foreign minister.

And the Sinai War, which broke out in October nineteen fifty-six, did one more thing: notable Israelis now went out for ice cream with former SS collaborators like Jeremias Himmelreich, ex-Wehrmacht generals like Reinhard Gehlen, or former National Socialist agent-runners like Franz Josef Strauß. They needed these men to save them.

Although with Strauß, we had excellent cold duck.

Yes, I once had to pay that short-legged, neckless, barrel-shaped Bavarian *Bazi* a visit. Peres had asked me when the best time would be to ambush a senior German politician, privately and unannounced.

And that time, of course, is Christmas.

On the twenty-sixth of December nineteen fifty-seven, we set off from the airport in Paris in the smallest car it was possible to rent, along icy, foggy roads, towards Upper Bavaria.

During the fourteen-hour overnight drive, both the car's heater and Peres' sense of direction failed, the latter having been knocked off-kilter by a small avalanche shortly before we reached our destination (it was actually just a slab of snow from a roadside spruce crashing onto the windscreen).

A few drifting flakes that the Israelis called 'a snowstorm' welcomed us to Rott am Inn, the snowbound birthplace of the mysterious and wonderful Hans Georg Asam, a church painter whom Papa had greatly admired. Of course, I led the overtired Shimon Peres and his two Ashkenazi companions into Rott Abbey. I explained everything to them, and showed them the altar sculptures by Ignaz Günther – the pinnacle of German baroque statuary. We were still talking excitedly about them when we finally reached the entirely unguarded farmhouse where Dr Strauß lived. We had to throw pebbles at the window to see whether he was even at home and, if so, whether he was alone.

The door opened and the defence minister, whom we found wearing long underwear and an open Bavarian waistcoat (modest flowers on green velvet), was pleased at the unannounced visit. A half-naked young girl ran up the stairs behind him. Marianne was in her mid-twenties at that time, late twenties at most, and had not long been married to 'Franzeljott', as she called him tenderly. It was she who later served up the cold duck and fetched beer from the local brewery's taproom, a delicious foundation on which to conduct secret negotiations of a highly explosive nature.

One of the two Ashkenazis, by the way, was Haim Laskov, an Israeli Army general who had taken it upon himself to hunt and scalp Nazi criminals in the Rhineland when he was stationed there as a British officer after the war. He told Franzeljott this story while eating a radish – in Hebrew, thank God, which allowed me to talk about skinning rabbits as I translated for him.

Peres' other colleague was Asher Ben-Natan, a Viennese Jew. He was one of the cleverest, shrewdest men I have ever met, tall, blue-eyed and the spitting image of the actor Curd Jürgens. Next to Colonel Harel, he was Israel's most influential secret agent, and I had discussed every step of the German–Israeli arms trade with him in advance. He quickly got to the point, since he was the head of the purchasing commission for Peres' defence ministry.

'My dear Dr Strauß,' Ben-Natan said in honeyed tones, 'our country urgently needs long-range bombers, artillery, shells and a fleet of warships, and Herr Dürer' – in Germany, Mr Himmelreich was of course Herr Dürer and no one else – 'is of the opinion that we might simply ask you directly.'

'Oh, you can ask directly all right, you hoodlums, you. And while we're being direct: what's in it for me? That I would like to know.'

Strauß let out a booming laugh at his half-joke, but it did not last long.

For then Shimon Peres explained that there was no money, really none at all; we were reliant on donations, for which reason we were asking for donations of long-range bombers, donations of artillery and shells as well, and we would also be grateful for a free fleet of warships.

Now Strauß was truly perplexed.

Just a few days earlier, the Knesset had denounced him as the head of 'a Nazi army of brutish murderers', and now here he was in his underwear, at Christmas, being hounded by begging Jews who wanted him to give away arms to the Middle East from the scant supplies of the new Bundeswehr. They were asking him to go behind the backs of the West German government, without the knowledge of the Americans and against the principles he had sworn to uphold.

Not that Strauß took these principles too seriously – it was just that he would only consider relaxing them if there was a healthy self-interest involved, particularly a financial one, and the complete absence of such made his chewing jaws slacken for a moment.

The global impact was also outlined, the fact that Israel had to stand firm as a bastion of the blah-blah-blah West against the blah-blah nations Sovietized by the Warsaw Pact, so that the Near East was not lost to blah-blah communism. But why Strauß was therefore supposed to steal tanks and munitions from his own Bundeswehr depots, where the fatherland had only just put them – at great expense – to defend itself against a Soviet invasion, was something that Shimon Peres could not explain to him even with the most sugar-coated blah-blah-blah.

'You lads,' Strauß grumbled, starting to pluck at the silver buttons of his waistcoat. 'We've said already, we aren't going to play Father Christmas wi' your weapons. *Manus manum lavat*, right?'

And then he asked flatly what good such a foolish trade would do the German people, such a foolish trade.

A kind of silence fell beneath the tinsel-laden Christmas tree. The only sound was of the scalper Laskov picking raisins out of the stollen with a knife.

And so, after a while, I cleared my throat, gathered my courage and said, 'It could bring the German people peace with Israel, Herr Minister. Peace forevermore.'

Now, as a hippy, sitting there on your stupid bench in the snow, you may doubt that these words ever passed my lips, but I swear to you that they did. Strauß looked at me quite askance; his reptilian tongue flicked in and out several times, and he placed his fork down beside his plate and reclined in his chair, making the back struts creak.

'Well, well, well, our man in Tel Aviv, quite the arrogant bore, isn't he.'

Shimon Peres looked at me as well – appreciatively, so I thought – and my only great fear was that he, too, would refer to me as 'our man in Tel Aviv', which of course was perfectly accurate, but would also have thickened the plot of my life as a double-agent to a dangerous consistency.

Franz Josef Strauß wanted to consider our offer. And to aid his consideration, he sought advice from three bottles of beer, tipped a few fruit brandies down after them and settled his stomach with the cognac pralines we had brought him. Then he suggested a postprandial stroll.

And so Shimon Peres, his two loyal assistants and I trudged after the swaying hulk in his bear-fur coat, back to the very abbey we had visited earlier.

How it gladdened the minister's good Catholic heart that Shimon Peres was already familiar with the magnificent ceiling fresco, even recalling the name of the artist (Matthäus Günther, not to be confused with Ignaz Günther). Peres admired its apotheosis, famed as the *Rotter Himmelreich*, the Rott Heaven, using the exact words I had spoken just a few hours previously, not forgetting the camel that represented Asia in a piece of moulding to one side, which might be the stupidest of all animals, but was also the most Arabian.

'Looking at that, it does make you want to be a Christian,' Asher Ben-Natan murmured – one of the cleverest and shrewdest men I've ever met, as I have said.

Strauß heard this and was charmed. He showed the admiring Hebrews the sculpture of Empress Cunegonde as well, a rococo masterpiece with a wry smile on her face, her left hand gathering up her skirts as if for a wild dance. Strauß insisted on explaining the drama of the scene: Cunegonde had been accused of adultery, and as proof of her innocence had to walk across hot coals, which she did gladly and without sustaining any burns, showing everyone that 'she was no tickle-tail', as Strauß said in a pleasantly inebriated tone.

'Tickle-tail?' Asher Ben-Natan asked.

'Moll,' Strauß said.

'Fallen woman,' I suggested.

Seeing the likeness of a dancing saint who was accused of having illicit sexual intercourse and met the accusation with a grin, at the foot of an altar in a house of God (albeit one belonging to the unbelievers, which automatically placed inverted commas around the phrase 'house of God'), was something of a provocation to us iconoclastic Jews.

Franz Josef Strauß, however, didn't notice that; he folded the church-proofed art historian Shimon Peres in his arms, whereby he was really folding me and my modest knowledge in his arms, at least I felt enfolded.

At the end of our visit, he gave us, firstly, four small wooden figurines of Mary holding the baby Jesus from Ottobeuren, and secondly, devastating precision weapons worth three hundred million deutschmarks.

*

So yes, I do think I brought peace to Israel. In a complicated and impertinent way, perhaps, but peace in Israel is not possible in any other way. The Hippy is still sitting in his place. You could form two medium-sized snowballs from all the snow on his hat and his fur coat and his pyjama bottoms, which are slowly changing from flowery to unflowery with each additional flake that settles there. Shall I give an answer to his scornful question? Will my answer undermine the self-encouraging hostility? Is that even possible?

'Yes, I did bring peace to Israel.'

'Thank you,' the Hippy says, as if in a dream.

15

My five years in Tel Aviv were my five years with Ev.

They were five years in which our souls (let's just think of them as a cluster of mental concepts, I don't want to argue with you, my dear Swami) found their way from the mouth back to the source – though our bodies did not.

And yet we were playful. In those five years, we sometimes played with one another like children playing doctors. In a resigned way, admittedly. Just as a child is surprised and fascinated as they explore another person's firm young flesh and its elastic openings, so we were each surprised and fascinated by the other's scars and scabs and fat deposits. They appeared in new places or refused to fade from old places, though you might wish them to with all your heart – like the thin white line on Ev's abdomen, torn into it by Anna's birth.

In those five years, we let this story take its course. For five years, we inflicted nothing upon one another but breakfasting together every morning and going to the beach together in the evening. Ev always swam ahead of me and a little to one side, her frog-like body hopping south towards Jaffa, and eventually I would overtake her and dive down at her side. Old images rose from the waters, memories of how this body, thin and bluish when seen from the seabed, and gliding like a shoal of small, wrinkled fish, once ignited like gas while baby Anna slept beside us in a Moses basket, in Hub's Standartenführer bedroom. Ev's arms had been turned away and her eyes fixed on mine, forcing me to look into them as they sank into me, almost to the end, as we vanished in the smoke of future events, the fabulous events promised by an approaching orgasm, though they don't come to pass when you are as good as fifty.

All the same, we were not only unhappy.

We were also anxious.

Because day after day, we faced the sword that Dionysus once suspended above his protégé Damocles' chest from a single horse hair. The thin hair might break at any time. At any time, somewhere in the world, the sword might plunge into us. It might, for instance, take the form of a photo showing the young Jeremias Himmelreich with dandelion hair and a nose that was not mine. It seemed entirely possible that one of the Jews he had studied alongside in Dorpat or Berlin was still alive. The man could be living three streets away. We would never feel safe from discovery. Never.

But more unsettling for me than this dangling, dormant, wholly invisible threat, was a very visible one: Ev was changing. She was changing mentally, and her soul was changing, too, now that she had joined me in my melancholy profession – a profession that for so long she had seen as merely a weakness of character.

She had no talent whatever for conspiracy. But she did for subversion. She had possessed that even as a little girl, and sometimes her childish temperament still asserted itself. While she could steal and lie in the name of anarchy just as she always had, she could never do so professionally, not under any circumstances.

She was not prepared to leave misery in her wake. Above all, she was not prepared to spy on her colleagues at the hospital, our neighbours, the other people who lived in our building. She was not even prepared to admit 'spying' into her vocabulary. She didn't put any files together (though later, she would come to love files). She had never denounced anyone, and considered it wholly impossible that I could ever have done such a thing, either. Nor had I, I swore to her – for this truth would have caused our breakfasts and evening swims together to suffer, and I didn't want that.

In those five years with the Mossad, the only thing that Ev considered sensible and appropriate was to hunt for Nazi fugitives.

This was an elementary need of hers that had been slumbering for a long time; all Colonel Harel had to do was wake it.

She began her hunt under his supervision, transforming herself into the moon-bright Artemis and roaming the forests of the SS blood-lands with her bow and arrow. She took me, erroneously, for her twin brother Apollo, urging me to pick up the scent and find the hiding places of the escapees. Their tracks almost all led to Pullach, down into that Hades with its population of elusive shadows that I knew so well.

'But, unlike you,' said the goddess of the hunt, the moon, the forest, the protector of women, children and anxious painters, 'the escapees seem to think of the BND as the Elysian Fields, and not as Hades at all.'

There were no clear indications, but I believe Ev had Hub in her sights even then. Perhaps she was hoping that eager pursuit might allay the sorrow of the years. She started speaking to me (often despite my own discomfort) about the Unspeakable. Many of the escapees had crossed paths with him.

Ev's knack for taking everything personally, her longing for some new goal, and the natural need for a sunbeam to drive away the black clouds of loss (is not the desire for revenge the only sunbeam that will pierce through any storm that torments you?) – all of these were fed with furtive rage until they were full.

This rage, since it was furtive, was expressed more in patience than impatience, in the almost feverish intensity and calm with which she could spend whole days studying the mass murderers who had been in contact with our brother.

Take Klaus Barbie, for example: a man you won't have heard of, so let me tell you his story.

One day, Ev lugged a Leitz lever-arch file of documents from the Barbie investigation home with her (which was strictly forbidden: Leitz, a company built on the German mania for order, was not wel-come in Israel). Our bright apartment grew noticeably darker. We sat down on the sofa and Ev began to read aloud to me, one page after another. I took her hand in mine, an old-couple way of trying to pro-vide a little calm and comfort.

But there was no calm or comfort to be had.

Klaus Barbie's talents – this much you need to know – were based on the exercise of immediate urges. In his mind, the sound of breaking bones was like a great flock of songbirds in God's blue sky. Their twit-tering brought him not only satisfaction but also a certain reputation, which Ev found confirmed in her documents by a confiscated telegram from the Unspeakable (I squeezed her fingers, and she squeezed back).

In nineteen forty-three, as this telegram set out in black and white, my brother had applied to have Barbie transferred to the Gestapo in Riga, though the request was denied. Hub wanted to reinvigorate his authority's rather uninspired interrogation methods. And word had clearly got around various SS offices, even as far out as the Baltics, that Untersturmführer Barbie was literally fizzing with a creativity that he had cultivated in high-class France.

For example, he came up with the unusual idea of carrying out interrogations not in gloomy Gestapo cellars, but in a luxury suite at the Grand Hotel Terminus in Lyons, where a world of possibilities opened up: once you had taken down the chandeliers and suspended Catholic priests upside down from the sturdy ceiling hooks, you could surprise them with electric shocks. In the *salles de bains*, imprisoned children existed on nothing but tap water until they were half-starved. Naked women were strapped to the French bed, beaten senseless, raped and forced to have sex with German shepherd dogs, while at the same time, champagne could be ordered from room service.

Ev's fingers did nothing more as she read these words. They lay like lead in my hand. Ev took the lead back and moved a little way down the sofa. She wanted to begin her vulture-like circling around the Unspeakable with the greatest possible objectivity. She tried to take me back to the day when the telegram – Hub's telegram begging for Barbie – had been written. She wanted to know exactly what day it was, what time, what the weather had been like; she wanted to know every single word that Hub had let fall like ashes that day. She also asked if I could recall the details of his clothing (come on, he always wore uniform), and finally started questioning herself: might she have been caressing her husband, or cooking for him, or cursing him that day?

Then it occurred to us that little Anna had been born three weeks after the message was sent, and up to that point we had slept together in every spare minute we could find, probably including the day in question – cautiously, so as not to disturb the foetus.

As the only alternative to weeping, Ev went on reading to me about Barbie, who had worked on his subjects himself, using blowtorches, red-hot pokers, boiling water and a whole collection of whips, tools and clubs. Shortly before the US Army's 45th Infantry Division marched into Lyons, it was time to wash up (in the language of our organization), and he erased all traces of his work by having the majority of his Gestapo colleagues shot, last of all his French lover – and you may believe that death by firing squad is impossible, transcendent Swami, but it is still unpleasant to the human eye.

Without wishing to pass moral judgement, I simply said that Barbie's actions were circumspect, but Ev strongly disagreed. My words seemed inappropriate to her, though I was just pointing out the expertise that made someone like Klaus Barbie of interest first to Hub, and later to the CIA, and even later to the BND. If you want to be successful in our profession, you need to develop an eye for quality and leave aside your emotions, however regrettable that might be in individual cases.

I took Ev in my arms. At first she resisted, but then we lay intertwined for a long time. Twice we missed our swim, and once we missed breakfast.

It was only days later, when she was feeling better, that I told Ev Barbie was now serving as a lieutenant-colonel in the Bolivian security forces, under the name Klaus Altmann. He advised them on interrogation techniques and anti-guerrilla tactics, and was a guardian of the Org as well, like Hub was. Like I was.

That was the thing she didn't want to believe.

And perhaps you don't, either, my dear Swami.

But in nineteen sixty-six, Barbie was still sending the BND dozens of situation reports from La Paz. I know because I saw them myself. And last year he killed Monika Ertl, a left-wing German liberation revolutionary who had made a rather touching attempt to abduct him with the help of a long-haired French philosopher. An unbelievably silly thing to do. Really. Ertl was thrown out of a police vehicle, still alive, and then – as she was struggling to her feet – shot dead in the middle of a slum, right there on the street. But before that, Barbie himself had tortured her at the behest of the Bolivian interior ministry – at least, that was the rumour circulating in the corridors of the BND.

It was difficult to close in on this truly glittering star among the Orcs (he was reminiscent of genuine Uruk-hai Orcs, who famously are not weakened by daylight), although Ev virtually quaked with the longing to sit opposite him in an interrogation room (on the right side of the table, of course). At that time, this question-and-answer fantasy ruled her life. I have never been able to understand it, but that was what fired up her two-stroke engine for the next few years.

A knowledge engine, which requires two strokes for every step of its work.

Question. Answer.

Question. Answer.

Question. Answer.

Question. Answer.

And for fuel, she had all these Orcs, who had to overlap in some way with the Unspeakable before they could be poured into the tank. Do you see?

I'm talking about people like Alois Brunner, who also arrived on our sofa inside a Leitz file. He made Ev's engine rattle along very nicely indeed.

I was introduced to Herr Brunner once, in Pullach, in nineteen fifty-three. He came over for a situation meeting from the Ruhr Valley, where he ran one of the Org's regional branches. While he was in Camp Nikolaus, he dropped in on Hub, his direct superior, with whom he shared some SS connection or other, as I gathered from various allusions he made.

We had lunch together in the Org canteen. Brunner had a prominent underbite and bad teeth, on which something was left clinging after every mouthful, I could hardly bear to look. Despite his pinched features he seemed affable, almost good-natured, with a ribald, Viennese sense of humour. Over dessert he trilled out a drinking song: '"Anna was a governess and very good to me, with a little slap and tickle I was happy as could be. But I'm not so merry now, no, my Anna's up and gone, oh my Anna, oh my Anna, oh my Anna's up and gone."'

A year later, the cheerful *chansonnier* was sentenced to death by a French court. As Eichmann's deputy, he had killed an unknown number of people himself (though in a less imaginative way than Barbie), and sent one hundred and twenty-eight thousand five hundred Jews to the gas chambers.

The trial, however, took place in his absence, and his continued (not to say permanent) absence from Europe seemed to be a matter of some importance. At least, it did to Reinhard Gehlen.

Through the strings he was able to pull, the Doctor organized his gifted agent's escape to Syria, where Brunner became the Org's representative in Damascus, at around the same time I was posted to Tel Aviv. He also hired himself out to the Syrian secret service, and worked there as an 'adviser on Jewish matters'.

'And that means,' Ev said, 'that he is helping to prepare Syria's future attacks on Israel.'

'What makes you think that?'

'There are scarcely any Jews left to wipe out in Syria. There's no need for any advice in that department.'

'Please, my darling, don't let it get to you like this.'

But unfortunately, Ev did let it get to her, because that was her greatest talent: taking things that caused immense pain and thrusting them under her own skin.

When it began to cause severe subcutaneous infections (infected dreams, screaming in the night), she asked me to procure Herr Brunner's address for Colonel Harel.

On the one hand, this was a much easier task than it would have been in Barbie's case; Barbie was a Bolivian secret service officer and therefore protected by a large security apparatus. Brunner, meanwhile, was running a sauerkraut shop under a false name in old-town Damascus (thereby knocking me and my art-supplies shop off the top spot for most grotesque BND cover business).

On the other hand, such a valiant denunciation brought great danger with it. Brunner was under the personal protection of Reinhard Gehlen, and the boss would set all the Orcs in the universe on me if he ever discovered that I had dared betray one of his outpost heads to the Mossad.

Ev and I spent a month discussing the pros and cons of giving Brunner to the Israelis. And if you were to imagine that Ev put forward her views soberly and sensibly, you would be wrong. Some of her arguments were cups and plates that shattered to my left and right on the kitchen wall. There was shouting and crying. She was driven by a moral indignation that stood in marked contrast to my own, of which there was no sign, since my primary concern was for our survival.

One day, Isser Harel called us into his office and showed us a photograph of an armchair-like monstrosity built out of metal pipes, steel plates and various hinges. Alois Brunner was standing beside it looking very dapper and cheerful, with a holiday complexion, linking arms with two Syrian officers. The officers were smiling at a major, who was sprawling in the uncomfortable armchair and giving a Hitler salute.

This was the *al-Kursi al-Almani*, the German chair.

'That's what the Syrians are calling it,' Harel explained. 'It's one of their newest instruments of torture.'

But really the contraption should have been called the *al-Kursi al-Brunneri*. It was Herr Brunner who had come up with the Brunner chair.

It was constructed from three adjustable metal plates, a back piece made of steel springs, a star-shaped foot and all manner of flexible structures. By means of a turning mechanism, you could deconstruct the body of a prisoner who was strapped to this device according to all the rules of art. It might take hours before the victim's spine snapped.

Two weeks later, Ev threw her arms around my neck in gratitude when I slipped Brunner's address into her pocket. I can't recall her ever being so childishly and purely happy about imminent excesses before. Her smile, her soft breath, her erratic joy all seemed to have a significance to me. She flew off on bat wings, with a dog's head, like the Furies.

The Mossad did not dilly-dally too long; they sent my BND colleague a parcel wrapped in gift paper and smelling of *Lebkuchen* from a Viennese address. Vienna was sorry to have lost Alois Brunner, who had once cleansed it of its Jews, and one might safely have assumed that the parcel had been sent in a spirit of guileless goodwill.

Had he opened it in a small room with solid stone walls, there would certainly have been no more Austrian drinking songs ringing out over the souks of Damascus. Unfortunately, however, he went up to his terrace, which had a view over the roofs of the old town all the way to the station, and the bomb did not meet enough resistance to exercise its full, vibrating passion. Unwrapping the gift paper, Herr Brunner therefore lost his left cheek and one inquisitive, *Lebkuchen*-desiring eye.

But that was all.

I believe that from that moment on, the moment that turned theory into an empty eye socket, Ev fully realized herself – a version of herself that emerged from a chrysalis fed by pain and anger. Perhaps that was what she'd meant when she spoke of wanting to 'birth' herself in Israel.

She now no longer shied away from compiling a dossier on Hub, and with that, her aversion to files began to crumble.

She found and showed me some translated witness statements made before a Soviet court, which described Standartenführer Solm as 'cool, energetic, intent on killing'.

She got hold of the telegram from his office requesting two new gas vans for Riga, 'including ten exhaust hoses, as the ones we have are no longer airtight'. Signed by 'Staf Solm'.

One evening, I caught her at her tiny desk putting together a statement of her own, line by line, which she titled: 'My experience with Standartenführer Hubert Solm at the Posen goods yard on the twenty-fourth of February nineteen forty-one (babies frozen to death)'.

Through all of this, she neither stopped swimming in the sea nor breakfasting on our balcony, and she went on playing with me in our resigned way, too, as we lay side by side in the evening, skin to skin, the window open because of the heat.

But her thoughts were with the dead, or those she wanted dead.

In the great chain of causes and effects, no person's role may be considered in isolation, not even Ev's. She did not enter into it on her own initiative; first and foremost, it was Colonel Harel who did all he could to encourage my sister, and she was quickly promoted to become his trusted expert on Nazi fugitives. That was also partly down to her predecessor having suffered a nervous breakdown, when no salary could be paid to her for seven months. In those days, the Mossad was truly not what one imagines it to be today, Basti.

For the time being, Ev had to house her rapidly growing archive in the crumbling basement of the lion's-head villa, in a pillared hall with an empty marble pool. Everyone called it 'the harem' because the joins in the walls still exuded the pleasant fragrance of decades-old massage oils. There, Ev's files took on the soporific scent of lavender, until she finally began to smell of it herself, when she came home at night and fell into bed.

She lugged the damned Leitz files around with her wherever she could, for inspiration. She looked things up in the newly opened Yad Vashem archives. She corresponded with young historians in Germany and the USA. The zeal lacquered her cheeks, she slept badly and gabbled the names of mass murderers as she dozed, counting them like sheep.

In the sea, she began to swim front crawl. She had taught herself the stroke overnight, a stroke that to this day I consider unwomanly and too fast for any flipperless mammal. She became a torpedo in red Trevira, which very soon shot away from me.

Eventually, she even gave up her hospital job in order to devote herself fully to venery. And of course, to her prey.

Although the luminaries of the medical faculty promised her a glittering future among their ranks, she was intent on squandering her perspicacity and focus, her efficiency, and all that you call *living in light and love*, Swami, on this deadly sticking-plaster.

The more information Colonel Harel asked Ev to compile, the more documents his informants in Eastern Europe's captured archives fed him, the more witness statements from survivors found their way to her and the more I shared my knowledge of BND staff, the clearer her impression became that the Org was little more than a giant sewage treatment plant for Himmler's SS cesspool.

'The way I see it,' Ev told the colonel, summing up everything she had discovered in a single sentence, 'we need to start taking much more radical measures than we have so far.'

Honestly, had this statement not been made in Yiddish, it might easily have been something uttered by Standartenführer Hubert Solm; even the determined tone of voice was much like his.

In alarm, I attempted to qualify Ev's dangerous fixation on the Orcs. But my words did not reach Agent Himmelreich; they were dispersed by her Artemis gaze, which stretched far into the future, into a world that would be fairly bursting with justice, swept clean of all evil with her diligent aid. She wanted to treat the BND in the same way she used to treat infections, viruses, cancerous ulcers.

She was on a mission.

'Give me some names, Ev,' Isser Harel muttered crossly. 'Some BND names.'

And Ev gave him some names.

Oh yes, she gave him some names.

16

Walther Rauff, for instance, former chief developer of Heydrich's gas-van fleet, surely a name that rang plenty of bells, at least in the ears of the Mossad.

In nineteen forty-two, Rauff had been the head of the SS's North

African unit, tasked with helping General Rommel to invade Palestine, raze Tel Aviv to the ground and kill all the Jews who had settled there. People like Colonel Harel were at the top of his list.

No wonder Isser had a lively interest in Rauff's current status as the BND's man in Chile, where he drew a service pension of two thousand deutschmarks a month. Once I had learned where he lived, he too received a Mossad gift box at Ev's suggestion. He didn't open it, though: unlike Alois Brunner, he was not a lover of sweet things.

The BND also held its protective employer's hand over BND names such as Otto von Bolschwing (Eichmann's adjutant, under whose leadership the Jews of Bucharest were killed), the Gestapo officer Hans Sommer (who had arranged the orderly demolition of the Paris synagogues), and Otto Barnewald, ex-head of administration for the Mauthausen, Neuengamme and Buchenwald concentration camps, with whom I had played the odd game of table tennis in Pullach. He had a remarkable serve.

BND name Hans Becher, a member of the Viennese Gestapo's Jewish department who was responsible for numerous deportations and some very thorough house searches (he liked to shoot into wardrobe doors before opening them), was dispatched to Egypt by Gehlen as an instructor for army and police units.

BND name Ernst Biberstein had been the head of the luminous SS-Einsatzkommando Six in Kiev, which ensured that the Ukraine was untroubled by Jews. The former pastor was sentenced to death at the Einsatzgruppe trial in Nuremberg, but managed to skip out of the hangman's clutches and straight into the arms of Reinhard Gehlen, who gave him a living as an informant.

The BND also managed to recruit a staff officer from Auschwitz, in the shape of Sturmbannführer Ludwig Böhne (Ev had a vague memory of him from her time as a camp doctor there, a fat little man with a Kaiser Wilhelm handlebar moustache).

BND name Hartmann Lauterbacher, meanwhile, had been deputy to the Reich youth leader Baldur von Schirach. In Pullach, he would show his wedding photograph to anyone who wanted to see it, with Joseph Goebbels standing beside him as his witness. Lauterbacher had been the Gauleiter in Lower Saxony during the war, and gave his name to the spectacular 'Lauterbacher Campaign' (the ghettoization of all the Jews who were still alive into 'Jewish houses', where they did not remain alive for much longer). Shortly before the capitulation, he threatened to execute any of his beloved Lower Saxons who absconded like cowards when faced with the enemy advance – though he himself was then the first to abscond, post-haste, along with one point seven eight million cigarettes he was heroically protecting.

In the late nineteen fifties, Lauterbacher was head of the BND's outposts in North Africa, first in Cairo and then in Tunis, meaning that he actually became my nearest colleague. I met with him covertly several times due to our physical proximity, in a first-class restaurant on the Nile for example, where we discussed this and that over kofta and kushari.

Herr Lauterbacher was someone else to whom Ev was keen to send a little surprise gift, but that would have led back to me (BND name Himmelreich).

In company such as this, the Unspeakable seemed like a relative light-weight, though Ev did discover his involvement in the Bikernieki Forest exhumation. Over those weeks that I had spent first sending Politov off to Moscow and then awaiting my execution in Riga's Gestapo jail, Hub had been in charge of pulling tens of thousands of partially decomposed bodies out of the ground. Soldiers dug them up, layered the bones and scraps of flesh on giant duckboards, covered them in petrol, oil and tar and burned them over several days, after which the carbonized human remains were pounded into earth, black crumbs in which our brother intended to plant birch saplings, but there was no time for that.

'No,' Ev summarized, 'there is no shortage of BND names. BND names flower along every wayside. I see no reason for us not to pull them up, root and branch. Your policy of picking the odd one here and there is no longer sufficient, Isser.'

Her tone was cool and blasé as she spoke to Colonel Harel, who rocked back and forth in his armchair like someone with a behavioural disorder, his lips pressed into a thin line. The three of us were sitting in his office in Jaffa. He had hung the lion's head on the wall behind his desk there, two-eyed now, the old white pebble with a pupil painted on it in the left socket, and in the right a brand-new glass marble, which stared down at me.

'Yes, you're right,' Harel eventually grunted.

Beside me, Ev gave a sigh of relief – of bliss, almost.

I know that sound so well. It was heard beneath the Christmas tree (the first time Ev was not given a doll, but tin soldiers painted by Papa, like her brothers), or on the telephone, when she loved my voice after the devastating air raids on Berlin. This exhalation that spoke of a worry suddenly allayed was such a curious response to Harel telling Ev she was right. Was she right that letter bombs cause too little damage? Was she right to declare open season on her big brother? Could she be right to wish the very worst on him? Was she a better person than he was for starting to do what he had once done? To dispatch? Liquidate? Eliminate? Pull up, root and branch?

Those were words that had suddenly begun to play a role in her life.

Not that I mean to raise myself above them; I, too, was using this vocabulary to drag myself forward, hand over hand. But believing oneself to be in the right at all times was something I had previously only associated with Hub. Ev was growing more like him in some ways. He had always felt himself to be a good person, and now she did, too, in the black, existentialist executioner outfit that I had zipped up at the back for her that morning.

'Jeremias!' Colonel Harel's stern voice shook me out of my fruitless thoughts. I hated people calling me Jeremias.

'Isser?' I said obediently, though I hated his real first name even more than my own false one.

'You will blow him up.'

'Sorry, who?'

'Reinhard Gehlen.'

A cardiac-arrest silence descended from the lion's jaws, flowing like cold air from its mouth. Where had he roared his last, I wondered. He was said to have been the last of his kind in Asia Minor, *Panthera leo persica*, killed by Bedouins in the Syrian desert; funny, the Latin that comes back to you at these moments.

'You want me to blow up the head of the BND?'

'It's the only solution.'

'General Gehlen is my boss.'

'I'm your boss.'

'I can't blow General Gehlen up.'

'But, darling, why not?'

'Please, Ev: stay out of this.'

Colonel Harel got up and walked over to the little balcony door. He looked out at the city that had been snatched from the Arabs, and if I had drawn his face, it would have been that of Laocoön, a sigh sculpted in white marble, astonishing the way that Isser could link emotions to principles in a fraction of a second.

'A former Wehrmacht general, who reported directly to Hitler, and is now appointing all these Nazis to the West German secret service?' he said, still facing the balcony. 'No, it just won't do. He's a constant threat to Israel.'

'How?'

'Take a look at your wife's collection of files!'

'I'm familiar with my wife's collection of files. They only became my wife's collection of files with my help.'

He turned back, Laocoön's pain still in his eyes, but now mingled with a very different determination to be rid of the snakes that were strangling and biting him.

'How does that man come up with such an insane idea, Jeremias? How can he install former SS people as his representatives in Egypt, Tunisia, Syria, Lebanon – all our neighbouring states? Is he working towards the final solution?'

'He installed me, as well, don't forget.'

'Yes, and honestly I'm amazed you weren't an SS man, too. That would be about right for Gehlen, planting a cuckoo's egg in my nest.'

'I believe,' Ev said hastily, 'that my husband has reservations on humanitarian grounds.'

'Humanitarian grounds?' Isser asked me, with a look of surprise. 'I thought you detested Gehlen?'

'Naturally I detest him. But . . . but all the arms deals are going through him. And those arms deals are bringing our two countries closer. You can't just blow up one of West Germany's most senior representatives. It's like blowing up the defence minister while he's giving you submarines!'

'Let me worry about that. I'll talk to Ben-Gurion.'

Ev smoothed her executioner dress and said ostentatiously, 'We need to light a beacon, to make it clear to the world once and for all that there is no safe haven for Nazis, wherever they might hope to find it.'

'That isn't lighting a beacon, it's self-immolation,' I scoffed.

'Isser,' Ev said, turning to the colonel, and I hated her patronizing nobility. 'You shouldn't give this mission to Jeremias. He's an artistic type.'

How could she call me Jeremias? How could she do that to me?

'An artistic type, am I?'

'Don't get upset. I understand your reservations.'

'An artistic type? I'm an assassin type!'

'Darling . . .'

'And I don't give a fig who I blow up. I would just like to be certain we aren't giving in to a paranoia that's going to end in people writhing in their own shit and blood.'

'We work for the Mossad, Jeremias,' Isser said gently. 'Of course we're paranoid. But just because we're paranoid, it doesn't mean no one is after us.'

With this old joke (which was certainly no *tav* joke), he turned back from the window, walked over and grasped me by my upper arms as if they were the handles of a mighty amphora filled with worry and reluctance.

'You're the only person who has Gehlen's trust, Jeremias. The only one who knows his house and is permitted to enter it. The only one who can get hold of explosives easily. BND explosives, even. You could probably dispatch him with his own supplies.'

He let go of the amphora and gave it a pat.

'Believe me, there are many things in your life that you might have done differently, and better. But what you will do now is far and away the greatest thing that dynamite can achieve.'

17

No one ever contemplated disobeying orders from Isser Harel. Though saying that, I have met few people who exuded less natural authority than he did. His wardrobe was legendary. He rarely wore anything but crumpled, sand-coloured cotton shorts, his one pair of sandals, and strangely patterned socks in colours you couldn't buy anywhere. He was incapable of knotting a tie. It was repeatedly explained to him – I, too, taught him a Windsor knot on several occasions – but he would always immediately forget the crucial first loop. Eventually, and for many years, he took to carrying a ready-tied tie around with him.

Originally dark green, with a greasy patina, it would be pulled over his head like a hangman's noose when necessary and tightened around his neck in front of all kinds of witnesses. He would then stroll with comfortable pride into any state banquets he was forced to attend; in marked contrast to Reinhard Gehlen, Harel hated banquets.

Gehlen also liked good German cuisine (roast venison! cordon bleu!), but did not spurn outstanding Italian food, or even better, French. In Pullach, meals were always served to him and his circle of high priests by junior agents in livery. Harel's lunch breaks, meanwhile, were spent entirely alone, in the most ordinary taxi-drivers' bars in Jaffa. He would survive for months at a time on nothing but the cucumber and yoghurt salad he loved so much, and English custard.

He refused to be driven around by a chauffeur, and always got behind the wheel himself, wherever he was going. He was a terrible driver, frantic and self-righteous, but for reasons of cover he always drove himself, with his chauffeur Yossi riding in the back. He believed this arrangement would greatly reduce the efficacy of any assassination attempt – at least for him, though of course not for Yossi. He had discovered this trick in an Agatha Christie novel. 'When you learn from Miss Marple, you learn how to win,' he often said.

Unfortunately, he didn't learn any English from her.

His Hebrew, too, was grotesque. He almost always spoke Yiddish, in the light, sing-song accent of the Latvian Jews.

We had discovered some time previously that he and his family came from Dünaburg. He was convinced that he must therefore somehow be related to Ev: in his opinion, all of Dünaburg's Jews were related.

The Mossad seemed to be staffed by no more than a handful of condescending layabouts; it was always in financial trouble, and was headed by a vexing gnome with no discernible leadership qualities (barring his most conspicuous quality, a choleric impatience, which doesn't get you anywhere on its own). I have always wondered, then, how this motley crew managed to become an efficient, intimidating and eminently useful intelligence service, and the exact opposite of the Org to boot. It may well have been because Isser Harel was prepared to think the unthinkable. Because his keen mind was no weaker than his will. And because personal preference, including the preference for morality (or, as he said dismissively, whatever morality one prefers), had no place in his work.

And for that reason, he also took the mission to kill Reinhard Gehlen completely seriously.

Naturally, my dear Swami, this was not the way for me to bring peace to Israel.

I was disturbed by Ev's level of dedication to this affair. By dedication, I mean a zeal that causes you to put all thoughts of yourself aside, a shedding of the self that I had never seen in Ev before; she had always been much too self-involved for that. Too convinced that she was a golden trophy in the game of life. From the outset, she had brought into our house something too infectious, too light, too funny ever to be fully extinguished.

She often felt dizzy, especially in Tel Aviv's hotter months, when she had to sit in the shade, though she no longer made a fuss about it. All her hypochondriac tendencies had drained away; you might say, all her entertaining tendencies.

I wondered why she had volunteered herself for this.

She was determined to have a hand in the planning of Project Gehlen, which was named Operation Thanatos. To work with me. Why? I asked her one morning. Why are you doing this?

She peeled a boiled egg in silence, murmured something about support and a testing time, and stuffed the egg into her mouth. But that wasn't an answer. That was distance. Having breakfast together in the morning and swimming together in the evening didn't help us to avoid the distance that comes with all marriage-like relationships – and is, in fact, inherent in their rituals.

Reluctantly, I started to think about Operation Thanatos.

I began by drawing from memory (and under protest) the floor plan of Gehlen's Starnberger See villa, and finding suitable places to plant bombs in 1) the pantry and 2) the basement boiler room. Calculating the blast radius, I considered various detonation plans, the brilliant result of which seemed acceptable for many a hateful thing (the tea evenings with the Silesian BND aristocracy, for instance, or the Labrador), but absolutely had to be revised for others (the slow daughters, or Frau Herta, who believed she was related to me).

Ultimately, the expected collateral damage brought us to a dead end. I scrapped the dynamite idea, and Ev and I considered whether a classic abduction might not be the best option for General Gehlen.

Ev was adamant that the Doctor should be brought up before a court, a plan that the unfortunate Otto John had already failed to carry out. When I confronted Ev with this fact, she was sitting at the table in our tiny kitchen, spreading some cheese onto bread for a change (we now only really spoke to one another at the breakfast table). She just wanted to see that piece of filth hang in front of everyone. At least, that's what she growled.

'But look, darling,' I began tentatively, and then for a while said nothing more. I had suddenly realized that, in all this time, we'd spoken very little about the hanging that was the ultimate aim of everything we were doing.

'What's troubling you?' she asked.

'Are you sure you want to go through with all this?'

'Of course I'm sure.'

'Ben-Gurion will never consent to it. You know that as well as I do.'

'We'll see.'

'But Gehlen has never done anything to the Jews. There are several denazification certificates for him. He even championed the reparations payments to Israel. And without him, you would never have come here.'

'*You* would never have come here without him.'

'And in return, I'm the one arranging for him to get a bag over his head and a rope around his neck?'

She turned to face me and put down the bread and cheese she had just bitten into. Her two small, overtired eyes caught me in a pincer grip.

'What are you getting at?'

'I think you're very hard, Ev.'

'I'm hard?'

'You've become ruthless since you started working for Harel.'

'And why does that bother you?'

'I don't know. Do you *have* to try and kill all these people?'

'What do you mean by people? Nazis?'

'Yes.'

'Very funny. And who gets hold of the addresses to send the gift parcels to?'

'It's what I have to do to ensure our survival. I don't like doing it.'

'You don't like doing it?'

'No.'

'I do. I like it.'

'You're changing, Ev.'

'They're bastards.'

'People like Gehlen are half-bastards, at most.'

She slapped the flat of her hand on the table, leapt up and thrust a forefinger at me (her right one). It extended towards me like a small sword. She wanted to say something, too, because otherwise such gestures make no sense, but whatever thought lay behind it, it had no time to ripen, and she laughed it away with a scornful snort. The forefinger-sword vanished and both arms were folded across her chest. Then she took a deep breath to calm herself down, paced back and forth for a while and finally stopped in the doorway, where she frowned at me as if baffled by something – perhaps by living with this mouse of a man, who was sitting at her kitchen table and staring at her bread and cheese.

'What's the sermon in aid of, Koja? Can you tell me that?' she barked at me. 'You're the one who encouraged me to start being active. I'm doing something meaningful again for the first time since Anna's death.'

'You were doing something far more meaningful as a doctor.'

'That was only half-hearted.'

'A person waking from a coma doesn't give a damn if his life has been saved half-heartedly.'

'Where is this conversation going?'

'I don't know. But we don't really have conversations any more – we negotiate, at best. We work together, and to be quite honest, I don't think that's a positive development.'

'Did you and Hub work together like this, too?'

'Like what?'

'The way we do.'

'You mean, talking about people who have to die?'

'That's not what I said.'

'It's what you meant.'

'Stop it.'

'I wouldn't be surprised if you'd started a dossier on me, too.'

'Don't talk nonsense.'

'Hauptsturmführer Solm! Born Riga, ninth of November nineteen-nine! Criminal charges as follows!'

'Now I know where this conversation is going. It's one of these conversations where what is said and what is meant have nothing to do with one another!'

'Do I feature in your files or not?'

'There are no charges against you! Not the slightest thing!'

'That's a yes, then.'

She sagged helplessly against the doorframe. 'Why are you asking me all this?'

'Because I'm one of those halves as well.'

She threw me a look devoid of all certainties.

'A half-bastard.'

It took a little time. But then her scepticism crumbled and made way for a thin smile, which sent small, concentric ripples across her face like a pebble thrown into water, until they reached her eyes, which grew very wide and bright.

'But, my love. That's completely different.' She pushed off from the doorframe with her shoulder and sat back down with me, putting her hand against my cheek, a gentle, warm hand divested of its punishing forefinger.

'You are Jeremias Himmelreich,' she said softly. 'You aren't Konstantin Solm any longer. And Konstantin Solm fought against the Nazis, even though he had to wear their uniform. He never killed anyone.'

That wasn't entirely true, but it was impossible to correct the error now, and so I just said, 'Exactly like Gehlen.'

'And Konstantin Solm never really harmed anyone, either.'

I saw the forest again in my mind's eye, the sunlight filtering through the branches.

'Did he?'

The tread of those unspeaking people.

'Koja? Is there anything you need to tell me?'

The screaming, and then the shots, and the baby lying next to the woman, that baby.

'Koja?'

'No. It's just that I don't understand how you can be so merciless. If you were consistent about it, you would have to show me no mercy, either, for passing myself off as a Jew. You would even have to be merciless with yourself, for leading a false life. You can send as many idiots to the gallows as you like, you're still leading a false life.'

'Thank God.'

'Thank God?'

'Thank God there isn't anything you need to tell me.'

She brushed something off my face – a lock of hair, perhaps, that had been there in childhood. Then she kissed me, with a sad, slow, lavish, deceptive tenderness that I was powerless to resist, and I almost testified to the picture that was hanging so clearly on the wall of my memory, painted in guilt, shame and fear, none of the colours that Ev knew as mine. Just then, if she had whispered that I could tell her anything, anything, even what was most terrible, because in her mind I was a human in the purest sense of the word and I had no need to wear a mask with her, then I would have shown her that picture. I felt choked, but she closed my mouth with hers, until I pulled away so that I wouldn't vomit between her teeth, and I heard her whisper how truthful I was, and then of course I couldn't say it.

After many weeks of concentrated preparation, Shimon Peres' very real veto slammed down into all the confusion, and was then backed by the prevaricating Ben-Gurion.

They both thought that assassinating one of West Germany's most important representatives – a representative of the state that was secretly donating arms to them, week after week, via the export harbour in Marseilles – was unlikely to have an exclusively positive outcome. To say nothing of violating international law. You know, the kind of thing politicians always say when it suits them.

Still, certain worries were lifted from my shoulders. Operational planning had never been a great strength of mine, in any case, and so I was relieved on that account, too.

Colonel Harel, on the other hand, whirled around his office like a Dervish, running his hands over his bald head, yanking the shirt out of his short trousers, even sinking his teeth into it (one of the reasons his shirts were always crumpled) and shouting over and over, '*A shande! A shande! A shande,*' his voice cracking.

'So then, you schemer,' he yelled down the telephone line, at the other end of which Shimon Peres was being deafened. 'So then, I'm supposed to just let these criminals get off scot-free, am I?'

The great, volcanic beacon that the colonel had hoped to light by getting the Doctor blown up or hung did not materialize.

The equally disappointed Ev proposed Hans Josef Maria Globke as an ersatz delinquent. He was Adenauer's poppet and the chancellery's chief of staff. Under the Nazis, he'd been an adviser at the ministry of the interior, where, as head of the office for Jewish affairs, he was responsible for the 'J' stamped in people's passports. It was also his ingenious idea to change any Jewish forenames that sounded too German, and replace them with 'Israel' or 'Sarah'. And he extended the concept of racial defilement so far that 'mutual masturbation' between an Aryan and a Jew became punishable by death – that same careful and yet luxurious act of love with which Ev and I liked to touch one another deeply on balmy Mediterranean winter evenings.

Colonel Harel, however, did not react well to the Globke proposal. He snarled at my wife, who was so unpractised in contrition, saying that she might as well have suggested assassinating Khrushchev. All of Ev's other proposals shattered on impact, too, hitting either his indignation at the insufficient prominence of her selected candidates, or an absence of address. The latter was the case with Martin Bormann, who had been Adolf Hitler's Hans Globke and was now thought to be on a hacienda in Mexico, associating with free-range chickens, though that was incorrect.

It was I who quietly reminded the raging Mossad boss that my own head of department, the precise Palestine Fritz, still had Adolf Eichmann's address in his desk drawer. Not that I hadn't mentioned it previously, of course, but no one had ever believed me. It is incomprehensible even to me that I didn't think of him sooner – perhaps because Eichmann, along with the famous Auschwitz doctor Josef Mengele (whom Ev didn't know; she had left the concentration camp before he began his work there) was the only fugitive to whom the Org had not paid the slightest attention.

Discovering that the BND had known for years where and under what name we might find the highest Final Solutioner, the lowest of all humans, the most corrosive prussic acid, sent Isser into a screaming rage that was impressive even for a choleric of his calibre.

He telephoned Shimon Peres on the spot and asked at the top of his hoarse, wheezing voice whether they could look again at the option of liquidating Reinhard Gehlen. The swine had withheld the ARCH ENEMY's address from the Jewish people, and when he said ARCH ENEMY, he meant ARCH ENEMY, Obersturmbannführer Karl Adolf ARCH ENEMY, head of the ARCH ENEMY department at the Reich Main Security Office in Berlin.

Peres reasoned with the colonel, expressed elements of purest sympathy, and finally suggested prioritizing the liquidation of Mr Eichmann far above the liquidation of Mr Gehlen, if only to avoid upsetting Defence Minister Strauß and his arms provision.

And so one thing eventually led to another.

It took me a whole year and two autumn visits to Pullach to tease the relevant information about the well-hidden Hebraist out of Palestine Fritz, taking a friendly approach (a little cunning, a little guile).

The way this story ended can hardly have passed you by, my peripatetic Swami. In his memoirs, Colonel Harel, the old fox, attributed that tip-off about Eichmann to a German state prosecutor – a clever move, a useful half-truth, especially as the prosecutor in question is long since deceased.

On the twenty-second of May nineteen sixty, the El Al plane with Adolf Eichmann aboard, disguised as a co-pilot and in the custody of a more than chipper special commando, touched down at Lod Airport. Ev and I collected our boss straight from the runway. And goodness me, he was in a good mood! Isser had led and carried out the capture in Buenos Aires himself, as befitted his temperament, taking with him a suitcase the size of a school satchel.

He chauffeured us off to see the prime minister, to whom news of the successful coup still had to be proudly announced.

From the anteroom, I could see Ben-Gurion's famous Einstein hair through the gap in the door; it seemed to be waggling in satisfaction. He was dignity incarnate as he offered me a sip from his champagne glass, once Isser had revealed my role in this drama to him.

In honour of the occasion, the prime minister saw us all out in person, and outside his official residence he was more than a little surprised to see his mighty *Memuneh* get behind the wheel of a Fiat to drive his two Yekke colleagues home – something which almost ended badly. On Bograshov Street a bus cut in front of us, and our brakes were not the best (particularly as Isser did not like to use them).

We continued the celebration with him for a little while in our apartment. But what kind of celebration can you have with someone who considers alcohol, cigarettes and anything sweet to be fripperies and distractions. He admired all our daughter's pictures on the wall, and later that evening I drew a caricature of him, or so he thought, though really it was a true-to-life depiction of his extraordinary visage.

But perhaps I was also a little out of practice.

In the five years since we arrived in Tel Aviv, I had barely drawn or painted anything. I had created a few pictures of heads split open or burning inside, with many eyes and mouths, but no ordinary landscapes or portraits.

The following day, Tel Aviv was a seething cauldron. Pedestrians ran shouting through the streets, the transport system broke down, and the whole country's telephone network collapsed. People clustered around transistor radios in bars and radio shops, and in the Knesset an ancient rabbi toppled off the benches when his wizened heart gave out at the news of Eichmann's capture. Car horns were deployed everywhere, and all the ships in the harbour sounded their foghorns as if celebrating King David's wedding. But it was just a beast who had been caught, a beast who not so long ago had queued with Ev at the baker's in Posen and, being a gentleman of the old Viennese school, let her go in front of him.

Five months later, Isser Harel called me and told me I was a piece of filth, a disappointing, ungrateful piece of filth, and that a catastrophe was about to unfold in Germany.

But I already knew that, because I was the one who had caused it.

18

It had begun when Ev and I arrived at the port of Jaffa, on the sixth of January nineteen fifty-six: the beginning of the end of the *herem*.

A few weeks later, it might have been the thirtieth of January nineteen fifty-six, the firm *Nein* to the use of the German language fell apart. The Yekkes were allowed to chatter in their own language again to their hearts' content. The general ban on performances by German musicians, actors and dancers remained in place. But exceptions could be granted. And the universities had permission to reintroduce technical literature in German, particularly if it related to the building of nuclear reactors, which would prove useful in future.

On the twenty-sixth of March nineteen fifty-seven, the first German VIP was officially permitted to fly into Israel – albeit only in a private capacity. And while Erich Ollenhauer, a candidate for West German chancellor, was not allowed to make a great song and dance, he was able to give a public speech – tolerated in silence and with little applause, but public all the same – about the beauty of social democracy (the Israeli rather than the German kind; it was the Israeli social democrats who had invited him).

On the fifteenth of September nineteen fifty-seven, Willi Daume, the head of the German Sports Federation, travelled to Tel Aviv, neglecting to mention the Nazi Party membership he had long since forgotten about. The first official representative of West Germany to visit, he started the wonderful tradition of atonement donations while he was there. In his case, it was a large number of bluish we're-very-sorry jerseys made by Adidas.

In this earliest stage of administrative rapprochement between the two countries, the 'fresh, free, fit and fair' image of sport led to members of the Bundestag being allowed to seep into Israel disguised as sports functionaries. A fat and severely rheumatic representative of the FDP, for instance, came as a table-tennis fan, bringing an appropriate donation for the Israeli association (fifteen thousand table-tennis balls, which were subsequently tipped into the sea by an angry Holocaust survivor – causing a poetic, if only brief and slight, raising of the swell).

On the first of December nineteen fifty-seven, the Weizmann Institute invited the Munich Max Planck Institute to Israel. Since institutes cannot travel, academics came, first and foremost nuclear physicists.

What they donated, nobody knows.

And the next noteworthy donation, arranged by Franz Josef Strauß in the wake of our very merry Christmas visit in nineteen fifty-seven, is to this day known only to a small circle of delighted defence experts.

On the first of January nineteen sixty, the ban on importing German cars finally became passé, when sales of Hitler's strength-through-joy car were (somewhat incredibly) permitted via Israel's first VW dealership. It sold in fabulous numbers (Volkswagen's donations must have brought tears to their recipients' eyes).

On the fourteenth of March nineteen sixty, David Ben-Gurion and Konrad Adenauer met at the Waldorf Astoria Hotel in New York, and discussed atonement donations of all kinds over glasses of advocaat, though these donations were referred to as trade agreements and personal cooperation.

By the first of September that year, the mollusc-like rapprochement of the two nations had picked up such a pace that the man very nearly condemned to death by Isser Harel, almost blown up by me and hanged by Ev, former general Reinhard Gehlen, also sensed the urgent need for German–Israeli friendship – a deeply shocking and worrying matter, of course.

My phone was ringing off the hook with calls from Pullach in search of good Jewish friends, and I decided that the essentially unbefriendable Mossad boss was not the first person I should inform about these enquiries. That was one of the greatest mistakes I have ever made.

A little while later, I was summoned to the Israeli defence ministry. In his office, Shimon Peres literally had his hands over his ears as Colonel Harel stood a metre away from him, yelling incessantly. It was a good few minutes before Isser was so exhausted that he had to knock back half a litre of water to prevent himself from dehydrating in the heat. Peres took advantage of these short, loud gulps to outline the benefits of the intelligence cooperation that Germany was offering.

'The BND,' he said, his outstretched arms indicating the size of Germany's pockets, 'are prepared to share all their information on the Middle East with us. They're offering to train our agents and help us to infiltrate Egypt.'

'I was sending agents into Egypt when the BND was still called the Gestapo.'

'The BND is not the Gestapo; the CIA is very closely involved in—'

'I know what the BND is, damn you! The BND is sitting just there, double-crossing me!'

He merely jutted his lower jaw in my direction, not wanting to dignify the ungrateful piece of filth with too much attention.

'My dear Isser. My friend. Mr Himmelreich is your most loyal agent – he's proved that. But he also works for the goyim. What is he supposed to do when they want to put out feelers here? You yourself know that you aren't the right man for that.'

'I'm the head of all the Israeli institutes, and when the head of an enemy institute approaches one of our institutes, then he should approach the damned head of it, and not some soft touch like you.'

'You didn't want to come when we went to see Strauß. You would never seek to make contact with Gehlen.'

'I would if I had enough plastic explosives with me.'

'You were quite right to come to me, Jeremias,' Peres said, turning to me politely. 'But until now, your people have been wishing luck to the Arabs. I'm not entirely clear on what lies behind this offer.'

'All I've been told to tell you,' I replied, 'is that Operation Blue Tit brings with it a broad package of aid.'

'Operation Blue Tit?'

'Mr Gehlen would like to fill you in on the details in person.'

Peres thought for a moment, closing one eye for the purpose. After a while he opened it again and his gaze, now padded with patience, rebounded off Colonel Harel.

'Listen to me, Isser, my friend: despite your reservations, I do think we should send a delegation (*kleyne delegatsye*) to Pullach.'

'You're welcome to send one, if you don't have so much as a spark of self-regard left in you.'

'With you at its head, of course.'

'Are you meshuga?'

'You're the head of all the institutes. And when the head of an enemy institute approaches one of our institutes, it should be the damned head—'

'You can French-kiss my arse, Shimon Peres! A director of defence can't tell me what to do! I'm going to Ben-Gurion!'

'I've already been to Ben-Gurion.'

This news did not please Colonel Harel one bit.

'You're so stuck up,' he hissed. 'Just because your grandfather was a rabbi? My grandfather was a rabbi, too.'

'Let's not argue over who was the better rabbi.'

'Do you think yours was the only family they killed?' Isser's hands flew from his sides like coiled springs being released. 'My uncles! My aunts! All dead! All blown away by *his* brother-in-law!'

He pointed at me, and while Peres did a good job of concealing his surprise, behind my eyeballs little ice crystals climbed up my optic nerve and cooled my retina, which fogged over like a windowpane. Apart from some wild arm-waving, I could see very little.

'My uncle Moshe! His brother-in-law killed my uncle Moshe!'

'Isser, I—'

'My dear uncle Moshe!' the colonel went on, cutting him off. 'His brother-in-law killed my dear uncle, Moshe Jacobsohn! And now he's in charge of the Pullach canteen, where your delegation is going to sit and have a cosy chat with a Nazi general we should be executing – you schmuck!'

My sensitive Swami. If someone had told me just a day earlier that I would ever come across Moshe Jacobsohn again, or rather his name, his memory, his contours solidifying before my mind's eye, the image of him searching through the birth register for Ev's name back in Dünaburg, the skullcap on his head; Moshe Jacobsohn inviting me back to his house for gefilte fish, stepping up to the edge of the pit in front of me as Stahlecker stared at him in amazement – 'You know me, Herr Youth Leader, please, my dear Herr Youth Leader, you remember me, don't you? Meyer and Murmelstein? You remember the names? Please, please no, Herr Youth Leader, please, please, ahh!' – if someone had told me this just a day earlier, I would have swum far out to sea, further than ever before, and sunk off the coast of Cyprus.

Instead, I now learned that Isser Harel not only came from Latvia just like me, and not only from Dünaburg just like Ev; his name was not just Harel but Halperin like his rabbinical grandfather on his father's side, while his non-rabbinical grandfather on his mother's side had been a Levin, and the largest vinegar magnate in St Petersburg.

And just as Opapabaron Schilling liked to pour wine for the Tsar when they played bridge together, Harel's grandfather Levin liked to pour vinegar for him: a small but charming thing we had in common. What will have tickled the Tsar's palate more, I wonder? I couldn't even give myself an answer to that; all I could do was submit to the biography of Isser Harel that was raining down on me. He had emigrated from Riga to Palestine with a pistol baked into a loaf of bread. I heard a lot of other strange things as well, as many as one can gasp out in the space of three minutes before one is defeated again by thirst and exhaustion.

Peres had not moved all this time, but he can listen very well when people start shouting. And when Harel sat down, panting, in the armchair in front of him, Peres asked him if he trusted me or not, that was the only crucial question.

'I don't trust anyone with a tongue in his mouth. But that piece of filth did give us the ARCH ENEMY. And he gave us Mrs Himmelreich.'

Peres gave a statesmanlike nod.

'Then put together a delegation with him, Isser, my friend, my dear man. As my grandfather always said: the man who can bend his knee can crawl forwards.'

'Crawling was all that little *rebbe* had?'

Remarkably, Peres did not get up, did not walk around his desk, did not stop in front of Harel and slap him. He simply stayed where he was, drew the back of his hand over his beautifully shaved chin in a well-rehearsed movement, and when he had finished, said, 'The man who has manners can tolerate rudeness.' Then he paused for exactly the length of time that made it seem not like a pause but like a new thought freshly plucked from the tree of knowledge, and added, 'I expect that was something your grandfather always said, the great *rebbe.*'

He was a very interesting man even then, that Mr Peres.

Ev ducked my questions when I spoke to her about it.

'Why do you do that,' I asked. 'Why do you tell the colonel everything about the Unspeakable? Why do you have to tell him he's in charge of the canteen?'

'It's all in the files,' Ev whispered.

It was the softness with which she said it that emptied the blood from my heart.

'Oh yes? And do the files also say he has a brother? And that the brother is hiding in Israel? And that he's created a Jewish identity for himself and will be convicted of high treason if anyone finds out? Is that all in the files, too?'

'I'm sorry,' she said. We were standing, stupefied, facing one another in our apartment, she with her back to the open balcony door, looking almost as though she was trying to stop me from running out and hurling myself over the balustrade.

'What if some photograph or other turns up, one with my head above a well-fitting SS uniform?'

'But you got rid of all those yourself.'

'There might be prints I didn't catch – how would I know? And now I'm going back to Pullach as a Jew. Do you know what that means?'

'Yes.'

'You have no idea!'

'You won't be able to be honest.'

'Honest? No. We can never be honest again. You can kiss goodbye to that once and for all.'

'You mustn't be afraid in Pullach. That's important.'

'I won't be afraid in Pullach. If I run into the Unspeakable there and he gives me a Judas kiss, or if someone else lets slip who I am, then my cover will be blown and I'll just stay in Germany. But you, Ev.'

'What?'

'You're here in Israel. They'll hang you.'

'Nonsense.'

'They'll hang you as a spy.'

She slid her hands around mine, as if warming a half-frozen bird.

'You will play this as cleverly as you always do. Credibly, and cleverly.'

'We can't be honest. You have to get that into your head. I want you to say you'll never be honest again!'

'Fine.'

She said nothing more, just turned round and pulled my hand to bring me close against her back, so that I could no longer see her face. I could not see her fearful smile, either, only the sweat on the back of her neck, and beyond it the open balcony. I was standing so close that I could see the hairs on her neck moving when I breathed.

'In the end, you're going to find me,' I said softly. 'I mean, that's your job here. Don't you realize that? You'll find me for Harel, in some file or other.'

'Stop it, Koja.'

'It can't go on like this forever. One day, something bad is going to happen.'

'Everything will be fine. I know it.'

In the final days before I flew out, she stopped speaking. No more breakfasts. No evening swims. No talking. Our bodies stopped moving like flesh and blood. She packed my suitcase. She gave me my kiss. She even drove me to Lod Airport, in silence, wearing the red dress dappled with white in which I had painted her twice, a long time ago. It gave her strength once I had disappeared through the check-in area.

I drag the long side of the black charcoal stick (it often breaks into small pieces, but I always carry it with me, even when I have to go for an X-ray) diagonally across the sheet of paper, shading the Hippy's dark zones. They are growing ever larger and deeper.

His face is falling in. His eyes are slipping back into their sockets as if being sucked into his skull by a vacuum. He has to lean on me as we shuffle to our new meeting place, the green bench in the main corridor. The hospital grounds shimmer like a crevasse in an ancient glacier and are just as inaccessible to us, and even in the corridor, with his hunched back leaning against the glass wall, he mostly just sits and breathes while I draw him in my sketchbook.

For a beginner, a dying man who offers himself up to the artist in endless repose, like a silent, dozing reptile, is seemingly easy to draw. But I would prefer a lively sparrow, or a capuchin monkey hopping from branch to branch. Perhaps the animals would listen more closely than the plant-like Hippy, too.

He doesn't listen.

He is driving me quite mad with his listlessness and his lethargy.

They need to treat it, quickly.

He needs an operation as soon as possible.

And I'll pay for the whole thing, if there are any problems with his health insurance.

I just want him to listen.

Is that too much to ask?

His sole interest lies in my portrait drawings, because they show him how his inner state is manifested in his appearance. His creeping demise is also changing his personality, of course, and I explain to him that portraits are not so much about similarity (because similarity is never perfect, the word itself tells you that), but about character. Hundreds of visitors come to the Galleria Doria Pamphilj in Rome every day, for instance, to admire portraits like Velázquez's painting of Pope Innocent X. But they don't do it for the similarity: no one is interested in that any longer, because no one is interested in Pope Innocent X any longer. The man himself is merely dust and a skull inside a marble coffin. What they are admiring is the *character* you can see in his former appearance, the eternal quality that at the same time is just one moment captured in oils. That is what constitutes its artistic value.

And I am attempting to characterize the Hippy in my sketchbook, in the very same way.

'But I don't look like a pope,' Basti whispers wearily, looking with disappointment at the likeness I am handing to him.

'You're a swami.'

'I don't look like a swami, either.'

'I draw what I see.'

'You see leftovers.'

'You are what you are right now.'

'I look like a figure of fun.'

'In everything we see there lies a caricature that we must recognize. As the great Ingres once said.'

The Hippy has never heard of the great Ingres, but he doesn't care.

'A painter,' I say, carrying on regardless, 'must have a good sense for a person's features, and discover the caricature in them.'

'I look like something out of *Asterix*.'

'You don't like the characterology aspect. You don't like my penetrating your mind.'

'You're not penetrating my mind.'

'You just don't notice my doing it. It doesn't hurt, after all.'

'You're not penetrating my mind. I'm penetrating yours – well, I thought I was. But I'm not penetrating your mind, either.'

'Because you aren't listening to me.'

'Hey, can I draw you?'

'I'm sorry?'

'Give me the paper? The sketchbook? I want to draw you.'

'You can't draw just like that. It's like thinking you can play the piano just like that.'

'Yeah, well, you're not exactly a piece by Beethoven or something.'

So now the Hippy is learning to draw. He always draws my face (he is drawing conclusions, as he says), in much the same way that little Anna did when she was five years old. One eye, two eyes, mouth and nose, that's the way the fuckface goes – the Hippy murmurs that sometimes.

Perhaps he thinks I can't hear him. Perhaps he's just very immersed in what he's doing.

It isn't as though he has no imagination.

Not at all.

His first portrait of me, for instance, had bars all around my head, and the Swami told me it was a birdcage.

Another time, he slashes my face with a razor blade, but then stiches it back together with safety pins pushed through my skin (he takes the real safety pins that Night Nurse Gerda has used to fasten the bandage around his head, and sticks them through the paper).

Then he puts my whole body in a ballgown, but with a hole where my penis is (he draws my circumcised Jewish penis) and embellishes me with a Hitler moustache.

I am also wrapped in a bloodstained nightshirt with the help of my red wax crayon. He has a bedside table dancing on my head, a cloud of butterflies rising from its open drawer. He particularly enjoys drawing winged death's heads.

I let the Hippy have his fun, listen to the eager scratching of his pencils (my pencils) on the paper, and go on with my story, because it's only when he's drawing that the exhausted Hippy can still concentrate on words.

'People who draw are often happy,' Papa always used to say. 'They spend so much time seeing.'

20

It was freezing, as if it must always be freezing when I come back to Germany, and it was even snowing, but only in those small pellets that the ice-cold wind uses to blind you. In Latvia, the snow had been called *sniegs*, we always said *sals un sniegs*, ice and snow, as if snow would never live alone, and *sals un sniegs* look most magnificent in the kind of bright, colourless noon light we had that day. They glittered to the left and right of the road ahead.

We were driving towards the large main entrance. It was barely recognizable.

The old wooden barracks had been torn down and replaced with a sturdy little brick guard house, slightly reminiscent of the entrance situation at the Buchenwald concentration camp. Yossi muttered as much – he'd had two years to study every architectonic detail there.

We waited with the engine running, staring at the new building. Modern bullet-proof glass windowpanes had been set into the corners. Behind the greenish glass, you could see some little cacti, a pot plant and two lizards, looking out at the snow just as we were.

Two guards came out. They weren't GIs any longer, but men wearing German police uniforms without any insignia. The words 'Bavarian Regional Office for Fruit and Soil' or something similar were embroidered on their sleeves. A cursory glance into the car (Yossi was trembling beside me), then the guards stood to attention.

The brand-new sheet-iron roller door squeaked open, and the two vehicles glided along the freshly tarmacked service road into what had once been Camp Nikolaus, past electric fences and sections of wall that were not mine.

The guard dogs barked, and the powerful Yossi couldn't stop shaking.

Colonel Harel pulled up outside the Doctor's villa and switched the engine off.

It was only the weather that had prevented him from arriving at this meeting in khaki shorts.

He reached across to the glove compartment, pulled out his unique, ready-tied green tie and went to put it on, but was so nervous that he accidently pulled out the ten-year-old permanent knot. I heard a muttered curse. He stared angrily at me in the rear-view mirror, as if this were once again the fault of Jeremias Himmelreich, who was still in a state of disgrace. He fiddled with the piece of fabric for a minute. Then he ceased caring about anything.

He slung the tie around his neck like a dead snake, got out of the car and tramped through the snow and wind in his much-too-large, open coat, towards a group of waiting men.

I recognized Reinhard Gehlen from some distance away. As ever, he was wearing a trilby and sunglasses, from which the windblown snow-flakes ricocheted like tiny, silvery metal filings. A black beaver-fur coat and dark leather gloves gave him the look of a cardinal. Flanking him in padded trench coats, ramrod straight and sheep-brained, Herr Sang-kehl and Palestine Fritz stood staring at us. Heinz Felfe was waiting off to one side, slightly hunched, but I only recognized him at the last minute.

There was no sign of a one-armed man.

Just before Isser Harel reached Gehlen, the latter took two paces forward, walked past him, pulled off both gloves and reached for the hand of our driver Yossi, who was still in shock. Perhaps because of his impressive stature, but quite certainly because he had been sitting in the back of our car, Gehlen had taken him for the head of the Mossad (one couldn't have taken him for the driver, since he wasn't driving).

'*Neyn, neyn, neyn, neyn, neyn*,' said Yossi, batting Gehlen's hand away. As he did so, Gehlen's gloves flew off and landed in the snow, where they looked like rather accusatory amputated hands.

The Doctor was more confused than angered, but I could see all kinds of things playing out behind the sunglasses. That was a good start, I thought, and Gehlen said, 'The pleasure is all mine!'

After that, there was a silence that allowed me to swiftly clear up the misunderstanding, by picking up the gloves and discreetly drawing Gehlen's attention to the short man standing a little to one side. He was in the act of throwing his green tie to the ground, and had been entirely ignored until that moment.

'Forgive me,' Gehlen said rather uncertainly, looking down at the gnome, who was nearly thirty centimetres shorter than he was, badly shaved, badly dressed and bad-tempered. His tie was so warm and drenched with sweat that the snow was melting around it.

'You are the one who?'

'*Vos zogt der goy in zayn mame-loshn?*' Colonel Harel asked me through gritted teeth.

'He wants to know if you're the leader of our delegation, Colonel.'

'*Ikh veys nit tsi dos iz klor: ikh red nor in mayn mame-loshn.*'

'What's he saying, Dürer?' Gehlen asked.

'He would like to communicate with you in his mother tongue.'

'Oh,' Gehlen said, looking concerned. '*I speak not English very good.*'

I explained to my official boss that my unofficial boss hadn't been speaking English at all, but Yiddish, since he wasn't an Englishman but a Jew.

That came as a surprise to Gehlen in one way, he said, but in another it didn't, for in the sounds he had heard, he recognized the word-roots that were common to both of those Germanic languages. Yes, well, I don't know if you can describe Yiddish as a Germanic language, at least not for the next two hours, I replied cautiously. I offered to translate for him, but, quite moved by his unifying linguistic epiphany, Herr Gehlen simply held out his hand to Colonel Harel.

And whether you believe it or not, dumbfounded Swami: Colonel Harel swung his arm back and smacked the BND president's hand just as hard as Yossi had (at least nothing happened to the gloves this time, which were firmly held in the Doctor's left hand and merely quivered a little).

Well, my speechless friend, it is not as though General Gehlen were subjected to this kind of assault every day, and certainly not a surprising sequence of them. But he managed to look as though he were.

He didn't seem put out in the slightest and, without any expression of immediate pain, went on standing and smiling in front of his guest, displaying all the outward signs of patient respect. The other guests and hosts stood around him, all waiting with the same level of interest to see what would happen next. And in fact, after a little while the Mossad boss raised his eyes to heaven; his childhood in Latvia had taught him all about the calming effect of *sals un sniegs*, and once a few flakes of snow had perished on the skin of his face, he offered the ritual of concord himself, extending his arm with a sigh and saying:

'*A hant vos me ken zi nit ophakn, darf men fest drikn.*'

'A hand you cannot hack off,' I translated after a moment's hesitation, 'you must shake heartily.'

'Of course, of course,' a bemused Gehlen replied, allowing his hand to be shaken heartily.

'*An arabish vertl.*'

'An Arab saying.'

'I understand, Dürer. Very good. My name is Schneider, by the way.'

'Schneider?' Isser asked, surprised. '*Nisht* Gehlen?'

'I'm known here as Dr Schneider.'

'*Dos heyst mit andere verter, az der goy zogt mir nor zayn indiander nomen?*' Isser asked me.

Don't worry, I hastened to assure him, all the names are false at the Org, always, your whole life long. People feel better when their true identities are protected or, let's say, when this rigmarole allows them to pretend their true identities are protected, even when the whole thing is patently ridiculous. No one would take it amiss if he introduced himself with an alias as well, I added – and so, having picked up the green tie and stuffed it into his coat pocket, Colonel Harel called himself Shalom and Israel (first and second name) for the rest of the visit.

Dr Schneider insisted on giving Shalom Israel and the other important guests a personal tour of his compound, which the winter seemed to have transformed into an icy grave.

Despite the increasingly heavy snowfall, we toured the large BND site in our hats and scarves, followed by a non-hibernating squirrel. The place bore very little resemblance to that homely Camp Nikolaus where Möllenhauer, my brother and I, and all the other Orcs had settled years before. The last tenants had long since moved out of Goethe's summer houses. Girl stenographers now typed up surveillance reports in our former bedrooms and living rooms. The agents' kindergarten, the agents' primary school and the agents' dairy shop were all gone, and the agent-daughter's swing I had once built for Anna had been ripped out to make room for new barracks, which now linked the older buildings to one another.

They were constructing new offices on the far side of Heilmannstraße, the road that cut the BND compound down the middle. The skeletons of modern buildings were already shooting up. I could see snow-covered construction sites everywhere I looked. Not even my old brick wall encircling the whole compound remained untouched; it had been gradually replaced with cheap exposed concrete (and ugly formwork joints).

The last remaining relic of the early days was the right of every agent to have a dog and keep it with them, meaning that on our tour we encountered a lot of dachshunds, terriers, cocker spaniels, schnauzers and even a German spaniel, being walked by their masters on the snow-covered grass. They left their droppings there, and 'Loki', 'Cutie' or 'Hexy' sometimes received vocal praise for it, much to the astonishment of the Israeli secret service.

Eventually we reached the Doctor's well-heated villa, which Martin Bormann had panelled with German oak and Semitic tropical timbers.

We took off our coats and contemplated Bormann's marble bathroom (now Dr Schneider's quiet room) and Bormann's bedroom (now Dr Schneider's office). We talked about Bormann's taste in art (bronze statues, rightly called Aphrodite and Galatea, out in the garden where snow was accumulating on their heads and breasts) and, most importantly, Bormann's current whereabouts, which the Doctor suspected to be Moscow, while Shalom Israel's money was on Tierra del Fuego.

When we had warmed up, we entered the ground-floor conference room, the far wall of which I managed to divest of its portrait of Admiral Canaris just in time.

The guests took their seats on the right-hand side of the conference table – the lively side, in some respects. In addition to Colonel Harel and Yossi, whose mountains of muscle had now ceased quaking, the Israeli delegation was made up of Shlomo Cohen and Champagne-Lotz.

Shlomo Cohen was a spindle-thin man who had once been a successful painter. He had the vague eyes of a morphine addict, and came from a family of Hamburg rabbis who had mostly been gassed. He never removed the Gauloise from his sticky lower lip. He represented Mossad's Paris outpost, and was responsible for terrorist attacks of all kinds in Central Europe.

Champagne-Lotz, a Haganah war hero – blond, blue-eyed, elegant, extroverted to the point of ridiculousness and proud of his intact foreskin – had been brought along as Harel's best Kidon agent. His mother had been a Jewish actress and his father a Westphalian impresario, from whom he'd learned all the Münsterland-dialect folk songs he'd tortured us with on the journey here.

I took a seat opposite this very Fauvist-looking delegation, whose dress was variously bad, slovenly, existential, and reminiscent of Prince Rainier of Monaco (Champagne-Lotz).

On my side of the table – the left-hand, boring side – were the Doctor, his adjutant Sangkehl, Palestine Fritz, and the head of the Soviet desk, Heinz Felfe, alongside four morose Germans all wearing the same glasses and the same grey cotton suits. Outwardly, the only link between the two delegations was the enormous ears displayed by both their leaders.

'I would like to welcome you very warmly to our home,' the Doctor said, finally beginning the official part of the programme, though I don't believe he should have said 'our home', because there were too many traces of chipped-off swastikas still visible above the doorways. 'The security of your thriving nation is very close to our government's heart, particularly that of Dr Strauß, who expressly asked me to pass on his best regards.'

The four Israelis received these regards in silence.

'As you may know, the deliveries discussed with your defence ministry will be taken care—'

'*Vos iz di* Operation Blue Tit?' Colonel Harel interrupted him. The lively side of the table raised their heads inquisitively.

'The colonel would like to know,' I translated, to horrified looks from the boring side of the table, 'exactly what Operation Blue Tit is all about.'

The Doctor put his right hand, which still bore delicate, fading traces of the punishment he'd received by way of greeting, to his mouth, so that no one would be able to read the expression of extreme disapproval on his lips. With the exception of Adolf Hitler, I suspect no one had dared interrupt him in the last two decades, or slap his hand. And the fact that he had now permitted both of these things to happen was an exceptional form of hospitality. That hospitality also resonated in his words as he explained, with a kindly sideways glance at me, how delighted he would be if our two countries could extend their commonality to the area of intelligence-gathering, bringing a close and trusting collaboration to beautiful fruition. This endeavour was what Operation Blue Tit was about – and then, believe it or not, he whistled a little birdsong melody (the boring side of the table doubled over with laughter; the lively side was merely baffled).

In the space of three minutes, the enchanting Doctor then offered the Israelis support in all areas. In the training of their agents, their military procurement, the financing of joint operations, and the acquiring of intelligence on all their neighbouring Arab states. Two more minutes, and the infiltration of the Egyptian secret service (which the Org had reorganized at President Nasser's request) was added to his offer. Another two, and he even proposed giving them copies of the daily briefings that the BND provided to the West German chancellor, the government's most highly classified document. And less than a quarter of an hour had passed before Colonel Harel was offered assistance and a completely free rein to conduct his secret-service activities in Germany.

'What secret-service activities are you talking about?' I said, translating Isser's mistrustful, lurking question.

'I think you know what I mean.'

A cloud of cluelessness hung over the lively side of the table.

'I'm sure you will have heard,' the Doctor explained patiently, 'that in recent times a series of German rocket scientists have been recruited by the Egyptian secret service?'

'Oh, that.'

'These professors are busy developing a missile programme in Egypt. A similar missile programme to that developed under Adolf Hitler.'

Colonel Harel gave a dismissive wave of his hand, as if to say so what, and glanced at the clock.

'The technology for the chemical and biological warheads comes from Baden-Württemberg,' Gehlen explained.

'We've heard about that.'

'So the Israeli cities that are earmarked to be wiped out first, as soon as the development is complete, won't have escaped your notice either?'

A strange joy bubbled up inside me as I realized that the BND had grasped the full extent of the threat posed to Israel by General Nasser's multi-billion-dollar missile programme. And no wonder: I had provided no shortage of hints, warnings and alerts. I also saw Colonel Harel nodding contentedly to himself, as he leant forward and presented a facade of heightened disinterest.

'With your help, our colleague here,' he said, indicating Champagne-Lotz, 'could be deployed in Cairo to take care of the problem. He speaks fluent German, French, English, Arabic, Yiddish and Hebrew.'

'Speaking six languages is very impressive, but it isn't going to prevent any missile attacks,' Gehlen replied brightly. 'Here is a list of all the people involved in the Egyptian research.'

For the first time that day, the Doctor flashed his famous alligator smile. Then he slid a document across the table which, on account of its bonbon colour, would soon come to be known by everyone as 'the pink list'.

'These are current addresses, are they?' the colonel asked in astonishment as he scanned the names.

'You can check for yourself how current they are.'

The only sound was Harel's forefinger moving down the list. The snowstorm outside the window made the room appear more silent still.

'You are aware, are you not,' the Mossad chief asked after a short pause, tapping his forefinger gently against his lips, 'that we must use every means at our disposal to prevent these people from completing their work?'

'The blue tit is a bird that can fly a long way,' the Doctor smiled.

'You know what I mean by "every means at our disposal"?'

'I don't believe I want to know the meaning of that phrase.'

Isser Harel took off his glasses, put them down on the table in front of him and washed his face with air, rubbing vigorously, raising his eyebrows and groaning. Then he lowered his hands again and they grasped the rolled-up green tie, tied it in a knot and threw it into the ashtray.

Finally, he said, 'Just to avoid any misunderstanding, Dr Schneider: you are offering to let us eliminate your own countrymen, on your own territory?'

'I am working on the assumption that you will be just as accommodating to us.'

'Believe me, I have seldom been so eager to know what someone will say next.'

The Doctor got up and stood behind his chair for gravitas, forcing the boring side of the table to crane their necks in a show of respect.

The lively side of the table just gave him a lively stare.

The Doctor said, 'The decisive confrontation with the Soviet Union is approaching. I can sense it. The will to attack everything that makes our lives worth living is currently tensing its muscles behind that wall, in preparation for a mighty leap.'

Everyone's eyes followed his finger as he pointed at the wood panelling, behind which was nothing but a lavatory, where someone was just then pulling the chain.

'Lenin set fire to your grandfather's vinegar factory, I hear?' the Doctor asked.

'That's right,' said Harel. 'But that was just the vinegar factory. It was some other gentlemen entirely who set fire to my grandfather himself.'

'Anyway,' the Doctor stammered, taken aback and a little confused, 'I can only imagine the energy with which you are now combating the global menace of communism.'

'You want to work against the Soviets with us, is that it?' the colonel asked impatiently.

The Doctor sat back down. He seemed glad of the chair, which lent him some stability.

'I hear,' he said, clearing his throat, 'that you have a very good information network in the East.'

'Well, yes, there is some potential there.'

'Would you let us have a share in it?'

All the life went out of the lively side of the table. It stopped breathing at a stroke, so it seemed to me. Shlomo's unlit cigarette hung like drool from his mouth. Champagne-Lotz straightened his gentleman-jockey frame. Yossi stole a glance at Colonel Harel. Harel, meanwhile, contemplated his German counterpart as you might contemplate a dewdrop that has formed in a curled leaf, which you hold in your hands and could obliterate between your fingers at any moment.

'You are asking me, in all seriousness,' Harel said warily, 'if you can take over our network in the Soviet Union?'

'Participate would be a more accurate word.'

Harel looked back at the pink list, read one of the names out loud (Professor Kleinwächter), shook his head and said, 'I've heard a lot of strange things in my life, Doctor. But never has another nation's secret service – and certainly not such an unusual nation as your own – asked us to provide them with our exclusive intelligence from the Soviet Union. Particularly as you are the country with the largest network of spies both there and in East Germany. What do you want with the few additional things we are able to tell you?'

The Doctor looked like he wanted to wind his neck in and slope off. But all he did was recline in his chair, pinched, almost defiant, his arms folded across his chest, saying nothing.

Sangkehl cleared his throat, leaned forward and said, 'We have our reasons for proposing close cooperation in this area.'

'And we do not.'

'That's regrettable,' Sangkehl sighed. 'Then we can't do anything about the weapons of mass destruction that our rocket scientists are wasting their talent on in Egypt.'

'We'll see about that.'

'There's nothing to see,' the Doctor chimed in. His tone had become more brusque and he was sounding like himself again. 'The political establishment is not going to come down on your side. That's completely out of the question. I know this from Dr Strauß himself.'

Isser's voice grew rough as a flame-thrower; he sounded like a man who was losing his patience.

'Can you explain just one thing to me, Doctor?' this voice hissed. 'You've toured us around a compound larger than the Pentagon in Washington. You have two thousand employees spying on the Warsaw Pact countries. You're the CIA's most important source of information. You have hundreds of informants on the other side of the Iron Curtain, endless resources at your disposal, and you can even afford every one of your agents the luxury of allowing his dog to crap in the most beautiful secret-service base in the Western world. And yet you want all of my modest institute's information, without offering us your own in return?'

From outside, there came the sound of a pneumatic drill. The most beautiful secret-service base in the Western world was in the process of becoming even more beautiful, and no one in the room said a word.

Finally, the Doctor clicked his tongue in disapproval. He was breathing heavily and seemed to be struggling with some internal dilemma. Then he unknotted his arms and whispered, 'We can't offer you our own.'

'Why not?' Harel asked, taken aback.

'We have a mole.'

Now both the no-longer-lively lively side of the table, and the suddenly lively boring side grew restless, although for different reasons.

But no one in the room experienced such an inner earthquake as KGB Agent Four-Four-Three, whose forgotten catacombs (he had not been active for a long time) collapsed into rubble. As I scrambled out of the ruins of my old self, abandoned since Comrade Nikitin's death, I still couldn't imagine that after all this time someone could have found the last little mole claw that might be left of me.

'What kind of mole?' I therefore asked, with seismological interest, although of course I should have waited for Isser to put the question himself.

The Doctor gave Heinz Felfe a nod, and he in turn appeared to wink at me. It almost triggered a second internal earthquake.

'For two years now, we've had scarcely any insight into the GDR's centre of political decision-making,' Felfe said, looking at me, before turning to Colonel Harel. 'The Stasi has obliterated almost all our information lines into East Berlin. And we have even fewer options for gathering intelligence in the Soviet Union. Most channels have collapsed, and many of our sources have been taken out of commission by the KGB. The mole is probably in my department. Eastern Europe. At the most senior level.'

An embarrassed silence filled the room.

'Herr Friesen is beyond all doubt,' the Doctor declared – because in the BND universe, Felfe's name was Friesen. 'And the same goes for everyone else in this room. But we've been infiltrated just below the top ranks.'

That was where the Doctor was mistaken.

For the underground, burrowing life of a mole (you might have followed this in the press, my well-read Swami), was one that Herr 'beyond all doubt' Friesen, alias Felfe, had cultivated to perfection. It was not just his face but his whole silky-soft appearance that was showing early signs of metamorphosis into his heraldic animal. There was his solitary existence, of course, and those six dioptres of visual impairment that were advantageous to his burrowing nature. Funny that for so long I had taken him for a cat – but then, he could probably assume any form. And that was how the head of counter-espionage for West Germany had managed to spend five years searching for himself.

Not that it has any bearing here, Basti, but according to a Yank memorandum published recently on the damage Felfe caused, this mole-cat betrayed more than a hundred CIA and BND agents, of whom at least thirty-four were executed. He also exposed ninety-four of the BND's informants, spread right across the world. He sent three hundred Minox microfilms containing fifteen thousand six hundred and sixty confidential photos to Moscow, which almost destroyed the BND. But the most impressive thing was that, at this fateful conference a year before he was unearthed, this industrious mole-cat mewed to Colonel Harel, 'We're already quite sure of this traitorous swine's identity.'

He even smiled at me after uttering these words, the mole-cat swine, and since neither Comrade Nikitin nor General Pertia had ever prepared me for this smile, my hands trembled so violently that I had to stick them into my trouser pockets.

'We are now moving from the surveillance into the planning phase for his capture,' Felfe grunted. 'But before we strike, we must test the waters.'

'That's precisely the point of this meeting, to test the waters,' the Doctor confirmed.

'There's not much water here,' Isser Harel remarked. 'It sounds like a barren desert to me.'

The Doctor said, 'We mean your waters, rather than ours.'

Felfe came to his aid. 'When we plug the security hole here and arrest this man, we're going to lose all the sources we still have behind the Iron Curtain,' he explained to the astonished Mossad. 'The Soviets don't hang about. If their mole dies, so do our rats. There are going to be a lot of dead rats.'

'To speak quite frankly,' the Doctor said, in a tone I would never have thought him capable of, 'we will lose the whole of our information network in Eastern Europe. That's why we are asking for yours.'

Just then, Gehlen's secretary Alo came sweeping in, asked if the gentlemen would like a little more tea or coffee or a biscuit, took the rubbish out, including the ashtray containing Isser Harel's tie, and closed the door quietly behind her.

Sals un sniegs now seemed to be falling in the conference toom, too, on every last one of us.

'This list,' Harel said after an eternity had passed. He tapped the pink paper. 'This list would be an absolutely vital precondition for such a, how shall I put it . . . such an exotic agreement.'

'Naturally.'

'Including all the final measures that Israel might feel compelled to take on German territory.'

'We have the greatest understanding for them.'

'Our man in Paris' – Isser gestured towards Shlomo – 'will plan and coordinate the campaigns. And you will place Wolfgang Lotz here' – Champagne-Lotz – 'in Cairo, as a BND agent attached to the German Embassy.'

'That's exactly what I would suggest myself.'

'Of course, I will have to speak to my government.'

'Please do,' the Doctor said, and followed this with a *'l'chaim!'* which he had evidently learned from Palestine Fritz, having asked him what 'cheers' was in Hebrew. He raised his water glass, and the boring half of the table did likewise with laboured grins on their faces, while the formerly lively half neither grinned nor raised anything.

'Another condition,' Harel went on, unmoved, eyeing the raised water glasses with interest (one of the glasses – mine – was trembling), 'is that we never have to look out at Bormann's garden again. We need a fortified house in Munich.'

'Of course.'

'And a permanent liaison officer.'

'Absolutely.'

Now Colonel Harel picked up his glass, to my surprise clinked it against mine, and said, 'Perhaps that should be Mr Dürer.'

21

If you wouldn't mind putting down that portrait, which doesn't bear any resemblance to my features (you really have read too many comics) – if you could lay aside the scribble, then, and sit up a little straighter (I'll help you, if you like) – then you'll see the chimney all the way over there, Swami. A little crooked, a little blackened, red brick, beyond those roofs. The fortified house is quite close to that chimney, in Schwabing, not too far from here. It would take us half an hour to walk there (if we had different feet, of course).

The house is almost always occupied. Even during the Olympics two years ago, two of our Kidon regulators were quartered there, people from a special unit, trained for assassinations, attacks and liquidation in all its forms.

They watched open-mouthed as – on television, with the whole world watching – a few stout German traffic policemen in bonbon-coloured tracksuits gave each other a leg-up and climbed (or tried to climb, I should say) onto the roofs of the Olympic village. They were intending to surprise the Palestinian hostage-takers, who of course also knew how to turn on a television set.

The Kidon people picked up their guns and were all for running over to the stadium, and I had to use every word of Hebrew I knew to prevent them – these young people don't speak Yiddish any more, you know.

And so we stood and watched as the Israeli Olympic team was slaughtered.

It was the first and only time that anyone has gone on the rampage in the fortified house. A wardrobe was broken, a mirror shattered, and the television and two windowpanes met their maker when one of the Kidon regulators gave them what for with an axe, in a whirlwind of rage.

One of our neighbours called the police, but the last thing the regulators wanted to see just then was the two moustachioed Bavarian sergeants who rang the front doorbell to talk to them about disturbing the peace and damage to property, when they should have been shooting some terrorists dead four kilometres to the north. And so one of the officers, a red-cheeked lisper with a rather inflated sense of self, ended up with the barrel of a Beretta M951 in his mouth, which afterwards necessitated a great many phone calls, and almost lost us this attractive residential property in a desirable area.

The fortified house, built in the late nineteenth century as a retirement property for an arms manufacturer, consisted of six apartments across three floors. It was accessed via a Jugendstil glass door that could be sealed off automatically with a hydraulic, bulletproof steel plate in the space of three seconds.

The offices on the ground floor gave the whole building an aura of public good, since they were occupied by the German–Israeli Association eV, an organization with charitable status. Ev had decorated these rooms with posters of the Negev Desert and an always ailing olive tree.

No one would have guessed that right next door was the secret Mossad communications and radio centre, the meeting room, and a small gym.

The accommodation for agents and instructors was on the first floor, along with a large recreation area and a munitions room with an armoured steel door, encased in a two-centimetre-thick layer of lead.

Ev and I lived on the second floor.

Our bedroom was directly above the arsenal. If the fifty kilos of TNT and the three boxes of hand grenades stored there had ever exploded, then steel and lead or no, we would have gone up in a fireball rising into the Munich sky, and rained down over our little garden, where the old apple tree would have caught us in its branches.

I often sat under that tree in summer. It bore the red autumn Calvilles that have sadly become such a rarity these days, a remarkable coincidence that meant Grandpaping was always near me, or rather I was always near him, and Mama (who stopped by from time to time when I wasn't having to be Mr Himmelreich) came to be close to him, too, though it still gave her terrible pangs of conscience.

And Hub was therefore always near as well; there was no avoiding it. For that reason, I never harvested the fruit in autumn, letting all the apples rot on the ground until they were just a brown mulch, tunnelled through by worms and mice. I inhaled their scent and, as one does with age, fattened up the images of my childhood on it: Riga's foaming beaches, the fermented Jugla, the lazy July sun in which Ev's immortal legs sat down.

I ran into Hub unexpectedly.

When Colonel Harel and General Gehlen had agreed the start of Operation Blue Tit, on that *sals-un-sniegs* day, we then had to traipse across the large, snow-covered lawns to the Führer's bunker. General Gehlen wanted to mark the occasion by holding a shooting contest with the Mossad men. That was his idea of an agreeable end to a day of negotiations.

I had set up the firing range years before on the lowest floors of the bunker, but now I hardly recognized it. Someone had tried to illumin-ate it indirectly. Pine panelling and the colour green had given it the atmosphere of a south German skittles alley. It smelled of forest, men's sweat and gun smoke, and on one wall there was a photo of last year's top BND marksman. Both he and the grinning men around him had black strips stuck across their eyes so that no one would recognize them.

When I stepped into the shooting booth, I saw a man at the far end of the range, bulky, bald and glowing in the light of a neon lamp mounted diagonally above him. He was changing the targets over, and it took him a little while. I recognized my brother by his lone arm before he recognized me, and so I saw the full extent of his unhappiness.

Colonel Harel was just taking the safety catch off his gun beside me, but he didn't look up. Nor did anyone else seem to notice that the former head of counter-espionage Eastern Europe, clearly ruined by alcohol, had been put out to pasture in the firing range. Hub was there to set up the targets, check the bullet trap, tot up the points and reload the Jews' magazines.

Lurching a little with every step, he didn't dignify me with so much as a glance.

By now, Colonel Harel and General Gehlen had grown accustomed to one another. They were in good spirits as they took it in turns to fire at cardboard cut-outs that bore Khrushchev's features. I had told Isser that on no account must the Doctor lose, and so he did not lose; in fact, he won a small silver trophy that he had commissioned himself, on which was engraved the Star of David and a crucifix, along with a kind of broiler chicken that was evidently supposed to represent the common blue tit (*Parus caeruleus*).

By the time we all left the Führer's bunker and gathered to set off, it was already dark. Led by the high-spirited victor, the whole group went over to the assembly hall, where a little reception had been arranged in the guests' honour. Gehlen had invited an army of his own relatives (sixteen family members very well looked after by the BND), who were always ready to put on an impressive party.

I stood in the rooms I had renovated myself a decade earlier, spotting old construction weaknesses and longing for self-criticism. I took a beer and, before the speeches began and the Orcs started applauding, drifted back over to the deserted firing range. There was a fizz of laughter behind me, and the image of Hub silently handing each of us the loaded pistols, putting the ear defenders on with his one hand and marking the crosses beside our names, mingled with memories of him from long-vanished times, in which there were at least traces of happiness to be found.

It had stopped snowing. The stars looked like bullet holes in a black paper wall with nothing but light behind it.

I went into the empty range and called out Hub's name. No one answered. I called again, louder. Something somewhere fell to the floor. I was about to go and see what it was, when I heard footsteps hurrying towards me from outside. Someone swung into the doorway and almost ran into me. It was Heinz Felfe.

'Where have you been?' the mole-cat swine panted indignantly. There was alcohol on his breath. 'I was sent to fetch you.'

I didn't understand his solicitude, and understood the urgency even less. A noise over in the cloakroom made Felfe flinch, and as I was trying to work out what the flinching signified and he was tugging at my sleeve with a starchy smile on his face, trying to drag me back outside, I had a sudden premonition.

I freed myself from his grip and walked towards the noise. The cloakroom door was pulled to. As I pushed it open, it took me just a fraction of a second to realize why Yossi had been brought all this way from Tel Aviv when there was no car for him to drive, and when Operation Blue Tit was something that could never have been borne forward on the tiny wings of his intellect. He had taken up a broad stance in front of my brother and was holding his fist like a rock. As I entered, it flew into Hub's face to transform it into shreds of flesh, a transformation that had already begun.

Colonel Harel was sitting on a cloakroom bench opposite, smoking a leisurely cigarette. He stared over at me with a kind of torpor in his eyes. Yossi, too, interrupted his beating. His dear stupid-boy face didn't know where to look. A bubbling fountain of blood was welling from the hole that had once been Hub's mouth, along with a few syllables. It took me a while to realize that they formed the sound of my name.

'Ko' – bubble – 'Ja.'

For half my life, Hub had protected me. He had always been there when I needed help, and to this day he is my acronym for audacity. Once, when we were still quite small and everyone still called him Hubsi, at Gut Poll where we spent the summer holidays, he had put a goose in a headlock because it had bitten my stroking hand until it was bloody. In so doing, he broke the animal's neck, which meant that Hubsi was punished and kept indoors for three days: the goose had not yet been fat enough for slaughter.

His eye, swimming restlessly in red liquid, was searching for me.

'Come with me,' I heard Felfe whisper at my back. 'You shouldn't be here.'

I looked at Harel, who turned his eyes away and nodded to Yossi. The latter pressed his lips together regretfully and, with the next punch, thrashed Hub's eye out of my line of sight. The one after broke something in my brother's jaw.

Moshe Jacobsohn must have meant a lot to Colonel Harel.

'You really shouldn't be here.'

I felt Felfe place a hand on my shoulder, the gentle hand of the KGB, which was soon to be discovered and sent off for amputation. But now, a year before his arrest and three and a half years before Reinhard Gehlen's political crucifixion, Felfe looked down without any apparent interest at this groaning, one-armed creature who was currently forfeiting his left eye, a man whom he had once usurped with the aid of a vengeful, deceitful, thoroughly wicked brother. His claws wandered further and he placed his whole mendacious arm around me, copying a gesture of Hub's that made the tears well up in my eyes.

And as he led me gently away, I heard Yossi complete his work behind me.

'Ko' – bubble – 'Ja.'

Felfe tried to pilot me back to the party, to take my mind off it. But I couldn't meet Gehlen just then, I couldn't even meet myself, and I absolutely couldn't meet Isser Harel, who was sure to be back mingling with the guests again later.

I ran past the lights, scattering a rainbow shimmer of ice crystals, kept running under Freddy Quinn's 'stars of foreign lands', which were issuing from the loudspeakers, ran out of the gate and all the way to the Pullach village church, where I got into a taxi and had it take me to a Munich Station brothel. There, I got myself thoroughly fucked by an old Italian woman, who demanded double the usual fee because she was a good Catholic and my absent foreskin alarmed her.

The morning after, saturated with booze to the very marrow of my swaying bones, I called Tel Aviv and told Ev – or at least my brain tried to tell her, though my tongue didn't necessarily comply – that Harel's price for cooperating with the Germans had been a personal one: our brother. His health. Perhaps his life. And Gehlen had paid the price and so had I, and she would pay it, too, because she was the one who had given them Hub, blood of my blood, with a stupid file.

I thought that Ev would say something to that, but she didn't say anything at all.

Then she heard that I couldn't go back to Israel, and still she said nothing.

He who remains has always survived others' catastrophes. That which is, is always just a pitiful remnant.

We die far beyond our means when we die in full possession of our potential, one must never forget that, especially in our profession. The bullet in my head, Hub's missing arm and his melted eyeball, not to mention your skull-screw, as grim as they all may be, are still mementoes of infinite beauty and greatness and perfection that has perished as, one blow at a time, we lost everything that once gave us meaning and worth or, at the very least, lustre. We could not achieve anything, anything at all, without ending up as leftovers.

There was especially little of Hub left over.

The events at the shooting range put him in hospital with injuries that, according to his own official statement, came from falling eight metres off the roof of the Führer's bunker (having had rather too much punch, do you see, punch, haha). Shortly afterwards, he lost his job with the Org after thirteen years of service.

At least they left him his pension – which I suspect was one of the reasons he took the real cause of his injuries with him into the intensive care ward.

Once discharged, he waited for me in the lobby of my hotel, a mummy encased in plaster casts and bandages, with a crutch and a black eyepatch – not such a rare sight at the Bayerischer Hof in those years.

I was alarmed to hear my full name come out of his mouth, with no bubbling, but also without the teeth one needs for the soft 'S' in 'Koja Solm'. The name that posed the greatest danger to me at that time.

I went over to the couch where he had been waiting for me since the early morning, and when I was standing in front of him, he told me what he thought of me. I had taken his wife and child from him, he said, and even his mother, who now barely spoke to him. I had taken his living, his dignity, his physical integrity and his future.

His past was all I had left him, he told me, and it was the same as mine. He had committed no more crimes than I had, and the ones I had not had to commit, he had borne in my stead. He'd been charged by the state prosecutor, and would have to answer for what had taken place in Riga. The Org wasn't protecting him any longer.

'But I won't spare you, Koja. I will give them your name, and that will be the only name I give them.'

He got up on his crutch with some difficulty.

'Your precious Jews are going to flay you alive. I can promise you that.'

He turned and stalked off, got stuck in the hotel's revolving door and, red with anger and shame, came limping back into the lobby. From the other side of the room, he called out to me, making the porters, the lift boy, the receptionists and several guests turn to look at him. 'You wanted me to die, but you're going to die first – and maybe I'll be able to help you along the way, little brother!'

I didn't take him seriously, although from what he had said my time was already running out. And that was partly why I noticed much too late that the noose was tightening around my neck.

22

Ev came a few weeks later.

She set up the fortified house.

She bought a beautiful double bed made from Canadian beech. She didn't bring anything with her from Tel Aviv. She said that, in the long term, she would have to stay in Israel if she wasn't to go mad.

But she did bring Anna's pictures. She framed them all and hung them on our wall in exactly the same sequence as in Graets Street (ponies on the top row, flowers on the bottom).

She also came to the cemetery with me every day. Our daughter's dust guided us to the ingrown Tlingit grave that Amama had tended well all these years, bringing fresh flowers every week and news of little Anna's parents, who had turned Jewish and gone mad, and were so seldom in touch from Israel.

It might be a cliché, but it was almost always raining when we entered the cemetery. I had forgotten what earth smells like when the rain sprays off a gravestone, forgotten what happens when a single drop keeps dripping on the same spot, gradually softening the earth until it becomes permeable and yields and a tunnel opens into the depths, and some days I risked tumbling down it.

In August nineteen sixty-one, on Anna's eighteenth birthday, Ev tried to celebrate our daughter's coming of age, at least in Israeli terms. She would have to be dead another three years before reaching her German majority.

Ev baked a Baltic birthday ring cake, bought candles and lit them, even purchased a red shift dress, which was the very latest thing. When we hung it on a hanger on the wall and saw how it would have emphasized Anna's slender figure, her liveliness and presence of mind, how pretty she would have become as a young woman, how the world of men would have lain at her feet, men with Caesar haircuts, reading

Camus and waiting for a Jean Seberg non-conformist like the one in Godard's *Breathless*, whom Anna would have led into the basement jazz clubs, we were comforted for a moment.

But it was a very brief moment.

It lasted only until Ev had cut the dress to ribbons and rolled herself up in our rug.

For a dead child is the end. A dead child doesn't admit any illusions or any present. There will never again be even one present-tense birthday party for a dead child. Only a curdled, irrecoverable past that cannot be assuaged by any future event. The child is gone from the world, and every way in which you failed that child is fixed for all time.

I could never tell Anna that she was my daughter. I never told her what it meant just to look at her, with her mother's throat and the sunlight in her eyes (truly a brief happiness), and so I will not tell her on her eighteenth birthday either, on her twentieth, on her thirtieth. I will keep it from her until my life's end. Until my life's end, I will carry that omission into the future with me. And this link to my child, a link of eternal omission that endures day after day (without ever calling up so much as an illusion of presence) will, I think, be difficult to bear.

But sometimes, miracles happen.

And the six years, nine months and six days ended with a miracle. Those six years, nine months and six days of rain that had been falling on me since Maya's end.

They ended on Anna's eighteenth birthday, because on the evening of that day, when I had unwrapped Ev from the rug and given her some hot tea and put her to bed, Anna came back to me.

Anna's voice was in my head. It was absolutely present and clear, and appeared just as I was about to fall asleep. She simply asked me if there was nothing I wanted to give her at what was such an important moment for her, not even a picture. Startled, I got up in the middle of the night, hunched over the desk and drew Anna's face, which I could still draw from memory, especially the amber colour of her watchful eyes. And I drew a body beneath the face, a nude Jean Seberg body; that was my birthday surprise, and I hoped Ev wouldn't see it, since she would have scolded me.

But the next day Anna spoke to me again, telling me I didn't need to worry. She quite liked her body, the rather too small breasts I had given her (they were large, but of course they seemed tiny to her), the protruding ribs that she had stupidly inherited from Mama, and her much too slender Baltic fingers, which she was surely going to break, so slender were they. I only became aware of how intense our conversation was when Ev gently pointed out that I was talking to myself at the breakfast table – or so she thought.

But really, Anna was talking to me. She came at the strangest moments, and of course I had to reply. Whether it was in a station waiting room, in the city library or the consulting room of the doctor who was treating my bad back.

Once, I had to go out on an operation: the Mossad had instructed me to oversee the execution of Professor Hans Kleinwächter. He was one of the rocket scientists from Harel's pink list, which was to be worked through meticulously, one name at a time (or *peu à peu*, in Shlomo's words).

Kleinwächter lived in Lörrach, a Baden border town within sight of Basel, to which he retreated every few months to recuperate from his work in Cairo.

In the early evening of an arctic February day, my commando and I were waiting for him to appear. We had positioned ourselves under dark blue pines on the edge of a mountain pass, the professor's preferred route home from the Research Institute of Jet Propulsion Physics in Stuttgart at the weekend, the loneliest, most richly forested route.

Our commando vehicle – a Mercedes packed to the gunnels with explosives – was parked across the road just before the turn-off for Lörrach, on the far side of a tight switchback bend. Kleinwächter spotted the car at the last minute and slammed on the brakes, their squeal echoing through the forest like the sound of a dying hog. He avoided the collision by a hair's breadth.

I stepped out of the darkness onto the road and walked up to the car, which smelled of burnt rubber. Kleinwächter, looking thoroughly tanned even by moonlight, wound down his window and peered out from under his shepherd's hat with concern in his eyes. Concerned people often seem a little reproachful as well, but Kleinwächter just looked like he wanted to know if I was all right. His concern was all for me, and not for himself. His questioning eyes, at least, seemed firmly convinced that some dreadful accident must have occurred and that I was in need of help. My answering eyes, however, told him that he needn't worry, and, without saying a word, I took the pistol with the silencer attached from my coat pocket and pulled the trigger.

But I missed.

The bullet hit the head rest a centimetre from the professorial ear.

Just as I was pulling the trigger, little Anna's voice had asked me what on earth I was doing. I am absolutely certain it was my daughter speaking to me, for even after all these years I recall her reticent tone, and several times she called me 'Papa'.

And so I must have spent a few seconds in dialogue with my disapproving daughter, explaining things to her while I lowered my gun and the man in front of me screamed and screamed, ducking into the footwell, covering his shepherd's hat with his hands and getting louder and louder until I could scarcely hear what Anna was saying.

Special Agent Number One leapt out of the second vehicle, the getaway car we had parked down a forest track twenty metres further on, and came up onto the road. He was pointing a sub-machine gun and shouting at me in Hebrew to step aside.

'Please don't step aside, Papa,' my daughter said, loud and clear. She had evidently been learning Hebrew, so what was I to do?

I stayed indecisively where I was, and Professor Hans Kleinwächter, who had now realized that his executioners were engaged in some kind of discussion, re-emerged from the underbelly of his car without his hat or his desert tan, engaged the reverse gear, stepped on the accelerator and drove off, still screaming like a singed sow.

Special Agent Number One tried to open fire as the face of the electronics expert, who would never again build a missile guidance system, never again even think about missile guidance systems (and who is now, so the papers say, researching the mysteries of solar energy) whipped past him. But the gun jammed. The scientist escaped, his tail lights quickly disappearing into the dark.

I have never believed in God, though of course I couldn't have said so to Grandpaping. But my daughter did not want Professor Kleinwächter to die: that's how I saw it at the time, and that's how I see it still, and she must have had certain options open to her, without forcing me to stretch to a belief in a higher power – quite unlike you, of course, my Swami, you who are so well-disposed towards the divine.

According to everything you have taught me, it would seem that my daughter's consciousness made contact with me, just as in your opinion Maya Dzerzhinskaya's consciousness resides in the teeth I have guarded so well. I don't know; I am largely baffled by the phenomena of life, and entirely baffled by the phenomena of death.

But at that time I had no interest in phenomena. I just wanted to get away.

I ran over to our getaway car and leapt into the back. A sweat-soaked Isser Harel was behind the wheel. He shouted at me as he started the engine and sped after our home-made Mercedes bomb, in which the remains of our contrite commando (there was a Special Agent Two as well, seemingly just to console Special Agent One) was heading for the border.

'So amateurish!' Isser shouted. 'I've never seen something so fucking amateurish in my life! How the hell do you miss someone? How? From the range of . . . a bagel? I wouldn't miss an ant from that range! So unbelievably amateurish! And what was there to talk about? Fuck! What do you talk to a target about when you've shot and missed him? Were you telling him to keep still? And what was wrong with Tevye's' – Special Agent One – 'Uzi? Why is this project so dogged by fuck-ups?'

I couldn't give him an answer to any of that.

Papa always said that the perceived colour of a body (by which he assuredly did not just mean women's bodies) did not depend merely upon what part of the visible spectrum it reflected, as those barmy physicists would have us believe; it also depended upon our own state of mind. We painters, in particular (among whose ranks you may also now number yourself, to some extent, my dilettantish Swami), may develop a specific preference for specific colours during specific phases of our lives. It is our soul showing us how we feel. With Papa, for instance, using a lot of pink was always an expression of general disgust with the world. 'My son,' he said, 'if there should ever be too much pink in your life, then you will be like charcoal on the inside, and you should go and spend a few weeks on the Riviera.'

He claimed that nothing in nature, with the exception of a woman's vulva, was naturally a rosy pink; even the lovely rose itself was only mauve thanks to human intervention, and the same went for all pink foods: meat, too, was only pink when you roasted it; it was a wholly artificial, sticky colour that must be avoided.

A strange attitude of Papa's, when he used no less pink in his work than Rubens or Fragonard. Like Papa, they had to paint a huge number of arses.

But actually, in those months I did come to love a light, warm pastel colour, a shade of apricot that my daughter would have liked, she told me so herself.

And Reinhard Gehlen's welcome gift, which I had to take care of – the list of prominent names, all those famous physicists and engineers – had been as pink as candyfloss, though as we worked down it it had darkened into a blood-red maelstrom of incomprehensible accidents.

Professor Kleinwächter, you see, was not the only one who had to be sacrificed to this piece of paper, as harmless and optimistic as it may have looked.

When I only think of Hassan Kamil! Egyptian arms manufacturer. Multimillionaire. Confidant of President Nasser. A perfect victim, since there was proof that Mr Kamil wanted to bomb Israel off the map, and was hiring great armies of German rocket makers from his home in Switzerland for this purpose.

The precision bomb that I had procured exploded as planned, high above the Teutoburger Forest in Mr Kamil's Air Lloyd charter plane. But it failed to pulverize the charmer himself; to our surprise, he was not on board. The only passenger was his wife, Her Highness the Duchess of Mecklenburg, Princess of Wenden, Schwerin and Ratzeburg, Countess of Schwerin, mistress of the lands of Rostock and Stargard, Princess of Mecklenburg-Strelitz and granddaughter of Kaiser Wilhelm II – who was, unfortunately, related to Gehlen's dear Frau Herta.

The letter bomb sent to the Hamburg-born head of the missile programme in Cairo Heliopolis, addressed to one Herr Pals, Puls or Pils, was not opened by the man himself, either, but by his secretary. Many parts of her were lost (eyesight, nostrils, top lip, four fingers), a dreadful business that weighed heavily on me, particularly as this lady had been wearing a pink dress.

Another, far more muscular parcel bomb, which would have blown away not just the secretarial staff but all the rocket scientists within a ten-metre radius (including the head of the project, barricaded into his adjoining office) was dropped in the distribution centre by a careless Egyptian postal worker (the parcel was marked 'Caution! Fragile! Do not drop!', though in German, idiotically), leaving a crater in the floor three metres across and a metre deep. Eleven Arabs and their various body parts were flung high into the air, a brouhaha that six of the men did, at least, manage to survive, though they were mutilated.

When it came to the largest German missile trader, then, the doctor of jurisprudence Heinz Krug, who had provided Egypt with special sheet metal, measuring and testing devices, machines and valves, nothing else could be permitted to go wrong.

I myself was there to witness Krug being asked to step out of his car, here in Munich. The two highly professional Kidon regulators (whom I liked very much; they were nice boys who always washed up their own dishes in the fortified house), were well prepared. They had gained access to a steelworks in Ismaning that was unguarded at night, and conducted some rather theatrical questioning there.

During the process, Dr Krug sustained some accidental damage from a two-ton steel pipe, beneath which he had really only been tied to create an impression and extract a few names from him. Unfortunately, however, the pipe slipped out of the cradle in which it was suspended, and afterwards Dr Krug looked so preposterous that he had to be entirely composted in an acid bath (even the caustic soda, which is actually colourless, had a pink tinge to it, I swear).

Gehlen's patience finally ran out when, on top of this, the children of Professor Goercke, an expert in electronic measuring systems, were invited to a hotel in Basel and asked to fetch their papa home from Cairo as quickly as possible before something terrible happened. The children had the most innocent names that German children can have: Heidi and Hans, and there can be nothing pinker than children called Heidi and Hans. You know, every country has its own national taboos. Just as Britain views treason as the most despicable villainy, or France patricide, or Italy sex before marriage, so the German soul regards violence towards pink children the number one capital crime. I was truly predestined to reach this conclusion from my own painful experience, and Anna's voice (calm and warm) confirmed it to me.

That must have been why I'd refused to carry out Harel's intimidation mission, which Shlomo therefore planned from Paris, using two incompetents who were stupid enough to get themselves arrested in the presence of little Heidi and little Hans.

Both men were taken into custody.

The Mossad was officially in the dock.

An intolerable notion to Colonel Harel. To be a perpetrator and not a victim. To receive punishment rather than meting it out. To be reliant on the mercy of the nation that invented the Shoah.

It gnawed away at Isser's composure and his self-image. He saw himself as a beardless version of Albert Schweitzer, with a pure heart and surgical instruments in his clean-as-a-whistle hands.

I met him for the last time in that period when his footsteps came drumming into the fortified house at an angry trot. He bellowed 'Shalom' as he ushered a whole pack of newly arrived Israeli journalists into the offices of the German–Israeli Association. The *Haaretz*, the *Maariv* and the *Yedioth Ahronoth* were all fed with material from Ev's archives. They gulped it down, feasting on the careers of Nazi rocket scientists who, in Harel's opinion, had forfeited their right to life.

The Israeli newspapers thought so, too, and within a few days a storm swept through the press, the offshoots of which quickly blew into Germany and shook the kingdom of the Orcs to its foundations.

23

Reinhard Gehlen was far from delighted.

'Tell Herr Harel that's an end to it.'

We were sitting in his office. His face was dark and almost as sunken as yours, Swami, the skin hanging from his cheeks like two lizards.

'Very good, Herr Doctor.'

The only other person in the room was Sangkehl, perching to my right on the edge of an armchair, the same worry-toad he always was. His face-and-neck bullet wound was glistening with anxiety (some kind of secretion oozed from the scar, as if a slug had crawled across his upper lip and into his nose). He was staring at the large pile of newspapers on Gehlen's desk as if paralysed. The headlines sounded like Perry Rhodan novellas.

'SOS from outer space: Nazi scientists plan death star for Jews'.

'Clouds over Israel: ninety years of radioactive pollution?'

'Germany lets its physicists travel to Hitler's cosmic castles at Egypt's behest'.

I'm exaggerating.

But it was something along those lines.

'This whole thing is a nightmare,' Gehlen growled. 'Come on, you live in Schwabing with these madmen. Can't you call a halt to it?'

'I'm just a liaison officer,' I lied. 'The Mossad don't really tell me what they're planning.'

'If this media witch-hunt doesn't stop, we'll shut down the fortified house. We'll throw the whole lot of them out. They won't get so much as a pocket knife from Germany in future. And Adenauer will put in an official protest; he'll take it all the way to the United Nations. We're this far away from doing it.'

He showed me how far with his thumb and forefinger. His thumb and forefinger looked strong; they had been trimming the sails of the family dinghy on the Starnberger See for years, but some time ago they had also started to tremble slightly, even when they were holding a champagne glass or one of his usual cigars, or thin air, as they were doing now.

'You tell that criminal. And I don't want to have to scrape one more dead academic off the roads. Is that clear?'

'Completely clear, Herr Doctor.'

'How did he even come up with this moronic idea?'

'Well, we gave him the pink list.'

'Yes, but which bag of nerves gave it to him?'

Sangkehl and I looked at the Doctor with respect and admiration. He was now sixty-one years old, but looked more like eighty-one. Hair sprouted from his ears. His hands rested Napoleonically on his stomach. Sangkehl was the first to pull himself together.

'I am sure,' he said, in his characteristically naive tone of voice, 'that it was Heinz Felfe.'

'Felfe!' Gehlen snarled poisonously. 'It really is a shame one can't pour petrol over him and set him alight. One of the democratic system's great disadvantages. Now he's sitting comfortably in prison, waiting for a spy exchange.'

'A disappointment to us all, this rule of law!' Sangkehl added.

'And you know, he was in the SS!' Gehlen roared. 'There isn't much you would put past the SS, but betraying your own fatherland? To the communists? That joker is betraying every single one of his comrades! Even his president, who invited him to his tea evenings twelve times. How often have you been to a tea evening at my house, Sangkehl?'

'Twice, Herr Doctor.'

'Dürer?'

'Once.'

'You see? And Felfe came to twelve!'

We nodded sadly.

'He even danced with my daughter. Swept her quite off her feet. I believe the word "marriage" was even bandied about. All these old SS men! Born traitors. Weren't you in the SS, too, Dürer?'

'The SS threw me in prison, Herr Doctor.'

'Outstanding. Absolutely outstanding. You know what? We'll shut down the fortified house now. Tell old Rumpelstiltskin in Tel Aviv that's an end to it.'

'Herr Doctor . . .'

'What?'

'We can't.'

'Why not?'

'The Mossad is giving us free rein with the Soviets. We give them free rein here.'

'Free rein, by all means. But no fortified house! And no pink list!'

'If I might be permitted to interject, Herr Doctor,' Sangkehl said gently, with a little cough, and I was truly grateful that this simple mind could still tell when things were getting serious. 'If the Israeli secret service stops distributing its information to us – if we lose the USSR intelligence – then in the medium term, the West German government will be blind in the East. Blind, deaf and dumb. It's going to take us at least three more years to build up our own team of staff.'

'Nonsense!' Gehlen barked. 'We can't be completely and utterly at the Israelis' mercy.'

He reached into the pile of newspapers in front of him, picked up a tabloid testily and waved it at us. 'It says here that the BND is supplying the Egyptians with poison gas. Eventually it's going to say "BND sells own grandmother". And all because Felfe handed the pink list to those Jews. What was he thinking?'

Shaken by such an abysmal lack of character, Gehlen got up to look for a place where he could breathe freely and, as so often, he found it right in front of his window. He stopped, stretched and looked out at the BND compound, which was growing unstoppably into the sky.

'Undermine everything that is good in the enemy's country! Implicate the representatives of the ruling classes in criminal enterprises! Do all you can to undermine their position and their respect! Expose them to public disgrace! Do not hesitate to use the lowest and most despicable men! Place secret scouts everywhere! Well, Sangkehl, who do you think said that?'

Sangkehl put an involuntary hand to his damp face-and-neck bullet wound. He blinked in surprise, caught out like a schoolboy who has not been paying attention and is suddenly asked for a trigonometry formula.

'Who said that?' he stammered.

'Yes, who said that?'

'I suspect it will have been you who said that, Herr Doctor.'

'Me?'

'Wasn't it?'

'You think I said: use the lowest and most despicable men?'

'No?'

'Get out of my sight, Sangkehl.'

'Very good, sir.'

The befuddled section head got up, very nearly clicked his heels together, gave the merest hint of a bow and disappeared out through the door into the grounds, looking red as a love apple.

It was not clear to me whether I should stay or go. The Doctor was quite still, a mere silhouette against the bright square of the window. I took courage and got to my feet.

'Not you, Dürer.'

'Of course.'

Stay, then. I sat back down.

A minute passed, during which my emotions were unable to choose between fear, disgust and sympathy, before he said that the correct answer was General Sun Tzu, and had I known that.

'I'm afraid not.'

'*The Art of War*,' Gehlen said, nodding. 'Two and a half thousand years old. Sounds like the guiding principles for global communist activity today.'

He had finally had his fill of the view; he turned back to his desk and took a seat behind it. He reached for his sunglasses and put them on. They made him look even more overbearing than his eyes themselves did.

'Waging war always relies on deception. When we are close by, we must make the enemy believe we are far away. When we are far away, we must make him believe we are close by. How close are you to me, Herr Dürer?'

'I'm not an enemy.'

'Your brother says you are.'

Fear. My emotions finally decided on fear, and I tried to get a grip on it with a disarming smile that was directed more inward than outward.

'Yes, my brother has surprised us all again and again.'

'He sent me a treatise. Confidentially, thank God.'

Reaching down, he heaved a mighty file out of the document drawer of his desk. He placed it on the newspapers, which crackled under its weight. The file contained papers, photos and dossiers, but I couldn't see any more than that; the Doctor was pressing his hand down on it.

'In here is every misdemeanour you've committed since you were a very small boy. He believes you worked for the KGB.'

I managed an elegant, disdainful laugh.

'I know that's nonsense. But I gather that charges are to be brought against your brother very soon. For war crimes in the East. He has already incriminated you heavily. We have a source in the police.'

'My brother put me in a Gestapo prison. He sentenced me to death. That's the truth.'

'Truth belongs to the victors, Sun Tzu says.'

'Herr Doctor,' I replied, choosing each of the words that followed with caution, 'my brother is not a victor.'

'And what about your sister?'

'I'm sorry?'

'Your brother writes about your sister here, too. Your wife. His wife. An astonishing sister, really.'

'Might I be permitted to have a look?'

Gehlen didn't react. All I could see in his sunglasses was the reflection of my arm, moving hesitantly towards him and the file, freezing in indecision and then retreating, like an adder that has found no food.

'And don't you agree,' his voice whispered, sounding suddenly weary and seeming entirely cleansed of its usual sharp tone, 'don't you agree that we have lost our equilibrium?'

'Equilibrium?'

'Well?'

'Who do you mean? The Firm?'

'The whole world. Morality. What is good, and what is bad. Everything has gone off the rails, you surely can't deny that.'

I had no idea what could be meant by 'equilibrium', and nor did I have any response for the deep sigh that escaped Gehlen's throat. Sighing was not something one could associate with the sunglasses and the thin moustache above the line of his mouth, which did not open a single millimetre to let out sighs.

'Is it true,' I heard him say after two more sighs, 'is it true that Frau Himmelreich has recently started working at the Institute for Contemporary History?'

I couldn't dispute that.

'And that under her Jewish name – yours, I mean – she is providing materials for . . . for Nazi trials?'

That, too, corresponded to the facts.

'For heaven's sake, Dürer! Has she become a communist, then?'

No, my wife had become an historian; an historian who occasionally surprised me, but who was completely neutral when it came to politics.

'An historian? Your brother writes that she's helping build the case against him.'

With the best will in the world, I could not imagine that, and that is exactly what I told the Doctor.

24

In truth, of course, I did know what was meant by 'equilibrium'.

Ev provided a lot of material for Nazi trials, but she particularly favoured the kind that plunged Hub into unhappiness. I have not yet told you this, my dear Swami; I omitted it out of shame or negligence or due to your peculiar lack of sympathy.

Ev had managed to get herself a position as an adviser at the respected Munich Institute for Contemporary History (with the aid of a history degree authenticated by the Mossad, and a forged doctorate from the University of Tel Aviv). In this capacity, she gained access to countless Nazi sources, travelled a lot (ah, she loved to travel) and brought back archive material, trial documents, witness statements and photos from all manner of countries. Pain and painkillers in one.

Everything had to be sent to Israel, registered there, archived and evaluated.

The Mossad headquarters was only able to withstand this flood of material by employing additional academics. Staff create departments, and departments create heads of department, and Colonel Harel had appointed Ev as head of the NS-01 information-gathering office, as the department for escapees was called. She naturally had to travel to Tel Aviv quite often, but in Germany she spent her days preparing for the trials, with the assistance of her documents and her practically Alexandrian library.

I know that Buddhists (if I may call you a Buddhist for the sake of simplicity) have no interest in legal disputes. And certainly not in jurisdiction. If one of you does something wrong, then your karma gets dragged through the dirt, and bang, next time around you're a grasshopper. That's your idea of 'equilibrium'.

But you need to look at it this way, Swami Basti: at that time, the head of public prosecutions in Berlin was preparing the largest criminal trial that Germany would ever see: the trial of the Reich Main Security Office, which at a stroke could turn a thousand highly respected citizens of the republic into a thousand grasshoppers.

To cope with this karmic transformation, the public prosecutors' office cleared out a whole wing of the Palace of Justice in Moabit. The ground floor was flooded with one hundred and fifty thousand ring binders. The remaining two floors were then occupied by eleven public prosecutors, twenty-three police officers, eighteen justice-department experts and secretaries, four drivers and couriers, two stenographers and four consultant historians.

'And I am one of those historians,' Ev had told me.

'You're not an historian,' I retorted, 'you're a con artist.'

'I am not.'

'You don't even know when the Principal Decree of the Reich Deputation was.'

'What's the Principal Decree of the Reich Deputation?' she asked, in a tone that suggested anything containing the word 'Reich' must refer to the Third Reich.

'You see? You're going to get caught out. It's all going to be very embarrassing, my love.'

We argued over tactics and strategies: the case against the Reich Main Security Office, to which Ev and her escapee archive were contributing (with witness statements from Israel, interviews with survivors in Munich, profiles of perpetrators and other documents pulled from the files) also affected my own karma.

I had, as you know, worked at the Reich Main Security Office myself a thousand years before, in that labyrinthine building not far from Haus Vaterland, headed by Herr Heydrich and known to everyone as THE OFFICE.

Elemental dukkha had emanated from the desks of this institution. THE OFFICE devised the slaughterhouses and stocked them with dukkha. THE OFFICE transported the calves and supplied them to the dukkha. THE OFFICE invented the technology, the legal structures and the bureaucracy of dukkha, and coordinated it all. THE OFFICE spoke to the Wehrmacht, telephoned the foreign office, conceived the Edenic disguise and the staffing structure that turned the slaughtermen into Eichmann-men and the Eichmann-men into a group of bureaucrats working in solidarity, so that there was no longer any trace of dukkha to be seen, except by those who meditated, of course, but I can tell you that, in the SS, very few people meditated.

Ev's mission was to shine a spotlight on the Reich Main Security Office, with all its attendant phenomena – the desks, the office chairs, the typewriters, the Einsatzgruppen, the concentration camps and the individuals.

The only thing that filled me with concern was that I myself might be lit up along with them.

'Darling, you didn't do anything,' Ev tried to reassure me. 'I haven't found a single mention of you and THE OFFICE anywhere.'

'Have you been looking for those mentions, then?'

'It won't affect you, believe me.'

'It will affect Hub, though.'

'Yes,' she said darkly. 'It will affect Hub.'

How do you explain German criminal law to a Buddhist – an

unorthodox Hindu-Buddhist mish-mash like yourself, at that? Even non-Buddhists have a hard time understanding it. In any case, it doesn't work on the principle of insight and self-criticism, Swami, I can tell you that much. German criminal law also seldom hands down reincarnation sentences. It doesn't seek out wandering souls who can be incarcerated in the body of a rat. It seeks a guilty party here and now. In the space-time continuum. As quickly as possible.

And who such a guilty party is, what he is, and why: that isn't easy to explain, either.

So let me tell you something substantive in the plain language of a non-legal mind: in German criminal law, the person who committed a crime is The Man In Whose Interest It Is.

It isn't necessary for the Man In Whose Interest It Is actually to have committed the crime. The person who committed it, if he committed it ignorantly and not for his own ends and therefore without it Being In His Interest, can be cleared of all charges. He is then just an accessory. An accomplice to The Man In Whose Interest It Is.

This interpretation of the law, my dear Swami, is a gift from God for every Nazi in the land. Because it means that Adolf Hitler, Heinrich Himmler and Reinhard Heydrich, Hihihey for short, are in fact The Only Three Men In Whose Interest It Is – the instigators, in other words.

But the people who did things at Hihihey's instigation, who worked in the SS-Einsatzgruppen or at Auschwitz and above all of course in THE OFFICE, were merely devoted helpers, accessories (to the most egregious excesses; excessories one might say). They were just selfless idealists, who presented themselves to the astonished German courts as almost Buddhist-like, for no one could have acted with less interest or will, or any hint of personal malice, than the SS death's-head commandos.

The millions of Jews they shot – and we are still following German criminal law here, which takes some getting used to, my dear Swami – therefore died exclusively at the hands of well-intentioned Buddhists, weary of their own actions, men who not only had never wanted to do what they did, but had actually been vehemently against it (though of course, as I've said, being for or against things was not their business, just as the enlightened Siddhartha counsels the wise).

And so if it could not be proven with absolute certainty that a defendant had slit throats or drowned Jewish children with full intent and passionate enthusiasm, then he could not be pursued for it. Even if, in some poorly run concentration camp, he should have been foolish enough to do a little slitting or drowning here and there, it was all right as long as it had merely been done out of a desire to help the Hihiheys, and not for the sheer hell of it.

The Red Cross themselves couldn't hold a candle to the blessed SS when it came to their desire to help (that first 'S' stood for *Schutz*, you know; 'protection' was their raison d'être). As a result, among those ranked below the Hihiheys and above the deplorable radical scum, there was no one to be found who'd had any desire for dukkha.

'That view of things is about to change,' Ev told me jubilantly – and now we have arrived at the part that has something to do with your own understanding of 'equilibrium'. 'This trial is going to rain on the parade of all those who got away with saying they just did office work. All the links are being uncovered. And that's why we have to put THE OFFICE in the dock. Then there will be no more accessories. Then we can prove that your colleagues knew what they were doing.'

It was with words like these that she usually fell asleep in the evening, often with a yoghurt pot still in her hand, and a yoghurt spoon in her mouth. As she began to snore softly, I would remove the spoon as gently as I would a thermometer, so that she wouldn't hurt her gums. Then I would slip carefully out of our bed, wash the spoon, throw the pot away and avoid going back, so that I wouldn't be infected by her suicidal mood, which was just beginning and would grow stronger as she slept.

Exaggerated zeal always has an aftertaste of despondency, as Papa used to say. He regarded Mama's zeal (when it came to the apple hosannah, for instance) as sad, pernicious and foolish – as a cause of death, in fact, where our Grandpaping was concerned.

I went downstairs, past our peacefully dreaming Kidon regulators, left the fortified house and felt a little better as soon as I had closed the front door behind me.

And as I walked across the deserted Münchener Freiheit square – warm, those nights were, and filled with the scent of lindens – I could resume my discussions with Anna.

That hadn't been possible in the bedroom. On those occasions when it did happen, Ev always thought I was talking to myself.

Such nonsense.

There was nothing more liberating than strolling through Schwabing by night, debating with my daughter the conflicts that were smouldering between me and her mother. Anna disapproved of Ev's fixation on the hunt. Mama is like a Jack Russell terrier, she sighed: a bird in the bush, a hare in the undergrowth, and she's off. Where did you learn what a Jack Russell is like, I asked her. But she reproached me, told me to stop treating her like a child. And yes, it was she who explained to me that, sooner or later, in some file or other, Mama was going to come across Hub, her father to an inexplicable degree – Pseudopapa, she called him, perhaps just to please me.

And if Mama put Pseudopapa through the mill, it would end badly.

All this was going through my head as I sat opposite General Gehlen and heard about the Chinese Sun Tzu for the first time, and then about my brother's treatise, which sat in a ring binder on the Doctor's desk awaiting further use. And finally, about my sister's efforts to destroy Hub utterly for the work he had done at THE OFFICE.

The Doctor let out another peevish sigh, leaned forward, took the binder with both hands and held it up like an auctioneer trying to raise the bidding on it.

'We are paying your brother a decent pension. And in return, he keeps his silence. Silence, Dürer. That's what we agreed. A thing like this breaks that agreement.'

The ring binder flew through the air into the waste-paper basket, which was too flimsy for such a tome and tipped over, spilling its load. A few sheets of paper slipped out and scattered themselves across the carpet. A photo, sandwiched between them. I saw Koja and Hubsi arm in arm in Riga, in their mid-twenties. In front of their starched white shirts was strung a little swastika flag, held by our sister, who was standing behind and exactly halfway between us, her chin resting on Hubsi's shoulder, her pretty Baltic fingers clutching the corners of the flag, all of us grinning into the camera, so incredibly young. And the eyes. Eyes armed with the purest happiness.

'You are living in Munich under a false name, Dürer. Under the roof of an institute you have to spy on. Your brother mustn't place you in any additional danger. We've told him that.'

He straightened up, regained his old arrogance and passed a business card across the table to me.

'This is the lawyer he's engaged.'

I looked at the card.

'Perhaps you could have a word with him.'

I was still looking at the card.

'Sneiper, his name is. A real spiv. Do you know him?'

25

At 'Sneiper', the Hippy shows a hint of reaction.

He is bemused to hear that name again, and his bemusement reflects my own.

He drops the pencil he is using to try and draw me in the shape of a sausage.

He can only manage scribbles now. His movements are those of someone who has just fallen over. His mouth hangs open. There is much about him that reminds me of Papa in his wheelchair, including his undisguised interest in new women.

'Coolumba.'

'Excuse me?'

'Coolumba musseen.'

I have no idea what the Hippy is trying to say, with the tongue that for the past few days has been frozen like molten lead in water. But he points to the pretty young student nurse who is dusting the corridor palms a few paces along from us. Her name is Nurse Sabine, and she arrived on our ward only recently. Night Nurse Gerda is instructing her. Unlike Night Nurse Gerda, Student Nurse Sabine is very shy, and she approaches us very shyly, picks the Hippy's pencil up off the floor and hands it to me. She doesn't like touching the Hippy, who sometimes suffers from spontaneous erections when she comes too close (she smells very good, perhaps that's why).

'Why aren't they operating on Basti?' I ask Nurse Sabine, giving the Hippy back his pencil.

'Oh, he's right at the top of the list,' she lisps sweetly. 'But he doesn't have private insurance, so, you know.'

'But any fool can see what's wrong with him. He can barely speak. He can barely walk.'

'Honestly, you need to ask the doctors about that. He's probably still doing too well. He's aware of everything that's going on.'

'Coolumba musseen, hmm Shny-ba?'

'What are you saying, Swami?'

'Hmm Shny-ba?'

'Sneiper?'

'Shny-ba, yeah.'

I turn to Student Nurse Sabine, who really is extraordinarily pretty. She is standing there like Botticelli's Primavera, her rather foolish countenance full of that nervous tenderness so typical of the Florentines, holding the duster like a sprig of fresh myrtle.

'I believe Basti likes you very much, Nurse Sabine,' I say. 'But there is someone he would like to talk to me about now, a mutual acquaintance of ours, you might say. And he begs you to excuse us while we do that in private.'

'Of course, I'm sorry.'

She hurries off with a look of alarm. I watch her go, floating all the way down the long corridor, taking her scent with her, and all her nakedness (for youth is always a kind of nakedness, something wholly transparent, while age is a state that no human eye can penetrate).

26

Dr Erhard Sneiper's Munich chambers were in the French quarter, not far from Orleansplatz. The address was to the west of the square, a mighty five-storey building with a theatrical baroque frontage that had been freshly painted.

There was a French restaurant on the ground floor. A waiter looked at me with friendly, bulging eyes, sensing a future customer. On the downstairs name plate, I read: 'Dr Sneiper, Mancelius, von Leyden & Partner, 2nd Floor. Please use the lift.'

Upstairs, the door looked like the hand-carved entrance to a Genoese royal palace, but it opened easily with an intercom button. It led into a reception that smelled of fresh chrysanthemums, and there I found some far-from-fresh chrysanthemums, along with green leather armchairs, several magazines (*Horse & Hound*; *Yachting*), a luxury chrome ashtray and a wall displaying the vanished Baltics. The map of the Russian Baltic Sea provinces (Meyer-Verlag, 1892) glinted behind glass in a gold frame, with an engraving of Riga right beside it. Even the cheerful secretary came from Goldingen, as she told me at once. She wore an amber pendant around her neck, the traditional jewellery for young Baltic women.

Erhard Sneiper received me two doors further on, in the modest ambience of the Biedermeier period. The rug alone was worth a fortune, the desk surprisingly modern, large, with a mint-green Formica top. We shook hands as two gentlemen from Riga should. The wood panelling on the walls suited his complexion, which had been freshened up with hearty Alpine hikes. His Jesuitical aspect seemed even more pronounced than before: unlike me, he had not gained a single gram of fat, just a kind of sly, hard-nosed energy. If I ever needed a ruthless lawyer, I would turn to him.

'Do take a seat, Koja. I'm glad you came.'

I wondered whether the silver cufflinks peeking out of his jacket sleeves were really decorated with little death's heads, as it appeared from a distance (they were butterflies, I realized when we said goodbye).

We chatted for a while about times past, about the French restaurant downstairs, which did quite excellent frog's legs, and what a nice neighbourhood this was. The streets were named after successful battles in France: Orléans, Balan, Lothringen, Metz, Paris, but also Woerth-Froeschwiller in Alsace, where the Prussian crown prince had trounced a whole brigade of French cuirassiers. 'Trounced,' Erhard said, reanimating the old duelling-fraternity jargon, which I swiftly killed off again with a few fragments of Yiddish.

Finally, my old ethnic Balt leader asked me if I would like a cola, and when I blinked in bafflement, he explained that he drank nothing but Coca-Cola these days, you always felt fresh and cheerful afterwards, and then I watched him drinking his Coca-Cola and asked if he needed me for anything else, since I didn't have all that much time.

'Your brother is angry with you.'

'I know. And he killed Ev's daughter.'

I saw a sad sheen come into his eyes.

'It is very regrettable when brothers withhold goodwill and forbearance from one another. Particularly when Hub has done so much for you.'

'I know what he's done for me. And what he hasn't done for me.'

I knew what he had not done for Erhard, too; he hadn't kept his dick out of Erhard's wife for Erhard. But I didn't want to think about Ev Sneiper that day, a day on which the sun even came out for a little while – it was summer, I forgot to mention that.

'There is absolutely no justification for the charges they're bringing against Hub. And I'm afraid the anger and the disappointment he feels over it have induced him to incriminate you.'

'If he does anything like that again, Gehlen is going to flay him.'

'Please, let's keep this civilized,' Sneiper rebuked me in friendly tones. 'Hub made a mistake. And I'm trying to find a good path for the two of you to take.'

His voice acquired a very lawyerly unctuousness – as if lawyers had a larynx full of rosin to apply to their vocal cords when needed.

'What kind of path would that be, then?' I asked, in as un-rosined a voice as I could manage.

'One that you can walk together.'

'Don't make me laugh.'

'The Auschwitz trial in Frankfurt attracted a lot of attention. Since then, left-wing state prosecutors have been trying to charge people in groups. That alone will put the two of you on the same path.'

'What Hub did was not what I did.'

'He will be prosecuted with the Riga group, because he worked in a particular office there at a particular point in time. Just as you did.'

'Yes, but I was visiting Latvian art exhibitions, Erhard. Not committing mass murder.'

'And then there is this other trial, I don't know if you've heard. It's a huge circus, focusing on the Reich Main Security Office. Our Reich Main Security Office.'

'It most certainly was not my Reich Main Security Office.'

'A truly outrageous affair. They mean to destroy entirely innocent people. People at the very pinnacle of our society.'

I showed him the weakest smile he had ever been given, but he was generous enough to overlook it.

'It's a political trial, Koja. If it goes ahead, it will open the door for a communist landslide in our country. Not even people like me will be safe, although state prosecutors in wartime acted entirely within the law.'

'What are you getting at, benevolent Erhard?'

'Is your-wife-who-was-once-my-wife not heavily involved in this matter?'

'Yes,' I said. 'Ev is looking forward to the trial against YOUR OFFICE tremendously.'

'You see. And that's why we need your help.'

You will understand my sudden desire to have a Coca-Cola in my hand. But I didn't say as much, because I would only have poured it over this man's head. He was now telling me, in his polite, kindly manner, that pacifying a nation was always a higher legal good than atonement, and that ever since the Peace of Westphalia a line could always be drawn under the unlovely side-effects of thirty-year wars.

I said there was no way I was going to help him. Neither him, nor my brother, nor any other prominent personalities. I couldn't do anything for any of them. For the murdered. For the instigators of murder. For the accessories to murder.

'Well,' Erhard replied, 'you may not be familiar with the legal niceties of that distinction.'

'Oh no, I am. There are people who were murdered. There are instigators of murder. And there are accessories to murder. But, of course, there are no murderers.'

Faster than I would have thought possible, Erhard pulled out a bundle of papers. This was a situation familiar to me; I had often sat at hostile desks across which life-changing documents had been slid towards me, and so I guessed that I was in for something thoroughly unpleasant.

But if I had known what was waiting for me *in nuce*, my dear Swami, then I most certainly would not have made such a foolish, naive, self-assured and condescending face, which was not at all appropriate for the papers at which I now found myself staring.

I read the declaration under oath of Finnberg, Emil, in the pre-trial investigation of Solm, Konstantin:

As I already mentioned in my statement of 10.5.1960, vol. X p.906, I was stationed in Riga from mid-July 1941 to the end of March 1942. In this time, I knew Konstantin Solm as one of the cruellest and most radical persecutors of Jews in the whole commando.

I read the declaration under oath of Haag, Edmund:

Obersturmführer Solm, Konstantin, always put himself forward to take part in as many executions of Jews as he could. In his words, he wanted to serve 'on the front lines of the race war'.

I read the declaration under oath of Hase, Robert:

Solm, Konstantin, was around 28–32 years old at that time, slim, neither broad nor narrow-shouldered, taller than average (around 175–180cm). I also remember Solm because he was always sitting under the pine trees, drawing, he liked to draw pines. At a mass shooting in August 1941, I saw Solm tear a child of about three years old away from its mother, throw it in the air and catch it on his bayonet. He always said we needed to save bullets.

Then I could read no more.

Erhard Sneiper had been leafing tactfully through a Porsche catalogue, evidently toying with the idea of getting himself a sports car.

I learned that none of the statements I had read about myself would ever have to be used in court. They had been written by my brother's comrades, who did not regard themselves as comrades of mine. And while the level of truth they contained might be negligible, their effect on a West German jury would not be.

I told Sneiper that Koja Solm no longer existed.

'Yes, your brother already told me that. Your name is Himmelreich, now. Jeremias, isn't it?'

'That's right. Koja Solm is dead.'

'He's only dead if your brother agrees to it.'

'Hub has clear official instructions about that.'

'The BND has dropped him. He doesn't care about instructions from the BND.'

'Believe me, Erhard, it would be a very bad idea to pick a quarrel with the government.'

'Oh yes, and you suddenly have the government's backing, do you, little Jew?'

There was an almost lascivious glint in his eyes. I wondered whether anyone before me had dashed his head like an egg against the desk with the mint-green Formica top, but I didn't utter another word.

'Let me put it this way, Koja,' my ex-brother-in-law purred

soothingly, 'your brother is waiting for us in the fabulous French restaurant downstairs. We should go down there now and discuss things in a manner befitting three Baltic gentlemen of the Curonia.'

I therefore had another encounter with the boggle-eyed French waiter who had greeted me in such a friendly and hopeful way half an hour before. His friendliness melted away when I ate and drank nothing, while Erhard ordered his precious Coca-Cola and coq au vin. On the wall to my right hung Jeanne Moreau, taking her elevator to the gallows. Beside my left elbow was Hub's right elbow. We had both put our elbows on the table, and neither wanted to be the first to take his off, especially not him: his was made of plastic.

'Friends, I will never be able to show my face here again. They won't tolerate people who don't eat. At least have a little foie gras.'

No one said anything. Hub, at least, had a glass of whisky sitting beside his prosthetic arm.

'Fine. Then let me make a suggestion.'

Sneiper dabbed a white breadcrumb from his lip with a napkin.

'Hub, you will leave Koja in peace. No more allegations against him. No more mad letters. No more Koja Solm. Long live Jeremias Himmelreich.'

Hub didn't react, merely fixed his eyes on me from the side.

'And you, Koja, will be helpful to the general amnesty movement.'

'The what?'

'Some very prominent people in this country are working to obtain a general amnesty for everyone actively involved in the war. That is to say, for everyone who, from the victors' point of view, may not always have behaved impeccably.'

'So what?'

'These gentlemen have a strong interest in a trial against THE OFFICE never coming to pass.'

'There's nothing I can do about that.'

'There's a great deal you can do, Koja. You can obtain various papers for us from your wife. Various papers from the BND. Various papers from the Mossad.'

'It sounds like the only papers you need are the ones admitting you to a psychiatric hospital.'

'Your brother tells me you are living in a Jewish house under your new name. Is that right?'

Surely, I thought, they cannot be blackmailing me so brazenly. I turned to Hub, or rather, to his plastic arm.

'You have no idea,' I gasped out, 'what will happen if you bring these things out into the open.'

Hub took both his elbows off the table, and the hand he was born with reached into his coat pocket and pulled out a revolver, which he pointed at me.

'Hub, don't do anything stupid!' Sneiper exclaimed.

Many years earlier, Papa had intended to shoot first us and then himself in the head, but foundered on his own indecision, and my brother had taken the enticing, silvery gun from him. But only now did I recall that Hub, my angel and constant supporter, discovered at that tender age what it feels like not only to look down the barrel of a loaded Smith & Wesson No.3 (Russian Model), but also to make someone else look down it, because that is exactly what he then did to me. There had been no hint of malice in his eyes, just a curiosity that I found disconcerting. Now, forty years and dozens of executions later, that curiosity had been sated – and I realized that, no matter what was about to happen, he wouldn't be capable of feeling regret or remorse; he had always been unreceptive to emotions that had their roots in the past.

The waiter returned to ask if we wanted to order anything else, but came to an abrupt halt when his bulging eyes lit upon this scene.

Hub, however, beckoned him over, put the revolver away and calmly asked if he would be so good as to bring him and his brother an apple, a red one if possible.

27

I went straight to see Ev.

I wanted to tell her everything.

Unfortunately, a few weeks earlier she had fallen in love with her psychiatrist, a youngish man in his late thirties, whom I myself had recommended to her. He had cured one of our Kidon people of his anxiety. 'A wonderful doctor,' the regulator had said, 'very sympathetic. He's got me shooting again with a completely clear conscience.'

When Ev confessed this to me one evening, she was lying in my arms. I closed my eyes and clenched my quaking jaw above her head, to suppress the rising sobs. She lifted her face to assure me that it was nothing to do with me, and I too was sure it was nothing to do with me. But it assuredly was to do with her, with the psychiatrist and all the other unwholesome things of this world.

Anna became an important prop to me at that difficult time.

She always answered when I called her, spoke in melodious sentences, reassured me, asked me not to question my relationship with Mama. She said her mother's brain had to release masses of morphine before she could feel happiness, to compensate for the sense of loss that had tormented her since her departure – Anna's departure, that is.

'Papa, I can't talk to Mama. Only to you. I can't reach her. Perhaps a dick has to reach her.'

I said crossly that she shouldn't use such vulgar language when talking about her mother. She apologized at once, but then I thought, why shouldn't she talk about dicks? She lives in my head, after all, sees what I see, hears what I hear, and knows about everything, all my physical infirmities, the constricted urethra, the bad back, the consistency of my stools. Children do get to know about these things eventually, if you get old and decrepit enough – or if they die before you.

I was astonished, however, at how expert Anna was in matters of the heart. Conjugal bonding, intimacy, cinema dates, jealousy. There was nothing we couldn't talk about.

'You were living like brother and sister, Papa,' she said precociously. 'If Mama has regained the ability to choose a young lover, it means her depression is receding. Isn't that brilliant?'

I had to admit that it might seem brilliant from many angles.

'Then let her come back to life, Papa. Let her have her little psychiatrist.'

His name was David Grün and he was a Schindler Jew, with an expensive practice in Lehel. The couch he tended there, it turned out, had a topography ideally suited to lovemaking. Ev called in one day, wanting to discover how the central mechanisms of her despondency functioned. But that was not what she said in the first session; instead, she explained to David Grün that she felt torn between the two countries that were important to her, and could he tell her which would make the better home, Tel Aviv or Munich.

David Grün, having dissected her unconscious in two afternoon sessions, described Ev as 'a pathological liar' who was experiencing 'chronically low mood'. Ev couldn't differentiate between dream and reality, he said, which meant that her dream (Tel Aviv, symbolized by a cup of black coffee in the analyst's left hand) and her reality (Munich, symbolized by a little jug of white milk in his right) flowed into one another like milky coffee and should be drunk in the same way, preferably hot and in Germany. (Naturally, that is precisely what then happened before Ev's still sceptical eyes.)

Ev had seldom heard or seen anything so inane, as she informed David Grün straight away, but he dismissed her objection: the metaphor was an artless one, but unfortunately so was the disorder. In some respects, he said, Frau Himmelreich was still in an adolescent phase, for how could she believe she was welcome in Israel: the ex-wife of a war criminal and current wife of a secret agent? She wasn't even especially welcome in his practice.

'When I explained to him,' Ev told me, 'that in my professional opinion he was a terrible doctor, he replied that I was a terrible patient. We shouted at one another. But two days later, he sent me a love letter. He said that he'd only treated me so poorly to avoid creating an emotional connection with me, but my absence had created that connection all the same, and it was a strong one. He had been attracted by my deep unhappiness at once, he said, and he wanted to see me again, soon. And so I did see him again. I hope you're not angry, Koja. You and I, we'll always be together, and I will always be honest with you, always, always.'

'Well, that's brilliant,' I said, using that unfortunate word of our daughter's, which of course she had got from me.

At night, when I lay silently beside Ev, repulsed by the regular, contented, sour breath that swirled from her open mouth (so much so that I toyed with the idea of taking the yoghurt spoon and, for a change, sticking it down her lying throat, then snatching up my pillow and pressing it down onto her skull, and preferably parking my fat arse on that pillow, with all the weight of my middle-aged spread on top of it), Anna woke up and asked me what I had always loved about Mama.

And it was always the smallest things that occurred to me – the way, for instance, that just before falling asleep she would lose the ability to pronounce the letter 's', and would whisper, ''leep well and no 'noring,' before tiredness overcame her. Or the way she had looked at me, aged sixteen, standing in the Baltic Sea, before letting herself fall backwards, away from the shore, as if the waves were my arms. Or her handwriting, which is on the one hand steeply slanted, and on the other looks like Jane Austen's, with fragile little curlicues over all the 'i's – beautiful, curly handwriting that has always inspired me.

But when I entered her room (on my return from the ominous meeting with the Unspeakable and Sneiper, completely exhausted, with the mark from the barrel of Hub's revolver still on my forehead), she was out shopping.

And I was in such a state of turmoil that I read the letter Ev was in the process of writing to David. It was lying there on her desk, and her handwriting inspired me to nothing but low sobs, for the aesthetics of the three little curls above the words 'I want you inside me' can only be enjoyed when it is oneself who is the 'you'. And my horror, my pain and my fear mingled with the horror, the pain and the fear I had brought with me like malevolent flowers from the chrysanthemum chambers in the French quarter. Bushes and borders of fear began to blossom until they formed an immense garden, and I decided to spend a few days mulling things over first, though Anna strongly advised me against it. Mulling things over is like liquid manure for fear, an excellent fertilizer.

Over the days that followed, I was oppressed by questions.

Was it really right to tell Ev about this wretched blackmail attempt? Would she actually believe me? Wouldn't she just be demoralized by those declarations under oath from my former SS comrades, who painted me as a monster? And didn't she always have David Grün on hand, who was so fresh and young and nauseatingly unassailable, a virtually flawless alternative to me? Wasn't he a better fit for her as a Jew? Wasn't he a better fit for her as a psychiatrist? Wasn't he a better fit for her in bed? Wasn't his penis larger, stiffer, more tenacious, more resilient (psychologically resilient, too) than mine?

But Papa, I heard Anna say at this point, please talk to Mama anyway. Confide in Mama. Have a little confidence in yourself. Mama loves you. She's your refuge and your shield. She's already bored with David. Sex is just the largest common denominator.

'No,' I cried out. 'You're mistaken. Go away! Leave me alone!'

'Darling, what's wrong?' Ev said, as I saw Anna flitting away.

'Nothing.'

'You were tossing and turning. You need to look after your heart.'

'Go back to sleep.'

'You keep groaning. There *is* something wrong, isn't there?'

She will always be the person who knew me best.

'Maybe.'

'Well then, what?'

The light went on. I blinked and saw Ev blinking next to me, her hand searching for her glasses. What on earth was I going to say to her? With a few foolish words, I could bring the hammer down on the anvil and shatter our whole world – or I could throw it in the air and catch it.

Something inside me decided on the second option.

'What is it you want to tell me, darling?' Ev asked sleepily, her hand (a still-dreaming hand) failing to find her glasses.

'The fact you are so keen on fellatio at the moment has something to do with the Mossad.'

Her body, still heavy and relaxed, righted itself a little. She rubbed her eyes, sticky elephant eyes.

'What did you just say?'

'The fact that you're so keen on fellatio at the moment has something to do with the Mossad. It stimulates you sexually. It turns you on.'

'It's two o'clock in the morning,' she groaned, flopping back onto the pillow. 'And anyway, I don't like fellatio all that much, darling.'

'I read your letter.'

Ev didn't say anything.

'I didn't mean to, Ev. I came home, and I wasn't feeling good, and it was lying on your table half finished. And I read it.'

Ev didn't say anything.

'You like fellatio quite a lot, these days.'

'You're reading my letters now, Koja?'

'Maybe you should ask me why I wasn't feeling good when I got home?'

'Why weren't you feeling good?'

'I'd been to see Erhard.'

'Erhard?'

'Sneiper.'

Only now did she turn to me, suddenly wide awake (her hand, too, incidentally).

'What were you doing with that fascist lawyer?'

I had the opportunity to come clean. Wasn't Sneiper putting pressure on me? Forcing me? Threatening me? All this I could have told her about the immaculately turned-out fascist lawyer. And yet, when faced with the choice of putting pride or truth first, pride always wins. And so I just murmured, 'He's your ex-husband, Ev. We talked about you.'

'So, you read my letter, and you went to Sneiper to talk about me?'

'Ev, I just wanted—'

'You know he's acting for those vile amnesty people?'

'Yes, but—'

'How could you go and see that scumbag behind my back? How could you expose me like that?'

'Come off it, Ev. Expose you? You're the one sleeping with other people here!'

'But not behind your back! I told you everything! None of that has anything to do with us.'

'Yes, maybe not for you.'

'You're too possessive.'

'I am not possessive.'

'David says the same, that you're too possessive.'

'Oh, so you're allowed to talk to David Grün about me, are you?'

'I am not *allowed* to talk to David about you. I *have* to talk to David about you. He's my psychiatrist.'

'David Grün is your damned stud horse, and I am letting myself be cuckolded because I love you, goddammit, and I want you to feel better!'

'Shout a bit louder, why don't you, then half the Mossad will start listening.'

'I can shout that I love you,' I shouted, 'can't I?'

Well, Swami, conversations of this kind always go back and forth for a while, and I don't want to bore you with the details. So, to cut a long story short: in the end, I chose one of the little escape routes that always exist in a marital argument. I made a cowardly excuse, because I simply wasn't in a position to take the major turn-off towards danger and the precipice, the turn-off I had already missed twice.

When Ev asked me later – pressed tight against me, the light switched off – why I had gone to see Sneiper, I just said he was organizing the Baltic German fraternity *Kommers* feast, and was still looking for helpers. And in memory of Papa, who had so loved the Curonia, I had agreed to design the invitation cards (inscribed with the fraternity toast: '*Ex est! Schmollis! Fiduzit!*').

'But you aren't Koja Solm any more,' Ev whispered, exhausted. 'You're Herr Himmelreich.'

'Yes,' I said, 'don't worry,' I said, and then kept very still as I waited for Anna to join us.

But she didn't come, not wanting to disturb us.

I have never felt happier than when I was able to hold Ev in my arms, as I did that night, though I already knew I was going to betray her.

28

Erhard Sneiper thanked me with an absent-minded smile when I paid my courtesy visits to him over the months that followed. He usually received me in his chrysanthemum office, and looked tactfully out of the window as I updated him on the progress of the Reich Main Security Office trial.

I convinced myself that in doing this I was protecting Ev. I was going behind her back, but for her own good. Without me, wouldn't Hub and Sneiper have resorted to other weapons entirely? Wasn't I ensuring my sister's well-being, by thwarting any probing investigations of her? What harm could my information do?

Ev told me which escapees were to be invited in for questioning.

I passed that on.

Ev complained about the public prosecutors.

I passed that on.

Ev was looking forward to upcoming arrests.

I passed everything on.

I helped the escapees to escape this, too. THE OFFICE was indebted to me. Even Sneiper said so several times, and as he was saying it, I looked him straight in the eye.

He was pleased. He informed his people.

I heard nothing more from Hub.

*

To distract myself from my infamy, I made an effort in all things. I showed Ev how much she meant to me. For example, I began to illustrate the cover sheets of her escapee archive. Generic terms like 'gas van' and 'T4 campaign' I depicted as you might imagine, but for 'concentration camps' I created artistic impressions of the tourist sights in each place (there were few sights in Sobibor, Treblinka and Auschwitz, it's true, but Riga had its beautiful cathedral, and for Buchenwald there was Weimar, so I could draw Goethe's summer house – insane, wasn't it?).

Anguish over the collapse of my already fragile moral maxims at least led me back to art. Probably a way to sublimate my grief. I had set up a small studio for myself in the attic of the fortified house. Dr Himmelreich, who had studied medicine and practised surgery, may have known every Jewish joke in the book and been able to recite whole chapters of Egon Friedell's *Cultural History of the Modern Age* off by heart, but he'd had no real creativity of his own. And so, as his revenant, I had to remain sadly talentless. I did draw from time to time, but only for the benefit of Ev, Anna and myself. Mostly elm leaves or flowers from the Munich parks.

It was the only scrap of peace I could find.

Papa had always warned me off elm leaves. Don't forget that life is movement, my son. That was his credo. Cross-hatch waves, why don't you. That's better than cross-hatching elm leaves. More difficult. Just look at Dürer. Or da Vinci. The great Leonardo could follow the water he was drawing with his eyes; even when it was bubbling out of a fountain, his eye bubbled with it. Not just elm leaves, Koja. Not just nature morte. And if you must, then at least touch them. Take hold of your elm leaf. When you've drawn it, watch how it disintegrates. Draw it again a few days later.

It disintegrates like your life.

The hardest thing in my disintegrating life was to remain Herr Himmelreich.

Munich's streets were paved with people who knew Koja Solm.

The Org, paved with people who knew Koja Solm.

A cobbled street stretched from here to Riga and the hellmouth of the Bikernieki Forest, and every cobble was a pearl-grey human head who knew Koja Solm.

Hundreds of swords of Damocles dangling from stallions' hairs above me.

Otto John, for instance. Escaped from the GDR. Convicted of treason before the Hamburg district court. Out again after several years in prison. Old. Broken. Lonely.

But back.

The return of the prodigal John, as Adenauer sneered.

Eventually, Otto also came to Munich, looking for me. He drove to the address of my old gallery. Galerie Solm on Salvatorstraße. He found a gentlemen's outfitters there. Baffled sales assistants foisted a summer suit on him just before the start of autumn. Galerie Solm no longer existed. And nor did the art dealer of the same name. He was nowhere to be found.

But since a former president of the Office for the Protection of the Constitution knows how to go about tracking down a missing person, Otto John made a few phone calls. He had people search for documentary evidence, papers, tax returns, cheques and bank withdrawals, court records and residency permits. He spoke to officials at the finance office, who had access to confidential files. He even telephoned Theodor Heuss, to see if he'd heard anything about me. He tried the SPD party headquarters, as Koja Solm had once been a member. He pieced together the movements of his old friend and faithful rescuer up to the winter of nineteen fifty-four. But after that date, all he had were rumours. The whereabouts of Konstantin 'Koja' Solm were a mystery.

Even when Otto John turned up at my mother's front door, all he learned was that one mustn't traipse all over her good carpet in one's outdoor shoes, and that in any case her son already knew where he was.

Finally, Otto discovered Ev's address, for she was my brother's sister.

I was on my way back from the Englischer Garten, where I'd been walking with Anna in a flood of clear morning light. I opened the front door (you know, the one with the three-second armour-plating) and only recognized the voice with the Hesse accent saying, 'Well, how very shtrange,' when I was already halfway across Ev's office. Otto was standing with his back to me. He was sloppily shaved, bloated, and in his little trilby and understated brown corduroy suit he still looked like a Brit – though a Brit who was down on his luck.

Ev gave me clear get-out-fast signals with her eyes. But it was already too late.

John turned towards me. His baritone voice sounded pleasant and calm; he went on speaking as he turned, mentioning my name and the fact that he was looking for me. His gaze was distracted, he scarcely met my eyes, and I had the feeling he was looking straight through me.

Perhaps he just wasn't concentrating, but he turned away again without any sign of recognition, taking me for a visiting stranger. I stood there, frozen in shock, and heard Ev tell him that it was a long time since she'd heard from her brother Koja; he was said to be in South America, Chile, maybe.

Then she asked why he was searching for Koja, anyway, and he replied, 'Ah, it's all right, I thought he might lend me a little money, that's all, I'm as broke as a pie crusht.'

I was able to dash upstairs unseen, my heart pounding, to our top-floor apartment. There, I scrutinized myself in the mirror. I looked at my hairstyle, which was beginning to turn from balding to a rather dishevelled version of a dandelion, with the aid of an expensive hair transplant. My grey beard was sparse around my chin, but full across my cheeks. I had Himmelreich glasses, a Himmelreich cane, even a Himmelreich gait, since you recognize people from the way they move as well as their faces.

There was no doubt that a lot of effort had gone into allowing me to remain Jeremias Himmelreich.

At the Org, Gehlen had even made sure that my permanent files were destroyed and replaced by Himmelreich files. Most of the people who worked there knew me by the name Dürer, which I retained. And the few who were aware that Hub and I were related had now retired, or were on the point of doing so.

Avoiding exposure meant avoiding most public spaces. I didn't even take Ev to the theatre or to concerts, and for these occasions she relied on David Grün.

The cinema was the only place we could scurry into together, always just after the main feature had started. I never saw the opening or closing credits of any of Fellini's films: as soon as we heard the first bars of the end music, we headed out into the night.

And as we walked home through the dark streets, threatened by lies and deception, shaken by my treachery, for which I could find no expression in my behaviour (because of course, I didn't want her to notice), we sometimes held hands. More than three times, I came very close to confessing that I was passing her documents on to THE OFFICE.

But I never quite managed it.

Man is weak, a cork in the current. Ultimately, everything depends on catching the right wave.

Although intelligence services are virtually obliged to conduct their business by not entirely legal means – which is to say, it's a point of honour with them – there is still a great general fuss when fountains of blood gush in plain sight. Prime minister David Ben-Gurion, at any rate, had been so badly damaged by the luckless assassination attempts on German missile engineers that he had to dismiss Colonel Harel from his position as head of the Mossad.

We heard this from Isser himself, when he called us to say good-bye. It was a beautiful March day in nineteen sixty-three. I remember a magpie cawing in answer outside the open window when Ev called me to the phone. Isser's voice in the receiver sounded even more high-pitched than it was in real life, and once he had outlined the perversion, uselessness and character weaknesses of everyone in his country's cabinet (including the head of state), he declared that he was at peace with the world and himself. His only complaint was an *Ulcus pepticum* in his stomach. When I didn't reply, he asked if I even knew what an *Ulcus pepticum* was.

I said how could I not know; I had been a doctor of medicine, a surgical specialist.

'If you're a surgical specialist, Jeremias, then I'm the baby Jesus,' Colonel Harel laughed, and hung up.

He was replaced by Meir Amit, an intimate enemy of Harel's. He was a technocrat, a sergeant-major type, and a connoisseur of all the subtleties of organizational hierarchy.

Meir's first official pronouncement was regarding the way he should be addressed. No forename, that much was clear, particularly as his forename was also one of the most common German surnames. Meir had people call him Ramsad. Chief Ramsad. He spoke of Isser Harel only as 'the previous guy'. He said things like, 'This is the previous guy's cock-up,' or, 'Such a lack of precision can only have been the fault of the previous guy.'

Chief Ramsad had the sharp, greyish-white, dead face of the polar fox muff from which Ev had once made my left winter boot, and I saw it for the first time in all its expressionlessness when Ev and I had to report to the new Mossad headquarters on Kaplan Street in Tel Aviv. Ramsad's poker face didn't show even a hint of surprise when we revealed who lay behind the Himmelreichs (the small, dark stains on our family history, I mean). Ramsad just muttered that this was more nonsense from the previous guy that he would have to straighten out.

But Shimon Peres protected us.

Ev's archive of escapees protected us as well.

And the fortified house in Munich gave Chief Ramsad the sense that he had an elite wigwam in the heart of the underworld. Effective. But light and unobtrusive. Unknown to almost everyone. Quick to take down. No waste. No getting off track. Fully financed by the Orcs. No direct responsibility. Acts of sabotage. High-risk interventions. Murder squads. Anything was possible. We could carry on working, just with greater restraint than before.

But what does 'restraint' mean. In both Tel Aviv and Pullach, radical secret operations were being planned. The missions were shared out fairly. The Mossad struck in Europe, in South America, then in parts of Asia. The BND provided the money, the weapons, the cover. And as coordinator, I inducted the Israeli assassins into German ways of doing things.

Champagne-Lotz, for instance. He stayed at the fortified house in Munich for a year, living in our spare room and getting his cover story from me. A former adjutant of Rommel's. Awarded the Knight's Cross of the Iron Cross. Then a farmer in Australia. That kind of thing. All of it verifiable. None of it true.

The BND organized his passports, the letters of thanks from Rommel (lovingly forged by my own hand), and even his Waltraud, a wife from Essen-Kettwig, pretty as a picture.

The Mossad took care of the communications, the infrastructure, and Shiva – another pretty wife from Haifa, who took her husband's betrayal very badly and only just survived a suicide attempt.

Champagne-Lotz and his Waltraud moved to Cairo, where he bred horses and got to know Egyptian generals, who were amenable to Arabian stallions, Oktoberfests, Waltraud's home-made Munich doughnuts, and all manner of questions.

Three years later, Champagne-Lotz single-handedly annihilated the entire Egyptian air force, by radioing Israel the coordinates of their secret runways.

So you mustn't think that I was solely occupied with fear, elm leaves and my wife's lover. And not just with innocence betrayed, either. I was the head of a Mossad outpost in the middle of Munich, and the head of an outpost always has his hands full.

To think of the work generated by Shlomo alone! My colleague in Paris channelled his regulators through our Munich house; I gathered information for him from the Org on the personnel of the Arab secret services; his payments of secret commissions to Syrian agents were made via me; and together, we coordinated the disappearance of a Lebanese businessman holidaying in the Bavarian resort of Füssen, from where he was planning an attack on a Parisian synagogue.

All legal operating costs.

All German–Israeli friendship.

All repaid with close-range surveillance in Moscow, and a light-brown house in a suburb of Leningrad, from which details of Warsaw Pact troop movements were transmitted to Tel Aviv using a converted UKW radio.

I performed all these tasks with passion and focus, and they were not detrimental to my inner peace. That peace was only dented by THE OFFICE.

29

It had been Palestine Fritz, of all people, who brought the Müllersche Volksbad by the Isar to my attention. Once a week he took his Labrador, bred from Gehlen's Labrador, to be bathed, soaped and coiffed by the dog groomer there, while one storey up he too cleansed himself, amid ostentatious decor (in a swimming pool with a bottom tiled like the floor of St Peter's Basilica).

I preferred the Roman-Irish steam room, the Irish aspect of which was always a mystery to me (perhaps it was the proximity to alcohol, for which there were plentiful opportunities in the Volksbad).

One evening, when most of the pool's customers had left, and the stern superintendent had announced that they would be closing soon, a blubbery body sat down next to mine (splatch). I ignored it at first, for I liked to sit on the little shelf above the round basin and sweat in peace. But then the man leant over to me, and I could smell his cigar breath (a peculiar aroma in a steam room).

'We need to talk,' he said quietly.

'Who is we?'

'You and me.'

I could barely make out his contours in the mist. A doughy, ageing, blackbird face, older than my own, with thick, black-rimmed spectacles halfway down it; beneath that, heavy, sagging breasts; and even further down, a flash of penis from under his belly – that was all I could see.

'I don't have any need to talk to you whatsoever.'

'Erhard Sneiper asked me not to come to you. But I thought it would be a good idea.'

'Do we know one another?'

'My name is Achenbach. Member of the Bundestag. Ernst Achenbach.' He lifted his reddened backside, slid a little closer to me, and whispered, 'FDP.'

The superintendent appeared again, said, 'Five more minutes, gentlemen,' woke an old man who had fallen asleep on his lounger, and shuffled off again.

'What do you want?'

'You won't believe how many people are taking their own lives out of sheer fright. Upstanding Germans who are now under investigation. Off bridges. Heads on train tracks. I've got photos outside.'

'Sneiper was right: coming to me really wasn't a good idea.'

'I've got photos of you, too, Herr Himmelreich.'

'I'm going for a shower.'

'Or should I say: Herr Konstantin Solm.'

I sat down again.

'You really do have no foreskin,' he grinned. 'You're pretty serious about this, aren't you?'

He had a smooth, clean-shaven, jowly face, which despite the fogged spectacles was a good fit for the baroque-ifying decorative flourishes behind him.

'Don't worry, your secret is safe with me. I'm a partner of Herr

Sneiper's. You're a partner of Herr Sneiper's. And a partner of Herr Sneiper's is a partner of mine.'

'What kind of partnership is that, then?'

'A political one. You're bringing us some very useful information. THE OFFICE has a lot to thank you for.'

For a moment, words failed me: it was only then that I came to my senses and fully realized that this stout frame belonged to the famous amnesty functionary and FDP politician Ernst Achenbach. He was always in the papers. And Ev had told me that, during the occupation of Paris, he'd been responsible for Jewish affairs at the German Embassy there.

'I'm glad you're supporting our efforts, Herr Himmelreich. But don't fail in your diligence. Diligence is the key to everything. With rather more diligence, you will also get rather more useful information.'

'You've come all the way from Bonn to sit beside me naked and talk nonsense?'

'Oh heavens, no. I happened to be visiting Munich, and I was in the taproom with the fabulous Sneiper, and he told me about you. And I thought, I'll take a closer look at this scoundrel, and the best way to do that is as God made him.'

'God did not make me this way. Nor you. God did not create a mountain of elderly flesh.'

The superintendent came back and began to turn off the heating pipes.

'Very well, Herr Himmelreich. You aren't in the best of moods. So let's make this brief: I would like you to assist us in another matter.'

He got up.

'Herr Sneiper will give you a telephone number. A telephone number in Bonn. You will call this number.'

'Call whom?'

'The federal justice minister is looking for a trustworthy adviser. Has to be someone who's been persecuted. A Jew for preference. And the fabulous Dr Sneiper thought of you and your good lady wife at once.'

The federal justice minister?

I drove out to see the fabulous Dr Sneiper in Grünwald, at his fabulous palace-of-a-thousand-rooms, in comparison with which his offices seemed positively modest. I rang the bell at the gate and, when no one answered, climbed over the fence and encountered a surprised miniature collie. I found Sneiper in his one-hundred-and-twenty-square-metre living room with its grand fireplace and asked him why he had not opened the door. Since I received an order rather than a reply ('Get out, this minute!'), I asked if he was particularly fond of the miniature collie, which was whining and struggling in my arms, and which could have done with a thorough wash at the Müllersche Volksbad.

But since all Erhard could come up with was foolish lawyer rhetoric, I took the Bowie knife off his wall – a gift from one Captain Miller, so I gathered from the engraving on the fifteen-centimetre blade.

And I used it to cut off the miniature collie's head.

That livened things up at once, and Sneiper confessed with deep regret that he had told several people about me, people such as Werner Best (never heard of him) and the well-upholstered Herr Achenbach, who had found me in the steam room and threatened me so unaesthetically.

The miniature collie's blood was now soaking the carpet, and I assured Sneiper that I was sorry for the animal, but he should never have given away my identity. Never. Erhard wept. He wept despite my declaring how much I hated to see his pain, but thank God his children were grown and out of the house. And his wife at a spa in Bad Doberan.

'I don't know why you're all so invested in this trial, Erhard. I'm giving you all the information about THE OFFICE. Everything I can get. I'm betraying my wife for your sake. And I don't like that. I love my wife.'

He sniffed and pulled a silk handkerchief from his waistcoat, embroidered monogram, with which to dry his tears. But I had urgent need of it for my blade, and as I wiped it clean I went on, 'But you don't have me under your thumb. I've told you this already: you have no idea who you're dealing with.'

Anna was angry with me for months afterwards. She loved horses, of course, and I tried to placate her by swearing that I would never hurt a horse, whatever its owner might have done to me.

'You know, my darling, I could just as easily have beheaded Erhard's Trakehner stallion. He was just a kilometre away in his stable. But I never could have brought myself to do it. I wouldn't kill any animal you're fond of.'

To make it up to her, I took Anna to the zoo in Hellabrunn, as I had done so often in the past, bought her favourite magazine, *Animals and Us*, visited the old elephant house, the hippos, the tigers, and Anna said you should try taking your Bowie knife in there with one of those tigers, you coward.

You are filled with rage, too, Swami.

That saddens me. Believe me, I'm not deliberately trying to make myself seem like a monster. I don't want to appear cynical, either. Please: I love and respect all creatures, I even respect grasshoppers, particularly since I myself may once have been a member of their species, what can I say.

But dogs, no, I simply find dogs abhorrent. I believe that secret agents will someday be reborn as dogs. Why else does the base BND man care so lovingly for his four-legged friend, take it to the office with him, treat it to a haircut in the most magnificent art nouveau jewel of a bath house in all of Europe, let it sleep by his stove as Gehlen does, treat it better than any of his fellow men? Perhaps because even the scruffiest mutt is regarded as loyal, a quality that so many of us long for in our profession and our lives, a quality we then buy with kibble and tripe.

That was probably why the shock was such a lasting one for Erhard Sneiper. Any further meeting at his office was now out of the question. And I certainly wasn't allowed back to his villa.

And so, in order to obtain the telephone number that would force me to Bonn, I had to go and see the Unspeakable. Erhard insisted on it. He wanted to make this as difficult for me as he possibly could.

Hub lived in a dingy back-courtyard apartment in Sendling.

It was dark by the time I arrived. Not a single light bulb worked on the staircase. I had to feel my way up four floors, along crumbling plaster and a greasy banister and through clouds of various odours. Outside his door, the air smelled of cabbage and tiled coal stoves. The doorbell had been ripped out. He answered after minutes of knocking. His stumbling gait looked even more unreal in the dark. Like a bat with only one wing. He was wearing a stained vest, and seemed uncertain whether to let me in.

'The telephone number,' was all I said.

He grunted and clung to the door with his arm. Then he reached for the wall beside him and switched on the light, a cloudy yellow forty-watt light. He walked ahead of me down a narrow hallway that looked like the inside of a sinking submarine. What was he spending that handsome BND pension on? The whole apartment was filled with rubbish and things in labelled plastic bags. They were piled on open shelves up to the ceiling. 'Long Johns', 'Trousers', 'Slippers', 'Misc. 1', 'Misc. 2', 'Emergencies'. I saw a small altar, sky blue the risen Christ, two candles, and wicks and wick-holders for eternal flames (hard to reconcile with the Protestant iconography). In the kitchen, he was hoarding bread. There was a bottle of vodka on the table and beside it, his unstrapped prosthetic arm.

He didn't offer me anything, or let me sit down.

'So, you're working for us now, little brother.'

'We shouldn't talk.'

'You and Ev, you're hunting the people who raised you. Who loved you. It's your own flesh and blood you're hunting. But you're still working for us.'

'Give me the telephone number, and I'll be out of here.'

'Your idiotic quest for justice. It's bringing much greater suffering than any injustice would. No matter. The important thing is that now a dog's been killed.'

'You think that's important?'

'It warrants attention.'

'I don't think it's that important.'

'That was very stupid of you. Sneiper is a powerful man. He loved that mutt. You'll be sorry, just you wait.'

He chuckled to himself and began to pull open the drawers of his kitchen cupboard, looking for the phone number. I saw that he had stuffed his socks into the knife drawer.

'This trial will never take place. You're not going to get THE OFFICE. And you're not going to get me, either.'

'We'll see about that.'

'They've called a halt to the investigation, in case you didn't know.'

I stared at him.

'They've stopped the investigation?'

'Insufficient grounds.'

He rummaged in a coffee tin.

'I'm glad for you.'

'You're a liar, Koja. You're not glad. I'll show you what'll make you glad.'

I said nothing.

'Come with me. I know where I put it.'

He disappeared off to the right, into a little room separated from the kitchen by a curtain. He switched on the light and I could hear him muttering. After hesitating for a moment, I went over, pushed back the curtain and saw a rope hanging from the ceiling. The rope was adorned with a hangman's noose, tied by a one-armed man and therefore not about to win any beauty contests, but just large enough to put a head through. Under the rope was a chair, and on the chair sat Hub, legs crossed, grinning drunkenly at me.

'I sit here every evening, for inspiration, and who knows, if you're lucky, one day I'll get up on this chair and set us both free.'

He glowered at me, swivelled around on the chair, opened the drawer of a dresser and pulled out an envelope. He thrust it at me disdainfully. I tore it open.

'That's a nice coat you're wearing, Koja. Excellent shoes.'

On Sneiper's notepaper I saw his pompous letterhead and, written in a delicate, girlish hand that probably belonged to the young woman from Goldingen, a telephone number with a Bonn dialling code: '0228/49336'.

Beneath it, the words: 'Gustav Heinemann, available daily from 09.00. Expecting Himmelreich's call.'

Four weeks later, I was the justice minister's honorary adviser on matters of National Socialist violent crimes.

30

A suffering and tormented lump of flesh.

The Hippy's steady decline fills me with concern.

He has stopped drawing. And he can barely follow my stories now; his teeth chatter, he sees beheaded miniature collies everywhere, even under his bed, and he believes that all the second screw in his head will do is control his dreams. His speech centre has completely decoupled itself from his brain and does what it wants.

Mrkstlwormblk.

That's what all his words sound like.

The Swami, pumped full of sedatives, is lying on a trolley in the corridor, waiting for his operation. I am sitting beside him. I have some hope for the procedure, especially with regard to Basti's sensory perception. He is wearing a surgical cowl made of green fabric, astronaut model, fastened under the chin like a helmet and giving the oval of his face an old-womanish aspect. His skin is in a catastrophic state. He hardly moves around now, and so it is inflamed and rotting, torn in many places, chapped. His body is covered in blotches and open sores.

Now and again, Night Nurse Gerda comes by to check on him. She tells me that it will be his turn any minute, and she's sure it is doing him good to feel my hand. My hand, which is holding his. I can hear him wheezing.

Our meetings in the hospital corridor have long since ceased. He has been suffering from sudden attacks of vertigo, which he claimed (when he was still able to claim things) I was causing with my appalling stories. But of course, that's nonsense. All these months in hospital have made his bones brittle. Their calcium budget is completely spent. When I tried to take him down to see the babies on the first floor one last time, he slipped out of my embrace and fell over. Perhaps he really shouldn't have had any Marrakesh Gold. Or at least not so much.

He hasn't got out of bed since his fall, and it's scarcely possible to talk to him.

Can he even hear what I'm saying?

'Can you hear what I'm saying?' I ask.

There is no reaction, though he must still be conscious in a fragmentary way.

'You know, Swami,' I whisper, 'when they wheel you in there and give you your second screw, you will get the gift of your radiant energy back. To start with, you might have to pay the price for what your brain will go through when it's shaken about like that. But through all its trials, Basti, your brain has reached such an unexpected level of maturity that I'm pleased at how well it has managed to grasp the momentousness of my tragedy. I wish your head the very, very best, and will communicate with it again once the operation is over. I will tell it what happened at the justice ministry, and the terrible time I had there. And if you should fall into a coma, then I will tell it a lot more than that.'

The Hippy's hand tries to wriggle out of mine, but I am holding it nice and tight.

Nurse Gerda approaches with a spring in her step and the beautiful Student Nurse Sabine in her wake.

Right, then, off we go.

They take the brakes off the trolley and roll it away, like one of Dalí's mad inventions.

31

I didn't want to go to Bonn.

What a miserable place.

The weather there is British, with high humidity and November fog in almost every season. In summer, it's like Bangkok, only curtained with cloud and roofed with tropical storms. No snow in winter. Puddles all year round. The cityscape eccentric, shapeless and sleepy, in the most boring baroque style in Central Europe. The prince-electors of Bonn never had any money, and the palace they built there was something Madrid wouldn't even have used as a jail.

Not wanting to create the impression of a proper capital city, the West German government spared every effort and expense to make 'the temporary seat of the federal government' look as temporary as they possibly could. The members of parliament were crammed into a former teacher-training academy until it was bursting at the seams. It looked a little like the CPSU headquarters in Minsk, but smaller and more makeshift. Bonn was an imposition, and an expression of the German political establishment's desire to get back to Berlin as quickly as possible.

That is why Konrad Adenauer's ambition had been to set up not only the most pitiable seat of government in Europe, but the tiniest. And in fact, only the capitals of Andorra (Andorra la Vella), Liechtenstein (Vaduz), Iceland (Reykjavik), San Marino (San Marino) and Monaco (Monaco) had fewer inhabitants than Bonn, though at least they were all either in the mountains or on the coast, rather than being sliced into two flat parts by the Rhine.

Ev, by contrast, was delighted. Both by the city and by Herr Heinemann, whom she came to trust so much on our first official visit that she called him 'Herr Heinzelmann' like the Heinzelmännchen from the fairy tale, though it was only a slip of the tongue.

Justice Minister Gustav Heinemann was a fantastic fit for Bonn: he was a jurist through and through, with his slick, white pomaded hair and his smooth, entirely scentless skin. He wore hideous glasses, but with dignity, and would have made a good stamp-gluer in a post office. He avoided music, poetry, novels, films, opera, theatre, dance, sunsets and any kind of exuberance. He loved Luther, theology, theorems, lists, playing *Skat*, church congresses, words such as 'ecumenical' and 'redemption', and above all he loved speeches that were as quiet and passionless as possible. He hated nuclear power, the rearmament and Dr Franz Josef Strauß; he scorned the BND, pompous asses and any kind of fuss. He talked to himself much of the time, was given to saying 'boy, oh boy' without any discernible cause, ordered himself to 'by the left – march' on leaving any room, and approached us in his office with the words: 'Well then, I believe this calls for a "good morning".'

Gustav Heinemann had once been a follower of Adenauer's. After the latter's rearmament venture and the founding of the West German Army, which in Heinemann's view was wholly absurd, he had left the CDU under protest. He started his own party, which failed, then went over to the Social Democrats, and had recently become the Federal Republic's first left-wing justice minister. His declared aim in office was to get the Great Criminal Justice Reform underway, a project for which I know you will have little sympathy, if only because it involves an aim, and an ambitious one at that. To achieve this aim, Heinemann needed colleagues who, as he said, were 'first and foremost beyond all moral doubt'.

Of course, I was the perfect man for the job.

Someone without a single black mark, who was being cheated on by the most attractive expert on escapees you could fuck anywhere north of the Alps – ah, these obscenities are always in my mind. They were then, too, as I sat beside Ev, feeling her enthusiasm, mistrusting the way she hung on every word that fell from the maverick minister's lips. She surely did the same with her paramour, particularly as David Grün's lips were much handsomer.

'You know, Herr Himmelreich,' the justice minister complained as he slurped his tea, 'my whole ministry is being ruined by old Nazis. All my heads of department were in the Nazi Party.'

'All of them?'

'Without exception. Sadly, you can't throw civil servants out on their ear just like that. But they're hatching some kind of plot.'

'I see,' I said.

'You'll keep your eyes peeled, won't you?'

'I'm afraid I have no legal background. And my wife is the historian here.'

'Ah yes, but you're a Jew. A Jew, hmm?'

'That's right.'

'You'll check the relevant correspondence here in the office. You'll advise me from an outsider's perspective, yes?'

'I will.'

'It isn't difficult. A layman's eye is what's needed. Good dose of common sense. Look out for people making odd suggestions. I'm sure you will have heard of the amnesty advocates?'

'Of course.'

'Achenbach?'

I could hardly say that I'd only met Herr Achenbach naked.

'A little.'

'That man has been trying to force through a statute of limitations for years now. He has a lot of friends here. We mustn't allow it. Mustn't allow it, I tell you.'

'And we won't,' Ev put in. 'We are very familiar with legal language. I'm currently advising the Berlin state prosecutors in the trial against the Reich Main Security Office.'

'That is a great ministration!' Heinemann gushed.

'Yes,' Ev said uncertainly, not knowing what he meant by 'ministration'.

'A great ministration, that work,' he therefore said again.

Every month, we went to Bonn for a week. We were given a small, draughty office in the Rosenburg, the grand villa where Heinemann's department was based, and spent our time there looking through files that related to the 'statute of limitations paragraphs' for a) murder and b) accessory to murder. We read the minutes from commission meetings for 'the Great Crim-Re', as the Great Criminal Justice Reform was known internally. I compiled dossiers on dozens of civil servants who Heinemann thought were compromised. Essentially, we were Heinemann's Jewish fig leaf, and perhaps his most secret secret police. He could not know that his secret police, or at least their more duplicitous half, were sharing their information with the Mossad, the BND and Erhard Sneiper's amnesty advocates – the whole bloody world, in other words.

Several times, I came very close (as I have said already) to inducting Ev into the ever-tightening net of conspiracies and intrigues that was wrapping itself around my ankles like humming underground electricity cables and slowly hobbling me.

At the same time, something threatening was visibly creeping towards us, like a poisonous dark blue cloud. But I was incapable of taking hold of Ev's chin, raising her eyes and pointing up into the rapidly darkening sky. I underestimated the approaching misfortune. The potential calamity of my being unmasked weighed heavier in comparison. Fear is seldom logical, or it wouldn't be fear. Why should a person be afraid of spiders, or their boss? Nothing that robs you of sleep is ever logical.

It does seem logical that a cause will always tow an effect behind it; you're entirely right about that. When the sun vanishes, it gets dark. When it rains, I get wet. When someone hits me, it hurts. When someone smiles at me, I am glad. Go ahead and call it karma, dear friend.

But I was not glad when Ev smiled at me. I felt jittery, not joyful. I thought about David Grün and Erhard Sneiper, and not about the power of certainty that dwells in every smile. The sun vanished when I sent the top-secret reports that Ev had written about Herr Achenbach, out of hatred for Herr Achenbach, to Herr Achenbach – yes, then the sun really did vanish. But it didn't get dark. I didn't get wet just because it was raining. That isn't what betrayal is like. There is no action-reaction. There's no logic, either.

The risk is that you will find yourself in circumstances beyond your control. And back then, in Bonn, everything was beyond my control. For I could see how happy Ev was as she sat across the desk from me in Bonn, believing she was making the world a better place. And I knew that I was making her unhappy when I passed on her information, gave away the paths she was taking, disrupted her hunt.

But she wasn't unhappy. She didn't become unhappy. She didn't hear about any of it. And so she didn't hear that she was being made unhappy. I hit her, but it didn't hurt. The cause had no effect. I was the only one who became unhappy, although I was actually happy:

after all, my wife and I were working together to catch fugitives, to democratize the country, to ensure justice was done, to minimize the dukkha.

Blah blah blah.

If only it weren't for David Grün, I thought.

If it weren't for David Grün, then I could confess everything to Ev.

How gladly I would do it. She wouldn't leave me; she would stay, as she had stayed with me in the days of the Bolshevik occupation of Riga. As she had always stayed with me.

I spent whole nights discussing it with Anna, because I had begun to think about certain things. All right, perhaps they were uncertain things, but they related to my knowledge of how to make people disappear. I suspect you would not call this connection karma, dear Swami. Although much of it also seems logical.

David Grün is hit. It hurts him (but not me).

David Grün vanishes. It gets dark for Ev (but not for me).

Anna wept.

She said I should never have cut that poor miniature collie's throat. No, I hissed, I should have cut Erhard Sneiper's throat. And David Grün's. It's his fault that all this is happening to Ev.

It was even his fault that I have Eduard Dreher on my conscience.

32

Heinemann had introduced us to Eduard Dreher just a few weeks after we first arrived.

'Well then, I believe this calls for a "good morning", Herr Dreher,' he said to the well-mannered gentleman with the arrogant horse face. He had knocked on Heinemann's office door and walked in as we were about to leave. The minister introduced us as 'internal architects', which left much room for interpretation, and asked Dreher at once what he had dreamed about the previous night. Dreher replied that his dream had involved half a giraffe journeying to the centre of the world. Heinemann found that a refreshing thing in an undersecretary. 'Herr Dreher is writing a little treatise about the world of human dreams, you see. What's the title, again?'

'*Here, Sigmund Freud is Wrong*, Minister.'

'Where is Sigmund Freud wrong?' Ev asked.

'Where he insists on the sexual nature of human dreams, dear lady.'

'You think so, do you?'

'We are not creatures driven by animal instincts. In humans, sexuality has evolved into a lasting, personal connection to someone of the opposite sex. That is what gives us joy.'

'And you don't encounter anything sexual in your dreams?'

'I actually only dream about criminal justice. And the beauty of nature.'

'Yesterday, it was a hare you were trying to arrest for aiding and abetting a burglar,' the attentive Herr Heinemann remarked brightly.

'It was, Minister,' Dreher smiled back.

'Well then, if you should ever dream of me,' Ev said, 'I won't have to worry about any nocturnal emissions.'

Herr Dreher blinked a little, as if he was cold, and Heinemann rocked forward and back on his heels just once. Then he said wasn't it nice, the informal level on which one could speak when one got away from the usual legalese, and that Undersecretary Dreher was the head of the commission for overhauling criminal law, which made him the head of the Great Crim-Re. His closest colleague. Thereupon he opened the door, ushered Ev and me out, and behind the re-closed door we heard a cry of, 'Glory be!' (Heinemann) and shortly after, 'How impertinent!' (Dreher).

Four or five weeks later, Ev came rushing into our office in a state of great excitement. The file she tossed over to me allowed us to draw some conclusions about Eduard Dreher's waking self as well as his unconscious. The old dreamer. During his hallucinogenic years as a Nazi state prosecutor in Innsbruck, he had given the little black sheep who were dragged before his judge's bench some unforgettable hours. In the magic kitchen of his criminal court, he turned up the heat on these delinquents with great skill. Numerous death sentences added some spice to proceedings, especially when they were passed for the most trifling matters.

Take the Karoline Hauser case. It was right at the start of the dream diary that I had now begun to leaf through in astonishment. Hauser was a forty-one-year-old factory worker, who the immaculate dreamer and Nazi prosecutor Dreher decided was 'harmful to the common good' and 'a dangerous habitual criminal'. She escaped the scaffold to which the dreamer tried to send her by a whisker, despite having sold a few dozen clothing coupons on the sly 'out of the most reprehensible self-interest and therefore with malicious intent'.

Or the Josef Knoflach case. He was put on trial as 'a habitual thief and violent criminal'. Knoflach, a fifty-seven-year-old labourer, had made 'unauthorized use' of a bicycle, in order to purloin a loaf of bread and a kilo of bacon. The special court acted on Dreher's recommendation and passed a death sentence. For serious pilfering. It was only an intervention by the Gauleiter of Tirol, who hated the Germans and wasn't going to let some Kraut behead any countryman of his for seriously pilfering a bit of bacon, that got the sentence watered down to eight years in jail.

Or the Anton Rathgeber case. Five weeks after an air raid, this booze-soaked old coffee roaster had taken a few grubby pieces of clothing from a chest that was lying around 'unclaimed' on a heap of rubble. Dreher prosecuted Rathgeber for 'harming the common good', because 'the act he committed should be regarded as looting' – although there was nothing in the statute books prohibiting people from warming themselves with other people's rubbish. The imaginative Dreher (for dreams are not the only place where the imagination is revealed) was not put off by this legal loophole. He fell back on a powerful pronouncement of Hitler's, according to which even the most trivial misdemeanours could be converted into crimes retrospectively, if 'healthy public feeling' demanded it.

Ten days after the start of the trial, the death sentence (a popular choice in those years) was passed on Dreher's recommendation. There was a last-minute petition, to which even the judges of the special court put their names, for 'a reprieve' that would see Rathgeber sentenced instead to twelve years in prison, but Dreher dismissed it out of hand as unwarranted clemency. The sentence was carried out two weeks later, and the time between the presentation of the victim to the executioner and the fall of the guillotine blade was one minute and thirty seconds.

No wonder that our guillotiner only saw half-giraffes at night, though the beautiful landscapes were a surprise.

'Now, hold on to your hat,' Ev said. 'Dreher has been working at the justice ministry since nineteen fifty-one. And I'll give you three guesses as to how he started his career there.'

'By reintroducing the death penalty?'

'Guess again!'

'Regulating prostitution?'

'Don't make stupid jokes. Guess again!'

'I don't know. Calling for higher salaries?'

'General amnesty!'

'You can't be serious.'

She slid the relevant passage across the desk. I followed her triumphant forefinger as it passed along the lines, and learned that Eduard Dreher had been refused admittance to the Württemberg North bar association after the war on the grounds of his involvement with the Nazis. After muddling through for a while as a lawyer in Stuttgart, he was taken on by the federal justice ministry's criminal law department. Responsibility: legal questions regarding the introduction of a general amnesty.

I was impressed.

'Here, have a read of this.'

Ev's finger disappeared; she needed it for chewing on.

Just by the by: Sigmund Freud saw dreams as vehicles for wishfulfilment, and as the shepherds of sleep, keeping the id's impulses in check.

'He corresponded with everyone?' I asked, reading the relevant passage with astonishment.

'Werner Best!' she said.

'Friedrich Grimm!' she said.

'Hugo Stinnes!' she said.

'Ernst Achenbach!' she not only said but hissed, at least my ominous ears perceived it as such. 'All of those vile men. All lawyers. And at the bottom there, that's a name you'll recognize.'

'Erhard Sneiper?'

'He's a member of the camarilla, too. Here you have it in black and white. So don't you go showing your face in his office again!'

She was pacing up and down nervously in front of me, her teeth nibbling at the nail on her forefinger. She moved like one of these TV detectives in their TV police stations: staged, almost artificial, free of depression and irony, with no interest in realistic dialogue or sparing a single thought for the junior detective who is so in their thrall.

'Dreher is a member of that *mishpokhe*,' DCI Himmelreich

suspected astutely. 'He's in contact with everyone, and he's sitting in the gut of the justice department like a tapeworm. He's the enemy!'

DS Himmelreich looked respectfully up at his superior officer. 'How does someone get to that position?' he asked, though he couldn't really care less about the whole thing. He was merely courting attention – and what could be more attentive than a swift answer.

'Good links with the SPD.'

'Dreher drives on the left?'

The detective chief inspector shook her head and began to lecture her less experienced colleague. The detective sergeant enjoyed this very much; he found it quite erotic, the way she got high on her own thoughts as she spoke (how he would have liked to make love to her thoughts, even the most banal of them).

'No, he's just jumped on the bandwagon,' she said. 'He's a fascist to his marrow. But a well-camouflaged one. And he couldn't join the CDU, because they collared him back in Stuttgart. Very smart.'

'And the Social Democrats are in on this?'

'Adolf Arndt has smoothed the way for him.' Now the DCI was putting her colleague through his paces. Would he know who on earth Adolf Arndt was?

'Willy Brandt's kingmaker?' he recalled, thank God, which pleased the DCI enough that she continued to share her razor-sharp deductions with him.

'But no one knows why,' she said, sounding surprisingly baffled. 'Arndt is a socialist, a Jew, and a member of the party executive. He's against a statute of limitations. He's against an amnesty. Why would a dyed-in-the-wool SPD man recommend Dreher to the ministry here? I have no idea. But he did.'

'Sympathy?' the detective sergeant suggested.

Oh, how he would love to ask the DCI to make him an inspector, to discuss all her investigative strategies with him and have the other detective sergeant, police psychologist David Grün, transferred to the vice squad.

'Desperation, more likely,' DCI Himmelreich said succinctly. 'There aren't any left-wing lawyers at the ministry. So the SPD will take anyone who hates the CDU, wherever he might come from. Everyone at the ministry knows what Dreher did in Innsbruck. But they all look the other way. Even Grandpa Heinemann is looking the other way.'

'So Dreher is sailing under a false flag?'

'And no one has noticed.'

'He's going to bring in a Trojan horse.'

'He is the Trojan horse.'

'We need to speak to Heinemann.'

'Oh yes?' the DCI said bitterly, and her loyal sergeant sensed just from the thinness of her voice that he had forfeited his brief moment of ardent attention, because then she contradicted him. 'Dreher is his closest colleague. And on top of that, he's a man who knows how to get rid of people. If we aren't careful, in the end we'll be the ones who are discarded.'

All the same, Ev did speak to Heinemann. She gave him our report, and was reprimanded.

And I spoke to Erhard Sneiper. I gave him our report, and was praised.

Meanwhile, Undersecretary Dreher now greeted us in the canteen with a politeness that was exquisite. Elegant. There's no other way to say it.

We didn't hear anything more about his night-time dreams.

The DCI and her sergeant laid low for months. For years. It was the sixties, Swami. You were a grown man by then. I expect you were in the midst of that party, eh? The full works? You know all this better than I do. Beatles and all the rest of it. Martin Luther King. Apollo 11. A crazily fast time. But not for the legal profession. Lawyers operate in a similar way to glaciers. Travelling another metre down the valley every year. Ice and legislation don't care that rock music is being invented.

The Great Crim-Re commission first met in nineteen fifty-one, and five years later it still wasn't finished. Nor ten years later, nor fifteen.

Original members of the commission died; the second lot stepped back because they didn't like the third. There were various stumbling blocks: retirements; the wording of paragraphs. New governments and old coteries.

We never encountered any suspicious propositions. Never stumbled upon attempts to conserve criminal law and adapt it to the needs of all the Nazis whose criminal trials were popping up all over Germany. On the contrary. What we read in the minutes of the commission meetings sounded like the liberalization of German criminal law, just as everything in those days sounded like liberalization.

But the DCI still thought something fishy was going on. She listened in to various telephone calls without saying anything to Heinemann. The detective sergeant even had two Mossad agents watch Dreher's house, but all they discovered was what time he went out to play skittles, and that his wife had a lover.

At that time, though, all wives had lovers. It was a phenomenon of the age. It made me feel closer to my fellow cuckold, undersecretary or no. I had to go back and re-read a few of his classic summations, which were composed in very clear, plain language ('disgusting, un-Germanic lowlife') in order to regain a proper sense of distance.

There was no Trojan horse galloping about anywhere.

The Reich Main Security Office trial also thrived, despite its lengthy title. After six years of preparation, the mammoth case was about to go to court at last. The final house searches took place. The first arrests were ordered.

And the office of DCI Himmelreich was firmly convinced that everything would proceed in a legal and orderly fashion.

33

Do you remember nineteen sixty-eight?

I have to say: it was the first good year since we'd left Latvia.

The first good year for two and a half decades.

A year of excitement and art.

I wondered how Papa would have felt, with his pastose bacchanals and his writhing nymphs in warm oil colours, amid all the Happenings, all the slogans and performances that jumped out at one that year.

Once, on the Münchener Freiheit square, a garishly made-up girl came wiggling up to me. She had a cardboard box attached to her front, with an opening in it through which you could access her bare breasts. She was accompanied by a shock-headed man with a megaphone, who shouted at me to hold his girlfriend's breasts for exactly twelve seconds, roll up roll up, my thumb and middle finger, roll up roll up. Eventually I complied, since this was a piece of performance art that took a titillating approach to the role of the female body in society – something Papa had of course done more or less all his life. He would have thoroughly enjoyed the performance, though he could have done without the cardboard box, and naturally the yelling boyfriend.

The streets were the wellspring of everything that happened that year. There was even a demo outside our fortified house, during which someone hurled a rock through the large office window of the German–Israeli Association eV.

We had just one Kidon regulator staying with us at that point, a rather chubby man, but agile with it. He was flabbergasted that, among all the American flags burning outside our building, a small Israeli flag was also set alight. The hot-blooded demonstrators shouted, 'Zionists are fucking fascists,' and in response to this delirious confusion the regulator went up to the munitions store.

It was a very good job that no second rock was used to smash a second office window.

Setting foot outside the front door always meant running into people like you, my dear Swami – and, unlike me, Ev quickly abandoned her initial reservations about that. She liked to be carried along by the Ho Chi Minh solidarity marches, because she saw a new, fundamentally democratic and anti-authoritarian Germany there. She could argue for hours over the word 'march', which some of the Maoists wanted to ban (along with the word 'shuffle', incidentally – everything should just be called 'forward motion', and none of mankind's many gaits should be discredited).

Ev volunteered to provide first aid as part of 'the first aid committee'. Her medical know-how was in high demand with the communist groups, whose noses had a range of impressions left on them by policemen's rubber coshes. She neglected her role as DCI Himmelreich criminally, and read nothing but books like Guy Debord's *The Society of the Spectacle* and Herbert Marcuse's *An Essay on Liberation*. These formed the basis of our morning breakfast ritual – while every evening, in the absence of the Mediterranean, we walked to the Englischer Garten, where Bob Dylan songs were sung at the Monopteros by splendid elocutionists, in the presence of stoned, dancing flower children, whose lives ran like sand through the fingers of young guitarists.

*

Nineteen sixty-eight was also the year when Reinhard Gehlen stepped down. He called me to his rooms one final time, apparently to extinguish the last memories of Koja Solm, to which end he handed me a bag containing the ashes of burned paperwork.

The general upheaval of those days, which extended from the metropolis right out into the countryside, echoed fretfully around the corridors of the Org. Gehlen's final internal memo instructed all male analysts to be equipped with Uzi sub-machine guns and a hundred rounds of ammunition each from the BND arsenal, to be used if they should come across any riotous anti-democratic assemblies on their way home. The memo was hastily ripped from the printing machine by his designated successor, and put through the shredder.

'That snot-nosed brat believes it's a youth revolt,' the Doctor snorted contemptuously.

'Isn't it?'

'Dürer!' he rebuked me. 'A long arm! A very long arm!'

'Moscow?'

'Of course. Uprisings all over Europe? Mass strikes in Britain and France? These things don't happen without Moscow's involvement.'

'You saw it coming.'

'From a long way off.'

'Your experience, Herr Doctor.'

'I offered to stay on.'

'Wonderful.'

'To ninety, I told the chancellor, happy to stay until then.'

'To ninety?'

'I sail every day. I swim. I have the heart of a student, my doctor says.'

'Your esteemed cousin?'

'Do you think, Dürer, that I would consult a doctor I am not related to?'

'Of course not, do forgive me.'

'Democracy, so the chancellor says, insists on sixty-six.'

'Sixty-six?'

'The age. Pension age. Time to strike one's colours.'

'Unbelievable. Sixty-six.'

'Blücher was seventy-three when he beat Napoleon at Waterloo.'

'I know.'

'Moltke was eighty-eight when he stepped down as chief of the general staff.'

'An ingenious strategist.'

'I can carry on till ninety with one hand tied behind my back.'

A dim light came into his eyes at the thought, like ship's lanterns in the fog, while the rest of him – the bony frame, the bald skull, the disdain and peevishness that had burrowed into the corners of his mouth – would not resist old age for much longer.

He got up from behind his desk, took a few paces over to the large display cabinet and opened up the richly decorated wooden map of the world that I'd had inlaid for him there.

'That was real art,' Gehlen murmured. 'Herta says you're a genius.'

'You flatter me, Herr Doctor.'

'I don't flatter anyone.'

He ran his hand over the Congo, for which I had chosen ebony, worth a fortune in the late forties. His fingers trembled slightly – with emotion, perhaps, though it might have been a calculated move. Either way, I will always connect this last sight of my map to the trembling, knotted hands hovering over the ebony.

Just four weeks after my farewell visit, the map's mahogany, satin-wood and cherry marquetry, slotted together in a sophisticated pattern from the west coast of America all the way to Japan – countries and oceans, even Pullach, and poor Maya, signified by the large 'M' over Moscow – was hacked into firewood when the old office was renovated.

We were already at the door when the Doctor told me that I would continue to oversee the fortified house under his successor, the snot-nosed brat. He had taken care of everything. I was a fabulous liaison officer, he said, not such a disappointment as my brother, although of course I didn't have a brother – I was Herr Himmelreich, not to say Herr Dürer, and I was to tip the paper bag of document ashes into the Starnberger See.

A week later, I put in an appearance at his official send-off. His old colleagues were all there: Scarface Sangkehl, Pinocchio Herre, Palestine Fritz. I couldn't be absent.

His secretary, Alo, was also there. It was only when I saw the fat tears sliding out from under her glasses like snail trails that I realized Gehlen was a man who drew deep satisfaction from being respected by secretaries, even if he had to love them in return. The affair that the two of them had been conducting for twenty years was only revealed towards midnight, when Alo fainted and in alarm, Gehlen let out a loud cry of, 'Pussy!' A number of those present were traumatized by hearing that word from his lips (first and foremost his wife, of course).

The event was held at the brand-new casino in the analysis building. Chancellor Kiesinger stayed away from the ceremony; an affront made visible by the empty chair beside the departing president of the BND. Ex-chancellor Adenauer couldn't come, because he had been dead for several months. The CIA sent only their B team, some old veterans who laughed too loudly. I could hear Donald Day causing a ruckus from some distance off; he was already drunk. Allen Dulles, the agency's former head, had even let it be known that he would consider it a personal favour if no reverence was shown for the occasion, or for the man at its centre.

The annihilation of the BND's good name, and the destruction of all the American intelligence lines on the other side of the Wall by SS mole-cat swine Heinz Felfe, had been neither forgiven nor forgotten. Bonn and Washington still hadn't fully compensated for the damage he'd caused, even five years after the arrests. Gehlen, whose dismissal John F. Kennedy was said to have called for himself, only managed to avoid being fired when the US president died in a hail of bullets in Dallas, just in time.

The intelligence from the Eastern Bloc, which trickled into Pullach via Israel as a result of my modest efforts, was too little to keep a secret service alive, and too much to let it die. The Mossad's internal sources in Russia were comparatively few, and almost all of them worked at the ministry of health in Moscow, so although the Org learned how many Russian tuberculosis patients were sent to Crimean sanitoriums every year, this did nothing to expand its knowledge about the potential military threat from the Soviet Union.

The BND itself couldn't recruit any more agents in the East. No one. Not a soul.

Its infiltrators were all gone.

No spy with any instinct for self-preservation was prepared to entrust his life to what was by far the worst secret service in the Northern hemisphere, in return for a few roubles. After all, there might have been more double agents than just Heinz Felfe slumbering in the Org. Me, for instance: there was always a risk I could be reactivated.

In a nutshell: the information that was washed to the BND's shores was a long way from being the Soviet Union's closely guarded political secrets. Quite honestly, my dear Swami: at that time, the government could just as soon have read *Pravda* and the *Neue Deutschland* every morning as kept two thousand people on the payroll.

The mood in the BND casino reflected this fact, when the Master of Disaster, as Donald Day liked to call the valiant Doctor, was waiting for his ovation, with wife Herta still at his side. (At the end of the evening, faced with the unconscious Alo, she would strike her husband for bending over his faithful secretary and bringing her back to her sad life using mouth-to-mouth resuscitation.)

But before that, the head of the chancellery and former SA man Karl Carstens gave the ceremonial address. He was a sleek, Hanseatic beanstalk of a man with dishevelled eyebrows, who had only been in his position since the start of the year and had never set eyes on Gehlen before.

The Doctor was so shaken by this complete stranger bidding him farewell (one can only be greeted or insulted by a complete stranger, never waved off), that he spent the whole speech leafing through his Sun Tzu breviary.

'You have certainly had your share of disappointments and setbacks,' Carsten was meanwhile reading from his eulogy, which had been written by someone in the chancellery keen to vent his blazing rage at the Felfe fiasco. 'But overall' – overall, dear Swami, meaning looking at the big picture, basically, ignoring all the failures and mishaps, that kind of 'overall') – 'overall, your achievement stands out as worthy of admiration and has been highly significant for our country's fate.'

There is no more polite way of extolling failure.

At the end there was a nice round of applause, and the Doctor's BND colleagues – including Jeremias Himmelreich, the heavenly creature he had created – gave the passionate Earl Grey drinker a magnificent tea set in polish-hungry silver as a retirement gift, along with two kilos of sugar. From the absent West German chancellor he received a Bible, his twelfth, as he told us. Donald Day handed him a Colt from the American Civil War on behalf of the Central Intelligence Agency. And a parcel had arrived from Tel Aviv containing a stuffed blue tit captured in a neighbouring Arab state (there are no blue tits in Israel).

Afterwards, I felt released.

The old man had gone.

The new world was demanding its rights.

The spring overwhelmed me. It was a wonderful spring, a spring of revolution. A feeling of boundless freedom that I thought I'd lost was pulsing through me. The last time I had felt it, I was newly released from the Lubyanka and standing outside its gates, though I'd been twenty years younger then and half-starved.

It was glorious to wake Ev before dawn and set off for Paris in our Citroën, just like that, at five o'clock in the morning beneath a Van Gogh sun. Spontaneous and light-hearted.

The last of the barricades were still smoking in the Latin Quarter.

The whole city was breathing like a newly healed animal awakened from its coma.

We borrowed its breath. We slept in a small bed and breakfast near the Bastille. In the morning, striking workers with their red flags, belting out throaty choruses, would pass by the cheese shop where we were gobbling down two croissants at a rickety bar table. Its owner had adorned his butter mountains, bowls of crème fraiche and pyramids of cow's, sheep's and goat's cheese with Mao's smile, and there was a twenty per cent revolution discount on every Camembert.

We ran across the Seine's bridges like children.

We thought of Bonn and Munich and were sure we were reaping a kind of 'both-and' happiness, meaning: we were winning on all fronts, because what was good and new (new *was* good in those days) was winning on all fronts.

I hadn't known Ev this happy for years. She was managing to sleep through the night again, even though the window was open and we could hear the riots until morning.

Her sweats, her sudden angry bouts of nausea, her panic attacks all ebbed away.

Anna was happy, too, to see fresh courage in her mother's shining, almost carefree eyes.

And the restaurants in the evenings.

We were not far off sixty, the best age for restaurants, with or without windowpanes (many were broken).

In the Louvre, which Papa had so loved for its Italian galleries, Ev spent three hours sitting beside me and watching as I drew the Nike of Samothrace. I told her nothing of my time in swastika-Paris, nothing of the listless SD Romeo agent I had been during the terrible weeks I spent stranded here, on the run from Ev's despair. Things were going so wrong for her then, so very wrong that she had tried to improve her lot by volunteering for Auschwitz.

Now things were going well. Really well. *Merveilleux. Excellent. Voilà.*

And so, in my opinion, she no longer needed David Grün.

I can even pinpoint the moment at which I became absolutely certain she no longer needed David Grün. We were sitting in the Tuileries, and she had spread her angular, narrow frame flat along one of these short Parisian benches. That morning, we had made love as we had not done for a long time. Forming a single surface of wrinkles and edges and sausage-shaped protuberances, and smelling our scents again, stronger than they used to be.

Now, on that Tuileries bench, I breathed myself in through her young blouse, knelt before her on the earth and laid my head on her belly, which was still firm, tested only by one futile birth. I breathed and smelled and felt her warm body and heard Anna whispering that I should stay there, just for a moment. And then Ev's hand stroked the crown of my head like it was the first time, and I flew back through the decades and saw, from a great height, two children below me swearing loyalty to one another in an enchanted gingerbread house, cross my heart and hope to die, and at that second I knew with absolute certainty that David Grün was no longer needed.

It was just that Ev didn't know it yet.

It was strange, but David had grown on me in the years leading up to that moment. Like a new shoot grows on an old tree. I had not protested, and she took that as assent. She thought me her dog, a little. I forgave Ev for that.

But I never assented to it. I just wanted her not to die. I just wanted her to be well.

And now she was.

Even Anna had to admit that Mama was doing well.

No one had to know how little I needed David Grün. It would only have made Ev sad.

My revulsion when I saw the threads of his long wavy brown hairs, with no hint of grey in them, clinging to her pullover. The quivering of my lip when he came to the front door and rang the bell like a postman, and I opened the door, and he said, 'Hi, Jerry,' as if we were in an American film. He even hugged me. The unbelievable Christmas when the three of us sat under the tree together and he gave me a home-made voucher for ten gratis therapy sessions. How I hated his home-made vouchers. Vouchers for day trips to Neuschwanstein Castle, vouchers for a good life. He drew like a five-year-old. I hate it when people can't draw; I hate that about you, too, Swami. I hated the sound of his footsteps, prancing up to the door of his villa when I went to collect Ev, and the farewell kiss she gave him. The mark of his teeth on her skin. Just once in all those years, on her neck; I couldn't sleep for weeks. The fact that he knew my name was Koja Solm. That he knew about my work and almost all my secrets, though I had never cashed in the ten-gratis-therapy-sessions voucher. Ev had told him everything. 'He's my analyst, darling, I can't play-act with him.'

My life was in his hands.

That was what I hated most of all. My life was in his hands, and on the day when Ev managed to find happiness without him, the day she left him, as people do leave their therapists, David Grün would be able to crush me with a telephone call or a home-made voucher for the arrest of a traitor.

There is no room in your world view for the level of hatred I bore for him, my fair-minded and (please) not-too-quick-to-judge Swami. But I want to be completely honest in these wintry times. And so I must concede: I hated and hated and hated that man and I wanted it to stop.

34

In the munitions room at the fortified house, we kept some substances in glass vials, locked inside a safe the size and shape of an accordion. Even today, the Amazonian Indians still stick small green frogs on skewers, set them alight, and collect the liquid that drips from the kicking creatures. This liquid was contained in five of my glass vials. No idea what it's called. One of those words that ends in 'xin'. Originally, in the blessed days of Colonel Harel, it had been intended for involuntary consumption by peckish rocket scientists. Now, it was just sitting there. Uncodified. Absent from the account books. In my custody.

I thought it perfect for David Grün. It could be blended with any foodstuff, had no taste, and left the recipient with a slight numbness on the tongue. A tingling face. Loss of coordination. Difficulty walking. Ataxia. Weakness. Muscle cramps. Slurred speech. Increasing paralysis. Fixed pupils. Sweating. Vomiting. Cyanosis. Falling blood pressure. Finally, cardiac arrest. It was not detectable in the blood, and it could be months before the final symptoms appeared.

When we returned from Paris, the happy Ev and her adoring husband, I had some heated arguments with Anna.

One got so loud that Ev knocked on the bathroom door. I set a lot of store by my daughter's opinion, but I found it difficult to agree with her in this case. She accused me of behaving selfishly. Of having no consideration. She said I was going to cross that Italian river that wasn't even a river, it was just a stream, and she couldn't think of its name right now (I gently reminded her it was the Rubicon; she had never been any great shakes in Latin or history).

We talked a lot about ethics. I showed her all the latest books that Ev left lying around everywhere, which spoke of violence against things and violence against people, and why, in an emergency, it could be legitimate to use regulatory methods. In order to change things, Anna. To change unbearable things.

But little Anna knew what she was talking about. She reminded me of all the Christian commandments that sloshed around in my family's genes, at least in her words. She conjured up the image of Grandpaping. She got the really big guns out.

But when she accused me outright of acting like a cowardly murderer (though I regarded myself as a clever urban guerrilla), I caved in. With a heavy heart, and I was still not wholly convinced. But Anna had threatened never to make contact with me again if I let myself go, or rather let David Grün go. And I bowed to her blackmail.

I took all five glass vials from the safe, put them in my briefcase, left the house and took a twenty-minute walk to Kleinhesseloher Lake. It was summer and, as always, half the militant proletariat of Schwabing was lounging about on the sunbathing lawns that afternoon. But the bench where Ev and I always took a little rest to look at the lake house on the opposite shore was unoccupied. I went down to the water, took the frog-back stuff from my bag, broke the vials and tipped their contents into the lake.

I had just emptied the fourth vial when someone placed a hand on my shoulder and said, 'Hi, Jerry.'

David Grün was standing in front of me, in sports kit, a sweaty endurance runner, beautiful and brown, as if sculpted by Michelangelo in frozen shit.

'What are you doing there?'

'Oh, er – medication.'

'You're tipping your medication away, Jerry?'

'Old medication.'

'You should never tip old medicines away. Ev didn't tell me you were seeing a doctor.'

'I'm better now.'

'She's worried, you know.'

'She's always worried.'

'She's in a good place at the moment. Paris did her a world of good.'

'Yes, it was lovely.'

'But she tells me you're quite unstable.'

'Rubbish.'

'Talking to yourself?'

'What?'

'She says you talk to yourself.'

'Not that I'm aware of.'

'That you have arguments, even.'

'I argue with myself?'

'With Anna?'

'Who's Anna?'

'Anna Solm?'

'Doesn't ring any bells.'

'I'm sure you know who Anna Solm is, Jerry.' He knitted his brows and smiled incredulously at the same time. 'Jerry?' he asked again.

'You mean Ev's daughter?'

'We both know she wasn't just Ev's daughter, Jerry.'

I said nothing, watching as a great crested grebe near the bank struggled to breathe, flapped its wings and tipped limply onto its side.

'I'm your friend, Jerry. And Ev is your friend, too. We're both doctors, and we can both be there for you.'

'Thank you, David. But Ev is my wife, not my friend.'

'There are dead fish floating in the lake back there.'

'Really.'

'The heat.'

'Must be.'

'Don't be so dismissive, Jerry. The thing that concerns me is Ev saying you sometimes put on another voice. You know what schizophrenia is?'

'Are you trying to make me angry?'

'Forgive me. I just want to help. You never took up your gratis therapy sessions. Why not?'

'I don't need them.'

'When a person talks to themselves over an extended period, it's a clear sign. Do you hear voices in your head? Do you hear the voice of Anna Solm in your head?'

'I have to get going now, David.'

'You've never addressed your grief. You know, that can make a person sick. It took me so many years before Ev could face her pain and her loss. And you can see now, she's doing better.'

'You healed Ev, did you?'

'There's no need to be sarcastic. Not healed. Started her down a path. A path that led to herself. You are such a long way from yourself, my friend. You need to learn to grieve. You need to allow yourself to grieve for your dead daughter.'

'She isn't my daughter.'

'You don't trust anyone, Jerry. No one at all. That's pathological. I'm on your side. Really. I would so like to help you. Ev has told me so many wonderful things about you. It would be terrible if you were to lose each other.'

'We'll never lose each other.'

'Your relationship might not be the way it seems to you.'

'And how does it seem to me?'

'Secure.'

A dog came out of the water, its coat dripping and a stick in its mouth. It was staggering slightly. As it dropped the stick at its master's feet, one of its back legs gave way.

'Nothing in this world is secure, Jerry. No emotion is ever secure. Ev is afraid of you. Of how you are. I think you ought to know that.'

'She's afraid of me?'

'She called me a few months ago. In the middle of the night. She even said she wanted to move out.'

'Move out?'

'Completely irresponsible. She'd had enough of you, she said. I had to do some very intensive work with her. She can't leave you just because you're going through a bad patch. I didn't leave her when she was going through a bad patch. And nor did you.'

'No.'

'You're smiling, Jerry. That's good. I like your smile.'

'I'm not smiling.'

'I thought that was a smile. I took it for one. Just look at all those dead fish, you wouldn't credit it. There must be at least twenty.'

'How do we begin our therapy sessions?'

'Jerry?'

'Hmm?'

'You want to take up the gratis sessions?'

'Yes, I just have this sudden feeling . . .'

'Thank you, Jerry. That's great. That sudden feeling is really great. Let it out, Jerry.'

'Do you fancy going over to the lake house for a beer?'

'Well, I'm a bit sweaty, and I'm not really dressed for—'

'Oh, that doesn't matter, David.'

'No, it doesn't matter.'

'No.'

'You know, my friend, we've never had a beer together.'

We walked halfway round the lake, past stark-naked hippies, past girls in miniskirts, past dumbfounded old Hubers and Meiers, and past the policemen running towards the hippies with their truncheons raised.

We sat down at a vacant table, from which David could not see the nutrient-rich lake, which was now dotted with tench, grass carp and pike.

When he went to the lavatory, I tipped the fifth vial into his *Weissbier*.

35

How nice that we're together again.

I crossed my fingers very hard while you were in the operating theatre.

And when you were in a coma, I told you about nineteen sixty-eight. Do you remember?

Night Nurse Gerda tells me that, unfortunately, you can no longer speak. Not at all. Is that right? Can't you speak now?

Aha.

But you can still hear me.

Look, here we are again. Our old pad.

The window over there. The washing facility back there. Fresh flowers from Night Nurse Gerda's little greenhouse.

There really can't be any more Marrakesh now. Like I told you before. Hash. Dope. Shit. No. Those days are gone.

Now the melancholy really has you in its grip. No more optimism, eh? Though this might very well be a stage-one melancholy you are suffering from. An illusion, created by the intravenous nourishment, this salt solution, I mean, that they're pumping into your blood. Or the salt you've got upstairs. Apparently, the brain thinks those screws taste of salt. The Greek doctor says.

And now there are two.

People with a greater intellectual capacity, of course, experience rather more advanced stages of unhappiness than you do. I despair of my own despair, while you sense only a simple despondency. But simple despondency is a good thing; it can pass (through better food, losing the skull-screws, life-lengthening measures).

Shall I tell you Herr Himmelreich's *aleph* joke again?

All right, I won't.

But you can move your head?

Good.

Do be careful, though.

I'll wheel you into this corner. You can get a nice view of the outside world from there. I'm afraid it's still snowing, but there is already a spring-like quality to the clouds, something clenched and powerful, I think. My motorcyclist died three days ago. His bed was vacant. That's why this opportunity arose, for us. Look, another one of those clouds. How fast it's going.

I really am glad to have you around again. Your silence makes you considerably more tolerable. I've brought a few birth announcements up from downstairs as well. Here, you'll like this little chap.

Why *do* you love the newborns so?

Is it their innocence?

That's what I thought.

I had a long discussion with Dr Papadopoulos, when you decided you didn't like me. Oh, no, you didn't like me, I know that. I asked the Greek about the possible reasons for your rejection. And of course, he doesn't know. But we spoke of melancholy and how it is expressed.

The key term is depressive realism. A depressive, Dr Papadopoulos says, at least a depressive of the higher orders, has a much firmer contact with reality than a so-called happy man. There are studies, the doctor has carried them out right here, honestly. Melancholy is a . . . a . . . a sign that someone has a realistic view of the world, in the generally accepted sense. Of its shittiness, one might say, its saturation with dukkha.

Depressed test subjects, for example, who were supposed to fly a rocket to the moon, were much better at estimating their chances of exploding than non-depressed subjects, who actually believed that a big crate with 'NASA' written on it could escape the earth's orbit. You and I, then, have a much more finely tuned ability to judge than any dull optimist. Just be glad that you are no longer one of those idiots.

So, if we both believe that we will die of our brain injuries, and soon – then on the one hand, that is an unsettling realization. On the other, it speaks for our intelligence, and for yours in particular, if we estimate the probability correctly.

You are not as cheerful now as you were in summer. Well, all right. But you can take a positive view of that, as well: you have become more intelligent. And that has happened through me. Dr Papadopoulos believes that intelligence is related to the severity of a person's depression. He is not especially depressive himself, but you know, why would he be, he's Greek. Ouzo and whatnot. Olive trees. Sunshine all year round. The theory is much more complex, of course.

Now, take your hands down for a minute. What are you trying to tell me? Paper? You want me to bring you some paper?

Here you are.

I can hardly read that. Is it a 'D'?

Oh, I see.

David Grün, and a question mark?

36

So then, to your silent question, silent Swami.

When we were in Paris, Ev and I, when we were celebrating the end of Reinhard Gehlen in that happily reeling, pubescent May of nineteen sixty-eight, rejoicing in all manner of upcoming victories, toasting the State of Israel's twentieth anniversary and revelling in a world turned upside down, the Bundestag was meeting in Bonn. It held no debates; it just passed laws. It was what Justice Minister Heinemann called 'a brown-bread meeting'.

On that memorable day, the first decree of the Great Crim-Re was also put to the vote. A trifling law. Like all laws, it had an unpronounceable name, and so we referred to it disparagingly as 'the parking-fine tosh'. Or rather, a few stultified journalists, spoiled by the revolutionary turmoil of those days, called it that – though of course the lawyers, who had spent forever and ever amen devising it, did not. Eduard Dreher, the efficient viper, had slithered up to Heinemann the previous winter and asked him to pass the regulation as quickly as possible; to put it ahead of all other canonical measures, in fact.

'Why should they do that?' Ev had asked the minister warily, confused by the sudden urgency. 'Why shouldn't they pass all the new criminal-justice laws in one go, when they're ready?'

'Because this one is about traffic offences,' Heinemann explained with a smile. 'It could be a long while yet before all the criminal-justice amendments are ready for submission.'

'It has been a long while already.'

'Quite. And petty crimes are an urgent matter. Boy, oh boy.'

'Why?'

'They constitute by far the largest group of legal infractions. There are a lot more people committing parking violations than there are serial killers.'

'So the serial killers can wait?'

'If we don't act at once, then five years from now, taxi drivers who do eighty on their way to the train station at midnight will still be treated the same as thieves and rapists. No one wants that, no one.'

'So, is it a good law?'

'Ah, *summum ius, summa iniuria*, my dear Frau Himmelreich,' the minister sighed, his hands folded in front of him.

Ev later asked me to pass the draft amendment on to the Mossad and have an Israeli criminal lawyer go over it with a fine tooth comb. That was both ridiculous, and entirely typical of her. My sister was panicking that some small detail might escape us. Her carefree lightness was gone. She would have seen the imprint of Eduard Dreher's poison fangs even in regulations on closing times for public houses. She wouldn't put anything past him.

I thought it excessive, but I still posted the paperwork to Tel Aviv.

However, the ignoring of West German traffic lights, et cetera et cetera didn't seem to have any particular bearing on Israel's right to exist. That was probably why weeks and then months passed without my hearing anything from Tel Aviv. Anything at all.

I didn't get so much as a confirmation of receipt.

At the same time, all the jurists at the Bonn justice ministry gave their assent to Dreher's submission. Assent is not really the word for it. Not a single criminal lawyer or politician in Germany had the slightest objection to anything in the parking-fine tosh.

Nothing at all.

And so the law was rushed through at top speed, and passed unanimously on the tenth of May nineteen sixty-eight.

And when I say unanimously, I mean that, of more than four hundred members of parliament, not a single one objected.

No one.

Not a blessed soul.

Some strange things happened over the days that followed.

Herr Achenbach ran into me in Bonn, this time in an exemplary fashion, fully clothed, at the Langen Eugen building site down on the bank of the Rhine – the only place in the capital where anything remotely new was happening. He enquired disgustingly after the health of my good lady wife. When I had answered him ('She's well, thank you, you creep!') he asked (his head tilted back to appreciate the top of the unfinished skyscraper, with a sigh of, 'Goodness, that's ugly,') whether I didn't fancy joining the FDP as soon as my work at the justice ministry was done – which, he could assure me, would be very soon.

I had scarcely arrived back in Munich when Erhard Sneiper telephoned. His voice was like honey in warm milk, and he invited me to take a walk with him in the gardens of Nymphenburg Palace.

'Whenever you have the time, Koja.'

It was the first time we had met since the unfortunate incident with his beloved miniature collie. Erhard brought his new dog with him, a well-trained, three-year-old Dobermann. The animal could do all manner of tricks; he begged and whined for me to throw a stick, and when he realized I wasn't going to, he chased rabbits. He caught a particularly stupid one, which must have taken him for a kind of uber-rabbit, or it would hardly have hopped after him. It was torn to pieces before our eyes.

Erhard told me how pleased he was that I was cooperating so well. If the parking-fine tosh came into force in the autumn without any problem, then I could rely on Hub's magnanimity, his tolerance and his Baltic upbringing to see me right.

'And on mine, too, of course,' he added graciously.

I said I was very glad of that.

'Though I'm afraid you will have to get bitten, just once,' he replied.

I didn't understand.

'By Heinrich.'

He indicated the Dobermann trotting in front of us, a small piece of white rabbit fur still hanging from his snout.

'But why?'

'Quid pro quo.'

'You don't seriously believe I'm going to let your mutt bite me.'

'Your Curonia honour demands it, Koja.'

He put his fingers in his mouth and whistled. The dog stopped, turned round and fixed watchful eyes on his master. Then he stood to attention. You could see every muscle under his black coat, and for a second it made me think of Mary-Lou. She had loved to bite me, too.

'Arm or leg?'

'There are walkers up ahead, Erhard . . .'

'Arm or leg?'

'You're really going to go through with this?'

'Let's just get it over with, and then we're quits.'

He still hadn't grasped who he was dealing with. He was one of the stupidest people I have ever met. Despite all his lawyerly perspicacity, all his rhetorical talent and all his analytical abilities, his brains would have been better suited to a chimpanzee's skull.

'What *has* happened to your hair?' he asked out of the blue.

'What do you mean?'

'Well, this new style. All that unkempt frizz. You've changed an awful lot in the last few years. It's intentional, I take it?'

It was probably those final words that made me realize things could not go on like this with Erhard. Someone who could testify to my painstakingly effected physical transformation; someone who knew so much about my identity, my cover, my history, my wife, and above all someone who had already blabbed about all this to people like Achenbach, presented an incalculable risk. And incalculable risks had to be regulated. That much, at least, I had learned in the Mossad.

'Leg,' I said at last.

Erhard took a few steps away from me, pointed an outstretched finger at my thigh and shouted into the large park, 'Heinrich, sic!'

At the hospital, they gave me a tetanus injection, picked the remains of the fabric out of my leg with tweezers and closed my gaping wounds with a dozen stitches.

The pain shook free my buried memories. How Sneiper had taken my brother from me and led me into Hitler's paradise. How he took my sister and tied her to his kitchen sink. How he even took my father from me, who effectively died during one of Sneiper's fanciful Home-to-the-Reich speeches, perhaps not assassinated by my colouring trick with Erhard's white shirt, but paralysed by the legendary stupidity of the Nazi slogans – why had I never considered this possibility, why had I always flagellated myself with recriminations, instead of bringing the real culprit to justice? And as all this was going through my mind, I thought of the munitions room in the fortified house. It offered endless variations on a theme. The Kidon regulators simply called them varieties, it sounded more genteel.

Hub himself also got in touch with me. That was the biggest thing. Had I been mulling over the conversation with Sneiper, he asked on the telephone.

'Why should I?'

'Does it hurt?'

'Yes, it hurts, Hub. I'm in pain, if that makes you happy.'

'It would make me happy if you couldn't walk again.'

'I'm afraid it isn't quite that bad.'

'Erhard is too nice to you. He has no idea what a cursed monster you are.'

'What do you want?'

'Fact number one: what he told you yesterday about my magnanimity was an exaggeration by a factor of twelve.'

'And what did he tell me yesterday?'

'I can play it back to you, if you like.'

'He recorded our conversation?'

'Including all the cries of pain. You really don't know what game it is you're playing, little brother.'

I wouldn't have any problem regulating this. That suddenly became clear to me. A Walther P1 with a light metal grip stock sprang to mind. The conservative, professional method, the one best suited to Erhard Sneiper.

'Fact number two: I won't blow your cover, as long as you pass on every last thing that happens in Bonn to Erhard, word for word.'

'Erhard isn't the only one being too nice to me. You are, as well. Why is everyone being so nice to me at the moment?'

'No one is being nice to you. They're all dragging you deeper into the shit.'

'What is this in aid of?'

'Why should it be in aid of anything?'

'This parking-fine-tosh business. Something isn't right there.'

'That is fact number three.'

'I'll take another look at it.'

I heard his rattling breath, could see his throat before me, a short, fat section of pulsating octopus tentacle a thousand metres below the sea, trapped in a crack in the rocks.

'If you do that,' he said in a strained voice, 'if you so much as attempt to stop the law or hold it up—'

'Careful, Hub,' I interrupted him. 'I've got a tape recorder going here, too. We get so many calls from lunatics threatening us Yids and wishing we were back in Auschwitz, you wouldn't believe.'

The octopus tentacle became very thin.

'Once a traitor to your people, always a traitor to your people,' he said.

Then he hung up. The shredded muscle tissue beneath the bandage was such agony I wanted to scream. But I didn't scream. I didn't make another sound; just listened to the dialling tone for a long time.

A few weeks later, a thick envelope arrived by courier from the Israeli Consulate in Munich. It came from a Jossele Rubinroth, professor of jurisprudence at the Hebrew University of Jerusalem.

Inside the envelope, I found copies of various legal commentaries, two articles from Israeli journals, and a very short letter, written in German:

Dear Herr Himmelreich!

Shalom and best wishes from Eretz Israel!

Please forgive me for taking so long to respond to you, in persona et in casu. *Unfortunately, I have been in hospital with cancer of the gall bladder, which has been something of a distraction. However, I have now received the amendment you sent to the German Introductory Act to the Act on Regulatory Offences (EGOWIG) and studied it with interest. It contains many elegant passages. It also gives a glimpse into the German soul, should one desire such a glimpse (the paragraph about the consequences of not keeping to the right-hand lane for mentally handicapped car owners in particular is not without a certain charm). Overall, however, it appears to be full-blown nonsense.*

Article 1, clause 6 of the Act contains a rephrasing of an important paragraph in the German Criminal Code (STGB). The current ruling in paragraph 50, clause 2, STGB states that the maximum sentence for aiding and abetting murder is life imprisonment. The new ruling makes a distinction based on whether the aiding and abetting of the crime is characterized by 'special personal qualities, relationships or circumstances'. In the absence of these 'special personal qualities, relationships or circumstances', aiding and abetting is treated as a mere attempt rather than a crime itself, and attracts a much more lenient sentence.

On the surface, this is good news for a German who, for example, is a passenger in a heavy goods vehicle at a red light, and without any 'special personal qualities, relationships or circumstances' aids the driver in deliberately butchering another road user, also driving a vehicle, by refusing to give way.

But ordinarily, such incidents are seen quite rarely on the roads, and in fact none has ever been tried in Israel. It therefore seems more than remarkable that this passage should be given such prominence in a legal text that deals with traffic offences and therefore quite rightly trades under the name 'parking-fine tosh' in Germany.

I am afraid I must inform you, however, that in my assessment, the shortening of the limitation period that necessarily follows from a reduction in sentencing, as is being sought here, can also be applied to every other conceivable offence in the German criminal code.

I would therefore strongly advise you to take all necessary steps to prevent this perfidious law from coming into force as a matter of urgency. It has already given a considerable stimulus to my gall bladder cancer. Otherwise, it is entirely possible (lex posterior derogat legi priori) *that all pending and future prosecutions of violent National Socialist crimes will be rendered invalid* de lege ferenda.

With very best wishes
Jossele Rubinroth

The Trojan horse had been wheeled past us, then, and was already standing, snorting, inside the city walls.

It had been built not of ship's timbers, but of dreams; the yearning dreams of Eduard Dreher first and foremost. He and all the other nocturnal Achaeans were just waiting for darkness, under cover of which they could sneak out of their Greek gift and set the world on fire. The sun would go down on the first of October. That was when the law came into force.

To this day, I don't know how Dreher the dreamer managed to smuggle the wording of that law past all the authorities, or rather through all the authorities, or better still over all those heads – wording that could allay all the anxieties of the escapees overnight, while the drunk Trojans were busy waving their flags.

Memor esto: a perfidious law, stimulating Professor Rubinroth's gall bladder cancer.

And at the same time, a harmless one.

How could that happen, Swami?

Happiness and unhappiness at the same point on the timeline.

Sukha here. Dukkha there.

What was the horrified Himmelreich to do? He was threatened by Sneiper's hellish hordes. And yet the parking-fine folderol could still be screwed up and thrown away. All I had to do was go running to Heinemann, show him Rubinroth's letter and change the course of history. The law would fall, and those hellish hordes could then take me away and skin me.

But I was attached to my skin, dear Swami.

I was reluctant to be parted from it, it was too sensitive.

How could I play the hero without becoming a tragic one?

It was impossible.

Either. Or.

But sometimes doing the right thing requires a good dose of madness. And I lacked it. I felt my mind was too intact to provoke my brother's revenge, the end of my existence, and to endanger my poor Ev, who would be crushed by Hub, Sneiper, Achenbach – anacondas, not vipers – all because of a few words of legal Latin. A bit of hermeneutical hair-splitting.

And although it tormented me, Swami, I capitulated; I hid behind my usual habits, left the EGOWIG alone, didn't shout out, didn't go racing in with sirens wailing, greeted Herr Heinemann every day, and forgot Jossele Rubinroth's lines. I waited for the days to pass and that sublime year of nineteen sixty-eight to lose its sublimity, its courage and its strong colours.

*

Before night fell and the legal madness came into force on the first of October nineteen sixty-eight, the only people in the justice department who realized its potential consequences were a few lowly officials.

Half a week before the deadline, a warning note from a meddlesome undersecretary landed on Ev's desk. It clearly hadn't been taken seriously by anyone else, and had a handwritten plea attached asking her to pass it immediately to the justice minister. I saw the words 'Urgent appeal!'.

Since Ev wasn't in yet, I picked up the note and carried it around with me uneasily all day; I kept it in my jacket until lunchtime, hit myself in the face with it that evening, tore it into tiny pieces that night and flushed the protest-confetti down the lavatory.

Then autumn arrived, and the Great Tosh became law.

Nothing in the world can unseat a German law (apart from a new German law, but these things take time).

Precisely one day after the perpetuum, the legal forever-and-ever, I went to Ev and told her that some things had been going round in my head overnight.

'I think, my love,' I said sadly, 'that this peculiar decree could have really catastrophic consequences.'

Then the world as Ev knew it collapsed.

Justice Minister Heinemann couldn't rant and rave. His temperament rendered him incapable of it. The slight raising of his glasses and the colour of his slappable face said it all.

'How on earth could this happen?' he lamented, when we hinted at the extent of the calamity. 'This is why I employed you, to make sure this didn't happen!'

Those authorities that had sent Jews to gas chambers and political opponents to prison cells, given fatal injections to Gypsies and the mentally ill, liquidated Russian partisans and British prisoners of war, and beaten Polish professors and French resistance fighters to death – those gentlemen who were so receptive to the *Ars Vivendi* – opened the champagne. The parking-fine tosh had the abracadabra effect of opening handcuffs and prison gates, emptying the dock, and ruining everything that DCI Ev Himmelreich had spent the last few years fighting for.

The bureaucrats who had worked behind the scenes (and what

terrible scenes they were), who were largely being investigated for 'aiding and abetting murder', escaped once again, and for all time.

At a stroke, their crimes had expired. Their raging and burning had lacked those 'special personal qualities, relationships or circumstances' that a road user also lacks when he leaves his vehicle in a no-parking zone without any malicious intent.

And that, my revered Swami, is applied jurisprudence.

Within a few weeks, Ev received the news that, on the basis of the new law, the mammoth case against the former heads and department leaders of the Reich Main Security Office, against hundreds of their loyal assistants, against the heart of the dukkha machinery, had been dropped.

There were no more investigations into Hub Solm, either.

THE OFFICE was off the hook.

Ev informed the media, with whom she had been cultivating relationships since the attacks on Nasser's rocket scientists. And although a few articles were published, they only appeared on pages 4 or 5 of the politics sections. *Der Spiegel* did at least remark on how incomprehensible the whole business was, and called it the Bonn republic's 'most embarrassing slip-up, a general amnesty brought about by fathomless stupidity'.

But the true background to the affair remained hidden.

'I never imagined such treachery,' a dumbfounded Gustav Heinemann told the press.

But no one called on him to step down. Every member of the Bundestag and all the legal experts in every party had given their assent to his legislation. Yes and amen. No ifs. No buts.

The official statement on the reason behind the fiasco: it had been an oversight. A faux pas. A regrettable lapse of concentration.

There were no popular uprisings.

Not a single Extra-Parliamentary Opposition activist, no member of the student socialists, none of the hundred thousand seasoned student protesters took to the streets because of the scandal. Vietnam had more napalm bombs for them to be horrified about. And better music.

It was what it was: a story of paragraphs and pedantry.

And I did not stop it; I opened the gates of Troy in the night.

*

Eduard Dreher managed to don the cloak of forgetfulness. His dreams must have overflown the most beautiful Elysian Fields. It goes without saying that he will have had a permanent erection while dreaming them. In any case, his authorship of the legislation went up in smoke (with my assistance). Ev didn't find any indication in the files that he was the one who had smuggled the crucial wording into the parking-fine tosh (I did my worst).

The minutes of the commission meetings remain lost to this day (having rasped through my shredder).

No one brought charges against Undersecretary Dreher, or even sacked him. Justice Minister Heinemann stood by him. And that, too, was down to my secret intercession, and Erhard Sneiper's discreet, viperous phone calls.

37

It was many years since Ev had dismembered the furnishings of an apartment so thoroughly. A porcelain cup now and then, occasionally filled with liquids, some of them hot. That, yes. Or cloths of all kinds, flung into faces (mine). But now, our apartment died as it had died after Anna's death: with the aid of saw, hatchet, baking shovel, hammer, nail file, nail-polish remover, whatever was to hand.

On Monday the kitchen was hammered to pieces. On Tuesday, our good Villeroy & Bosch vases with flowers on and in them. Wednesday was the day for shredding curtains. Ev underwent a dramatic regression to her blackest hours. She stopped sleeping and leafed maniacally through her documents at night without switching the light on.

I heard her rustling, through mountains of paper, rat-like, aided only by the light of the moon.

Then there were phases of madness, actual insanity. She poured raw eggs into her eyes, babbled about 'eggy-eyes', the yellow liquid ran down her face, she was amused by it and afterwards lapsed into total apathy.

She lay in bed trying to click her tongue in time with the alarm clock, for hours, until I managed to get her some neuroleptics from an emergency pharmacy to sedate her a little.

*

One day – I had just got back with the shopping, which she could not be expected to do – I found her standing at the kitchen stove, stirring a large blue cooking pot with a wooden spoon. She was boiling to a pulp the flowers I had given her two days before, to replace their predecessors from the smashed Villeroy & Bosch vases. I went over and turned off the gas.

'Have you gone mad?'

'What's this?' She was holding out the letter; it trembled between her fingertips.

'Why are you going through my drawers, Ev?'

'WHAT IS THIS, YOU FUCKING BASTARD?'

'It's the letter from the legal expert in Jerusalem.'

'THE LETTER FROM THE LEGAL EXPERT IN JERUSALEM? YOU TOLD ME THERE WAS NO LETTER FROM A LEGAL EXPERT IN JERUSALEM!'

'Please calm down, my darling. It's not what you think.'

She had been crying, and now she wiped her eyes and turned away from me. Her back an armoured carapace.

'Explain it to me, Koja!'

Her hair an abandoned bird's nest. Her dressing gown all coffee stains and mustiness.

'In a second.'

I took the blue cooking pot in both hands, scalding them quite thoroughly in the process, went out to our balcony, poured the stewed flowers over the railing and saw them hanging in the bare apple tree down below. The tinsel of desperation.

I thought for a minute.

Then I went back into the apartment.

In the kitchen, I said, 'The professor's misgivings shocked me just as they did you. And naturally, I called him at once.'

'When?'

'On the day the letter arrived.'

'You called him?'

'Yes.'

'On the day the letter arrived?'

'Yes.'

'I want to see.'

'What do you want to see?'

'I want to see the list of all the calls that were made from here on the day the letter arrived.'

'I called him from a phone box.'

'You're lying.'

'In Kaiserstraße.'

'You're lying.'

'I was very upset. I had to know what was going on.'

'And what was going on?'

'I reached him.'

'And?'

'Nothing. He told me he'd made a mistake.'

She laughed. The way she had laughed when she was cracking raw eggs over her face.

'I'm telling you, that's what happened.'

'How can you lie like that, it's incredible.'

'He had overlooked the passage in paragraph five. He told me to throw his letter away.'

'I want to speak to Professor Jossele Rubinroth on the telephone right now.'

'Ev, you can believe me.'

'Now! This instant!'

'Let me talk to him first.'

'No.'

'He doesn't know you. He can't gauge your mood.'

'That doesn't matter.'

'He was under instruction from the Mossad. He won't tell you anything.'

'I have instructions from the Mossad, too.'

'Ev, please don't do this.'

She put her glasses on, searched the letterhead for the telephone number and plodded out of the kitchen to the study. The door banged like a guillotine. I heard her first sobbing and then speaking quietly on the phone, and sobbing again, and speaking quietly again. I put the shopping away in the fridge. I washed up. I mopped the floor.

Then she came back.

'He's dead.'

'Oh my goodness.'

'Gall-bladder cancer.'

'So soon?'

Her face a tin bucket filled with all kinds of liquids.

'You knew, didn't you? That he was dead? And that's why you fed me this pack of lies?'

'I swear to you, Ev, I would never keep anything from you.'

'You frighten me, Koja. You frighten me, the way you talk to yourself, the manoeuvring, the deception, and all your madness.'

'My madness? Take a look at yourself! Take a look at our apartment!'

'Don't change the subject – you've been pulling the wool over my eyes, Koja!'

'I'm sorry for not showing you the letter. I didn't want to unsettle you. I really am desperately sorry.'

'Do you know how implausible that sounds? Someone writes to tell you that the whole parking-fine act is a crime, and you don't say a word to me? When we *knew* that Dreher was planning something.'

'We all made mistakes in this affair.'

'You didn't say a single word to me about this bloody letter! Not a word! David warned me about you.'

'How is he?'

'Not good.'

'Did the milk cure help at all?'

'He likes you, Koja, but he says you're dangerous.'

'He's confused.'

'He is not confused. He's sick. I'm afraid something terrible is going to happen.'

'Please, my darling – speak of the devil and he'll appear.'

She started to cry again. It was something I was familiar with. At times like these she could start to cry in the way other people might start to speak. I went over and rubbed the armour of her carapace. She pulled away, went and sat on the couch. I had to keep going; I sat beside her, proffering my good shoulder so that she could lean on it at any time.

'I just don't understand it,' she wept. 'He's been going downhill for months. None of his doctors can find anything wrong. Why are the doctors so useless? It's just not possible.'

'Could he have poisoned himself with something?'

'They've ruled that out. His blood results are normal. His liver, too.

But the paralysis. And he has sleep apnoea now. It's getting worse and worse. As if his nerve pathways are dissolving. I blame myself!'

'But you're taking such loving care of him, my darling.'

'I'm not taking care of anything. I'm lying here like a corpse. I'm going mad. What can it be? I thought he was just overworked.'

'David will get back on his feet. A fit and healthy man like him.'

'It keeps getting worse.'

'I brought a large marrowbone back from the butcher. I'll boil it up and make a nice broth from it. You can take it over to him.'

'That's good of you, Koja.'

'Don't mention it.'

'This letter from the professor in Jerusalem – I don't know if I can forgive you for it.'

'And then we'll have dinner at that nice Italian place.'

'You're not lying to me, are you?'

'You're my life, Ev.'

'You won't ever lie to me?'

'I'm here for you. I'm always here for you.'

'I think I hate you. I'm so sorry, but I hate you.'

She spoke the last words very softly, almost wistfully, in a kind of trance. Her breath was sour; it carried on it a note of longing that reached far into the past and belonged entirely to me, to an image of me that she was seeing at that moment. And that image had nothing to do with my manipulative shoulder-turning, my deliberate placement beside her, the present warmth of our bodies. It was a crazy tone she had chosen for those words. They were a dismissal, a beautiful, calm, agony-white dismissal that touched my heart deeply, a goodbye that merely anticipated the goodbye that was to come.

You always know in advance when something is over.

It was one of those presentiments that your Buddha spoke of, when countless streams of consciousness suddenly flow into one another. Something is happening, but it has already happened or is only about to happen. And I looked at Ev from the side, saw her profile; the hair-fine lines at the corners of her mouth; the little bird's feet by her eyes, more hummingbirds than crows; the mouth that once so liked to laugh, now cemented up, with cement lips; and the little mole to one side of her chin, where a soft fuzz grew.

I knew it was over, although the causes were still to come.

I got up from the couch, leaving her with Rubinroth's letter, which she read over and over inside her bell jar of madness, and went down to the apple tree. I picked the stewed flowers from its branches, leant against the trunk and thought long and hard about David Grün, the Schindler Jew, the sporting ace with the sharp mind beneath his curly hair, the hyper-analyst, who still owed me all ten of those gratis therapy sessions.

He held out for another three weeks – kept alive only by Ev's devotion – before his organs failed, and he shuffled off this mortal coil.

He was apparently asking after my well-being until the very last.

This by way of answer to your mute question about David Grün, ah, silent Swami.

38

Nineteen sixty-nine was the escalation of nineteen sixty-eight and, for me, despite spaceships landing on the moon and a hallucinogenic age billowing around me, it brought a host of elemental, one might say archaic, experiences.

For example, Dr Erhard Sneiper was found dead in his car. That was extremely archaic.

Someone sitting in the rear seat had shot him in the back of the head with a Walther P1. Afterwards, that person had detached what was left of the head (largely emptied of brain matter) with a saw and placed it in his lap, beside the head of his Dobermann, which was fully intact, but also removed from its trunk.

Since there was no evidence to be found, the police assumed it was one of these Neapolitan contract killings, which happened from time to time in the course of the shady arms deals in which the Italophile *avvocato* seemed to be involved (I had no idea he was an Italophile – why had he drunk so much cola, then?).

The tabloid press took an interest in the case over three editions. They also printed the biography of this man who had passed away so suddenly, mentioning his marital status, lover, favourite brothels, his history and his homeland: the bygone Baltics. The beautiful old Hanseatic cities of Riga, Reval and Dorpat shone out from a special page featuring photos of all their sights. (The next day there was another special page on Naples, an unfair duel with unequal weapons.)

Days later, Ev received a long letter from the Unspeakable, which gave her all manner of reasons to leave. It said that three years before, I had been planted in Gustav Heinemann's office at the Bonn justice ministry on Erhard Sneiper's instructions, a placement arranged by Herr Achenbach, where I had worked covertly on behalf of the amnesty faction.

There was a tape enclosed with the letter: the recording (indistinct and repeatedly interrupted by a Dobermann's joyful barking) of a conversation I'd had with Erhard Sneiper in the grounds of Nymphenburg Palace. You could also clearly hear Erhard saying, 'Heinrich, sic!', followed by my screams.

As a postscript, Hub mentioned that he held me responsible for the murder of his old friend, Ev's ex-husband and my once-so-beloved ethnic leader, Erhard Sneiper.

Post-postscript: *Quod erat demonstrandum.*

Ev left me the same day.

I had been expecting it, as I've told you already.

But it's still different when a thing actually happens.

I ran down the street after her. I knelt before her in the rain. I threw myself onto the bonnet of the taxi (four hundred and fifty-three deutschmarks in repairs to the paintwork). She remained composed and didn't look me in the eye even once, as if I were Medusa, fiery eyes, scaly armour, long fangs, look her up in the Glyptothek Museum, you'll see what I mean.

Ev went back to Israel.

I haven't seen her since.

She gave up her position at the Mossad, probably no longer seeing any sense in it once the escapees had escaped on all fronts.

I believe she is now working at the Schneider Children's Hospital on Kaplan Street. She hung on to our old apartment on Graets Street. She took all Anna's pictures back to Tel Aviv with her. But not the Alaska watercolour of the Tlingit queen Anna, Baroness von Schilling, surrounded by her Indians. Not that.

*

I never heard from Anna again.

I have called on her often in recent years, called her name in every tone of voice I can muster into the empty vault that is my heart. In vain.

Sometimes I believe I can feel more than see her smile, and then I sleep better. But it might be my imagination. Every day I would go to her Indian grave, always taking something with me: a sweet, a gemstone, a little meerschaum pipe bought at the flea market. Once, a drawing vanished overnight, although I had placed a pebble on it and there had been no wind and no rain. I thought she might have taken my little effort up or down to her, because it was a drawing of her mother's eyes.

I stayed in the fortified house. I did as I was told. I remained alone and became the man I am now.

39

Two and a half years ago, on the morning of the fifth of September nineteen seventy-two, a Palestinian commando calling itself Black September (for this September was to be the blackest that Munich had seen in many years) stormed the Olympic Village in Milbertshofen. Eight terrorists took almost a dozen Israeli athletes hostage, intending to escape with them to Cairo on a Boeing 727.

That night, I received a phone call from the Fürstenfeldbruck military airfield. It was Zvi Zamir, the successor to Chief Ramsad, the successor to Isser Harel, all-powerful head of the Mossad, official observer of the German crisis team and my ultimate superior. In a voice boiling with rage, he ordered me to send our two Kidon regulators out from Schwabing. Down the telephone line, I could hear assault rifles being fired in the background. I pointed out that the agents were steaming drunk, since in sheer frustration at not being deployed that morning, they had assassinated my supplies of vodka.

'However drunk they are,' Zamir growled darkly, 'they'll still be able to shoot better than these German halfwits.'

In the background, I heard someone with a Bavarian accent shout, 'Oh, give it a rest, lads!' Probably Strauß, the leader of the CSU. Zvi Zamir was calling from the office of the crisis team in the air control tower, which was under fire from the terrorists. And then no one spoke as I heard explosions and a windowpane shattering somewhere close by. The connection was interrupted. And then the line went dead. And because one of my regulators had thrown the television out of the window that morning in a fit of impotent rage (you remember, Swami, I've told you this already), we had to follow events on a transistor radio as the policemen's attempt to free the hostages by force ended in a massacre.

Several officers were shot and wounded, including a helicopter pilot. A sniper hit one of his own colleagues in a barrage of fire and badly injured him. Another policeman was killed by a ricochet. Five terrorists lost their lives. None of the hostages survived. They all bled or burned to death, or were torn to pieces by grenade shrapnel.

Two days after the catastrophe, I was invited to appear on a television chat show. A large studio in Unterföhring, on the outskirts of Munich. The walls were white and so were the people. Their faces, I mean.

The political parties that made up the Bundestag had been asked to suggest participants for the discussion, and the SPD had put me forward because of my Jewish background. Gustav Heinemann remembered me; he was now president of West Germany. That evening, the goyim needed an approachable Jew. They begged Herr Himmelreich to fly the flag for Germany in this discussion, despite the burning helicopter and the failure of the German authorities. Black-red-gold. A good German state (the better German state, more importantly, compared with the hammer and sickle over the way).

Before the recording began, I spotted an Israeli foreign correspondent on the panel, very young, as young as Maya had been, and just as beautiful, her face framed by a mop of wild, tousled hair. She came from a kibbutz near Caesarea and was full of German sounds (her mother had probably escaped from that city of spires, Cologne).

Perhaps I was gripped by sorrow because she wore an 'M' at the start of her name. Mandolika, autumn is here. Though I expect I was also sad because the Olympic fiasco was burning in me as it did in all of us. Or it might have been the roaring in my head, which had given me no peace since Ev disappeared, but was suddenly silenced by this journalist, completely silenced, just by her sitting opposite me and staring at me. The cameras hummed, the presenter hummed as well, and all I could see was a pair of wide-open eyes with a look in them that burst me apart.

The Mossad had tasked me with representing Israel's position on the chat show, highlighting the disgraceful ineptitude of the Bavarian police force, and making the most outrageous comparisons with the Holocaust that I could. The BND, meanwhile, had pressed me to do the exact opposite, to defend the German side and refuse to let anyone use the disaster as leverage.

But what I actually said was something entirely unexpected – or rather, something entirely unexpected came out of my mouth. It flowed out, so to speak, like honey, sap or maybe pus. I had not intended to say it, no, really, it just happened. When Herr Himmelreich was called upon as an expert on Israel, in the midst of a discussion about terrorism and deaths, I said that I was not Herr Himmelreich at all.

'Aren't you?' I was asked.

No, I said, for many years I had gone by another name entirely, my rightful name.

'And what was that?' Mandolika put in.

My name was Solm, first name Koja, born in Riga like Herr Himmelreich, that much was true, but otherwise the descendant of German barons and a stubborn pastor, whom the Bolsheviks had put in a sack and held underwater, like kittens. I had never been a Jew. But the BND had made me one. I had been a BND Jew, a civil-service Jew, but not a real one.

Imagine the effect that had in the studio.

And I pledged my love to Israel.

Though I am German to my marrow.

The presenter sweated and rifled through his stack of little cards.

A journalist from the *Frankfurter Allgemeine*, a stout hedonist with a fine silken blue in his eyes (sent by the FDP), asked if that meant I had been a secret agent under a false name, working for Reinhard Gehlen. And who *was* Herr Himmelreich, then?

I wept so freely that even the cameramen started to sob. And the audience on their benches. Then I also spoke of my deep German guilt. And everyone in the studio believed I was talking about the general stuff that was in fashion then, and not about what Koja Solm had done partly of his own free will.

Only that young journalist, Mandolika from Cologne and Caesarea, leaned over to me, put a hand on my arm (the pressure so soft, almost like an animal's warm mouth) and said in front of the rolling cameras that I was a significant man, very significant. And the new, democratic, social-democratic Germany should be glad to have men like me, who spoke the truth quite unsparingly – especially in the face of those terrible events in Munich, events that could make an Israeli lose their faith.

Their faith in a good Germany.

40

The Greek doctor says that we need to act like a sports team if we're going to make it.

Few sports teams, of course, consist of two members. But there are some: table-tennis players, for example. When they play doubles, one stands to the left and the other to the right behind the table. I've always liked table-tennis, because selecting a table as a piece of sports equipment is a poetic idea. I mean, there are bars, asymmetric and high, there are boxes, hurdles, poles, foils, there are a thousand kinds of bats and balls, there are nets and tracks and skittles, there are ropes, racehorses, arrows and all kinds of incredibly fast vehicles. But a table? Mankind invented tables to sit at, to eat, work, draw at, to play chess (not a sport!), or *Skat* (not a sport!), to place their elbows on and think (also not a sport!), to put things on, like carrots, apples, beer bottles or body parts for dissection. The table is the least suitable thing in the world for any kind of sport, with the possible exception of the bed. But there is nothing I would call a sport that happens in bed, although two people do sometimes form a team there.

That, in any case, was certainly not what Dr Papadopoulos meant.

I believe that table-tennis would be the perfect sport for the Hippy, if he could still move. I am good at attacking and smashing; he's an excellent defender. And hopefully he won't say that Buddhists don't attack or defend. Excuse me? Buddhists are the world's best table-tennis players, the world champions all come from China or Korea.

But Dr Papadopoulos was talking more about the spirit of the thing when he spoke of a sports team. We should stick together. Not eat alone. Not go to the lavatory alone. Not read alone. Not do our occupational therapy alone.

All right, the Hippy can't speak or get out of bed, but his arms are still fully functional. Well, perhaps not fully functional, but he can move his fingers. Little, darting fingers, like Horowitz. Like Rachmaninov. Oh, how Papa loved his Rachmaninov. If he makes a real effort, the Hippy, then his arms will soon improve, and his legs. In two or three years, I tell him, you can be living the life of a snail again. It's a joke. But he doesn't laugh. His laughter, his cheerfulness, all of that has of course receded a long way into the background.

There is one thing I must say: Dr Papadopoulos is a good fellow. He even finds it droll when I call him Dr Frankensteinoulos. I mean, he really has turned the Hippy's head into that of Boris Karloff, the sad monster. Plugs everywhere, and this huge line of stitches from the temple to the ear. I tell the Hippy this. I show him photos of *The Bride of Frankenstein* that I find in a television magazine. I am only making fun. Trying to cheer him up.

He always used to say I was a wonderful person. It was he who said that, not I.

Somehow, I almost started to believe it myself. But now that I have explained things to him, it looks more complicated, no?

I don't know how much good and bad karma I have accumulated. David Grün was most certainly not good karma. I regret the vial in his *Weissbier*, although not as much as the Swami would evidently like me to. He had tears in his eyes. He actually had tears in his eyes for that busybody. Hard to believe.

But I have also produced some good karma. I was a Jew for a very long time. That is extremely good karma now, in social-democratic Germany, and we all know what shitty karma it was for a thousand years.

I also accumulated good karma through my work with you, Ev. And the regulation of the rocket scientists? I don't know if you can really call that bad. Perhaps it was bad that we failed. Perhaps it was bad that the wrong people suffered. Wives, depot workers, two secretaries. I would say there is a certain equilibrium to the karma there, wouldn't you? The karma books are balanced.

But when it comes to the chat show, the one after the Olympic massacre – well, I do believe I worked my way a lot further towards nirvana with that. The overwhelmed presenter, the charming Mandolika, the other studio guests and many members of the audience came up to me after the programme had finished. They embraced me, they patted me on the back and told me I had really moved them and taken them with me a little way on the beautiful, sad plane ride into my soul.

Some well-meaning moron even asked about my foreskin.

Only the BND man, who was present as a matter of routine (standard practice when Orcs appear in public), stared silently at me from narrowed eyes, and then marched into the control room with an air of determination to demand they hand over the tapes. It was not a live broadcast. That would have been all we needed. The chat show was never aired. No one saw me bawling on television.

That evening, I was summarily suspended.

Betrayal of official secrets.

Disclosing a protected identity without permission.

Endangering internal intelligence lines.

It was wonderful.

It was not quite so wonderful having to move out of the fortified house.

The Mossad, too, had learned what I'd said that evening, principally because it had sent me there with a clear objective. The charming Mandolika was also working for foreign intelligence, though she had chosen to stay at the luxurious Vier Jahreszeiten Hotel rather than my modest fortified house in Schwabing. What a false minx.

Mandolika's report on my behaviour was a stream of invective ('Himmelreich vulgo Solm: typical semi-intelligent German ... highly self-reflective, egocentric personality ... manipulative character, deeply dishonest despite all his revelations').

Since she could not know that I was essentially her superior, and that my role at the German–Israeli Association eV was by no means confined to playing the Munich hotelier for regulators, her verdict carried very little weight.

The Mossad boss, Zvi Zamir (Chief Ramsad had moved on to the happy hunting grounds of politics years earlier), summoned me to Tel Aviv to give an account of myself. He told me just how disappointed he was to discover my true and extremely un-Jewish background. But I had been a loyal servant to Israel for many years. That was taken into consideration when judging my actions.

Instead of putting me up against the wall, Zvi Zamir merely reduced my pension. I was also prohibited from ever revealing any information about my operations, the fortified house in Munich and the identity of my colleagues.

I received my full pension from the BND, since civil service legislation made anything else impossible. It all worked out quite nicely. From a material perspective. Who manages to rake in pensions from Germany and Israel at the same time? Really, only Holocaust survivors.

I'm not just telling you this, Ev. I tell the Hippy as well. I tell him that I can provide for him, yes, that I can see he gets all the support he needs, when he gets out of here. I'm sixty-five years old now. I have a detached house in Bogenhausen, not too large, not too small. A holiday home in Ticino. I started running a gallery again last year, as well, very close to the Pinakothek art museums. Focusing on the German modernists.

I've given up the painstaking business of forgery. My eyesight isn't what it used to be, and I stay away from anything illegal, anyway. My reputation is also excellent as Koja Solm. The police may still be sitting at the door after all these months (though less and less frequently now, one might even say occasionally), but that's just what they would do for anyone. The security services have to take care that any projectile lodged in the head of a respectable citizen isn't joined by a second. They're simply protecting me, you understand? I'm not under any kind of surveillance. Why would I be? The death of Herr Himmelreich (original edition) was never connected to me. He did not want to be in the world for us fucking apes, us false madmen, as my poor Hebrew teacher called me and all the other Orcs. So he wrote in his farewell note, before hanging himself in the German woods. But he *was* in this world for us, and for us alone. When my brave joke-collector strung himself up all those years ago, above a carpet of bluebells, he did a great service to German–Israeli relations. And with that, he vanished from the account books of the here and now.

And so I am doing quite nicely. I have been able to make arrangements for my private needs, too. Until my accident, ladies from the Ariadne Agency were coming to see me twice a week, discreet, clean, professionally caring.

I loved to have them urinate in my bathroom; I have an ideal lavatory for this purpose, into which one pees loudly, at least from female genitalia. How did I get on to that? No matter. The Hippy can be sure that in me he has a reliable, well-off friend of steadfast character. My God, he could be my son.

Unfortunately, anything he wants to tell me now has to be written down on small cardboard tablets. Night Nurse Gerda has bought him a whole pile of lined cards from a stationer. Green, yellow, blue and red. Along with green, yellow, blue and red felt-tipped pens. He has made a blue card with a blue QUESTION MARK and a yellow card with a yellow EXCLAMATION MARK. How does one come up with such a combination? On the blood-red cards that lie on his chest and are intended for communicating with me, he has written the following words, in red letters, of course:

'PIG!'

'MURDERER!'

'GET OUT!'

'NO THANK YOU!'

'NO!'

'NEVER!'

I tell the Hippy that this won't get us anywhere, and is a very long way from sports-team-like. No table-tennis player would say these words to his partner (unless he was a truly terrible partner, but I am not).

'FUCK YOU!' the Hippy writes with trembling fingers on a new red card.

'Please don't misunderstand me, Swami. I have nothing against your anger. I understand your anger. You are horrified. You are disappointed in me. But we can still work with that.'

He just looks at me.

'We can work with that as a sports team. Train together. Prepare together. As Dr Papadopoulos says: work towards a common goal!'

He laughs as if he is trying to cough up small pebbles, to gather them in his pharynx ready to spit at me.

'You see, Swami. You've told me so much about Buddha. But you didn't tell me that even Buddha had to die. Though, since Buddha was no common-or-garden person, his death was not a common-or-garden death.'

The Hippy takes a red card and writes 'NIRVANA' on it.

'He entered nirvana – yes, why not. But I don't care whether he did or did not go on existing after that. What I am getting at is this: he was eaten by worms, just as you or I will be eaten by worms. And then he transformed himself into something special.'

He writes: 'SPECIAL?'

'Of course something special. But if the special Buddha could die like a human being, then he could also live like a human being. And in that case, he, too, must have known what anger was.'

He writes: 'ANGER?'

'I know that the Buddha did not approve of the passions. But he must have known immense rage, and hatred, too.'

He writes: 'HATRED?'

'He must have known hatred, but since he was not a common-or-garden person, he did not feel a common-or-garden hatred. He felt enlightened hatred.'

I have to wait for five minutes while the Hippy writes.

The card says: 'READ THE MAHAPARINIRVANA SUTRA ABOUT PARI-NIRVANA AND REALIZE THAT HATRED DESTROYS YOUR WHOLE SELF, YOU BASTARD!'

'What I'm talking about is an enlightened hatred that doesn't destroy the self, but leads you to yourself, to what you really are. The power of the storm to cleanse and renew is something you realize only in hatred.'

I read: 'FUCK YOU!'

'You see, you hate me, too.'

He keeps holding up the 'FUCK YOU!' card, but at least he also starts picking his nose with the little finger of his other hand.

'You hate me. We both know that. And it's a good thing. And now we have to make the good thing even better. We have to make it better as a doubles pair. Me with the forehand, you with the backhand. Ping. Pong. Ping. Pong. Gold medal!'

I can still see 'FUCK YOU!' as the Hippy closes his eyes.

'When you hear about how I caught my bullet, then enlightened hatred might not seem like such an impossible concept to you.'

He lets a little frozen time roll down over his eyebrows to his closed lids, where it stops, melts, and – because of the high acidity – burns his eyes open. The look he gives me is pure craving. He wants to know. He wants to know everything. He looks at me, and I fear that the region behind his eyes is populated by creatures from his imagination, all of them shooting at me. The 'FUCK YOU!' card sinks slowly back down onto the sheets, like the fan slipping from the grasp of a poisoned Cleopatra.

But I don't say anything else.

I go back to my bed, switch on my reading light and turn my

attention to a biography of Camille Claudel which has been gripping me for days. I let the Hippy stew, let the acid penetrate deep into his brain. Night Nurse Gerda comes in, puts a tray of hospital what-passes-for-food down in front of me, then goes over to the Hippy and tries to feed him a spoonful of yoghurt.

He writes a card.

She reads: 'TASTES SHIT!'

She nods sadly, straightens his bedclothes and says she would prefer it if he didn't speak to her like that, though he isn't speaking at all.

He is upset and sore and has gone half-blind, and so I give him the night.

41

The Haus der Kunst. Do you know it?

You've lived in Munich for twenty years and you don't know the Haus der Kunst?

On the Piazzale Michelangelo, the Führer once looked out over the roofs of Florence and sighed, 'Finally, finally I understand Böcklin,' and that was when he decided to have a magnificent temple of the muses built for the city of Munich, and to stuff it full of bronze con-querors, plaster does and a triptych called *SS Man, SA Man, Fatigue Duty*.

Now this granite and limestone thing – cleared out, empty, a gigantic building with twenty-one Titan thighs for pillars along its front – stands at the edge of the Englischer Garten. I'm sure you will have sat on its steps before. People sell joints there, so I gather, and much worse things. All marble inside: the doorframes, the staircases, the skirting boards. Really, all of it marble. And proper German marble, too: red marble from Kelheim, yellow from Saalburg and the yellowest of all from Tegernsee.

Swastikas shimmer on the ceilings, real gold leaf on pink mosaics. In the galleries, you feel you are inside a majestic steamer. They hold art exhibitions there, openings, sometimes they put on performance art. The Neue Pinakothek, pulverized in an air raid and with no fixed abode, shows its collection of what was once called degenerate art in these rooms.

A few months ago, a chance encounter with Ignatius Kirchmaier, the major collector from Starnberg, opened up an undreamed-of opportunity for me to see a retrospective of Papa's work.

Kirchmaier, a gifted erotomaniac, brought to the project a collection of Solm pastoral scenes purchased by his father. Dear Ignatius contributed portraits of girls, women and fine ladies that I had never known existed. Mama, two other patrons, and the national museum in Riga also loaned pictures. And from the Pinakothek collection came Baltic landscapes rich in birch trees, their emotions incarnated in the bodies of evanescent nymphs.

I stood like a dishevelled old cloud, saturated with rain, before the feminine nude of my lost Ev at the age of fifteen, sixteen at most, before she was very feminine at all. Papa had posed her lying down in his studio, as the goddess of holy meditation. Her head was propped in the corner of the sofa where I, too, had loved to lie as a child, and she was wearing a mere nothing made of silk.

But Mama recognized it as her old negligee. She was entirely opposed to the picture, which she thought indecent: the beauty of youth and its eternal laws (namely that it is difficult to renounce contemplation of it) were veiled only by Ev's ancient eyes, and not by her clothes. There was a scepticism in her smile, a scepticism that also whispered in her dark eyes, and I was not at all surprised that Papa had called the picture *Melancholia*.

More than three hundred visitors came to the opening of the exhibition, perhaps more. And whether they knew Jeremias Himmelreich or Koja Solm or even Herr Dürer, they had all been very warmly invited by me, in my newly regained Solmhood.

But not Hub.

Hub had a court appearance, where he had to explain the gas vans from Riga, or rather where the gas vans from Riga had to be explained, along with the question of why the former SS- Standartenführer had set such great store by their availability.

Mama came dressed to the nines, a hawkish spectre longing to have Papa back with her. I saw the marcel-waved Herta Gehlen there, too, with a thoroughly morose Reini in tow. He walked past Papa's works with a look of revulsion. I even thought I spied Otto John in the crush of bodies. And then, craning my neck in astonishment as I looked through a cloud of charming, buzzing and humming art-lovers, I caught a glimpse of Isser Harel's large ears. Was that possible? Could that be possible? I had sent him an invitation, too, but had not hoped to see him. Israel was so far away. And he hadn't responded to the postcard.

The sensitive curator, a Grand Guignol if ever I saw one, called his exhibition *The Art of the Old School: Eros, Thanatos, transcendence and pose. The allegorical work of the Baltic artist Theo Solm.* At the start of the opening ceremony, he stalked over to the sturdy box-shaped lectern, breathed a few preliminary words into the microphone and then introduced me as 'the artist's son, and not without some talent of his own'.

And so I stepped forward, armed with my best suit, and gave a lecture about my father for the first time in my life. About my father and his typical Solm style. It is, however, a very peculiar thing to speak about one's own father in public, it feels impossible, like the light bulb having to explain who Thomas Alva Edison was and why he was important.

I said what a joy it was for me to see so many people there, on this almost Baltically warm – that is, not hot – Sunday morning. I wanted (I went on) to say a few words about *Melancholia*, Papa's portrait of his beloved daughter, which was hung behind me so that everyone could see it as I was speaking.

With his insight into human frailty and his creative ability to turn those deficiencies into advantages (I said), Theo Solm was also able to draw from the features of this girl, whom he had painted in nineteen twenty-four or nineteen twenty-five, the very essence of longing and loneliness (I faltered). Please notice how pale he has kept the whole face. And the bluish tinge to the lips (I gave an insight into the colour blue, the colour of depth, which never leaps out at us like red or monop-olizes our attention like the sun-soaked yellow beloved of children). The model's eyes appear sick, helped by a tiny dab of crimson here around their edges. The melancholy temperament, which according to medical lore arises from the dry humour of black bile, can be seen in the black of her pupils and the shadows of mortality they cast, in such shattering contrast to the freshness of her flesh and her young life. I would claim (I claimed) that this juxtaposition can be found in all my father's pictures, however kitschy and melodramatic or even wanton they might be: he himself was a melancholic, a melancholic through and through. And fully aware that man, with all his abilities, his capacity for abstract thought and his unimaginable knowledge, can still only orient himself reliably and confidently in the realm of the visible.

'And yet – is not the invisible the only valuable thing about a person?' I asked the room. 'In any case, ladies and gentlemen, my father's art may well have brought the invisible qualities of this half-child as close to the realm of the visible as one can get. And this is precisely why I cannot, unfortunately, suppress a degree of emotion now' – please forgive my lack of composure – 'for in the last fifty-five years, I have not truly known this young woman – my sister, Ev was her name, and will be her name for a little while yet, I hope – for a single second. And yet all I had to do was look at this likeness of her, which my father kept from us, kept from all of us, including my mother, who is standing down there and weeping just as I am. Instead, he sold his work to a collector, a complete stranger to him, the father of our noble (in the truest sense of the word) Herr Kirchmaier. For mere peanuts, he sold a work that depicts mankind's sadness at his temporal, earthly existence, at his limitations and unrealizable potential, all contained in the face of a pretty girl. A bad deal. But I shan't complain. Because if Herr Kirchmaier senior had not made that spur-of-the-moment decision to buy it, then Ev, Eva-child as she was then – the world was breaking her apart, and she knew it – is someone I would never have seen in these colours behind me, with this smile that she never showed me.'

Then I thanked the city of Munich, the Herr Kirchmaiers both late and living, the Haus der Kunst (but not Adolf Hitler), the Munich Pinakothek, the Riga Art Museum, the Soviet Embassy in Bonn, the SPD, the BND (these thanks conveyed only via a nod to Herr Gehlen), my mother, the many guests and friends who had come (I also spotted two ladies from the Ariadne Agency there), and not least the curator, who had another important contribution to art history to make now, namely the main address of the day.

I hadn't considered that what now followed, the dismaying and horrendous thing that now followed, might be present among the possibilities for how that day would evolve, even just in trace elements. The mood seemed so convivial, a trifle bored perhaps, but also distinguished and buoyant, dampened only by this mild apprehension about the curator's speech, which was guaranteed to be very alien, and in fact began with, 'Ladies and gentlemen, honoured guests, let *ars longa* guide us on our sentimental journey towards a *scientia* of the Solm oeuvre – and in so doing let us ask ourselves: is what we see here art at all?'

I went and stood in the front row with Mama, who was ashamed of the tears welling out of her. She was also put out by my words, which were too public for her liking. And she wanted to rest, by which she meant escape from the mob. I led her ninety-five-year-old bones to the marble benches at the back of the room, where she sat down, turned herself into a bolt-upright statue and said, 'Leave me in peace, child.' I was now a long way from the action, a big mistake.

The curator was talking himself into a groove, or so he thought. But the fizzling sparklers of his thoughts fell like ashes onto the strained heads in front of him. The audience was soon radiating a restless, hard-to-suppress desire to get away. An old gentleman who was leaning on a pillar even seemed to have fallen asleep. Papa did not deserve that.

Suddenly, from the corner of my eye, I saw a young man step forward, a bearded fellow in a Mao cap. He somehow produced a megaphone from his checked dungarees and switched it on. It crackled threateningly once or twice. Having just uttered the words: '*haut goût* of naturalistic kitsch', the curator broke off in alarm, a speechless faun, and stared at Dungarees. The latter brought the megaphone up to his wildly woolly mouth and, raising a clenched fist, cried out, '*Achtung, Achtung!* Art, art!'

At least no one was bored now – which, stupidly, I took for a good sign. This predisposition might well explain the almost fatal reaction times I displayed later. Dungarees blew into his megaphone again, before shouting, 'This is a Happening in remembrance of the art-citizen Solm! You are now watching an autonomous action by the Art and Revolution group!

Six more young desperados suddenly appeared beside Dungarees. They whipped off their clothes at lightning speed. The only confusing thing about this for the guests seemed to be that these people were Austrian: someone next to me whispered disapproving words to this effect when Dungarees began to read out Mao quotes in a Viennese dialect. Fired up by the Great Chairman, the naked people shoved the curator aside and gave the skinniest activist, who looked like Woody Allen, a leg up onto the metre-high lectern, which wobbled dangerously. Once he was up there, he squatted down with his reverse side facing us, his arms bent, stark naked – a rather lovely image, actually, full of Solmesque creatureliness. With a look of intense concentration, he began to squeeze a sausage out of his anus. At first, it peeked out like a shy mole, retreated for a moment, and then emerged from its burrow in one flowing movement, drawing no comment at all from the breathless audience, not even when it slapped onto Hitler's Solnhofen limestone floor (the colours went quite well together).

Now, at the latest, the dimensions of this event should have been obvious to me; they were suddenly obvious to everyone who, just moments before, had thought these good-natured and gregarious visionaries were simply here to liven things up a little.

Before anyone could react, another artist positioned himself in front of Papa's *Melancholia* and began to masturbate diligently, while in the background two young women whipped one another – though, to avoid hurting themselves, they struck my father's painting instead. The masturbator took a step closer to my sister, who was filled with longing and sorrow, but did not look particularly shocked (that was very like her). He was quite evidently intending to mix his ejaculate with the dammar varnish my father had applied fifty years earlier. And then Reinhard Gehlen suddenly appeared at my side, handing me the small pocket pistol he always carried with him, which was perfectly suited to incidents of this kind, and saying, 'A truly unforgettable event, Dürer.'

He added that I should shoot the slacker in the heart.

Here we have reached a suitable point, my dear Swami, at which to contemplate enlightened hatred, for in view of the circumstances it did not seem advisable to renounce all my desires and passions just then. I took Gehlen's kindly pistol, stuck it in my pocket and started moving, as a member of the audience shouted, 'Where are the police?'

As if on cue, the dedicated artists started chanting, 'Call the pigs, call the pigs, someone call the bourgeois pigs!'

The hall now began to seethe, the crowd's reactions varied but still sluggish. I ran past Dungarees, slamming the megaphone full-force into his teeth as I went, saw him start to bleed, reached the masturbator, grabbed him by the throat, got him in a headlock, though without any great success, as he simply went on masturbating, and hung off him like a scarf with nothing but cotton wool in my sixty-four-year-old arms. Someone started tugging at me, and then I felt a blow to my head. I exploded.

When my eyes came to, the whole of the grand hall that Hitler had hewn so beautifully in stone was reeling and spinning. Ahead of me, among the dancing feet, I could see a tooth. It might have been one of mine, and so I crawled towards it. A little way off, in front of the lectern, someone slipped in Woody Allen's shit, but managed to right himself quite elegantly, like the black swan in *Swan Lake*.

I snatched up the tooth and tried to get back on my feet.

Around me there was uproar, snorting, screaming, gurgling.

Art and Revolution came streaming in from all sides. Art-citizens lashed out. The artists let themselves be struck. I stumbled again, and saw one of the young whipping girls slash my sister with a huge machete. The masturbator was getting a kicking. Dungarees, his face empty like a burst blood blister, was going from one Papa-picture to the next entirely unchallenged, throwing what was doubtless caustic soda or something similar at the colourful shadows.

From a long way off there came an exultation of police sirens.

Then Yossi appeared beside me.

As if it were the most natural thing in the world.

I had not invited Yossi to the opening – and why would I have invited a chauffeur who couldn't even drive? But before I had time for any questions, he helped me to my feet, slid my left arm over his golem shoulders, gripped my waist with his right and fled the melee with me.

I didn't want to flee.

And yet flee we did, through a series of quieter rooms, to a staircase that we descended into the darkness, ending up in an enormous labyrinth of cellars that had barely been used since the war.

I didn't want to be in any cellar labyrinth, either.

I told Yossi that I didn't want this, but he held me in his vice-like fists until we reached the air-raid shelter. He pulled me through the gas doors, heaved the final steel door closed behind us, slid the heavy iron bar across and switched on the light.

42

The room was illuminated by a single bulb hanging from the ceiling.

Bunker aesthetics.

I saw reinforced concrete on all sides. I saw the words 'Silence Please', written in old-fashioned white Sütterlin script on the dark grey reinforced concrete. I saw Yossi, waiting by the steel door. I saw a single chair with Colonel Harel in it, his Mickey Mouse ears casting expressive shadows. I saw a washbasin with a briefcase in it. And above the washbasin I saw an old enamel sign, also bearing the words 'Silence Please'.

I heeded it, and was silent.

Isser Harel said, 'Many thanks for the invitation, Jeremias.'

It was strange not to see him in sandals, or in short trousers, or in crumpled cotton, or in Tel Aviv. It was strange to see him, full stop.

I greeted him and said that I had to go back up.

'No, you don't.'

I had to go up and rescue my father's paintings, I repeated, and I would be glad if he and Yossi could help me.

'There's nothing to be done for them, Jeremias,' Isser Harel said flatly. 'We're not going to help you. We had the artists up there flown in so that they could help *us*.'

I was starting to realize that the tooth in my trouser pocket might indeed have come from my own jaw.

'Help us do what?'

'Not you. Just us. They're helping us by doing what they're doing. They're just artists. And what they're doing is just art.'

His voice was high-pitched, but calm and firm, as if he were telling me the time. Then he looked up at the ceiling with an expression that said the whole thing was self-evident.

'They are going to destroy every single painting up there,' he said, 'until there's nothing left.' He sounded lost in thought.

As I followed his eyes, I noticed how quiet it was. Two metres and fifty centimetres of reinforced concrete quiet. Not a sound from above. But silence doesn't always make for a quiet mind.

'So you're the one behind this whole spectacle?' I asked, bewildered.

He lowered his eyes, ran a hand over his forehead and gave me no reply.

'Why? What had those pictures done to you?'

'They're your father's.'

'Yes, but what had they done to you?'

'Your father was no Jew. Your father's name was not Himmelreich. Your father didn't die in a concentration camp. That, Jeremias, is what the pictures did to me.'

I showed him my contempt by turning wordlessly to the gas doors and limping towards them. But when I got there and tried to open the first one, Yossi appeared and slammed his fist into my chin. I fell to the floor and felt him kicking me with all his might, in my abdomen, my ribcage, in the face. I was gripped by the wrists and dragged across the rough concrete, then dumped like a sack in front of Isser's chair. This was a serious matter.

'The picture up there, the one you grew sentimental in front of,' I heard Colonel Harel's voice musing, after a while. 'Was that Mrs Himmelreich I recognized in that picture?'

I nodded. One or two of my ribs were broken, and I was spitting blood.

'She's a paediatrician in Tel Aviv now, I hear?'

I nodded and struggled slowly upright.

'And the two of you are no longer together?'

I shook my head.

'That's good. We would miss her.'

'Is that supposed to be a threat?'

'There's no need to make threats. You are here. We are here. Things are happening.'

'The Mossad gave me an honourable discharge.'

'The Mossad gave you an honourable discharge?'

'I'm drawing a pension.'

'He's drawing a pension, Yossi.'

'I'm going now.'

'Not yet.'

'Now.'

I started moving again.

'Jeremias, we've been through this already.'

I kept shuffling forward.

'When you reach the door, Yossi is going to break your arm.'

I was making good progress.

'It hurts him to use his fists on you. His fists are not as young as they were.'

I didn't get the impression it hurt him to hit me in the face. I landed on the floor again, and stayed there.

'What do you want?' I asked, exhausted.

Isser got up.

That always had a surprising effect, because unlike almost everyone else who got up from a chair, it didn't make him any taller. At the same time, it gave his appearance a grotesque aspect, which he intensified with explosive gesticulation. He paced up and down in front of me, though his voice was unchanged.

'You came into my institute. Came under a false name. Came with a false identity. Under false pretences. With a false wife. As the son of this pornographic painter. As the brother of a mass murderer. And you think you're going to get away with that?'

'She wasn't a false wife.'

'You stood and watched Yossi punish your own brother. You were there. You watched him punch one of his eyes out. I hate that man. But not even he deserves a brother like you. You are scum, Jeremias Himmelreich, Koja Solm, Heinrich Dürer, or whatever you want to call yourself.'

What I felt, alongside a sense of humiliation that overwhelmed everything, was my mouth, populated with wobbly teeth, and the right side of my chest, where Gehlen's pistol, safely stowed in the inside pocket of my suit jacket, had bruised or broken my ribs through some kind of impact. But it also brought a seductive quality to the situation, giving me the power to change the dynamic whenever I wanted.

'I was a loyal servant to you, Isser,' I said, sitting up with some difficulty. 'For many years. I hunted the big beasts for you, and you nailed up their pelts in your office. I killed people for you, though I'm not proud of it. And I'm not proud of the day when you beat Hub to a pulp and I had to watch, either. But what of that? Does pride have any place in our profession? No. Never. Are you proud to be here, doing all this? Yes, I think you are.'

He looked at me, slowed his pacing. I clung to Yossi to pull myself up, and he, with his dear donkey face, didn't know what to do about it.

'Pride is what brought you here! It's pride that drew you to Hitler's Haus der Kunst. Go and piss in that corner, if you're proud of pissing on the Führer's concrete.'

Colonel Harel paused. He wasn't moving at all, now. He was like a torpedo that had been shoved into the launching tube with great haste, and was now just sitting there, waiting to be fired.

He gave Yossi a sign. Yossi grabbed me and dragged me over to the washbasin, where the briefcase was. He seized it, shoved me back under the light bulb and opened the case there.

The last time I had seen the photos, thirty years before, Comrade Nikitin had shown me only high-contrast prints, cheaply produced. Now I saw what it was possible to extract from old negatives in nineteen seventy-four. The laboratory had done themselves proud. The grainy quality was hardly an issue; you could see every nuance of the facial expressions.

'One of our sources works in the KGB archive,' Isser said, walking up behind me. 'They sent us this three months ago.'

On the fourth photo, I spotted Moshe Jacobsohn. He was looking into the camera with no expression on his face, besides a haunted look of mortal terror. I was there in half-profile.

'What do you have to say about this?'

I didn't say anything about it.

'What was it like, when my uncle died?'

I simply couldn't say anything about it.

'The sun was shining. You can see from the patches of light here that the sun must have been shining.' His finger tapped the paper. 'Was it nice when he died? Was it a nice day, when my uncle died?'

It was bad. But that was not the worst of it, I said.

The worst were the pictures still to come.

The colonel let out a roar. Then he walked around me, stopped straight in front of me, pulled himself up to his full height and spat in my face. Being so short, he had to spit from below, and his saliva hit me in the nostril. He was breathing loudly. He might have been weeping.

After a long, uncomfortable silence, he turned away.

'We will not regulate you, Jeremias,' he said quietly, still not looking at me. 'The new Mossad leadership raised an objection to that in light of your service. They won't even reduce your pension.'

He took the pictures from Yossi, sorted them into the correct order and put them back in the briefcase.

'But I am going to send these photos to everyone they might mean something to. The German authorities. Your brother. Your mother. All your fine friends up there.'

He turned back to face me with deliberate slowness.

'And of course, to Mrs Himmelreich.'

Angry? Yes, Swami, Isser Harel was angry. He was so angry, he had to adopt a sardonic tone of voice to avoid bursting with rage. He would have made a crummy Mossad boss if he hadn't stayed angry for decades. You have to admit that being angry for decades is different from being just and righteous for decades. Wanting to be just and righteous sounds much better than being angry. But there is one thing I would ask you to consider: you can be driven by hunger, by thirst, by the longing for love. But you cannot be driven by the longing for justice. Unless you call this longing by its proper name. And then it is called anger.

Anger, of course, doesn't sound special. And of course it would look better if a former head of the Mossad set off from Tel Aviv in a spirit of pure and peaceful and shall we say Buddhist enlightenment, to see that justice was done.

But it was not this noble sentiment that brought Isser to Munich, to this damp, musty Nazi bunker, risking an international scandal if Dungarees should object to going to prison and start mentioning contacts – contacts that were murky and anonymous, yes, but also contacts that were in Israel.

The truth is that the old colonel was simply angry, fiercely angry, and that is the sole reason he had come. For it is anger that drives us and sets us in motion. Ev, too, had always been driven and set in motion by anger. She hunted the escapees out of anger, not out of love for the human race. This enlightened anger, my dear Swami, this enlightened anger is an engine, and if you use it for something meaningful, it can give you a purpose. It's that simple. I cannot imagine that the Buddha sees it differently.

Sadly, it is something I myself have never managed. I should have learned anger, for perhaps my lack of it might have been the essential cause of all the calamities that my presence in the world has brought about. Perhaps there was just too much of the good in me. No man's a sage without some rage – a little rhyme you may remember. Enlightened anger is a necessary quality. Not these attacks of fury that come on like a fever and only make everything worse.

For that is precisely what happened to me, as I stared at this man who was so confident in his anger, in this purest form of anger, a man who despised me in his anger, who did not recognize me, who knew nothing of my love for Ev and Anna and Maya and Mumu and Mary-Lou and Mandolika and all the 'M' women, this fucking gnome who had come all this way just to humiliate me, and to rob the world of that picture, the girl on my father's sofa, a picture I will always miss.

And I reached into my jacket, pulled out Reinhard Gehlen's pistol, a pocket pistol, it's true, but still good for a surprise. Yossi looked quite taken aback. He will take that childish aspect to the grave with him. An owl in an ivy bush. And even Colonel Harel had a moment of confusion. I screamed at them both and they stood there like tin soldiers in a high heat. Then Yossi sprang forward two paces, reached the light bulb, jumped up and smashed it with both hands, squashing it like a giant fly. Tinkle.

And everything went black.

I waited too long in the darkness, my heart pounding, perhaps one second or two.

Then I fired a shot in Yossi's direction. But the bullet missed. Instead, it hit a half-open steel door that led into the old bunker complex. From there it ricocheted off a corner, which did little to slow its speed, but gave it an eccentric spin, then hit the gas door, which directed the shot so artfully that it merely grazed a concrete pillar and from there, now travelling not much faster than a small bird, found its way back to me like a boomerang, a billiard ball, a black one, that's all.

With the last of its momentum it pierced my skull – it was so tired now that I could actually feel its impact – and then burrowed through the liquid core of the planet, a firework of colours, and stopped at a diagonal to the wall of my skull, yes, perfect, and that was that.

43

The Hippy opens his eyes wide.

I fetch him the envelope.

It's the envelope that Hub brought me.

That was a long time ago now, goodness me.

I have kept the envelope under the mattress ever since, slept on it every night, though there is no tooth fairy to thank me for it in the morning with a piece of chocolate, something sour or some crackers.

I bring the photos into the light and show Basti each and every one.

His fingers tremble, his eyelids tremble, the last of his hair trembles between the Frankenstein skull-screws.

He sees me, afraid, standing in a group of SS men in the sunlight.

He sees Moshe Jacobsohn, and he sees my profile.

He looks at the photos again and again.

He sees me with the pistol, standing at the edge of the pit with my arm outstretched, a rare amount of space between me and that gloved hand.

I keep both eyes open as I take aim, because in the SS it is regarded as cowardly to squeeze one eye shut.

He sees the woman.

He sees the baby.

He sees the baby transformed by all the bullets.

I shoot off the whole magazine into that baby.

He sees my face up close as well.

My face on the paper and not the other.

I tell him he should go ahead and let the anger come.

The anger lights our way to a better world.

Buddha will understand, beneath his Bodhi Tree.

I tell him he should get really angry now.

Then it's night.

I fetch the scalpel.

I lie down with him in his bed.

I show him where he needs to cut me, and how deep.

No person is better than any other.

But I don't tell him that.

Just let the anger light the way.

But the next morning, quite unexpectedly, I wake up.

Beside me, the Hippy is glowing in an early sunbeam. He's cold.

His mouth is open like a piranha's.

His head has leaked out in the night; the pillow is wet.

From the screw, I expect, what a useless piece of junk.
The scalpel is lying on the floor.
In a minute, I will call Night Nurse Gerda.
But before that, I see the little yellow card.
He must have written it in the night.
The handwriting is shaky, and it's lying under his neck.
Yellow writing on yellow card.
It says: 'PEACE!'

Glossary

THE THIRD REICH

Einsatzgruppen: SS special action groups, which followed the army into Poland and Russia to murder Jews and political figures during the Second World War.

Gauleiter: district leader, the senior Nazi Party administrator in a *Gau* (administrative region).

Horst Wessel Lied: a Nazi marching song, written by Horst Wessel, a Nazi 'brownshirt' who was killed in 1930 in a street fight with communists.

Kampfkommandant: battle commander, the highest-ranking military officer in an embattled area or city. They were appointed on Hitler's orders starting in 1944, as Germany was losing ground.

Reichssippenamt: the Reich office for genealogical research, charged with determining whether people were of Jewish or non-Jewish origin, and issuing 'Aryan certificates'.

SD/Sicherheitsdienst: security service. The Nazi Party's own intelligence and security body, created in 1931 to protect the Party.

SS/Schutzstaffel: defence unit. Originally Hitler's personal guard, it was transformed into a huge army and a 'state within a state' by Heinrich Himmler.

SS ranks mentioned in *The Bastard Factory*:

Scharführer: squad leader, an NCO rank, roughly equivalent to a sergeant.

Untersturmführer: junior assault leader, the lowest of the officer ranks and equivalent to a second lieutenant.

Obersturmführer: senior assault leader, equivalent to a lieutenant.

Hauptsturmführer: head assault leader, equivalent to a captain.

Sturmbannführer: assault unit leader, equivalent to a major.

Obersturmbannführer: senior assault unit leader, equivalent to a lieutenant colonel.

Standartenführer: standard leader, equivalent to a colonel.

Brigadeführer: the post held by Walter Schellenberg, equivalent to a brigadier.

Reichsführer-SS: the highest rank of the SS and the equivalent of a field marshal. Himmler held this position from 1934 until late April 1945, and during the Second World War was responsible for all internal security in Nazi Germany, including concentration camps and the Einsatzgruppen murder squads. He reported directly to Hitler.

PLACE NAMES

A number of towns and cities outside Germany are known to Koja by their German names, either from his Baltic-German roots, or because they were occupied by the Nazis.

Breslau: Wrocław, post-war Poland, a city in the historical region of Silesia

Dorpat: Tartu, Estonia

Goldingen: Kuldīga, in the Courland region of Latvia

Pleskau: Pskov, north-western Russia

Posen: Poznań, Poland

Reval: Tallinn, capital of Estonia

Warthegau (Reichsgau Wartheland): an area of Poland annexed by Germany in 1939, including the city of Poznań and named for the Warta, the main river flowing through it.

ACRONYMS

BND: Bundesnachrichtendienst, Germany's Federal Intelligence Service

CDU: Christian Democratic Union (German centre-right political party)

CSU: Christian Social Union (Bavarian centre-right political party, allied to the CDU)

FDP: Free Democratic Party (German centre/liberal political party)

NKVD: The People's Commissariat for Internal Affairs (USSR interior ministry, in charge of secret police and public order from 1934 to 1945)

SED: Socialist Unity Party (the founding and ruling party of the former East Germany)

SMERSH: an umbrella organisation for counter-intelligence agencies in the Red Army during the Second World War. The name is a portmanteau of a Russian phrase meaning 'death to spies'

SPD: Social Democratic Party of Germany (German centre-left political party)

UNRRA: United Nations Relief and Rehabilitation Administration (international relief agency, 1943–1948).

Acknowledgements

Many books had an impact on the form and content of this novel, which is to a large extent founded on the work of other authors. I would like to express my heartfelt thanks to them all, even if I cannot do justice here to all the influences that made this book possible.

In 2002, my late mentor Heinz Kroeger introduced me to the historical subject matter, and made his ample private archive available to me for the years of research that followed. I also have him to thank for pointing me towards the study *Deutschbaltische SS-Führer und Andrej Vlasov 1942–1945* by Matthias Schröder, without which *The Bastard Factory* would never have been written (and nor would the extensive and unpublished family history that I wrote in parallel to the novel. In its bibliography are listed those academic books without which the world of the Western and Eastern secret services and their National Socialist equivalent, the SD, would have remained closed to me. See http://diolink.ch/krausbibliographie).

Over the years, the most vital expert assistance was provided by the journalist and historian Anita Kugler, whose wonderful biography *Scherwitz. Der jüdische SS-Offizier* reveals the ambivalence and contradictions inherent in a figure who was both victim and perpetrator. If my novel can help this multi-layered work on Fritz Scherwitz, who was both a member of Einsatzgruppe A and a saviour of the Jews (a bizarre character in every sense, gifted with criminal energy), to reach a wider audience, it would be a particularly welcome side-effect of my efforts. It is to Scherwitz that my protagonist, Koja Solm, an SS officer who speaks fluent German, Russian and Yiddish, owes a hypothetical fatherhood, at least.

Jörg Friedrich's seminal work, *Die kalte Amnestie. NS-Täter in der Bundesrepublik*, which is still shocking more than thirty years after it was written, also had a lasting effect on me, and a very direct effect on the plot. Its theses, including individual sentences, are incorporated into the final chapters of my book. I am also particularly grateful to *Die 'Endlösung' in Riga* by Andrej Angrick and Peter Klein, from which (along with Andrew Ezergailis's *The Holocaust in Latvia*) several details on the history of occupied Riga were taken.

Michael Wildt has edited a volume on the SD (*Nachrichtendienst, politische Elite und Mordeinheit. Der Sicherheitsdienst des Reichsführers SS*) and has also written a monumental overview of the leadership corps in Heydrich's Reich Main Security Office (available in English as *An Uncompromising Generation*). These books give rise to the question of how it was possible for West German society to find its way to democracy despite the former Nazi personnel working in its institutions – a question that drove forward the story you have in your hands. I knew about Operation Zeppelin from family connections, and was able to make an in-depth study of the state prosecutor's investigations of this complex of crimes using files held at the Ludwigsburg Zentrale Stelle, but it was the work of Michael Wildt and a book by Klaus-Michael Mallmann (*Der Krieg im Dunkeln. Das Unternehmen Zeppelin*) that alerted me to the existence of these files, for which I am very grateful.

Studies on National Socialism that have had a particular influence on this novel are, among others: those by Götz Aly (whose investigations range from *Biedermann und Schreibtischtäter* to *Die Belasteten*, and trace the after-effects of the Nazi state all the way into the present political landscape); Christopher Browning (*Ordinary Men*); Alexander Dallin (*German Rule in Russia, 1941–1945*, which was written in 1958 but remains a benchmark to this day); Peter Longerich (*Politik der Vernichtung*); Raul Hilberg (*The Destruction of the European Jews*, a constant companion for me) and Saul Friedländer (whose work *Kurt Gerstein: The Ambiguity of Good* brought home to me the insoluble ambivalence of people facing moral dilemmas).

For the immediate post-war period and the integration of former Nazis into the Bonn republic, works by Christopher Simpson (*Blowback: America's recruitment of Nazis and its destructive impact on our domestic and foreign policy*); Norbert Frei (*Karrieren im Zwielicht. Hitlers Eliten nach 1945*); Gerd R. Ueberschär (editor *of Der Nationalsozialismus vor Gericht*); Christina Ullrich (*Ich fühl mich nicht als Mörder*) and Annette Weinke (*Eine Gesellschaft ermittelt gegen sich selbst*) were especially significant sources.

*

The main part of this book focuses on the German intelligence service, the BND, as well as the CIA, the Mossad, the Stasi and the KGB. It is impossible for me to single out just a few of the many published and unpublished sources on these organizations as especially important to my novel, since they all seem of equal value to me. However, I owe a particular debt of gratitude to Tim Weiner's startling reckoning with the American foreign secret service (*Legacy of Ashes: the history of the CIA*), from which details of Operation Red Cap and various others were taken.

Among the many works on the early history of Israel that I used for writing the fourth part, 'Black Red Gold', I found books by Tom Segev (*1949, the First Israelis*); Michael Bar-Zohar (*Spies in the Promised Land*) and Ari Shavit (*My Promised Land*) especially helpful. The last of these inspired specific details relating to the arrival of my protagonists in Israel. Dan Diner's *Rituelle Distanz* provided details of the German–Israeli negotiations in Wassenaar. Isser Harel's account of the capture of Adolf Eichmann in Buenos Aires (*The House on Garibaldi Street*) was an important source for the chapters on the former head of Mossad. I took several jokes from Josef Joffe's delightful book on Jewish humour (*Mach dich nicht so klein, du bist nichst so gross!*).

I have quoted liberally from the writings of various historical figures who appear in the novel, using them to create partly fictional conversations. These include quotations from Heinrich Himmler, Reinhard Gehlen, Isser Harel and Shimon Peres.

The classic work by Heinz Höhne and Hermann Zollig on the history of the BND and the involvement of many of its employees in violent Nazi crimes (*Pullach intern*) was published several decades ago, and since then the subject has received increasing attention, especially in recent years. The Independent Commission of Historians Researching the History of the Bundesnachrichtendienst 1945–1968 is currently bringing out a series on the early history of the BND that will eventually total thirteen monographs. Eleven have so far been published. Even though these unfortunately came too late for the information contained in them to be incorporated into *The Bastard Factory*, I have found nothing (in Gerhard Sälter's monograph *Phantome des Kalten Krieges*, for example) that speaks against the novel's thesis. On the contrary, Sälter's meticulous study proves to an even more bewildering degree that the line of personnel from the Third Reich to the BND continued unbroken into the 1960s. This institution's aversion to any kind of democratic, anti-fascist clean slate is astonishing. 'The Gehlen Organization', Gerhard Sälter writes, '[had been] from the very start not merely an intelligence service, but a political organization working against former victims of National Socialism.'

I built the Otto John affair, which was controversial at the time, into the novel's plot as an emblem of this trend. Like the Dreher affair or Egypt's missile programme, my version of this story was distilled from a multiplicity of studies, reportage, specialist books and background reports from the daily press of the time.

There is one more name I would like to mention in relation to the novel's historical background-painting: Harald Welzer, a cultural studies expert whom I admire greatly, and who wrote an astonishing, clever book that I cannot praise highly enough: *Täter. Wie aus ganz normalen Menschen Massenmörder werden* ('Perpetrators: how quite ordinary people become mass murderers'). His title would fit my novel well.

Aside from the factual research, the novel also owes thanks to numerous literary role models. The repertoire of its ideas, language and dramatic twists was enriched in many respects by reading my favourite authors. First and foremost, without the monumental work *Celestial Harmonies* by Péter Esterházy, I might well not have found the courage to write a fictional epic with such personal foundations. Several facets of Grandpaping Solm's story are indebted to Esterházy's work, along with a few metaphors. I have also, at the end of the second part, 'The Black Order', allowed myself to paraphrase an invention of Gabriel García Márquez from *One Hundred Years of Solitude*. I hope the master of magical realism will forgive me for this, from his cloud above Macondo. Here I also use Wilhelm Busch's poem, 'Es sitzt ein Vogel auf dem Leim'. And if elsewhere there should be traces of the works of Oda Schaefer, Vladimir Nabokov, Henry Miller, Uwe Johnson, Don DeLillo, John Irving or hundreds of other authors, then it is because everyone who writes is a dwarf sitting on the shoulders of giants, who guide you through the world in such a way that something of them always remains in your memory. I hereby give thanks to my giants, both the living and the dead.

*

The story of the Solm family only saw the light of day because the publisher Tanja Graf was accidentally given the manuscript when it was nothing more than material for my next feature film. I am heartily grateful to her for her rock-solid conviction that there was a literary project in this paper brick, which she luckily took to Diogenes Verlag. I would like to thank the publisher at Diogenes, Philipp Keel, for his courage and his unshakable optimism, which everyone who knows him experiences as boundless enthusiasm. Silvia Zanovello insisted on corrections and improvements to the book for so long and with such meticulous care and gentle firmness that they were actually made – the hallmark of a sensational editor. I am grateful to Tamar Lewinsky for being kind enough to read over and correct the Yiddish passages. My agent, Uwe Heldt, had confidence in me generally and in this book in particular, and I am deeply saddened by his death. Thanks to Rebekka Göpfert for the great energy and loyalty with which she took on and continued to guide the project as my agent. My cousin, Sigrid Kraus, largely financed and enabled the exploration of our shared family history some years ago, and thereby helped plant the seed of this literary work, for which I cannot give her enough credit. I am deeply indebted to my producers and combatants on the battlefields of the film industry, Kathrin Lemme and Danny Krausz, for generously releasing me from my obligations in the middle of a critical production phase of our film, *Die Blumen von gestern*, in order to finalize the novel. *The Bastard Factory* caused them, and everyone else involved, plenty of stress throughout.

This is especially true of my wife, Uta Schmidt, who has had to tolerate the cast of crazed and lost characters who populate this book in ever-changing variations for the past fifteen years, and whom I want to thank from the bottom of my heart for her love, companionship, patience and shrewd judgement. No one has believed in this story more than she, and no one conveyed this belief more strongly to me in my hours of doubt (which sometimes filled whole days).

The transformation of historical events into a novel always comes with distortions, abbreviations, instances of laxity and negligence, the occasional bending of the facts and deliberate interventions, and I alone must take the blame for these, along with all errors, inconsistencies and lazy artifice.